Praise for *Something to Hide*

"In *Something to Hide*, Elizabeth George delivers another intelligent, intricate mystery starring Detective Inspector Thomas Lynley of New Scotland Yard."
—*The New York Times Book Review*

"Superlative . . . This is a memorable addition to [the Inspector Lynley] series." —*Publishers Weekly* (starred review)

"'Abso-bloody-lutely' good! That would be DS Barbara Havers's verdict on this one. . . . An unsettling and thoroughly involving narrative." —*Booklist*

"A skillfully spun yarn of murder and mayhem."
—*Kirkus Reviews*

Praise for Elizabeth George

"Another reliable presence in bestsellerdom."
—Elisabeth Egan, *The New York Times*

"[George] is an essential writer of popular fiction today."
—*The Washington Post*

"[George is] one of the reigning queens of the genre."
—*Milwaukee Journal Sentinel*

"Elizabeth George is a superstar of the crime-fiction world."
—*The Seattle Times*

"It's tough to resist the pull of [George's] storytelling once hooked." —*USA Today*

"Ms. George can do it all, with style to spare."
—*The Wall Street Journal*

"[Lynley is] one of the great character portraits in contemporary crime fiction." —*The Boston Globe*

PENGUIN BOOKS

SOMETHING TO HIDE

Elizabeth George is the *New York Times* bestselling author of twenty psychological suspense novels, four young adult novels, two nonfiction books on creative writing, and two short story collections. Her work has been honored with the Anthony and Agatha awards, two Edgar nominations, and both France's and Germany's first prize for crime fiction, as well as several other prestigious prizes. She lives in Washington State.

ALSO BY ELIZABETH GEORGE

A Great Deliverance
Payment in Blood
Well-Schooled in Murder
A Suitable Vengeance
For the Sake of Elena
Missing Joseph
Playing for the Ashes
In the Presence of the Enemy
Deception on His Mind
In Pursuit of the Proper Sinner
A Traitor to Memory
I, Richard
A Place of Hiding
With No One as Witness
What Came Before He Shot Her
Careless in Red
This Body of Death
Believing the Lie
Just One Evil Act
A Banquet of Consequences
The Punishment She Deserves

YOUNG ADULT
The Edge of Nowhere
The Edge of the Water
The Edge of the Shadows
The Edge of the Light

NONFICTION
Write Away:
One Novelist's Approach to Fiction and the Writing Life
Mastering the Process: From Idea to Novel

ANTHOLOGY
A Moment on the Edge: 100 Years of Crime Stories by Women
Two of the Deadliest: New Tales of Lust, Greed, and
Murder from Outstanding Women of Mystery

Something to Hide

A LYNLEY NOVEL

ELIZABETH GEORGE

PENGUIN BOOKS

PENGUIN BOOKS
An imprint of Penguin Random House LLC
penguinrandomhouse.com

First published in the United States of America by Viking,
an imprint of Penguin Random House LLC, 2022
Published in Penguin Books 2023

ISBN 9780593296868 (paperback)

THE LIBRARY OF CONGRESS HAS CATALOGED THE HARDCOVER EDITION AS FOLLOWS:
Names: George, Elizabeth, 1949– author.
Title: Something to hide : a Lynley novel / Elizabeth George.
Description: [New York] : Viking, [2022]
Identifiers: LCCN 2021029231 (print) | LCCN 2021029232 (ebook) |
ISBN 9780593296844 (hardcover) | ISBN 9780593296851 (ebook)
Subjects: GSAFD: Mystery fiction.
Classification: LCC PS3557.E478 S66 2022 (print) |
LCC PS3557.E478 (ebook) | DDC 813/.54—dc23
LC record available at https://lccn.loc.gov/2021029231
LC ebook record available at https://lccn.loc.gov/2021029232

Printed in the United States of America
1st Printing

Set in Bembo Std
Designed by Cassandra Garruzzo Mueller

For those who suffer,
Those who endure,
And those who fight.

For the human soul is virtually indestructible,

And its ability to rise from the ashes

Remains as long as the body draws breath.

ALICE MILLER

For Your Own Good

PART I

21 JULY

Deborah St. James came at Sanctuary Buildings by way of Parliament Square on one of the hottest days of what had so far been a blazingly hot summer. She'd been asked to meet with one of the secretaries at the Department for Education as well as the head of the NHS. "We'd like to talk to you about a project," she'd been told. "Are you available to take something on?"

She was. She'd been casting round for a project since the publication of *London Voices* four months earlier, an undertaking that she'd spent the last several years putting together. So she was happy to attend a meeting that might turn into a new project, although she couldn't imagine what sort of photography the Department for Education in conjunction with the NHS might have in mind.

She approached a guard at the door with her identification in hand. However, he wasn't so much interested in that as was he interested in the contents of her capacious bag. He told her that her mobile phone was fine, but she was going to have to prove that her digital camera actually was a camera. Deborah obliged by taking his picture. She showed it to him. He waved her towards the door. He said just as she was about to enter, "Delete that, though. I look like crap."

At the reception desk, she asked for Dominique Shaw. Deborah St. James here to speak with the undersecretary for the school system, she added.

After a discreetly murmured phone call, she was handed a lanyard with VISITOR printed on the card that hung from it. Meeting Room 4, she was told. Floor 2. Turn to the right if she chose the lift. Turn to the left if she chose the stairs. She went for the stairs.

When she arrived at Meeting Room 4, though, she assumed she'd been given the wrong number. Five people sat round a polished conference table, not the two she'd been led to believe wished to meet her. Three floor fans were trying heroically to mitigate the temperature in the room. They were only creating something of a scirocco.

A woman rose from the end of the table and came towards her, hand extended. She was smartly dressed in a manner that shouted "government official," and she was decorated with overlarge rimless spectacles and gold earrings the size of golf balls. She was Dominique Shaw, she said, parliamentary under secretary of state for the school system. She introduced the others so quickly that for the most part, Deborah only caught their positions: the head of the NHS, a representative from Barnardo's, the founder of something called Orchid House, and a woman with the name Narissa, whose surname Deborah didn't catch. They were a diverse group: one was Black, one looked Korean, Dominique Shaw was white, and the woman called Narissa appeared to be mixed race.

"Please." Dominique Shaw indicated an empty chair next to the representative from Barnardo's.

Deborah sat. She was surprised to see a copy of *London Voices* in front of each of the people who were there. Her first thought was that the book was causing difficulties somehow, that she had created a volume that had turned out to be politically, socially, or culturally incorrect, although she couldn't imagine how any of that would involve the Department for Education. For the book comprised portraits of Londoners taken over a period of three years. Each portrait was accompanied by some of the subject's words, recorded by Deborah during the photographic session. Included among the portraits were depicted at least two dozen of the increasingly large homeless population, people of all ages and races and nationalities who ended up sleeping in doorways along the Strand, stretched out in the subways beneath Park Lane, curled next to wheelie bins—and sometimes inside of them—and behind hotels like the Savoy and the Dorchester. These parts of the book didn't deliver London as the glamorous global city it made itself out to be.

She demurred on the offer of coffee or tea, but happily accepted tepid water from a glass jug on the table. She waited for someone to bring up the subject of the meeting—preferably clarification on the topic of what on earth she was doing there—and once Deborah had her water, as well as her own completely unnecessary copy of *London Voices*, which Dominique Shaw passed to her, the undersecretary for schools began to elucidate.

She said, "It was Mr. Oh who brought your book to my attention," with a nod at the man from Barnardo's. "It's impressive. I've been wondering, though . . ." She seemed to cull through various options of what she was wondering while outside and below the window what sounded like a lorry with a very bad transmission screeched in the street. Shaw glanced at the window, frowned, then went on. "How did you manage it?"

Deborah wasn't sure what Dominique Shaw meant. She looked at the cover of the book for a moment. The publisher had chosen an inoffensive image: one of the many elderly people who regularly fed the birds in St. James's Park. Peaked cap on his head, he was standing on the bridge over the pond, hand extended, bird on his palm.

It was his deeply lined cheeks that had interested her, how the lines mapped the distance from the eyes to his lips, which were very chapped. The photograph wasn't one she would have chosen for the cover of the book, but she understood the reasoning behind it. One *did* want the prospective buyer to pick it up and open it. A photo of someone sleeping rough in the Strand wasn't likely to be as effective.

Deborah said, "D'you mean getting people to pose? I did ask them. I told them I wanted to make a portrait and, to be honest, most people are willing to have their picture taken if they're approached and given the reason. Not everyone, of course. There were some people who said no, absolutely not. A few unpleasant remarks here and there, but one can't be put off by that. Those who were happy to let me shoot them where they were . . . ? If they had an address, I sent them a copy of the photo I chose to use in the book."

"And what they said to you." Mr. Oh was speaking. "Their remarks that you've included?"

"How did you get them to talk to you like this?" the woman Narissa asked.

"Oh. Right." Deborah opened the book and leafed through a few of the pages as she spoke. "The thing about taking someone's photograph is to get them not to think about the fact that I'm taking their photograph. People stiffen up in front of a camera. It's human nature. They think they're supposed to pose, and suddenly they're not who they really are. So the photographer has to devise a way to catch them in a moment when they . . . I suppose you'd say in a moment when they reveal themselves. Every photographer has to do this. It's easy enough if I can catch them unaware of being photographed in the first place. But for something like this—I mean for a book or for any formal portrait, really—one can't do that. So most photographers talk to them as they shoot."

"Tell them to relax, tell them to smile, tell them what?" Dominique Shaw asked.

Deborah saw how the undersecretary had misunderstood her explanation. She said, "I don't tell them anything. I ask them to tell me. I listen to them and I respond and they carry on. For this"—she indicated the book—"I asked them to tell me about their experiences in London, about how they felt about living in London, about what London feels like for them, about the place where the picture was taken. Naturally, everyone had a different answer. It was the exploration of the answer that ended up giving me the moments I was looking for."

The founder of Orchid House said, "Wha's this, then? D'you think you have a special gift for getting people to talk to you?"

Deborah smiled as she shook her head. "Lord no. I'm completely inarticulate if the subject veers away from photography, dogs, or cats. I *can* do gardening, I suppose, but only if it deals with weeding and only if I don't have to identify the weed. For this"—again she indicated the book—"I settled on the same questions in advance and I asked them as I took the pictures. Then we went from there. I built on what they gave me as answers. Whenever people hit on the subject that triggers them, their faces alter."

"And that's when you take the picture?"

"No, no. That's what I'm looking for, but I take the pictures all along. For a book like this . . . I culled through . . . I don't know . . . p'rhaps three thousand portraits?"

There was a silence round the table. Glances were exchanged. Deborah's conclusion was that she certainly hadn't been called here for reasons having to do with *London Voices*, but she still couldn't work out what they wanted with her. Finally, the undersecretary spoke.

"Well, you've done quite a job with the book," she said. "Congratulations. We have a project we'd like to talk to you about."

"Something to do with education?" Deborah asked.

"Yes. But I daresay not in the way you might be thinking of it."

MAYVILLE ESTATE
DALSTON
NORTH-EAST LONDON

Tanimola Bankole had been clinging to the hope that the fourth straight week of misery-inducing summer heat would disrupt his father's train of thought, which had been steaming along the railway track of Tani's irresponsibility for the last thirty-seven minutes. This wasn't a new subject for Abeo Bankole. Tani's father was fully capable of banging on, both in English and in his native Yoruba, for forty-five minutes, and he'd done just that on more than one occasion. He saw it as his paternal obligation to make certain Tani fully took up the mantle of manhood as defined by Abeo, and Tani could do this only by embracing all of manhood's attendant duties, also as defined by Abeo. At the same time, he saw it as Tani's filial obligation to listen to, to remember, and to obey his father in all things. The first of the three, Tani generally managed. It was the second and third that caused him trouble.

On this particular day, Tani couldn't argue against a single point his father was making. He *was* lucky to have regular work made available to him by virtue of being the son of Abeo Bankole, proprietor of Into Africa Groceries Etc. as well as a butcher's shop and a fishmonger's stall. He *was* privileged that his father allowed him to keep one-eighth of his wages for his personal use instead of depositing all of them into the family pot. He *did* enjoy three meals each day provided for him by his mother. His laundry *was* delivered to his bedroom spotlessly clean and perfectly ironed. Et cetera, et cetera, and blah blah blah.

Instead of taking any kind of notice of the waves of heat rising from the pavement, of the trees—where there were any in this part of town—losing their leaves far too early into the year, of the remaining ice in the fish stalls in Ridley Road Market melting so quickly that the air was thick with the smell of hake and snapper and mackerel, of the meat in the butchers' stalls sending forth a stench of blood from the simmering organs of sheep and cows, of the fruit and veg having to be sold at discount before they rotted, Abeo merely strode onward in the direction of Mayville Estate, oblivious of everything save Tani's failure to arrive at work on time.

Tani was completely at fault. His father said nothing that wasn't true. Tani *couldn't* keep his mind on what he was supposed to be doing. Tani did *not* put his family first. Tani *did* continually forget who he was. So he didn't say anything in his own defence. Instead, he thought of Sophie Franklin.

There was much to think of: Sophie's gorgeous skin; her soft, cropped hair; her smooth-as-silk legs and glorious ankles; her luscious breasts; her lips and her tongue and all the rest of her . . . Of *course* he was completely irresponsible. When he was with Sophie, how could he be anything else?

His father might have understood this. Although he was sixty-two, he'd been young once. But there was absolutely *no* way that Tani was about to tell him about Sophie. The fact that she was not Nigerian was only one of the reasons Abeo Bankole would have a stroke there on the pavement if he knew of Tani's relationship with her. The other was sex with Sophie, the very fact of which was more than Abeo would ever be able to take in calmly.

So Tani had been late to work at Into Africa Groceries Etc. He'd been so late, in fact, that the daily restocking of shelves was in progress when he'd finally arrived. This restocking—along with reordering and general clean-up—was Tani's job once his college duties had been fulfilled each day, and the only other employee of Into Africa, Zaid, was not intended to do anything but direct customers to whatever they were looking for and otherwise to work the till. Zaid wasn't happy to be doing everything on this particular day. He'd expressed this unhappiness via mobile to Abeo just along the way in the butcher's shop.

Tani had rushed dutifully to take over the restocking of the shelves when he finally arrived. But Zaid had done the general cleanup, and he cast a number of baleful looks in Tani's direction before Abeo walked in and told Tani he was to come with him.

Tani had understood he was in for it. But he recognised that this might be a very good opportunity for him to put his father in the picture as to Tani's future. He hated having to work in either one of his father's two shops, *or* the fishmonger's stall, and he hated even more that he was intended to take over the running of Into Africa Groceries Etc. as soon as he finished his catering course at sixth form college. *This* was not for him. Truth about it? This was bollocks. What he meant to do was to head to uni for a degree in business and in no one's dream world was he going to waste that degree by taking employment in a shop. Abeo could call upon one or more of the Bankole cousins for a shop manager. Of course, that would mean allowing a family member from Peckham into the constricted life Abeo had designed for his wife and his offspring in north-east London, and Abeo wouldn't like that. But Tani wasn't going to give him a choice. He meant to have the life he wanted.

The walk to Mayville Estate after work hours followed a zigzag pattern north through the streets. Late afternoon and there were pedestrians and cars and buses and bicycles everywhere as inhabitants of the area headed home. Among a very few Nigerians in this part of town, in a mixed-race community that was transitioning from African to West Indian, the Bankoles lived on the grounds of Mayville Estate in Bronte House, a building that comprised five floors of the undecorated London brick that was ubiquitous on the housing estate. The structure had the distinction of being directly across the lane from an asphalt play area, shaded from the scorching sun by enormous London plane trees. There were basketball hoops and goalposts at either end of it, and it was fenced to keep children chasing balls from going into the street.

Concrete steps led up to the doors of the ground-floor flats in Bronte House, while outdoor corridors marked the route to those on the upper four storeys, which were accessed by a stairway or a lift. Nearly every door was open in the futile hope of catching a breeze that was, at least for now, nonexistent. So from gaping windows television noises and dance music along with rap issued forth, accompanied by the fragrance of a multitude of meals being prepared.

Inside the Bankole flat, the temperature made the place feel like an overheated sauna. Tani felt blanketed by a pall of nearly liquid air that forced him to squint against his own sweat. There were fans running, but they did nothing to mitigate the roasting air. They merely moved it around like sluggish swamp water. One could breathe, but it wasn't pleasant to do so.

Tani caught the scent almost at once, and he glanced at his father. Pa's expression showed that he wasn't pleased.

It was Monifa Bankole's job to anticipate many things. At this time of day, she was to anticipate not only the hour that her husband would walk into the flat, but also the meal that her husband would prefer. He usually told her neither. In his head, they had been married for twenty years, so he should not have to broadcast information to her like a newlywed. During their first years together, he'd made her well aware of many things, among them his requirement that his tea be ready no more than ten minutes after his return from the day's labour. This day, Tani saw, things were looking good for the *time* of tea if not for the substance. His sister, Simisola, was laying the table for all of them, which meant the meal was imminent.

Simi bobbed a hello instead of speaking, but she shot Tani a grin when he said, "You baffed up cos your boyfriend's coming to tea, Squeak?" She quickly covered her grin with her hand. This hid the appealing little gap between her front teeth, but it did nothing to stifle her giggle. She was eight years old, ten years Tani's junior. His principal interaction with her was defined by teasing.

"I don't *have* a boyfriend," she declared.

"No? Why?" he asked her. "In Nigeria you'd be married by now."

"Would not!" she said.

"Would too. Tha's what happens, innit, Pa."

Abeo ignored him to say to Simi, "Tell your mother we are home," as if this were necessary.

The girl swirled round, danced past one of the nearly useless fans, and called out, "Mummy! They're here!" And then to her father and brother and just as her mother would, "Sit, sit, sit. You want a beer, Papa? Tani?"

"Water for him," Abeo said.

Simi shot Tanimola a look and swirled round again. It came to Tani that she was doing all the swirling in order to show off a skirt. It was an old one, looking like an Oxfam special, but she'd decorated it with sequins and sparkles and her headband—from which her short dark hair sprang up in twists—she had decorated as well. It sported more sequins, and she'd added a feather. She dashed into the kitchen, nearly knocking into their mother, who was emerging with the *gbegiri* soup Tani had smelled. Steam rose from it, fogging her specs, beading moisture on Monifa's forehead and cheeks.

He couldn't imagine even trying *gbegiri* soup in this heat, but he knew what mentioning that would trigger. Abeo would embark upon another saga of how things were when *he* was a boy. He'd been in England for forty of his sixty-two years, but when he spoke of his native Nigeria, one would think he'd arrived at Heathrow only last week. How things were "back home" had long been his preferred topic, whether he was holding forth about the schools, the living conditions, the weather, or the customs . . . all of which seemed to exist in a fantasy African homeland born from watching *Black Panther* at least five times. It was Pa's favourite film.

As Monifa placed the serving bowl in the centre of the table, Abeo frowned. "This is not *efo riro*," he said.

"In this heat, I worried," Monifa said. "The chicken. The meat. We had none here, just a bit of beef. And I wondered how fresh could the other meats stay if I bought them in the market. So I thought *gbegiri* soup might be wiser."

He looked at her. "You have made no rice, Monifa?"

"Here, Papa!" Simi had reappeared with the beer. She had a frosty can in one hand and a frosty glass in the other, and she said, "It feels *so* cool. Feel how cool it is, Papa. C'n I have some? Just a sip?"

"You can*not*," her mother said. "Sit. I am serving the food. I am sorry about the rice, Abeo."

Simi said, "But I've not got Tani's water yet, Mummy."

Abeo said sharply, "Do as your mother tells you, Simisola."

Simi did so, casting an "I'm sorry" look at Tani, who shrugged. She ducked her hands beneath the table and cast a look at Tani, who gave her a wink. She cast one at her mother, who kept her gaze on Abeo. After a long moment of observing Monifa, he gave the sharp nod that indicated his wife could begin serving.

He said to Monifa, "Your son failed to show up at work on schedule once again. He was able to give the shop only thirty minutes of his valuable time. Zaid had to do nearly everything at closing, and he was not pleased." And then he said to Tani, "Where were you that you failed in your responsibilities?"

Monifa murmured, "Abeo . . . ? Perhaps later you and Tani . . . ?"

"This, what I speak of, is not your concern," Abeo cut in. "Have you made *eba*? Yes? Simisola, bring it from the kitchen."

Monifa spooned a large portion of *gbegiri* soup onto a rimmed plate. She passed it to Abeo. She scooped up more and gave it to Tani.

In a moment, Simi emerged from the kitchen with a large platter of *eba*. To accompany the swallows and in a bow to "being English," she'd tucked under her arm a bottle of brown sauce. She placed this in front of Abeo and returned to her seat. Monifa served her last, as was their custom.

They ate in silence. Noise from outdoors along with the smacking of lips and swallowing of food was the only sound. Halfway through his meal, Abeo paused, shoved back his chair, and performed what Tani thought of as his father's nightly ritual: He blew his nose mightily into a paper napkin, balled this up, and tossed it to the floor. He told Simi to bring him another. Monifa rose to do this herself, but Abeo said, "Sit, Monifa. You are not Simi." Simi scampered off, returning only moments later with an ancient tea towel so faded that it was impossible to discern which royal marriage was being celebrated on it. She said to her father, "I couldn't find any but there's this. An' it will work, won't it, Papa?"

He took it from her and used it on his face. He placed it on the table and looked at them. He said, "I have news."

Instantly, they all became statues.

"What kind of news?" Monifa asked.

"Things have been settled well," was his reply.

Tani saw his mother shoot a glance in his direction. Her expression alone was a trigger for his anxiety.

"It's taken many months," Abeo said. "The cost has been more than I expected. We start at ten cows. *Ten* of them. So I ask can she breed if I am to pay ten cows for her? *He* says she is one of twelve offspring, three of whom are already producing. Thus she comes of breeding stock. That is of no account, I tell him. Just because her mother and siblings have bred so well, this does not mean *she* will do the same. So I ask for a guarantee. Ten cows and there is no guarantee? I say this to him. He says, Pah! What sort of man asks another for a guarantee? I say, A man who knows what is important. We go back and forth, and in the end, he says he will settle for six cows. I say it's still too much. He says, Then she can stay here, because I have other options. *Options*, he says. I tell him I know he bluffs. But the time is right, her age is right, she will not last long if he puts the word out. So I agree, and the thing is settled."

Monifa had lowered her gaze to her plate and had not lifted it again during Abeo's speech. Simi had stopped chewing her food, her expression telegraphing her confusion. Tani felt lost within his father's story. Ten cows? Six? Breeding stock? He felt something very bad in the air, a gust of tension flavoured with the scent of dread.

Abeo turned to him, saying, "Six cows I paid for a virgin of sixteen years. This has been done for you. Soon I will take you to Nigeria where you will meet her."

"Why'm I meeting some Nigerian girl?" Tani asked.

"Because you are going to marry her when she is seventeen years." That said, Abeo went back to eating. He broke off a piece of his swallow and used it to scoop up a small piece of beef. This appeared to remind him of something he wished to add, for he addressed Tani with, "You are lucky in this. A girl her age is usually given to a man of forty years or more because of the cost. Never to a boy like you. But you must settle and take up your manhood soon. So we will go, and while we are there, she will cook for you, and you will get to know her. I have seen to that so you do not end up with someone useless. She is called Omorinsola, by the way."

Tani folded his hands on the table. The room seemed several degrees hotter than it had been upon their return from Ridley Road. He said, "I'm not doing tha', Pa."

Monifa drew in a deep breath. Simi's eyes became as round as old pennies. Abeo looked up from his food and said, "What is this that you just said to me, Tanimola?"

"I'm not doing it is what I said. I'm not meeting some virgin you've picked out for me, and I'm definitely not marrying anyone when she turns seventeen." Tani heard his mother murmur his name, so he faced her. "This isn't the Middle Ages, Mum."

Monifa said, "In Nigeria, Tani, these things are arranged so that—"

"We don't live in Nigeria, do we. We live in London and in London people marry who they want to marry *when* they want to marry them. Or at least I do. I will. No one's picking out a wife for me. And I'm not getting married anyway. Not now and definitely not to some guaranteed African breeding virgin. Tha's mad, innit."

There was a tight little moment of the kind of silence that echoes round a room. Abeo broke it, saying, "You will do exactly what you are told to do, Tani. You will meet Omorinsola. You are promised to her and she is promised to you, so we will have no more discussion."

"You," Tani said, "are not the ruler of me."

Monifa gasped. Tani heard this and said, "No, Mum. I'm not going to Nigeria or to any other place just because he decided it."

"I head this family," Abeo told him. "As a member of it, you will do as I say."

"I won't," Tani said. "If you thought I would do, then you're mistaken. You can't force me to marry anyone."

"You will do this, Tani. I will see that you do it."

"Really, eh? Tha's what you think? D'you plan to hold a gun to my head? Tha'll look good in the wedding photos, innit."

"You watch what comes out of your mouth."

"Why? What will you do? Beat me up like—"

Monifa quickly said, "Stop this, Tani. Show your father some respect." And then, "Simi, go to—"

"She stays," Abeo said. And to Tani, "Finish what it is you wish to say."

"I've said what I wanted to say." At that he rose from the table, his chair screeching on the lino. His father did the same.

Abeo's fist clenched. Tani stood his ground. They stared each other down across the table. Abeo finally said, "Get out of my sight."

Tani was happy to do so.

THE NARROW WAY
HACKNEY
NORTH-EAST LONDON

Detective Chief Superintendent Mark Phinney wasn't surprised to find his brother waiting for him. Paulie had arranged everything in the first place, so he had a vested interest, more or less, in how Mark liked what he'd found waiting for him inside Massage Dreams. Besides, Massage Dreams wasn't far from either one of Paulie's two pawnshops, and well within convenient walking distance of their parents' house and Paulie's own. At least, Mark thought, his brother wasn't lurking inside the damn place, in its tiny lobby. Instead, he'd taken himself the short distance from Mare Street to The Narrow Way, and there he was sitting on one of the benches in the middle of the pedestrian precinct. Mark saw him at once as he rounded the corner. On Paulie's face was that knowing leer with which he'd always greeted his younger brother whenever—as an adolescent with spots on his face—Mark had returned from what Paulie had assumed was a date but actually was hanging about with a group of mates from school, all of them misfits like Mark himself, three of them girls. Paulie's words then were always the same when Mark arrived home: "Get any, mate?" to which Mark would reply, "If I did, you're not hearing about it."

Today's leer, though, had nothing to do with adolescent girls, although it did have to do with getting some in one of the back rooms of the day spa, which happened to be more than a mere day spa if one had the right currency, as they did not give change *or* accept credit cards when a man purchased this particular service.

Paulie said, "So . . . ?" and when Mark didn't reply at once, "It took long enough, Boyko. What'd you do? Have more than one go?"

Mark said, "I had to wait twenty minutes for her. Let's go. Mum'll have dinner nearly ready."

"That's *it*?" Paulie said. "Just 'I had to wait twenty minutes for her'? I went through a lot of favours to get you an appointment today, lad. That's how popular the place has become. So was it good? Worth the money? Was she young? Beautiful? Haggard? No teeth? What'd she use? Hand, mouth, tongue, some other body part? I reckon between the tits would do nicely, eh? No? Hmmm. P'rhaps under her arm? Or did you go the full monty with her?"

Mark tuned him out. He walked in the direction of St. Augustine Tower, the crenellated top of which overlooked The Narrow Way. A group of kids appeared to be playing an imaginative form of kick the can at the base of the tower, a sight he hadn't seen since mobile phones, texting, gaming, and PlayStations had obliterated the ways children had entertained themselves for generations.

They entered St. John of Hackney churchyard, just to the right of the ancient tower. They headed east, on a route that would take them along a paved path the distance to Sutton Way. There Paulie and his family lived in a structure unappealingly reminiscent of the hasty architecture that grew out of the 1960s, all angles and picture windows looking onto very little of interest.

Paulie said, "Well, it was better than internet porn, I wager. More costly, yeah, but it's the woman's touch that does it, eh? It's special, that. Another human being. Warm flesh. Shit, Boyko, if Eileen hasn't always known what I want before I even want it, I'd've been in there with you having my own go." His voice altered to meditative. "That woman's a sex machine, our Eileen is. Most days she doesn't wear knickers, and if the kids aren't in the room, she lifts her skirt every chance she gets. She's even done me in one of the shops. Have I told you that? Right behind the counter, this was, three days ago, with the shop full open for business. I'm surprised I wasn't taken to the bill to answer questions about wife abuse. *That's* how much noise the woman was making when I got her going."

Mark said nothing. He'd heard about Eileen's sexual antics before. Ad nauseam, in fact. The silence extended until Paulie said, "Pete coming to dinner? Or is it just you?"

Mark glanced at his brother, who was looking straight ahead as if there were something in the distance that wanted memorising. He said, "Why d'you ask that? You know it's impossible just now."

"What about that Greer person? Isn't that her name? Greer? Pete's friend? The one she sees so much of? Greer could stay for an hour or two. She'd know what to do if anything happened."

"Pete doesn't like to leave Lilybet," Mark told his brother.

"I know she doesn't *like* to. We *all* know she doesn't like to, Boyko."

Again Mark made no reply. While it was true that his misery was deep, it was not about Pete, who did the best she could, given their circumstances. Instead, his misery was more about what he couldn't anticipate, and that was what the future was going to look like for all three of them: Pietra, Lilybet, and himself.

They walked across the lower section of the churchyard. It was mostly empty at this time of day, so close to dinner. A few benches were occupied, but mostly by people who were staring at the screens of their smartphones. There were dog walkers as well, and one woman in a scarlet sundress appeared to be walking a large tabby cat on a lead although the cat's slinking along a scarce inch from the ground indicated his lack of enthusiasm for the activity.

As they drew closer to the other side of the churchyard, the smell of frying burgers created a fountain of scent in the air. The source was a small café just to their side of the wall that separated the churchyard from the neighbourhood beyond it. The café catered to the area's multiracial, multicultural populace, as its posted menu indicated that on offer were not only burgers but also crêpes, samosas, kebabs, chicken shawarma, and various vegetarian dishes. The place appeared to be doing a brisk business. There were people tucking into numerous cartons at the several picnic tables set on the lawn. There was also a long queue waiting to order and another waiting for food to be packed up for takeaway. They wore the martyred expressions so typical of Londoners, most of whom spent their lives waiting in a queue for something: a bus, the underground, a train, a taxi, their turn at the till.

"Can't believe that place is still here," Paulie commented as they passed. "The grandkids must be running it by now."

"Must be," Mark said. They walked by the café and then through the far exit from the churchyard, which took them into Sutton Way, where Paulie snatched up a discarded cigarette packet and shoved it into his pocket. They went not to Paulie's house among the string of 1960s-looking structures, but to the house in which they had grown up. It was across the street and down the way a bit, in a terrace of soot-soiled brick houses in need of a thorough scrubbing. They were all identical. Each had three floors, a slightly recessed arched doorway, fanlights above the doors, doors themselves painted ebony. Wrought-iron railings defined the house fronts; two windows on each floor gave an idea of size. Nothing distinguished one from another except the window coverings and the brass door knockers, their originals having been replaced over the years by whatever the occupants fancied. In the case of Mark and Paulie's childhood home, the knocker of choice was a brass jack-o'-lantern, and the window coverings were the creation of Paulie's kids, with assistance from their gran, who'd supplied the paints. There was a primitive charm to the finished product, as long as one didn't attempt to identify the animals that the kids had decided to depict.

Paulie didn't use a key as the door was seldom locked during daylight hours. He opened it, shouted, "Hiya! The conquerors have arrived!" and dropped to one knee to receive the embraces of his

offspring, who came storming towards him. Yells accompanied the
pounding of their feet. "Dad's here!" "Mummy! Gran!" "Granddad,
Dad's here! So's Uncle Boyko!"

Mark looked for his godchild among them. His niece, Esme, was
his favourite. She was also his wound. Two weeks younger than Lilybet, she offered a contrast between them that had always been a rapier
to his heart.

Chaos tsunamied round them as the kids demanded "something
special from the shop, Dad!" This would be the odd item never redeemed by its owner and, as it happened, not particularly sellable either. Today there was only one object, a dull-edged and tarnished
cigar cutter. Paulie handed it to his oldest boy. He told all of the
children that they each got one guess as to what it was. Write it on
paper and deliver it to your dad, were the rules. Whoever got it on
the money would also get to keep it.

His and Mark's own dad was in the sitting room, watching telly
with an enormous set of earphones on his head to save the rest of the
household from whatever headache the telly's intense volume would
otherwise cause them. He waved a hello at his sons; they waved in
turn. They went on to find their mother in the kitchen. Paulie's wife,
Eileen, was stirring something in a large pot on the stove while their
mother, Floss Phinney, was engaged in tossing a salad.

Eileen came at once across the room and wrapped her arms round
Paulie's neck. Paulie squeezed her bum as they shared the kiss of lovers
who've been apart years instead of ten hours. Mark looked away. Floss
was watching him. She smiled fondly. Paulie and Eileen broke it off and
Paulie went to the stove and lifted the lid of the pot steaming there. He
sniffed. He said, "Jesus in a handcart, Mum. You've not let our Eileen
do the cooking, have you? This smells like something she'd make."

Eileen slapped his hand away, saying, "We'll have none of that,
you," while Floss turned her attention to Mark. "Pietra's not with you,
Boyko?"

"She may be along later," Mark told her. Paulie went to the refrigerator and did what he'd done since childhood: opened the door and stared into it like someone divining the future from the various leftovers of previous meals. Mark said to his mother in a lower voice, "She's interviewing."

"Is she indeed?" Floss asked. "Well, that's good, eh? We can hope things turn out a bit different this time." She looked past him to where Paulie was still inspecting what was on offer inside the fridge. She said, "Paulie, fix us a beverage, there's my boy. Eileen, make sure he's not stingy with the ice this time round. I hate a beverage that's overwarm, I do."

The kids were raising a ruckus in another part of the house and Paulie shouted at them as he went to the sitting room's drinks cart to make his mother her favourite, gin and tonic, very light on the tonic. The kids' voices lowered—it wouldn't be for long as it never was—and during the relative peace and semi-quiet, Esme slid into the room. She came to Mark and slipped her hand into his. She leaned her head against his arm. She said just above a whisper, "Passed my maths test, Uncle Mark." She was the only family member, aside from his wife, who didn't call him Boyko.

"That's grand, that is, Esme," he told her.

"Lilybet would pass it if she could," Esme replied. "She'd prob'ly do better'n me."

He felt a tightness round his eyes. "Yes. Well," he said. "Perhaps someday, eh?"

Floss asked the girl if she wouldn't mind laying the table for everyone. Esme pointed out that her mother had already done it, Gran. "She did, did she?" was Gran's response. She smiled fondly at the girl and said, "Then c'n you give me a moment with your uncle?"

Esme looked from Mark to his mum, back to Mark. She said, "That's why you asked me to lay the table, Gran. It would've been okay for you to ask me direct."

"I stand corrected, darlin'. Sometimes I forget you're quite the big girl now. I'll be d'rect with you from now on."

When Esme nodded and left them, Floss said to Mark, "How many this time?"

"Applicants?" He shrugged. "I've not asked her. She does her best, Mum."

"She needs time to herself now and then."

"She does take time, some two hours every week."

"That's hardly taking time, is it. She can't keep going along this way. If she tries that, she'll be dead before she's fifty and then where will Lilybet be? Where will *you* be?"

"I know."

"You have to insist, Boyko."

As if he hadn't, Mark thought. As if he hadn't and hadn't and hadn't till the words were rote and their meaning long robbed of importance. He said, "Pete wants to do right by her."

"Well, of course she does. And so do you. But you must also want to do right by yourselves, eh?" She stirred Eileen's concoction and then turned back to him, wooden spoon in hand. She observed him in the way only a mother observes: a silent comparison of the boy he'd been and the man he'd become. Clearly, she didn't like what she saw. She said, "When was the last time you two had relations?"

She'd never gone in this direction before. Mark was taken aback. He said, "Jesus . . . Mum . . ."

She said, "You tell me, Boyko."

His gaze slid away from her to the open window upon which a line of terracotta pots grew the fresh herbs she liked to have on hand. He wanted to ask when they'd been last watered. The basil was looking a bit limp. He said, "Last week," and prepared himself for the moment when she accused him of lying, which indeed he was. He didn't know the last time they'd had relations. He only knew it could be measured in years, not in weeks. For this, he couldn't possibly blame Pete. Even when she was there, she wasn't there, so what was the point? Every sense she possessed was tuned into Lilybet's small bedroom and the noises emanating from it on the baby monitor: the hiss of oxygen, the puff that indicated the rise and fall of Lilybet's chest. One couldn't make love to a woman who isn't there, he wanted to tell his mother. It's more than mere friction, two bodies rubbing together in a growing frenzy of pleasure that would lead to release. If that's what it was, anyone would do. An anonymous foreign "masseuse" would do. Hell, a blow-up doll would suffice. But that wasn't what it was. Or at least that wasn't what he wanted. If nothing else, his interlude this day at Massage Dreams had demonstrated that. Orgasm? Yes. Connection? No.

Floss regarded him with sadness in her eyes. But all she said was, "Oh, lad."

"It's fine, Mum," he replied.

KINGSLAND HIGH STREET
DALSTON
NORTH-EAST LONDON

Adaku Obiaka had dressed to blend in, and she blended in well. Where she stood, she was anonymous, forgettable, and largely out of sight. She'd taken up a position in the recessed entry of Rio Cinema from where the smell of popcorn and coffee—what a strange combination, she thought—fought for neighbourhood dominance with odours wafting from across the street. There, Taste of Tennessee was belching forth a mixed miasma of scents: cooking oil, fried chicken, ribs, and burgers. The very air felt greasy with the smell.

She had been there coming up to three hours, watching the action along the street in general, watching the lack of action in one set of

disreputable-looking flats in particular. These were positioned above
what once had been Kingsland Toys, Games, and Books, an establishment announcing itself with a garish violet sign wearing equally garish letters of twelve different colours. The business was no more, and
nothing had taken its place although the COMING SOON sign lent a
hopeful air to the empty storefront.

The defunct shop stood directly between Taste of Tennessee and
Vape Superstore, and like most of the businesses along the street, it
possessed two doors. One of them gave customers access to the shop.
The other, always locked unless one possessed a key, gave inhabitants
access to the flats above. Six decrepit windows marked the position of
these flats. There were two on each floor. The top-floor windows
showed bright lights behind dingy curtains. The middle floor seemed
dark behind Venetian blinds. The first floor stared blankly out at Rio
Cinema, reflecting its marquee, which promised yet another tired,
dystopian universe that had to be restored to decency by a cinematic
adolescent heroine, preferably one with white skin and blond hair.

During her three hours on watch, no one had entered or left
through the locked door giving access to the flats. But Adaku had been
told confidentially that someone would, and it was that prospect that
had kept her there past the rumbling of her stomach longing for dinner. It had taken her far too long expending far too much energy in
order to dig up Women's Health of Hackney. Although she could
easily have come back another day to position herself in the cinema's
entry, the lights in the uppermost flat told her someone was there. All
she had to do was to wait them out, even if it took till morning.

In the time Adaku had maintained her position, the street noises
had altered from pedestrian chatter and crying babies and children
shouting as they zipped by on scooters to what they were now: rumbling traffic, violin practice coming from a flat somewhere, a busker
playing the accordion in front of Snappy Snaps, a few paces away from
a Paddy Power betting establishment, the busker no doubt hoping that

some lucky punter had a few extra pound coins to toss in his direction after a successful day at the races.

Adaku wished she'd brought a sandwich along. Even an apple and a bottle of water sounded good. But she'd not thought to stock up on provisions. Nor had she the time. A phone call leaving the message "She's there" had taken her from West Brompton underground station to the Rio Cinema, and only another phone call would change her location till she saw someone emerge from the building across the street.

Her fourth hour was ten minutes old when her long observation was finally rewarded. The lights in the topmost flat were extinguished and in a minute the door leading to the flats above Kingsland Toys, Games, and Books opened. A woman stepped out. Unlike Adaku she dressed English in close-fitting trousers and a thin jersey, white with horizontal red stripes and a boat neck. She wore a red baseball cap at a jaunty angle, and she carried a shopping carrier bag over her shoulder.

The woman had probably changed in one of the flats above for her work that day. There, she would have worn garments that looked more professional, as a way to reassure her clients. Dressed appropriately, *all will be well* would be her unspoken message. Wasn't it the truth, Adaku thought with a derisive shake of her head, that desperate people are ready to think and believe exactly what others tell them to think and to believe?

The woman headed briskly north in the direction of the railway station. This suggested that she might not live nearby. That being the case, Adaku needed to make her move in advance of her quarry's catching a train. So she crossed the street quickly, and once on the pavement, she picked up her pace. Soon enough she drew even with the woman. Adaku slid her hand through the other's arm, saying, "I must speak with you."

The woman's lips formed a perfect O. Then, her words naming the UK as the land of her birth, she said, "Who're you? What do you want?" and she tried to pull away.

"As I said, I need to speak with you. It will not take long," was Adaku's reply. "I was given the name of this place. It is Women's Health of Hackney, yes?"

"No one stops me on the street like this. What d'you want from me?"

Adaku looked round for listeners and lowered her voice. "I was told only the location. Coming upon you like this was the only way I had. I don't have a phone number that I could ring. So it was this or nothing. *Will* you speak with me?"

"'Bout what? If you're hoping for medical advice handed out on the pavement, you definitely got the wrong idea."

"I want only five minutes of your time. There's a Costa Coffee just along the high street. We can go there."

"D'you need to have your hearing checked? I just said—"

"I have money."

"For *what*? Is this a bribe? D'you have the slightest idea what you're about?"

Adaku said, "I have money with me, here in my bag. I'll give it to you."

The woman laughed. "You're that daft, aren't you? Like I said, I don't even know you, and I sure as bloody hell don't talk 'bout medical matters on the street."

"I've fifty pounds with me. I can bring more later. Whatever you say."

"Whatever I say, eh?" The woman gazed long at Adaku before looking left and right as if trying to decide if this was some sort of trick. She finally said with a sigh, "All right. Grand. Let me see this fifty."

Adaku reached into her shoulder bag, more a carrier for groceries than a secure container for her possessions. She brought out an envelope, half crumpled, with a coffee ring on it. She opened it and took out the money, which the other grasped quickly between her fingers. Fifty pounds did not comprise many notes. Still, the woman made much of counting it.

She looked up and said shrewdly, "Five minutes. It will be two hundred fifty more if you want anything from me *other* than five minutes of my time."

Adaku wondered how she was going to come up with two hundred and fifty pounds while still keeping her plans a secret. She also wondered what it would gain her, when all she actually wanted was allowance to step into the inner sanctuary above the erstwhile Kingsland Toys, Games, and Books. She said, "What will I receive for this three hundred pounds I'll be giving you?"

The other woman frowned. "Receive?" she asked. "I've no idea what you're talking about."

"Is it a deposit, this money?"

"For what? This is a women's health clinic. We care for women's physical problems. We're paid to do so. When you got the additional funds, we'll see you. Bring your medical records along."

"Why do you need them?"

"You want a medical service, don't you? Isn't that why we're talking? Or is there some other reason?"

"It's the matter of paying so much in advance."

"Well, I can't help with that. It's how we do things."

"But will you guarantee—"

"Listen to me. You just used up your five minutes, and we're not speaking of anything further standing here on the pavement. You gave me fifty pounds. You can top that up to three hundred when you have it."

Adaku felt the sweat on her back. It was dripping to her waist. But she nodded. Then she said to the woman, "I don't know your name."

"You don't need to know it. You won't be writing me a cheque."

"What do I call you, then?"

The woman hesitated. Trust or distrust. She finally chose. She dug a card from her bag and handed it over. "Easter," she said at last. "Easter Lange."

25 JULY

Mark Phinney was awakened by Pietra's voice. She was murmuring darling, darling, darling, and these words had intruded on his dream: her finally willing body beneath his, and himself so ready that his bollocks ached. But as he swam to full consciousness, he realised the aching bollocks had to do solely with his morning erection, and Pete's words came from the baby monitor as she talked to Lilybet in the next room. As he lay on his side beneath a single sheet—the thin blanket having been kicked off sometime during the night's unremitting heat—Pete began to sing quietly. His wife had a genius for making anything into a song. She never used the same tune twice, and she managed to make up rhymes on the fly.

He could tell from the accompanying sounds exactly what Pete was doing as well: changing out Lilybet's oxygen tank, after which she would see to her nappy. He remained in bed till the nappy song began, at which point he threw off the bed sheet and rose as Pete sang gaily: "Oh we've got a stinky mess, yes we do, yes we do . . ."

Mark smiled in spite of himself. He so admired her. His wife's devotion to Lilybet had never wavered in the ten years of their little girl's life. She was attentive, educated, and unceasing in her efforts to help their daughter, especially to give her more of a life than the mess of her birth had condemned her to. He was sick at heart about what amounted to his own devotion to the girl.

His mobile chimed on the bedside table. He saw it was a message from Paulie: *Beer tonight, Boyk?* He thought about what *beer* was probably a euphemism for. He replied with, *Need to be here. But ta.* Paulie replied with an emoji thumbs-up.

Mark stared at the mobile's screen for too long. He realised afterwards that if he'd set the smartphone back on the table, he'd have been safe. No chain of thoughts leading his mind in the wrong direction and therefore no temptation. But he wasn't fast enough. Both were instantly there: thought and temptation. He scrolled through his contacts to one of three that had numbers with no name given. He tapped the message *thinking of u.*

He waited for a reply. He wondered if it was too early. In a minute, though, the chime signalled and he looked down to see that there was a link. He tapped on this to hear their song, although he knew the entire idea of their having a "song" was completely mad. Except . . . this one's refrain was so dead apt—"No, I don't wanna fall in love . . . with you"—in a voice so deep and mellow the song sounded more like a meditation.

Mark understood why she'd sent it. Her heart ached as his heart ached, and their pain described the complete impossibility of their situation. He closed his eyes as he listened to the song, mobile pressed to his ear.

He was thinking about how to respond when, "Mark, is it work?" Pietra had come into the bedroom.

He swung to her and saw that she must have been up and about for quite a while as she was fully dressed: blue jeans, trainers with no socks, a white T-shirt. He called it her uniform, and it altered only in cooler weather, when the white T-shirt became a white dress shirt, usually with the cuffs rolled up. When he told her to buy something new and different for herself, she responded with the same declaration. "I don't *need* anything else, love," which was more true than false in that she rarely left the flat and when she did, it was most often with Lilybet in her heavy chair, the emergency oxygen on its stand behind her. If the subject of dinner out or taking in a film came up—just the two of them, and Greer could stay with Lilybet for a few hours, couldn't she?—the response remained the same. I do so hate to ask her, Mark. She already does so much.

Pete said again from the doorway, "Mark? Is it work?" and he realised he hadn't replied the first time round.

He said, "Meeting today in Westminster," which was actually true, and with inverted air commas he added, "Someone thought I needed reminding."

She smiled fondly. "That will be the day, eh?"

When she started to leave the room, he saw she'd got some of Lilybet's poo on her shirt. He said her name and nodded at it. She looked down and exclaimed, "Good Lord, how disgusting!" with a laugh as she hurried to the bathroom to wash it off.

He could hear Lilybet on the baby monitor. He could tell that she was manipulating the mobile that hung above her hospital bed. In a moment the television began to blare. She cried out, startled. He called to his wife, "I'll see to her," and yanked his trousers up. He went to their daughter's bedroom.

It wanted a good airing, and he opened the window onto The Mothers Square, which was actually oval-shaped, not quadrangular, and reminiscent in a very down-market way of the Royal Crescent in Bath. A car's engine coughed among those parked between the line of pergolas in the oval's centre, and Mrs. Neville came dashing outside, waving her husband's lunch bag. She ran to the car, the window was lowered, she ran back inside, clutching her dressing gown at its throat.

Mark turned back to the bedroom. With the hospital bed, Lilybet's massive wheelchair, the oxygen tanks, the chest of drawers, and his father's old recliner, there was very little space in which to move. Much of it was taken up with extra nappies, the pail for used nappies, and all the other accoutrements of having an infant. Except, of course, Lilybet wasn't an infant but rather a child who would only grow bigger, the single constant that defined her parents' lives. She couldn't speak, although she could both see and hear. She couldn't walk, although she could move her legs. He had no clue whether she understood him when he spoke to her, so he made it enough for himself every day that she seemed to know who he was.

She cooed as he approached her bed. He bent over her and, fresh nappy in hand, wiped her face. He said, "Up?" and she gurgled. He raised the bed. He said, "So what's planned for today, little one? Birthday party? Trip to the zoo? Madame Tussaud's to see the wax people? Library? Shopping for a party dress? Girls your age have birthday parties. Have you been invited to any? Who do you want to come to yours? Esme? Esme would love to come."

A coo in reply. He smoothed her wispy hair behind her ears and allowed himself a moment of what-ifs. These were so much more welcome than the what-will-bes. The what-ifs were sad, but that was all they were. The what-will-bes were terrifying.

"I'm so sorry." Pete spoke from the doorway, where she was pressing a hand towel to her T-shirt where the poo had been.

He looked up from their daughter and caught the expression on his wife's face, which told him she'd heard his words to Lilybet. "It's not anyone's fault," he said.

"Except she's not an it. Not to me."

He straightened from the bed. "You know I didn't mean Lilybet."

She looked at their daughter, then back at him. "I do know," she admitted. She dropped her hand and her shoulders sagged. "I'm sorry. There're moments when I just want to say something hateful. I don't know where that comes from."

"This is hard. You're owed," he told her.

"*You're* owed. I've lost the part of me that you loved."

"That's not true," he said, although they both knew it was. "We've got a rough path here, Pete. That's all this is. No one's to blame."

"I wouldn't blame you if you *were* to blame." She came fully into the room. She joined him at the hospital bed's raised rail, and she curved her fingers round this as she gazed at their daughter. Lilybet seemed to be studying them, although her eyes didn't appear to be focused properly. Mark found himself wondering what it was she saw. Pete went on with, "You've been saddled with both of us, haven't you."

He'd heard this remark so many times before. There were a hundred and one answers to give but there was only one that she wanted to hear. He said, "I couldn't do without my two ladies right here and there's an end to it, eh? Have you had breakfast?"

"Not yet."

"Shall we have something, then?"

Her gaze went automatically to their daughter. He quelled his impatience and said gently, "She can do on her own for fifteen minutes, Pete. She does longer than that at night." But not much longer, he realised. Pete was up and down all night, checking on her, terrified that her breathing would stop while her mother slept, no matter the alarm that would begin to blare and the supplemental oxygen they could easily supply if Lilybet stopped breathing.

Pete said, "Let me check on her, then. You go ahead. I'll be there in a moment."

He knew she would already have checked her before she'd left the room a few minutes earlier, but he said nothing. She couldn't help herself. She had to record something—anything—on the clipboard at the end of the bed. He hadn't looked at it when he entered the room and walked to the window, but he hadn't needed to. It was a monument both to Pete's sense of responsibility and to the guilt she carried for what had happened to their daughter. And this despite the fact that none of it was her fault. Pete was culpable only for being human, for wanting the best for Lilybet, the best for their marriage, and the best for him. The fact that all of this was far too much for her was merely a twist of fate.

He acceded to her wishes and went to the kitchen. He pulled three cereal boxes from the cupboard and chose one at random. He fetched the milk. He didn't feel like eating, but he knew he had to go through the motions. If he didn't, Pete would see it as a useful ploy to eat nothing herself. And God knew she needed to eat. She was virtually skeletal.

He ate standing, leaning against the draining board, listening to Pete explaining to Lilybet where Mummy was going and how long she would be and after that, "Mummy's going to give you a bath, darling, a *proper* bath. I cleaned you up but when one poos in a *certain* way, more is required. *You* know what I mean, my love." Which, of course, Lilybet did not and never would and what the hell were they going to do when she hit puberty because facing that was going to be like—

His mobile chimed. He looked at the message. *Tough morning?*

A bit, he replied.

It was a quite long moment before she sent him, *I'm so sorry. U have my heart.*

He wanted more than that, though. He wanted all of her and all of the life they could have if his life were not impossible. *See you soon* was all he could give her.

Soon was the limit of what she was willing to give to him.

"Paulie this time?" Pietra was in the doorway. Mark wondered what she'd managed to read on his face. She smiled. Was it warm or determined? He could no longer tell. "I expect he's offering a beer after work."

"Ah. That's our Paulie," he said.

"Please go. I can handle things here. Greer's coming to have our book talk this evening anyway. I'll ask her to bring along some Chinese."

"I'm out enough as it is, Pete."

"You aren't, at all. You need to be good to yourself, Mark. You can't be good for us if you're not good for you."

"And isn't that the pot and the kettle?"

"It sounds like, but I'm truly fine."

But she wasn't fine. Both of them knew how long it had been since she'd been anywhere close to fine.

He said, "Well . . . an hour, p'rhaps. But only an hour."

"Make it two at least," she replied.

CHELSEA
SOUTH-WEST LONDON

Deborah St. James had drawn a stool to the central chopping block-cum-table in the basement kitchen, and there, she was slowly going through the first set of portraits she'd taken at Orchid House to find the best representation of each of her subjects. She jotted the occasional reference number on a legal pad as well as on a printout of the lengthy transcribing she'd done over the past several days. Behind her, her father was banging round the kitchen as he put together breakfast, while on the worktop next to the cooker a smallish television was broadcasting the morning's news. She was giving idle thought to asking a question about why the word *news* when applied to television generally meant something bad was happening, when her husband joined them, accompanied by Alaska, their great grey cat. In a corner, Peach had been dozing in her basket—preparing herself for a determined round of begging for bacon—but sensing the feline presence, she lifted her head and narrowed her eyes.

"Don't even think of it," Simon told the dachshund even as Alaska teased the poor dog by sashaying—as only a cat can do—in front of her basket while waving his tail like a country's flag in a parade of Olympic athletes.

Peach growled.

Deborah said, "He's tempting her, Simon. You can see it yourself."

"Stay where you are," Simon told the dog. He scooped the cat from the floor and deposited him by the door to the garden. Alaska made use of the flap, after which he made use of the outdoor window sill and leapt up to it, gazing solemnly into the kitchen.

"Eggs done how, you two?" Joseph Cotter asked.

"Boiled for me," Deborah told her father as Simon replied, "No time, I'm afraid."

"What d'you mean 'no time'?" Cotter demanded. "At this hour? It not gone half seven. *And* we've not yet seen to your leg."

Deborah glanced at her father. He could cope with Simon's ir-regular mealtimes but not with his missing a session that dealt with the atrophying muscles of his damaged leg.

"It can't be helped today."

"Where're you heading so early, then?"

"Middle Temple. I've a meeting. Sorry."

Cotter harrumphed. Simon came to Deborah's side and gazed at the photo she was studying. "That's a gorgeous piece," he noted.

"You're my husband. You're meant to think it's gorgeous," she replied.

". . . gone missing from her home in north-east London and fears are rising . . ."

They both swung round. Cotter had used the remote to turn up the sound on the news, which was showing the photograph of a pretty, young mixed-race girl—little more than a child—with gold studs in her ears and her hair in miniature twists. She wore a school uniform and an impish smile. On the bottom of the screen *Boluwatife Akin—Missing—Boluwatife Akin—Missing* ran across in a banner.

"What's this, Dad?" Deborah asked.

He waved her off as the newsreader went on to ". . . did not return from the Yoruba Cultural Centre where she had attended her weaving class. She is the daughter of barrister Charles Akin and Dr. Aubrey Hamilton, an anaesthesiologist closely associated with Doctors Without Borders. Their daughter—who's called Bolu by her friends and relations—was last seen entering Gants Hill underground station at half past seven last evening in the company of two adolescents, a boy and a girl. They were documented by CCTV inside the station and once again aboard the westbound train. They debarked prior to Ealing Broadway, and film from CCTV in all the stations prior to that is being inspected. If we can have a look at the film that we have . . . ?"

The CCTV from Gants Hill underground station appeared on the television screen. It was, as usual, grainy. Also as usual, it rendered the film's subjects unrecognisable to anyone who did not know them personally. This was followed by another grainy film in which three individuals—who appeared to be the same as those in the previous film—sat side by side in one of the carriages of the westbound train. The child was between the adolescents. She didn't appear to be under duress, but considering the nature of the film, it was difficult to tell.

The newsreader concluded with, "Anyone with information about Bolu Akin should contact the Metropolitan Police at the number now appearing on your screen. Once again, her parents—Mr. Charles Akin and Dr. Aubrey Hamilton—are asking for her safe return."

The screen altered, showing a mixed-race couple on the front steps of what was apparently their home. The woman was holding a framed photo of the girl, this time wearing a red jersey and a striped summer skirt. The man had his arm around his wife. Their faces reflected both their fear and their anxiety.

Aubrey Hamilton said, "Please don't hurt her. She's our only child. She's very young for her age and very innocent. We will do anything to have her back with us. Please contact the police. Anyone at all with information please, *please* ring the police."

The picture then went to the two regular presenters of the programme, ensconced on their peacock-blue sofa, for their comment. Cotter muted it. He said to Deborah, "Never said, did I, but every day you went off to school . . . ? I worried something'd happen to you, jus' like that."

"How could anything at *all* have happened?" Deborah replied. "You walked me there and you walked me back at the end of the day. Someone would've had to hit you over the head with a polo stick to get to me."

"Not a laughing matter, girl. And *then* off you went to photo school in America when you could've stayed right here in London, eh? And how much of a worry was *that*? There you are in the land of guns-for-all-and-all-for-guns. Anything could've happened. So I worried, which is 'bout ninety percent of what a parent does."

Deborah didn't ask what the other ten percent was, nor did she mention that worrying as a parent was probably not ever going to be part of her life, no matter how she would have welcomed the opportunity.

Cotter went on with, "And *now* we got child sex trafficking and perverts on street corners. You ask me, it's an ugly world, it is, and it's getting uglier."

"On that excessively happy note," Simon put in, "I'm off." He kissed Deborah on the forehead and began to turn.

She grabbed his arm, saying, "Be a proper husband, please."

He kissed her mouth, saying, "You taste of chocolate."

"Dad's already been to the bakery. *Pain au chocolat.* You know I must have it once a week. Will kill for it if necessary."

"Let's hope it doesn't ever come to that."

He kissed her again and headed for the doorway to the garden steps as Cotter called out, "Turbot for dinner?" and Deborah added, "We can eat in the garden, under the tree."

Simon said, "Peach will doubtless be wildly in favour of that."

He left them, then, and they heard him climb the steps. He would cross the garden and go through the gate to access the garage on Lordship Place. Inside, the true love of his life sat parked: an antique MG TD, altered to accommodate his need for a hand-operated clutch.

Cotter said, "Wish he'd get rid of that motor, I do."

"Whyever?" Deborah said, looking again at the portraits she'd taken.

"Safety features," was Cotter's reply. "He doesn't need a second car crash. The first was bad enough. An' I don't like it when he skips his sessions on the leg."

Deborah said, "Hmmm. Well, if that's the biggest of your worries, I expect you're actually quite a happy man."

"An' what about you, girl?"

Deborah tilted her head to consider the idea. "I expect I'm as happy as I make myself be."

Her father put eggs, bacon, and toast in front of her. Alerted, Peach decamped from her basket and approached, tail wagging enthusiastically. Cotter said, "I know what'll make this one happy, I do."

"Don't you dare," Deborah said.

RIDLEY ROAD MARKET
DALSTON
NORTH-EAST LONDON

It was midday when Monifa turned into Ridley Road. She could feel the pavement through the soles of her sandals, so blazingly hot it was.

There'd been former potholes filled with tarmac along her route from Mayville Estate, and in the searing sun the tarmac was going soft. There was no breeze and, in the sky, not a cloud to be seen. In the market, a few electric fans were whirring, extensions on their flexes running into nearby shops. But they provided relief only to those who stood directly before them, having sweated through their clothing.

As if impervious to the temperature, the stalls and barrows were colourful as always: the peppers red, the plantains green, the bananas yellow. There were pyramids of ripe tomatoes, Puma yams lined up like removed appendages, aubergines so shiny that they looked artificial, strawberries, blueberries, and leafy greens. The air was awash with battling scents: turmeric and garlic, clove and parsley, incense and offal. Here was palm oil, there was boxed *fufu*: flour, plantain, cassava, and cocoyam. Meat was on offer from butcher shops like Abeo's and from stalls: every kind of meat someone would ever want. Cows' legs? Right. Goat's head? Yes. Tripe, heart, liver, kidney? They were available. Just point out what you want and someone will wrap it for you for tonight's dinner.

There were also takeaway food stalls selling crab claws, rice, and chicken. All with chips and each one for a fiver.

And then the music. It blared at such a volume that anyone wishing to have a conversation had to shout or duck inside one of the shops and close the door. These lined the street on both sides, directly behind the stalls: Ghana Food Store, Boboto from the Congo, Into Africa Groceries Etc., Rose Ebeneezer Afro Hairstylist. There were establishments where one could have eyebrow threading done, places for waxing any part of the body one might wish to wax, shops selling fashions, bakeries selling naan, both shops and stalls selling meats and fish.

Simisola's destination was normally Cake Decorating by Masha, a bakery that extended the length and breadth of the upper storey of The Party Shop. She earned money there to contribute to the family pot: setting up for classes and cleaning everything afterwards. But a stop there had told Monifa that there were no cake decorating classes today, so she headed to Talatu's Fashions for the Head, which was situated dead in the middle of the market. Simi also earned money from Talatu, supplying her with ready-made head wraps in various styles, and Monifa had learned that her everyday turbans had been popular for the entire season. Indeed, several customers had placed specific requests, Talatu informed her: two more ready-made turbans using the lion pattern and three more of the material featuring lilies.

Simi had been there, Talatu told her. She'd collected her money and headed off in the direction of the hair salons. "Wants a braided bob, was what she tol' me," Talatu said. "Saving up her money for extensions, she says. Try Xhosa's Beauty. I seen her there las' week."

So that was where Monifa took herself next, and that was where she found Simisola. She also found two stylists. One of them was a gum-popping mixed-race woman with long plaits that flowed from cornrows and were held away from her face in a ponytail. She wore a bright red pencil skirt and a blouse with a neckline showing far too much cleavage. The other stylist—also a woman and for that, at least, Monifa could be thankful—was African head to toe in a complicated bright orange head wrap and a loose-fitting dashiki print tunic. Beneath this, she wore dashiki trousers in a contrasting print, and she'd decorated herself with wooden bracelets that clacked together as she moved, and four beaded necklaces. She was much more acceptable to Monifa than the other woman, save for being heavily made up, to include false eyelashes and deep red lipstick. As she worked, she drank from a glass that appeared to be holding champagne.

Everywhere there was clutter and smell. The clutter existed at the two workstations, inside a glass display case, on the counter with the till, on the windows where handbills were posted on virtually every inch of glass, and in the dozens of photographed hair styles, each one more complicated than the last. The smell came not only from the products being used but also from the fish in a stall not far from the door to Xhosa's Beauty. The fishmonger was pouring more ice onto the seafood, but he was fast losing his battle with the heat.

Simi was watching the red-skirted woman with complete absorption, so she did not see her mother in the doorway until Monifa said her name and added, "Talatu told me where I might find you. What are you doing here?"

Simi spun to the doorway. She said brightly, "Mummy!"

"What are you doing in this place, Simi?" Monifa asked once again. "If Masha has no work for you, you're meant to come home straightaway."

"Oh, I like to watch. I'm saving up for extensions, Mum. Tiombe's going to do a bob for me. Here, let me show you the colours. They're ever so pretty."

Tiombe, it seemed, was the ponytailed, mixed-race woman. She gave Monifa a nod and gave the other stylist a glance in which they exchanged some message that Monifa could not interpret and did not want to. For her part, Simi grasped a sample of hair extensions with colours woven into them and held up one that was shot through with pink.

"See? Mum, isn't it pretty?"

"You must speak to your father about this," Monifa said. When Simi's face altered, Monifa tried to change her tone, attempting to sound encouraging despite knowing there was little hope of Abeo's ever agreeing to his daughter's plans. "Come with me now, Simi," she added. "I must speak to you."

"But sometimes Tiombe lets me help, Mum."

"Today that will not be the case. Come."

Simi cast a look at Tiombe, who inclined her head in the direction of the door. The other stylist nodded at Monifa and said, "Nice to make your—"

But Monifa had stepped away and Simi followed her. They strode from the market, passing Talatu, then Abeo's butcher shop with the fishmonger's stall out front, then Cake Decorating by Masha, then they were at last in the High Street. Once there, however, Monifa paused. She hadn't thought through where to take Simi for the talk they needed to have. She'd only been intent upon finding her.

She looked left and right, rejecting the shopping mall and ultimately settling on McDonald's. It wasn't an establishment she would ever frequent, but the day was so hot that any place with air-conditioning was a haven. She led her daughter there and directed her to a table inside, far from the noise of diners, of ordering, of numbers being announced, and of the tills. At all of this, Simi's face showed her surprise. She knew that her mum would never have brought her here unless she absolutely had to. It wasn't a place the family stopped in, at least on the few occasions when they were out as a family. Out and about with Tani in times past, Simi doubtless had been the purchaser of more than one baked apple pie.

Monifa asked her daughter what she would like. Simi blinked. She sucked in on her lip in that way she had, which ended up with her two front teeth showing. She said that if she could have a cheeseburger . . . ? When Monifa said of course she could, Simi added French fries and a Coke.

Monifa went to order, returning to the table with a handful of paper napkins. She took from her bag a small bottle of spray sanitiser and used it liberally on the surface of the table. She wiped this off with the napkins, fished out a packet of sanitising wipes, and used these on the chairs. She used another one on her hands and gave one to Simi for the same purpose. When she was satisfied, she nodded at the chairs and both of them sat.

Monifa folded her hands. She considered the best way to begin. She wondered if she should wait for the food. She decided that, as there was much to say, she ought to make a start. She began in a voice she kept quite low, saying, "You are approaching nine years old. What do you know of becoming a woman, Simi?"

Simi frowned. Clearly, she hadn't been expecting this. She slid her gaze to the street and then back to Monifa. She said, "Lim's mum told her about babies and Lim told me."

Monifa felt alarm race along her spine. Four years Simi's senior, Lim had been Simi's only Nigerian friend in Mayville Estate, but for weeks they hadn't spoken of her. "What did Lim say?"

"That a girl can't have babies till she's a woman and a man puts his thingy inside her somewhere. We couldn't work out where, me an' Lim, except Lim said babies come out of a woman's stomach, so I said maybe the man puts his thingy in her mouth cause that's where food goes to get into her stomach as well."

"Did Lim not tell you she'd become a woman?"

Simi shook her head, but she looked intrigued, which was very good. "Is that why she's gone to her gran's for summer hols?" she asked Monifa. "She *will* come home, won't she?"

Monifa answered the only way she could. "I do not know and her mother has not said. But I *do* know that Lim had begun her bleeding and you will also, not so very far into the future. It's the bleeding that says your womanhood has arrived."

"Bleeding?" Simi asked. "Mum, Lim was *bleeding*? But how . . . ?"

A number was called. Monifa went for Simi's food. For herself, she'd purchased nothing. She had no appetite for this sort of thing. She set the tray on the table, removing each item and placing it in front of her daughter on three paper napkins that she opened to serve as protection against the table she'd already cleaned. She nodded at Simi to eat. Her daughter took a French fry and nibbled on it.

Monifa spoke quietly, bending towards Simi so that no one could overhear. Home would have been a better place to talk about this, but the truth was that she couldn't risk it. "When a girl bleeds between her legs—which she does monthly when she reaches womanhood— her body is speaking to her, saying that she's ready."

"For babies?"

"Yes. But *until* there are babies, she prepares herself to grow them, and she also prepares herself for the man who will plant them in her."

Simi had picked up her cheeseburger but she didn't take a bite. Instead, she said, "Mummy, I don't want babies. Not now. Really, Mummy. I don't."

"Of course not. Not yet," Monifa told her. "That comes much later for a girl, after she is able to declare herself both pure and chaste. In Nigeria, this usually happens in her village. But for us—for our family—it is more complicated."

Simi finally took a bite, but first she said, "Complicated? Why, Mummy?"

"Living apart from our tribal village means that we must *declare* ourselves Yoruba. And this happens through an initiation. A ceremony must be performed to take you into the Yoruba tribe. Then, after the ceremony, you will be able to meet your aunts and uncles and cousins."

Simi's small brow furrowed as she took this in. She thought about it and finally said, "Oh. You mean I have to be really and *truly* Yoruba, so that I can meet them."

"This is exactly what I mean."

"Mummy, is that why we never see our family in Peckham? Because I'm not part of the tribe yet? But *you're* part, aren't you? And Papa? And Tani?"

"We are part because we were born there, all three of us. Being born there makes things different. As to Peckham, we will go for a visit once you're made pure. Would you like that, Simi? You would be so welcomed by your cousins."

"I would ever!"

"Then that shall happen when you are ready." Monifa tucked an errant bit of hair into the scarf Simi was wearing like a headband. "There will be a grand celebration. You will be the guest of honor, and people will come to celebrate your womanhood and to bring you presents and money. Only when you are ready, though."

"I am!" she cried. "Mummy, I am!"

"Then we shall make it happen. But you and I, Simi . . . ? We must keep the initiation a secret between us until everything is arranged and the clothing is purchased and the cake is ordered, and the food is chosen. Then it will be a surprise for your father and for Tani and for everyone who has not yet met you. Can you keep all of this a secret?"

"I can! I can!"

27 JULY

Tani had learned about Simi's "initiation" from Simi herself, the very night of the day when Monifa had revealed it to her. He didn't know what the hell she was talking about, so he barely attended to her chatter until the next evening when she was fairly bursting with more exciting information. She first swore him to secrecy, saying, "Cos I'm really not s'posed to tell *anyone*." But everything was to happen soon, she said, now that she was—in her words—"almost becoming a woman." She wasn't altogether sure *when* the initiation would occur and she couldn't 'member *everything* Mum said, but there *would* be an initiation—"It's a ceremony, Tani!"—and then lots of people would come for a celebration. There would be gifts for her, and food and drink for everyone and even music and prob'ly dancing. Mummy was taking her to Ridley Road Market to find some suitable clothes for the celebration, Simi had informed him. And Mummy said she—Simi—could choose *everything* all by herself.

"She tol' me you didn't get initiated," Simi said, which was the moment when he started to listen to her even more closely. "She said when someone's born there like you, they're automatic'ly Yoruba. Which is sad cos I expect you didn't get to have a party, did you."

Tani had never heard the word *initiated* used in reference to anything Nigerian. He asked her what the bloody hell she meant and she reported additional details of what their mother had told her. There was a lot of it and most of it was rubbish: not being Yoruba unless you were born on Nigerian soil, becoming a woman, becoming a pure and chaste woman, never having seen their family in Peckham in all these years *because* one had to be pure *and* initiated into the tribe in order to meet them. A ceremony would make all this happen, followed by a party, and new clothing. And course, there would *not* be babies till one was ready to have babies . . . Tani's head felt stuffed with explosive cottonwool by the time his sister had finished her recitation.

He decided, however, not to confront their mother at once. He decided to wait in order to see how—or even if—this whatever-the-bloody-hell-it-was progressed. As things turned out, that did not take long.

The afternoon after that conversation with Simisola, while he was working at Into Africa, Tani saw his mother and sister browsing in Ridley Road Market. He wasn't affected by the sight of them. Monifa came to the market often for the African food—especially greens and spices—that she couldn't get in the local supermarket, and Simi frequently dropped by with a delivery of ready-made head wraps and turbans for Talatu's stall. But during that evening, he began to see their trip to the market in a different light when Simi—bouncing with excitement on her bed—announced that she and Mum were "getting things ready."

"Let me show you, let me show you, let me show you," she sang.

He was on his bed, earphones on, listening to Idris Elba read *A Prayer Before Dying,* when Simi finally secured his attention. It was towards the end of the novel and Simi's interruption wasn't welcome, so he was irritated when he said, "Hey! Squeak, I'm listening. You c'n see that, can't you?"

Her face altered. He felt immediately guilty. She did that to him. He said, "Okay. Sorry," and removed the earphones. "What d'you need?"

"I want to tell you and show you," she said. "It's really good, Tani. You won't be sorry."

He put the earphones on his bedside table next to his iPad and said, "Tell and show away. I'm all yours."

She brought two shopping bags from her part of their shared clothes cupboard. She emptied the contents onto her bed in a jumble of colour as she chatted away, saying, "Part's a big secret. Mum made me promise. But I c'n show you *this*. You must look, Tani. See what Mum bought me. It's all so pretty!"

He roused himself from the supine position he'd been in, swinging his legs to the floor and joining his sister at her bed. She was sorting through items, and he saw among them two head wraps, three colourful wrapper skirts, four bright shirts, and a tangle of African jewellery: necklaces of wood and beads, earrings fashioned from seeds and pods, bracelets, two brooches of bone. His first thought was, What *is* this shit? His second thought was, Why's she got all this crap meant for grown women?

It got worse when she dumped onto the bed a variety of makeup and the brushes to apply it. Christ, did she even have false eyelashes? Lipstick as well? What the hell?

She was chattering and he'd failed to attend. He tuned in when she was saying, ". . . all decorated with *Congratulations, Simi!* on it. Plus we ordered balloons, Tani. Helium balloons! And best of all—the very extra special best—I'll have the money and Mum says I can spend it however I want. I'm having extensions braided in a bob. I want dark extensions with pink in them. Tiombe is going to do them. At

Xhosa's Beauty. I have to pay, an' it's a lot but . . . A bob, Tani." She sighed. "Just think!"

Tani felt a sinister rush flooding his body. He looked at everything, picked up a necklace, rubbed his fingers on the tatty fabric of one of the skirts. He said, "This is crap, this is. Why'd you want to wear it? Girls your age don't go about in shit like this, Squeak. It's for grown ladies, not for little girls."

She was silent for a moment. He knew he'd hurt her feelings, but hurting her feelings was beside the point. The point was the clothing, the jewellery, the makeup, and what the hell was going on.

"I won't be a little girl any longer," she said in a confidential tone. "I'll be a woman. That's what Mum says."

"Except you're not ready to be a woman. No eight-year-old can be a woman. Being eight years old is the *opposite* of being a woman, Squeak."

"I *will* be. Mum says. An' Easter tol' me how it happens. She said she gives me a jab that makes me a woman *and* makes me initiated into the Yoruba tribe."

"*Wetin dey happen?* Who the hell's Easter?"

"She's a lady Mummy took me to see. This is before we went to the market today. I wasn't s'posed to tell you. But I will. She put me on a table—did Easter—an' she checked my heart 'n' stuff an' then Mum came in an' held my hand an' then Easter looked at my . . . well, then it was over an' she told Mum three weeks an' Mum took me to the market to pick out clothes and the other stuff. D'you want to know about the cake? We haven't done the food yet, me 'n' Mum, but we talked to Masha about the cake. D'you want to know? I c'n tell you."

Tani was thinking too rapidly to follow all this, but he managed to nod as his mind continued racing. He barely heard:

"It'll be lemon. That's what I want. Lemon cake with chocolate icing and yellow letters for *Congratulations, Simisola!*. I think I want daisies on it as well. Mum said roses would be better but *I* said daisies an' I'm the one gets to decide. So maybe there'll be like a daisy chain round the whole cake and on the daisy petals there'll be sprinkles. Gold sprinkles are best, I think. Or maybe pink? I'm not sure yet."

Tani listened to all of this with growing confusion. He couldn't work out what his sister was really talking about, but it sounded to him like, for whatever reason, Monifa had spun a bizarre sort of web round Simi.

He decided to speak to his mother. The purchase of clothes and Simi's report about this Easter person made it more than time to have a conversation about his sister. The next morning, with Simi still asleep in her own bed across the room from his, he got up quietly, threw on jeans and a T-shirt, and went to find Monifa.

She was in the lounge, sorting through a very large mound of laundry. It didn't look like any of it belonged to them except several of his father's bloodstained shirts. The rest were clothes meant for small children along with articles of the kinds of women's clothing that Monifa would never allow herself to wear. She was, he concluded, taking in laundry. He wondered if this was his father's idea: more money for the family fund.

It was stifling in the flat. Monifa's wrapper was a longer one, tied at one side of her chest. It left her arms bare—which Abeo wouldn't like—but this was doing very little to cool his mother's body. She was sweating and also murmuring to herself. He couldn't catch what she was saying.

She didn't see him, so he watched her. He realised that he had no idea how old his mother was, and he would have to start from his father's age to work back to hers. What he did know was that she looked old to him. Although her face was unlined, everything about her—her posture, her movements, the way she held her head and worked her hands—suggested age.

"Who's Easter?" he said.

She started with a little cry, dropping the small T-shirts she was holding and gathering them and the rest of the laundry into a pile. "Tani! I did not see you. What is it you ask?"

"Who's this Easter that Simi's going on about?"

She didn't answer at first. Instead, she took a pillowcase up from the floor and began to stuff the children's clothing inside. When she had that done, she put the women's clothing in a separate pillowcase. Abeo's shirts she left where they were.

"What did Simi say?"

"She was telling me 'bout some daft 'initiation,' Mum. Easter's s'posed to help her be Yoruba now tha' she's becoming a woman. Those're her words, not mine. So who's this Easter and how's she helping an eight-year-old get to be a woman?"

Monifa gave a fond little laugh. "Oh goodness. Simi has become very confused."

"'Bout what? An' why the bloody hell does she think she's got to be 'initiated' to be Yoruba?"

"She said that?"

"There's some big ceremony in her future is what it is. She's got a pile of new clothes and jewellery. She showed it all to me. Then she went on 'bout this person Easter who's giving her a jab so she can be a woman. She said there's a ceremony and a celebration and why the hell di' you tell her she has to do all this in order to meet the family in Peckham when you bloody well know Dad will *never* let her or me or you meet them because that means he might lose power over us."

Monifa sat on the lumpy sofa. She gestured at a chair for Tani to sit as well. The last thing he felt like doing was sitting, but he cooperated. He flopped into his father's armchair and waited, fastening his gaze on his mother's face.

"There are things," she began.

"What things?" he demanded.

"Things that are of women, Tani. They are personal and difficult to explain to a child."

"Difficult to explain to Simi is what you're saying. So . . . ?"

"So I tell her a little story to smooth the way."

"The way to what?"

"The way to being examined for the first time. This is what Easter did. She listened to her heart and her lungs and then she looked to make sure everything was in order . . . inside Simi. Do you understand?"

"Her girl parts? Tha's what you mean?"

"Yes. Her girl parts."

"Why's an eight-year-old need her girl parts looked at?"

"As I said, Tani. It is important that a girl be right."

He took this in. He followed the path his mother was treading to its logical conclusion. "You mean you're checking to *see*, innit. You told her 'bout initiations and ceremonies but what you're in'erested in is if she can . . . Wha's the word Pa uses? Oh, yeah. *Abi*. Breed. So this Easter looked her over to make sure her parts are right. There's no jab and no initiation and no ceremony or anything else. There's just wanting to know can Simi breed."

Monifa said nothing. In her silence, Tani saw the truth.

"An' if she can, which is what you wanted to know, Pa can put her up for auction. He can take her to Nigeria, or he can put her face on a website, or he can what*ever*. He wants a big bride price for her, I wager, prob'ly more than he paid out for Omorinthesalad or whatever she's called. Tha's wha' this is all about. And you're goin to let it happen."

"This is *not* true."

"Yeah. It is. Why would it be anything *but* true? You're happy for him to buy some random virgin for me to plug, so why would I *ever* think you might do something, say something, or *be* something to stop him from finding some bloke with big money who likes the idea of buying himself an eight-year-old guaranteed to be learning from her mum how to be a proper Nigerian wife?"

"Tani, your father would *never*—"

"I don't wan' to know what Pa would or what Pa wouldn't. He's just a bloke thinking he can get away with whatever he wants. But you don't see that, do you? I jus' hope you wake up, Mum, before he wrecks all of our lives."

―――――

TRINITY GREEN
WHITECHAPEL
EAST LONDON

During her first photography sessions at Orchid House, Deborah had discovered that there were going to be a few stumbling blocks to her success with the project. Most notably, she learned that she wouldn't be allowed to begin photographing the girls until Narissa Cameron arrived. The girls didn't know her, they had no reason to trust her, so this was how it had to be. On this day, though, when Deborah entered the room with her equipment, only the girls and the filmmaker's associates were there. They were setting up for the day, and while Narissa's digital camera looked ready to go, Narissa herself wasn't present.

"She's down below," the sound technician told Deborah in answer to her unasked question. "She said she needed a word with Zawadi and that was . . . I dunno . . . thirty minutes ago? We're on the clock, so it doesn't matter to me or Elise here, but I don't know how long we can keep this lot waiting." She tilted her head towards the girls.

"I'll see if I can fetch her," Deborah said. She didn't want to lose a day of work, which she would do if the girls decided they'd waited long enough and drifted away.

She left the erstwhile chapel that Orchid House occupied at the far end of Trinity Green, a walled-in collection of seventeenth-century almshouses in Mile End Road. As she descended the chapel stairs, she caught a glimpse of an antique bloke watching her from a window in the nearest cottage along the green. She gave him a jaunty wave and, quick as that, he ducked away from the window. She went to a door that was tucked beneath the stairway and opened it. Here were the offices of Orchid House, among them the one belonging to Zawadi, Orchid House's brusque and rather intimidating founder.

Deborah wasn't anxious to interrupt whatever Zawadi and Narissa were doing, as the former had greeted her arrival for the first round of taking photos a few days earlier with a dislike she didn't bother to veil. "Let me tell you this, eh? I don't want some do-gooding, privileged white cow on this project at *all*," had been her greeting. "Jus' so you know, I want a Black photographer and I mean to find one and when I do, you're gone. You understand?"

Deborah's slowly spoken "Right," and her snappy "I don't blame you at all," had seemed to surprise Zawadi. But the surprise lasted only a moment, after which she narrowed her eyes and said, "Go take your bloody pictures, if you can."

It wasn't exactly the hearty vote of confidence and approval that she'd hoped for and she'd wondered at first if Zawadi's displeasure was something she intended to communicate to the girls. But that had not seemed the case, as once the girls had been given—from one of the adult volunteers—an example of what Narissa Cameron wanted from them in front of the camera, the project lurched forward, with Deborah photographing some of the girls while Narissa was filming others. Aside from Zawadi's marked dislike of her, there had been very little to impede Deborah's project until this morning.

"Two more days is what I can manage," was what Deborah heard as she approached Zawadi's office. "I'm sorry, Zawadi. It's just that I've a contract with my parents. As long as I stay clean, I can use the basement flat. If something violates that, upsets them, offends one of my sisters or my brother . . . ? Who *knows* what it will take? But if that happens, I'm out on the street. And then I'm done for."

"Just *talk* to them. Be up front, be above board, be whatever. They're reasonable people, yes?"

"I don't want to make things more difficult than they already are."

"Things're always difficult. Haven't you worked that out yet?"

Deborah coughed to alert them of her presence. She popped into the doorway. Zawadi was sitting behind her desk albeit shoved back from it in her wheeled office chair. She had adopted a position that indicated no compromise: arms beneath her breasts, no hands visible, stoic expression on her face.

"Sorry," Deborah said to them both. "We're ready above, Narissa. I'm a little concerned the girls might scarper. Everything all right?"

She knew as soon as she added that last bit that she shouldn't have, for Zawadi rolled her eyes and came back with, "'All right?' Really? When was the las' time things were all right for *any* of us?"

Narissa said firmly and—it had to be said—kindly, as if to make up for Zawadi's hostility, "Everything's fine. And you're right: I've got to see to my work. We can talk later, eh?" She directed this last to Zawadi. "If you'll make a few more calls in the meantime . . . Please. I can only do what I can do."

Zawadi huffed and turned her desk chair so that she didn't need to look at either of them. As she did so, Deborah followed Narissa to the stairs.

"Try to ignore her," Narissa said as they ducked outside and round the corner of the building to the stone steps up to the chapel. "She's been at this for over a decade, and she gets out of sorts when things aren't running the way she wants them to run."

"I suppose she's got a lot on her mind," Deborah noted. "I can understand."

Narissa halted, third step from the top. "Don't *ever* say that to her."

"What?"

"That you can understand. You can't. You don't. You never will." Narissa sighed, looking out over the summer-dead lawn that gave a

name to this place in other seasons. "You probably have good intentions. But what's bad in Zawadi's life . . . ? It's not something she can
take a holiday from, at least not in the way you probably can."

Deborah followed Narissa up the rest of the steps. The filmmaker
stopped again, this time at the entrance to the old chapel. Deborah
said, "What am I to say to her, then?"

"Clueless," Narissa said. "That's me, not you. Half the time *I* don't
know what to say to her, and at least I'm mixed race, so I've got an
advantage."

"I do know she wants someone else to take the portraits," Deborah
said.

"Sure. Can you blame her? I mean, no way is Zawadi going to make
like she's happy Dominique Shaw chose you. Doesn't make sense to
her. Doesn't make sense to me either. It's not like there aren't any Black
photographers in London. But Dominique's white and she thinks
white, which is to say most of the time she doesn't think at all because
she doesn't *have* to think. She never thought we might be better off if
we hired someone without marshmallow skin, no offence. She liked
your book, which meant you were the one to do the job. Zawadi tried
to argue the point before you ever came to the meeting *and* after you
left, but Dominique said, 'This is more important than political cor-
rectness, culture wars, and white privilege.' So here we are, after one
hell of an angry debate, by the way, during which Dominique learned
more than she probably considered possible about white privilege."

Deborah saw how the entire project—as envisioned by the
undersecretary—might have benefitted from having only Black people
affiliated with it. But she also thought about the size of the battle they
were mounting through Orchid House, through other organisations
like Orchid House, through Narissa's documentary, and through her
own photographic project. She said, "Could it be that Dominique's
intention is to enflame as many people as possible, from all races and
all walks of life?"

"Are you suggesting that Black people wouldn't be able to do that, that only a white project made by white people is capable of it?"

"That's not at all what I mean."

"No? Then *think* about what you're saying when you say it."

Deborah felt at a loss. She finally said, "I *do* want to help. Does she know that? Do *you*?"

"Oh. Right. You want to help. *Everyone* wants to help till it comes down to it and help is solicited. People say this is a righteous cause. Always. What else are they going to say? But words're nothing because when it's time to step forward or write a cheque, things turn different."

"I'm not like that," Deborah told her.

"Really?" Narissa sounded scornful, but she adjusted enough to say, "Well, at some point you'll probably have a chance to prove it."

That said, she entered the building, calling, "Who's ready to talk? Come to the filming room. Take a seat."

KINGSLAND HIGH STREET
DALSTON
NORTH-EAST LONDON

Adaku had rounded up the required two hundred and fifty pounds. She phoned the number from the card that Easter Lange had given her, made the long journey to Kingsland High Street again, and used the unmarked buzzer next to the door to ring the bell. When a disembodied voice demanded to know who was at the door, she said, "It is Adaku. I have the money."

The response was, "I don't know what you're talking about."

"Are you Easter?"

"If I am, that doesn't mean I know what you want." And she ended their exchange abruptly.

Adaku wondered what had gone amiss. She concluded that Easter was not alone. She wasn't sure if she was meant to wait or meant to come back another time. Then, some thirty seconds into her wondering, footsteps pounded towards the front of the building. Two deadbolts were released, the door cracked ajar, then swung open, and Easter stood in front of her, a white lab coat buttoned over her street clothes. She made no courteous preamble. Instead she said, "Show me."

"Once I'm inside. Not before."

Easter's eyes narrowed speculatively. She kept one hand on the knob of the door and her body blocked any attempt on Adaku's part to enter. She gave a slow and studied look round the area: across the street, windows and doorways on their side of the street, the same. She said, "Why are you really here? I have a very bad feeling about you." She looked beyond Adaku again. A street sweeper had rounded the corner, and he was desultorily removing debris from the gutter. Then back at Adaku, she said sharply, "You're the police."

Impatiently, Adaku shifted her weight from hip to hip. "Do I *look* like the police to you? What do you think? I'm an undercover agent who throws money round?" She rustled in her bag and brought out the envelope holding the cash. She said, "Here's the money you asked me to bring. Two hundred fifty pounds."

Easter glanced at it, on her face the expression of a woman who suspected that the notes were likely to explode into a shower of red dye if she put her fingers on them.

"Isn't this what you asked for?" Adaku said. "Two hundred fifty pounds?" When Easter still did not reach for the envelope, Adaku took the notes from it and fanned them in her face.

Easter looked over her shoulder in the direction of the stairs. Once again Adaku thought there must be someone above who was unaware of what was going on below. This had to be straight-out bribery.

Adaku added, "I can get a referral for you as well. It won't be easy, but I'll do it. If the money and the referral aren't enough for you, though, I will have to take my business elsewhere."

"It is five hundred pounds in total," Easter said. She snatched the envelope. She shoved it into the pocket of the white lab coat she was wearing, and said, "Two hundred more if you want to proceed."

"And if I do not wish that?"

"Are you asking if your money is then returned? No. It isn't. Not once you've stepped inside. So what's it to be? In or out?" She opened the door wider. With a curse beneath her breath about money she would lose if things went wonky, Adaku entered.

The foyer wasn't a great deal larger than a draughts board, with lino in a draughts-board pattern. It bore at least a week's worth of post lying round. Most of it appeared to be rubbish adverts.

Easter led Adaku towards the back of the building, where stairs were covered by dusty, threadbare carpet worn completely through in places. The handrail was sticky here and there and marked up by past encounters with furniture. Adaku touched it only briefly.

The first floor revealed one door, presumably to a flat. It wore a steel plate and had three deadbolt locks, although from the street the place had looked uninhabited. Easter led her past this and up another flight of stairs. Here a newish-looking door also possessed a steel plate and two deadbolts, along with a sign reading PRIVATE. Up the final flight of stairs, they came to a door standing open to a reception area furnished with a desk, its chair, two filing cabinets, and two additional plastic chairs against one of the walls, with a small table between them. This held a lamp, a woven grass basket containing miniature chocolate bars, and two dog-eared home decorating magazines. On the desk stood a computer's monitor along with two stacked in-and-out trays. Nothing was in them, and aside from Easter, there seemed to be no one present.

Adaku said, "I would like to speak to the doctor."

"You're speaking to the doctor," Easter told her.

"If that's the case, why is no one else here?"

"Procedures occur only as requested. Is that somehow important to you?"

Adaku frowned. This wasn't what she had expected. She said, "How do I know you *are* a doctor, then? How do I know you're qualified?"

"Because I've just told you. You can choose to believe me or you can go. It's all the same to me. Now, do you want to see the establishment for your three hundred pounds or was the climb up the stairs enough for you?"

Adaku considered her options, which appeared to be limited to losing her money or at least being shown the premises. She chose the second option. Easter led her to a room that opened off the waiting area.

To Adaku, it looked like every examination room in the country: exam table, scales, small credenza, the top of which held cotton wool, swabs, thermometer, rolls of gauze, a stethoscope, a sphygmomanometer, a speculum. Everything was pristine, not a smudge or a fingerprint anywhere. There was nothing on the walls save a chart that indicated the optimum weight for a particular height. In one corner was a chair upon which, Adaku assumed, the patient—or client, she supposed—left her clothing. In another corner a wheeled stool made it easier for the doctor to conduct examinations.

It was all very orderly, Adaku thought. Indeed, the room was considerably more orderly than her own GP's office. That told her a great deal.

Easter opened a second door, and this gave onto a small operating theatre, with lights, the necessary table, several large canisters—presumably for the purposes of anaesthesia—two monitors, and a credenza holding sterile gloves, instruments in cases, and everything else to suggest that medical procedures were conducted therein.

Adaku asked Easter who administered the anaesthetic. Easter said a nurse anaesthetist joined her as needed. "Do you want to see below?" Easter asked her. She didn't sound enthusiastic about showing Adaku anything else.

"What's below?"

"A recovery room. The patients remain overnight."

"Who stays with them?"

"Their mothers or another female relative. I check on them as well."

Adaku wondered at this. Easter appeared to be a woman-for-all-medical-seasons. Why, then, wasn't she working at a hospital instead of here, hidden away in a decrepit building in north London? She asked the question.

Easter said, "Because I believe in the work of this clinic."

But anyone could make that claim, Adaku thought. "Have you lost any patients?" she asked.

"Of course not."

"But that's what you would say, eh? You're hardly going to tell me otherwise."

Easter opened her hands and moved her shoulders in a way that said, Believe what you wish.

"Where do we go from here? I mean, after I see the recovery room."

"After that, you make your decision." Easter led the way out of the operating theatre and opened a drawer of the desk. From this she took a card, identical to the one she'd supplied earlier. Printed on it was only a telephone number. No name, no employment, just a phone number. She handed it to Adaku. "If you decide to go ahead, you phone that number for an appointment."

"Then?"

"You're given a date for the procedure. Two weeks after, there's another exam."

"It sounds very thorough," Adaku noted.

"It is. What is done here is always swift, hygienic, and without any danger of post-surgery infection."

"And if that happens? Some kind of infection?"

"Then you're better off having come here in the first place. I expect you're not looking for a butcher."

STREATHAM
SOUTH LONDON

She'd designated the Rookery for their meeting that evening. Part of Streatham Common, it was all that remained of a once-flourishing estate: a large house, and its gardens that had stood on a slope overlooking much of London. Part of the place was walled and formal: neat paths laid out, beds delineated, flowers and shrubbery thriving. Part of it was wild and wooded.

She'd told him she would meet him among a grove of juvenile chestnuts. They were easy enough to find, she said, as they stood on the north side of the Rookery at the end of a wide paved path that bisected the entire area. This path was sided by a long row of wooden benches set against each other cheek by jowl and facing a sloping lawn upon which an enormous cedar of Lebanon stood. There were steps down this slope, she'd told him, but don't use them. There will be no need. The chestnut grove is above.

Mark Phinney had waited ten hours to see her. When she hadn't been there as he'd ducked into the grove of chestnuts, the panic he'd felt had nearly—and stupidly—done him in. Foolishly then, he'd phoned her. Foolishly then, he'd texted her. Then, he'd cursed her. Then he'd cursed himself, his life, his desire, and everything that could be cursed save Lilybet. Lilybet, he told himself, did not deserve as a father the kind of man he was fast becoming. No. That last bit wasn't true, was it? She did not deserve the kind of man he *was*. He wanted to leap into his own head and scour his brain of every thought that did not have to do with his daughter. That, he decided, was the only solution to what was happening to him.

And then she was there. She came through the trees quietly, and as quickly as an act of magic, everything else was forgotten because she was his anchor and the better part of his soul. He began to kiss her. His abject hunger humiliated him.

But her need seemed to meet his. She removed her blouse and her bra and her breasts were what she offered. He squeezed her nipples till she moaned and then he took one into his mouth as her hands found his waist and his buckle and the zipper and God God God he shoved her against one of the tree trunks and freed his cock and grabbed her again and felt for her skirt and raised it raised it raised it but no she said no Mark no not yet let me and she knelt and took him into her mouth then she rubbed him between her breasts then into her mouth again then her breasts and he wanted to weep and he wanted to hurt her and he wanted to make her want him as much as he wanted her and she couldn't stop she must not stop she must never stop because for this entire day for every moment when he couldn't think because of this this *she* was what was waiting for him.

He gasped as the pleasure surged through him. He wanted to own her the way a man wants to own a woman in a moment like this.

She murmured against his cock. Was it good?

He was drained of tension. He was full of nothing, just the fact of her in his life.

She rose. She cradled his cheek. He kissed her palm and said, "Let me. I want to—"

She placed her slender index finger against his mouth. "Was it good?" she asked again.

He laughed softly. "What do you think?"

"I'm glad of it." Both her blouse and her bra lay discarded on the ground, and she picked them up. When he said, "No, don't," she shook her head. When he said, "Please. I just . . . All right. I'll only look. I swear. If you won't allow me . . . I've got to *see* you, at least."

"I can't," she told him. "The park will close soon. Someone will be along in a moment to make sure no one's locked inside."

He wondered if she'd set things up that way. This was the part of town where she lived. She would know where and at what time they could meet, the sort of place where the hour of the day allowed only what had just occurred between them. He said, "I've gone straight round the bend. You're all I think about. I can't do my job properly any longer. And I'm not going to be *able* to do it properly if we go on like this."

She was buttoning her blouse. The light was nearly gone. He couldn't see her face as well as he wished. She said, "Are you saying you won't be able to do your job unless you've had your penis inside my vagina?" She laughed sharply.

"This isn't a game," he said, and when she didn't reply, he added, "D'you know that I could have you right here if I chose to? Or I could show up one night at your flat. But I don't do that, do I? I let you set the rules."

"Do you mean you're owed something because of that?"

"You know that's not what I believe."

"Then what do you believe? What do you imagine? You come to my flat, force your way inside, I submit and we fuck—"

"Don't say it like that."

"—and then you go home to your wife and child and I'm left with what? Watering my plants? Is that how you see it?"

"Is this how *you* see it?" He gestured round the grove. "This feels . . . filthy is what it feels."

"And in my flat—perhaps in my bed?—it would feel less so? With your wife and your daughter at home while you and I are naked in a bed together?"

"Not *a* bed. *Your* bed."

"Which makes it less tawdry? My bed where at least we can control the freshness of the sheets?"

"I love you," he said. "It's killing me. There's nothing for me there. Pietra and I . . . there's nothing. Just Lilybet and even she . . . without you . . . Christ, I think I'm going mad. And with you not letting me be with you the way I want to be with you . . . ? That makes it all worse. Not better. *Worse*."

"Then we should end it."

"Is that what you want?"

She moved to him. She kissed him deeply, pressing against him. "I don't want either of us to make this into something we both end up regretting," she said.

"I won't regret anything. There *is* no regret for me. There's just this. Us. But I can't cope any longer with the way it's going."

He strode away from her, ducking beneath the chestnut branches to come out on the path above the slope of lawn. She was right about so many things, he thought. She was wrong about so many others. But they were caught, the two of them. They had been caught the very moment he found himself looking at her long, crossed legs—so smooth, they were—and then allowed himself to look at the rest of her, quite slowly, taking her in and wondering and imagining. Had there ever been a bigger fool? he wondered. Paulie's recommended way was also the way of wisdom: massage with benefits administered by a woman whose full name he would never know, let alone pronounce correctly. It was a business deal with nothing attached to it save money, while this was like a structure on fire, doing what unmanaged fires do: consuming everything in its vicinity.

He heard her emerge from the trees behind him. She took his hand. He raised hers to his face and pressed it to his cheek. They walked in silence, out of the Rookery and in the direction of Streatham Common. He said, "I don't know how to continue as we are because I can't see a life without you in it. I can't even imagine a life without you in it. What I have now is a life by halves, by quarters, even."

"Our life together—yours and mine—can only go so far," she said. "If it goes farther, we both face ruin. We have other people we must protect. Or at least you do. And I must also protect myself."

Of course she was saying only what both of them already knew. He could no more desert Pete and Lilybet than could he cut off his right arm without pain. Through no fault of their own, they needed him, and though he needed this woman standing next to him, his hands were as tied as his future was set.

They were halfway across the common when she said, "Over there," and indicated lights in the distance, across the wide and open space. "The Mere Scribbler," she said. "Let's end this evening with a drink at the pub and say goodnight. Just goodnight and nothing more."

He nodded agreement. No matter his wishes—and they were plenty—it was, in truth, the only plan that could be acted upon.

28 JULY

"*Wetin dey happen*, Monifa, that you not do what you are meant to do?"

Over the phone the voice came at her, as clearly as if her mother were standing in the very next room. Indeed, it came to her as clearly as it had done for months on end.

"How you expect her to marry, Nifa? You got no wish for it there, you send her to me. *Abi?*"

The words continued to ring in her ear long after Monifa ended the call. Her mother had phoned from her home in Nigeria, and while one would think that after twenty years of marriage and two children, one simply could not be pressured by one's mother into any kind of action, Monifa had been finding herself on the receiving end of such pressure from Ifede via phone at least once a week, sometimes twice for the last seven months. The subject matter was invariably the same: no matter she was only eight years old, Simisola had to be marriageable. And Monifa's mother wasn't the only woman saying this.

While she might have successfully fought off Ifede's oft-voiced concerns, Monifa was finding it difficult to do anything at all about the concerns of her mother-in-law. For Abeo's mother included Abeo himself in her harangues about Simisola, and "You want him to leave you, Monifa?" was generally where every conversation between Monifa and Folade both began and ended.

Easter Lange was the answer, but Monifa had not yet heard from her. She'd hoped for a cancellation in her upcoming schedule of appointments, but when she explained this first to her own mother and then to Abeo's, neither woman was mollified. From Ifede had come growing concern that began to border on tearful anxiety. "Simisola will be shunned. She will have no friends. You know tha', yes? She will never have a home of her own. She will get no *ozzband* to protect her, no chil'ren to care for her in her old age."

From Folade had come, "Women they bleed, they serve, they produce chil'ren, and then they die. That is what God intended, Monifa. That is why woman was created *out* of Adam, not Adam from Eve. Man came first. Man still come first. Woman's wants and needs get met through *ozzband*. Your mother she would have taught you this. If you not been pure, you think Abeo would pay the bride price your father ask?"

So Monifa had rung Easter Lange. Had there been a cancellation? she asked. If not, was there anyone on the schedule who might be willing to give up her place to Simisola? Surely there must be *someone* among everyone scheduled who would understand that Monifa Bankole had a critical need.

After speaking with her mother and her mother-in-law, Monifa rang Easter Lange yet again. She'd lost count of how many times she'd tried to reach the other woman. This time, she finally met with success, and when Easter answered, Monifa offered her a compromise. If Easter would give her—Monifa—the details of each client who had a future appointment at the clinic, she herself would ring every one of them and beg each one's willingness to allow Simisola to take the place of whomever they'd made the appointment for.

Easter said in a quiet, calm voice, "That in't possible, Mrs. Bankole. You're asking for confidential information, you are."

"Their numbers alone, then. Do not give me any names. Just the phone numbers. I will introduce myself to them. I will tell them that I do not know their identity. I will explain why my Simi must have an appointment. I will tell them to ring you if they are willing to give up their space for me."

Easter sighed. "Mrs. Bankole, this's something I can't do. It's a betrayal, it is. I wouldn't do it to you and no way can I do it to them."

"But you are the only one who can help me. Please, you must listen. Let me tell you why this is important."

"You got to try to understand . . ." Easter Lange's voice drifted off. She paused. This was followed by a long sigh. Then she said, "Right. Let me ring a couple 'f people, Mrs. Bankole. Not promising, mind you, but I'll try my best. Keep your phone nearby today."

"Oh thank you, *thank* you," Monifa said. "You do not know how important—"

"Right. I'll ring you."

CHELSEA
SOUTH-WEST LONDON

It was during a morning stroll with Peach that Deborah picked up a copy of *The Source.* Someone had left the tabloid lying on the bottom step of the stairs leading up to the blue double doors of what once had been Chelsea Town Hall. This was a distinguished place of Corinthian columns, dog-toothed cornices, double-hung windows, and a shallow balcony that would have done excellent service for the wily Duke of Gloucester waiting for the citizens' appeal to his royal blood. But it was now, dismally, what was referred to as an "event space," that event generally being an amateur art show, a jumble sale, or a fair offering either vintage clothing or dubious antiques. She'd left her father seeing to Simon's bad leg and Alaska seeing to his post-breakfast bath atop one of the window sills in the kitchen. With a good amount of time before she intended to leave for Whitechapel, she decided that walkies were in order.

Peach preferred the Embankment because she knew the route and hence its length and the time required for her to accompany Deborah before returning to the comfort of her bed and the hope of something edible falling to the floor. But Deborah preferred the sight of people to the rush of traffic, so she urged the dog in a crisscross to Old Church Street and from there up to the King's Road.

Peach took her time, naturally. Walking the dachshund was like attempting to walk a hoover: every inch of the route had to be sniffed and sorted. These things could not be rushed.

Deborah was grateful when she saw the tabloid. Peach's progress being more the tortoise and less the hare, along with her complete unwillingness to be hurried in any way, meant that her companion on the walk either needed the patience of Moses waiting for the Pharaoh to wise up or, better yet, had brought reading material or earbuds connected to soothing music. Deborah, alas, had neither, so *The Source* would have to do.

Thus she saw the front-page headline and its accompanying pictures. The tabloid was continuing to feature the disappearance of Boluwatife Akin as its main story. The concentration on this day, however, gave the reader copious background information on the girl's parents, revealing to the reader that Boluwatife had come into the world via IVF, and the girl's mother, Aubrey Hamilton, had undergone four rounds of the procedure to have the child. Her relations were coming forward to share further details. The child was the centre of her parents' lives, they said, she was a treasure, and her parents were devoted to her.

A sidebar accompanied this on page three, where the story continued. It revealed background on the girl's father, Charles. Born in Nigeria, he possessed a first-class degree in geography from Oxford. The veracity of this was examined, as was his time at Lincoln's Inn, where he'd completed his pupillage and where, at present, he was a barrister associated with an international chambers. He was high profile, according to the sidebar, within the field of civil law. Nothing he'd done in court was either controversial or glamorous. He was not flashy, and if he was said to have ambition, it was to take silk one day.

He'd spoken to a reporter about his daughter's disappearance, saying that he wanted to believe that Bolu was only lost in town somewhere. If not that, he wanted to believe that she was being held for ransom and, although he was not a rich man, if it was money that was wanted to bring Bolu back to them, he and his wife would find it. He wanted, in short, to believe *anything* that was not the worst fear a parent faces when a child goes missing.

Accompanying the story, both on the front page and on page three, were half a dozen pictures that the parents had handed over for publication: Bolu as an infant in her mother's arms, Bolu as a toddler gripping her father's fingers, Bolu perhaps six years old on the lap of Father Christmas, Bolu on her father's shoulders, Bolu on her mother's hip.

Deborah closed the tabloid, but she didn't toss it into the nearest rubbish bin. Instead, she took it with her.

Peach picked up the pace once she realised they were heading in the general direction of home. Home was where the treaties were. Home was where the bed was. Home was where that obnoxious feline dozed, just out of reach of fierce canine jaws.

It was the fact that Charles Akin was born in Nigeria that gave Deborah pause. She realised that she was tossing him into a basket in which he very well might not belong, but there were several considerations that the tabloid wasn't touching upon, and this seemed out of character in a paper known for its proclivity to dig up dirt and smear it across the face of anyone who might have earlier garnered the public's sympathy. England's tabloids had always lived by a single creed: build 'em up and tear 'em down. In other words, if a tabloid loved an individual highlighted by a front-page story, there was a virtual guarantee that the same individual would be vilified by that same tabloid within seventy-two hours.

With Peach safely at home and ready to doze, Deborah collected her equipment and set it by the door. She dashed up the stairs, where she found her husband just finishing the buttoning of a blazingly white shirt. He had on trousers, and the matching jacket lay on the bed along with a tie. She said, "Giving testimony?" and to his wry response of "Now how the dickens did you guess?" she responded with, "There's no other earthly activity worthy of a shirt like that. You could do with a haircut, Simon," she added, and when his gaze met hers in the mirror above the chest of drawers, "Honestly, I've never known anyone as afraid of barbers as you. Never mind. I'm off as well. Peach has been walked and fed, so don't let her beguile you with her dachshund eyes."

"She holds no charm for me," he said.

"Right. I *mean* it, Simon. She mustn't get fat. It's not good for her."

"Nor for any of us." He turned from the mirror and took up his tie. "I swear I shall pass her by with nothing falling loose from my hand," he said. "Are you off to Whitechapel, then?"

"I am."

"Not enough photos yet?"

"This is something else. I mean, more or less it's something else."

"Suitably vague, my love," he pointed out. "You sound more like me than you."

"I'll take photos, as well. But there's . . . Never mind. It's not important." She kissed him. She eased her fingers into his hair. It was soft as it curled against her palm. She gave it a tug and said, "Leave off going to the barber for now. It's nice."

"As you've been looking at it since you were seven years old, I'm gratified it maintains its appeal." He kissed her back.

She headed out, pausing only to scoop up her equipment. A quick drive down Cheyne Row to Cheyne Walk and she was on the Embankment. Like nearly everyone else, she drove along the river in the direction of Westminster. She wondered how she would ask what she wished to ask. More, she wondered to whom she could address her question in a situation that could truly be called none of her privileged-white-lady business.

It turned out to be Narissa Cameron, who was mulling over a large map of London spread over the table in the reception area of Orchid House. This once had been the vestibule of the chapel, and it was the only part of the building that was separated from the chapel by a wall.

Narissa turned as she entered. She looked beleaguered by worries. She said, "Oh. You," in a way that was less than welcoming. But Deborah was not to be put off, since less than welcome had so far been all but the youngest girls' stock in trade.

"You look a bit wrung out," Deborah said. "D'you want a coffee?"

"I've had four. One more and you'll have to scrape me off the ceiling. Christ, this is *such* a bitch."

"Difficulties?"

"That just about says it."

"Anything you care to . . . I mean, not to intrude or . . ."

"Stop treading on eggshells, Deborah. I'm not going to punch you if you say the wrong thing."

"Well, that's a relief. What are you trying to come up with, then?" Deborah nodded at the map.

"I'm trying to settle where the narrative moments are going to be filmed. Although it would be bloody nice to *have* a narrator in the first place. Who would've thought *that* part of the project would be the most difficult?"

"If I may ask . . ."

"Stop it! I swear . . ." She sighed. "Forget it. Please. You *can* talk to me person-to-person. You don't need my permission just because you're white."

"Sorry. It's just . . . Never mind. What sort of narrator are you looking for?"

"A woman. Black. With a commanding appearance and a compelling voice. A celebrity would be best—actor, pop singer, athlete—although I'd settle for a politician if I could manage that. Thing is, I should've listened to my dad. He told me to get on that first. These people have packed schedules, he said. But of course I went my own bloody way. Which is what I always do. Or at least always did and am trying not to do any longer."

"Zawadi," Deborah said. "Commanding presence and compelling voice?"

"I've thought about her, more than once. She's not a celebrity but the rest is definitely there."

"And?"

"I'm giving her . . . let's call it 'space' for the moment. She's not happy with me, and flexibility is *not* her middle name." Narissa bent over the map. She was holding a red felt-tip pen, and she used it to mark smallish dots on various sites. She said, "Peckham Common will work. The Somali Community Centre, Myatt's Fields Park in Camberwell, St. Thomas' Hospital, Middle Temple. No. Not Middle Temple. Stupid idea. *Not* Myatt's Fields. *What* am I thinking? Brixton Market is better."

"What'll they provide?"

"A backdrop for the narrator so she's not sitting behind a boring desk or in front of an equally boring bookcase. Also footage to be used when the narrator's off-camera and doing a voice-over."

"In front of a schoolyard with children—all girls—at play. A children's play area?"

"There *was* one on Camberwell Green. There's another at the far end of Peckham Common."

"Children playing, children's voices. The voices fade out as the narrator speaks?"

Narissa glanced in her direction and gave her a smile that appeared only halfway reluctant. "You could be good at this," she said.

"Thanks. Nice to know there's a second career waiting out there for me. Can I ask you something?"

Narissa capped her red pen. "Ask away."

"Can we . . . ?" Deborah indicated the out-of-doors. Narissa followed her outside and onto the green. It was lined with pollarded acacia trees, oddly umbrella-like in appearance. Deborah led her to one of them. She said, "I've been thinking a bit about this girl who's disappeared, the one with the long name but they call her Bolu. Do you know about her?"

Narissa was silent for a moment before she said, "I saw it on the telly. What about her?"

"I was struck . . . Well, this morning I saw a copy of *The Source*."

"You were lining your dustbin, I hope."

Deborah smiled. "Walking the dog. I found *The Source* along the way. There was a story—on the front page and inside—about her parents."

"What about them?"

"It's just that when Bolu first disappeared, she was with two teenagers and they were on the Central Line, coming from Gants Hill."

"And?" Narissa was distracted momentarily by the arrival of her two technicians. She called to them, "I'm set up already. I'll be along directly." And then to Deborah, "What's your point?"

"Just that the Central Line goes through Mile End, and if they changed trains there for the District Line? And then got off at Stepney Green?"

"The girl's at risk," Narissa said.

"So Zawadi—"

"All you need to know is that she's at risk, Deborah. The girl said something. Someone overheard. The pieces were put together. That's all it takes. So *if* you want to prove yourself more than a white Lady Bountiful snapping away with her expensive camera, you'll keep everything you know and everything you think you know to yourself."

That said, Narissa turned and made her way to the chapel. When she got to the steps, she turned and said, "Do you understand what I'm talking about?"

Deborah nodded. She walked back to the chapel, back to her pictures.

THE MOTHERS SQUARE
LOWER CLAPTON
NORTH-EAST LONDON

Mark Phinney knew that he couldn't go on in this way. He had responsibilities coming at him from every corner of his life, and, while he was meeting them at work, he wasn't meeting them with a decent degree of professionalism. He also wasn't meeting them with a surplus of compassion, empathy, love, or whatever else at home. At Empress State Building he was fast mastering the art of listening without listening, as well as taking in and reading reports on activities without actually digesting a thing. He attempted to hide his growing indifference to the job at hand as well as his grudging acceptance of his duties to his wife and his daughter. But whereas he was fairly competent at hiding his lack of interest at work, at home he could hide virtually nothing when it came to Pete.

He didn't wish to be read by his wife. He wished to be free. He wanted desperately to be out in public, finished with clandestine meetings that left him feeling three times the traitor to everything he once believed in, and to everything else he'd once held dear. He could cope with the guilt, with the betrayal of his marriage vows, with the many ways he was failing his colleagues, with the entertaining of unspoken wishes about his only child. What he could not cope with—and had not even once anticipated—was falling in love and having to suffer the consequences of that love in a situation in which any move he made was going to crush someone.

Yet he wanted to make the move. He could, at least, admit that. He wanted to walk away from Pete and Lilybet and into the waiting arms of the woman he loved. She was his soulmate. They were in effect a single person cleaved in two by . . . who knew, really? Fate, a hopeless situation, his failure to act upon what he knew to be real and true? And while that failure didn't need to define his future—or their future together—he couldn't see a way to trigger events in his life so that they led ineluctably where he wished them to lead. Pete would never allow that to happen, and who could blame her?

She'd read him well enough to hire a helper, at least and at last. He was a retired male nurse called Robertson, who did not wish to spend his pension years becoming less and less useful to society. He was seventy-one, but in his case the seventies were the new forties. He spent his holidays walking various pilgrim trails in Europe—his favourite being the Rome-to-Santiago route, which he'd done an amazing three times—and his free time in England was dedicated to getting physically prepared for the next pilgrim walk. Mark felt like a sloth next to him.

Robertson was there days—to give Pietra a few hours of free time—so several of them passed before Mark actually met him. When he arrived on this particular evening, however, the bloke was still there, as there had been "a wee bit of a scare with baby girl's breathing this afternoon," as he put it. "I got to her directly the alarm sounded, but I haven't liked to leave her without someone else here besides Mrs. Phinney." Someone else meant Mark, and he was home later than usual. A new member had been assigned to his team—Detective Sergeant Jade Hopwood, she was called—and he'd been meeting with her each day's end to bring her up to date on what had been either planned or achieved so far and to put her more fully into the picture of what they were trying to do next. She was a quick student—praise God—and she was equally good when it came to suggestions, but there remained many reports of actions to be gone through as well as much to discuss.

Mark asked Robertson at once about Lilybet's breathing. What had happened? When? How?

Robertson's reply was, "I'll let the missus explain it." Then with a glance at Lilybet's room, he lowered his voice and went on. "Baby girl ought to see her specialist, though. This thing that happened? It came without warning. She was fine and then she wasn't. She was breathing and then she wasn't. Best have her checked." And off he went, stopping at the front door to put on his hiking boots and to take up the walking poles he used to keep his arms in shape.

Mark went to Lilybet's room. Pete was sitting on the bed with her, her arm round their little girl's thin shoulders, Lilybet's head on Pete's breast. Both of them had their eyes closed. Only Pete opened hers when he entered.

"Robertson told you?" She paused to clear her throat. "For a moment I thought we'd lost her."

"Did you ring 999?"

"I did, but you know how it is. They take so long. By the time they arrived, we'd resolved everything, Robertson and I. But Mark, she was turning . . . Her lips were going purple." Her eyes brightened with tears as she spoke.

"Robertson says she should see the specialist."

"What good would that do? She'll say what she always says. 'Her system's compromised. In a situation this grave, she needs round-the-clock care.' Anything can happen, she'll say. Choking, suffocation, a stroke, an aneurism, cardiac arrest. *But*, he'll add, the worst can still be avoided if she's put into a care home with full-time medical staff."

Mark looked at Lilybet, her head lolling against her mother. The television on the opposite wall was showing one of the *Frozen* films. The sound was muted. Only the bright colours remained. If her eyes were open, he wondered, would the vibrant hues be enough to stimulate her brain? Could her brain even *be* stimulated? Was Pete spending her life—these vital years—attempting to scale a mountain that could not be scaled?

"She might do," he said to his wife. "But one way or another, we should take Lily to see her. Someone needs to assess her after she's had an incident."

"Assess her for what? Brain damage?" she asked derisively.

"You know what I mean, Pete."

"I don't want to hear the words another time."

"What words?"

"The 'put her away' words. The 'no one will blame you for making a decision like that about her care' words. As if I'm *worried* about being blamed. As if I'm desperate to hand her over to someone who'll put her in a bed in a ward and check on her three times a day so that I can be relieved of a burden, carefree, able to . . . I don't know . . . go to a gym? Learn to play golf? Start swimming again? Have my hair styled monthly? Play tennis? Study French? This is my *child*, Mark. This is our little girl."

"No one is putting Lilybet anywhere," Mark said. "But we need to understand what happened today and how to prevent it from happening again. Ring the specialist tomorrow, Pete. We'll take her in, both of us. Robertson can go as well."

"I don't want—" She stopped herself.

"What?"

"I *can't* put her into a care home. Please, Mark. I know this is difficult but you must see . . ." She began to weep. This roused Lilybet, who lifted her head. Pete pressed her back into her former position. "No," she said. "I can't."

Mark said, "Pete, you're exhausted. Let me stay with her for a while. Have a long bath. Have a glass of wine."

"I'm her mother." The tears on her face looked hot and burning, not like tears at all but rather an acid capable of singeing whatever it touched. "I want to remain her mother. She's my only chance to *be* a mother. I *want* that. Mark, she's my life. Isn't she yours?"

Lilybet defined Pete's world, but he had defied the claim his daughter would make upon him if he allowed it. So the answer was no, she was not his life. She was part of it, yes, an important part of it. But she wasn't everything. Not as she was for Pete.

Still he said, "Of course, she's my life," because he knew that was what Pete needed to hear and because he also knew it was the only way to get her off the bed in order to see to her own needs for at least half an hour. He touched Lilybet's baby-fine hair. He touched Pete's short dark curls. He added, "As are you, Pete. As you always will be."

She looked up at him, into his face, into his eyes. "Do you mean that?" she asked.

"As much as I've ever meant anything, love." He breathed deeply to absorb his lie, to make it into a truth that he could live with. He said again, "Have a bath and a glass of wine now. I'm happy to stay with her."

"Truly happy?"

"Of course."

Slowly, she eased away from Lilybet, moving her gently back against the stack of pillows that supported her. Mark took her place on the bed. He reached for one of her storybooks, opened it, and read aloud, "'It's a funny thing about mothers and fathers. Even when their own child is the most disgusting little blister you could ever imagine, they still think that he or she is wonderful.'"

He sensed as he read that Pete hadn't left the room. He could feel her watching him. Minutes passed. He continued to read. She continued to watch. Finally he looked in her direction.

"Bath and wine, Pete? It'll do you good."

She nodded but she didn't turn away.

"Mark," she said, "I know who she is."

29 JULY

KINGSLAND HIGH STREET
DALSTON
NORTH-EAST LONDON

Adaku considered her ability to wait one of her finest qualities: waiting for something to happen, waiting for things to be different, waiting to feel different, waiting to believe that something just round the corner would swing her life in another direction. So waiting for someone to show up and to enter the door to the flats above Kingsland Toys, Games, and Books was nothing to her. Her circumstances had undergone a change, and she now had unlimited time to wait.

She had rung the number printed on the card given to her by Easter Lange on her earlier visit. She'd thought everything through, she'd told Easter, and she was now ready. She had the additional money that Easter had demanded and she wished to hand it over in order to reserve a place on the schedule. So they made arrangements for Adaku to part with the cash and for Easter to part with an appointment.

Easter set the time for 10:00 a.m., and now here they were, on the day itself. In advance, Adaku had made the necessary acquaintance of a young musician whose bedsit was across the street and two doors down from Kingsland Toys, Games, and Books. This had not been difficult once she explained her purpose. He was on board at once and introduced himself to her as Richard. Dickon, he was called, he told her. She could call him Dickon if she preferred.

That very day he'd given her a key to his flat in the event she needed to enter while he wasn't there. He composed background music for films, he'd told her. Mostly he worked here, at home, but there often were times he had to go into the studio. Make yourself at home, he'd said, such as it is.

Dickon, she'd seen upon that visit, might be casual about handing out keys to his flat, but he was serious about his music. He owned an expensive-looking keyboard and a sound synthesizer. He also had a guitar, a set of electronic drums, a trumpet, and a violin. Living in his vicinity must be an interesting auditory experience, she thought. But as long as she had access to his window overlooking the street, she was happy.

He'd still been in bed when she'd arrived this morning. It was just before seven, and she'd let herself in. Like all bedsits, there was no actual bedroom. In the case of this bedsit, there was merely a fairly deep alcove where one could keep a futon, a mattress or some other furniture. He appeared to use an IKEA bed covered with a sleeping bag for his nightly slumber. She could see the top of his smooth, shaved head as she moved with near silence to the window.

She tilted the venetian blinds to give herself a good view of the street. She'd planned carefully. She only hoped she'd been careful enough.

Shortly before eight, Easter showed up, as expected, coming from the direction of Ridley Road. Before she reached Kingsland Toys, Games, and Books, however, she was caught up by a woman with a child in tow. The three of them finished the walk in each other's company, the women talking intensely with their heads together, as the child with them looked about. Adaku froze. At first she discounted what she was seeing, telling herself that the other woman was merely a friend of Easter's, yet the presence of the child suggested to Adaku that her long-range plan was already happening and it was happening directly in front of her. She was astonished at such a piece of luck.

Easter unlocked the door that would allow access to the flats on the second and third floors of the building. She held the door open for her two companions, making a "you first" gesture. When the woman and child had entered, Easter then looked right and left and across the street, which made Adaku quickly drop her fingers from the venetian blinds covering Dickon's window. But she didn't move from the window itself, so she was able to see Easter go into the building and close the door behind her.

Adaku stood still and silent. This was not how anything was supposed to happen, not according to how she'd developed the plan. But if she made no move now—when conditions were astonishingly perfect—would she ever have another chance like this one?

She pictured how long everything would take. She went through preliminaries as she envisioned them. Then she fumbled in her skirt for her mobile, and she made the call.

"Kingsland High Street," she said when her call was answered. "It's time. Now."

That done, she placed the key to Dickon's bedsit on top of his electronic keyboard. Quietly, she let herself out and descended the stairs. On the pavement once again, she went to her earlier observation spot at Rio Cinema. She wanted to be there watching when Easter and the others were taken from the building and hauled to the nick. The women would lie and deny, of course. But everyone was more than ready for that.

MAYVILLE ESTATE
DALSTON
NORTH-EAST LONDON

That night Tani found it impossible to sleep. The heat in the bedroom was deadly, which was bad enough. His brain wouldn't quiet down, which was worse. Near teatime, Abeo and Simisola had preceded Monifa into the flat, and it seemed to Tani that whatever had brought them to Mayville Estate in a group, it was not good. Abeo's "Get out of my sight" was accompanied by a slap against the back of Monifa's head as she moved past him in the direction of the kitchen. As for Simi, she went to their bedroom and didn't say another word from tea onward.

Tani had been lying there sleepless for hours, listening to Simi's breathing from across the room, so he was fully awake when the whispering began, long after midnight. There'd been whispering before—the flat's walls were tissue paper—but generally he could ignore it. This time, though, it sounded fierce, like a bitter argument being kept under wraps. When a low cry from his mother was cut off suddenly, he sat up and swung his legs out of bed.

He padded to the bedroom door and eased it open. He listened more carefully. He heard his father's voice. He hadn't ever before heard such fury expressed in a whisper. "You will *not* defy me, Monifa."

"Why will you never try to understand?"

"*What* did you say to me?"

Monifa's tone shifted at once, becoming conciliatory, even weepy. "Abeo, I cannot allow—"

"You will do what I say. This costs a pittance."

"But everything cannot be about money."

"If you dare to disobey me, Monifa, I swear before God—"

"Please. You must listen to me."

"You do not question my decisions. I have heard enough."

"You have *not*. How much do you expect to receive as a bride price if Simisola is dead? Sometimes I think you will not see things as they truly are. You can't—" A rush of footsteps and then she cried out, "No! Abeo! Stop it!"

Tani took a step towards their bedroom door, fired up as much by "bride price" as he was by his mother's cry.

"Do not *ever* speak to me in such a tone." Abeo's voice was louder now, no further attempt to stifle his words.

"I *must* speak if it means the protection of our children."

"There is no *must*. You must nothing. Do you understand me? *I* protect our children."

"Stop it! You're hurting—"

"Oh, you hurt, you hurt. What do you expect from me, eh? You and your father and the lies you told. What do you expect? I was meant to have a breeder, but here I am with you, with your pain and your tears and . . . *Enough. Enough*. You need to be shown . . . You *make* me do these things, Monifa . . ." The sound of tussling ensued, feet shuffling on the floor, a heavy thud.

"You're hurting me. *Please*, Abeo."

At that, Tani grabbed the knob and shoved the door open. His father had pushed Monifa to the edge of their bed, but she was still upright. He had the back of her neck in one hand and her chin in the other, and he was squeezing so hard Monifa's face was inflamed. "Leave her alone!" Tani said.

Abeo didn't loosen his grip on Monifa's chin, but he released the back of her neck. He swung round to Tani, his free hand clenched into a fist, which he raised.

"D'you want to hit someone? Hit me," Tani said. "Do it, because I want like hell to break your nose. You got that, Pa? Come *on*. Or is it only women you hit?"

"Please! Tani! You cannot speak like that!"

But there was no fight for Monifa to worry about. Abeo snarled at her, "You know what to do," and shoved Tani aside. No fool, Tani thought. His father demanded complete respect, but he knew damn well what awaited him if he struck Monifa in Tani's presence. He followed Abeo out of the room.

Monifa cried, "Let him go! Tani! Just let him go!"

But Tani had no intention of doing so. Any peace they had with his father's departure would last only till morning and then everything would start again. It needed to be finished, and he understood that he was the only person who could possibly do that. A door slammed. Abeo had left the flat.

He had a head start on Tani because Tani had to check on Simisola. He saw that she was awake. She was sitting up in bed, her eyes huge and dark, clutching her pillow to her chest. Tani said, "Go to Mum. I'll be back," and he left the flat before her fearful protest kept him with her a moment longer.

Outside, he looked left and right. There was no telling where his father was headed. No pub would be open at this time of night, and it was doubtful his men's club was available to him either.

Dim lights shone down on the tarmac pitch across the lane. Tani gazed through the trees, but the pitch was unoccupied. He looked round and saw that no one lingered nearby. His father had managed to disappear into the hot ether of the night.

31 JULY

He'd not been able to keep his mind where it needed to be when it came to his courses at college, so Tani had skipped three lectures and one supervision. He had to talk to someone, but the only person he really wanted to talk to was Sophie. Only . . . there were things he didn't want her to know, things about his family that he could hardly stand to let stay in his mind, let alone share them with anyone else. But he finally gave in to the pressure building inside his brain. He needed a plan in a situation in which he saw no way to come up with a plan. This suggested to him that, like it or not, two minds were indeed going to be better than one.

He found Sophie working on an essay in the college library. She was wearing her noise-cancelling earphones and chewing thoughtfully on the end of a pencil. As he watched her, she read a bit from a text and scribbled a few lines on a piece of paper. He put his hand on the open book.

She looked up, smiled, and removed her earphones. He could dimly hear white noise issuing from them. It sounded like rain. He swung his leg over a chair across the table from her and straddled it.

She looked at the institutional wall clock above the checkout desk. "Where've you been, Tani? And don't you have a lecture just now?"

"I get plenty 'f lectures at home."

"Very funny." She leaned across the table and kissed him. She made a business of it. He was more than willing to let her. When she drew away from him, he pulled her back till they were forehead to forehead and he could lock his stare onto her dark gaze.

She whispered, "What?" with a smile.

He whispered back, "What *what*?"

"Tani, you missed your lecture. You *never* miss a lecture. So something's going on with you. I can see it." She touched his cheek. "And I can feel it. You've gone all tight in the face. Have you gone at it with your dad again?"

He moved back so he could see her properly and speak to her the same way. Still, he glanced away from her when he said, "It's mostly Simisola."

Her expression altered. "Your sister? What's wrong?"

Tani said, "You got time enough to go outside?" and she agreed, scooping up her rucksack and leaving the rest of her things behind in order to follow him. He used this time of leaving the library to seek a way to explain, and he wondered whether he could possibly tell her what he suspected was going on without completely betraying his parents. He couldn't find it. It felt like walking into the middle of an inadequately frozen pond. He settled on not looking at Sophie as he said, "Few nights ago? She showed me all this rubbish, did Simi. Shit Mum bought her. Up Ridley Road Market? Clothes and jewellery and makeup, this was."

"Really? Jewellery? Makeup? Your sister? That's odd, isn't it? For her age, I mean. And from what you've told me about her, it doesn't sound like your mum. I got the impression she's sort of traditional."

"Yeah. But this is . . ." He paused, thought about it, switched gears just a bit. "See, Simi thinks it's all for a celebration. *The* celebration, she says. Which follows *the* initiation."

Sophie frowned. "What's she being initiated into?"

"Into being Yoruba," he said. "Mum's told her she has to be initiated cos she was born here, not in Nigeria."

"Is that how it is? I mean, do people get initiated if they're born here and their family is Nigerian?"

"'Course not. It's all rubbish, tha'. I tried to explain, but Simi wasn't having it. All's she's thinking is that there'll be a cake and people will be giving her money an' she's got this shit she c'n wear from Ridley Road Market an' she gets to paint up her face. I tried to talk to Mum 'bout it, but she said Simi misunderstood what she told her cos the only thing happened was that they went to a place where she got inspected by a doctor or a nurse or whatever. Mum told her it was to make sure all her parts were intact."

Sophie looked away from him as she considered this. Her gaze was on the fountain in the middle of the courtyard where they sat on top of a retaining wall. She said at last, "Is this, like, a regular thing that happens to Nigerian girls? Getting their parts inspected is what I mean."

"Sure as hell, I don't know. They're meant to have lots of babies, they are, so I c'n see how the first question to answer is *can* they have babies."

"But she's only eight years old, right?"

"What I thought 's well. An' here's something else. I heard Mum and Pa arguing las' night. I think it's to do with Simi. Mum was saying she's trying to protect her."

Sophie raised her fingers to her lips, and she gazed at him as if to read his face. She said, "From what?"

Tani was reluctant because of what it would reveal about his family, but he went on. He found that he needed to talk to her. "From letting Pa get a bride price for her."

Sophie said, "A *bride* price? Is your dad planning to *sell* her? That's so *totally* against the law. You might have to phone the police, Tani, if that's what he intends to do."

"There's no point. They'll just deny it. Or at least Pa will."

"Then you have to be ready to get her out of there the instant you hear *or* overhear *any* plan to get money from someone willing to pay for her. If your mum's been buying her clothes and all that rubbish, like she's going to be presented to someone, that means whatever is being planned is going to happen soon."

"So where do I take her if I get her out? Like I said, there's no point to going to the police and where the hell else is there?"

She looked from him to the building across the courtyard. He followed her gaze. Someone was busily opening windows, hoping for the best, which would be the sudden manifestation of a stiff and cooling breeze. Sophie was silent, and in her silence birds twittered as they dipped and fluttered in and out of the nearby fountain, where water burbled pleasantly. Everything was going on as normal, except in his life and Simi's. Sophie finally replied with, "If there's really no point to ringing the police, when the time comes, you can bring her to me."

"No way I can do that."

"Why not? You never told them, did you? Your parents? About us, I mean."

"No, but we've been in the market together, Soph. *Someone* would've seen us and you c'n bet on that. Market's the first place they'd look for her. And when Simi's not there, Mum's going to know I'm behind it cos Simi's been dead chuffed with everything she's been told about her 'initiation,' so she bloody well isn't going to run off on her own. All it'll take is jus' one person in Ridley Road saying, 'What about that girl been seen with your Tani?' And then tha's that. A few more questions and they have your name and off they go. No, I need to find a place for her where she can't be got to."

"Care might be the answer."

"I can't do that to Simi."

"What other answer is there?"

"I don't know, but I can't have her going into Care cos what happens next? When does she come out? Does she *ever* come out?"

"She comes out when your parents agree not to find a husband for her."

"They won't agree to anything. Ever. My dad won't agree and my mum ends up doing whatever he tells her. So Simi goes into Care and gets punished for something *they* want to do."

"Care isn't a punishment, Tani."

"Bloody hell it isn't. And how's *she* supposed to see things? How's she goin' to feel other than scared out of her mind?"

"But you'll have to get her out of their control, your mum and dad, at least till someone can talk to them about whatever plan they have in mind for selling Simisola."

"Yeah? Who's going to talk to them?"

They were silent again, considering this. Sophie scratched her head, found a pencil she'd stowed behind her ear, brought it out, played with it between her fingers. She tilted her head with a sudden thought, saying, "Tani, do you think . . ."

He waited. When she didn't go on he said, "What?"

"Well, it's this and could be it's too dumb. But is there anything you can hold over them? Either one of them? Both of them? To keep Simisola safe from being sold for a bride price?"

"Hold over them how?"

"Like blackmail. P'rhaps something they're doing that they don't want anyone to know they're doing? Only you *do* know and you tell them you'll not say a word to anyone about it long 's Simisola's kept safe."

"What would they be doing? Selling drugs out 'f the butcher shop? Running a sex ring? Tha's not on. And Mum hardly ever leaves the flat."

"Could there be something your dad's doing on his own, then? Something he doesn't want your mum to know?"

Tani considered this. There *was* the fact that his dad left many nights, returning only in the early hours of the morning. He'd always reckoned his father had gone down the pub or to his men's club, but could be he was up to something. Gambling, betting on horses, bringing immigrants illegally into the country, smuggling something heavily taxed.

"Could be," he said. "He's gone at night. A lot, this is. Gen'rally he comes back in the morning, though."

"What if you followed him?"

"I could do that. But what if what he's doing in't secret or illegal? Then what?"

"Then you and I think what to do next. Meantime and just in case, you must get Simi's things together so you can get her out of there fast if you need to."

MAYVILLE ESTATE
DALSTON
NORTH-EAST LONDON

As things turned out, Tani had the opportunity for discovery that very night. Abeo was a brooding presence at the evening meal. Even the egg rice went no distance to alter his mood. Nor did the *asun* Monifa had plopped onto the table as a starter, despite the ram meat she had managed to find and the *ewedu* soup she'd also prepared. She had everything ready for the moment Abeo came into the flat, his shirt heavily bloodied from a day in the butcher shop. Whatever he'd been cutting up had given him the unappetising appearance of a forensic pathologist after an autopsy. It would have been more pleasant for the rest of them to dip into the meal had he changed his shirt, but no one was about to recommend he do that. Or ask him. It seemed that— without consulting one another—the three other members of the family had decided that averting their eyes was a better course of action. So aside from the moment when Abeo pushed back from the table for the stomach-turning ritual of blowing his nose and tossing his paper napkin onto the floor, there was no other noise save chewing, swallowing, and whatever voices reached them from beyond the windows and open door of the flat.

As far as Tani could tell, nothing had changed since the night his parents had argued. Abeo still wanted something from Monifa. Monifa had not given it to him. Both of them were stone when it came to each other.

After the meal, Abeo shoved his chair back from the table and left them. He disappeared into the family bathroom and the water began noisily filling the tub. Monifa stood and started to clear the table of their plates and the remains of the food. She said, "Simi, you will help me," and Simi scampered off to do just that. She cast a glance at Tani as she snatched up glassware in the crook of her arm. He could see she was uneasy with the change that had come upon their family: everyone avoiding conversation, their parents at some mysterious odds, and her coming "celebration" a topic no one seemed willing to bring up any longer. That part was just as well, he thought. He would have hoped everything to do with that was fast becoming a distant memory.

It was an hour before Abeo left the bathroom. He went from there to the bedroom he shared with Monifa, and Tani thought at first he would not emerge again that night, punishing all of them with a silence that contained a fury he couldn't adequately conceal.

Tani went to his own room, and from beneath his bed, he found the rucksack he'd used in secondary school. He emptied it and went to the clothes cupboard he shared with Simi. He was reaching for one of her summer dresses when she came into the room. He dropped his hand and turned to her. No way could he tell her what he was doing.

She said, "Papa is cross, Tani."

He said, "Yeah, but it's got nothing to do with you."

"What's it got to do with, then? Is he cross because you tol' him you won't marry that girl?"

"Omorooki or whoever she is?" Tani said. "Tha's part of it, that is."

"An' the rest? Is it about . . . Tani, is it about me?"

"You jus' stay out of everything having to do with Mum and Pa, Squeak. Less you're involved in wha's going on, less anyone's thinking about you. Which, lemme tell you, is a good thing jus' now."

"I don't un'erstand."

"Tha's just as well."

He heard his parents' bedroom door open. He cracked the door to his own room, wide enough to see Monifa going inside to join his father. The sight of her made his muscles go tight. He didn't know what she was willing to do to keep the peace, and he didn't want to know.

It was dark when he heard their door open again. He was sitting on his bed, waiting for Simi to fall asleep so that he could pack up some of her clothes without her knowledge. He heard his mother say, "Abeo, can you not—" before the door shut again. He eased open his own door in time to see his father crossing into the lounge, fully dressed, and trailing the scent of aftershave, the signal he was leaving for the night.

Tani turned to Simi. He whispered, "I'll be back. No noise, you got that? Mum's not to know."

"'Kay," she said. "But where . . . ?"

"Don't know. Like I said, I'll be back. Go to sleep." He waited till she'd settled in, at least to try.

He traced his father's steps and went out into the heavy humid night. He didn't see Abeo at once, so he listened carefully. A dog barked, and he followed that sound.

Closer to the barking dog, he saw the unmistakable burly shape of his father. He was in no apparent hurry, looking merely like a bloke out for a walk in the hope of escaping the heat inside his home. He was strolling towards Woodville Road. There, he turned left, and Tani jogged to catch him up. He was in time to see Abeo heading in the general direction of Kingsland High Street. But the route he was taking took him to deserted streets, with housing estates and tower blocks defining the places where families slept, doing their best to cope with the temperature that even darkness had not relieved.

Finally, Abeo came to the high street. Here, too, no one was about. The air felt thick with the heat, as if the temperature wished to be absorbed into the storefronts, invading shops long closed for the night. The exhaust fumes from the day's heavy traffic seemed to ooze from the pavements, and wheelie bins puffed out foetid clouds from rotting vegetables and the remains of takeaway meals.

Abeo crossed over, throwing a glance back the way he'd come. Quickly, Tani faded against the navy-painted grille that covered the entry to an Asian furniture shop, with the hope that this would be enough to camouflage him from his father's gaze. It seemed sufficient, as Abeo continued on his way, and minutes later he made the turn into Ridley Road.

For a moment, Tani entertained the thought that his father—sleepless in the night—intended to do some work inside Into Africa or the butcher's shop. There seemed to be no other reason why he'd be setting this course. There was nothing else in the area. Everything was closed and locked, and in the dim light from the streetlamps the day's rubbish waited for someone to sweep it away. They were hours from this happening, though. The street sweepers would come with the dawn, as with the dawn would come the market traders.

Abeo made no stop in Ridley Road. Instead, his pace increased. There was now something of a furtiveness to his movements as he darted into Chester Crescent and from there into Dalston Lane. Up ahead in the distance Tani could dimly see the viaduct that carried the railway tracks across the lane, and for a crazy moment he thought his father was going somewhere via rail, despite the hour, which was one when no London train would be travelling anywhere.

Tani felt a quickening of excitement as he acknowledged the brilliance of Sophie's idea. His father did indeed have something to hide, and if it was good enough to use against him, Simi was free from *whatever* their parents had in mind for her. Tani had never before thought much about his father leaving the family on the nights he chose to do so. He'd just considered it part and parcel of what married men did when they wanted the company of other married men. But this—what he was witnessing now in Abeo's night-time stroll—this had nothing to do with wanting the company of other married men. He was up to something, and Tani reckoned he had it all put together by the time he'd trailed his father past Hackney Downs station and then Amhurst Road, to follow him into The Narrow Way.

There were pawnshops here, which told Tani that some kind of exchange was about to occur and that exchange ultimately would result in money. There would be contraband involved, and either Abeo was in this place to receive it for selling from the butcher's shop or from Into Africa or he was here to hand over part of the profits. One thing was certain, though: no matter what was happening at this time of night, whatever the exchange was, it was probably illegal. But by the time Tani had worked through this scenario, his father had reached the top of the street. He crossed over, where on the corner stood his apparent destination.

This turned out to be Pembury Estate, an enormous collection of red-brick blocks of flats. The estate sat at the junction of Dalston Lane and Clarence Road, conveniently close to a Paddy Power betting shop for any hopeful punters who happened to occupy one of the hundreds of flats on the estate itself.

Tani paused at the corner as his father entered the grounds of the housing estate. It looked larger even than Mayville Estate, and because Abeo's route involved no hesitation and required no studying of the estate plan posted just beyond the entrance, Tani understood that his father had been there before.

He shortened the distance between them, keeping to the edge of the paths Abeo took so that he could leap into the shadows on the chance that Abeo would turn round and look for followers here. But Abeo didn't turn. He merely paced through the warren of buildings till he came to the one he sought. He strode to a panel on the lift shaft. There were buzzers on it, but it seemed that none were necessary, for Abeo removed something from his pocket that gave him access to the lift. It came, he stepped inside, and up he went.

Tani retreated in an effort to see where his father left the lift. Soon enough he was rewarded. On the third floor, he saw Abeo stride along the outdoor corridor. He went in the direction of a door that opened. In the doorway Tani saw the woman, and from where he was, he could hear her voice.

"You're very late tonight," was what she said.

For Tani, this was quite enough.

1 AUGUST

Tani spent the rest of the night just there, on Pembury Estate, thinking about his choices. He waited within sight of the lift that had taken his father to the third floor of the block of flats. When he'd followed Abeo here from Mayville Estate, he'd reckoned something useful could come out of it, but he'd not had the least idea that he'd be handed such an opportunity as the one that lay before him now.

Several people came out of the lift at 5:30. Several more at 5:45. It was just after 6:00 when Abeo appeared on the third floor's outdoor corridor. He went to the lift and used it. He walked jauntily towards Tani as if expecting him to be there. He carried a large manila envelope. Once he stood in front of Tani, Abeo used this to gesture with as he spoke.

"I thought it was you who followed," he said. "You were careful, yes, but not careful enough."

Up close, Abeo smelled of sex and sweat. The odour was so strong that Tani stepped away. At this Abeo smiled slyly. He began to retrace his route of the previous night.

Tani said to his father's retreating back, "If you're going to fuck some nasty bit on the side, a shower wouldn't hurt when you finish with her."

Abeo made no reply. His gait looked youthful, as if he was proud he'd been found out.

"Can't be bothered to wash?" Tani demanded. "But wait. Right. You *want* that stench because how else will every person within twenty feet of you know you had it off last night? And tha's the important bit, innit, Pa? People have to *know* Abeo Bankole's getting some."

At that, Abeo paused, but he didn't turn completely. He just moved his head so that Tani could hear him when he said, "You will speak to your father like this?"

Tani approached him. "Who is she? How long has this been going on?"

"The answers to those questions are not your affair," Abeo said. "When I think something is your concern, I will tell you." He resumed his walk, slapping the manila envelope against his thigh. He began to whistle tunelessly.

Tani followed close behind him. "Third floor," he said. "I can get in. Is that what you want? Your son showing up at the minge pie's door? And who is she? Haven't you made Mum miserable enough without finding some greasy bag to spread them open for you?"

A street sweeper approached, clearing the pavements and the gutters. He glanced between them and gave them a sharp nod. Abeo nodded back. Tani did nothing.

They continued on their way. Traffic was building. Buses were grinding along the streets. The air sucked up exhaust fumes greedily, and the sun promised yet another day of blazing heat.

Tani saw his father unfasten the clasp on the manila envelope. He drew from it a piece of heavy paper. He handed it to Tani. On it, a very young hand had drawn and labeled a group of stick figures and had given them each spiralling hair. Two of the figures were large.

Two were small. Above the group of them was printed *My Family*. Beneath the two smaller figures a more skilled hand had printed *Elton* and *Davrina*. Beneath the two larger figures that same hand had identified *Mummy* and *Daddy*. There was nothing else of note save the stomach of Mummy, which bulged. An arrow pointed to it and along that arrow's shaft was printed *Baby*.

Tani said, "You're fucking some bloke's *wife*? And she's up the spout? What's wrong with you?"

Abeo said nothing. He merely handed the envelope to Tani. At first Tani thought he was meant to return the crude drawing there, but then Abeo said, "Turn it over," and Tani saw that *For My Daddy From Elton* was printed on the front.

Tani looked from those words to his father and back to those words. He said, "What the hell? Who are these people?"

Abeo said, "My children and their mother. Elton is six. Davrina is four. There will be a third in December. A man is meant to have a family. Children and grandchildren. Your mother is ruined. Lark is not."

"Lark?" Tani asked. "She's called *Lark*?" Then he twigged. "Christ! She's *English*. All your talk about Nigeria and shit and you're fucking some English woman."

"She is Black English," Abeo said. "She gives me children. There will be more. Children are a man's proof of who he is."

"That's your story, is it? Mum had two but that wasn't enough, so you went out and . . . what . . . *advertised*?" When his father said nothing, Tani went on. "You *did*. You advertised. Internet, I expect. And it wasn't about having kids, that advert. What does she think about us, then? And where does she think you are when you're not with her?"

"She knows where I am. And with who. She is happy with the arrangement and it suits me as well."

Tani felt lightheaded. He wanted to sit, to think things through, but he had to keep walking because he wanted to pull from his father every detail he could use against him.

"What if someone gives Mum the word about . . . whatsername . . . *Lark* . . . and she walks away from . . . from this, from you, from this whole rotten life? What if Mum divorces you?"

"She will not do that," Abeo said. "She has no reason. Should she and Lark ever meet, she will thank Lark for her . . ." Abeo seemed to search for the word. He chose, "For her services. And Lark has done them well."

His father was bluffing. Tani could see it in the way Abeo's eyes shifted as he spoke, his glances going from Tani to the pavement, from Tani to the vehicles that passed them in the street.

Tani said to him, "Really, eh? Okay, I'll tell her and we'll see how she feels."

"If you must." Abeo was, it seemed, without embarrassment, shame, or guilt, without anything at all. He merely *was*. Everything about him was saying to Tani, This is who I am and you can cope or not. It is of little matter to me.

Tani reckoned Abeo was trying to pull whatever wool he could get his hands on. He said, "I'm telling her, Pa."

Abeo replied, "As you wish."

"You'll lose Mum, Simi, and me. You'll lose half of everything you own. Is that what you want? Because I swear I'm going to tell her. Unless."

Abeo glanced at him then. He cocked his head, interested to hear what followed *unless*.

"Unless you swear to leave Simi alone. You swear to it here. Now. You leave her alone, you leave her in London, and no way do you *ever* sell her to some bloke in Nigeria."

Abeo crossed the road. Tani followed. In the distance the sun was striking the tops of the tower blocks of Mayville Estate. More and more people were in the streets: on bicycles, in cars, on foot, on motorbikes. Shops would soon open and the market traders would be arranging their wares.

Abeo said to Tani, "That is your price?"

"Tha's my price. Simi's my price. Simi staying in London is my price. Simi being left alone is my price."

Abeo nodded thoughtfully. The right side of his upper lip twitched. "I will think about it if you say nothing for now."

"Decide by tonight," Tani told him.

"Tonight," Abeo acknowledged.

When they reached Bronte House, neither Monifa nor Simisola had yet awoken. Tani expected his father to head to the bathroom straightaway, to wash the smell of Lark and sex and sweat from his body. But instead he went to the door of the bedroom he shared with Monifa. He opened it without ceremony and said, "Nifa, come here."

Tani could hear his mother stirring. He heard her say, "What is it?"

"I said come, Monifa. Did you not hear me?"

There was rustling from the room, and then in a moment Monifa appeared in the doorway. Her face was swollen with sleep or lack of it. Her eyes looked hooded. She saw Tani, and she looked from him to Abeo as she brought one of her hands to her throat.

Abeo said, "Show it to her, Tani," and he handed Tani the manila envelope. "You wish so much to do it, yes? So do it now." And when Tani did nothing, "Tani, I said show it your mother as you said you would do if I did not follow your wishes in this matter." And still when Tani didn't move, Abeo snatched the envelope and thrust it at Monifa. "Look," he told her. "Your son wants you to see this, so look at it."

Monifa shifted her gaze from husband to son to the envelope she held. She did not have to be told again what to do. She opened the envelope and drew out the paper and her gaze fell upon what Tani himself had seen. Slowly she raised her head and looked at Tani. Slowly she covered half of her face. "I'm sorry," she told him. "I didn't want you to know."

Abeo lifted his head and tossed it in a way that unaccountably reminded Tani of a bull. But when he spoke, it was to Monifa. "Make coffee," he said. "I will be in the bath."

TRINITY GREEN
WHITECHAPEL
EAST LONDON

Narissa Cameron's efforts with the girls were not paying off in the way she seemed to desire. Although one of the adult volunteers had done a brilliant job two weeks earlier of demonstrating exactly the storytelling style Narissa was after—indeed, Deborah had photographed her and recorded her words as well in the hope she could use both when she put together her book—there wasn't a single girl who so far had been able to emulate that. Instead, whether it was rehearsing or filming, the girls depended upon recitation, becoming automatons in front of the camera.

Narissa's reaction to this was made worse by the fact that with Deborah—a bloody *white* woman, for God's sake—the girls seemed natural. Deborah knew the reason was not that she had a magic touch of some kind. It was merely that she had more experience. Part of what she'd learned both in photography school and over the years making portraits was how to draw her photographic subjects out of themselves. It seemed to her that Narissa didn't yet have that ability, which came mostly from experience, and her frustrated intention was at war with her passionate desire to dig into the girls' stories.

Deborah paused as she was leaving Orchid House when she saw Narissa on her mobile, at the bottom of the steps. She heard her saying, "It's bad. It's *truly* bad. *Hideously* bad. Victoria, you *must*—"

Victoria evidently cut her off at some considerable length, after which Narissa said hotly, "I know what I need. You're *not* helping. Are you my sponsor or my mother?"

And then she listened. But she didn't seem to like what she heard because she said, "I can't get there. It will take too long. I won't make it, and—"

More from Victoria and then, "All right. Yes. All right."

She ended the call. She saw Deborah and said, "*What*? Why're you lurking round? Aren't you on your way home? Go away!" Without waiting for Deborah to cooperate, Narissa strode onto the bone-dry and dying lawn that extended the length of the two rows of cottages. But she stopped in the middle and then swung round. Deborah hadn't moved, so Narissa shouted, "Do you ever listen to *anyone*? What's wrong with you?"

Deborah descended the steps and walked to her. She said, "Is there anything . . . ? You seem . . . I'm just . . . Can I help at all?"

"Do I look like someone who needs your help?"

"To be honest? Well . . . yes."

"So what are you? Some supercilious Madonna of the . . . Christ. I can't even think what you're the bloody Madonna of."

Deborah chuckled. Then she said, "Oh, sorry." And then she clapped her hand over her mouth.

Narissa rolled her eyes. "Does anyone *ever* slap you and your privileged white arse into another time zone?"

Deborah thought about this. There were certainly possibilities. She replied seriously with, "I'm sure there are those who want to, but so far all of them have restrained themselves."

Narissa began to walk towards the boundary wall and the street beyond. Deborah accompanied her. Narissa shot her a look. "*What*?"

"The filming seems to be . . . well . . . not going as well as you hoped."

"Sherlock has arrived," Narissa said to the sky.

"So if I can say it? You're having something of a time of it."

"I'm having a meltdown is what the fuck I'm having."

"Definitely another way of putting it," Deborah noted.

"Do you *ever* curse?" Narissa demanded. "Are you always so nicey-nicey? Forget it. Don't answer. I need a bloody meeting is what I need. That or a drink. Or a pill. Or something."

"Conversation?" Deborah offered. "I mean, I know I'm not what you need. And of course I don't know and can't pretend to know what it's like. I mean, your meetings and everything? But I can talk. I mean, I can listen. And you can talk. And I can respond if you want a response."

Narissa shot her another look. Deborah knew she was being evaluated. There was nothing for it but to wait for the other woman to decide. Finally, Narissa brusquely said, "Oh fuck it. I'm getting everything but the outrage. I keep asking myself why do they show no outrage? We've heard about the betrayal, the lies, the loss of innocence, the degradation of and subjugation of women, but why are they not outraged about it? *I* am. I'm bloody, sodding, bleeding outraged. And that, just there—the outrage—is *completely* missing when I look at each day's work. And yet, when the girls talk to you, I can *see* it then. And why they talk to you like they do . . . I mean, you're white, you're lucky, you're charmed, you're whatever the hell you are. So what am I doing wrong?"

They continued their walk towards the wall that bordered the pavement. When they reached the end of it, Deborah paused in the shade of one of the mop-headed acacias. She said, "You seem—I don't know—rather hard on yourself?"

Narissa laughed harshly, without humour. "I'll recover from *that* soon enough. Believe me. It's my stock-in-trade."

"Joke if you want, but if I can ask: How many documentaries have you made?"

"I've worked with my dad and he's been filming documentaries for something like forty years. So I know what I'm doing if that's where you were heading. I *know* the routine. I've heard it from the cradle."

"What?"

Like a long-ago memorised recitation, Narissa said, "That the smoothest route to success lies within the filmmaker's ability to remain objective, that everything comes down to the filmmaker's being a disinterested but nonetheless sympathetic witness when shooting."

"But still, this *is* your first documentary?"

"That doesn't matter. I should be able to—"

"What? And why?" When Narissa didn't reply, Deborah went on with, "Why *should* you anything?"

Narissa paused and seemed to consider this for a moment. She finally said, "Because I bloody *want* to."

"So? Look, I know nothing about making documentaries, but perhaps you're looking at this the wrong way round? It sounds like you want the outrage to come from the girls. But shouldn't it come from the film's viewers? And shouldn't the filmmaker have faith that the viewer will actually feel the outrage? I mean, isn't outrage something that builds over the course of a film? Isn't how the girls tell their stories—the simplicity of their telling—going to speak more loudly than . . . I don't know. Tearing out their hair? Beating their heads against the wall? Sobbing? Weeping? You know, you might be getting in your own way, Narissa. It's like you've got all these voices in your head, telling you not to bother because you're going to fail."

"I *don't* like amateur psychologising. And frankly? You're fucking patronising me, so stop it."

"I won't. I'm white and you're Black and I get that we live in a racist world. But I'm saying this anyway: I think you're setting yourself up to do badly because you don't have faith. Not in the girls and how powerful their stories are, not in the viewers' ability to understand what you're doing with your film, and definitely not in yourself."

"I've got piles of faith in myself, and *you're* talking like there's something wrong with wanting to make a difference," Narissa said hotly. "These girls who come here . . . ? They face pressure like nothing your sort have ever seen. From birth they've been taught that women have to be transformed into vessels of chastity and purity for men. It's all about becoming worthy of some bloke who's willing to shoot his semen inside you. Doesn't that make you want to bloody well scream? And it continues to go on and on and on with virtually *no* one doing a thing to stop it."

"How can you say that? Zawadi is. You are."

"Brilliant. Two of us."

"I am," Deborah said. "And there're others who, I expect, feel the exact rage you're looking for and probably belong in your film as well."

"I've got several," Narissa admitted, rather grudgingly, after a moment. "Before I started filming here."

"Who are they?"

"Some coppers trying to end all this."

"And?"

Narissa walked through the pedestrian gate and onto the pavement beyond which the traffic roared ceaselessly up and down Mile End Road. "They were good, the coppers. They were ready to talk, spread the word, crack skulls together, whatever. They put me on to a surgeon who's working on this as well."

"Was there outrage? I can't think a surgeon wouldn't be outraged."

"I expect she is, but I didn't get an interview. I barely got a returned phone call. She would've been brilliant on film, but she won't do it. Which is too bloody bad because I could use her just before the film finishes. One of the coppers ended up saying that stopping everything that's being done to women is like trying to bail out a canoe with a teaspoon, so it would be nice to end with a bit of hope." Narissa looked at the traffic. Her expression became thoughtful. Deborah wondered what she was contemplating. She learned soon enough when Narissa went on with, "In fact, you should talk to her for your project, the surgeon. Her name's Philippa Weatherall. I got the impression she's paranoid as hell, so she probably won't let you take a photo of her, but an interview with her as an introduction or a conclusion to the book you're planning . . . ? Or both introduction *and* conclusion? She might go for that."

Deborah shifted her weight from one leg to the other and observed Narissa Cameron. She said, "Hang on. Have you just handed me a way to structure the photo book I want to do? Bookended with interviews with this surgeon?"

"Christ! Have I? What does it mean? We're trying to help each other? You and me? Why the hell would we do that? We've got nothing in common. We can't be friends. I don't even *like* you."

"And I don't like you. So we have something in common after all."

Deborah smiled and Narissa laughed. Her mobile phone rang. She looked at the caller. She said, "My sponsor. She was looking for a meeting nearby. AA or Narc-Anon. I need to take this."

"Of course. I'm due at home anyway."

"Where d'you live?"

"Chelsea."

Narissa hooted and rolled her eyes. "Why, of *course* you do."

RIDLEY ROAD MARKET
DALSTON
NORTH-EAST LONDON

He told Sophie. Her comments were, "Oh my God. I can't believe . . . Is your mum . . . ? Do you even know why she . . . ?," all of which came tumbling out of her. But he had no answers to anything, so it was just as well that she could not even articulate the questions. He'd revealed to her that, yes, there *was* something in his father's life and yes, it *could* have been used to force his father to cooperate except it wasn't illegal, and his mother knew all about it.

Sophie couldn't understand it. She couldn't get her mind round it, she said. Neither could he. But once it became clear to him how pointless it was to threaten his father with blackmail over Lark, he knew he had to start thinking in another direction.

Tani considered bringing Simi into the picture at that point, telling her about Abeo's second family, about Monifa's knowledge of the second family, and about the plan to offer Simi to some Nigerian bloke willing to pay a bride price. But he knew there was a risk involved. To reveal all of this to her very likely would prompt her to go directly to their mother and ask her if what Tani had said was true. Monifa would deny it. And that would be that. Simi trusted their mother one hundred percent. It was Tani's job to create a fissure in that trust, and he had no idea how to do that.

What he could do, though, was to make his sister ready to disappear in preparation for the moment when he made her understand that she *had* to disappear. That meant first packing up some of her belongings into his old rucksack. He went to Simi's end of their clothes cupboard and fished there for garments suitable for the summer heat. He went to the chest of drawers and scored underthings and T-shirts. From beneath her bed, he brought out some of the items she used when making head wraps or decorating her charity-shop clothing. In each case, he took just enough so as not to raise Simi's suspicion should she rustle round her clothing or her decorative supplies prior to his removing her from Mayville Estate. All of this went into the rucksack and the rucksack itself went into his side of the clothes cupboard, pushed to the back, ready to be grabbed at a moment's notice.

Then he had to ponder where to take his sister when the time was right. There didn't appear to be many options. The best seemed to be in Ridley Road Market. Simi knew any number of people there. He merely needed to speak to them carefully in order to ascertain if one of them would temporarily hide his sister until he could come up with a better plan for her safety.

He walked to the market. He understood that he had to be careful. Conversations in the market were water in a sieve, and *confidential* had never made it into anyone's vocabulary. He reckoned that the people most familiar with Simi would also be the people most familiar with Monifa and Abeo. It wasn't likely that those people would help out with removing Simi from her home for the simple fact that doing so crossed a line among them, one that differentiated market business from family business. Thus, he had to cross Talatu off the list as well as Masha and anyone else who worked at the cake decorating place above the party shop.

When he arrived, Ridley Road was a din of music, conversations, haggling, and bagging. It was crowded this early in the day. Half the street was in shadow from the nearby buildings, and perishables had been moved to this shade even though neither the hour nor the shadows were doing much to mitigate the heat.

Tani decided upon the hair salon. He knew that Simi had gone to the same salon any number of times to watch the stylists fashion cornrows, add extensions, and create styles with braided hair. His problem was that there were four salons in Ridley Road, and he couldn't remember which of them Simi had visited.

He got lucky on his second try. Inside Xhosa's Beauty, he discovered two stylists who were acquainted with his sister. One of them was called Bliss, the other Tiombe. When they saw Tani in the doorway, Bliss whistled appreciatively and Tiombe looked him over head to toe and said, "Mmmm, *mmmm!* Look what's for lunch." Everyone laughed.

Obviously, these were women who were not cowed by men. This was a good thing because once Abeo started looking for Simi, the kind of person who was sheltering her couldn't shrink in his presence or in the face of his anger.

He said, looking from Bliss to Tiombe to Bliss, "Wondering if I could have a word?"

To which they responded in unison, "*Now*?"

"We don't look busy to you, gorgeous?" Bliss added.

"It's important," he said. "But I c'n wait."

"Hmmm. Well, tha's what you're going to have to do, innit," Tiombe said.

"Or you c'n come back in an hour," Bliss added.

"Your choice," Tiombe said. "Is this about your hair, cos we don't gen'rally work on blokes."

"It's about my sister," Tani said.

"An' who's your sister?"

"Simisola Bankole. Simi."

"Simi Bankole?" Bliss raised a perfectly shaped eyebrow. "We know Simi. I buy turban caps off her. Got two head wraps 's well. She's your sister?"

He nodded. "It's important."

"She's all right, innit?" Tiombe said.

"Not exactly," was his reply.

Tiombe and Bliss exchanged another glance. Tiombe put her hand on her client's shoulder and said, "You mind, Missus Okino?" And when Mrs. Okino indicated that she didn't mind, Tiombe nodded towards the door and she and Tani went outside.

There, she lit a cigarette, offering him one, which he refused. She smoked the way they did in films, a fag between her fingers and her lungs dispelling the residual smoke through her mouth as she spoke. She said, "How's Simisola not exactly all right?"

He said, "I got to find a place for her to stay."

"Why?" Tiombe's eyes narrowed. She was mixed race, Tani realised, and it looked to him like one of her parents was from China.

He looked round. He didn't want his parents to have police troubles, so he didn't know how far he could trust Tiombe. On the other hand, he also wanted to protect Simi. He had to come up with something that did both.

He settled on, "My dad's setting something up for Simi in Nigeria. She doesn't want it."

"Why not?"

"Because of what it is."

"Which is what?"

"A bride price. I mean he's promising her to some bloke who's willing to pay a lot of money to have her."

Tiombe's eyes widened. "You mean your dad's going to marry her off? How old's Simisola?"

"Eight." Tani didn't add that Simi would not marry straightaway. He could see that Tiombe was stirred by the idea of an eight-year-old girl being promised to anyone, no matter how much money changed hands. And this was a more powerful point. He said, "See, he paid a big bride price for a girl in Nigeria that I'm meant to marry. I think he wants to recoup the money, and he figures getting a bride price for Simi's the best way to do it."

Tiombe took a long, hard hit of her cigarette. She shook her head. "Tha's disgusting, that is," she said. "What c'n I do?"

He looked round. At this point it was crucial that there be no eavesdroppers to their conversation. "You c'n hide her," he said quietly. "It would be for only a few days till I find something more permanent."

"Care's more permanent," Tiombe said.

"Care's going to rattle her. I don' want that."

Tiombe looked past him. Her forehead became lined. "In't there someone can talk to your dad? This 's madness, innit. Where's your mum in all this?"

He shook his head. "She won't go against him. He makes the decisions for the family. Full stop."

"Hmph. Your dad's Abeo Bankole, right? He's got the little African market and the butcher's shop along the way?"

"How'd you know that?" Tani asked her.

"He flirts with the ladies, he does. An' Bankole's not an everyday name."

Tani couldn't imagine his father flirting with anyone. Most of the time he seemed either angry or impatient, but nothing else.

"Asked me 'n' Bliss for a pub drink twice, he did. Maybe three times," Tiombe said. "We went once. He's a friendly bloke, your dad. Only I don't like friendly when a bloke's married, and Bliss neither. I 'xplained it to him, and he was, like, okay with how we felt. Seen him since, we have, but he's always shown respect. So if you want me to, I c'n go to him and—"

"No! It's dead important he doesn't know we've talked, you and me. He'll work out what I'm trying to do. He'll make it impossible for Simi to get away. Like I said, it's only for a few days. Will you?"

Tiombe nodded. She dropped her cigarette to the pavement. She ground it out with the toe of her stiletto. She ducked back into the salon and returned to him with a scrap of paper. She'd scribbled a phone number upon it. "My mobile," she said. "When you're ready, you ring me and I'll fetch her to my place. She like animals, does Simi?"

"Animals? Like dogs?"

"Like goats," she said. "I got one as a pet."

PART II

5 AUGUST

Detective Inspector Thomas Lynley sat in his car, staring at the unattractive concrete wall of the underground car park, its unimposing grey expanse begging in vain for a Banksy. He was completely exasperated. He wanted to be exasperated with Daidre Trahair, the woman with whom he'd been involved—if that's what one could actually call it, which was something about which he had serious doubts—for more time than was reasonable considering how far along their relationship was. Or wasn't, actually. But the truth of the matter was that, if he had to be completely honest, his exasperation was with himself. The conversation they'd had on the previous night had not even needed to happen. He had been its instigator. And the argument that had arisen from it—identical to the previous arguments they'd had on the very same topic or a variation thereof—had been completely unnecessary. But he appeared to be incapable of letting pass what looked to him like a viable opening merely posing as an inadvertent comment.

In this case, though, it wasn't an inadvertent comment at all. It was part of a reasonable conversation, the topic of which had been introduced by Daidre herself. This involved her two younger siblings, twins

Goron and Gwynder, whom Daidre had insisted take up residence in her holiday cottage in Polcare Cove on the west coast of Cornwall. They'd been living with their parents until then, with Goron helping their father futilely stream for tin and Gwynder helping nurse their mother in the final years of her life. Once she had passed after a long and—it had to be said—unrealistically hopeful battle with cancer that had included crystals, visits to Catholic and Celtic shrines, drinking water from holy wells, Eastern medicine, and two spiritualists, Daidre's sole desire was to get her siblings out of the disreputable caravan that was the family home. She knew that her father would never leave the caravan himself. Although he might position it on another stream in Cornwall, he'd never abandon it. But she didn't know about the twins. In their late twenties, it was time for them to have some positive life experiences, she thought. It was time for them to develop and achieve some goals. They needed this. But it couldn't happen from an isolated caravan site, and although her holiday cottage was isolated as well, it was a brief drive from there to the hamlet of Morenstow and not much farther to the town of Casvelyn.

So she'd managed to get them to agree to the change of home— Goron being the more difficult of the two as he was generally fearful of any sort of change—but she didn't have the funds to support them once she got them there, which meant they were going to have to find employment. In multiple trips to see them, Daidre had managed to secure both of them jobs on a local cider farm: Goron as a handyman, ciderman, and appleman, and Gwynder as one of the cooks in the farm's jam kitchen.

But as the weeks went by, the twins decided that they wanted to return to their father. Goron did not like the work he was given, maintaining all the farm machinery, and a future watching over great vats of jam wasn't what Gwynder had in mind for herself. Daidre, however, was clinging to the belief that all the twins needed was time: time to get used to their new accommodation, time to meet people in the larger community, time to recognise and acknowledge the severe limitations their previous life had placed them under.

"They're just afraid," Daidre had said to Lynley on the previous evening in her flat in Belsize Park. She'd only just returned from Cornwall and he'd come to her directly once he could get away from New Scotland Yard. He'd brought a takeaway curry with him, which they'd ignored. Instead, they had decamped to the bedroom.

They were sitting up in Daidre's bed afterwards when she brought up Goron and Gwynder and their declaration of intent about returning to their father. "They don't want to believe me when I tell them that they *will* adjust and that if they run back to that caravan, they'll never know what kind of lives they could have had. Their father—my father, although I stopped thinking of him as that once we all were taken from him and my mum—is not going to live forever, and what will they do then, when he's gone?"

"Perhaps you moved too fast with this," Lynley offered. "I mean getting them out of the caravan so quickly after your mother died."

"There was never going to be a good time to do it, Tommy. And if they return now, it will just reinforce the idea of running away from whatever they fear. It seems to me that, when one is afraid of something, the only way to change that—to become unafraid of it—is to face it head-on."

And there it was, his opportunity. He should have avoided it like an enormous sinkhole on the landscape of his life, but instead he seized on it. He began with, "As to that, Daidre . . ."

"As to what?"

"As to facing one's fears head-on . . ."

"Yes?"

She was not about to pick up the lead. He could tell by the set of her jaw, which he was looking at as she was in profile, her back against the headboard and pillows piled behind her.

"I very much want you to be in my life," he told her.

"I *am* in your life. Look where we are, Tommy."

"Yes, of course. But I mean . . ." What *did* he mean, he wondered. What did he want from her beyond what he already had? A declaration of love? A commitment to some sort of future with him? She'd never once used *love* to describe her feelings, but was that so important? He lowered his gaze to the sheet that covered them both, to the hillocks made by each of their bodies. He realised that it *was* important. But then he was forced to ask himself why. And to that, he didn't have an answer. "Because I want it" was utterly insufficient unto the day. He settled on, "I suppose I want there to be a we, an us, an our. I love you and I want to take another step forward."

She shifted her position then, turning to face him directly when she said, "I'm here for you. I'm available to you. I want you in my life. I love having you in my life. Why isn't that enough?"

"Because it leads us nowhere."

"Why must it lead us somewhere?"

"Because that's what love does. At least that's what my love for you does. Or wants to do." Again, he thought, there was the opening. She could walk through it or she could slam it shut.

She shoved her sandy hair back from her face. She reached for her glasses on the large cardboard box that was still serving as her bedside table. She put them on. She said nothing, and a wise man would have let the conversation go at this point. But . . . Lynley sighed. When it came to Daidre, he was not a wise man. He said, "Why are you afraid?"

"I'm *not* afraid." She rose from the bed and gathered from the floor the T-shirt she'd been wearing, as well as her underwear. She put these on. When she'd done so, she said, "To be frank—"

To his credit, Lynley did not take this coming frankness as a positive sign.

"—where we are just now—you and I, Tommy—in this moment, is where I've always ended up with men. Men want something from me, and I don't understand what it is. Nor do I understand why what we have isn't enough." She placed her hand on her sternum and searched his face. She said, "This is who I am. Who I am at this moment is who I'll always be. I've tried more than once to explain this to you, but you seem to believe that if you continue to bang away at the bloody topic, to *delve* inside me, to . . . I don't even know what to call it. But you seem to think that if you keep on with these discussions, there will be something more you'll knock loose from me. But there just isn't."

He, too, swung off the bed and began to dress. He said, "And *you* continue to believe that there's nothing inside you intent upon keeping you at a safe distance from the rest of humanity in general and from me in particular. That's living a half life, Daidre, and I don't believe that all you want is a life by halves. You're afraid of moving into a future with me, and I don't know why, and I *won't* know why if you refuse to tell me."

"This isn't about fear. This whatever-we-have isn't about fear. Who I am isn't about fear."

"What is it, then? How can you get past it if you don't know it and can't name it?"

"Honestly, Tommy." She put on her jeans and began to walk towards the bedroom door. Instead of leaving the room, however, she turned back to him and said, "What are you, then? My analyst? My psychiatrist? My vicar? My . . . Oh, for God's sake. I don't even *know*."

"I'm the man who loves you," he told her.

They went a few more rounds on this general topic, and they did not part happily. He thought it best—and told her as much—that he not spend the night. She replied with, "You must do as you wish."

As before, nothing was resolved. But unlike before when he left her, she did not see him to the door.

And now in the underground car park at New Scotland Yard, he stared at the wall, calling himself every which way a fool. He wished he had not given up smoking. He very much wanted to take it up again.

As if she were a genie who'd popped out of a nearby brass bottle having heard his wish, his long-time partner Detective Sergeant Barbara Havers appeared at the driver's window of the Healey Elliott, sucking down the smoke from a nearly spent Player's. He waited for her to stamp it out before he opened the car's door. She stepped out of the way, and he got out. She was dressed with her usual flair: too-short trousers that she had to have found in Oxfam, her usual red high-top trainers, and a T-shirt reading "Being cremated is my last hope for a smoking hot body." He sighed when he saw this. At least, he thought, she had some sort of jersey tied round her neck. She could put it on in a hurry should an officer more superior and less tolerant than he encounter her.

She peered at him shrewdly. "Knackered or cheesed off?"

"Neither." He set off towards the lift, and she followed, hard on his heels.

She said, "No? So why d'you look like you just dropped beans and toast down the front of your shirt?" She stepped in front of him to examine this garment. "Did you, by the way?" she asked him.

"Metaphorically, I suppose the answer is yes." He punched the button to summon the lift.

"Ah. That means Daidre," Havers noted.

"She won't appreciate being compared to beans on toast."

"I'm not telling her. Are you?"

"When we begin speaking again, I might do. But probably not. And not to put too fine a point on it, Barbara, I generally don't tuck in to beans on toast for breakfast."

"Bloody hell!" she crowed. "I've converted you to Pop-Tarts!"

He shot her a look. The lift doors opened.

Up above, the first person they encountered was Dorothea Harriman, the department's redoubtable civilian secretary. Unlike Havers, she was dressed to the nines as usual, although Lynley wondered how she managed to teeter round the building comfortably on high heels that looked like the tools of some mediaeval oppressor. She said upon seeing him and Havers, "Ah. Acting Detective Chief Superintendent Lynley, you're wanted by his knighted nibs. Judi-with-an-i rang"—here she checked her wrist, upon which she was wearing one of those complicated watch-like affairs that apparently did everything but cook one's meals—"about twenty minutes ago. Shall I give her a bell and tell her you're on your way? Stephenson Deacon's with him, she told me. A word to the wise, I expect."

"Better you than me," Havers muttered to Lynley. She loathed the head of the Press Office nearly as much as he did.

He said to Dorothea, "Do we know what this is about?"

"It's all hush-hush and extremely *sotto voce* but the grapevine has it"—and Dorothea was born vintner—"that something dodgy's gone on at Empress State Building."

That didn't sound good, Lynley thought. Empress State Building was one of the three large policing centres that were in charge of groups of boroughs as more and more cutbacks were making the London police consolidate by doing away with local stations. If New Scotland Yard was being called in on something, it was going to be serious. If the Press Office was involved in some way, it also wasn't going to be pleasant.

Havers voiced what he was thinking. "Someone's done something they're about to regret. That is, if they don't already."

Lynley said, "I'll put you in the picture as soon as I'm in it," and he set off to the Assistant Commissioner's office.

WESTMINSTER
CENTRAL LONDON

Lynley had not been out of their presence for ten seconds before Dorothea turned to Barbara, giving her T-shirt a critical eye and doing much the same to her trousers and her trainers. She shifted her weight from one hip to the other and said, "Barbara . . ." in a tone that Barbara knew presaged a lengthy sartorial conversation that she didn't wish to have. She said hastily, "I know, I know. I've got a change of clothes in the car. I was out running earlier and this was what came to hand."

"You were out running," Dorothea said. "D'you expect me to believe that? And why did you not show up for tap dancing last night?"

"Ingrown toenails?" Barbara said with hope.

"*Un*amusing. Next week I intend to drag you by your hair if necessary. How much weight have you lost?"

"Don't know," Barbara said. "The bathroom scales and I have not been intimate lately. But I've probably lost nothing, Dee. Whatever I lose, I make up by eating curry for the rest of the week. And naan. Absolute piles of naan."

"Oh bother," Dorothea said. "You're impossible."

"That sounds good."

"Don't cross me, Barbara. I simply *refuse* to let you cross me. Now. Let's get to a computer. I've found something spectacular for us."

To Dorothea *spectacular* meant having the potential to line herself up—and, unfortunately, Barbara as well—with a man. In this case, however, it appeared that her intention was to line them both up with herds of men. It was a website called GroupMeet, and Dorothea brought it up on Barbara's computer the moment they reached her desk.

"This is simply the bee's knees," Dorothea said.

The bee's knees? Wasn't that something from . . . Barbara wasn't sure. The 1920s? Dee had been watching period television again.

"What is it?" Barbara asked over Dee's shoulder. Bright colours, photos of laughing, smiling, chortling, giggling people from thirty-five to seventy engaged in various activities. Men with women, men with men, women with women, old with old, young with young, older men with younger women, younger men with older women. They were all playing tennis or boating or working in gardens or riding horses or attending the opera or the ballet. And everyone was having a smashing good time. "What the hell, Dee?" Barbara repeated. "This isn't some dating site, is it?"

"Lord, no," Dorothea said. "Heaven forfend and all that. This is an activity site. What one does is scroll through the various activities—Look! Here's one for tap dancing!—and click on whatever appeals. That takes you to where the next round of that activity will be taking place. Here, let me do it."

As Barbara watched, Dorothea clicked on Rambling. Up popped various photos of ramblers along with a list of upcoming rambles. Dorothea then clicked on *Pub Rambles,* which took them to a dozen different walks to and from pubs that were scheduled in various parts of England. She clicked on Oxfordshire and found two rambles listed, both to take place in the following week. She chose one of them and a list of names popped up. "One adds one's name to the list and then just shows up for the activity," she announced. "Isn't that brilliant? Name the activity and there's someone doing it. Look." She took them back to the main page and began reading off the various activities: Sketching, Plein Air Watercolours, Rock Climbing, Crewing, Ballroom Dancing, Amateur Theatricals, Choirs, Chinese Cookery, War History, Architecture, Inigo Jones Landscapes. "It goes on and on," Dorothea told her. "We *must* do one of these together, Barbara. It sounds like *such* fun."

It sounded to Barbara like various levels of the Inferno.

Dee was going on, however. "Of course, we still have our tap dancing, you and I. But there's more to life than that."

"Right. There's curry *after* tap dancing as well."

"Don't be silly. I'm signing us up for something." She peered at the terminal's screen again. "Sketching," she decided. "I'm signing us up for sketching. I've always longed to sketch, haven't you? Never mind.

You'll just say you've never given sketching a thought. But I know you better than you know yourself, so sketching it is. And, oh! Look at this, Barbara. There're language groups as well. French, German, Cantonese, Hebrew, Arabic, Italian, Spanish, Finnish—heavens, does anyone actually *speak* Finnish these days? Are you interested in Italian at all, Barbara? It can be a very useful language when one travels, you know. Conversations with the locals and all that."

Barbara narrowed her eyes. Dee was very clever. She was leading to a topic that Barbara had been avoiding for weeks. Inspector Salvatore Lo Bianco of the Lucca police had been in England since early July—was still in England, as far as she knew—to study the language, and Dorothea had decided straightaway upon meeting him that he was the answer to a young girl's dreams, or at least to Dorothea's dreams for Barbara. Only Barbara wasn't a young girl with dreams nor had she considered Salvatore as someone she might set her cap at. Whatever setting one's cap meant and from where on *earth* had she dug up that expression? Possibly one of her Regency romance novels. Time to switch genres, she told herself. Horror, perhaps. Yes. Horror sounded good.

She said, "Two dinners at a wine bar in Holland Park. European cheek kisses at the end of the night."

Dorothea blinked. "What?"

"Dee, please. I know you better than you know yourself, as someone once said to me. You want to know if I've seen Salvatore Lo Bianco since he's been here—other than at our dance concert, although to call it a dance concert makes it sound like we actually were able to *dance*—"

"*Which* we absolutely were and you know it."

"Right. Whatever. So I've had dinner with him twice, once with Lynley and Dr. Trahair, so that barely counts." That had been the limit of her intercourse with the Italian policeman, and Barbara intended to keep it that way. But Dorothea was nothing if not determined to move a man into Barbara's future as well as into her own. "And anyway, I already know Italian," Barbara added.

"Oh my God! You *do*?"

"*Ciao, grazie, pizza,* and *prego,* but don't test me on what any of that means. Except *pizza,* of course. I've got that one bloody well down."

"Very funny," Dorothea said. "Hilarious. I'm bursting my buttons. I'm also signing us up for sketching. If you don't behave yourself, I'll sign us up for Chinese cookery as well."

"Fine. Wonderful. A-okay and all the rest," Barbara told her. "Look up sketching and tell me what you discover. I'll start pinching paper and pencils."

She wasn't long at her desk when Lynley returned. He was carrying a small stack of manila folders. He indicated with an inclination of his head that he wished to see her in his temporary office. He gestured at DS Winston Nkata as well. Nkata appeared to be buried deeply in the mind-numbing boredom of a CCTV film taken inside Gloucester Road tube station. He also appeared to be barely able to keep his eyes open for whatever it was for which he was meant to search. Barbara had to call his name three times before he looked up. Then she did the same as Lynley, inclining her head in the general direction of his office.

Winston rose from his desk. He was quite tall, six foot five, so standing from a seated position required some adjusting of his spine. As soon as he was on his feet, Barbara set off towards Lynley's office. If Lynley wanted to see them both, chances were good that the game was afoot.

As she entered, she noted that the acting DCS—Lynley—had still done nothing to alter the office. Its usual occupant—DCS Isabelle Ardery—was on personal leave for at least eight weeks, taking the cure on the Isle of Wight. The state of the office served to indicate Lynley's confidence in Ardery's ability to get herself in order regarding drink before she bollixed up her life for good. Personal items—like photos of her twin boys—had been removed by the DCS herself. Everything else was as it had been. Even the furniture had not been moved so much as an inch.

Lynley gestured to the circular table at one side of the room. He said as he did so, "Dorothea was correct. We're dealing with something from Empress State Building."

"Something dodgy happening there, sir?" Barbara asked.

"A murder," Lynley told her.

"Why's the Press Office involved?"

"The usual: to keep things quiet, calm, and, they hope, out of the papers for as long as possible."

EMPRESS STATE BUILDING
WEST BROMPTON
SOUTH-WEST LONDON

Empress State Building stood massively on Lillie Road, not far from West Brompton underground station, as well as the lichenous Victorian monuments of Brompton Cemetery. The building was staggeringly tall, vaguely clover-shaped, and dressed in the uninspiring grey-and-glass of so many of London's modern buildings. Like New Scotland Yard, it was heavily protected. One didn't simply wander in off the street to chat with the local bobby.

Lynley was expected. After a five-minute wait opposite Peeler's Café, a ginger-haired man of middle age came out of one of the lifts and then through the turnstile, saying, "DCS Lynley?"

"Thomas," Lynley said. "And the DCS is acting only. I've been asked to step in for a few weeks while my guv's on leave. You're DCS Phinney?"

"Mark." He offered his hand. He had a firm grip, Lynley noted.

Phinney said, "They've given you a visitor's badge, I see. Good. Come with me. We're on the seventeenth but I'll take you to the Orbit. Spectacular views up there."

He badged Lynley through the turnstile and led the way to a bank of lifts that went only to the upper floors of the building. It was a quick trip. The lift was fast and silent.

The Orbit turned out to be part lounge and part café, with the cooking done in the middle area, which would be the spine of the clover. The views were just as Phinney had described them: spectacular. Lynley felt as if he could see straight into the Home Counties in every direction.

He accepted Phinney's offer of coffee, and he found a vacant seating area close to one of the floor-to-ceiling windows. These encircled the entire Orbit and it wasn't long before he realised that the lounge itself rotated slowly. Sit long enough and one would see the entirety of Greater London as one inched by it.

Phinney returned with two cups and two croissants. He placed these on a coffee table and sat opposite Lynley, saying, "What can I do for you, Thomas?"

"You can tell me about Detective Sergeant Bontempi."

"Teo?" he said. "She's on the upswing, isn't she? I've not heard."

An odd response, Lynley thought. He said, "When did you last see her?"

"I saw her in hospital. Three nights ago."

"Had the hospital rung you?"

"No. Where is this heading, Thomas?"

"I'm afraid she's dead."

Phinney stared at him, as if an attempt he'd made to read Lynley's lips had come to nothing. "How can that be?" He could easily have been speaking to himself. Before Lynley responded, he said, "I saw her. She was very much alive. I found her."

"Where?" Lynley asked.

"At her flat. I went inside and found her in bed. I couldn't rouse her, but . . . *Christ,* she was absolutely breathing. I rang 999. When they finally showed up—"

"Finally?"

"It was at least thirty minutes. They took her vitals, got her on a drip, put her on a stretcher, and took her to hospital. I followed in my car."

"Were you able to speak with her at all?"

He shook his head. "The last time I saw her, they were taking her into A and E. I waited for word but there was none. After two hours, all I was able to learn was that they'd moved her from A and E into Critical Care and they'd contacted her next of kin. I don't know whether that was her husband, her parents, or her sister, although I reckon it was her husband. I left before any of them arrived." He got to his feet. He walked to the window and placed his hand on it, his palm flat against the glass. He said to his dim reflection, "She was in bed when I found her. She was in her nightclothes. How could she have died?"

"How did you manage to get into her flat?" Lynley asked.

Phinney turned from the window. Lynley noted that his ruddy face had become quite pale. He said, "I showed the concierge my warrant card and explained the situation."

"Which was . . . ?"

"What?"

"The situation. What took you to her flat in the first place?"

One of Phinney's hands made a fist and gently hit his other palm as he spoke. "She'd recently transferred to one of the MITs in south London, but she'd requested some days off before starting there. When she was due to begin, she failed to turn up. I was called for confirmation that the date of transfer was correct. It was and as Teo—DS Bontempi—was nothing if not dedicated to her job, it made no sense that she'd failed to turn up. I thought at first something had happened to her father. He had a stroke earlier in the year. But when I rang her parents, all was well. So I began to ring her mobile at intervals. There was no reply. After a few hours, I went to her flat."

"There was no one more local that you could have rung?"

"Probably. Of course. But I didn't think to search anyone out. I just made my way there and got the concierge to let me inside the place."

"You knew where she lived? Had you been there before?"

"I drove her home one night after something of a booze-up that the team had at our local. A morale-boosting thing. She had no car, and, as I'd had only a glass of wine, and as it was late, I thought public transport might not be the best idea."

"She was drunk?"

"Tipsy, but not drunk. Look, what's actually going on? Why's the Met become involved in this?"

Lynley saw no point in obfuscation. "She was murdered, I'm afraid."

"Murdered." Phinney said the word in a manner that managed to be both numb and disbelieving simultaneously. Then, *"Murdered?* In hospital?"

"She died in hospital, but the cause of her death seems to have occurred in her flat."

His brow furrowed. "How is that possible? What *happened?*"

"Epidural haematoma," Lynley said. "A blow to the head had fractured her skull. She was in a coma when you found her. Hence the reason you couldn't rouse her."

"You said murder, though. But she must have fallen and caused the fracture herself. What I mean is, she was in her nightclothes. She was in bed. And there was no sign. I mean, there was no indication of a blow. There was nothing to suggest . . . Who else knows?"

"That it was murder? The family only know she's died, as they authorised her being taken off the respirator. And that she died was actually all anyone knew prior to the post mortem examination. I've officers heading out now to tell her relations that it wasn't a natural death."

"But *murder* . . . ? With no overt sign of a blow to her head?"

"The blow was on the back of her head, so you wouldn't have seen it, and it didn't break the skin. There was also a weapon. The skull fracture indicated that."

"What was it?"

"We don't know just yet. Everything that could have been used is being removed from her flat by SOCO to go to forensics. If nothing among all that would have served, it's safe to assume that whoever hit her also brought the weapon to do so. And took it away afterwards."

"Then why do you assume she was hit and not . . . ?" He answered the question he hadn't bothered to finish. "The autopsy, of course. As you said. There would have been one. My God, I could have *done* something for her. I'm trained to see things, and I saw nothing."

"You couldn't have known what had occurred, Mark. As you've said, she was in bed, she was in her nightclothes. What were you supposed to think? The DS herself probably didn't know she was so badly wounded. She was given a blow, but it's altogether possible that she didn't actually lose consciousness immediately. Or if she did lose consciousness, the regaining of it would have made her think it had been a glancing blow, and that's all. She might have been dizzy. She might have had something of a headache, for which she took paracetamol. Or she had no immediate memory of what had happened in the first place. She got herself into bed without a complete understanding of the danger she was in. Then her condition worsened, she lost consciousness, she went into a coma. The only way she could have been saved was if someone had found her in time to get her to hospital so the pressure on her brain might have been relieved. That didn't happen, and it's not the fault of anyone who knew her, save her killer."

"You're saying she knew her killer, then?"

"If she'd been attacked in the street or in another public place, she would have been quickly found. The fact that she wasn't suggests that she admitted her killer into her flat."

"Or the killer was someone who had a key."

"Or that. Yes."

"Her family might have keys. Her parents, her sister. Perhaps even her husband. Ross Carver."

"'Even'?"

"They were separated. Two years? Perhaps longer? But they'd lived together in the flat during their marriage. He may still have a key."

Phinney returned to the sofa where he'd sat initially. He tore his croissant in half, raised it, couldn't seem to find it within himself to eat it. He set it back on the plate and took up his coffee. His hand shook, Lynley noted. Not so badly that it would be noticed by someone not looking for signs, but quite obvious to anyone who questioned villains on a more or less regular basis.

Lynley said, "What can you tell me about her transfer? Was it voluntary?"

Phinney hesitated. Lynley saw him swallow. "Sadly, no," he said. "I initiated it. She would have preferred to remain here."

"You mentioned a team. I assume she was part of it."

"She was," Phinney said. "She was a good officer and a fine detective."

"Why did you have her transferred, then?"

"It's difficult to explain, and I would have had it otherwise. But there were issues with *how* she worked. She preferred going off on her own if she uncovered what she thought was a lead. She'd come up with her own activities as well, so she wasn't a team player in the way I need everyone here to be. When something popped into her mind— even if it was beyond our remit—she did it and reported on it afterwards, if at all. We had any number of run-ins, she and I, over what was best for the project."

"What were you working on?" Lynley asked. *Project* suggested something ongoing, possibly of long duration.

"Abuse of women," Phinney said. "But primarily FGM. She was

passionate about rooting it out and putting a stop to it. Well, of course, anyone would be. But the difficulty was that she insisted on forging ahead, in whatever direction took her fancy, in an investigation that's monumentally difficult to run anyway."

Lynley took up his own croissant and broke off a piece. It was, he found, actually quite good. As was the coffee. "I can understand her passion," he said.

"Right. Of course. As a woman, she—"

Lynley cut him off with, "She was more than merely a woman in this particular situation."

"What do you mean?"

"She herself was badly mutilated. It was discovered in autopsy. I can't think she would have told anyone about it save her husband."

Mark's gaze dropped as his mouth opened. But he made no sound for several moments, into which a boisterous group entered the Orbit, apparently on their way to their elevenses. He finally managed, "No, of course she never told me." He nodded at the folders that Lynley was carrying. He went on with, "You said it was bad?"

"Infibulation."

"Jesus." Liquid came into Phinney's eyes. He raised a hand as if to shield them from Lynley's view. Because of the project he was heading, he obviously knew exactly what infibulation was.

Lynley said, "According to the Home Office pathologist, it would have been done many years in the past, possibly when she was an infant. All we know is that it was badly done. At some point she'd been almost completely sewn up."

Mark raised his other hand to indicate no more. Lynley couldn't blame him. The woman had been his colleague. The surprise of learning, the horror of knowing. And Mark Phinney himself had been the one to force her transfer. As if he'd read Lynley's mind, Phinney said, "I would *never* have transferred her. Why the hell didn't she tell me? She could have *told* me why she . . ." He seemed at a loss.

"Why she didn't play by your rules?"

"Everything would have been different had she only told me."

"You would have had to have her wholehearted trust for her to tell you, I daresay," Lynley pointed out. "After what had been done to her, it stands to reason that she probably trusted very few people." He picked up his coffee, finished it, and stood. He said, "We'll need to take a look at everything she's done on your team and everything she may have done on her own. That means her files, her notes, her computer, her reports on her actions, digital photos, digital recordings, and anything else she may have documented and given to you or squirreled away. I'll need to talk to her colleagues as well."

"Aside from myself, we have only two DCs and Teo's replacement, DS Jade Hopwood."

"Four people in total?" Lynley was incredulous. "How do you intend to put an end to the abuse of females with only one sergeant and two DCs?"

"That's all the Met would give us," Phinney said. "So I expect you see the difficulty we face."

NEW END SQUARE
HAMPSTEAD
NORTH LONDON

DS Winston Nkata knew that one of the reasons he'd been tasked with telling the family of Teo Bontempi that she had been murdered was that he was Black, as had been the detective sergeant herself, as would be her family. He didn't mind this, although he did wonder if his guv—Lynley—thought that hearing horrible news from a person of the same race somehow would make the blow less grievous. But he accepted the assignment without question or remark, although he didn't relish it. No one ever truly wanted to be the carrier of this sort of news.

He was surprised by the family's address in Hampstead. Hampstead meant money by the bucketful and money by the bucketful meant either an inheritance that the death duties hadn't completely eaten up or employment with serious remuneration. Having grown up on a housing estate in an area of south London still waiting to be called fashionable, he was used to immense tower blocks, multiple ethnicities, gang warfare among youths who were often Black, and parents—his own, especially—who allowed him out of their flat during his childhood only if he had a destination he could name and a path to that destination that didn't take him onto anyone's declared turf. That hadn't mattered much. He'd been recruited into the Brixton Warriors anyway, just as had been his brother, Harold, who was languishing in prison at the monarch's pleasure and would be doing so for at least seventeen more years. Winston had been plucked from the Warriors through the kindness and interest of a cop—Black like the Nkata family—and he had ventured onto a new path as a result. And although his life had altered radically over the years, he'd long ago concluded that the only members of his race who ended up living in Hampstead were celebrities: film stars, well-paid athletes, and the like.

The Bontempis' address took him to New End Square, an area of shaded pavements and wisteria-draped porches. There the Bontempi family had impressive digs: a red-brick mansion, which appeared to be the largest dwelling in the area. It sat behind a black wrought-iron fence. Between the fence and the house was a flourishing garden. The house stood three floors—five multipaned windows on each—and from its roof sprang a multitude of chimneys. It even had a single-storey extension built onto it, although why a house this large would need an extension was a mystery to him. One vehicle was parked in front of it, a Land Rover of recent vintage. He stowed his own Fiesta just behind it.

Once he'd climbed out, he made his way to the gate. Although both the fence and the gate were no more than four feet tall, the gate was nonetheless locked to discourage easy entry. He pressed the single button. It took more than one try. Finally, a woman said, "Yes? What is it?" in what sounded to Nkata like a boarding-school voice. He identified himself and the lock on the gate was released. He proceeded inside and headed in the direction of a massive cave of wisteria, which he assumed was overhanging a porch. It was. It grew in three directions from a substantial trunk that looked as if it had come from the Garden of Eden, at the spot where Adam and Eve were shown the door. It covered the porch, draped over every ground-floor window, and was climbing avidly towards the roof.

The door was opened before he had a chance to mount the steps. A tall and extremely attractive woman stood there, her hand on the knob. She looked close to his own age—which was twenty-seven—and she wore a white sundress tightly cinched at the waist and printed with sunflowers. The material provided a marked but pleasing contrast with her skin. Her feet were bare, he saw; her toenails bore red polish; her hair was straightened, and it fell to her jaw in a bob that well became her. As did her careful makeup and her jewellery. Both were understated. She looked put together by a professional stylist.

She said hesitantly, "New Scotland Yard?" She made no effort to hide her perusal of his lengthy facial scar. Perhaps it was that which made her look wary, he thought.

He produced his warrant card. She looked it over, then looked him over, then said, "How d'you say your surname?" as if it was a test of some sort.

"N-sound plus kahta," he told her.

"African then."

"My dad's from Africa. My mum's Jamaican."

"You don't sound either."

"I was born here."

"You're really Metropolitan Police?"

"Tha's how it is. I need to have a word with your parents."

She turned with a bit of a swirl that showed off her frock as well as her legs. She disappeared into the house proper, but she left the door open, so he stepped inside. He stood in an entry with a glossy black oak floor. On this lay faded Persian rugs. There were antique tables, polished brass fittings, and landscape paintings framed in gold. As Barb Havers might have put it, the Bontempis weren't exactly hurting for it.

The young woman returned. She was carrying a large bottle of San Pellegrino and four glasses on a tray. She said, "They're coming. It's just this way," and she took him into a sitting room, which looked like something out of a home decorating magazine: overstuffed sofas, overstuffed armchairs, upholstery printed with flowers and vines, shining mahogany tables, a curio cabinet holding a strange collection of small porcelain figurines of women cut off at the waist. He couldn't imagine what their use was or had been.

The young woman said, "I'm Rosalba, by the way. Rosie, that is. Have you come about Teo? I'm her sister."

Nkata turned away from the curio cabinet, saying, "Right. Yeah."

"Pellegrino?" she asked, holding forth the bottle.

"Sounds good. Ta." And then because he was dead curious about how a family such as hers had ended up in a place such as this, "C'n I ask? What's your parents' occupation?"

"What a terribly rude question."

"Yeah. Sorry. It is. I was jus' wonderin'."

She frowned but said, "My father has a veterinary hospital near Reading. It's like a regular hospital? Twenty-four hours a day, I mean, with specialists, operating theatres, and all of that? Mum's a private pilot." Rosie rolled her eyes. "She flies the bored wives of big-money executives to buy their shoes in Florence and have lunch in Paris."

"Don't be judgmental, Rosie." The woman's voice came from the same direction Rosie had come with the water and the glasses. She spoke with an accent that sounded French. Nkata swung around. He was quite surprised. Rosie's mother was, he saw, as white as a white person could get, her skin a stark contrast to her black, pinstriped suit. She would have done Dee Harriman proud, he thought: slim trousers, crisp white shirt with the collar turned up to frame her face, jacket cut to fit her perfectly, flat shoes with gold buckles. Her jewellery was also gold, and he reckoned it was the real stuff: rings, earrings, and a chain with a pendant that he couldn't make out. She said to him, "I'm Solange Bontempi. Rosie says you've come about our Teo."

She didn't strike Nkata as the grieving mother. He wondered about that. Then he wondered about himself for wondering that. Because of his job, he well knew that people had different ways of grieving. He asked himself if he was doubting her because she was white. Probably, he decided.

Before he could answer, Rosie said, "Does *Papá* need help?"

"Yes, but don't offer, Belle. Today, it is . . . as it has been." And then to Nkata, as if she'd read his doubts about her. "Cesare—my husband—is taking Teo's death very hard. Rosie and I try not to burden him further with our own loss. And just now it seems less than real, as if it has happened to someone else. And no one will give us permission for her body."

"Tha's due to the postmortem exam. I 'spect it'll be a bit 'f time yet."

"This is something I do not understand," Solange said. "And no one will tell us anything."

"That's why he's here, *Maman*. This is Sergeant Nkata from the Met."

"And why has this Sergeant Nkata from the Met come to see us?" A man speaking this time, another accent that was not English. It was also not French. He was coming from the same direction his wife and daughter had used, but with a difference. His progress was quite slow and he used a Zimmer frame. One of his legs, Nkata noticed, did not work well.

"It's about Teo, Cesare," Solange Bontempi said.

Cesare Bontempi said to Nkata, "I do not understand why we're forbidden from bringing her home. We want a funeral. We want our friends around us. We want our priest to—" He stopped himself. He waved away more words.

"*Papá*, sit," Rosie said. "Please. Here. Let us help you. *Maman*?"

He flung out an arm to keep them both at bay. He continued his agonised progress into the room. There was sweat on his forehead and his upper lip. They waited in silence until he joined them. He collapsed into—rather than sat upon—one of the sofas. He shoved the Zimmer frame to one side.

He said to Nkata, "Why can we not have our daughter returned to us?"

Nkata waited for the women to sit. They didn't appear to want to. Indeed, Rosie looked like someone wishing to flee: she kept glancing in the direction of the open front door. He gestured to two of the armchairs. He sat at the other end of the sofa from Cesare. He said, "'S not good news. I'm sorry to have to tell it to you."

"There is something more?" Solange's hand crept to her throat in that defensive manoeuvre some women employed, but her gaze went quickly to her husband. "Cesare, perhaps—"

"No! You tell it, Mister Sergeant Whoever You Are."

"Nkata," he said, "Winston Nkata. I'm come to tell you tha' looks like she was murdered, your daughter. Which is why, see, they won't r'lease her body to you."

"Murdered?" Cesare said. "Teo is *murdered*? She was police. Who murders police?"

Solange got to her feet and went to him. He waved her away again. Solange said, "Cesare, please. You must—"

"What must I? Stay calm? Teodora is murdered, and I must be calm?"

"You are not well, my dear. Rosie and I are afraid for you."

Cesare cast a glance at Rosie. Her head lowered, her gaze on her lap, on her hands clasped tightly.

Solange said to Nkata, "I do not understand. *Who* has decided she was murdered? And why? And how?"

Nkata explained how it would probably have happened, based on the report Lynley had shared with him and Barbara Havers. He did not rehash the details that they would already know: the discovery of Teo Bontempi by an officer she worked with; the hospitalisation; the examination, the scans, and the X-rays revealing the epidural haematoma; the futile effort to save her by drilling into her skull to reduce the swelling; the autopsy conducted by a Home Office pathologist once it was determined that she couldn't have injured *herself* in the way that she'd been injured. He spoke merely of the conclusion that the pathologist had reached. All of this would soon be presented before a coroner's jury, he said. But everything about her injury, her subsequent coma, and her death suggested murder.

The three of them remained silent. They appeared stunned, each trying to work out how this could have happened. Solange was the one to break the silence.

"Who would have wanted to do this to Teo? And why?"

"Tha's what we'll be working on," Nkata told her. "Tha's part 'f why I'm here. We start with who."

"You think that one of *us* hurt her?" Nkata saw that Rosie's hands remained clenched tightly in her lap as she spoke.

Her mother said, "You cannot think—"

"Are we supposed to supply *alibis*?" Rosie cut in.

"Matter 'f form, but yeah," Nkata told her.

"And you will want to know if she had enemies," Solange said.

Cesare Bontempi scoffed. "Teodora had no enemies."

"Tha's hard to tell from the outside looking in, innit," Nkata said. "So we'll need names of her friends, names of anyone she might've been seeing. We got her husband." He looked through the notes he'd taken during a phone call with Lynley and Havers prior to setting off. "Ross Carver. But tha's the limit so far."

All three of them exchanged glances at the name Ross Carver. Nkata was about to ask them about the nature of Teo Bontempi and Ross Carver's relationship prior to her death, when Rosie spoke.

"You'll want to know when we last saw her as well."

"Tha'd be a good place to start."

"She was here . . . I think it was three weeks ago," Solange said. "She called in to see about her *papá*."

"We watched that film, the old cowboy one where they jump off a cliff," Cesare said.

"*Butch Cassidy*, yes, yes. I remember. You two love that film, don't you. You have seen it so many times together." She smiled briefly, perhaps at the thought of father and daughter sharing this love of a particular film. She said to Nkata, "It was difficult for Teo to call here as often as she wished. Her work with the police kept her quite busy."

"She lived for her work," Rosie added.

"Lots 'f cops do. It's why cop marriages go bad."

"Hers did," Cesare said. "Her marriage. It ended."

"When was this?"

"Over two years ago." Rosie was the one who answered, and she added, "They've been apart that long, but they haven't . . . they hadn't yet divorced. Teo thought it was time, though. Well, it was when you think of it. There's really no point to hanging on when a marriage has gone dead between two people."

"They both—"

"Ross—"

Solange and Rosie had spoken at once. Rosie was the one to complete her thought. "They both wanted it," she said. She kept her gaze fixed on Nkata as she spoke, and her parents kept their gazes fixed on her.

Nkata said, "She seeing anyone?"

"She could have been, but Teo never talked to me about private things. Perhaps that was due to the difference in our ages? She's seven years older."

"Her husband, then? He seeing anyone?"

This question was met with silence until Solange said, "You speak of Ross?" as if her daughter had practised polyandry and Ross Carver was only one of her many. She looked at Cesare, then at Rosie. Then back at Nkata when she said, "We see Ross occasionally, but this is something he wouldn't have told us."

"Because . . . ?"

"I expect he wouldn't have wanted Teo to know. As they were still married."

That made not a jot of sense to Nkata. They were divorcing. They'd been apart two years. What difference could it have made if Teo Bontempi had been told the truth about her estranged husband? He stirred restlessly for a moment as he studied them until he could feel it straight to his fingertips: he wasn't close to the truth with these people. Something was going on in the family, something more than the death of one of the daughters.

He let a silence hang, as he'd learned from observing Lynley. Most people, he knew, couldn't cope with silence. But these three, he discovered, were not most people.

Cesare finally said, "I have fatigue. I leave you now," and his wife was on her feet at once to help him to his.

She said to Nkata, "If you don't mind, Sergeant? Belle, please give him our mobile numbers. You'll want them, won't you, Sergeant?"

He acknowledged this and watched as she helped her husband from the room. He could hear the murmur of their voices. A door opened and shut in another area of the house and they were gone.

Rosie, however, was very much there. He had a feeling about her, a basic uneasiness telling him she was good with secrets: her own and others'. She knew far more than she was saying, he reckoned. What he couldn't work out was whether what she knew was about her parents, her sister, or her sister's husband.

HACKNEY
NORTH-EAST LONDON

His employer had told him to take a few days, which was why Barbara Havers found Ross Carver at home. She'd not needed to beat any bushes to locate him. She rang the mobile number next to his name in one of the files and there he was. Could she speak with him about the death of Teo Bontempi? she asked. She could meet him somewhere or she could come to him, wherever he happened to be.

There was a significant pause before he said heavily, "Teo?" with what sounded peculiarly like resignation. And then, "Of course." He gave Barbara his details and she set off.

It turned out that he had a flat in a large block that was part of a collection of similar blocks running the length of Goldsmith's Row, in Hackney. Most of these displayed bleak visages of dreary and long-unwashed London brick. Only one, however, appeared to be of more recent vintage and its concrete façade hadn't yet fallen victim to exhaust fumes, dust, and other grime.

This being London, there was, of course, no place for her Mini. Indeed, for reasons obscure, all traffic into Goldsmith's Row had been blocked by means of three bollards. One could walk or one could bicycle in the lane. But that was the extent of it. So she pulled onto the pavement alongside a wrought-iron fence nearly overtaken by shrubbery, and she fished in her rat's nest glovebox and found her police placard, dog-eared though it was. She positioned this to be clearly seen by anyone peering into the windscreen. She did hope that noticing the placard would preclude anyone's noticing the plethora of takeaway cartons on the floor of the car and an overfull ashtray in need of clearing. She reckoned she could get away with the Cadbury wrappers that she habitually tossed over her shoulder.

Out in the air, she was immediately assailed by the stench of manure. Lots of manure. The area was a veritable manure-palooza that the summer heat seemed to be cooking into a grossly malodorous stew. That, together with the crowing of an overstimulated rooster, the quacking of many ducks, and the braying of a donkey, told her she was in the near vicinity of Hackney City Farm. Indeed, when she peered through the shrubbery on the other side of the fence, she found herself looking into a ramshackle flower and vegetable garden, beyond which she could make out the top of a barn. As she observed the garden, two young women entered from the barn side of it, wearing tall gumboots on their feet and sun hats on their heads. They carried gardening tools with them and trugs as well. Harvesting time, Barbara thought. Doubtless Hackney City Farm put its copious manure to very good use.

The smell didn't fade as she walked along Goldsmith's Row, checking addresses. She couldn't imagine living directly across the lane from the farm. One probably couldn't open a window ten months of the year.

Ross Carver's block of flats was nearly at the end of the lane, but its position didn't do much to improve the air. She found that she was trying to hold her breath. The stench was so bad that she reckoned breathing through her mouth might expose her to two dozen forms of bacteria previously unknown to science.

A buzzer releasing the lock gave her access to the building. She took the lift to the topmost floor. Ross Carver, she decided, must have been watching for her. She had barely lifted her hand to knock before the door swung open and a nice-looking but swarthy man—Carver himself, presumably—was standing before her.

She knew little about him other than that he was a structural engineer. At the moment, he appeared more like a wannabe rock star. He was unshaven, his sumptuous, dark curls were swept back from his face with some kind of gelatinous substance, and he wore a manbun at the back of his head, two small hoop earrings and a diamond-looking stud in one ear, and that stud's mate in the other. He had on a waistcoat that had seen far better days on a much larger body, as well as blue jeans. He wore no shirt. Prince Charming he wasn't.

She said, "Ross Carver?"

He said, "DS Havers?"

Their identities more or less established, he opened the door wide to a flat so meagerly furnished that she wondered if he lived in it at all. An adolescent boy came out of another room as she entered. Behind her, Ross Carver said, "My son, Colton." She nodded at the boy. He nodded back, did that teenage-boy thing of flipping his overlong hair off his face, and said, "I should go?" to his father.

"Could be for the best," Carver said. "She's here to talk about Teo. Ask your mum about the Gibraltar trip. Tell her I'll give her a bell tonight."

"She'll just say no."

"I'll try the sweet talk."

Colton snorted. "As if." He slouched in the general direction of the door.

When it was closed upon his departure, Carver said to Barbara, "I'm having a lager. You?"

"Too early for me. A glass of water'll do it."

"Give me a minute," and he disappeared round the corner of the room into what she assumed must be the kitchen.

She walked to the window. She wanted to open it as the room was tipping the scale at ten degrees beyond stifling and her deodorant was sending extremely threatening messages from her armpits, but she reckoned the smell from the farm might knock both of them over. She said, "You ever able to open these?" with reference to a set of glass doors to her left. They gave onto a balcony. It held at least two dozen taped-up cardboard boxes, a bicycle, and a set of free weights.

He came back to her, a bottle of water in one hand and a Stella Artois in the other. He said, "I signed the lease in the dead of winter. Rain keeps the smell down at that time of year, and I didn't notice. I was in a bit of a hurry. And now?" He indicated vaguely towards the south. "I'm going back to Streatham."

"Back to Teo's flat?"

"It was ours together when we *were* together."

"You've been packing." She nodded at the balcony with its boxes.

"I never unpacked." He took a swig of his lager. "I always hoped I wouldn't have to. Teo wanted the split. I didn't. I hoped she might have me back." He used the cold of the bottle against his forehead. Barbara wouldn't have said no to sharing it, if only for that purpose. "You wanted to talk to me about her."

Barbara plunged her hand into the depths of her shoulder bag to bring out her spiral notebook and a mechanical pencil that she'd nicked from Nkata's desk. As she did this, she followed Ross Carver to what went for the sitting room: four deckchairs positioned round a card table. He was, she thought, a real minimalist. The only additional piece of furniture was a floor lamp. There were no bits and bobs— presumably they'd never been unpacked—no magazines, no tabloids, no broadsheets, no umbrellas, no discarded shoes or articles of clothing. There were photos, however. Photos galore. Most of them stood along one wall. Some of them looked like wedding shots of him and his estranged wife.

She said, "C'n we sit?"

He said, "Help yourself. The accommodations are spare."

"Not so the photos," she noted.

He looked at them, ranked like soldiers at the Trooping of the Colour. He said, "Teo didn't want them when we split. But I like looking at them. They're reminders."

"Of what?"

"Who we were. Happier times. What you will." He gave the photos a glance. "We grew up together. Our parents were friends from before we were born."

"How'd they get connected?"

He seemed to think about this for a moment, after which he said, "You know, I haven't the first clue. It seems like they were always there, Teo's family. I can't remember a time when they weren't. It can't have been a church thing. My parents—all of us really, and by that I mean my family, not Teo's—we're lifelong unbelievers. Teo's family, they were—they still are—Roman Catholic."

"Teo herself?"

"Christmas and Easter and only then if she was invited to attend with her parents and her sister. Otherwise, no. Teo doesn't . . . She didn't like the trappings of anything."

"She seemed to like the trappings of a wedding," Barbara noted, acknowledging that particular set of pictures.

"Most women do, I expect, even if they start out thinking it's all fuss and nonsense. Besides that, her mum insisted. I would have preferred just the registry office and lunch in a fancy restaurant afterwards. Champagne and chocolate-covered strawberries. But Solange—Teo's mum—she likes tradition, and it was easy enough to please her."

"How'd she react to your split, then?"

"The same as everyone else. Surprised. Sad. We'd been together so long that TeoandRoss had become one word to our families."

"To you as well."

He looked at the bottle he held and, after a moment he nodded slowly. "Like I said, I didn't want the split. But at the end of the day, I'm the one who caused it."

"Some other woman?"

He shook his head. "There's always been only Teo for me."

"But Colton . . . ? Doesn't he represent when some other woman was just fine for you?"

"Colton was the result of turning competitive ballroom dancing into this-is-meant-to-be. I was eighteen, so was my partner, and we took doing the salsa to a higher level. Latin dancing tends to mess with the mind. At least, it messed with mine. She came up pregnant. She reckoned we would marry. I reckoned different."

"Did Teo know about Colton?"

"He's been part of my life since he was born. I rejected his mum—I'm not proud of that, by the way—but never him. Teo knew all that."

"Where's his mum now?"

"Hammersmith. Married, two other children, and perfectly happy with her life." He tipped his bottle and took several more gulps of beer. "I'm just guessing that last part," he admitted. "But I can't see why she wouldn't be happy. Colton never reports otherwise, and he and Kieran—that's the stepdad—get on well. He's quite a decent bloke is Kieran."

"Did Teo never feel betrayed?" It all seemed so adult to Barbara, so *au courant*, if that was the term, although it could well have been *a la mode*, she reckoned.

"Because of Telyn's pregnancy? She wouldn't have done. She's three years younger, Teo is. She was only fifteen when all this happened—when Telyn and me happened—and we'd not yet ever been a couple, me and Teo. Then once we were, I never looked at another woman. I never wanted to."

"If that's the case—you never doing the dirty outside your marriage—how were you the one to throw a spanner?"

"I loved her too much."

"Too much?"

"One can do that, you know." He looked towards the doors onto his balcony as if what he wanted to say resided outside. He settled on,

"It's like overwatering a plant. One means well, but the plant can't cope and it dies."

That, Barbara thought, was a strange analogy since Teo Bontempi—Teo Carver who had been—was at the present moment awaiting burial. She said, "When did you last see her?"

"It would have been two nights before she went into hospital."

"Where?"

"In Streatham. At the flat."

"Your idea or at her invitation?"

"Her invitation. She said she needed to speak with me."

"Needed?"

"Needed. Wanted. I suppose both add up to the same thing: conversation. She asked me to come over for a word. So that's what I did." He paused, drawing his dark eyebrows together as if trying to recall his wife's exact words. "She wanted to . . . 'go over a few things' was how she put it. She asked if I would come to Streatham. I had nothing on, so that was fine with me. When I arrived, though, she didn't bell me into the building."

"So you left?"

"I had a key so—"

"Had she given you a key?"

"I'd never given up the one I had. When we split up, I made four trips? Five? To fetch my clobber. She never asked me for the key because she wouldn't always be home when I needed to stop at the flat."

"You never handed it over once the move out was finished?"

"Didn't. So that night I let myself into the building. I reckoned she'd only stepped out, gone to the shops or something. She knew I was on my way, so I decided I'd wait as I never knew when I'd have another chance."

"For what?"

"To see her." He drained the bottle of beer. He said, "I'm having another. You don't want one?"

Barbara demurred. When he returned, however, he brought two bottles. He set one in front of her, already opened, "Just in case," he explained. He sat. He was silent. Barbara reckoned that fetching the beer had been intended to buy him time.

She said, "Have you any clue what she wanted to talk to you about?"

Before he could answer, his mobile rang. He dug it out of the back pocket of his jeans and looked at the screen. He said to Barbara, "Sorry. I'm meant to take this."

She nodded with a gesture towards the mobile. He said into it, "Yeah?" and mostly what he did after that was listen. He rose, mobile pressed to his ear, and went to the balcony's door, which he opened. He stepped outside, closed the door behind him, and continued listening. Barbara saw his expression change. He looked at her, saw her looking at him, turned, and, head lowered, seemed to speak. It wasn't a long call, less than two minutes. When he came back into the flat, his expression was grim.

He said to her, "She was *murdered*? When the hell were you planning to share that detail?"

"Who gave you the information?" she asked.

"Does it matter?"

"Since it's a murder, yeah, it does."

"Why don't you tell me what's going on, Sergeant . . . What was your name again?"

"Havers."

"Sergeant Havers. Why don't you tell me what the hell is going on? Teo was in hospital. She was—"

"—in a coma after a blow to her head."

That stopped him for a moment. Then, "A blow to her head? A bloody blow to her head?" He glanced at his mobile but it seemed the look was inadvertent.

"Who was on the phone?"

"Teo's sister. Rosalba. She said the police had called in and had given them the news. Why wasn't I told? Because we're estranged? Because you think I did something to her? Is this what you were leading up to? You listen to me, eh? I let myself into her flat. I found her on the floor in the loo. She'd been sick into the toilet. She said she'd been nauseous and dizzy. I wanted to take her to A and E, but she wouldn't have it. She said she just needed a lie-down, so I helped her to bed."

"Documents indicate she was in her night gear. Is that how you found her when she was in the loo?"

He swigged down more lager. He said, "No. I . . . Look, I undressed her, but it's not what you think."

"What do I think?"

"That this was some kind of sexual thing. My taking advantage of her. It wasn't. That was over. That was how she wanted it. But I cared for her, so I got her into her night things. I fished two paracetamol from the medicine cabinet, gave them to her, and put her into bed."

"And then you left? You were never able to learn from her why she wanted to see you?"

"No."

"Which is it? No, you didn't leave, or no, you weren't able to learn why she wanted to see you?"

"She never told me what it was she'd wanted to talk about."

"And once she was tucked up in bed, you left?"

"I didn't. I spent some of the night with her."

"You spent some of the night with your estranged wife."

"I didn't want to leave her alone, so I put her to bed, I lay next to her, and I fell asleep. I didn't intend to but that's what happened. When I woke, it was . . . I don't know . . . round half past three? She was asleep, and I didn't want to wake her. I put her mobile next to the bed, and I left."

"Why didn't you try to wake her?"

"Why would I? Like I said, she was *asleep*. It was the middle of the night and I had no reason to wake her."

"Not even to speak about whatever it was that she had you dashing to Streatham to hear? Weren't you curious? Seems to me that you'd've been curious."

As she spoke, Barbara observed the line of damp at his hairline. It was hot enough in the room to make an iguana sweat, so he certainly had an excuse for the dampness on his forehead. But this seemed more the product of anxiety than the product of the ambient temperature.

He said, "If I'd not fallen asleep . . . if I'd insisted on taking her to A and E like I wanted . . . ," and then after a moment and quite as if she hadn't been pressing him about his lack of curiosity regarding his wife's desire to speak with him, "You said it was a blow to the head. What sort?"

"A fracture-your-skull sort. She was hit with something heavy. D'you know what a epidural haematoma is?" And when he nodded, "That's what killed her."

He looked at her directly. "It wasn't me. There's no way in hell, on earth, or anyplace else that I would have struck Teo. I *loved* her. I wanted her back."

"How did you learn she'd been taken to hospital?"

"From her parents. They rang me. They said she'd been brought to hospital, that she'd be having a scan. When I got there, she'd been moved to Critical Care—"

"Did they ask you to come, her parents?"

"What? Ask me? No. But I had to go. I needed to be there. I couldn't understand how a simple fall might lead to brain scans, a coma, and . . . and all the rest."

"All the rest being her death."

"And everything leading up to it: a ventilator, monitors, heart machines, life support."

"And brain death," Barbara added bluntly, trying to read him as she said the words. She wanted them as bald as she could get them, and she wanted to dig for what he knew. He seemed genuine but so did most psychopaths. Projecting normal was their speciality.

She said, "Anything you want to add, then? About your wife? About your marriage?"

Carver shook his head. "I want to wake up and find this is a nightmare, frankly."

"People generally do," Barbara said.

PEMBURY ESTATE
HACKNEY
NORTH-EAST LONDON

Tani knew that he alone was what stood between his sister and Abeo's intention to offer her to some ancient Nigerian rich enough to pay his asking price. He also knew that Monifa was going to let it happen when all she had to do was pack a suitcase for Simi and one for herself and leave Mayville Estate while Abeo wasn't there.

And he wasn't there most of the time. Now that his second family was out in the open—or at least out in the open to Tani—Abeo had apparently made the decision to spend more of his time with them, certain for some reason that neither Monifa nor Tani would tell Simi about them. He came by the flat only to drop off his bloodstained shirts and aprons, which Monifa dutifully washed and ironed. Indeed, upon reflection, Tani had realised that Abeo had been bringing to Monifa his second family's laundry, and true to form, his mother had also been obediently washing and ironing it, which explained the mound of clothing Tani had seen her working on.

It hadn't taken him very long to come up with a second way to approach his father. So, late that afternoon, he waited for Abeo's arrival

at Pembury Estate in order to make his move. He'd not gone to Into
Africa Groceries Etc. on this day or the day before. He did not want
to get into it with his father before he knew what he wanted to do.
Now that he did know, he was ready. So he kept himself out of sight
on Pembury Estate but within spotting distance of the lift that Abeo
would have to take to reach his other family's flat. When this happened, at the end of the day, Abeo looked done-in, but he nonetheless
wore a freshly washed and ironed shirt so that Lark and her children
would not be confronted with the unappealing sight of animal blood
on his clothing, on his chest and his hips. Tani waited. He wanted to
give his father time to settle in before he confronted him.

Twenty-five minutes after Abeo had arrived, Tani strode to the lift.
It was late in the day, so other inhabitants of the building were coming and going, and it was in the wake of a woman with too many
carrier bags that he entered, nodded hello, pushed the button for floor
3, and rode upwards.

Most of the doors along the external walkway were open. So it was
with his father's other family. He could hear children chattering and
Abeo's voice answering and then a woman saying, "There just there.
Oh, you *are* a love, you are." And then with a laugh, "That tickles!
No, no! Abeo, stop!"

"This then?" Abeo's voice was followed by more laughter and the
woman saying, "Elton, come! Make your father stop!"

Tani went to the doorway. His father's lover was supine on the sofa,
a wet washing flannel across her forehead and her feet in Abeo's lap.
Abeo was play-acting at biting Lark's instep, making growling noises
as she laughed and their children giggled from a nearby table where
they were kneeling on chairs and building something green from a
mountain of Lego pieces. Abeo stopped the mock biting and began
rubbing cubes of ice on the soles of Lark's feet and between her toes.
A towel and a bottle of lotion were on the floor next to his feet.

"Better?" he said.

"You're an angel," she sighed.

She was the one to see Tani. She took the washing flannel from her head, saying, "Davrina, Mummy needs more ice, there's a love," as she glanced in his direction.

Davrina jumped from her chair, but then she saw Tani as well and said, "Who's *he*?," which caused Abeo to turn his head towards Tani.

"Did that for Mum as well, did you? When she was pregnant, eh?" Tani's words felt like pincers in his throat.

"What do you want?" Abeo asked. "Why have you not been at work?"

Tani sauntered into the flat. He went to the table where the children were sitting. He said to Abeo, "Sh'll I tell them who I am or d'you want to?"

"It is a matter of indifference to me," Abeo said. Then to the children, "This is your brother by my wife Monifa, or so she says. He is called Tani. Say hello and go back to your game," just as he went back to massaging Lark's feet.

Tani saw that the children were building a T. rex. He picked up a Lego and examined it. He wondered what it would look like shoved into his father's eye.

"D'you like to play Lego?" Davrina asked him.

"Never had any," Tani told her.

"Not *any*?"

"Not any. You got a sister, by the way. She's called Simisola. She's never played Lego either." And then to his father, "Same thing in store for this one, Pa? When she's a bit older? Or is it just Simi that you got plans for?"

Lark, he saw, looked at him and then at his father. She seemed confused.

"Lark is English," Abeo said. "Our children are English."

"Yeah? What does 'Lark is English' mean when it comes to selling little girls—little *breeders*—to the highest bidder?"

Lark sat up. Her expression altered. It was mostly in the eyes, Tani noted. Caution came into them as she gazed at Abeo.

"She's half Nigerian through you, right?" Tani went on. "Davrina is. An' Nigerian girls're meant to get husbands who'll pay big bride prices, right? Least that's what you've been banging on about when it comes to Simisola." Then to Lark, "Hasn't he tol' this to you?"

"Abeo, what is he—"

"Since she's only half English, I s'pose you c'n only sell part of her, eh? So which half of Davrina's going to be sold? Top or bottom? Left side? Right side? Or should I just guess?"

"Leave us," Abeo said to him.

"Abeo, what's he talking about?" Lark asked.

"He talks of nothing. He overhears nonsense and believes he knows what is meant by what he hears. Then he accuses. This is how he is."

"Accuses who? Of what?"

"He's going to sell Simisola," Tani told her. "D'you know what I mean? She's meant to produce babies for a bloke in Nigeria and soon 's she's able, he's handing her off to be made pregnant by whoever's willing to pay what he wants for her. Won't happen till she can actually *get* pregnant, but she'll still be a kid when it does and she probably won't know what's in store for her." He shot a look over to Davrina who, along with her brother, was watching Tani with round and apprehensive eyes.

"Go to your room, Davrina," Lark said to her daughter. "Elton as well."

"But the T. rex—"

"Go!"

"Daddy!"

"Do what your mum tells you. We need to speak to this person."

The children scampered off with a fearful look from each of them cast in Tani's direction. A moment passed and then a door shut somewhere inside the flat. After this, Abeo launched himself with,

"You are no son of mine. I blame your mother for who you have become with your English ways and your English attitudes towards our people."

"Tha's right, Pa. We're *English*, innit? So if you didn't want us to be English you should have stayed in Nigeria. But you came to London and you expected it would all be the same. All of us'd be doing just like you want so you can feel important, dictating everyone's futures to benefit yourself." He swung to Lark, who'd raised a hand to her chest where she fingered a silver crucifix that shone brightly against her skin. He said to her, "He does what he wants, does my dad. An' what he wants jus' now is money. See, he d'n't tell you about buying a virgin for me to marry, did he? Right? Well, tha's what he did, and the only way he c'n get back some of what he paid is to get a good bride price for Simisola."

Abeo shook his head slowly in a display of his sadness and disappointment. He said, "Monifa said this person is my son, Lark, and eighteen years ago I decided to believe her. But he and I . . ." Abeo rose. He gestured to himself and then to Tani. "Look at us. See how we differ. He has long known he is not my son, and for this he blames *me*. He has spent his life seeking to destroy my marriage with his mother, and he now wishes to destroy what we have, you and I: our family. This story he's told you . . . Let me ask: Why would I do this to my daughter Simisola? Or to our daughter Davrina? Of course I would not do it. So why does he say it? Here is the answer: If he can make you believe I would ruin Simisola's life or that of Davrina, you will leave me, he thinks. You will take our children and this new child inside of you, and you will disappear. This, he thinks, is what I deserve for allowing him to believe that he is my son."

Tani's mouth felt as if he'd swallowed a cup of sawdust. He couldn't put his mind round the sheer audacity of his father's words. Abeo was the incarnation of hypocrisy, and surely, surely, his lover saw that. He looked at Lark. She was watching Abeo. She'd risen from the sofa and she was cradling the new life she bore. She went to Abeo. She put her hand on his cheek, and he tilted his head towards her.

She said, "I'm so sorry you must bear this pain, Abeo," and Tani knew she'd made her choice.

He couldn't really blame her for taking Abeo at his word. Two children and another on the way? She needed Abeo more than she needed to hear or accept the truth. Tani had thought he could win her to his side, and he'd been wrong.

But he had a final card to play. He said to Abeo, "I'll marry the girl."

Abeo's eyes narrowed. "What is this?"

"As long as Simi is left alone to be herself and to grow up, I'll go to Nigeria and marry Omorinsola. That was her name, wasn't it? Omorinsola, the guaranteed breeding virgin? I'll marry her. I'll give her babies. I'll bring her back to London. Your daughter-in-law and your grandchildren, Pa. I'll do what you want. I'll take over Into Africa as well."

Abeo chuckled. "Since what you've said about Simisola being sold is a black-hearted lie in the first place, why would you offer to do anything at all?"

"Oh, there've been plenty of lies told round here, Pa. But what I said about Simi wasn't one of them."

Abeo snorted. He said, "Get out," but in his eyes Tani saw that Abeo intended to consider his offer.

BELGRAVIA
CENTRAL LONDON

Lynley had always loathed the political part of police work, and this first day of investigating the murder of Detective Sergeant Teo

Bontempi stood a very good chance of becoming political. Unlike the politics that related to governing, however, where opposing sides met, debated, discussed, argued, and pounded out a compromise in the form of legislation, the politics that related to policing generally involved controlling whatever information was given to the press. In his morning meeting with Assistant Commissioner Sir David Hillier and the head of the Press Office, Stephenson Deacon, the political concerns of both men had been writ large enough and dark enough for a mole in sunlight to have read them. To wit and per the carefully worded explanations of Hillier and Deacon, Teo Bontempi was not only a police detective, she was a *Black* police detective. Not only was she a Black police detective, she was a *female* Black police detective. The last thing the Metropolitan Police needed to have hurled at them was an accusation that not enough was being thrown into the investigation because the officer in question was Black or a female or both. Racism, sexism, misogyny . . . There could not be a *whisper* of any of this during the investigation and did the Acting Detective Chief Superintendent understand what was being said?

Before Lynley could offer his thoughts on the topic of treating this investigation no differently than he'd treated any other, Deacon whipped two tabloids from his briefcase and held them up for Lynley's perusal. On the front page of each, the story of a missing child was featured. She had been gone from the care of her parents for a number of days, there had been a significant hue and cry, the father was a barrister, the mother was a physician, and the daughter had last been seen with two teenagers in Gants Hill underground station. There were pictures accompanying the story, which made the jump to the inside pages. Lynley knew about the missing child since he'd seen the story featured—with far less garish panoply—in his own morning newspapers when the girl had first gone missing. He wasn't sure what the girl's disappearance had to do with Teo Bontempi's death, and he asked that question of the two other men.

Their answer was nothing at all, *but* the moment the tabloids decided to put a full stop to the story, they would be onto Teo Bontempi's murder like rats on a rubbish tip, and *when* they made that switch, the Press Office wanted to be sure that DCS Lynley would have mountains of information available, the sort of information telling the press that the Metropolitan Police were holding back not a single resource in order to bring to justice the person who murdered one of their own, no matter the gender or race.

"Speaking of resources . . ." Lynley explained that they were probably going to need more officers involved.

Deacon assured him that he would have exactly what he needed. Hillier shot Deacon a look that mixed outrage and incredulity. His was not to assign manpower. That was the outrage. Who the hell do you think you are giving that assurance? That was the incredulity.

Lynley left them to battle it out.

He was unlocking the front door of his house in Eaton Terrace when his mobile rang. He had hopes that Daidre might be phoning after the way they'd left things on the previous night. But he saw it was Barbara Havers, and as he opened the door and stepped inside, she launched a rocket of information.

"Th' estranged husband was with her the night she got coshed, sir. For most of the night, as it turns out. Claims she asked him to come round because she wanted a chat."

"About what?"

"No clue. That's me *and* him. All he offered was she asked him to come for a chat, he agreed, and the rest is the rest. Easy enough to check out, you ask me. Their mobiles are going to show us."

"Hmmm." Lynley picked up the day's post. Charlie Denton had placed it on the walnut demilune table in the entry, inside an empty and ancient Tupperware container standing in place of the silver tray of old. Clearly, he'd forgotten to take them—the day's post and the Tupperware—down to the kitchen. "Anything else?"

"He says she was the one who wanted the divorce, not him. Says he 'loved her too much,' and she couldn't cope with it, whatever all of that means. He's got photos of her—and of them together—all over his sitting room 's well. Says he likes to look at them, he does."

"Obsession?"

"Could be."

"Stalking that turns into if I can't have you, no one else can?"

"I wouldn't say no. He's intending to move back into the flat, by the way."

"That's an interesting detail."

She related the rest: Ross Carver's possession of a key to that flat, how he'd found his estranged wife, what she said, her nausea, her dizziness, her inability to remember—or perhaps her unwillingness to say—exactly what had happened prior to his arrival. She added, "He's a white bloke, in case that matters."

Lynley wondered if that fact would please Hillier and Deacon or send them straight round the bend. He said, "She could have moved on, had another lover, the husband not liking it?"

"S'pose. But if that's the case, he's not saying. The family might know. Have you heard from Winston?"

"Not yet."

"What's next, then?"

"Streatham. We need to have a thorough look at the scene tomorrow. Has SOCO finished up there?"

"They've had enough time. I'll give them a bell. Where are you? Belsize Park?"

"Home for the night. I'm letting Belsize Park cool down a bit."

"Ah. Think that's wise, do you?"

"Wise? Barbara, it should be obvious to you by now that I have no idea what constitutes wisdom in male-female affairs of the heart."

6 AUGUST

Deborah slid her car into a vacant parking bay across the Thames from Eel Pie Island just before dawn. She'd never been to this place before. Indeed, she'd never heard of it, despite having lived in London since just after her seventh birthday. No one had been trying to hide its existence from her, of course, but the heyday of the island had been long ago, as she'd discovered. Even its history as a quite small mecca or the rock 'n' roll of the 1960s had not saved it from the virtual obscurity it enjoyed now.

When she'd recommended that Deborah speak to Dr. Philippa Weatherall, Narissa had advised her to make this early morning journey, one she herself had made when searching out the surgeon in the hope that having a real face-to-face conversation with her—bearded in her home before she set off for her day's work—might convince her that her appearance in Narissa's documentary would give crucial hope to any girls who might be in danger and to women who had already been harmed. As things turned out, Narissa had explained to Deborah, she'd gained nothing from her effort. She'd lost several hours' sleep, she'd driven for an hour, and she'd used up petrol and valuable time.

Dr. Weatherall had told her she was not willing to draw attention to herself for fear of reprisals.

"You can give it a go," Narissa had told Deborah. "Since your project isn't a film, you could have better luck." She'd handed over the surgeon's details, which had turned out to be the product of sixty minutes online with various search engines and data banks prior to her own visit there. "You c'n ring her first, but I wouldn't. That's what I did and I wager she had already written out her refusal and memorised it."

Deborah would find Dr. Weatherall's home on Eel Pie Island, Narissa had told her. Cottages there had no addresses—they hardly needed them, considering how few there were—so what Deborah needed to know was Mahonia: a cream-coloured cottage with a blue-tiled roof, set back some twenty yards or so from the main path bisecting the island. It had no name on it, but it did have a picket fence in front of it, an arbor in serious need of rehab, a dead lawn, some dying shrubs, and a few ornamental grasses.

Deborah had asked Narissa how one actually got onto the island if, indeed, it sat in the middle of the Thames. Narissa's answer of "You'll see. Don't worry about it," didn't inspire confidence, but Deborah decided to trust her. Putting a note on the kitchen chopping block table, she'd left everyone still asleep and made the journey to Twickenham, where she saw exactly what Narissa had meant. An arched footbridge led to the island, its railings hung with colourful miniature petunias that draped red and white blooms along the way.

From the footbridge, where a slight early-morning breeze on the river made a false promise of an end to the heatwave, Deborah saw that Eel Pie Island wasn't large. There were cottages along its edge built with direct access to the river from their back gardens, and in the breaking dawn, she could see small jetties as well as simple bollards where motorboats bobbed along with kayaks, rowboats, and canoes. The island was thickly treed. Enormous willows grew close to the water. Poplars, chestnuts, and limes threw shadows along a paved path that curved and seemed to disappear round a bend. No one was about. Birds were stirring and doves were cooing, though. In another hour Eel Pie Island would doubtless be fully alive for the day.

The cottage with the blue-tiled roof, Deborah found, wasn't far along the hard-surfaced path. Narissa had described it well. She'd left out the empty window boxes and a trellis upon which nothing grew, but otherwise it was as she'd indicated it would be. It was also, however, completely dark. The surgeon had either already left for the day or she wasn't yet out of bed, or she was in the back of the building from which no lights could be seen from the path. Deborah decided that, having come this far, she would try her luck. She went through the gate, which hung lopsided from only one of the two hinges that held it to the fence.

There was no porch: just a single-step landing and the front door. She looked for a bell. She saw that knocking would have to do the job, so she forcefully applied knuckles to wood. The only response she received, though, was that of a slender orange tabby. The cat slinked round the side of the cottage and began to weave around her legs. A few plaintive meows accompanied this. Then a light came on above the door, although the growing daylight made it likely that Deborah was completely visible from inside. The door swung open. The cat took the opportunity and dashed into the cottage.

"Who the devil are you? And what the devil are you doing knocking me up at this hour?"

It wasn't an auspicious way to begin.

"Dr. Weatherall?" Deborah said.

"What d'you want? Who *are* you?" The surgeon stepped forward. She wasn't tall—Deborah reckoned five foot four, no more—and she wore black, tight-fitting neoprene clothing. She carried in her hand a thin windcheater of the sort meant to be seen in the dark when struck by lights. She had nothing on her feet. "Wait." The word was sharp, a command. "Did that bloody filmmaker send you? That Marissa Someone."

"Narissa Cameron. Actually, I'm—"

"No means no, and you can tell her that from me. Full stop. Nothing to be added."

"This isn't about her documentary," Deborah said. "I'm a photographer. Will you talk to me? This will take five minutes. I promise you it has nothing to do with Narissa's film."

"I don't care what it has to do with. And I haven't got five minutes. I'm already late to the river." She turned quickly from the door and for a moment Deborah thought this meant she was going to have it shut in her face. But, just as quickly, the surgeon turned back, having picked up the cat. She tossed it outside. It gave an outraged yowl and darted back in. "Damn it! That bloody cat."

In the light from the porch, Deborah saw that on one side of the step upon which she was standing were two empty bowls, both of them shaped like cats' heads. She said, "It seems to be out of food and water?"

"It's not even my bloody cat!" Dr. Weatherall snapped. Then she added, "Oh *damn* it." And from inside and just to the left of the door, she brought out a water jug and a bag of dry cat food. She said, "Get out here if you want something, Darius," as she filled both bowls.

Darius? Deborah thought as the cat reappeared, looking quite smug.

"I can't abide cats," Philippa Weatherall said.

"Then if I can ask: why do you feed this one?"

"It's obvious. I'm a fool." Dr. Weatherall returned the food and the jug to the interior of the cottage, took up a pair of trainers, stepped outside, and shut the door. She bent straight from the waist—no flexing of knees or squatting for her, Deborah noted—and put on the shoes. Head to toe, she was in excellent physical condition.

She said to Deborah, "If you want five minutes, you can have them while we walk," and she headed towards the picket gate. Once on the path, she strode to the right, the opposite direction from the footbridge.

Deborah followed. Dr. Weatherall, she saw, had a don't-mess-with-me way of walking. She moved rapidly and Deborah did likewise. She was fairly certain that whatever else Dr. Weatherall was going to give to her, it probably wasn't going to be a full five minutes. So she began to talk: about the project she was working on for the Department for Education, about Orchid House, about the photo book she wished to produce, about the bookending idea making use of interviews with her. She ended with, "Narissa spoke highly of you."

"Well, that's very nice of her, isn't it," the surgeon said. "I can hardly mind being spoken highly of, can I. But I've given Narissa chapter and verse on why I prefer to remain as deeply in the background as possible. I'm hardly a popular figure when it comes to those parts of the Nigerian and the Somali communities who practise disfiguring women, not to mention those insecure men looking for women who've been cut up and sewn up to assure them that their technique—such as it is, which I daresay it isn't—will never be compared to another bloke's. Have you spoken to these women?"

"I have. I've not been accepted with open arms—hardly a surprise considering the nature of the issue, not to mention the nature of our society, but I have spoken to them. If I may ask: As a white woman, how did you become involved in reconstructive surgery?"

"I trained for it in France. It was pioneered there, so I went to the source."

"Was that always your focus, reconstructive surgery?"

"It wasn't. I was as ignorant about cutting women as most of the population. I'm a gynecologist and obstetrician by training."

"So how did it happen that you moved from that to what you're doing now?"

They'd reached a tall gate, on it the sort of lock that required a code to release. Dr. Weatherall punched in a set of numbers, shoved the gate open, and headed towards the water. "I was called in to advise on a special case," she said. "A child in hospital had a rampant infection, and nothing was stopping it. It would slow, then it would seem to be gone, and then back it would come stronger than ever. She'd been cut about ten weeks before I saw her."

"What happened to her?"

"She died. They'd waited too long, her parents, to take her to hospital."

"That's terrible."

"It's far worse than that. She was three years old."

"Oh my God. That's . . . I don't even know what to call it."

"Ghastly, horrible, inhuman, disgraceful, disgusting, appalling, hideous, despicable. Words fail to do the job, don't they?" the surgeon said. "When it happened, I decided I had to *do* something. But as you helpfully pointed out, I'm a white woman, and an English white woman at that. I knew it would be next to impossible to explain to any woman from one of the immigrant Black communities still practising FGM that her culture—or at least some members of her culture—is adhering to an ignorant tradition that threatens a girl's welfare, her future, her ability to bear children, and possibly her life. And anyway, I'm very bad at talk and persuasion and all the rest. So I offered my services instead, to women who'd already been damaged."

They walked along the side of a building and came out on a wide concrete boat launch. The building was a boathouse. Lights were on inside and someone had rolled a tall rack of sculls out onto the top of the launch. She hoisted one off effortlessly, setting it gently on the ground. She said, "I had to work for ages to gain anyone's trust, but Zawadi helped me with that. She saw the point of what I was doing and of what I *could* do. She began referring young women to me. She still does."

"How did you find your way to Orchid House?"

"The internet. Isn't that how everything's done these days? I began to contact the various anti-FGM groups that I discovered online. Orchid House was one of the first to respond. Others have since. I explained what I do: repair the damage, try to restructure, and—if whoever butchered a girl left the nerves of the clitoris intact—I rebuild that as well. Or as much as I *can* rebuild it so that the patient may experience at least some degree of sexual pleasure." Dr. Weatherall looked at the river and said in a tone that indicated their conversation had concluded, "There may be more savage things being done to women on this wretched, dying planet of ours, but I'm not yet aware of what they are. Still, I've learned over time that even as far as one allows one's imagination to go when it comes to the abuse of women, someone is out there already doing it." She nodded sharply at Deborah and took two oars from the rack. These she carried to the water's edge. She returned and said, "I wish I could help you, but it's just not on. For the sake of these women, I can't afford to be taken out of commission by someone or a group of someones who might disapprove of my work."

Deborah knew the value of having Dr. Weatherall's work represented in the photo book, however. It was a beacon of hope for the thousands of women who'd been disfigured, either in the UK or before their arrival. She said, "I do understand, but I'm wondering if we can compromise. What about an interview accompanied by one or two photographs during the surgery? You'd be fully covered. And I wouldn't use your name."

Dr. Weatherall hoisted the scull again. She carried it to the water's edge where she'd placed the oars. She said, "What's the point of that?"

"Hope," Deborah said. "Garnering support. Gaining the interest of other surgeons who could then train like you."

The surgeon considered this, although she was beginning to seem impatient with Deborah's tenacity. Still, after several moments of thought, she said, "No names? Not mine, not my anaesthetist's, not the nurse's, not the patient's? And the patient might well not want to be photographed at all, so this conversation we're having could be for nothing. Would you accept that?"

Deborah was hardly in the driver's seat. But she'd got further than Narissa, at least. She said, "I'd be happy to accept that."

STREATHAM
SOUTH LONDON

The building that housed Teo Bontempi's flat was situated on Streatham High Road, on a section that featured broad pavements and leafy London planes with their distinctive peeling bark. These provided ample shade, although the lack of summer rainfall had made their leaves dusty and looking stressed.

Lynley parked the Healey Elliott in as large a space as he could find, directly in front of Maxwell Brothers Funeral Directors and a few doors down from Carpetright, a business apparently having a half-price sale on laminate flooring. The block of flats in question sat directly across the road, as architecturally uninspiring as grey concrete, nondescript shrubbery, and a few scattered balconies could make it. The structure was reminiscent of those in former Eastern Bloc countries, rectangular and unforgiving, with plain steps and plainer handrails leading up to plain front doors.

He crossed the street. Havers, he saw, had managed to reach Streatham before him. Her banged-up Mini was parked directly in front of the building and with her usual panache: three of its wheels on the pavement and a faded police placard propped up on the steering wheel, eating up sunlight.

Next to the front doors were plain mailboxes and a column of buzzers. Above these buzzers hung a CCTV camera, that ubiquitous feature of modern London.

When he pushed the buzzer next to the name *Bontempi*, Havers's disembodied voice called out, "Yeah? C'n I help?"

"I earnestly hope so," he replied.

"Right," she said. "Second floor, sir. Lift's a bit wonky, so I'd give it a pass. Stairs're at the end of the corridor."

She buzzed him in, and he saw that, like its exterior, nothing distinguished the building inside. Institutional yellow-speckled grey lino squares covered the corridor floor, and the doors to each flat bore black metal numbers, two locks, and one peephole each. The stairs— separated from the corridor by a hideous fire door of the sort one saw in every multi-unit residential building in the country—were concrete like the front steps of the building, the handrail some kind of metal once painted shiny black but now badly chipped. Lynley climbed to the second floor and found Havers waiting in the corridor in front of an open door midway down. She wore paper shoe covers and her latex gloves put him in mind of Minnie Mouse. He didn't mention this.

"How long have you been here?" he asked her.

"'Bout twenty minutes. I've just been through the kitchen. Nothing in there of interest 'nless rotting iceberg lettuce means something crucial. Mind the fingerprint dust when you go inside, sir. The crime scene blokes were dead liberal with the stuff as per usual." She handed over a second pair of latex gloves along with shoe covers. He donned these and followed her into the flat.

He saw that it was quite a decent size. Midway down the corridor and to his right he found a door opened to a large bedroom with capacious clothes cupboards and en suite bathroom. To his left two large cupboards provided storage, and directly ahead was a sitting room with a balcony overlooking Streatham High Road. The balcony's door stood open—in hope of a breeze, he reckoned—and a fan was running. This disturbed a stack of papers on a dining table that were weighed down by an African cookbook.

"Let's have a look at all that," Lynley told Havers. "I'll see to the fan."

As she moved the cookbook out of the way, he shut the fan off and walked out onto the balcony. There, he found a collection of very thirsty-looking plants and eight bonsai trees of various species. Beneath these stood a toolbox. He opened it to see gardening implements as well as the wire and small scissor-like shears that were used to shape and prune the bonsais.

Inside again, he noted that a large, unsealed cardboard box standing in front of a credenza and beneath a flat-screen television held various personal items that had ostensibly come from the detective's desk in Empress State Building. Among the items were a pristine coffee mug with *Hooray George!* and *It's a boy!* round its middle circumference, a cheese knife, a pair of scissors, a small collection of envelopes banded together, a calendar, two boxes of Earl Grey tea, and several framed photographs. These appeared to be of her immediate family—mother, father, and two young girls—as well as the family dogs. One of the photos depicted the family at Christmas, the other seemed taken on holiday in a sunny clime. The parents were white; the sisters were Black.

While Havers went through the papers on the table, he turned to the bedroom. It was furnished only with a king-size bed, a chest of drawers with a mirror above, two bedside tables, two matching lamps. There was also a bookcase on one side of the room, opposite a clothes cupboard. It held biographies—Winnie Mandela, Mary Prince, Efurunoye Tinubu, and Harriet Tubman among them—as well as novels by women whose names he did not recognise: Chimamanda Ngozi Adichie, Leila Aboulela, Ama Ata Aidoo. There was nothing inside the drawer of one of the bedside tables. In the other, there was little enough: a packet of tissues, a container of silicone earplugs of the type swimmers often wear, an eye mask used for sleeping, lip balm, and a tube of lotion meant to be applied to one's feet. In addition to the lamp, the table's surface held only a mobile phone charger. On top of the chest of drawers, on a small, vintage tray featuring the Guinness toucan, five gold bangles rested along with a set of keys on a ring with a scowling Tweetie Bird, and what he assumed were the victim's wedding and engagement rings. This last seemed verified by the initials engraved inside the band: RC and TB, separated by an engraved heart. Inside the chest of drawers, jerseys were neatly folded along with underclothes, nightwear, and copious amounts of costume jewellery.

A canvas shoulder bag hung from a hook on the back of the bedroom door, but, upended onto the bed, it offered no joy. A purse held forty-five pounds in notes, various coins were contained in a leather pouch, and a purpose-made hacker-proof holder accordioned out to display a cashpoint card, two credit cards, an Oyster card, a driving licence, and a card indicating her wish to have her organs donated should she die unexpectedly. He was returning all this to the shoulder bag when Havers appeared at the bedroom door, saying, "Sir, here's something odd."

He saw that she looked perplexed. When he said, "What is it," she replied, "It was with everything else that was under the cookbook. How'd Teo Bontempi end up with it, d'you reckon?"

She handed him a business card. He read it, felt a jolt of surprise, said, "I haven't the least idea," and slid the card into his pocket, saying, "I'll look into it. Let's get Nkata over here as soon as he can manage it. We need chapter and verse about Teo Bontempi's life, both here and where she was working. That means whoever's been seen here coming or going, whatever's been heard, and whoever's been caught on CCTV ringing the front buzzer to get into the building. And we'll need to view the CCTV film from the nearby neighbourhood as well. Everything from the day and the night she was attacked. People, cars, number plates—ANPR footage if there's a camera nearby. Have we got her mobile?"

"Her ex—or soon-to-be ex—told me he left it on her bedside table the last time he saw her. It wasn't there?"

"It wasn't. Are you certain about the husband?"

"What he said about the mobile?" she asked, and when he nodded, "I've got it in my notes. S'pose he could be lying."

"Track it down. SOCO might have bagged it. Do we have a list of what else they've taken?"

"They're sending it along. I reckon they've taken anything and everything that she could've been whacked with and delivered it to forensics."

"Make sure we have that list." They left the bedroom and Lynley followed her back to the sitting room. He said, "Laptop?" and she said, "I expect it's in that credenza-whatever-thing under the television if she's got one. I haven't got over there yet."

He went to the credenza-whatever-thing. It looked very Danish and it featured three drawers along the length of it and three cupboards beneath those drawers. The middle drawer cleverly opened into a desktop that held a PC. Its battery was dead, however, so he bagged it along with its flex and set it aside for Nkata to handle. On the same surface, a small appointment diary was open to several days before Teo Bontempi had been struck. He gave it a look and set it aside as well. This would go to Havers, he thought. They needed to trace Teo Bontempi's final days.

Finished with his overview of the place, he rejoined Havers, who was in the kitchen. He gave her the word about Teo Bontempi's appointment diary and said that what they needed next were interviews with everyone who lived in the building. When she finished up here in the flat, she could get on to that. When Nkata arrived, he could join her. Meantime, Lynley said, he was going to attempt to discover why a business card belonging to the wife of his closest friend was in the flat of a dead detective.

MAYVILLE ESTATE
DALSTON
NORTH-EAST LONDON

Tani reckoned his dad thought he wasn't at home because, if Abeo had known, there was no way in hell he would have brought the woman to the flat. Monifa wasn't there and neither was Simi, which in and of itself was a worry for Tani. But because of this, Abeo must have assumed that Tani was out and about as well. He generally was at this time of day. But then so was his father. For his part Abeo should have been in Ridley Road Market, either inside the butcher shop supervising his assistant butchers or keeping ice on the fish outside in the stall.

At the very first, when he'd heard his father's voice, Tani had reckoned his mum was with him. His reasoning was simple: Abeo was talking about money. Of course, that wasn't unusual. Abeo always was talking about money. But this time, he was talking about a specific amount: three hundred quid.

He was saying, "Three hundred bloody pounds, it was. I swear to you, she needs to see the flat of my hand if she doesn't—"

A woman's voice interrupted, sounding vaguely amused. "Just the flat of your hand, it is? You no get sense, Abeo. It is crazy you think that ends it," in an accent that made Tani's stomach feel like liquid. It wasn't a voice he'd heard before. But the accent was Nigerian, like Abeo's and Monifa's.

"So it will be the buckle of the belt," Abeo said. "I don't know where this wife of mine gets her ideas."

"Ah. That. We all got to have our disciplining done on us from our men," the woman said. "Tha's how it is. An' this 's our nature. Do you not know that?"

Tani moved from his bed to the doorway and from the doorway into the short corridor. When the corridor ended with an arch into the lounge, he paused, held his breath, and eased his head into sight just far enough to see who was speaking. Abeo was responding with, "Yes, yes. And perhaps it is that I let her go her own way without discipline for too long." The woman to whom his father was speaking was older than Abeo, in her late sixties, at least, with short, iron-grey hair. She was not wearing African garb, despite her distinct accent, which had led him to expect her to do so. Instead, she was dressed in plum-coloured linen trousers and a jacket with a cream-coloured blouse. Her shoes were black, as was the briefcase she carried. She wasn't at all what he'd expected to see, so Tani backed out of sight and listened.

She murmured in answer to Abeo's admission, "And here you are today, eh? You should have consulted me at once. If you had, it would be finished, no *wahala*."

"I'm putting my foot upon it now."

"If I come to you, you must know the cost will be greater."

"What do you mean 'greater'?"

"It's a larger risk I do it here. It needs a larger payment. You have aunties will come?"

"No aunties."

"Means more cost. The girl must be held down. Aunties will do this."

"*I* will take the place of the aunties. *And* we agreed upon the charge."

"*Abeg* you hear me. We agreed. But that was before I knew that Monifa—it *is* her name, yes?—tried to make other arrangements. Even if she agreed to this that we will do here, I would still have the need for aunties. They must attend me."

"I will attend you."

"*Abeg* no vex me! I allow *no* man. Some others do, I do not."

"But I told you about her mother's wishes, so how can you now say—"

The woman cut in, as if Abeo were not in the act of speaking. "If we do not agree on the charge, Abeo, you must look elsewhere. In the Somali community, you will find—"

"All right. We agree." Abeo seemed to spit the words out. Tani was not surprised when his father went on with, "No filthy Somali will touch my daughter."

"Then we now talk of what must be done by you in advance. I leave this information for you. Certain requirements must be met."

At this, Tani faded back to his bedroom. He was sweating heavily. His palms were tingling. The pounding in his chest told him how stupid he'd been. How bloody seriously he'd misunderstood what was going on between his parents. This today—what he was hearing from the sitting-room conversation—went far beyond finding a husband willing to pay a high bride price for Simisola. This today was being engineered to make Simi worth the high price.

Tani understood from the overheard conversation that there had never been a real chance for him to strike a deal with his father regarding the virgin chosen for him to marry. He had been a fool to think otherwise. He'd left Pembury Estate presuming Simi was finally safe. Now all bets were off. He moved in silence back into his room, pulled out of the clothes cupboard the rucksack containing some of Simisola's clothes as well as her sequins and glitter and glue, and climbed over the bed to open the window.

Once out of the flat and round the corner from the play area across the lane from Bronte House, he phoned Sophie on her mobile. She was at home, she told him, memorising her lines for a very small the-atre company's production of *A Midsummer Night's Dream*. She was one of the fairies accompanying Titania. She'd wanted Helena—she'd *longed* for Helena—but had to settle for Mustardseed. Mustardseed said virtually nothing, she explained. The main requirement of the actor playing any one of the fairies was to flit around and to look enthusiastic whenever directed by the fairy queen to do something.

Their respective worlds could not have been more different. Still, Tani made what he hoped were sympathetic noises directed at her world before telling her what was going on in his. When he was finished, Sophie said, "Oh my God! They're going to *cut* her? Tani, are you certain? Did you hear them say it?"

"I heard this woman sayin' she needed aunties to hold Simi down."

"This's madness. I didn't even know it was still going on in this country. When's it supposed to happen?"

Tani didn't know. If they'd set a date, it was after he'd climbed out of the window with Simi's things. But now was the time to hide his sister, he told her, and he'd made arrangements to do just that.

"Ring me when it's all set up, 'kay? And be *careful*, Tani. I expect your dad'll work out who managed to get Simisola away from him so fast."

They rang off. Tani picked up his pace. He decided he'd go directly to Xhosa's Beauty to give Tiombe the rucksack to hold while he started looking for his sister. Simi would be somewhere in the market, and leaving the rucksack in the hair salon would prevent her from clocking what he had in mind. If she realised what was up, Tani knew, she might well refuse to go with him.

He was careful about the route he took to Xhosa's Beauty. He didn't want to risk being seen by anyone who knew him. He chose to dart along the pavement on the opposite side of the street from the butcher shop, ducking behind each stall he came to, keeping his face hidden from view.

Opposite Xhosa's Beauty, he looked right and left before he darted across the market street. He muttered "Shit!" as someone called his name. He glanced behind him and saw that it was Talatu, the woman who sold Simi's head wraps. She called out, "Where's that sister of yours? She's s'posed to deliver more turban caps."

He waved and shrugged. The interpretation of this was meant to be "Clueless on that score," and Talatu was shouting, "You tell her Talatu needs those head wraps, you hear me, Tani?" as he swung round and stepped inside Xhosa's Beauty.

Tiombe, he saw, was not there. He scrambled in his head for the other woman's name. Happiness? Joy? No. Bliss, he thought. Her name was Bliss. He said, "Tiombe? She somewhere in the market, Bliss?"

Bliss was leaning on the salon's glass countertop, a chat magazine opened in front of her and a takeaway cup sweating beads of moisture set to one side. She looked up and it seemed to take her a moment to clock who he was. She said, "Nowhere in th'market 't all."

"I got to talk to her. Where is she?"

"Wolverhampton. Mum broke her hip. This's last night and Tiombe's up there. She went straightaway she got the word. Surgery and rehab and Tiombe's the only one who c'n care for her. Got sisters and a brother, Tiombe does, but they got families and she doesn't, so off she goes."

"When'll she be back?"

Bliss flipped a page of her magazine to a two-page spread with the title "What Were They *Thinking*?" and a line of female celebrity pictures beneath it, each featuring a different choice of clothing more outrageous than the last. "Don' know, do I?" Bliss said. "She don' know either. Least, tha's what she said."

"When?"

"This morning, she rang."

"She rang you?" and when Bliss nodded, "Did she mention my sister? Simisola?"

"Not a whisper."

"But we had a 'rangement, me and Tiombe. Tiombe was set to look after Simi till my dad and mum come to their senses. They want her to be cut, they do."

Bliss took this in with little reaction beyond a momentary widening of her eyes. She said, "Cut? Tha's a nasty business. You certain?" And when he nodded, "You ring the cops?"

"I don't want to do that. I just want her to be someplace safe while I reason with them."

There was a cigarette packet on the countertop, and Bliss shook out a fag and lit it. She offered him one. He declined. She took a good long hit. She said, "You think you got tha' kind of reasoning power in you?"

"Don't know, do I? But the first step was going to be Tiombe looking after Simi."

"Then I'm tha' sorry that she i'n't here."

"What about you?" Tani asked without thinking. He could see the question gave Bliss pause. She seemed to consider it before she shook her head. She said, "Not like I don' think *any* cutting done to girls is bloody-minded and wrong. I's double both and it makes me sick. But truth is I got a business to run here and I believe in good relations with everyone in the market, which 'ncludes your daddy. There's also my clients, see. I can't have them thinking I'm running some sort 'f underground escape route for girls wanting to get 'way from their parents. I'm tha' sorry 'bout it. And I do wish Tiombe was here. But she's not and—"

A woman and girl entered the shop, stopping Bliss from saying more. The girl looked about twelve years old. Bliss smiled at them both and said, "Alice here wearin' you down, Fola?"

Fola, the adult, said, "As far as cornrows jus' now. No extensions till she's fifteen."

"Tha's just *mean*, that is!" Alice protested.

"Yeah? Well, mean is as mean does," Fola replied. "I c'n show you mean if that's your decision."

Sulkily, Alice flounced over to Bliss's station and flopped herself into the chair there. Apparently she'd realised quick enough that she was caught in a beggars and choosers situation.

"Ta for stopping by, then, Tani," Bliss said as she crushed out her cigarette. "Got to get to work now but if Tiombe rings, I'll tell her you were here."

CHELSEA
SOUTH-WEST LONDON

With Havers finishing up in the flat and awaiting Nkata's arrival in Streatham, Lynley drove to Chelsea, where parking was always a horrendous prospect once the locals began arriving home from their day's employment. He finally managed to deposit the Healey Elliott in Paultons Square, and he walked from there to Cheyne Row, removing his jacket en route and slinging it over his shoulder in the steaming early evening.

At the corner of Lordship Place, he mounted the steps of a tall brick building and rang its single bell. Generally this invited the enthusiastic barking of the resident long-haired dachshund, but on this day Peach was apparently elsewhere, and the door was opened after a few moments by Simon St. James. He carried with him what looked like a written report, but, upon Lynley's questioning, this turned out to be a monograph that he was reading for a fellow scientist prior to its submission to a journal for publication.

"You're still working, then?" Lynley said. "I won't stay long."

"Rubbish. I'm achieving very little. My thoughts have been turning to whiskey for at least thirty minutes. What's your pleasure?"

"A single malt, as always."

"Lagavulin or the Macallan?"

"I wouldn't say no to either, but I'll have the first."

"Always a wise choice." St. James led him into his study, to the left of the entry where, at one time in the home's Edwardian heyday, a dining room would have been. An open window suggested St. James's wish of catching a breeze should one develop, but not much joy was coming from this owing to the position of the house and its lack of cross ventilation. It was only slightly less hot in the study than it was outside. Nonetheless, the room was psychically comfortable if not physically so. It possessed a display of Deborah's black-and-white photographs, along with overfull bookshelves, worn leather furniture, and a completely disordered desk. An Anglepoise lamp shone down on the clutter here, shedding a cone of light on a toppled pile of manila folders along with what looked like several days' unopened post.

St. James poured two fingers of Lagavulin into each of two tumblers and handed one over, with "Cheers, then," and after they'd both had a sip of the whiskey, "Why do I think this isn't a social call?"

"Clearly, I have no poker face," Lynley said. "But it's Deborah I need to speak to, if she's here." He fished from his pocket the business card that Havers had found, and he passed it to St. James. "This was found among the belongings of a murder victim. I'm hoping Deborah can shed some light."

St. James looked it over, then handed it back. "She's in the garden," he said. "Peach was requiring some exercise and she's giving it a valiant effort. Deborah, that is. Peach would do nothing of the sort. Doubtless the dog will be more than thrilled with any interruption."

Lynley followed him from the room into the corridor, where at the far end a set of stairs led down to the house's original kitchen. It was fitted out with all the mod cons now, but time was when three or more household servants would have spent half their day washing, chopping, roasting, serving, and washing again. Now, a chocolate sponge stood on the room's central chopping block cum table and next to it, dinner plates were stacked and cutlery was laid out, ready to be taken above to the dining room.

At the far side of the room, a door was open to a set of stone steps leading up to the garden. From there, the sound of Deborah's voice came to them. "She wants to believe she's too old, Dad. Honestly, she ought to wear a sandwich board: *Will Only Play for Treats.* Don't you dare give her one unless she goes after the ball."

"A cruel mistress," St. James said to his wife as he reached the top of the stairs. "I've brought someone who wishes to speak to you."

"Well, Peach will be pleased, and I'm not far behind."

When he reached the top of the stairs, Lynley saw that Deborah was crossing the lawn to a small teak table. Her father joined her, as did one very recalcitrant long-haired dachshund. A bucket on the table held water—previously ice, he supposed—along with two bottles of Fanta orange and several small bottles of San Pellegrino. Both Deborah and her father went for the water, and Deborah offered one each to her husband and to Lynley. As they both still had their whiskeys, they demurred.

Deborah said, "You're sure?" And before he replied, she went on with, "How are you, Tommy? How's Daidre?"

"Ouch," he replied with a smile.

"On that note, I'm going back to work," Simon said with a laugh, and Deborah's father joined him, scooping up the dog and returning to the house.

"Have you been misbehaving again?" Deborah asked Lynley.

"It appears to be my stock-in-trade, although I never intend it. I've found something of yours." He reached into his pocket and brought out her card again.

She took it from him, looked at it, cocked her head, and said, "And . . . ?"

"It was with the belongings of a murder victim. Barbara found it when we were looking through her flat."

"A murder victim? Who is it?"

"Detective Sergeant Teo Bontempi. She worked out of Empress State Building."

"How extraordinary." Deborah turned the card over, perhaps to see if she'd written upon it. She could observe, as he'd done, that the card wasn't dog-eared, suggesting that DS Bontempi had come by it recently. Deborah said, "I've no idea why she had it, Tommy. Or how she came by it. Teo Bontempi, you said? I don't know the name. Someone must have passed the card along to her."

"You've given out no cards yourself lately?"

"Oh, I have done, yes. I attended a meeting at the Department for Education last month. There were . . . let me think . . . five people there? I gave all of them my card. But no one was called Teo Bontempi."

"Anywhere else?" he asked her.

She frowned, tapping her fingers on the arm of her teak chair. "Well, there's Orchid House. I gave my card to the women who work there and to the volunteers. But I know everyone there and no one is called Teo."

"Orchid House?"

"It's a group protecting girls from FGM. I've been taking their photos for a booklet the Department for Education wants to use: photographs of girls who are trying to escape FGM, photos of some girls who've had it done to them and others who've managed to escape having it done to them. I'm recording their statements as well: whatever they want to say to me. It's meant to be given to girls through schools all over London."

"That's the commonality, then."

"What is?"

"Teo Bontempi was on a team working to end the abuse of women,

FGM in particular. I've been told she went to schools and to community centres in the Nigerian and Somali communities, speaking to girls and to their parents. She could have come to Orchid House at some point."

"If she did, it would have been when I wasn't there. I would have remembered a policewoman, Tommy. And no one has mentioned a policewoman visiting. I daresay she came by my card another way."

"Any ideas about that?"

Deborah considered this. "Not really." She drank some of the Pellegrino and removed the sun hat she'd been wearing. She had stuffed her heavy, copper-coloured hair inside, and, now released, it fell thickly round her shoulders and down her back. She poured some of the water onto her head. She said, as water dripped down her cheeks, "Sorry. It's this beastly weather."

He smiled, saying, "That's one way to handle it," and he laughed and demurred when she extended a bottle of Pellegrino towards him to do the same.

"It's something that needs sorting," Lynley said.

"The heat? I couldn't agree more. But you're probably talking about my card amongst Teo Bontempi's belongings, aren't you? Let me think for a moment. When I gave out my cards initially at Orchid House, I gave one to Narissa Cameron. That would be a second card, as I'd given her one at the meeting at the Department for Education."

"She is . . . ?"

"She's a filmmaker doing a documentary, also for the Department for Education. Now that I think of it, I gave another card to Zawadi, and that would be her second card as well."

"She was at the same meeting?"

"She was."

"Her surname?"

"She doesn't use one, as far as I know. And . . . Oh yes. I also gave a card to Adaku. She's one of the volunteers. She was helping with the documentary filming, and the girls were finding it rather difficult to tell their stories in a natural way for the camera, for Narissa's film. So to make it easier for them, Adaku told her story first." Deborah was thoughtful. She lowered her eyes for a moment to say, "It was horrific, Tommy. She was completely mutilated, years ago, in Africa."

"May I ask why you gave her your card?"

"I've decided to do a larger photo book—like my London book?—but this one on the subject of FGM. I want to include her portrait. When I asked her, she was very reluctant, so I showed her some photos I'd snapped of her while she was speaking, just to illustrate what I had in mind. I gave her my card so that if she changes her mind, she can ring me. I may have frightened her off, though."

"Why do you say that?"

"She's not been there to volunteer for a few days. I've learned that Adaku has quite a special touch with the girls."

It seemed something of a coincidence: African, mutilated, missing for a few days. He said, "Teo Bontempi was African, Deb. She was also brutally circumcised."

Deborah looked down at her sandal-shod feet. Then she said slowly, "Tommy, you said she worked on a team, yes?" And when he nodded, "Could the team have placed undercover officers in the community? Women, I mean?"

"Teo Bontempi was the only female on the team, and her superior didn't mention anyone working undercover."

"Could Adaku be a police informant? She was born in Nigeria. If she's one of Teo Bontempi's sources and she's learned Teo's dead, that could explain why she's not turned up at Orchid House."

"It could do, yes. Have you any idea how to contact her?"

She shook her head. "Zawadi will have a number to reach her, I expect. I do know she has family in the area because she spoke of them and of being adopted."

Lynley homed in on the word. "Adopted?"

"She mentioned that when she was telling her story for the film. Her parents are white, and I think she might have had some . . . I don't know . . . some issues with that."

"Teo Bontempi was adopted, Deb. Her parents are white."

She looked into his face but seemed to be looking elsewhere, because in a moment she put her hand on his arm and said, "Tommy, come with me." She rose and made for the house at a rapid pace, striding across the lawn, through the kitchen, then up the stairs. At the front door, she snatched up a black metal case and took it with her into Simon's study, saying to her husband, "Are we disturbing . . . ?"

He made a gesture of get-on-with-it and scribbled some notes on the paper he was reading. Deborah put her metal case on one of the leather chairs and opened it.

Lynley saw it contained her digital camera and an additional lens. She turned the camera over to its screen and switched it on. She began going through its photos, so quickly that he didn't have time to register them. But when she came to one in particular, she stopped and turned the camera so that he could see the screen: a haunted-looking woman in African dress, turbaned, with a substantial necklace carved from wood and large gold hoops in her ears.

"This is Adaku," Deborah said.

"This is Teo Bontempi," he told her.

7 AUGUST

By phone Lynley had made certain that DS Jade Hopwood knew he would be coming to Empress State Building. He didn't want to waste time through having her not expect him, but more than that he didn't want to have to wait for her and thus inadvertently give himself any time during which he might be forced to think. If he did that, his thoughts would take him directly to Daidre, and if his thoughts took him directly to Daidre, one of the many subjects with which they would present him was the one that had him questioning why he hadn't yet phoned her.

He asked himself if his reluctance had to do with owing her an apology. He wasn't sure if this was one of those gentlemen-typically-do-not kinds of moments in his life, during which his conscience took up residence in his brain till he behaved by rote exactly as he'd been brought up to behave, or if this was one of those moments in which he merely needed to clarify all that had passed between them, particularly what had been said and which part of that was his responsibility.

Admittedly, he did seem to choose the most extraordinary women with whom to fall in love. They always turned out to be far more complicated than he reckoned they would be. He couldn't work out why this was the case, unless it meant that he simply didn't understand women at all, which seemed ever more a distinct possibility. He was, perhaps, expecting them to be Jane Bennet to his Mr. Bingley (because, after all, he knew he couldn't possibly cope with an Elizabeth), which meant his unspoken and unacknowledged wish was for a woman who blushed, made conversation when necessary, knew all the appropriate social niceties, was gentle and submissive, expressed her opinions in ways that he found both acceptable and supportive of his own opinions, and otherwise didn't occupy his mind other than when she was playing the piano and even then she would exist merely as an object for him to own and admire. But surely that couldn't be the case. Could it? No. It absolutely couldn't. He wanted a life companion, a woman with her own mind who was more than merely a piece of set decoration with a vague talent for arranging flowers and embroidering handkerchiefs with his initials. So how the devil was he going to manage it? That was the conundrum he faced with Daidre, because the very last thing Daidre Trahair was, was a decorative object to be shown off to the world, and when it came to flowers, she'd probably be far happier feeding them to one of her zoo animals than placing them in vases. As for the handkerchiefs . . . one could only expect so much of another human being. There remained, however, the reality he was facing: while he could identify with a fair amount of precision what Daidre wasn't, he still hadn't been able to put many pieces together that would tell him what she was. And in those infrequent moments when he *did* discover something new about her, he was proving himself completely incapable of dealing with it.

Lynley headed for the entrance to Empress State Building, where he found DS Jade Hopwood waiting for him, a visitor's badge in hand. He knew from doing preliminary legwork that she was fifty-five years old and a grandmother twice over, but she looked far younger, her dark skin unlined, not a strand of grey in her hair. She wore this in a multitude of braids that encircled her head. She was sporting three stud earrings on one side of her head and a large gold hoop on the other, and she was very smartly dressed. She was also unsmiling and all business. When he introduced himself, she offered a brusque nod and led him—much as Mark Phinney had done—towards the lifts that serviced the higher floors of the building. But unlike Phinney, she didn't take him to the Orbit. Instead, they rode to the seventeenth floor, and when the lift doors slid silently open, she strode to her desk, snatching up a plastic chair on the way. This she plopped down at the side of her desk. She gestured Lynley to it and sat herself.

He saw that her desk had no bare surface. It was a mass of manila folders, internet printouts, newspapers and tabloids, books, brochures, and CDs. Two framed photos sat atop a set of overfull metal in-and-out trays. One held a picture of two small girls clutching between them a very large Winnie the Pooh and the other held a picture of these same girls with, he assumed, their parents. They were a handsome group.

The detective sergeant saw him looking at the photos and said, "Three more on the way. My daughter's due next month and my son's wife—not that son in the picture, mind you—is having twins in December. If she lasts that long. To hear her, you'd think she's been carrying septuplets for a year. Now. DCS Phinney wants you brought up to speed. 'Tween you and me, I think he'd be the better one to do it since I'm still getting up to speed myself, although he's been good at helping out when he can. But this"—she pointed a slender finger to the surface of the desk—"is mostly how I'm having to do it. Reading every file and report I can put my hands on. So I'm not sure how much I can help you, but I'll give it a go."

"Is all of this from DS Bontempi?"

"She left everything behind. Only took personal items from her desk. The way DCS Phinney tells me, she wasn't exactly over the moon to be transferred. I expect she left in a huff and reckoned she'd let someone else deal with her mess. I don't blame her. She'd been working on this team for years."

"Did you speak to her once you took her place?"

"Oh yeah. By phone, this was. I asked her first what she wanted to keep from what she'd left. She said nothing. I could have it all and do with it whatever I would. I could bin it if I wanted. I rang her with questions a couple more times after that and she rang me once as well."

"Did she help bring you on board?"

"She was good about that, she was, especially with all my questions. You ask me, she did a good job entire time she was here."

"Anything you can tell me about her and about her activities is enormously helpful. Just now, we don't know much."

The detective settled back into her chair and folded her hands in her lap. She said, "Way I understand it, she was involved in a big way with individual communities, mostly through community centres. She also talked to assemblies in schools and she made contact with various support groups for girls across town. And she'd managed to get fairly close to the Nigerian community: knowing people by name, developing relationships with them, and the like. She's Nigerian herself—but I expect you know that—so she made a good fit. Th' way the guv tells it—the DCs as well—she was that good with people."

"Is there anything in all this that's caught your eye?" Lynley put his hand on a pile of manila folders. "Any names, dates, places, reports that might give someone a bad shock if it came out that DS Bontempi had some sort of relevant information or that she was also a cop? Did people know that, by the way, when she was at work in the community?"

"Not sure 'bout that. But she didn't hide it, far as I know. She was going to schools and to groups, like I said. Can't think she would've been allowed to do that without telling head teachers that she was a cop."

Lynley nodded. It made sense. "Anything else?" he asked.

Hopwood looked as if she was considering the question, her gaze on the mass of material in front of her. She said, "Y'know, there was this one thing . . . ," and she reached into the lower of the in-and-out trays and grabbed a sheaf of papers held together by a large black clip. She unfastened this and fingered through the information till she came to what she wanted. This was a card the size of a business card, but blank on both sides save for a line of numbers printed across it. It was stapled to a piece of white paper. There was no indication what it was aside from what it appeared to be: a mobile phone number.

"Have you rung it?" Lynley asked.

"Twice," she replied. "All I get is one of those computer voices telling me to leave a message. Which I've also done. No joy, though."

"Did you ask DS Bontempi what it was, this number?"

"Didn't get a chance. I hadn't even got to it yet. I only found it last afternoon when I was pulling out all her reports and the like for you."

"You've not started a trace?"

"Like I said, no chance."

"And that's the only thing that leapt out at you?"

"Even that di'n't exactly leap. More like it slithered." She chuckled. Then something seemed to strike her because she went on. "Oh. Wait. Right. There'd been two arrests not long before she left us, so that could be something."

"What sort of arrests?"

"Let me see . . ." She stood as this made it easier for her to shift things around and find what she was looking for. She said, "Two women got hauled to the local nick for questions. A DC there wrote th' initial report. It's here somewhere—" She pulled out a folder from the stack and opened it, saying, "Here. Happened in north London. Stoke Newington Station dealt with it, but DS Bontempi got the paperwork on it. Like I said, she went to community centres and the like, and I expect she developed some decent informants. Anyway, what she says in an attachment to the report is that there's community cutters in north London who're being paid by families when they can't go to Africa to have it done. These cutters're African women, who did the same back there and support themselves now by doing it here."

"They can't be broadcasting that."

"Don't need to, do they. It's all word of mouth."

"And the arrests you mentioned? The two women?"

"Looked hopeful at first—seems there was a little girl with one 'f them—but turned out to be sod all in the end. One woman runs a clinic in the community, for women who don't want to see a male GP for things like antenatal exams, birth control, breast checks, smears, and the like. The other just happened to be there when the cops arrived and carted both of them off. Could be something, could be nothing. Lord only knows."

"The women's names?"

"In the report as well." She handed it over and looked at all the material on her desk. She said, "D'you know how many African immigrants're in London? Somali and Nigerian, 'specially?"

"I don't," he said.

"Neither do I. But that's where this maiming's going on. Not everyone does it, 'f course, but I swear to God, I got no idea how we're going to stop those who do."

Lynley tapped the edge of the folder on his palm, observing the detective. He heard anger in her voice, but he also saw resignation on her face. He said, "Sergeant Hopwood, did you know that DS Bontempi had herself been cut?"

She looked perplexed only for an instant before she realised what he meant. She said, "Holy God, no. I didn't know that. But I wouldn't have done, would I? I mean, we only spoke on the phone and there was no reason for her to tell me." She shook her head slowly and added, "I'm dead sorry to hear it, but it 'xplains a few things, that does."

"Does it?"

"Way I heard things, she was one hundred and ten percent committed to this work, like the very idea of it set her on fire. It was personal for her, wasn't it?"

"Very personal," he agreed. He gestured with the folder she'd given him, saying, "May I take this?"

"All yours," she told him. "You ring me if you end up with more questions than answers. I'm happy to do what I can."

He thanked her and headed to the lifts, where he descended to the ground floor and made a stop at Peeler's Café. There, a double espresso gave him time to read the report written about the arrests made in north London. There was very little to it, he discovered. A phone call had led the local police to a clinic where two women—one Easter Lange and one Monifa Bankole—were arrested. A child had been with them, as Jade Hopwood had indicated to him, the daughter of Monifa Bankole. It was this child's presence that had evidently prompted the phone call.

In advance, the local police had been led to believe that this particular clinic was providing something called medicalised FGM. Translated, this meant the practitioner was able to render the "patient" unconscious during the mutilation. But the Stoke Newington police had no proof of this, and they could hardly raid the place on a whim if nothing was in the process of going on. On the morning in question, though, the presence of the child suggested something was about to occur. Hence, the raid.

Ultimately, the report confirmed everything Jade Hopwood had told him, Lynley saw. The place the locals raided was a women's health centre, and everything therein attested to this: filing cabinets filled with patients' information and most of it dealing with breast checks, cervical exams, postnatal issues, and on and on. Easter Lange ran Women's Health of Hackney on her own, and she was certified to do so. She was also a midwife.

For her part, Monifa Bankole had had an appointment to deal with what she referred to as "troubles down there." The child was with her for the simple reason that her mother had not liked to leave her at home alone. From A to Z, every detail had checked out, and the local police were apparently philosophical about the entire cock-up. They put it down to an informant who was determined to be helpful. Only in this case, she'd been too helpful. She'd jumped the gun and wasted everyone's time.

That was the limit of what the report contained. When all was said and done, there was nothing the women could be charged with, so off they went once things were sorted. Lynley wondered about it all, however. Who was the confidential informant who'd passed the information along to the local police? More, how had Teo Bontempi come to have possession of the report?

STOKE NEWINGTON
NORTH-EAST LONDON

Tani rang Sophie the next morning. With Tiombe gone and Bliss unwilling to shelter his sister, Tani saw no other possibility, although he'd spent most of the night trying to come up with something. He couldn't trust his mother, obviously. There was no deal he could strike with his father. He needed another way to look at the options, and, as far as he was concerned, Sophie was that other way. So he asked could they meet for some talking, but he didn't tell her the subject of their would-be conversation.

She said of course, and she told him she was inside Abney Park, which was going to be the site of her star turn as Mustardseed in *A Midsummer Night's Dream*. The park was one of London's great Victorian cemeteries, long ago allowed to grow wild and go to seed. It was a close-to-perfect setting for the play, with all the greenery and trees and whatnot.

She'd meet him at one of the cemetery's side entrances, she said, this one on the High Street. It was not far from her parents' house and far, far cooler. All night, her bedroom had felt like a firepit made for roasting pigs.

Tani went there at once. It wasn't close by, but he found her patiently waiting for him at the High Street entrance, just as she said she would be. He came from the rail station a short distance north, and when she saw him, she came towards him with the bright smile that always gave him a quick burst of joy.

"Hiya," he called to her.

"Hiya yourself. Listen to this, Tani: I got the understudy for Titania! Director rang just after you."

"Tha's excellent," he told her. "Now you only got to think of a way to poison th' other actress, eh?"

"Just what I was thinking. Are you going to kiss me, or am I going to have to manipulate you into it?"

"Don't need manipulating, do I," he said, and he kissed her in the way he knew she liked, softly at first, then a flick of his tongue and her lips parted.

After a moment, she said against his mouth, "Missing you, Tani."

After another moment, he said, "Same for me." It was, he thought, a blessing in life to know that someone was truly yours. Omorwhatever-in-Nigeria had been a potential problem to his future. But with the revelation of Abeo's plan for the cutter, Nigeria had ceased to exist. Now there was just Sophie.

She took his hand. "Let's go inside. We can find a place to sit, I can show you the old chapel 's well. Most of the play's happening round it."

He wanted to talk, not to see. But he found he couldn't disappoint her. He followed her inside Abney Park Cemetery, along a narrow path among graves long given over to nature through the means of shrubbery, brambles, vines, and wildflowers. Enormous trees sheltered the place, and the air had an almost tangible scent of fresh oxygen, so unusual in London. As they went along the path, Sophie continued to talk about the play, Titania, and the director while Tani made appropriate noises. When they finally reached the chapel—which was more a ruin than a chapel and he couldn't see how this was going to work and what did it matter because he wasn't there to talk about acting anyway—she turned to him, saying, "It's sort of a strange idea, isn't it. But if it works, the production will run through September."

He did his best to appear enthusiastic. He said "Cool," but he obviously wasn't able to be genuine. Sophie knew this because she walked over to a nearby stone bench, sat, and said, "Tell me."

He sat next to her—his shoulder pressing hers, he feeling comforted by the contact—and explained what he'd set up with Tiombe and how that was now impossible. He didn't mention the failure of the deal he'd struck with his father: marriage in Nigeria to a guaranteed-to-be-a-virgin. That was finished, thrown into the rubbish—courtesy of Abeo's finding a Nigerian cutter here in London—so Sophie didn't need to know about Omorinsola. He understood that not telling her everything was something of a risk, but the other risk was telling her and having her desert him for not telling her from the start. Just now he needed her more than ever, because Simi had to be spirited away from Mayville Estate as soon as he could manage it.

Sophie's eyes grew rounder as she learned about Tiombe's absence. She said at once, "Then bring Simi to me. We'll come up with an excuse. It's the only answer. And it's time we met anyway, Simi and me." He started to make a reply to this, but she put her hand on his arm. "Tell her it's my sister's birthday and she's invited."

"Is it her birthday?"

"'Course not."

"So when I get Simi to your house and there's no birthday and no party, you don't think she's goin to want to go straight back home? Listen, she doesn't understand what's going to happen to her. She doesn't even know what being cut means."

"How can she not know? She *has* to have been told. The schools are making sure of it now."

Tani shook his head. "My mum's home educated her, is what it is, Soph. She did the same with me, but tha' was just infants' school. I always thought it was cos Pa didn't want our minds 'polluted' or something. I reckoned he didn't want us to be English."

"Then you must explain what'll happen to her if she doesn't stay away from home. *And* you must give her the details." She seemed to read something—like the truth—in his expression, because she said, "You *must*, Tani. You don't have a choice. You tell her about being cut and then you bring her for my sister's 'birthday' tonight. Between now and then, I'll tell my mum and dad what's going on so they'll—"

"Don't tell them! Sophie, you do that an' . . . " Tani didn't know how to finish the sentence. He'd met her parents, but he'd been careful to be seen as English as they were, as English as Sophie was. If they learned the truth of who his parents were and the primitive act that his father intended to subject Simisola to, they would probably want Sophie to end things with him, deciding he was completely the wrong person for their daughter. And who could blame them? "Jus' please don't tell them."

"But if she stays with us, they're going to wonder what the hell is going on, Tani."

"So she can't stay. I can't have her stay and have them ask you about her. There's got to be something else, somewhere else."

Sophie frowned. "All right, then. I'll think of something to tell them. *And* I'll start looking online for . . . I don't know. There's got to be a way to protect her."

"I don't want her in Care!"

"I don't mean Care. I don't even know *what* I mean. But I'll start looking. In the meantime, we've got to get her away from your parents, Tani. One of them is going to hurt her."

OXFORD STREET
CENTRAL LONDON

"It's a simple enough answer." Rosie Bontempi took a moment to smooth down her linen pencil skirt. As far as Winston Nkata could tell, it didn't need smoothing, but the gesture did draw attention to her legs. It also drew attention inevitably to her ankles, which were as fine as any he'd seen, made finer looking still by the dizzyingly high stilettos she was wearing. He and she were leaning side by side against the ledge and front windows of a café on Oxford Street not far from Selfridges, where Rosie was working—she confided—until something more suitable came along, hopefully as one of the makeup artists on an ITV police drama that was scheduled to begin filming soon in Norwich.

She'd agreed to speak with him a second time, but only during her morning break and only if their encounter did not occur inside Selfridges. She'd named the café and the time she could meet him. He'd arrived there early.

"Teo went completely African," she continued. "She wanted me to do the same. I wouldn't. And she didn't bother to *try* to understand why I wouldn't." She gave a sharp, humourless laugh. "Like, our parents snatched us out of a bloody African *orphanage*, for heaven's sake, so one would think she'd be grateful for that. At least grateful enough that she wouldn't want to hurt them by cutting them out of her life. Believe me, they'd still be cut from her life if *Papá* hadn't had a stroke."

"You're saying tha's what you argued 'bout?" Nkata asked her.

"Not exactly," was her reply.

She watched the taxis and buses as they jockeyed for position in the street. It was not yet blazingly hot so the fumes of the vehicles were not as oppressive as they would be later. Nkata was thankful for this. Give it another hour, and walking on the pavements of Oxford Street would be like slip-sliding straight into hell.

He'd come to Rosie Bontempi directly from New Scotland Yard, where he and Barbara Havers had spent the first two hours of their workday dealing with the telephoned instructions of DCS Lynley. They'd written up their activity reports from the conversations they'd had on the previous afternoon and evening with Teo Bontempi's neighbours and sent her laptop off to the digital forensic techs. Neither of them had looked at any of the CCTV film from the building that housed her flat, though, and Teo's mobile had not turned up. For his part, Lynley put them into the picture of Teo's dual identity: as Adaku the volunteer at Orchid House and Teo the detective sergeant working with a team dealing with various forms of the abuse of women, prior to her transfer. As a result of all this, Nkata had been tasked with having another go at Rosie Bontempi, while Havers headed to east London to uncover what she could at Orchid House.

A phone call to Rosie had brought him here. At her request he'd obediently brought her a takeaway macchiato. To her, "No coffee for yourself?" when she saw him, he'd lifted his fizzy water and replied, "Caffeinated enough from my mum's kitchen. Her coffee's like mud on speed."

He was there to ask her about the argument she'd had with her sister, just two days before Teo had fallen into a coma. It had apparently been a fracas for the ages, as all four flats with adjoining walls, floors, or ceilings had, upon questioning, given either him or Barb Havers chapter and verse about two women going at it at full volume.

When two of them reported a shouted "Get out of here, Rosie," prior to the crash-slamming of a door, it was no major effort to suss out the identity of one of the arguers. To his question of what they'd been arguing about, Rosie's response had been, "I'm not surprised someone heard us. We've been arguing for years." He'd asked why, arguing about what? Her statement about her sister "going African" had been her reply.

Did she know that Teo also called herself Adaku? he'd asked her.

'Course she knew. Adaku was her birth name. Adaku Obiaka. "I just *said* she went African, didn't I?" Rosie declared. "The clothes, the hair, the jewellery . . . She, like, *disappeared* behind a new persona. We were lucky she didn't make us all *call* her Adaku. Not that it matters, because once she became Adaku, we barely saw her. And *that*, by the way, is what she and I were arguing about. I'd gone to her because she'd not been to see *Papá* in weeks. He had a stroke—well, you saw him yourself—and one would think she'd be just a little concerned about him. Even re*mote*ly concerned. I mean, she even could have *pretended* to be concerned, couldn't she? But he's not Black—our dad—so he doesn't count. *Maman* doesn't either. They don't register with her any longer. It was like she woke up one day and looked in the mirror and made a decision and that was that. It was, I mean, totally stupid. I think she wanted to punish them."

"For what? Being white?"

"There's that, yes. No one could possibly deny that they've got to where they are today because they're white. But for her the bigger issue was that they *had* to take her from the orphanage or they wouldn't've been able to adopt me. I was a baby and they wanted a baby. She was just something on the side that they had to put up with."

Nkata glanced at her as she said this. He caught the twitch of her lips that appeared to rein in her smile. "Seems harsh, that."

"Yes. Well. The facts often are, aren't they." She looked at him. She seemed to evaluate him. She said, "Why's your face scarred? Were you attacked somewhere?"

"Knife fight," he told her.

"Oh my God. How awful!"

"No God was involved. I was willin' enough to be part of it."

"Were you arresting a criminal or something?"

"I was in a gang," he told her.

Her eyes widened. "A *gang*? Did you lot have . . . what do they call it . . . turf wars or something?"

He shook his head. "We jus' liked to fight."

"You're quite big, though, aren't you. I'm surprised anyone was willing to take you on."

"So was I," he replied. "Then I got myself more surprised when the bloke turned out to have a blade and know how to use it. I 'as lucky not to lose an eye."

"So you left the gang?"

"That would've been way too clever and clever was not my middle name. Three more years of it but I got better with the knife. Then I met a bloke an' he got me out of it an' I never went back."

"Are you gay, then?"

He shot her a look. "Sayin' what?"

"Are you gay? You said a bloke got you out of the gang life. And you don't even flirt, so that made me think . . . I mean, you looked at my legs but that was all. Do you not like Black women? Are you married? And don't tell me it's because you're working a case because you aren't working a case twenty-four/seven. We could meet for a drink if you'd like that."

"I'm not gay," he told her. "An' I 'preciate the offer, but I gen'rally don't have drinks with . . ." He wasn't sure what to call her. The correct word was *suspect*, but he didn't like to apply it to her.

". . . with people who might be murderers?" she finished for him. She downed the rest of the macchiato and walked over to a rubbish bin to toss the cup, thus affording him another opportunity to give her shapely form a look. She was beautiful in every possible respect, no doubt about it. She was also sexy as bloody hell. But his antennae for trouble were finely tuned. And Rosie Bontempi was trouble squared, no question.

"So how'd she work it out?" he asked Rosie when she returned to lean against the window with him.

She rubbed a nonexistent spot on the arm of her blouse. This was the colour of cream, and it looked like silk. She said, "Who?"

"Your sister. How'd she work it out that your parents took her only because otherwise they wouldn't get you?"

"I don't know. P'rhaps one of them told her. Or Ross. He might've known from his own parents."

"This's your brother-in-law, right?"

"More or less. We all grew up together. His parents and mine were extremely close."

"'More or less' meaning what?" Nkata asked her.

"They were divorcing, Ross and Teo. We did mention that when you came to speak to us. He was on his way out of being my brother-in-law."

"Way I hear it, he wasn't 'xactly on board with that."

"With the divorce?" She dropped her gaze to her stilettos. There was very little to them, he saw, just a few pieces of leather and a heel that looked like a rapier. He couldn't imagine what her feet felt like at the end of the day.

"Look. It's like this," Rosie said. "Teo threw Ross away. He wasn't African, and, like I said, she'd gone *completely* African. He's white and she can't—she couldn't—abide anyone white once she learned why she'd been adopted. It was a dreadful blow for her. What else can I say?"

She could say that she was the one to tell her sister the adoption story, Nkata thought. He reckoned sharing that sort of news would be right up her alley.

TRINITY GREEN
WHITECHAPEL
EAST LONDON

Barbara Havers thought it was a good bet that she was going to have two big problems with paying a call on anyone at Orchid House. The first was that she was a cop and, as such, a life force sure to freeze her out of everyone's heart once she stepped foot in the place. The second was that she was white, and although Lynley had explained to her that Deborah St. James had already made an inroad in the white woman department, Deborah St. James had not been there to ask questions but merely to take pictures. So her first reaction to the activity Lynley had assigned her once his meeting with DS Hopwood had finished was, "Shouldn't Winston do this, sir?"

"According to Deborah, men aren't welcome inside," Lynley said. "Rein in your tendency to say the first thing that pops into your mind, and you'll be fine."

"And when I tell them that one Adaku Obitami—"

"Obiaka, Barbara."

"Obiaka, right. How d'you expect they're going to greet the news that Adaku Obiaka was a cop?"

"I doubt that's where you'll begin," Lynley said. "By the time you reveal the information—*if* you must reveal the information—I feel certain you will have won them over with your abundant charms."

So she crisscrossed the City to get to London Wall and from there to Mile End Road. What she knew about the location of Orchid

House was limited to "You'll find it inside the chapel in Trinity Green," from Deborah St. James via mobile phone. "It's two rows of almshouses—Trinity Green—behind a brick wall. If you find you've come to the statues of the Booths—which is what I did—you'll have gone too far." She'd added the completely unhelpful information that the Booths—a mister and a missus—had founded the Salvation Army and there appeared to be some sort of Salvation Army building in the vicinity, which, if she came across it instead of seeing the Booths, would *also* tell her she'd driven too far.

With that in mind, once Barbara managed to get herself and her Mini to Mile End Road, she began to keep her eyes open for brick walls and almshouses or, if it came to that, the statues of the Booths. It was, she thought, not the sort of area one would expect to find almshouses, behind brick walls or not. This part of Whitechapel appeared to be a commercial area exclusively. Lorries by the dozens barrelled through it, trundling goods to and from their destinations as they belched diesel fumes into the day's growing hot air. The traffic noise was teeth grinding, and it wasn't the sort of steady motorised roar that one might become used to, at long last fading into the background in such a way as to become unnoticeable should one live nearby. It was certainly ceaseless enough to qualify as white noise, but it was also accompanied by the grinding of gears, the squeaking of brakes, and the occasional blaring of a horn, and all of this at a volume just shy of deafening.

Along the pavements on either side of the wide road sat every sort of business establishment, from hairdressers to ethnic restaurants to failed ventures with their front grilles pulled down and tagged in a multiplicity of colours. The ubiquitous rug shop was having its expected Going Out of Business sale, and a Chinese takeaway was accepting the delivery of an impressive number of cardboard boxes featuring green dragons shooting nostril flames. Next to this, a fish and chip shop was offering a two-for-the-price-of-one discount.

There was no indication what the product was, aside from its being edible, but that was good enough for Barbara. She made a mental note to stop inside the place once she'd concluded her trawling for details at Orchid House. Meantime, the sun beat down on everything, as if getting its own back on people who'd spent decades complaining about the grey, damp weather of summer in England. Barbara could see shimmering waves of *something* rising up from the Mini's bonnet. She frowned and held to the hope that it was just the day's heat.

As Deborah had warned, Barbara saw the statues before she located Trinity Green. The Booths stood facing each other on the greenway between the pavement and the road. Catherine Booth, gowned and bonneted and clutching what had to be a Bible, was positioned so close to the traffic that she might have been hitchhiking. William Booth, arm raised and preternaturally long index finger pointing towards the heavens, appeared to be preaching. The building in front of which they stood bore a sign identifying it as Tower Hamlets Mission. Just beyond it the greenway widened, and Barbara pulled onto it.

On foot, she headed in the direction from which she'd come. Trinity Green turned out to be a short distance to the south-west. It stood off the road and behind the tall brick wall that Deborah had mentioned. This was easy to overlook because only a small, enamelled metal sign on this wall indicated Trinity Green's existence beyond it. There were two means of access to the place: through a set of large wrought-iron gates that were at present padlocked and through a smaller pedestrian gate that was standing open. Both sets of gates were painted bright green.

The almshouses comprised two terraces of small cottages facing each other, with the eponymous green in the middle, its dried-up lawn shaded by two lines of moptop trees. To one side of the pedestrian gate, a bronze memorial plaque announced that the seventeenth-century buildings therein were houses built originally for "decay'd masters and commanders of ships or widows of the same." The cottages themselves were redbrick with white dog-tooth cornices along the rooflines and decorative corbels holding up narrow porch roofs that offered scant protection from the elements. Stone quoins punctuated each end of both terraces; worn steps led up to each front door. To the side of these steps were small patios that acted as individuation for the dwellings: some were filled with plants, others with toys, still others with barbecues and seating for outdoor summertime meals.

Barbara reckoned that the chapel she sought was the distinguished-looking building at the far end of the lawn, facing in the direction of the road and featuring a handless blue clock face with golden numbers to indicate the hours. Access to Orchid House was up a wide flight of stone steps and through open chapel double doors, above which a curved pediment was going green and black from years of ignoring moss, mold, and mildew.

Barbara entered an octagonal vestibule. Here four large notice-boards were hung with a variety of posters indicating upcoming diverse events in the neighbourhood: from a performance by an acrobatic group to a weekly class on meditation given somewhere in this building. Just inside the chapel proper, a table of the sort one found in school lunchrooms held boxes of stationery, filing folders, and office supplies, along with a hand-lettered poster board name plate upon which someone had neatly printed RECEPTION. There was, however, no receptionist present.

Barbara looked round to see if anyone was lurking nearby. Finding no one, she wandered farther into the chapel, which, while serving at one time as a place of worship, was subdivided now with unappealing temporary walls some nine feet tall, behind which voices could be heard. Still, the chapel had managed to retain a few decent features, no doubt in keeping with its age: A carved and gilded wooden cornice as well as cream-coloured paneling were the most noticeable. At one time there had been chandeliers as well—crystal, brass, silver . . . who knew?—but they'd been removed, with only their chains hanging disconsolately from the ceiling to mark the place where each had hung. The lighting now consisted of grim fluorescent strips, two of which were flickering badly, and whatever the flooring once had been—stone or oak or tiles—it was now institutional carpet of a particularly depressing shade of blue. This was, admittedly, one step above carpet squares, but it was equally hideous nonetheless.

"Can I help you? What d'you want?"

Barbara turned. She found herself facing a tall, heavyset woman wearing a complicated magenta and gold headpiece and a matching gown that flowed and draped over her body. She stood in the unmistakably unwelcoming posture of one hip thrown out and both arms crossed beneath her ample breasts.

"DS Barbara Havers." Barbara fished enthusiastically in her dilapidated shoulder bag and brought out her warrant card, which she handed over, saying "New Scotland Yard. This is Orchid House, right?"

Barbara could see caution alter the woman's face. "It is," she said, handing back the warrant card. "What is it you want?"

"Conversation." Out came her notebook as well, along with the mechanical pencil she'd nicked from Nkata. "I'm here about one of your volunteers. She's called Adaku." Barbara didn't use the surname. She reckoned women called Adaku weren't exactly dropping off the trees outside.

"What's she done?"

"Unfortunately, she's got herself murdered."

As the woman echoed her with "*Murdered?*" Barbara looked round and said, "Would there be a place we could talk? Who are you, by the way?"

"Zawadi. I'm the founder and managing director here. But did Adaku—"

"Could you spell it? Zawadi, not Adaku. I've got that one down."

Zawadi did the honours. She added that she had no surname. She'd dropped it legally years ago, she explained, when she decided she wanted no further communication with her family.

Bit harsh, that, Barbara thought. But on the other hand, there had been a time when she'd felt that way herself. She jotted the name and then repeated her request, as she had no interest in speaking with Zawadi where anyone might be able to overhear them.

Zawadi told Barbara to follow her. She led the way back outside the chapel, where beneath the wide steps that had given Barbara access to the place, a door allowed one to enter the basement. This was subdivided as above.

Zawadi ushered Barbara into a corridor and from there into what seemed to be her office. It was a small room, and it was already overcrowded with three women: mixed race, Indian, and Chinese. Zawadi made short work of the introductions, using her hands to flip casually at each one of them as she said their names. Barbara caught only the first one, Narissa Cameron. She was a filmmaker. The other two were apparently a lighting technician and a sound engineer.

"Adaku is dead," Zawadi announced baldly. "You'll have to muddle on without her."

The other women were rendered momentarily wordless. Then Narissa repeated, "What *happened*?"

"She was murdered." Barbara gave the answer. "I'll be speaking with everyone here who knew her. I'm starting with Zawadi. The rest of you, don't leave the premises."

Narissa's gaze went to Zawadi as if for further information or a recommendation regarding what she should do. Zawadi said, "Carry on. Tell the girls Adaku has been delayed."

That was certainly one way to put it, Barbara thought.

When the three other women had left both the office and the basement that contained it, Zawadi sat behind her desk and gestured in the direction of the most uncomfortable-looking folding chair that Barbara had ever seen. She carried it from where it was leaning against a wall and opened it at the side of the desk and not in front of it as Zawadi might have wished her to do.

Zawadi said, "Why did they send you?"

Barbara planted herself on the seat of the chair, saying, "We talk to everyone the victim's been associated with."

"That's not what I mean. I mean why *you* and not a Black officer?"

"You'd've preferred a Black officer?"

"What do you think? You'll find I'm not the only one with that preference here."

"We've got one on the team, another DS, but he's a bloke. My guv reckoned if it came to race or gender, you'd see gender as the better alternative for an interview."

"Are you telling me you have *no* Black female detectives in the Metropolitan Police?"

"I'm saying there aren't any in this investigation. Matter of fact, there aren't any other *women* in this investigation. Adaku was a cop, by the way. She'd been working on a team that deals with genital cutting and all the other crap that's being done to women in the name of God knows what. We're trying to work out whether she was murdered because she was Adaku or because she was the cop Teo Bontempi."

That piece of news, Barbara saw, snagged Zawadi's complete attention. She said, "She didn't come to us as a policewoman. Her name wasn't Adaku?"

"Adaku was her birth name. It got changed to Teo Bontempi when she was adopted. As a cop—she was a detective sergeant—she used the adopted name."

"Why did she never tell me that?"

Barbara shrugged. "Could be she didn't trust you. Could be she was looking for something here that she knew she wouldn't find if she identified as a cop. How'd she show up? Wander in off the street or what?"

"The local schools know about us. She would have learned about us there, *if* she'd told us the truth when she said she'd been doing some speaking to the female pupils about FGM."

"That part was on the up and up."

"So she came here, she spoke to me, and I could see she had something to offer the girls."

"D'you mean she could offer them the fact that she'd been mutilated?"

"I mean she could offer them the fact that she was a woman willing to speak of it." Her face bore a look that seemed to challenge Barbara to ask for more personal information.

Barbara went with, "Christ. Did it happen to you as well?"

Zawadi looked across the room to a large calendar on which activities were scrawled, along with the name of the leader of each activity. *Adaku Obiaka* was printed three times. Looking back at Barbara, Zawadi said without a hint of emotion, "I was six years old. It was supposed to be a holiday with my extended family, but it turned out to be something else. I was held down on the floor at my gran's house and gone at with the blade of a pair of scissors. With everyone telling me what a privilege it was that a newly sharpened blade was being used instead of the usual."

"Which would've been what?" Barbara asked.

"A razor blade, a knife, a piece of glass. Anything that cuts."

Barbara felt somewhat lightheaded. She said, "I'm that sorry, I am."

"I have no need of your pity," Zawadi told her.

Barbara waved her off. "Believe me, pity's not what I feel. Sod it, why's this *happening* to girls?"

"Because no one has been able to stop it completely. It's outlawed, people are arrested and go to trial and to prison because of it, but no one has managed to end it. And the only thing we're able to do— Orchid House and organisations like it—is to keep the girls safe if they're able to make their way to us."

"Do they?"

"They do. Adaku wanted to help with that. At least that's what she said, and I believed her. As to her life as a policewoman, I know nothing about that and I expect no one else here does either. Now, if there's nothing else?"

"I'd like to talk to that woman Narissa and the other two. If they knew Adaku, they might know something about her that hasn't been uncovered."

THE MOTHERS SQUARE
LOWER CLAPTON
NORTH-EAST LONDON

Because of her chair and her emergency oxygen, getting Lilybet from The Mothers Square to Great Ormond Street—for an appointment that had taken days to arrange—had required the use of a special van kitted out for her wheelchair, as well as a seat for whoever was going to attend her during the transport. Mark knew that his wife would not consider anyone except herself attending Lilybet, so once they had her tucked up in the van—strapped into her chair with the chair itself fixed in place on the floor—Pete belted herself into the attendant's perch while he rode in the front with the driver. Robertson elected to stay in The Mothers Square. He would be there to assist when Pietra and Mark returned with their daughter. "Don't mind the time," Robertson said, waving them off. "I'm happy enough here, and I want to be in the picture of what the specialist says as well."

So off they went. It was a silent journey.

His wife had gone through his iPhone while he slept, something which, as far as Mark knew, she'd never done before. She'd found the messages. She'd found and listened to the refrain from "their song," after which she'd tracked down the song itself in its entirety and listened to it, hearing so much more than "No, I don't wanna fall in love . . . with you." From there, she'd found the relevant voicemails, which, stupidly, he'd not been able to bear deleting. So she'd heard her voice, and while she would not have recognised it, she did recognise the import behind *Mark darling* and *I feel the same* and *I want to be with you as well*. He'd kept all of it because he was so caught up in the rightness of what he'd felt, in the mad this-is-bigger-than-both-of-us, which was always the lie that one told oneself to justify surrendering to the libido. It could never just be a case of "I want what I want and I mean to have it," which was, at least, an honest reaction to lust. Instead, it had to be written in the stars, an embracing of fate, a headlong rush into what seemed so extraordinary that it obliterated any memory of having been at this place once or twice or three times before. This was *truly* a case of I've-never-felt-like-this-before. Everything preceding it in one's life had been mere dress rehearsal for This Big Moment. It was incontestably real. Because of that, one could not bear to eliminate a single item that, looked upon, fired up the senses once again, reassuring oneself that, yes, it was decidedly real this time, and one was finally alive in ways that all previous *finally alives* were rendered meaningless.

When confronted by Pete, he swore that he'd not broken his vows to her, and while this was technically true, he accepted the fact that in saying this, he placed himself among the rogue husbands who told themselves that being blown by a woman did not constitute having actual sex with her. For only *actual* sex equated to full-on infidelity, and *actual* sex comprised taking a position between the legs and pumping away. Anything short of that meant he could look Pete straight in the eye and say with impunity that "nothing" had happened between them. He'd *wanted* something to happen between them, true. He'd wanted the real something to happen, but as his wife did not ask him a question that would have required that admission, he was at least in the clear when it came to telling her an outright lie.

At first he felt lucky that there was nothing that would tell her who the other woman was. She was attached to a number on his smart-phone, but the number had no attribution. This, however, had not presented a problem for Pietra. From his own smartphone, she texted the number with the message *Ring me, it's urgent*, and when Teo had rung, her first words had been, "Darling, what's wrong? Has something happened . . . ? Mark . . . ? Did you not just text me?"

So she'd heard the voice, and while at first she couldn't attach that voice to a face, she did manage to attach the mobile's number to a Teo Bontempi, with whom he worked. After that, finding her online had been child's play. Nothing having to do with one's identity was difficult in the age of social media.

"It was just that we were working so closely together," was his lame excuse to his wife. "And then, there were times . . . There *are* times, Pete, when the loneliness . . ." But really, how could he finish up with that kind of reasoning, no matter its truth. Besides, she *knew* he had the occasional release—as he termed it—and she understood that "going out with Paulie" sometimes meant more than a few pints down the pub. Which, after all, she encouraged.

But this thing with Teo was different to paying for a massage's happy ending. That, his wife could cope with. That, she could even encourage. That, indeed, was her salvation. "Going out with Paulie" relieved her of the double anxiety with which she lived: that Mark might one day leave her and Lilybet to fend on their own, that he might give her an ultimatum about making her body available to him, her husband, with a husband's ostensible rights. "Going out with Paulie" obviated her need to worry, to think about, to plan, to . . . anything.

Still, her response to his excuse had astonished him. "You don't need to pretend with me, Mark. I know how difficult all of this is, especially with me being like I am. And I want you to have a sexual life. I'm happy for you that you've found someone. I want you to have this."

"This? What d'you mean?"

"The passion, Mark, the fulfillment, what you and I once had and have no longer. I don't blame you for anything. This is helping you be good for Lilybet. And your being good for Lilybet is your being good for me."

But now there was no Teo Bontempi. There was, instead, Teo's death, and what it meant once "death by misadventure" had been altered to "homicide."

Pete said suddenly and in a low voice, "I still can't work out how it happened."

For a moment, he thought she'd read his mind and was speaking of Teo's death, something that he hadn't yet shared with his wife. He didn't reply.

She said, "Mark, are you listening? Did you hear what I said?"

"Sorry, love. No," he told her. "I was in the clouds."

"I said I can't work out how it happened when the alarm went off. I left her for not even five minutes. She was perfectly fine. She'd been watching *Beauty and the Beast* again. You know how she loves it. I stepped out for—"

"Where was Robertson?"

"Just in the kitchen. He was making tea, getting juice for Lilybet. I stepped out of the room just to use the loo."

"Did you not put the cannula in?"

"She'd been fine all morning. I was leaving her for a moment, only. The oxygen's supposed to be supplemental anyway. As needed. I know it's a safeguard as well, but that's for the night, and I knew I'd be out of the room for less than five minutes. But then the alarm went off. Robertson reached her before I did. He put the full mask on her straightaway and started the oxygen. If he hadn't been there, if he hadn't got to her so quickly . . . One small mistake is all it takes and I'm the one who made it."

"No harm done, Pete." He turned in his seat to look at his wife, then at his daughter. Lilybet was watching what went for scenery in the busy London streets: buses, taxis, cars; women with pushchairs; boys wearing hoodies and baggy jeans; a crocodile of children heading somewhere; a woman in hot conversation with a lanky teenager while two toddlers clung to the woman's hands and an electric scooter lay on the pavement. He said to Pete, "I think we can trust her specialist. If she says Lilybet's not got worse, I think we can rely on that."

"I'm so sorry. I feel like a criminal."

"Don't say that, Pete. These things happen."

"But they shouldn't happen," she countered. "We both know that."

TRINITY GREEN
WHITECHAPEL
EAST LONDON

Barbara Havers was drawing the conclusion that, whatever had happened to Teo Bontempi to prompt someone to kill her, it didn't seem likely that its genesis was at Orchid House, unless the organisation was run by a first-class liar in the person of Zawadi. That was always a possibility, of course. But still . . .

As far as Barbara could discover from those she interviewed in the place, Teo-as-Adaku not only had been admired but she also had served as a source of solace to some of the girls, as inspiration to others, and as a role model to the rest of them. She'd volunteered extensively: leading group discussions; engaging in community activities; speaking to parents; devising projects to keep the girls coming back to Orchid House; being a resource for information about the long-term effects of FGM, physical, emotional, and psychological. She'd not told a soul that she was also a cop, which was perplexing at first, till Barbara understood how reluctant the girls would probably have been to leave their families in the first place and how frightened they would probably feel knowing that, should things go wonky, one or both of their parents could be arrested, put on trial, convicted of a crime, and sent to prison if they—the daughters—were not careful about what they revealed and to whom they revealed it. Out of all of this, it seemed to Barbara that only Teo Bontempi's contact with the parents of girls who'd already been placed with sheltering families might have prompted someone to dig around a bit, discover she was not the Adaku who visited them but rather a Metropolitan Police detective, and as a consequence want to do away with her. But unless a parent had come upon her unexpectedly in her police persona, Barbara couldn't see how anyone would have sussed out that she was a cop.

Barbara still wanted to have a word with the filmmaker, Narissa Cameron. She hadn't intruded on the filming itself but instead waited till they had a gap in their work. Then she joined the three other women whom she'd met earlier. None of them seemed happy with how things had gone without Adaku there to offer the girls her supportive presence.

They'd heard her story firsthand, Narissa told Barbara, and that had opened them up to telling their own stories, especially since not one of them was as remotely horrifying as hers.

Barbara asked if Adaku's story was still available on the digital camera. Narissa said that it was. Barbara made a request to see it. Narissa, not unreasonably, asked why.

Barbara opted for honesty. "I'm not sure. But there might be something in what she said on film . . . One never knows. That's just the point. It can be a word. It can be a look. It can be anything. But it sets us in a direction, which is how we got here, to Orchid House. We found Deborah St. James's card in Teo Bontempi's flat. My guv spoke to her—to Deborah St. James—she explained, and here I am. Your film may get me somewhere else. That's all I can tell you."

Glancing at the camera, Narissa said, "She wanted me to delete this, Adaku. But I was hoping that she'd change her mind and let me use it. I kept filming after she was finished speaking. She didn't know that. But it illustrates this . . . I don't know what to call it other than this power she had with people. It was like she *knew* she could make a difference while most people only hope they can."

Narissa had a monitor, and she told Barbara it would be easier to view the film on that rather than on the camera's much smaller screen. Barbara sat while Narissa got things rolling. Then the filmmaker joined her as, on the screen, the woman who'd been known at Orchid House as Adaku took her place on a stool and began to speak.

She began with her name, Adaku Obiaka, and the age at which she had been cut, less than three years. She said, "I learned later that the age I was at the time of the cutting is called prememory. What that means is that I was cut before I could form memories of the cutting while it happened, which is supposed to be merciful. But there have always been fleeting memories, even today."

Barbara studied Adaku's face. What she saw was infinite and abiding sorrow. Grief seemed to be deep in her bones, no transitory thing but something that was part of the fabric of who she was.

Adaku was African in many ways, but she was English in many ways as well. Perhaps that was part of what made her compelling. She told her story with marked dignity.

The worst that could be done to a female child had been done to her, she explained. "It's called infibulation. But those who do this to girls—and those who did it to me—don't call it that. They call it a rite of passage or female circumcision or making you a woman or cleansing you of the nasty bits or preparing you for eventual marriage or increasing your value to a man or increasing that man's pleasure when he takes you, which is your duty as a woman. But it's all the same at the end of the day. It's being mutilated."

Infibulation, she explained, consisted of the clitoris being removed, the vaginal opening narrowed, a covering seal created for that opening, the labia cut and repositioned. Everything then was either sewn up or sewn together, leaving a single small opening through which urine and menstrual blood were supposed to pass.

"Christ." Barbara felt her palms begin to sweat.

Narissa said, "Should I stop the recording?"

"No," Barbara said fiercely. She would not say she had heard enough. She owed it to the dead woman to hear it all.

Adaku was saying that, before she knew the facts of what had happened to her and because she'd never seen what uncut genitals looked like, she'd not realised what had been done to her. It was only when her period hadn't begun by the time she was fifteen that her adoptive mum took her to the family's GP for a check-up. It was during that check-up that she'd learned the truth. There was little to be done at that point, so many years after the fact.

She had reckoned this practise was something that went on only in the land of her birth. But then she'd learned that this vile procedure sometimes went on here, in the UK. So she did what she could do to stop it and she would continue to do so.

She said, "I'm Nigerian. We're a very proud people. But there are times when—out of ignorance—we do to our girls what was done to me when I was so young, what was also done to my mother and to her mother. It once was merely the way of things amongst our people, and since my mum had also been cut, she knew no different than to pass along what she saw as a 'tradition.' But then she died in childbirth when I was seven, and I was sent to live with my aunt, my father's sister. The baby that my mum died giving birth to went with me. Our father did not believe he could care for us, and as it turned out neither could our aunt. She had seven children already, so she delivered us to a Catholic orphanage. We were lucky. A husband and wife adopted us and brought us to the UK. Because I was eight years old at the time I arrived here to my new home, and because I was healthy, no one had any reason to inspect my genitals. Why would they? So no one knew, and it was only later when I was a teenager that the truth about me came to light. I don't know who cut me. I only know that in places where FGM still occurs, it is something done almost always by women. Let me say this again: It is done *by* women *to* women. To ensure we're chaste. To rid our bodies of the parts that were put *on* our bodies so we might know sexual pleasure. We are not meant to have that pleasure because, in the minds of many tribal men, a woman's ability to have sexual pleasure increases the possibility that she will stray. But what I want you to know is this: much of my life has been made unbearable by what was done to me, and I often feel like half the person I ought to be."

Narissa stopped the recording and the picture froze on Adaku's face, Teo Bontempi's face. Barbara found she couldn't move her gaze as she tried to sort out what the woman must have felt at the time she was describing for the listening girls what had happened to her. Superficially, she seemed to feel nothing. When it came to anger, rage, despair, or whatever, she looked like a woman who'd worn out those passions long ago. If this was the case, then, perhaps what remained within her was only her willingness to speak to those who were also damaged, to those who ran the risk of damage, and to those who still insisted this mutilation *had* to be done because if it wasn't, the child the girl the woman in question might actually have a life beyond whatever role her husband-to-be decreed she was to play.

"What happens to the girls who come here, then?" Barbara asked.

"If the girl is in danger, Zawadi puts her into hiding."

"Where?"

"There're homes spread across greater London. I don't know them. It's all kept secret. Families take the girls in and protect them till their parents can be dealt with." She began to unhook each piece of equipment as she spoke.

Barbara focused on *dealt with*. She said, "What's that mean, then? Who deals with the parents? And how?"

"Zawadi at first, usually with a social worker," she said. "They visit the parents and try to reason with them; they warn them of the criminal nature of what they're intending to do. It takes several visits, but if all goes well, the girl can return to her family, although she maintains her contact with Orchid House."

"And if the family goes ahead with the plan anyway?"

"That's the issue, isn't it. It's difficult to trust that a girl's well-being has been absolutely secured. But the parents are put on a watch list. They agree to attend some meetings here. The girl attends activities as well and they agree to that."

"Sounds like they lose control, eh?"

Narissa turned from her equipment box, where she'd just deposited the camera. Her assistants returned to the room, doing their part with the sound and lighting equipment. Narissa said, "You're thinking this would give a parent a motive to kill, aren't you?"

"What d'you think?"

"I think most people don't want trouble with the police. The parents are caught, more or less. The rock and the hard place? If they harm their daughter, they go to prison. If they harm someone else, the result's the same."

RIDLEY ROAD MARKET
DALSTON
NORTH-EAST LONDON

Tani had the rucksack he'd packed for his sister ready. He now needed Simisola herself. He returned to Bronte House to fetch both. His mum was on her knees in the kitchen, yellow Marigolds on her hands, a pink bucket at her side. She was wielding a large sponge, scrubbing away at the lino.

She didn't notice Tani enter the flat, nor did she hear him, and he took care not to reveal he'd come home. He slipped into the bedroom he shared with his sister, but she wasn't there. That meant she was in the market. With her friend Lim gone, she had no place else to go. He fetched the rucksack into which he'd already stowed some of Simi's things. He wasn't sure that he had everything that she would need, but he reckoned Sophie or her sister would fill in the gaps as and where they could.

He didn't want to risk being seen, so he went for the window. He tossed the rucksack outside and followed it. He set off in the direction of Ridley Road Market, and there, accosted by a thousand and one rank odours from various types of meat and fish, he scooted behind the stalls on the opposite side of the street from the butcher shop. He caught a glimpse of his father going at an enormous disemboweled pig inside the shop as one of the apprentice butchers watched and another did a typically bad job of keeping the flies off a pile of sheep's legs and another of organ meats soaking up the sun.

Tani knew of Simisola's various haunts, so he found her easily enough in a large room above the party shop Cake Decorating by Masha operated from this location. When Tani walked in, he saw that cleaning up after the most recent class was giving way to setting up for the evening class. Simi was at the washing-up sink. To her right, colourful mixing bowls joined a number of baking tins on a drying mat. Inside the bowls were measuring spoons and measuring cups in multiple sets. Beaters from the electric mixers still displayed the colours chosen for their concoctions by Masha's eager students.

The centrepiece of the room was a long, chipped green table, its surface speckled with the remains of various doughs and icings. Masha was walking along the table, spraying it with some kind of cleaner. She wiped up as she went, after which she headed towards what appeared to be a storeroom. When she emerged, she had numerous spices and such held in the clasped, curved lap of her apron. She clocked Tani and said, "'Fraid there's not another class till half past seven and it's filled. You have to wait till next week."

"Come for Simisola," he said.

Hearing his voice, Simi swung around. "Tani! Are you walking home with me?" She looked delighted.

"Yeah," he said, because they would indeed be walking together, although their destination wasn't going to be Bronte House.

"I got to finish up first," she said. "But you'll wait, won't you? Won't you wait till I'm done?"

He looked at the wall clock. He reckoned that she wouldn't be missed for hours and neither would he. His father would know he hadn't been at work, but that was of no matter since he—Tani—had been burning bridges in that regard as quickly as he came upon them. But, still, he and Simi needed to move with speed in order to get her to the Franklins' house.

"Hey," he said to her, "Sophie wants to meet you, Squeak. And she wants you to come with me to her sister's birthday celebration."

"Oh, I *love* birthdays, Tani. Will there be cake? When is it?"

"Tonight. I came to take you over there."

"Tonight? Oh no! I can't go tonight. Mum and I 're going to do sketches for my celebration cake. An' Masha's going to make it. 'Member? I told you. It'll have special decorating on it. We'll have it for after the initiation."

"Yeah. We need to talk about that as well, Squeak."

"Why?"

"We just do. Let's finish up and get out of here."

She was intrigued enough, he saw, that she picked up the pace, and within twenty minutes she had her bit of earned cash from Masha, and they were back in the market. He needed to keep Simi out of sight of their father's butcher shop and fishmonger stall, as well as Into Africa. So they kept close to the shops abutting Masha's and the party store beneath it, and they emerged at the market's far end. There, he bought a small order of chips and a Coke for Simi. He bought only a Coke for himself. These they took farther along Ridley Road to where the market ended and a dusty-leafed beech tree provided shade. There was no bench, just the tree itself. They leaned against its trunk.

His sister politely offered him a chip, which Tani took. He chewed it thoughtfully and watched her do the same. He opened both of the Cokes and handed her one of them.

He said, "It's dead important that you go to Sophie's, Squeak. The Franklins? Like I said, they want you to come."

"But Mummy and I—"

"Squeak, listen." He drank down some Coke as if it were something that could bolster his courage. "There i'n't any initiation. There never was. Mum means something totally different, but she's calling it an initiation because she thinks you'll go for it if you don't know what's really meant to happen."

Simi was chewing slowly, and she turned to look at him, round-eyed. She said, "Mummy said . . ."

"Yeah. I know. But she said it to trick you, so you'd think it was part of being in a tribe. But you're already Yoruba, Squeak. You're born Yoruba. There's not an initiation, and there never was."

"There *is*," she said. "I told you, Tani. I went to the place where I'm gonna *get* initiated. Mummy took me there. I met a lady, Easter. She said she would give me a jab and that would make me initiated."

Tani tried to decide what to tell her without destroying the world she shared with their mother. He said, "It's this, Squeak. Mum doesn't want you to know it all because she doesn't want you to be scared. But what they want to do to you is what some of the tribes do to girls in Nigeria. An' other places 's well."

She looked at her dusty feet in her dusty sandals. Then she looked at him. She said, "But what they do is jus' to initiate them, Tani."

He shook his head. "It's not, Squeak."

"What is it, then?"

Tani looked away from her for a moment. He needed a woman to explain this to her and he realised he should have found one to do it. Sophie would have, but it would have had a bloody sight more power if the explanation came from someone who'd been cut. He looked back at his sister and tried to give her details. "They muck girls up is what they do. They muck girls up between their legs. It's real bad, Squeak. It happened to Mum and now she wants it to happen to you. Cos it's like this mad tradition they got some places in Nigeria. And tha's why you got to come with me to Sophie's now. Because if I don't get you out of there, they're going to muck you up between the legs 's well. Squeak, you'd know all about this if Mum had let you go to school. Didn't you ever wonder why you got taught by Mum at home? It's cos at school they teach about this an' all sorts of other things. You c'n ask Sophie. She knows all about it. She doesn't have to worry whether it will happen to her because she's English. But you and me, we're Nigerian, and—"

"What about my celebration?" she asked, her voice rising, her eyes growing bright with tears. "Lots of people're coming, Tani. Even our cousins will come from Peckham. Everyone's giving me presents and eating cake and—" The first of her tears began to drip down her cheeks. Her lower lip was trembling and Tani felt struck. His stomach was turning into liquid.

He said, "Mum's not lying about that part. There'd still be that: the cake and presents and the rest. Only . . ." Shit, he thought. She was only eight bloody years old. She was ages away from understanding the significance of the plan to cut her: what it would do to her now, what it would do to her later, and what it *could* do to her if things went south. Even he wasn't clear on all that. But Sophie's reaction to the Nigerian cutter coming to Bronte House had lit a fire that he wasn't going to allow anyone to douse.

He said, "I bet no one's told you the truth about Lim, right?"

"Lim's with her gran, Tani. She's having a holiday for th' summer. She's coming home in—"

"She won't be coming home," he said.

"Why?

"Because she's dead."

Simi's eyes grew enormous. She shook her head. "She's with her gran. That's what Mummy said. She'll be back for school. I don't know where her gran lives, 'xactly, but she'll be back for school. Mum said."

He touched her cheek, wiping the tears away with his thumb. He said, "She killed herself, Squeak. She was 'initiated,' if that's what you want to call it, just like it's meant to happen to you. But it went bad, really and truly bad, and it stayed that way, and she couldn't cope. So she unwound one of her mum's head wraps and she used it to hang herself."

Twelve years old she'd been, Tani thought. Simisola's friend and idol from Mayville Estate. With an infection attacking her rampantly till she couldn't endure the pain another moment, till death seemed the better alternative than to go on in a life that had been destroyed in the name of purity, in the name of chastity, in the name of bloody-hell-who-knew-what?

Simi said, "She didn't! She didn't! Mummy said—"

"*Listen* to me. Mum lied to you. About Lim, about this initiation rubbish, about everything. Squeak, you *got* to come with me. Pa invited a Nigerian woman to come to the flat. She's meant to cut you. Mum wasn't there when he arranged it, and he didn't know I was there. He reckons he can plan the whole thing and no one will know till the cutter shows up. He'll make it for when I'm not there. He'll make it for when Mum's not there. There'll be some women to hold you down and—"

"No!" she shrieked. "No! No!"

She threw the chips to the ground and the Coke as well. Before he could stop her she began to run, straight through the market with no mind as to crashing into anyone who stood in her way.

BELSIZE PARK
NORTH LONDON

It was late when Lynley arrived in Belsize Park. He'd rung Daidre earlier, settling for voice mail instead of the real person. Coming at this hour was, thus, something of a risk. But they hadn't spoken since their unhappy conversation about fear and whatever-else-it-had-been-about, and he didn't like feeling unsettled about her, about who they were to each other, or about where they were heading. At this moment, though, it was only the end to their previous conversation that he wanted to do something about, although, truth to tell, he wasn't at all sure what he could do about it other than say sorry. For his part. Which, of course, had been to bring up the topic in the first place, taking her words about her brother and sister and turning them on her in a fashion about which he wasn't proud.

His final meeting of the day with Havers and Nkata had gone on longer than he'd anticipated. Both of them had reports for him, and all of them wished to sort through what they'd uncovered in order to make sense of it.

The missing smartphone meant one of several things: that someone had gone to Teo Bontempi's flat to do away with the mobile once she had gone into hospital—knowing the mobile contained some sort of incriminating evidence—or Ross Carver was lying about the smartphone being there on her bedside table when he'd spent the night, or Mark Phinney had grabbed it when he found her unconscious in her bed. The first option suggested that whoever had struck the detective sergeant had returned later for the phone, although it begged the question why the killer had not removed the phone from the premises immediately after the blow had been struck. The second option suggested that Teo Bontempi's estranged husband had something to fear from what the phone might reveal about him. And the third option was that Mark Phinney had wanted to investigate what was on that phone. There was, of course, a fourth possibility: Someone else had removed the smartphone from Teo's flat for reasons they'd yet to uncover.

According to Barbara Havers, she'd had a look at the dead woman's appointment diary taken from her flat. The word *evaluation* was written in it on July 24, and that wanted clarification. The fact that the word appeared by itself with only the hour of the day indicating when she was to have or do the *evaluation* suggested that it was for something in a location with which she was familiar. That, in turn, suggested Empress State Building, especially since her transfer to another job occurred almost immediately afterwards.

Nkata brought up his morning's encounter with Teo's sister. Nothing about it seemed right to him. She didn't sit well, was how he put it. He explained the source of the row between Rosie and Teo: Teo's infrequent calls upon their father as he was rehabilitating after a stroke. That didn't quite smell like it should since Teo's mother had related her daughter's visit three weeks prior to her death. But it was more than just that, Nkata said. Rosie's declaration that Teo had "gone African" and thus had rejected her husband because he was white didn't fit in with what Barb had already said about Ross Carver's explanation regarding the cause of their separation: that he'd loved his wife "too much." One of them seemed to be massaging a few details: either Rosie or Ross. Both of them wanted further looking into.

Had he started the CCTV films? Lynley wanted to know. Nkata said that he'd viewed a few hours of film, but it was a gargantuan task. Dozens of people were in and out of Teo's building all day and into the night. It'd be helpful if he had a narrower window of time as well as some idea of what or who he was looking for.

"Got hours more of recording to look at," Nkata said, and since he'd not personally put eyes on anyone connected to Teo Bontempi aside from Rosie and the parents, he was working in the dark. He *could* isolate images of anyone entering or leaving the building alone on the day and the night when Ross Carver had said he'd found his wife, and he could view the CCTV recordings from nearby businesses on Streatham High Road. There was no ANPR camera in the vicinity, so he was in for a monumental slog.

"I could do with some help on this, guv," he concluded. "There's got to be a few DCs we can call in to lend a hand, innit."

Lynley said he would do his best. But, he cautioned them, as the request for help had to go through Hillier, he wasn't sure that his best would be good enough.

What was agreed upon by all of them at the end of the meeting— during which an appearance by Dorothea Harriman informed Barbara that their first sketching session would be at the weekend, 10:00 a.m. sharp at the Peter Pan statue in Kensington Gardens—was that Barbara would return to Ross Carver for further conversation the following day, Nkata would see to producing isolated images from the night Ross Carver paid his call to Streatham, and Lynley—after an attempt to pull in some additional help—would have another word with DCS Phinney as the last person to have been in Teo Bontempi's flat before she was hospitalised.

And the phone number that Jade Hopwood had handed over to Lynley? Havers wanted to know. He was expecting a result on that in the morning, he told her.

Now in front of Daidre's flat, Lynley paused. Daidre had not responded to his message, but he decided not to take that as a sign of anything save how busy she was at London Zoo.

He mounted the steps. He had a key but the way of wisdom suggested he not use it, so he rang the bell. Since the door to her flat was just inside the building's entry, she generally came personally. But that wasn't the case tonight. He heard her voice instead, and she sounded completely done in. "Can you bear me?" he said in reply to her *who is it.* "Or is sleep preferable?"

"Sleep with you is more preferable still," she replied. "Shall I buzz you in? Do you not have your key?"

"I have it."

"Ah. You weren't assuming. I like that. Come in." She hit the buzzer to allow him to enter the building.

With his key he let himself into the flat, and he found her looking over some paperwork in her kitchen. A bottle of red wine was open.

"It's very cheap plonk," she told him. "I don't recommend it. Your teeth and tonsils will never be the same."

"Luckily, I've no tonsils to speak of," he said.

"Teeth, then. Really, Tommy, it's godawful swill. I'll avoid the Oddbins two-pound special henceforth. There's white in the fridge. Open that."

He said, "I wouldn't think of it," and poured himself a glass of the swill. He took a mouthful. "Good Lord, Daidre."

To which she replied, "Do you never take advice?"

"One of my character flaws, of which there are literally dozens, as you're learning."

"Hmm. I am indeed. Please pour it out. Pour mine out as well. Open the other."

"Only if you're certain."

"I'm completely certain. *That* one cost six pounds. A real step up. How bad can it be?"

"No doubt it's a vintage year." He went for the wine and joined her at the table, bringing fresh glasses with him. She said, "Have you eaten?"

"A sandwich from Peeler's. At least that's where Barbara claimed it was from. Egg salad. Aside from coronation chicken, it's the only filling that's virtually impossible to ruin unless the entire lot's gone bad. What are you working on?"

She shoved the papers into the manila folders from which they'd apparently come. "Staff reviews. Not my favourite thing to do, so I've been procrastinating."

"That's not like you." Neither, in fact, was the terrible wine. The white was much better, though. She'd obviously been joking about the price.

"I know," she said.

"You're worried about Cornwall."

She looked at him, obviously reluctant to go there in conversation another time. She took up her glass and drank. "I ought to eat something," she said.

He got to his feet. He went to the fridge. She said, "Oh God, Tommy, I didn't mean for you to cook."

"I'm delighted to hear that. No doubt you've been warned off by Charlie Denton."

"Well, he *has* given me a word to the wise. Why does he insist upon calling you 'his lordship,' by the way? He manages to make me feel like someone in a Victorian costume drama but without the costume."

"Consider it role-playing. He's always onstage in one way or another. I did try to break him of it, but I've long since given up in exchange for his cooking and dusting. His hoovering skills are rather hit-and-miss, but the man does know how to launder shirts and wield an iron."

"There are things such as laundries for that."

"Hmm. Yes. He likes to be useful between auditions, however. I humour him. Ah. You have cheese. Are there biscuits? Apples? No. Stay where you are. Really, Daidre, I *can* handle this."

He did so. Apples, cheese, savoury biscuits. He even unearthed an unopened bag of mixed nuts as well as a box of currants. The two peaches he found at the bottom of the fruit bowl had given up the ghost, but there was a banana that looked as if it had something edible left to it. He assembled all this and carried it to her, along with two plates and appropriate cutlery. He sat.

She said, "Yes."

He said, "Hmmm? Oh. Cornwall?"

"Cornwall. I thought at first that the isolation of the cottage would actually appeal to them. They couldn't have been any more isolated than they were in my father's caravan, so I told myself they'd feel more comfortable in lodgings where they didn't have to interact with anyone. Of course, working on the cider farm as they do puts them into contact with people."

"Perhaps that's what's not working well for them."

"But they have to do something, Tommy."

"Were they doing something with your father?"

"Goron was." She stared at nothing. It had grown dark outside, and he watched her reflection in the window overlooking the garden. Its upper panes were open and he could smell the night-blooming jasmine she'd planted beneath it. A cat mewled plaintively nearby. Daidre slid from her chair and went to the door. A black-and-white cat strolled in. In the way of all felines, he assumed ownership at once, leaping onto one of the kitchen chairs and looking expectant.

"Have you adopted a cat?" Lynley asked.

"He's adopted me. Mostly for the food and fresh water, although every now and again I catch him eyeing me adoringly."

"A cat? Adoring you? That seems like a contradiction, not that you lack the necessary adorable qualities."

"Cats do adore, Tommy. It just looks different coming from them."

Daidre rustled in a lower drawer next to the stove. She brought out a bag of dried cat food and poured it into a bowl on the floor next to the door, beside a bowl of water. Lynley had not noticed either before. Too focused elsewhere, he thought.

She patted the floor and said, "Come along, you. I know you're hungry."

Lynley watched as the cat jumped silently from the chair to investigate the bowl. Daidre's gaze was on the cat, so this left Lynley free to study her.

There was something that radiated from Daidre's face that seemed to be lacking in other people. It drew him to her. It was, possibly, why to see her was, for him, to want her. He'd shared quite a long history of friendship with his wife prior to their more personal involvement and then their marriage. But with Daidre, he wanted to create a history, and to have that history carry them into a future that he couldn't quite describe.

He was wise not to mention any part of this. Instead, he said, "Have you named him, then?"

"I have." She sat back on her heels and brushed her sandy hair from her cheeks. She tucked it behind her ears and anchored it there with her specs.

"And?"

"Wally. To me, he looks exactly like a Wally. Don't you agree?"

Lynley examined the cat. He'd tucked in to the food, tail curled round his body and a loud purr emanating from him. "He's decidedly a Wally," he said. "Only a Wally would purr like that."

She began to rise. He extended his hand. She took it and allowed him to help her to her feet. They stood virtually chest to chest. He wanted to kiss her. He didn't do so.

She said, "You've not told me what you're working on."

He made it brief: a murdered police detective, assigned to Empress State Building, an investigative team at work on preventing the abuse of women and girls. "Genital mutilation, among other things," he told her.

"That's dreadful, the mutilation."

"It's meant to keep them pure for their future husbands."

"Are the future husbands required to remain pure for their future wives?"

"What do you think?"

She gave a short laugh. It had nothing to do with being amused. "Why am I not surprised?" She went to the table and picked up her wineglass. She took a sip and said, "Sometimes I wonder how you can possibly do the work you do, Tommy. *Homo sapiens* is such a sick species. We should have stopped at *Homo habilis*. Everything past that is iffy. Doesn't it ever make you want to throw in the towel? On humanity, I mean. Animals are fine. They do what their natures direct them to do. They don't have to abuse or destroy others of their kind in order to do it."

"Save during mating season," he pointed out.

"Yes. But even that is according to their nature. It's about survival. The weak males *are* driven off, aren't they. The strongest dominate in order to preserve the group. A weaker male can't protect the rest of them. A strong male can."

"Perhaps they're better than we are, then."

"The animals? Indeed they are. There's no subterfuge with them. They are who they are. They are what they are."

He drank some of his wine. She picked up a piece of cheese and placed it on a biscuit. She took a bite, seemed dissatisfied, returned the biscuit to its plate.

She said, "Tommy, I know we need to—"

At the same instant, he said, "Everything should be—"

Both stopped at once. He nodded at her. "You first, then."

"I was going to say that I know we need to talk about many things, you and I."

"And I was going to say that everything should be easier between us. I love you. I suspect you love me. I keep attempting to manoeuvre you into admitting that. But I'm going at things the wrong way round.

It's as if I've come to believe that only a baring of your soul will suffice to reassure me that . . ." He sighed.

"What?"

"Truthfully? I'm not entirely certain. That's the devil of it. Am I trying to reassure myself that the struggle is worth it?"

"I can't answer that for you, can I. But I can say that sometimes we're forced to accept that there's too much damage inside a person, that no repair is possible, that the person is just who the person is."

"You're speaking of yourself, but I can't make myself believe that. I believe that you—that I as well—are the sum of many parts and our pasts are just one of those parts. We carry it all with us, naturally, but we don't have to stagger under the load."

"I'm damaged, Tommy. Perhaps irreparably. I just don't know. But *if* I am, what it is for me is . . ." She hesitated. He saw her swallow. She looked down at her wineglass and then up at him. "I've thought about this so much. I've looked at us—whatever we are—and I've tried to come up with a plan of action. Or at least an answer."

"You don't sound as if you've been successful."

"I don't want to hurt you by pretending, Tommy, by trying to be the Daidre you wish I was. That would reassure you for a time, but it wouldn't be who I really am and eventually that person—that real Daidre—would emerge and break your heart. I don't want that to happen. And if we carry on, I don't know how to prevent it."

"Are you saying we should end this, then?"

"I'm saying that I don't feel as other people feel. I would like to, I want to, but I don't. You call it fear, but I'm not afraid. I truly am not. Believe me, there are times when I would *love* to be merely afraid. Instead, I'm just . . . inside . . . I'm stone and you can't want that, Tommy. You *mustn't* allow yourself to want that."

"Daidre." He said her name on a breath.

"No. Please."

"Do I actually appear so weak to you?"

"This isn't about weakness."

"But it is. It seems to me you're thinking that heartbreak—my potential heartbreak, caused by you—is something that might well destroy me. But you and I met at the worst moment in my life, having lost Helen. My wife, pregnant with our child, murdered on the front steps of our home, shot in the chest, with shopping bags at her feet. She was just trying to unlock the bloody door. She had the key in her hand. In another ten seconds, everything would have been different for her. For me. For our child. But it happened and they were taken from me. And here I am."

"You adored her."

"I did. I would never say otherwise. She was completely maddening at times and utterly frivolous at other times. She wasn't perfect. She wasn't even the person I'd thought I would marry. But life doesn't look at the plans we make or the intentions we have. Life just happens. I happened to you. You happened to me. And neither of us can possibly know how this life between us is going to end."

She sat again. She still held the wineglass and she twirled its stem in her fingers and watched the liquid as the ceiling lights hit it. On the floor, Wally had finished his meal. He was engaged in the washing up ritual of every cat, at present attending to his face and his whiskers. He suddenly stopped, blinked, and looked from Daidre to Lynley. He jumped gracefully into Daidre's lap. His purr was so loud that it easily could have been heard in the sitting room, in the entry, in the street. He was, Lynley saw, content. Food, water, a lap to sit in. That was all it took. Daidre was so correct in what she'd said: Animals did what their natures told them to do.

She bent and rested her cheek on Wally's head. He accepted this, endured it as long as his cat nature would allow, then jumped off her lap and sashayed back to the doorway to be let out into the night. Lynley did the honours, then turned back to her.

"That's something of a relief," he told her.

"What is?"

"Wally's departure."

"Whyever?"

"He looks particularly possessive. I didn't fancy our sharing the bed with him."

"*Are* we sharing the bed, Tommy?"

"I hope so. You?"

"I too."

8 AUGUST

A phone call to him on the previous night had revealed to Barbara Havers that she would have to meet Ross Carver in Streatham in the early morning. He would be dropping off a few boxes at the flat on his way to a job site, a large project in Thornton Heath. She agreed to this. She even eschewed her normal breakfast, which on this particular morning was truly a sacrificial move on her part since her local shop had begun offering a new flavour of Pop-Tart—Wildlicious Wild Berry—and she'd bought half a dozen on the previous evening and was eager to tuck in. She could have consumed one as late dinner, but anticipation was half the fun of a prime culinary discovery, and it had to be said, she did know how and where to draw the line. Breakfast-for-dinner at any hour was where she drew it. It seemed the thing of ancient spinsters living in poorly heated accommodation, sitting in a threadbare chair in front of two bars of electric fire, dining on a single depressing soft-boiled egg and a slice of equally depressing unbuttered toast. Perhaps she indeed had that to look forward to, but Barbara reckoned that while she had her wits, her career, and sufficient means to keep herself rolling in takeaway dinners from the local chippy, the boiled-egg-and-toast route was one she did not immediately need to take.

She did make herself a morning coffee—from powder, alas, but at least topped up with real milk and sweetened with a heaped spoonful of equally real sugar—and she downed this as she drove, not an easy feat since her antique Mini did not possess an automatic transmission or—logically, considering its vintage—cup holders. But over time she'd become proficient at grasping a mug between her thighs, and in this particular instance she spilled on her T-shirt and not between her legs as she'd done occasionally in the past. Wisely, however, she'd worn black and its message—*In my defence I was left unsupervised*—seemed, if not inspired, then at least prophetic.

Getting to Streatham turned out to be relatively easy since no Victorian water main had burst in the night, no one had hit a cyclist before dawn, and most of the traffic was headed into town anyway, and not out towards the suburbs. So once she made it over the river, she arrived with no difficulty other than the coffee spill, and she parked across Streatham High Road from the building that housed Teo Bontempi's—soon to be Ross Carver's—flat.

She crossed the street and let herself in to the block of flats. The lift was still not reliably lifting anything, so once again she clomped up the stairs, managing to slosh coffee only once en route to the flat. She let herself in, opened the balcony door to allow the relatively cooler morning air to relieve the stifling conditions inside the place, and set her coffee on the kitchen worktop. She did a small recce round the room on the chance that she and Nkata had missed something. She was just completing the removal of everything hanging on every wall—preparatory to checking each article for signs its backing had been tampered with—when she heard a key scraping in the lock. The door opened and Ross Carver stood there.

Seen before, he'd been rather piratical in appearance. Now he was dressed more formally, although he managed to demonstrate that three-piece suits, bowler hats, and rolled-up brollies weren't going to reappear in London anytime soon. He was khaki and cotton with a casually knotted necktie. No earrings or manbun, just an elastic band gathering his curls at the base of his neck. Three cardboard boxes formed a neat stack next to him. He gave Barbara a nod of hello, picked them up, and carried them inside.

He was even wearing designer sunglasses, which he removed once he'd shut the door.

"You're working early hours, then," she said to him.

"It helps. I'm not one hundred percent present every moment, but it's a distraction to be back, which I bloody well need just now. What've you lot found?" He slid his sunglasses into the pocket of his shirt.

"Adaku Obiaka."

"Teo's birth name. It wasn't a secret."

"At times she was operating under it. African togs head to toe. The full Monty this was. The team she was part of out of Empress State Building didn't know about any of this, so she wasn't working undercover for them. She was on her own. Any idea why?"

He walked into the living room and sat at the dining table. Barbara joined him. He looked away from her in the direction of the balcony, with its shelf of neatly arranged bonsai trees. "Was she taking back her birth name officially?" he asked, and his tone—which tried and failed to sound indifferent—made it seem to Barbara as if her reply would have a deeper meaning to him than merely a factoid about his estranged wife.

"We haven't checked. Could be that she was using it only when she went to Orchid House as a way of being undercover. But her sister's claimed to one of our lot that she'd 'gone African.' So, I reckon, the name she was using could have something to do with that."

"What's Orchid House? I don't know it."

"A group sheltering girls who're at risk of FGM. Teo—as Adaku—was a volunteer there. It doesn't seem to have had anything to do with her regular job, but that can't be ruled out."

He was silent for a moment, as if tossing this information round in his head. Finally, he said, "That makes sense, that she'd volunteer there."

And then with a look that seemed to interpret Barbara's facial expression, he went on with, "I expect you know by now she'd been cut."

"From the autopsy."

"Right. Of course. There would have been an autopsy." He was quiet for a moment. He'd begun to perspire but so had Barbara. She got up, switched on the fan for the little good it would do, and returned to the table. He said, "She told me years and years ago, when I wanted sex. We were teenagers with all the hormones doing their thing, you know. I pressed her for sex without knowing what was wrong. I *kept* pressing her till she told me."

"And when she told you . . . ?"

He sighed. "Are you asking how I felt, what I did, what went next? I was nineteen, Sergeant. I was randy as the devil, and I wanted her. I didn't even know what she meant about the cut. I was more, like, 'Yeah, yeah, we'll sort it but, look, I'm dying for you and I want us to start doing it.' Then, of course, I learned exactly what she meant when she said she'd been cut."

"How'd you react?"

"It didn't matter to me, and I made sure she knew it. I wouldn't *let* it matter. I was careful and she didn't have pain. So we went along like that for years, acting as if nothing was wrong. Then we married, still acting as if nothing was wrong. And then, finally, I couldn't act any longer. I knew she was just going through the motions for my sake, but she got no pleasure from it. How could she?"

"P'rhaps the closeness was enough for her? The intimacy between you, I mean."

"Would it be enough for you?" And then less than a second later, "Sorry. I shouldn't have said that. The thing is, I began to dread sex. I started feeling like I was just using her to have what I wanted. Roll on, grind her, orgasm, roll off. The whole thing started to seem de-humanising, and I felt rotten. I just couldn't continue."

"But she was the one who wanted the break-up?"

"Yeah. That's how it was."

"When I came to your flat, you said she left you because you loved her too much. What did you mean?"

"I wanted to *do* something so that she could . . . I don't know . . . enjoy being with me."

"Sexually enjoy."

"Right. So I began to search for some kind of solution. Any kind of solution. I didn't even know what I was looking for. But when I found it—"

"What was it?"

"Plastic surgery to repair where she'd been cut. I told her about it. I'd found a specialist. But Teo wasn't having any of it. She wouldn't even make an appointment to be evaluated. I mean just to see if something was possible. I couldn't work out why she didn't want to know what could be done. Or not be done, as the case might've been. Because there was a *chance*, see. I wouldn't let go of the subject. I *couldn't* let it go. My whole focus was, 'I want you to feel something. I want you to want me. I want you to want it, sex, the act, whatever.' Ultimately, she'd had enough."

Barbara nodded, but she was struck by something. "An evaluation?" She went to her shoulder bag where she'd left it on a chair in the sitting area. She brought out Teo Bontempi's diary and opened it to the relevant page: July 24. She rejoined him and handed him the diary.

He looked down at it, then he looked up. "You're thinking she went to someone? You're thinking she actually was evaluated for surgery?"

"She got in touch with you. She wanted to speak with you. Is there anything else she might have wanted to speak with you about?"

"I don't know. All I can tell you is that she wanted to talk face-to-face."

"Good news? Bad news? Anything like that?"

"She didn't give me a clue." His gaze went unfocused again, as if he were putting together pieces of information. Barbara waited. He continued in that posture of thinking. Finally he said, "I could do with . . . Is there water?"

Barbara went to the fridge. She brought out an opened bottle of fizzy water. She poured him a glass. It had long ago gone flat. But he took it from her and drank it down. He stared at the credenza. Then he stood and walked to it, saying, "Where are the sculptures? The collection wasn't stolen, was it? Teo has . . . she had . . . a collection of African sculptures."

"They'll be with forensics, being tested for evidence."

He turned to her. "Was that what was used on her?"

"Don't know. We're waiting to hear."

He was silent, looking thoughtful. He said, more to himself than to her, "Yes. They're heavy enough, aren't they. I expect anyone could use one as a weapon."

As if in illustration of Carver's point, the flat door opened. A slim young Black woman stood there, stylishly dressed in a crisp white blouse, navy trousers tapered to show off shapely ankles, and red stilettos that looked like something capable of taking out an eye. She was also quite pretty. She said brightly, "Concierge let me in. I thought I might be able to help."

"Help with what?" Ross Carver said to her and then to Barbara, "This is Rosalba, Teo's sister."

MAYVILLE ESTATE
DALSTON
NORTH-EAST LONDON

"Tani, what happened? Where are you? Why didn't you bring Simi here last night?"

"My mum worked it out that I told her. No initiation, just being cut up. She di'n't want to believe me, so she made a run for it. Straight to Mum, this was."

"But why didn't Simi believe you? She has to know you wouldn't lie to her."

"It's cos I added Lim, I expect." He told Sophie about Simi's friend Lim. He added the fact that Lim's mum, Halimah, was there—with Monifa—when Simi reached Mayville Estate. She had confronted them both—Halimah and Monifa—with tears, accusations, and rising hysteria. And Monifa had managed to use the hysteria as a weapon against her. One hard slap across the face had been enough to quiet her. Halimah had departed quickly, Monifa had soothed Simi with Ribena and loving words that managed to reassure her that *wherever* she had heard *whatever* she had heard, it was vicious and false and "Look at me, my dearest Simisola. Would I *ever* hurt my beloved child?"

"She reckoned I was the one told her about the cut. Di'n't take much, did it, since I'm mostly who Simi sees. I mean, she knows Masha from the cake decorating shop in the market and a couple other people there, but they got no reason to tell her and they're not Nigerian anyway. So there was no one else."

Tani went on to explain what he'd found upon returning home: Monifa was in the process of moving everything of Simi's from the bedroom she shared with Tani into Monifa's own bedroom, where she would henceforth sleep. No problem with this since Abeo had taken up residence with Lark. When Tani had demanded to know what was going on, his mother said, "I know what you have planned. But if you try to prevent this, all of us will pay."

Tani had said in return, "Tha's it? All of us will pay? Then *all* of us got to get out. What we got now i'n't any kind of life and you know it, Mum. And let me tell you straightaway, *no one* is hurting my sister. She i'n't being sold for a bride price and she sure as hell i'n't being cut."

Now he said to Sophie, "But I don't know how I'm making that happen cos what I can tell you is that a madness 's come on both of them, an' no way do I un'erstand why Mum's doing like she's doing."

"There's got to be a way to get her onside, Tani."

"It's jus' not a go."

She was quiet for a moment before she said, "I wish you'd managed to bring Simi here."

"Same," he said. And then he added, "I can't hand her over to Care, Soph. But I got to do something cos the cut's going to happen if I don't."

"Agreed. I thought I'd bought us some time. So let me get back on it," was her reply.

They rang off. Tani had rung Sophie from his bedroom and now he swung out of bed. He left the room and saw that his mum's bedroom door was closed. Either Simi was still sleeping or Monifa had managed to lock her in somehow. It would be a psychological locking-her-in, however. There was no real way to secure the bedroom doors. Abeo had seen to that long ago.

He knocked softly on the panels. He said, "You wake, Squeak?" but he heard nothing. His trepidation prompted him to open the door. He saw both his mother and his sister still in bed. Monifa was awake. Simi was not.

His mother got up swiftly and silently. She put on a thin dressing gown. She motioned him away from the door and then followed him to the sitting room. There, she stood with arms crossed.

"I will slap you till you're black an' blue," she said tersely. "You bother Simisola again."

"Slap me like you slapped her, Mum? I told her the *truth*. You wan' to hear it?" She made no reply, so he went on. "Pa found a cutter. She was here, right in the flat. He di'n't know I was home, so they made their plans an' I heard 'em and the *only* thing makes this diff'rent from cutting Simi in Nigeria is that this pa'ticular cutter might actually know what a scalpel is. Or, at least, she might have a package of razor blades 'stead of just one she uses over an' over an' cleans with a rag in between. You followin' this, Mum?"

Monifa said nothing. Her eyes narrowed.

He went on. "She told Pa she'd bring aunties to hold her down. Pa said fine, jus' fine, fine, fine. So I went off an' I found Simi and yeah, Mum, I told her. Everything. Cos no way can I get her to leave if she thinks there's supposed to be some fucking initiation and celebration, eh? No way will she cooperate with me. But I need her to cooperate, see. Jus' like I need *you* to cooperate, but we both know—you and me—tha's not about to happen when it comes to cutting her. *You* want her cut 's well, innit. It's only that you want it your way, right? But in the end, it's all the same."

Monifa took this in. She let silence hang between them before she replied, saying, "There're things you don't un'erstand. Some things get done that we don't wish done but they have a purpose."

He blew out a breath. "Oh, right. I file that away, Mum. Some big purpose I don' un'nerstand. So tell me, then. Wha's the big *purpose* for slicing up an eight-year-old 'tween her legs?"

"You don' call it that. Have sense, Tani. This . . . this cut you call it solves a problem for her."

"Oh, I 'spect it does. It keeps her a virgin, right?" He sputtered a laugh and went on. "You lot mus' think girls're sex machines: hot and ready for it twenty-four/seven. So let me ask you this, okay? Tha's wha' you were? Tha's all you thought of? Couldn't get your mind off some bloke sticking his dick inside you?"

"You do not talk to me like—"

"I mean, you lot mus' think girls'll jus' have anyone comes along, so you got to make the whole thing a real terror for them, eh? Do you know how backward thinking tha' is? How stupid? How ignorant? How bloody-minded cruel?"

Monifa looked over her shoulder, in the direction of the bedroom.

She said to him, "You talk lower if you want to talk. This's about your sister's future."

"You're *destroying* her future. Maybe she doesn' want to marry some old Nigerian with money to buy himself a virgin. Maybe she wants a bigger life 'n that. Maybe she wants to go to uni and have a career and—"

"This preserves her."

"*Preserves* her? Like a tinned tomato?"

"This increases her value to her husband. This makes it possible for her to marry well."

"What the *fuck*? You talk like Pa. This's all about what someone will *pay* for her."

"That is not what I mean. It is not about money or goods or land or anything else 'cept being cherished by her husband. What we do tells him she was willing to have herself seen to in order—"

"*Cut*, Mum. At least use right words. Cut. Mutilated. Come out an' *say* it."

"She is made clean this way. She becomes a vessel for her husband's love. His desire is heightened and so is his pleasure."

"Oh. Well. Right. How'd that work out for you? You enjoy being the vessel of Pa's love, do you? An' before you answer, let me tell you 'bout these walls here. They're thin, they are. So I spent *years* listening to how much you enjoy this vessel-of-his-love business."

"No woman's place is to enjoy."

"Tha's rubbish! An' fuck but you *know* tha's rubbish. So why're you sayin' it? Wha' are you so bloody afraid of?"

She finally hesitated. Tani thought briefly that she might actually answer his questions. He also thought her answers—whatever they might be—could set her on a path that might lead to her safety, to Simisola's safety, even to his own.

"I *tried* to do it right and safe," she said in a voice so low that he had to take a step closer to hear her words. "You truly think I want her to suffer like me?"

"Well, tha's what's happening, Mum. So *do* something."

"That is what I was doing. But then the police came so now I must wait until the clinic—"

"I'm not talking about some fucking clinic or *whatever* it was. I'm talking 'bout getting Simi away from here. You got two feet las' time I looked. Why'n't you standin on them? What's the worst he c'n do? Kill you? Kill me? Kill Simi and forfeit his fucking bride money, Mum?"

"Kill?" she said. "Abeo will not kill. But everything short of that . . . ? Yes. He *will* do. He has done."

"So divorce him!" Tani shouted. "Divorce him! Divorce him! Wha's stopping you?"

The door opened as Tani asked the question. He swung round as his father entered the flat.

STREATHAM
SOUTH LONDON

"It's Rosie," the young woman said to Barbara. "Ross is the only person who calls me Rosalba."

"What are you doing here?" Ross Carver asked her.

Her smile faltered briefly before she answered him. "I did say, Ross. I thought I might be of help." To Barbara, Rosie's eyes looked as if they were shooting something at her late sister's husband. His eyes looked as if they were shooting something right back. But as to what those somethings were, Barbara couldn't have said but she reckoned she was going to learn at some point and she hoped it would be soon.

"Aren't you meant to be at Selfridges?" Carver asked his sister-in-law.

"Not till noon today," was her reply. "We've plenty of time." She shut the door behind her and came to them in the dining area. She kept her attention fixed on her brother-in-law as she said, "*Maman* and *Papá* are worried they've not heard from you. *Papá* especially, and we don't want him worried. So I told them I'd seek you out to make certain you were coping with everything." She lowered her gaze. "We all thought you might come to Hampstead, Ross. You must know that." She raised her eyes and looked at him, then at Barbara, then at him again. She went on with, "All of us loved her, Ross."

Barbara reckoned she would need a backhoe to excavate the conversation for the hidden meanings in what the young woman was saying. She also wanted to ask her how she'd known to find her brother-in-law here. There seemed only one way that she could have known: he'd told her. This suggested she'd rung him or he'd rung her. But this also suggested she'd been with him when Barbara had phoned him the previous night about wanting another chat. If that was the case, what was going on between them at the moment was performance art.

She considered Nkata's report about Rosalba Bontempi. She'd claimed that both her sister and Carver had mutually wanted to divorce. So once again it was an either/or situation. Either Rosalba had lied to Nkata about the upcoming divorce or Ross Carver had lied to Barbara.

Ross said, "I should have phoned them, at least. I will do."

"And what will you say?"

"That's the question. I don't know what to say."

"They don't blame you for what happened between you and Teo. The divorce. All that. They know things change between people. You and Teo were young. You hardly had any time to explore the world before you and she decided to be a couple. You'd not met other people or tried other ways of being together. I think you know what I mean."

She certainly meant something, Barbara thought. What she couldn't sort out was whether Carver read between the lines of what she was telling him. She had the distinct feeling that he did.

He said to Rosie, "The police have taken Teo's sculptures."

"Whyever?"

"For testing."

Rosie directed her gaze to the credenza where the bronzes had stood. "Do they think one of the bronzes was used for something?"

"Forensics are looking at everything that could have been used as a cosh," Barbara told her.

Rosie said, "I'm surprised she never got rid of them, all things considered."

"What things would those be?" Barbara asked her.

"When people are divorcing . . . ?" Rosie lifted one shoulder. She made the movement look elegant. "Or when they're ending a relationship? Mementoes can cause pain, can't they. The sculptures were mementoes. They represented a connection to Ross that she no longer wanted."

"So to follow that line of thinking, if she kept the sculptures, it was owing to her wanting to hang on to a connection to Mr. Carver?"

"I'm merely suggesting how things could have been under different circumstances, not how they are."

Barbara scoffed inwardly. She found herself idly wondering how strong Rosie was because there was a disturbing undercurrent to everything she said and the way she said it, and Winston had reported the same reaction to her.

She said to Ross, "Her mobile's still missing."

"I don't see how that's possible," was his reply.

"We're going to need its number. I presume you have it."

"Of course." He recited it and Barbara took it down in her notebook. Afterwards, she looked up and said, "You didn't take it?"

"I wouldn't have done. I had no reason to."

"Are you certain it was here when you spent the night?"

"Completely. It was recharging on—"

"Ross, you didn't tell me you spent the night," Rosie cut in. "Why did you spend the night?"

"Teo couldn't remember what had happened. She'd been sick. She was dizzy. I didn't want to leave her alone. I was worried about her."

"I would have come to be with her if you'd phoned. Or *Maman* would have done. I don't understand it. What's going on?"

"Nothing's 'going on.'" Ross sounded testy.

"But something must—"

"Stop it, Rosalba!" He snapped the order like an officer to his underling. "Your sister's dead and we're trying to work out what happened to her."

Rosie said nothing. Neither did Barbara. She waited and watched and what she saw was Rosie's eyes filling with tears. Ross apparently saw this as well. An expression of what appeared to be exasperation fleetingly crossed his face. He strode to the balcony door and breathed in the morning air deeply. After a moment, he turned back to them and said quietly, "She was still my wife, Rosalba. Despite everything. Still. I was here because she'd texted me. She'd asked me to come here as she'd wanted to talk to me."

"About what?" Rosie asked the question quietly.

"I don't know. She never said."

"You were here as well, two days earlier," Barbara said to her. Then she quickly added before Rosie could reply, "According to the neighbours, you two argued."

Rosie could hardly lie about this, Barbara thought. She wasn't stupid, and she would know that Nkata had shared the information she'd given him about the argument she'd had with her sister. But Barbara reckoned that Ross Carver didn't know about the argument, and from the way he began to say something then stopped himself abruptly, she saw that he'd been clueless.

"She hadn't been to see our parents," Rosie told her. "She *should* have gone to see them regularly, but she didn't. I was angry about that. And she was angry that I was angry. It was all very stupid. Like arguments generally are."

"Argued a lot, you and your sister?" Barbara said.

"That's what sisters do."

"Shout at each other, you mean? Loud enough for the neighbours to hear? Sounds like a real set-to, to me. When was the last time she'd been to see your parents?"

Rosie pressed her lips together. Clearly, she saw the trap, but she had no choice. She could walk straight into it or she could sidestep briefly by asking her parents to lie for her. In either case, the coppers would be checking. And, in this particular situation, the truth wasn't going to be difficult for them to uncover.

———

CHELSEA
SOUTH-WEST LONDON

Deborah heard the telly as she descended the stairs to the basement kitchen. An educated voice was saying, "Please understand my point. To submit to *any* arbitrarily dictated step is to allow our lives to be tainted by an allegation that is not only false, but also reprehensibly so. Such submission will result in a blackening of our reputations as individuals and as a couple. We absolutely refuse to countenance this denigration of our characters. We're being targeted because one of us is an immigrant."

"What's going on?" Deborah asked. Both her husband and her father were in the room. Simon stood with arms crossed, leaning against the edge of the worktop and munching a piece of toast while her father put slices of cantaloupe on a serving platter. Both of them looked in her direction.

Her father said, "Sky News's talking to that girl's dad and her mum, the one 't disappeared."

"Have there been developments?"

"Just switched it on," her father said.

". . . unreasonable, considering where she went, Mr. Akin." The journalist—an Asian woman with gorgeous hair, shapely lips, and disturbingly exophthalmic eyes—was making a point.

"What we know is this," Charles Akin said, "and we would appreciate the story being reported *accurately*. Bolu did not go to this organisation on her own. Bolu was taken there from the cultural centre. We don't know why. We don't know by whom. All we know at this point is that the director of this organisation is demanding that we meet with her and a social worker. And *that* is something we will not do."

"You do see, though, how your refusal to cooperate makes it appear that Orchid House has taken the appropriate decision not to reveal—"

"I'm not interested in what my refusal looks like. I'm interested in having our daughter returned to us. She's been taken. How can I possibly make that any clearer? She did not flee. And her mother and I have no intention of cooperating with anyone until the police arrest the director of the anti-FGM group responsible for hiding Bolu. That is false imprisonment. The police should speak to Bolu herself. They will then see that there is nothing for anyone to learn about this family."

"And yet the director of Orchid House believes otherwise. Why would she place Bolu out of harm's reach without Bolu herself giving her a reason?"

Simon looked at Deborah. "Did you know?" he asked.

"What?"

"That Orchid House is involved in the girl's disappearance. The director of Orchid House, it seems."

She glanced at the window. The sun was beating on the garden, announcing another steaming day. She said, "I suspected because of some things that were said. But that's all."

On the television, Charles Akin's wife was saying to the journalist,

". . . a rash act that's been committed against us because my husband's Nigerian. Yes, FGM is still practised in some few parts of Nigeria, but the Nigerian government, like our own, has outlawed it."

"Yet it remains a practice in London amongst some families in the Nigerian and Somali communities," the journalist pointed out.

"We would not *ever* allow any such thing to be done to our daughter," Aubrey Hamilton said. "We're being discriminated against because of my husband's place of birth."

On that note, the interview ended, the programme shifted back to the studio, and there suddenly was Zawadi, sitting with the presenters, one of whom said to her, "There you have it. Any comment?"

To Deborah, Zawadi looked completely uncowed by the interview she'd watched or by the question from the presenter, a woman in red with a helmet of blond hair that looked as if it would stay in place in the midst of a hurricane. "It's very simple," Zawadi said, sounding more than reasonable. "My comment is this: *If* parents have nothing to hide and desperately want their daughter returned, they will cooperate. They will do anything it takes to have her back. Our remit at Orchid House is to protect girls from harm and from the potential for harm."

"Does that mean you maintain your belief that the Akin child will come to harm without your protection?"

"I maintain that Boluwatife is perfectly safe at the moment—as other girls who come to Orchid House are—and she will remain where she is until such a time as we are certain she will not be harmed."

"But if she didn't come to you on her own, if she was brought to you by two adolescents whom you refuse to identify—"

Cotter used the remote to switch off the telly. He looked at Deborah. He looked at Simon. Deborah saw their wordless exchange. "What's going on?"

Simon poured both of them a coffee as her father went to the fridge and brought out eggs. As he passed the sugar and milk to her, Simon said, "Deborah, you do see that there's a chance this woman's a blind crusader, don't you?"

Deborah became immediately hot when she heard his maddening paternal tone, the main trigger to every argument they had. "No, I do not see that. *And* she isn't. Unless this woman's passionate commitment to a cause equates to blind crusading these days."

"A figure of speech. I apologise. And I do know you hate being lectured to or advised, particularly by me."

"True. But you're going to lecture and advise anyway, aren't you."

Cotter cleared his throat. Deborah knew very well that—despite the fact that she was his daughter—his first loyalty was always going to be to her husband. So she was not the least surprised when he said, "Could be that lady sees only what she wants to see, Deb. 'F you know something 'bout where the girl is—"

"I've already *told* you I know nothing."

"How is that possible?" Simon asked her. "You've been there daily since—"

"For God's sake. I'm *white*, Simon, which I presume you've noticed. That doesn't exactly make me a figure of trust. London didn't turn into a Utopia of racial equity while I was otherwise engaged, did it?"

"The girls are speaking to you, aren't they?"

"That's completely different, and you know it."

A silence. The cat's door flapped, announcing Alaska's intention to join them. Peach was asleep in her basket and did not notice the nearly silent feline intrusion into her domain.

Simon looked down at his shoes, then up again. "Do you believe that those people—one a barrister and the other a physician—actually intended their daughter harm?"

"I don't know. I'm not meant to know anything about this situation. But Orchid House exists to keep girls safe, and *someone* brought her to Orchid House for a reason. That needs to be sorted."

"Shouldn't cops do the sorting, Deb?" her father asked.

"I've no idea. Neither do you. You said it yourself, Simon: I've been with those girls at Orchid House. I've heard their stories. I've seen their fears. So I say this: if two parents have to be inconvenienced because they won't agree to speak to someone with Bolu's interests at heart—"

"Bolu?" Simon asked the question.

His sharp emphasis was infuriating. Clearly, Deborah thought, he'd spent far too much time at the Old Bailey being questioned by barristers during trial. "*Bolu*," she said. "That's her *name*. That's what she's called. They just said it on the television news. My saying it means nothing beyond my saying it. Stop trying to read between the lines where there are no lines, for God's bloody sake."

She left them then. She'd lost her appetite for breakfast. But it seemed that neither of them was finished with her. Her father stopped her on her way up the stairs to tell her that he *was* concerned with "tha' sweet little girl" as he called her, but he was also concerned with how the sweet little girl's father would be feeling and what he would be thinking because he kept imagining what he *himself* would think and what he *himself* would feel if Deborah went missing. "Half mad with worry, is what tha' bloke is," was her father's conclusion.

As for Simon, it turned out that his concern was the fallout: what it could do to all of them if she knew something and did not reveal it. "You're placing us on the wrong side of the law if you keep silent."

"I'm not placing anyone anywhere," she countered. "And what law is involved? I don't know where she is. All I know is that she's at risk."

"The girl is being kept from her parents. The police are searching for her."

"Instead of what they *could* be doing."

"Which is what?"

"Stopping the abuse of girls. Which is more important than harassing a woman who's committed her life to their protection."

So she'd parted from them—Simon and her father—without any of them feeling at peace with what was going on. For the two of them, there seemed to be only one resolution: to discover who was holding Bolu and to hand that person over to the police. But connected to that were a score of scenarios that Deborah didn't want to consider.

ISLE OF DOGS
EAST LONDON

Deborah decided to stop at Trinity Green on her way to the Isle of Dogs. She wasn't at ease after her argument with her husband, and she concluded the only way to *become* at ease was to learn the truth behind what had prompted two adolescents to escort Bolu Akin to Orchid House. She had no hope of Zawadi's confiding in her. But she reckoned Narissa might.

She found the filmmaker inside the chapel reviewing some footage she'd taken to be used during periods of voice-over narration in the documentary. Seeing Deborah entering their filming space, she said, "I can't tell if this works. Are you willing to give me your honest opinion?"

"Will you believe it's honest?" Deborah asked her.

Narissa considered this. After a moment, she said, "That's an interesting question. It forces me to decide if you're a patronising white cow, doesn't it?"

"I hadn't thought about it in quite those terms, but yes. I suppose it does."

Narissa nodded, gave Deborah a head-to-toe-to-head, and said, "I'll risk it."

She'd filmed four sites so far, Deborah saw: an adventure playground, a street market, a group of uniformed schoolgirls, and St. Thomas' Hospital. After she'd watched the footage of each, Deborah said, "The market and the girls, I think. The other two, no."

"Not the playground?"

"It doesn't seem to work. Do you think it does?"

Narissa looked at the screen for a moment before she said, "My dad—"

Deborah interrupted with, "He'd be a much better judge, Narissa."

"—said the same thing." She glanced at Deborah. "You might be good at this."

"It's just a photography thing. I couldn't tell you *why* something works. It's just how it feels."

Narissa nodded. "Wouldn't I love to get back to that."

"What?"

"The way to . . . It's just that . . . never mind."

"I 'wouldn't understand'?"

"That's the size of it, yeah."

Deborah nodded. She said, "Right," and reckoned her next best step was to say nothing more on the subject.

But Narissa said, "This?" with a gesture at the monitor she'd been using but clearly referring to more than that. "What I just said? It's not a Black and white thing this time. It's a drugs and alcohol thing. You reach a point where you can't feel. Or know what you're feeling. At least that's how it is for me."

"Ah."

Narissa shot her a quick smile. "Ta for not saying 'I understand.'"

Deborah felt moderately encouraged, enough to say, "I saw Zawadi on the news this morning. The Akins as well."

Narissa grew quite still, as she'd done before when the subject of the Akins came up. When she didn't reply, Deborah went on with, "They're quite compelling." Still no reply. "Have you seen them? On the telly?"

"What's this about, then?" Narissa asked sharply. Unmistakably, a portcullis had been lowered.

"Nothing, really. I was just wondering—"

"Stop it. You're not wondering. You're fishing."

"I suppose I am. Why did they bring her here, those kids? Do you know?"

"Not a clue. She probably said something to them. If you want to know, you'll have to ask Zawadi."

"Are you on board, then? With what's happening with Zawadi and the parents?"

"If Zawadi says some girl's in danger, that's all I have to hear."

"And then what?"

"Then . . . ? Like other people in the community, I help where I can. I wouldn't be making this film otherwise. And anyway, cutting girls is only part of what can happen to them. I expect you know that by now."

Deborah frowned as she thought about the implications. "Are you saying that just because her parents won't have her cut, they might do something else? What?"

"How about ironing her breasts for a start?"

"*Ironing*? What on earth . . . ?"

"Breast flattening. To make sure boys don't start looking at them."

"But how old is Bolu? Does she even *have* breasts?"

"Christ. That's not the point. Look. It's like this: A girl's mum takes her out to buy what she'll need for her monthlies and that's the signal. She's on her way to womanhood and that means she has to be cut."

"That can't be the case for every girl."

"Of course it's not the case for every girl. But for those girls whose families follow the old ways, monthly bleeding can trigger the process of being made pure. Those girls don't know this. Others do. And those others take action to keep her safe."

"Are you saying that's why Bolu was brought here? Her mum took her out to buy what she'll need for her monthly bleeding? That's *all* her mum did? That's what she told Zawadi? Narissa, that could mean—"

"Forget it," Narissa said. "Shit. Hell. Look. I need to work. I need to think. Go away. Okay?"

Deborah did so. But she was more uneasy than she'd been before. She left Orchid House to make her way to the Isle of Dogs, where she used her GPS to locate Inner Harbour Square.

She found Philippa Weatherall waiting for her, and the surgeon was all business: a nod of hello to Deborah, and then, "We're in my office. It's just this way." Deborah followed Dr. Weatherall from reception through a door into a corridor from which three doors opened. The murmur of voices along with the sounds of preparation drifted from one of the rooms. This, she was told by Dr. Weatherall, was the clinic's operating theatre, where two volunteer surgical nurses and a volunteer anaesthetist were readying everything for the coming procedure.

She gestured Deborah into her office. Inside, a Black couple waited, and the surgeon introduced them to Deborah. Leylo was the name of the woman, and she appeared to be no older than Deborah herself. Her husband was called Yasir. He seemed perhaps a decade older than his wife, and he also seemed far more nervous. But both of them were willing to be photographed. They signed the appropriate releases, which would allow Deborah to use both the pictures she took and their words as well as their names if she felt that naming them would strengthen the project's intent.

Yasir rose politely and offered Deborah his chair. She demurred. She began to unpack what little equipment she needed, chatting to them as she did so. On her lap, Leylo held a brightly wrapped package with an artful bow. Deborah assumed that it was a gift from the couple to Dr. Weatherall, a thank-you for what was to come, which, if successful, would end Leylo's chronic pain at the same time as it altered the couple's life together. But she learned the very opposite was the case. Along with the gift of life-changing surgery, it was the surgeon's habit to acknowledge the courage of the women who sought her out by giving them a token present.

"Going under the knife is never a small thing," she told Deborah before she left the office to scrub for the surgery. "We're fighting an antique belief system that damages women, but we're also asking women to battle their fear."

Leylo said she was not afraid. Yasir added that he was afraid enough for them both. All of them chuckled, Dr. Weatherall disappeared to prepare herself, and Deborah began as she always did: with a camera ready to shoot what she saw as she spoke to the couple and a digital recorder to document their words.

They'd had a grim time of it, she discovered. Leylo had undergone the cut as a six-year-old. Four other girls had been mutilated that day. She'd tried to run when she heard the screaming, but she'd been caught by her uncle. He'd carried her back and handed her over. She remembered that he said, Do her next, stupid woman, or she'll run again and I'm not chasing her if she does.

Yasir took his wife's hand. He spoke quietly of what she'd gone through for the twenty years since she'd been cut: abscesses, poisoning of the blood, bladder infections, cysts. They'd had a child and it had nearly killed her. The child did not survive. "She is a good wife," he said. "I have not been so good a husband."

Leylo tutted. This was not altogether true. He had not understood. Neither had she. But now they saw a way to make their lives better.

It was a nurse who came for Leylo. Yasir rose. He took the package his wife had been holding, placed it on the chair she'd been occupying, and put his hands on her cheeks.

"I know that God will be with you," he said.

While the nurse prepared Leylo for surgery, Dr. Weatherall explained what Deborah would see. She would be rebuilding and repairing the labia, both major and minor, using the young woman's own flesh. She would also be carefully cutting through the scar tissue left from the removal of the clitoris in the hope, she said, that there were nerves left. If there were, this would allow Leylo to experience some sexual pleasure. If there were not, at least at the end of the surgery and the repairs, she would no longer have a catalogue of reproductive and other issues that had led to excruciating pain for so long.

She concluded by saying, "Leylo's husband has never seen the damage, you know. It's not unusual for women to be unwilling to allow it. In Yasir's case, he knows what was done to his wife and what the physical results were. But as to the visual, no."

"D'you find that common?"

"Very. The women are often both shamed and ashamed. The shaming is done by those people within their culture who tell them they have to be cut. Then they become ashamed."

"Of their bodies."

"Yes."

"Even though it's not their fault? I don't expect any one of them has *chosen* to be cut up."

"It has nothing to do with choice. It has to do with comparison, and comparison starts when they finally see what a whole woman looks like."

EMPRESS STATE BUILDING
WEST BROMPTON
SOUTH-WEST LONDON

After the team's regular morning meeting, Mark Phinney went up to the Orbit. His claim was a belated breakfast. He knew that he would be believed because the other officers were aware of Lilybet's disabilities and how often her condition called for an alteration in his daily schedule, with breakfast being part of that schedule. Thus when he told DS Hopwood, "You'll know where to find me, Jade," she looked up from her computer and gave him a friendly nod. "I could do with a coffee when you've finished," she told him. "No hurries, though, guv."

He offered a smile. It was a weary one, produced with effort. He liked Jade. It was not her fault that she did not match up to who Teo had been.

He had no real appetite, but for appearances, he bought a mass-produced biscotti wrapped in plastic that he could pretend he intended to open. Along with it, he purchased a coffee: nothing fancy, nothing possessing a foreign name, but a good old coffee—white—into which he dumped a packet of sugar. He took this to one of the windows, and he tried not to think of the last time he'd been here with Teo. He failed at the effort.

He'd brought her up from the seventeenth floor to unveil the news of her transfer. He'd done so with the belief—foolhardy as it might have been—that she would not do what she could have done, which was to turn him over to those who dealt with allegations of sexual harassment, sexual impropriety, sexual anything at all as long as the adjective *sexual* was applied to it. He would have been guilty of every single term she might have chosen to use. The fact that he could not and had not been able to escape *sexual* when it came to Teo was largely why he knew he had to pull whatever strings necessary to place her far, far away from him.

From the first, it had been impossible for him to ignore her sensual power, although she never used it. She had, in fact, done absolutely nothing but her job. She was a member of his team and she was passionate about their work, full stop. But she was not passionate about her superior officer, and he fully intended to keep his distance from her. He told himself he *could* admire her: the skin, the hair, the eyes, the hands, the arms, the legs, the lips, the . . . He couldn't, he couldn't think of her breasts and the dip of her waist and the shape of her arse. He couldn't think of what he didn't have with Pete and what he wanted and what it meant about him if he made the wrong move.

And yet he finally did just that: he made the wrong move. It was an after-hours knees-up at the local, something he occasionally suggested for everyone on the team, plus a few extras from Empress State Building joining them. Teo went along. He hadn't sat with her, nor had he sat near her. Neither of them ended up drunk. They'd become tipsy, perhaps, but not to the degree that one's laughter was a bit too loud, that an inappropriate joke or comment seemed perfectly in order. Neither of them was tipsy enough even to place a hand on a shoulder, let alone to put it where it never would have been mistaken for a gesture between friends. The hour was late, though, and as Teo didn't have her car and as her journey to Streatham from West Brompton on public transport would be a long one, and as he did have a car, it seemed polite to tell her he would drive her to her flat. It was not a problem, he did say, despite the fact that he lived in the opposite direction.

So he'd taken her there, to Streatham, to her flat. They'd spoken on the way and they'd spoken upon their arrival. All of it was business . . . until it wasn't. And that was down to him. She was so intelligent, she was so beautiful there in the darkness with part of her face lit from a street lamp near the car, she was so female, she was . . . she simply *was*. Still he intended nothing.

After a few minutes of business talk, she'd thanked him graciously for seeing her home, she'd said goodnight, she'd reached for the door handle, and he said her name. Just "Teo . . . ?" and she turned back to him and he felt something break inside his mind and attack whatever sensibility he had left. He had a moment of *do not do this*, but like all moments, it did not last.

He kissed her. She let him. The kiss went on. He had to touch her. Just her breast, he thought, just long enough to feel the gratifying sensation of her nipple hardening beneath his fingers. Would that be doing too much or asking too much or wanting too much in a situation like his in which he had nothing? Or so he asked himself.

These sorts of things never ended well. He knew that now and he'd known that then, but he had not cared to speculate upon the fact. He'd only acknowledged that he wanted her and he'd convinced himself that *if* he had her just once in the way he wanted to have her, that would be enough.

It might have been, but she would not allow it. He'd assumed—like the idiot he was—that her refusal was about power and control. If she did not submit, she had the power, and as such, she controlled whatever happened between them, no matter what his passion dictated or where his animal instincts tried to lead. In all of this, he'd seen only his need and her determination—as he named it—not to meet his need. In all of this, he'd completely failed to see that there was something she did not want him to know, let alone to see or to touch. It was only in her death that he understood, and only her murder had made it possible.

He'd tried to explain to her that her transfer from the job she loved and did so well had nothing to do with her unwillingness to give him access to her body in the way he was desperate to have. It was her very presence, he'd said. It was the fact that he couldn't think straight, that when she was in the room with him or when they were in a meeting together or when he saw her at her desk or speaking to someone on the phone or standing at the copier machine or *anything* at all, he could no longer properly do his job. He'd asked her to try to understand what it was like for him. He had not bothered to advance his own knowledge about what it was like for her.

She'd said, "Why don't *you* request a transfer, then? Having me transferred is sexual harassment, Mark."

He'd replied, "You can go that route. I hope you don't, but I know you can."

She'd said, "It would be a completely different situation if I had you in my bed, wouldn't it? There'd be no transfer."

He'd said, "Teo, please. Try to understand."

To which she'd bitterly replied, "I'd've had you in my bed and you'd've had what you want. And off you'd've gone to your wife afterwards and what sort of life would either of us have then?"

What he'd thought then was how it always came down to this moment when one strayed outside the culturally and religiously imposed boundary of marriage. It always came down to one of the individuals wanting more and the other unwilling or unable to give it. What he'd told himself was that he should have known it would come to this moment, and he'd put his entire career on the line, and if he couldn't somehow smooth over the entire situation he would have thrown everything away because he'd wanted her in a way that she clearly did not want him. He'd been and he still was a fool.

She'd left him then—alone in the Orbit as he was now—and he'd waited for her to make a move against him. But instead she'd departed quietly, as he'd obliquely requested. She'd given him that. She'd worked to bring Jade up to speed, she'd completed the action she'd begun in Kingsland, and after requesting a few days to sort herself out before reporting to her new job, she'd gone from his life.

Only she hadn't, apparently. Not entirely.

He set his smartphone on the coffee table and he stared at it for a very long moment before he accessed his texts. He saw the trail he hadn't wanted to see, one he hadn't wanted to believe might even exist.

I think of you. It's mad. I can't stop

It can't be over. I know how you feel. I know how I feel

I dreamed of us. I was searching for you. I couldn't find you. Please. Will you see me?

Darling to be inside you once more once more

She'd not responded to any of them. But in the end, that had not mattered.

From his pocket he removed the rectangular, sturdy little ticket that he'd found. He placed it next to his smartphone. He'd needed some money that morning and he'd not had the time to stop at a cashpoint. So he fished in Pete's bag, calling to her as she changed Lilybet's nappy that he was taking two twenties. She called back to him, "That's fine, Mark. You know where to find them," and so he had. The ticket was tucked at the back of the notes.

He'd known at once what it was. He'd seen tickets such as this one all his life. Beige, they were, printed with a row of four numbers, serrated at the top for easy removal from a companion ticket upon which would be written a name, a date, an amount, and a generic description. Neatly filed away, this would be. Easy to locate when called upon to do so.

He wanted to rip it into pieces and to toss those pieces into the rubbish. It would be so easy to do it, there in the Orbit, which was, he forced himself to admit, what he'd intended to do when he'd come up to the building's top floor with its spectacular views of the city he had bound himself to protect and to serve, as one among many, some of whom had given their lives doing their duty.

He took the ticket from his pocket, and he felt its near weightlessness in his palm as well as the burn of its presence. He considered the possible implications attendant to where he'd found it. He thought about loyalty. He thought about obligation. He compared both of these to responsibility.

Finally he stood and took up his smartphone. He put it into his pocket, and he left the Orbit. The ticket and what it meant went with him.

WESTMINSTER
CENTRAL LONDON

When Barbara Havers arrived at New Scotland Yard from her meeting with Ross Carver, she joined Lynley and Nkata in the former's office. It turned out that Lynley had managed to corral two DCs from one of his colleagues, in this case DI Hale. This was all done on the down low, he explained to Barbara and Nkata. Assistant Commissioner Hillier was of the belief that having two detective sergeants—Barbara and Winston—should equate to having four DCs, and four DCs should be more than enough to deal with this matter of murder. This, from a man who'd never investigated a murder in his entire career.

Lynley assigned the DCs to Nkata. They would join in the thankless and wearisome task of viewing the CCTV footage. Their objective: to isolate the images of any faces of individuals ringing for entry into the building in which Teo Bontempi had lived, as well as to note down the number plates on cars captured by CCTV on the two closest businesses across the road from that building. Had there been an ANPR camera in the immediate vicinity, this would have been the easiest of all their activities relating to the death of Teo Bontempi, as the ANPR system offered real-time data on cars and their number plates. Since they had only CCTV available, however, the number plates would be sent to Swansea for identification. It was anyone's guess whether joy would be produced from faces seen on CCTV or number plates captured by the camera, but watching what was available from the cameras had to be done.

For his part, Lynley had finally dug up a name that went with the mobile number given to him by DS Jade Hopwood at Empress State Building. The phone was the possession of one Easter Lange.

It hadn't taken him long to work out why this name sounded familiar, he told them. Easter Lange was also the name of the woman who had been arrested in Kingsland when the Stoke Newington coppers had descended upon Women's Health of Hackney. Easter wasn't a name one stumbled upon often. So when the putative owner of a mobile having a number that Teo Bontempi had passed along to Jade Hopwood turned out to be someone called Easter Lange, Lynley had sought out the reports made by the officers who'd arrested the two women at the clinic. There she was at the top.

She'd been taken to the Stoke Newington police station in the company of a woman called Monifa Bankole, who'd been present with her daughter at the clinic when the police had arrived, Lynley explained. Both Easter Lange and Monifa Bankole had undergone a few hours of questioning, but this had proved useless. However, now this same Easter Lange had a connection to a dead woman, and that needed to be dealt with.

"How have you done with the CCTV footage so far?" he asked Nkata, who was leaning against the door jamb.

"Frozen treacle," was how he put it. "Don't think this's the best use of my time, guv."

"Leave it to the DCs, going forward." Lynley looked over the top of his reading specs. "You're going to be needed elsewhere." He gestured to the report and said, "Monifa Bankole, address in Dalston. Since Teo Bontempi was gathering information about this clinic prior to her transfer, Monifa Bankole wants talking to."

Nkata took the address with a grateful nod. He said, "Anything else as to the CCTV?"

"Have the DCs send any moderately decent images to tech for improvement. Otherwise everything remains the same."

"Will do," he said, and began to leave when Barbara interrupted with, "Hang on. I've met Rosie Bontempi."

She gave them chapter and verse on her encounter with Ross Carver and his sister-in-law. She pointed out the two facts that she saw as salient: Rosie appeared to have taken issue with her brother-in-law's spending the night with her sister. And somehow Rosie had known that Ross would be at the Streatham flat that morning. Barbara concluded with, "She tells the same story she told Winston about the argument heard by Teo's neighbours, sir, but I'm smelling something and it isn't roses."

"You're thinking the two of them might be involved?" Lynley asked.

"Not necessarily with the murder."

"With each other? The husband and the sister?"

"If they're not, I wager she wants them to be. Why else give a toss that he spent the night there? Why give a toss where he spent the night at all?"

Lynley looked at Nkata. "What do you think?"

"We prob'ly need to have another go," he said. "I don' like to think she killed her sister, though."

"Did she get to you?" Barbara asked him, and, as he began to reply, "I'm not accusing, by the way. I've got the feeling she's on autopilot when it comes to pulling men."

"She is, that," Nkata agreed. "But I don' see as she has a reason to hurt her sister. They were splitting up, Teo an' Carver. He was due to be a free man, innit."

"Except according to Carver, Teo wanted to have a natter with him," Barbara said. "That's why he went there."

"But we jus' got his word on that, right?"

"Right. Yes. Till we put our hands on her mobile. But the fact is, we've just got everyone's word on everything, don't we?"

"No one's been crossed off the list," Lynley noted. "Back to business, then. Barbara, you'll come with me."

THE NARROW WAY
HACKNEY
NORTH-EAST LONDON

They were stretched thin as it was, so Barbara wondered why Lynley wanted her company. When it turned out they were headed for a Marks & Spencer, though, she reckoned his lordship was in terror that his very lordshipness would not survive the polluting atmosphere of that establishment should he go inside solo. At least, that was the thought with which she entertained herself. And she needed something for entertainment, not to mention distraction. For Lynley's motor—circa 1948—had no air-conditioning to ameliorate the summer heat, and he'd given her the stink eye when, despite knowing full well the answer in advance, she'd asked him if she could have a smoke as they drove.

Once those issues had been dealt with, he asked her how the sketching was going.

At first she was clueless until she recalled GroupMeet or Group-Grope or whatever the bloody hell it was called, along with Dorothea Harriman's intention to involve her in it. The sketching, she informed Lynley, wasn't going at all. At least not yet. To this she added, "And if I have my way, it never will. *Why* does she think I need a love life, sir? Do I look like I need a love life? And what does someone who needs a love life look like anyway? *And* how the bloody hell is sketching supposed to lead to a love life?"

"I wouldn't presume to answer a single one of those questions," Lynley admitted. "Obviously, I have difficulty enough in the love-life area myself."

Barbara harrumphed. "I need someone to pose as my lover, I do." She thought of her acquaintances, most of whom were her fellow cops. Then she had it. "What about Charlie Denton, sir? D'you think he'd be up for the job? It could take a massive amount of acting, 'course. But on the other hand, there's every chance that a little sighing along with flowers and boxes of chocolates and looking at me with cow eyes could do the trick. Dee's not met him, has she? He's not been round to see you at work, right? Of course, there *is* the problem of Denton not being my type, but p'rhaps we can get round that some way." When Lynley didn't reply, she went on with, "I mean, you do agree, right? Denton isn't my type."

"Have you a type?" Lynley asked her.

"According to Dee, we all have types. We're just meant to devote some serious time sorting the wheat from the whatsit."

"The chaff?"

"Is that what it is? And is the wheat supposed to be my type, or is it the chaff? *And* what the bloody dickens is chaff when its home with its mum?"

"Flotsam and jetsam of the corn world, perhaps?"

"Oh, that's very helpful, sir."

They found Easter Lange at her regular place of employment. This had been something of a surprise to them, as they'd expected her employment to be oriented towards the clinic at which she'd been arrested. But they ended up instead at the top of Mare Street in Hackney, where a Marks & Spencer sat in a pedestrian area, just across from a crenellated tower, which marked the near end of a small park. This immediate area, they learned, was called The Narrow Way and it was crowded with shoppers who appeared to be preparing scores of children with uniforms, shoes, and school supplies for the new school term, which was fast upon them.

Upon making an enquiry at the department store, showing his warrant card, and using his plummiest accent to smooth the potential for difficulties inherent to speaking to an employee during her working hours, Lynley was able to unearth the information that they would find Easter Lange in ladies' wear, particularly undergarments, even more particularly knickers and brassieres. Barbara allowed herself a small snicker. She reckoned that while Marks & Spencer wasn't exactly Lynley's usual stamping ground, the department featuring ladies' knickers and bras was even less so. Nonetheless, he impressively girded whatever needed to be girded, and he led the way.

Easter Lange turned out to be a stout figure somewhere in her sixties. She had shockingly red hair, which was unexpected, but she carried it off well. She was rounded everywhere: arms, legs, arse, breasts. Her hands were dimpled and so were her cheeks. She would have looked quite pleasant and utterly approachable should someone have a question about ladies' undergarments, but she looked dead angry when Lynley introduced himself, introduced Barbara, and said they'd been given permission to have a word.

"You lot took your time," she snapped. "What're you doing to catch those bloody kids?"

Lynley and Barbara exchanged a look. Easter Lange seemed to clock their confusion because she said, "Police, right?" Then, "You di'n't come about the raid last evening?"

"We did not."

"Well, tha's just the bloody limit, that is. We had more'n one hundred kids in here, doing a raid. Had it all planned, they did, and in they came in a swarm and there was *nothing* to be done to stop 'em. Tha's when we needed you lot, innit. Stuffing all sorts of clobber into bags, they were, with no one to hold 'em back but shop assistants and two security guards. This whole place was a tip by the time they finished their fun. Oh, they're all on CCTV, the lot of them, but how's that goin' to help? We still got to put this place in order." She indicated the lingerie department, which seemed to have taken quite a hit during the invasion. She continued what she had been doing, which Barbara saw was hanging up bras where they belonged. Knickers were easier as they were mostly in packages. "They lef' saying 'there'll be more of us tonight,' and laughing like this was the local asylum. They do it all by mobile, y'know. They message the time and they message the place and they storm it, taking everything they can get their maulers on. I ask you how're we meant to stop 'em when they come at us like that? 'S that what you come to tell me? You're here to say how I'm s'posed to prevent this? An' why *me* when there's other departments got hit as well? Shoes got hit worse, I hear it."

Lynley apologised for the local police, who were already under-staffed and certainly outnumbered by teenagers up to mischief of an evening. He went on to tell Easter Lange that he and Barbara were there to talk to her about her mobile.

She looked as astonished as a peeved woman could, saying, "Wha's Scotland Yard got to do with my mobile?"

"A police detective had your mobile's number," Lynley explained.

Barbara added, "A police detective who's now dead."

Easter had been crouched in front of a wall display of bras in a multiplicity of riotous colours, but now she stood upright, one hand on her hip. She said, "I don' know about tha', do I. I don' know *any* police detective at all, I don't."

"This is someone you may have known as a Nigerian woman called Adaku Obiaka. You might not have known her as a police detective."

Easter gave a half snort, half laugh. "As to that," she said. "I *defi-*nitely don' know some Nigerian woman called . . . What did you say?"

"Adaku," Barbara put in. "Surname Obiaka. Or she might have been calling herself Teo Bontempi when you met."

"I never talked to any Nigerian woman or Nigerian police detec-tive or *any* police at all or anyone like it."

"But you probably would have done before you were arrested and taken in for questioning," Lynley pointed out. "And Adaku—Teo Bontempi—was the person who gave the police information about the clinic that brought the local police to it."

Should Easter Lange's eyes have been on springs, capable of bounc-ing out of and back into her head, they no doubt would have done so when Lynley spoke. She said, "*What*'re you lot on about? I never've been arrested in my *whole* life. And I don' know one thing at all 'bout some clinic. *Clinic*? Why'd I supposedly get arrested at a clinic, eh? And where's this clinic anyways? What the bloody hell is this? I never even got a parking ticket."

Barbara exchanged a look with Lynley. Easter Lange was righteous indignation made flesh and given voice. Lynley produced the card on which the mobile number had been written and apparently intended for Adaku Obiaka. He said to Easter, "Is this not your mobile number?"

She gave it a look and shook her head. "Uh-uh. No it most certainly i'n't."

"If it's not the number of your mobile—"

She turned back to her work and set upon it with even more industry than she'd shown before. "You c'n ring it yourself an' see, but it i'n't mine." She glanced in their direction and said, "Go 'head and ring it. It's like I said and you'll see that soon 's you punch in the numbers."

"Mrs. Lange, the phone's registered to you."

"There's no mister. Never been, never will be."

"Miss Lange, as I said, the—"

"*Ms.* Lange," Barbara put in. "There's a policewoman dead. She gave this number to another detective. Whoever this number belongs to is someone using your name. We need to know who she is."

"Using my *name*, you say? Ah. Tha's quite another thing. Tha's Mercy, that is. And that's her mobile number, I expect."

"Mercy?" Lynley said.

Barbara took out her notebook and waited for more details. "My niece, she is. Did it once before: using my name. Don' ask me why she did it with a mobile cos I don' know and, believe me, I don' want to know. But tha' girl? Mercy? Swear to God, she's been trouble for years she has, an' sent her mum to an early grave. Forty-five, she was. Dropped dead in the launderette. Rest 'f the family, we thought *that* sorted Mercy. An' it did for a while. She went to school and got herself a first in some kind of science. She was meant to take up nursing las' time I heard. She's got a good head on her, so she prob'ly did jus' that. Off she went into her life and I never talked to her since. But I 'spect for sure she's the one you want to talk to about that mobile. Prob'ly 'bout the arrest 's well cos it wasn't me got hauled off to the nick."

"Do you have her details?" Lynley asked.

"Full name's Mercy Hart."

"Her address?"

"I got an old one I can give you. Happy to do it. But you got to know she prob'ly i'n't there. She never liked one place long. Said she got bored of it, is what she said. But she'll be in London if she was working in . . . What sort 'f clinic was this and why'd she get arrested for workin' in a clinic anyways?"

"We're trying to sort all of that," Lynley told her. He reached in his jacket for one of his cards. Barbara reached in her shoulder bag for one of hers.

"Ring one of us if you hear from her," Barbara said. "It's important."

Easter Lange took the cards, read them both, and stuffed them into the pocket of her tunic. She said she certainly would ring them, and she'd certainly give them the only address she had for Mercy, but she hadn't spoken to her in forever, and she didn't expect to be speaking to her anytime soon. She didn't know what sort of help she'd ever be able to give them.

"Any help is quite a lot better than no help at all," Lynley told her.

KINGSLAND HIGH STREET
DALSTON
NORTH-EAST LONDON

Lynley and Havers reached the same conclusions when they arrived at the location of the clinic, where the arrests of Mercy Hart—posing as

Easter Lange—and Monifa Bankole had occurred. Their first conclusion was that, for a women's clinic, it wasn't doing anything to advertise its presence since the only sign indicating anything at all at the address they'd found in the police report was one that announced the establishment as Kingsland Toys, Games, and Books in bright letters on a purple background, all of it done in plastic. Their second conclusion was that the clinic was apparently closing down. A large van stood blocking the traffic travelling south, its rear doors gaping open and a ramp descending to the street. This appeared to be a grossly unpopular exercise, for a tailback had formed and the drivers affected were not being shy about sitting on their horns or shouting from their open windows. A traffic warden was definitely wanted. Unfortunately, none was evident.

"Ah London, a place of boundless tranquillity," Havers said to the sky, and jerking her thumb at an establishment next door to the putative clinic, she went on with, "Taste of Tennessee would do well to start taking orders from all that lot, you ask me."

"Is that the source of the horrific stench?" Lynley asked her.

"Grease and exhaust fumes, sir. Some people call it the fragrance of the gods. I could do with a nosh, by the way. I missed breakfast and we're way past lunch."

"Have you given much thought to the condition of your arteries?" Lynley said to the DS.

"I'll eat veg tomorrow, sir. Breakfast, lunch, and dinner. All raw. With water. No fags either. Scout's honour, nun's vow, oath taken on the Bible, or whatever you like. I'd suggest the first option, though. Something tells me you don't carry a Bible round in the boot of your car."

Lynley glanced at her wryly. "You don't expect me to believe any of that, do you? I mean the part of eating only raw vegetables and drinking only water."

"I don't see why you wouldn't."

"Havers, the word *incorrigible* does not do justice."

"Have a heart, Inspector."

"Exactly," he replied. "Heart, yours. Clogged arteries. Sudden death."

"Oh good bloody grief."

"Which we, whom you leave behind, would feel. Come along, Sergeant."

They crossed the High Street and paced back to Kingsland Toys, Games, and Books where two men in blue boilersuits with *Pack 'n' Go* forming an embroidered arc on the back were just coming out of a door propped open for ease of access and egress. They were carrying an upended desk with gaping holes where its drawers had been. Lynley stopped them, identified himself, and asked for a word.

It was brief and given only after they had the desk loaded into the van. Yes, they were emptying the clinic, they told him. Yes, it was closing down. Yes, they'd been sent to do the job. No, they didn't know who had made the arrangements. They just went where they were told to go by their guv'nor, and this was where they were told to go. They were taking everything to a storage facility "out Beckton way." They'd made one delivery there already and "the guv'nor being so tight with the money, he won't buy something larger for bigger jobs like this one," they might even be forced to make the trek to Beckton one more time. There was nothing for it but to soldier on, which was what they were trying to do. This last was said more meaningfully than that which had come before it.

"My colleague and I need to have a look round the place, I'm afraid. Have you had your lunch?"

They both guffawed at that, which suggested they weren't allowed lunch when they were transporting items. When Lynley encouraged them to have a lengthy break from their labours and to use the advent of the Metropolitan Police as their excuse if their guv questioned them, they were only too happy to comply. They didn't bother to ask him for a warrant. It seemed that the siren smell of Taste of Tennessee had been working its magic upon them as efficiently as it had done upon Havers. They made fast tracks to that establishment and disappeared inside.

"Not worried about *their* arteries, I see," Havers groused.

"At the very least, I do need to know someone's name, Sergeant, before I consider their vascular system and the imminence of their shedding their mortal coil, et cetera." Lynley gestured to the open doorway. "After you," he said.

The entry smelled musty with disuse, and there was a scattering of post lying on the floor. Lynley picked this up and riffled through it. Nothing of interest and nothing directed to a clinic.

"Stairs back here, sir," Havers called. "Look decrepit, but I expect they still do the job."

He joined her and saw that the stairway was indeed old if its condition was anything to go by. Banister badly scratched and dented here and there, balusters occasionally detached from the railing above them and the steps below, carpet on the treads worn through. All of this served as a very strange welcome for anyone coming to this place.

The only door inside the building that stood open was on the top floor, and as its furniture was in disarray, Lynley reckoned they were at the clinic, which was in the process of being dismantled. Aside from the names of the two women who'd been inside the premises when the police showed up, what they knew of the clinic was limited to what the local police had been able to wrest in the form of information from those same two women: that it served ladies in the surrounding communities and that it dealt with women's health.

Women's health, Lynley thought, casts a very wide net. He reckoned it included everything from reproduction to hormonal imbalances to various types of cancers. He indicated two four-drawer filing cabinets that stood against one of the walls. They had apparently been separated from the waiting area by the previously departed desk, the drawers of which now sat upon the floor. Wordlessly, Lynley went for the filing cabinets. Havers took the drawers: two standard size, one for filing and one that would have fitted just above the kneehole.

Lynley quickly saw that one of the two filing cabinets contained supplies: both office and medical. They were neatly ordered with the medical materials in the upper two drawers and those for the office in the lower two. What files still remained in the office were contained within manila folders in the drawers of the second cabinet. These were marked with patients' names. None of them were anywhere close to bulging with the kind of physician's notes one would assume were kept to be held in a medical surgery. He chose ten of them at random and carried them to a corner chair that had not yet been removed for transport. He sat, opened the first of them, and began to scan the documents it held. There were few: a medical history, a release form, a perfectly unreadable scrawl of notes that seemed to be concerned with three different appointments. The next folder was much the same, as was the third. All in all, the files asked for the conclusion that, whatever women's health issue was being addressed, the clinic had solved it quickly.

"Here's something, sir." Havers was crouched on the floor where the desk drawers had been stacked after their removal from the desk. She held up a black spiral book, and he saw it was a desk-size appointment diary. Havers began to go through it.

"Just names, sir," she said. He watched as she read the appointments for one day, then another, then a third and a fourth. She looked up, and he saw that her expression was puzzled. Her gaze was fixed and focused on nothing.

"Barbara?" he said.

She looked at him. "I don't know, sir, but it seems odd."

"Something in the appointment diary?"

"This area's mixed race, right? I mean, everywhere in London is mixed race. Well . . . not Belgravia and Mayfair and wherever there's big money—no offence, sir—"

"Go on."

"But you know what I'm saying, don't you?"

"I do."

"Then here's what's strange, you ask me. This's a clinic for women. It features women's health from A to Z. But there's not a name in here that isn't African. What d'you make of that? I mean, Easter Lange wasn't African, sir. She's as English as me. P'rhaps not as English as you with . . . what is it? . . . six hundred years of family history barking at your heels."

"That would be the Percys," he told her. "They've been around forever. The Lynley roots are appallingly shallow by comparison."

"Not compared to those of us whose roots are planted in a Saxon hut somewhere."

"Those are very deep roots, Barbara."

"Too right they are. But I was talking about the appalling part of it."

He chuckled. "As to Easter Lange?"

"Oh. Right. My point is that Easter Lange is English, which means Mercy Hart is English as well, I expect. So what's she doing working in a women's clinic that only African women come to? Especially since, like I said, there are all *sorts* of non-African women in this part of town. But only Africans come here?"

"English Black women. African Black women. This obviously suggests something to you."

"Did you notice there's no clinic's name on the door? Not this door and not on the door that got us into the building. What kind of clinic doesn't want to advertise itself as a clinic?"

"One run by a fraudulent physician?"

"Or one doing something illegal. Let's look at what we've got. Teo Bontempi was part of a team working on the abuse of women. Somehow she ended up with the arrest reports on two women connected with this particular place. How did she know about it?"

"The clinic? She could easily have had an informant inside one of the African communities."

"Okay. An informant. It's possible. I see that. But while an informant might have told her that this place was *here*, there's no way the clinic is going to be raided by the locals or anyone else without someone checking on it first."

Lynley thought about the timeline involved. Then he said, "She *was* in the midst of working on an action just before her transfer, Barbara. DS Hopwood mentioned it."

"I'll put down a fiver, sir. This was it. She learns about this place but then she gets transferred *before* she knows whatever she needs to know and then what? She does some research with her free time? Then she puts the locals into the picture? They show up and make arrests."

"All right. I see how that's possible. And she did ask for a few days before she was intended to show up at her new posting."

"But then her part in it gets sussed out. She dies soon after, which is to say she's murdered soon after. I don't know what that tells you, but it tells me that, setting everything else aside—Ross Carver, her sister, and anything else in her personal life—there's a connection between what Teo Bontempi was working on and how she died. And that connection runs directly through this clinic."

"Are you suggesting that FGM was being performed here by Mercy Hart, an Englishwoman?"

"Sounds spot on to me. Plus, according to Easter, she's some kind of nurse."

"Which hardly qualifies her for—"

"That's just the point, sir. She's a far sight better qualified than some old lady with a razor blade. Look, FGM doesn't end where the UK begins. If it did, we wouldn't need a team established by the Met to work on the problem. Like I said, this so-called clinic for women's health doesn't have a sign on the building and it doesn't even announce itself on the door. I reckon there's a reason for that, and someone in here"—she lifted the large appointment diary—"or somewhere in one of those"—she indicated the manila folders, which he'd been examining—"is going to be able to tell us."

MAYVILLE ESTATE
DALSTON
NORTH-EAST LONDON

After hour upon hour closely watching CCTV films, Winston Nkata was more than ready for a change of scenery. So far on his own, he'd managed to isolate, enlarge, and send on to tech fairly decent images of three people who'd entered the apartment block in Streatham on the evening and night of the attack on Teo Bontempi. He'd been concentrating on those who entered or left on their own. With the help of DI Hale's DCs, they could now move more quickly through the recordings. If none of the resulting images bore fruit, he and the DCs would go back and work on those who had companions when they entered. The Met couldn't afford to ignore anyone in the footage captured by the cameras since, as far as he knew, nothing at the scene indicated that Teo Bontempi had met her end at the hands of a single person. Additionally, current residents of the building could not be ruled out. In short, it seemed to Nkata that there was no possibility that could be left without exploration.

When he reached north London, Nkata left his car near a sign that identified the buildings on the grounds of Mayville Estate. He knew he was looking for Bronte House, and after perusing the posted map of the estate, he was gratified to see that the route was simple. As he approached Bronte House, he was equally gratified to see that most of the flats offered open doors because of the weather, and included among these was the flat whose number Monifa Bankole had given to the police upon her arrest.

He'd had a call from Barbara Havers en route to this place. "There was no Easter Lange," she told him. Then she corrected herself by saying, "What I mean is: there *is* an Easter Lange but she's not the person got herself arrested."

"Say wha', then, Barb?" had been his reply.

"The real Easter Lange works at Marks and Sparks and her size thirty-eights have never darkened the doorway of the bill. She thinks it's her niece got hauled off. Called Mercy Hart, she is. Black sheep of the family or something like. Anyway, Auntie Easter hasn't a clue where she might be—Mercy Hart—so we'll need to get on that."

"The guv want me on that 'nstead of what I'm doing?" he asked.

He heard Barbara saying something to Lynley and then, "He says to carry on with this other woman. And Winnie . . ."

"Yeah?"

"We think the situation may have to do with FGM, which we also think could have been going on at the clinic where the two women got arrested. It's closed down now, but the guv says to bear that in mind when you're having a chat with this Monifa Bankole."

Now he mounted the steps to a line of flats comprising the ground floor of Bronte House. Unlike the building in Streatham, no key was required to reach them. From the flat in question came the sound of voices: a woman and a man. She cried out, "I tried. I could not. I have *told* you. Abeo, you're hurting me!" and his reply was "Can you not be good for something? I have told you what I want. Now you *will* do it." Both of them appeared in the doorway. The man had the woman by the arm. He appeared ready to shove her from the flat. She appeared to be trying to stop him. Neither of them saw Nkata, nor did the teenager who followed them. He was shouting, "Leave her the *hell* alone!" And then a child, crying, "Papa!" from somewhere inside the flat.

Rapidly, Nkata mounted the steps. He had his warrant card at the ready. He said, "Police," and he made certain his voice carried above the chaos. Neighbours had come out of the flats above, and some of them were leaning over the railing to see what the commotion was.

At this, the man shoved the woman in Nkata's direction and turned on the teenager, shouting, "You disrespect me, your father," to which the boy replied, "Oh jus' try it, Pa. Punch me in the face, you—"

"Tani!" cried a little girl who'd come to the door while the woman shouted, "Abeo, Tani, do not!" as Nkata put himself between the boy and the man and said, "Police. You both think twice b'fore you make a decision results in handcuffs, got it?"

"I am the head of this family," Abeo said.

"Whatever you declare, man. You sound jus' a bit like a foreigner so let me make somethin' clear 'n case you never heard. Assault i'n't part of heading a fam'ly in this part of the world."

Abeo thrust the teenager back inside the flat, away from the door. The little girl followed, crying, "Tani! She made me and I di'n't want to."

Nkata was left with the couple who, he assumed, were husband and wife. He said, "Monifa Bankole," to the woman. When she nodded, he gave his name and rank and said, "I need a word."

Abeo Bankole said, "I do not allow this. She speaks to *no* man out of my presence."

Nkata said pleasantly, "I don' care wha' you allow, man. You c'n do a disappearing act for me or I c'n take your lady to the nearest police interview room, which, I 'magine, you'd not much like me to do, eh? But you c'n decide. My car's not far. Jus' make it quick, eh? I got a lot on my plate today."

Abeo looked long at Nkata, who, at six feet, five inches, was ten inches taller than he was. Then he looked at his wife, who shrank from his gaze but stood her ground. He said, pointing a finger into her face, "You shame me. Look at what you have become. Fat and stink, hanging with flesh that no man of sense would—"

"Tha's enough, that is," Nkata said.

Abeo produced a snarl. He turned on his heel and went back inside. Nkata hated to expose the bloke's children to him because he seemed the sort who only went after people less powerful than he was, especially when his day turned sour. But he had a sense that the boy, Tani, would protect the little girl at the same time as he would defend himself against his father if it became necessary.

Since Abeo had gone into the flat, Nkata sought a different location to speak to the man's wife. For her part, she was trembling but doing her best to hide it. She clutched at her bright wrapper dress. She'd had a scarf of sorts on her head, but it had fallen to her shoulders.

Nkata had spotted a children's play area across the lane, shaded in part by two London planes. He led the woman there, entering through the chain-link gate and taking her to what looked like an overturned wine barrel. There were four of these and they did service as benches. He sat her upon one and squatted in front of her. He saw that she'd begun to weep. He dug for his handkerchief—embroidered by his mum, who liked to keep her hands busy when she watched telly—and he handed it to her. She gazed at it and then at him. She began to thrust it back at him but he said, "You go 'head and use it. Tha's wha' it's for."

He waited while she took off her specs and pressed the handkerchief beneath each of her eyes. He tilted his head towards Bronte House and said, "Not a very nice bloke, tha' one."

She said, "He is crazy sometimes. But not always. More now, yes, but when I was young no."

"He hurt you much?"

She glanced at him quickly and then away. She didn't answer.

"Yeah. Wager he does. There's places you an' your kids c'n—"

"No!"

Nkata held up his hands, palms out. "Right, right. But b'fore I leave, I'm giving you my card. An' if you decide to leave that bloke, you ring me. I know people who'll help."

She turned his handkerchief in her hands. She traced the initial on it: *J.* Seeing this, he smiled and said, "Jewel. Tha's what she calls me, my mum. I got others with my reg'lar initials but tha' one's special, like a joke between her and me. I'm not much 'f a jewel, 'specially not with this scar on my face, but I let her call me that cos she got a lot of grief from my brother and I don't 'ntend to give her more."

She raised her head and gazed at him. Nkata found himself considering how afflicted she seemed, like someone bearing life rather than living it.

He said, "You were at that clinic when the cops came, eh? That clinic over Kingsland High Street. What's that meant to be, that clinic?"

"I gave her some money," she replied. "Abeo didn't know. He wanted me to fetch it back."

"You mean tha's why you were there? To get money returned to you? From who?"

"Easter, she is called. Abeo wasn't to know I took it, but before I could replace it he went into the family money for Lark. She needed to get the children school uniforms. That's how he saw some was missing."

Nkata jotted down the name Lark and asked for a surname, which Monifa didn't have. Nor did she have any other details on the woman save that she was Abeo's lover and that Lark and Abeo had children together.

"Where'd the money come from?" he asked. "This money you took, I mean."

"From all of us. We all put money into the box."

"Your kids 's well?"

"All of us. The children keep a portion for their own use, I keep a portion for doing the weekly shop, the rest goes into the family money."

"Lark's meant to be part of the family, then?"

Monifa looked away, to one of the two basketball hoops in the playing area. "She bears more children for Abeo. I cannot. But with Lark, Abeo has two. Another is on the way."

"An' you lot here? You're meant to support them?"

"The children—my children—they did not know. They thought the money was for our family."

"You went along with that, did you?"

She returned her gaze to him. "There was not a choice."

Nkata wanted to tell her that there was always a choice, but he saw little good in doing that, and for her there probably hadn't been one anyway. Instead, he said, "So you took the money and gave it to this woman Easter? She need it like Lark?"

She looked back to the doorway of her family's flat, across the playing area. He followed her gaze, but no one stood there. Still, she looked threatened, a woman who knew she faced displeasure, danger, and disrepute no matter what she said.

He told her what Barb had told him. "Tha' clinic, Mrs. Bankole . . . ?" and when she looked back at him, "It's closed down, it is. I got the word from my guv 'bout half an hour back. He and 'nother officer went there and met the removals men hauling everything away."

She turned back to him, saying, "That must not . . . that cannot happen."

"'Fraid it did. Someone made a decision about it, I expect," Nkata said. That Easter person, p'rhaps."

"But I gave her money . . ."

"Hmmm. Right. But seems th' only thing left when my guv arrived was some boxes and chairs and part of a desk. I gotta think your money's gone. Permanent, I mean. So's the woman called herself Easter Lange. She's ackshully Mercy Hart, by the way."

"Gone." She said it numbly. And then with a narrowing of her eyes, "Talk true."

"Tha's wha' I'm doing, Missus Bankole. And what I'm thinking 's this: Cops show up, cops bang about tha' clinic and make 'n arrest 'f two ladies, cops ask questions 'f someone who gives them a false name. No charges end up being made, but clinic closes straightaway. Now I don' know, do I, what all tha' suggests to you. But what it suggests to me is someone un'erstanding real fast tha' they been lucky as the devil and they i'n't likely to be lucky as the devil twice. An' *tha'* suggests something illegal going on in tha' clinic cos there's no other reason to shut it down. Wha' d'you think?"

"Now he will hurt her," was apparently what she thought. Or it was, at least, what was on her mind and what she was willing to say.

"Someone hurting this Mercy Hart?"

"He will hurt her. I cannot stop this."

"Missus Bankole, you got to tell me who. I can't help you if—"

"You can't help at *all*. *No* one can. And now he will hurt her and none of us can stop this not even I can stop it and she's my *daughter*."

Nkata put this together with what Barbara had reckoned was going on at the clinic. He said, "Mrs. Bankole, tha' little girl . . . ? One that came to the door . . . ? Was something going to happen to her?"

"Go!" She cried, and jumped to her feet. "Now! Please. Go."

THE NARROW WAY
HACKNEY
NORTH-EAST LONDON

Mark Phinney made one stop before heading to The Mothers Square and home. He went to Sutton Place and parked not far from his parents' house. He wasn't there to see them, however. He wasn't there to see anyone at all on Sutton Place. But it was conveniently close to The Narrow Way, and that was where he was heading. He reckoned

Paulie would still be at work. Mark himself had left West Brompton with enough time, in fact, to ensure this.

Paulie had two pawnshops in The Narrow Way. He'd taken over their dad's shop at the bottom of the lane, on the junction of Mare Street and Amhurst Road, and when a knitting shop had closed its doors at the top of The Narrow Way four years past, he'd signed a lease and opened a second pawnshop there. The first bore the family name. The second did not.

Paulie was generally inside Phinney Pawn, mostly because it was the shop closer to his house. Not that the second one was any great distance at the end of a long day, but Paulie's belief was that the less energy expended on working and walking, the more energy he had for Eileen and the children. Mostly for Eileen. As for the other shop, Eileen's brother ran that one. Paulie had put him in charge out of the goodness of his heart and with significant cajoling from Eileen. Stuart—the brother—was the family's ne'er-do-well. He was a charity case, as far as Paulie was concerned. When it came to his brother-in-law, his options were to lend Stuart money incessantly or to give him a job and pay him for showing up at the appointed hour and not bollixing up too badly when it came to the merchandise.

When Mark arrived, he found Phinney Pawn closed and a sign on the door that said CALL IN AT HOWE's, which was the other shop. So he walked the length of The Narrow Way, past the scent of burgers that seemed to be mechanically pumped out of McDonald's as an enticement, dodging last-minute shoppers from the Pound Shop, and glancing into the brightly lit supermarket where the customers comprised mostly women making purchases of Afro-Caribbean food.

The overhead bell rang when he went into Howe's. No one was about, so he called out his brother's name. In reply, he heard Paulie's voice, although he wasn't speaking to Mark. Instead he was saying loudly, "I'm asking you something here, Stuart. Right? How many chances d'you need?" No reply. Then Paulie: "Let me tell you something, brother-in-law, the world does *not* owe you a thing. Nor does any person—and that would include me—who's scraping together a living. You are one lucky devil to be Eileen's brother."

"Hiya," Mark called when Paulie stopped long enough to take a breath. "That you, Paulie?"

"Boyko?" Paulie came through the curtained doorway that led to the back of the shop. The unfortunate Stuart lurked sheepishly behind him.

Stuart said, "Hiya," to Mark and "Sh'll I bunk off now?" to Paulie.

Paulie said with an expressive rolling of the eyes, "Surely, yeah, Stu. It's what you do best."

"Sorry again," Stuart said as he made tracks for the front door. He'd come on his bicycle, which he had left inside the shop only partially out of the way of customers. He swooped his helmet over his thinning hair, put clips on the legs of his trousers, and rolled out of the shop.

"I am," Paulie said, "a bloody saint to put up with him."

"What's he done this time?"

"He breathes." Paulie looked round the shop with a scowl. "He was meant to put the place in order. Do some dusting up. Hoover. Sweep. Instead he takes two hours for lunch and claims he's been to the dentist about his 'roots.' The man talks crap, I swear. If he wasn't Eileen's baby brother, I would have put my booted foot into his bum crack long ago."

"Ah well. You're a softy, you are, Paulie. Always were."

"Bloody too true, that." Paulie set about closing up the shop, beginning with lowering the window blinds and removing jewellery from the cases in the windows. It always seemed sad to Mark, people pawning their wedding rings and engagement rings and bracelets and medals and whatnots. Paulie had told him long ago that most of these objects were never redeemed, but instead they were purchased by someone hoping to find a bargain. Paulie's prices were always fair. He wasn't greedy and never had been.

Mark watched him and made no move until Paulie had the jewellery stashed in the safe that stood behind the curtain to the back room. He followed that up with the money from the till. He came back out front and leaned against the glass counter. The odd piece of silver was displayed in this case: serving pieces, snuff boxes, card cases, powder jars.

"So," Paulie said. "Another visit to Massage Dreams? I c'n ring 'em. Do you remember her name?"

Mark said, "Not here for that."

"No? I wager you're due. Am I right?"

Mark avoided answering by taking from his pocket the beige ticket he'd found inside Pete's wallet. Its companion would be in this shop or in Phinney Pawn at the bottom of The Narrow Way. Paulie looked down at it then up at Mark. His expression was blank, neutral. Mark wanted to see wariness in his brother's eyes but he saw nothing.

Mark said, "What did she pawn?"

Paulie said, "No."

"No she didn't pawn a thing, no you won't tell me, or no this ticket isn't one of yours?"

"You know the rules, Boyko. It's confidential."

"As a policeman—"

Paulie barked a laugh. "Don't try that. First you need a warrant, which no one is going to give you. Second, what I said before and what you know because you worked at the other shop summers and so did I when we were in school."

"In this case, that can't matter. It's important, Paulie. Pete hid it from me and it could mean something crucial."

"Crucial to who, Boyko? Crucial to what?"

Mark couldn't bring himself to tell him. He just needed to know what his wife had pawned. The date on the ticket was August 3. That might have been insignificant were it not the day after he'd found Teo unconscious in her bed.

When Mark didn't speak, Paulie went on with, "You want to know details, Pete's the person to give them."

"What she pawned, though. It's here? It's in this shop? If I have a look round, will I see it, Paulie?"

"You asking me to play cold-warm-hot with you? That what's going on? Boyko, it's not going to happen."

"For Christ's sake, I'm your brother."

"Not likely I'll forget it."

"So you've got to—"

"Boyko, I've got to nothing. She trusted me and I'm not breaking that trust and that's where we are. Now. Want to go over to Mare Street for a pint? Or something stronger if that suits you? I'm paying the tab."

Mark shook his head. A drink with his brother was the last thing he wanted from him. What he wanted was the truth but he knew he wasn't going to get it.

9 AUGUST

Winston Nkata arrived at the Bontempi home before seven in the morning. It had been years since he'd engaged in an all-nighter at work, and he was fairly done-in despite the three cups of coffee he'd had before leaving New Scotland Yard. These were in addition to the numerous coffees he'd had while gazing at the Streatham CCTV footage along with the two DCs that Lynley had borrowed from DI Hale. The result of their efforts consisted of nineteen images they'd captured of individuals who'd either aroused their curiosity or, on the day or the night of her attack, had needed to ring the buzzer in order to enter the building in which Teo Bontempi lived. The images weren't great. They weren't even particularly good. But they were the best he and the DCs could come up with until such time as the Met's tech wizards were able to improve them. Before he left New Scotland Yard, he instructed the DCs to sleep for two hours and then get on to their next activity, tracking down the patients whose files Lynley and Barb Havers had taken from the clinic in Kingsland High Street.

When he pulled his car in front of the Bontempis' impressive house, he felt that a kip wouldn't go amiss, but instead he finished listening to the weather report, which was promising more of that which the country had been enduring for weeks. At least, he thought wryly, the railway hadn't yet shut down. It was known to do so for any number of weather-related events including—memorably—an excess of autumn leaves on the tracks one year. But the trains were running nicely for now, albeit not exactly on time. And although the Circle Line was down for work on a section—but, really, when was the Circle Line not down for work on a section? he wondered—all the rest of the London Underground lines were operational as well.

He took a moment to ring his mother, who by now would have risen, made coffee, and begun to wonder why he hadn't shown his face at her breakfast table. When she learned he'd spent the night at work, she wasn't happy—"You are eating properly, are you, Jewel?" being her first question—but once he assured her that he'd have a hot lunch in place of the hot breakfast at home that he missed, she was happy. At that, he got out of the car into the morning air. It was still cool, and it smelled of lawn clippings from an adjacent property whose owner was either ignoring the hosepipe ban or somehow using dish or laundry water to keep the grass growing.

The pedestrian gate was off the latch, so he entered and went to the door. He carried with him the stack of images from the CCTV footage. He rang the bell and waited for a bit before he rang it again, twice this time. He heard footsteps on the entry floor, bolts being drawn back, and then he was face-to-face with Solange Bontempi, dressed neatly in a slim trouser suit, a conservative blouse buttoned to her throat. Her hair was neatly done as well, a bun from which no hair escaped, low on her neck.

Solange looked surprised to see him, but she seemed to realise what his visit could imply because she quickly said, "Detective. You have brought us news?"

"Got a few questions only, 'm afraid," he replied. "C'n I come in?"

She held the door open. "Yes. Of course. I'm assembling a breakfast tray for Cesare. Is it Rosie you wish to see? Me? My husband? Come with me, please."

Nkata followed her into the kitchen, where several packages wrapped in butcher's paper sat on the worktop along with a bowl of fruit, a large wedge of cheese, and a basket of hard bread rolls. A quite small, strange-looking double-decker coffee pot sat on a burner of the stove. It was hissing and emitting steam, so he reckoned Solange was cooking up an espresso.

She pulled a tray from a nearby cupboard and said, "Cesare, he has never become English when it comes to his breakfast. Well, come to think, he has never become English in his eating at all." She began to take some unidentifiable and presumably Italian meat from the butcher's wrapping and she placed this on a plate along with a slice of extremely aromatic cheese that, to his surprise, caused Nkata's mouth to water. She took a tin from inside the unlit oven, opened it, and removed what looked like a poppy seed cake. This she sliced, shot Nkata a glance, and sliced a second piece for him. Then came the bread—two rolls—both for Cesare. She raised an eyebrow at Nkata but he demurred. Once she had added fruit to the tray, she covered the entire thing with a tea towel and looked at the clock. "His carer is late," she said. "Usually she comes at half-past six. I thought it was she at the door, having forgotten her key." She turned off the heat beneath the strange coffee maker, but she left the pot where it was although she fetched a small jug and filled it with milk. She said, "He won't use the milk but if I don't include it, he will wonder why." She sighed. "Men. Now tell me your questions."

"You don't want to take the tray . . . ?" He tilted his head the way they'd come, which would give her access to the stairs.

"It can wait a few minutes. He's still asleep. Or he was when I left the room. What is it you wish to ask me?"

"When the last time was you talked to Teo." He consulted his notebook to make sure of the details. "You said she came here three weeks past to visit her dad. Did you talk to her af'er that?"

Solange glanced at a calendar on the wall, hanging above a telephone. She said slowly, "Yes, but the answer is more difficult. I cannot be sure . . . I think ten days ago?" Solange explained that while Teo had made an effort to see her father once or twice each week since his stroke, there had been times when she couldn't because of her work. But whether she was coming to Hampstead or not, she generally rang once a day. "We worried when we did not hear from her in the days that followed her last visit. There was only one phone call. And then we discovered why."

"When she was found in her flat, you mean?"

"Yes. You did not know her, of course," Solange said with a small sad smile, "but Teo was the daughter any parent would want."

"An' did you?" Nkata asked.

"What?"

"Did you want her?"

Solange drew back, and her expression was clearly confused. "I am not sure what you mean," she said. "Of course we wanted her."

"But th'way I un'erstan' things, you wanted a baby to adopt but you ended up with more 'n' that. So I'm wond'ring if tha's something you could've done without. An older girl."

"Oh no," Solange replied. "No, no. We wanted a baby, of course, and we learned the baby we'd arranged to adopt had an older sister. We were hesitant about that at first. But then we met her—Adaku, as she was called then—and really, to meet her was to be immediately enchanted, and even if that hadn't been the case, we wouldn't have separated the girls. They'd already lost so much: their mother, their father, their aunt, their cousins. It would have been cruel to take from either one of them the last blood tie they had."

"Di' she know that?" he asked.

There was a door to the outside at the far end of the kitchen and it had opened as Nkata was speaking. In came a young woman whom Solange greeted with, "Here is Katie at last," to which Katie responded, "I am *so* sorry, *Madame*. Please. Let me take over."

"We are lucky he's not roaring by now." Solange took a smallish china coffee pot and into this she poured a viscous brew that resembled long-exhausted motor oil. This she put onto the tray, which Katie then took and, with a friendly nod at Nkata, left the kitchen.

"Your question again?" Solange said to Nkata.

"If Teo knew she was wanted."

Solange placed a cube of sugar into a cup and poured another espresso. She offered it to Nkata, but he had no intention of downing any more caffeine. She stirred the espresso and said, "We told her often. I am certain she knew. And she was the very heart of Cesare. They were . . . that expression . . . thieves in the night? No, no. That is not it."

"Thick as thieves?"

"Yes, this is the one. But I have never understood what it means."

He smiled. "Nothin' far as I know. But I get your meaning."

"Yes, they were very—"

"*Maman!*" Rosie burst into the room. She said something to her mother in rapid French as she more firmly belted the yellow dressing gown she was wearing. "Why didn't you *tell* me?"

Apparently understanding the implication, Solange said, "I did not wake you because the detective asked to speak with *me*."

"Wanted to bring your mum into the picture of where we are in the 'vestigation," Nkata said. "I been asked to keep you in the picture. The family, I mean."

Rosie said, narrowing her eyes, "And where are you, then?"

"Your mum's been telling me how you and Teo got adopted. And I got to say: Seems like you been interpreting things a bit wrong."

Nkata saw a pulse beating in her temple. He decided she was trying to test the wind: like which direction was it blowing and how strongly and was there anything she ought to be doing before it turned into a gale. Finally, she said, "Have I? How odd."

"We c'n agree on that. So I'm wondering why you tol' me that your parents were forced to take Teo when all's they wanted was you. How'd that get all mixed up in your mind?"

"Heavens, Rosie," this from her mother. "How could you ever have thought that? Did Teo think that? Did she say something to you?"

"We can talk later," Rosie said. "I have to get ready for work just now."

"Can't let you do that till we've talked, you 'n' me," Nkata told her. He handed her the stack of photos he'd brought. "Anyone here familiar to you?"

She looked at the first and the second and frowned. "I don't see how anyone could be identified from these." She squinted at them, as if that would make the photos sharper. After she'd gone through them all, she shook her head and passed them back to Nkata with a "sorry," to which he said, "Tha's fine, innit. We're working on making the images better. Takes time, that. You can give another look when we get better ones." He took note that she didn't appear excited by the prospect. He said, "I need to know bit more 'bout your thing with your sister."

"What 'thing' is this meant to be?" she asked him.

"Well, seems to me you're not telling the story of you an' Teo the way it's meant to be told. If tha's the case, somethin's going on. 'Specially in light of the row you two had."

He gave Solange a glance. "Seems things 'tween Rosie and her sister weren't like how she wanted them to look. Seems like Rosie's not telling the story like it should be told. That the case, something's going on. 'Specially since they had a row heard on all sides of Teo's flat."

"A row? Rosie, what is this?"

"Rosie tol' me it was 'bout Teo not coming round to see their dad often enough. But from talking to you, seems like that's not the case, either."

Solange took a step back from the worktop where she'd been standing since Katie's arrival. She said, "Rosie, did you . . . ?" And then after a moment for thought, "Whyever would you lie to the police, Belle?"

"Because," Rosie said, "what Teo and I talked about was none of their business. She'd thrown him away, *Maman*. She didn't want him. All she wanted was Africa. *Africa*. And whatever else Ross ever was to her, he wasn't Africa and he couldn't begin to pretend he was. That mattered to her. It didn't matter to me. It doesn't matter to me and it never will."

"What do you mean with this 'doesn't matter to me' you speak of, Rosie?"

"Reckon it goes back to her sister's marriage and to her splitting up with her husband," Nkata said.

"Is that true?" Solange asked her daughter.

"He was over her," Rosie said. "She didn't want him, and he was finally over it, he was over her. I wouldn't ever've thrown him away. He knew that and he still knows it. *We're* together now and she can't abide that. She didn't want him but I wasn't meant to have him, either. Only it doesn't matter now because it's too late."

Solange went to the table beneath the kitchen window. She sat. Nkata remained where he was, leaning against the stainless-steel cooker, his arms crossed. Rosie clutched her dressing gown at her throat. She said, "I loved him first, *Maman*. He saved me. Remember? I would've drowned in the sea, but he saved me. He saw and he came into the water and I was floundering and *no* one saw but him. And he said 'No worries, Rosie, I've got you,' and from there, he saved me. I knew we were meant, after that. From that moment, I *knew*."

Solange said, "You were six years old, Rosie. Everyone went into the water to help you. Ross got to you first. That's all."

"No! It was Ross. We were meant, him and me. And then Teo got in the way and she didn't even love him. She never loved him and he threw away all his love on her. But that's over now and I'm here, and I'm with him, and she can't stand it. She never loved him but she doesn't want me to love him either. But she's too late to stop us from what we want, Ross 'n' me. I can do what she can't and what she never could and what she didn't want to do anyway."

Nkata looked from Rosie to Solange and then back to Rosie as Solange said, "What did Teo not want to do?"

With a glance at Nkata—perhaps evaluating his response to what she would say—she said, "I'll tell you but we meant it for later, after all this, after Teo . . . It's got all mixed up. We were both going to tell you. Me and Ross together. Ross and me with you and *Papá*. Teo didn't want a baby, not Ross's baby, not anyone's baby. But I did and I do and it's finally happening and that's what I went to tell her."

Nkata said, "You went to tell Teo that you and Ross're having a baby?"

"Yes! That's exactly what I did." Rosie gave a defiant toss of her head, of the sort one saw in television dramas. It seemed more for effect than anything else. She said, "She was going to know sooner or later that Ross and I are together. We've been together for months and months. I wanted him. He wanted me. I'm giving him the baby he wanted from her."

Solange, Nkata saw, had closed her eyes. She was sitting in the same position, save for her right hand, which she'd raised to her forehead. She murmured, "Rosie. *Mon dieu*, Belle."

"What?" Rosie demanded. "Ross and I are giving you the grandchild you want and don't lie and say you don't want grandchildren because I know you do. Ross's parents are just the same and they'll be over the moon once we tell them."

"What did you say to her?" Solange asked her daughter. She dropped her hand from her forehead.

Rosie replied with, "*Maman,* she was dangling out hope to him. That's what she does. I wanted her to stop it, so I told her. What difference does it make? She didn't love him. She didn't want him. She didn't want a baby with him, she—"

"Of course she wanted a baby with him!" Solange cried. "They tried and tried but she was damaged. She'd *been* damaged for nearly thirty years."

Rosie stared at her mother. She looked at Nkata. He kept his face without expression. Rosie said, "What do you mean, damaged?"

Solange began to weep. She tried to speak. Failing, she got to her feet and hurried from the room.

Rosie turned to Nkata. "What did she mean?"

He saw no purpose in keeping her in the dark, so he said, "Your sister got cut bad b'fore you were born. In Nigeria."

"What d'you mean, cut bad?"

"She got circumcised. Or whatever you want to call it. Serious bad, this was. I expect they"—with a nod at the door to indicate her parents—"di'n't want you to know. Or she di'n't want you to know."

Rosie swallowed. Her lips looked quite dry. "You're lying," she said. "That's what the police do. They lie to people to get them to talk about things they don't want to talk about."

"Not the case," he said. "On the telly, p'rhaps, but not for real. And with this, there wouldn't be any need to lie."

"But Ross never said. He would've said. He would've told me."

"Could be he di'n't want you in his private business. I mean his business with your sister. Could be he knew she di'n't want you told. Could be he respected that."

"She didn't *want* him. He was *over* her." Her gaze dropped from Nkata's face to the floor. She added, "Oh . . . please."

THE MOTHERS SQUARE
LOWER CLAPTON
NORTH-EAST LONDON

Changing the soiled sheets on Lilybet's bed gave Mark Phinney the opportunity he wanted. It was always a two-person job, this morning made exigent because of the foul-smelling excretion that had seeped from Lilybet's body and her nappy during the night. So disgusting was the odour that he found he could not breathe through his nose. Pete managed to, despite the smell. He couldn't understand how she was able. But then, she had always been a woman fully capable of rising to whatever occasion needed her to be involved in it.

She looked as she always looked, despite the early hour. She was calm and composed, her white T-shirt tucked neatly into her blue jeans and her hair swept back and fixed behind her ears. There were grey strands in it here and there. She would never be bothered to colour them.

They'd done the cleanup of Lilybet together, one of them stripping her of her pyjamas and nappy as the other held her upright. He had sponged off the residue of her accident—as they always called it—while Pete murmured and comforted her with a soft song comprising nonsense words set to "*Con Te Partiró*" by that blind Italian bloke whose name he could never recall. After the sponging, they transferred Lilybet to the bath, and they were in the midst of washing her from head to toe when Robertson arrived. He called out a hello, to which Mark responded, "In here," and the nurse searched them out. Mark heard him pause at Lilybet's bedroom door and say, "Oh dear," and then call to them, "Shall I handle this or help with the bath?" It didn't matter to Mark as both needed to be done. It mattered to Pete, who said, "The bed please, Robertson," because she didn't want Lilybet to be humiliated by what was going on despite no one knowing if humiliation was in her repertoire of reactions.

It was fine with him, Mark thought. It gave him more time to consider what Pete might have taken to one of Paulie's two pawnshops. It also gave him more time to consider why she'd needed—or wanted—to pawn anything in the first place. He didn't know which worried him more: the what of it or the why.

He asked himself if he truly needed or even wanted an answer to either of the questions. Was it any of his business? Under normal circumstances he might have said it was not. Under the circumstances of her having known about Teo and having also communicated with Teo, he had to say it was.

He knew the physical part of his relationship with Teo would not bother her. Whether it comprised actual intercourse or something short of intercourse, she would not worry. She'd been encouraging him for years to find—as she put it—a release. And while she didn't know that the way he'd wanted Teo and fantasised about Teo had come to very little in the end, what she'd apparently worked out was exactly to what extent his heart—rather than his body—was compromised. Here was her terror set before her: that her own encouragement of his sexual infidelity may have led him to find someone with whom he could have a complete relationship, that he might then leave her—Pete—because he'd come to see that the half life she offered was far less than what he'd thought he could endure. He knew that the fear of desertion had long been the reason that Pete shouldered most of the burden of caring for their daughter. More than anything, she wanted to seem fully capable of handling everything so that he wouldn't leave.

"Up?" Pete was saying to Lilybet. "Ready to get out of the bath, my love?" She lifted their daughter, who was mostly dead weight. The years had made Pete quite strong.

Mark reached for the big towel in which they wrapped her post-bathing. It was a childish thing with a duck's head and the fixings to turn it into a cape. While Pete held Lilybet steady, he tucked the towel round her thin body and plopped the duck upon her head. "Look at you!" he said, striving for lightness.

"We forgot her chair," Pete said to him. "Can you fetch it, Mark?"

He could and he did. Robertson was just finishing up the bed, and when he saw what Mark had come for, he said, "Let me do it. You've work today, yes?"

"Eventually," Mark said. "No rush."

"Then you get yourself something to eat. Set yourself up proper for a long day, eh?"

Mark agreed. He went to the kitchen. He put on coffee and brought cereal from the cupboard. He set everything necessary on the table.

As he went through these motions, he asked himself what truly would have happened had Teo not died. Would he have left Pietra? Would he have eventually harboured a terrible hope that Lilybet might die so that he *could* leave Pietra? He didn't want to believe that he ever would have come to that: wishing for his daughter's death so that he might be free for a woman other than her mother. But the truth was that he didn't know. Nor had he been tested because Teo had never asked a single thing of him.

Perhaps, he thought, the reality was that Teo was and always would have been a mere fantasy. Perhaps she was, during his worst moments, merely a way to occupy his mind with stories drawn from his image of what a life with her would have been like: the two of them, deeply and permanently in love, setting out on the great adventure of openly being a couple, this stunning woman on his arm and all eyes turned towards them as they . . . what? Took a skiing holiday? Dined in expensive restaurants in town? Walked in any number of London's public parks? Supported each other, listened to each other, developed interests that they could share? Men who saw them together would feel desire. Women who saw them together would experience jealousy. His family would embrace her for her warmth. Her family would embrace him for his devotion. They would have a house in town and a cottage in the country where they would . . . what? Raise vegetables? Walk their dogs? Go to the village fete hand in hand and greet their neighbours? Set off fireworks on Guy Fawkes Night? He'd entertained himself with all of these possibilities and more, because in the end it was all about what *he* wanted and never about what Teo was suffering. And why was that? Because he hadn't known she was suffering, because she hadn't told him she was suffering, because while he could easily imagine every one of his dreams being fulfilled by her, he never once asked himself what her dreams were or even if he was remotely capable of fulfilling them.

He became aware of a conversation Robertson and Pete were having. Robertson's voice came to him first, saying, "You got to watch that, you do. Could be she's building an intolerance to something and not the reverse, eh? What does the GP say?"

"I've not phoned him."

"Well, you best do it before things get worse. That's what you got to keep in mind, Pete. With special conditions like this one, things c'n always get worse."

Mark understood that they were talking about Lilybet and that he hadn't a clue what their concern was. In this too, he was at fault. He hadn't been paying close attention to anything beyond himself for at least a year. His sin hadn't been the act of wanting something, though. It had been the act of *blindly* wanting something, which rendered him ignorant of everything else.

He needed to speak to Pete directly, he thought. He needed to read her face for the truth or a lie. Pete didn't lie well—in his experience hardly anyone did save psychopaths—so if he spoke to her, he would know both the what of it and the why. Even if it took them to the truth of his feelings about Teo. Even if it took them to the truth of what could happen to destroy their world, as pathetically small as it was.

"Here we are, Daddy!" Pete called out as she rolled Lilybet into the kitchen. "Someone wants scrambled eggs and toast this morning. With butter and strawberry jam. Doesn't that sound good? Can you make that for this someone, Daddy? Or I can do it. It's easy as anything. Matter of fact, you sit down. Just cereal for you? That's not good. Let's have a real breakfast for once, all three of us together. Robertson too, if he wants. Robertson," she called in the direction of Lilybet's bedroom. "Eggs and toast? Strawberry jam?"

"Let me do it, Pete."

"Nonsense. You've always done more than your share. Hasn't he, Lilybet? Hasn't your daddy always done more than his share?"

Lilybet lolled in her wheelchair. She waved her hands.

"She's clapping!" Pietra said. "She understands."

"Pete, we need to talk," Mark said.

"But look at her clapping! She's clapping! She's *never* done that."

"Robertson?" Mark called. "Will you join us?" And when the man appeared in the kitchen doorway, laundry bundled against his stomach, "I must speak to Pete for a moment. Will you see to Lilybet?"

"'Course," Robertson said. "She c'n help me make scrambled eggs, can't you, Lily?"

Lilybet waved her hands.

Mark took his wife's arm and led her to their bedroom. He closed the door. He faced her.

"Can we talk about the pawnshop?" he asked.

She cocked her head. "What about the pawnshop? *What* pawnshop? One of your brother's?"

"I expect it's the one Stuart runs in The Narrow Way. You know him, Pete: Paulie's brother-in-law. Paulie runs the shop at the bottom of the street; Stuart runs the shop at the top." Mark was carrying the pawn ticket in his trouser pocket, and he brought it out, centred on his palm, and showed it to her. "I've been wondering what it is that you pawned. I've also been wondering why you pawned it."

She stood quite still with her gaze on the pawn ticket. He waited. She said nothing at all.

"Pete?"

"Nothing," she said. "I don't know what that pawn ticket's for or where it came from. I haven't pawned anything. What on earth do I have to pawn?" She gestured round the room, by which he took it that she meant the entire flat. "Honestly, Mark. I mean it. What have I to pawn?"

"If you needed the money, why didn't you come to me? I've never held back, have I? When you've needed something, when Lilybet's needed something . . . Pete, d'you want to tell me what's going on?"

"Nothing's 'going on,'" she said, making inverted commas in the air as she used his own words. What could possibly be 'going on'?" The air-sketched inverted commas again. "And when on earth would I have time to go to one of the pawnshops anyway?"

"This was in your purse," he said.

"Are you actually going through—"

"I told you. I was pinching a couple of notes from your wallet. That's where I found the ticket."

"So why didn't you ask me straightaway?"

That was the question, wasn't it? And he knew the answer well enough: he hadn't actually wanted to know. So why was that, Mark? he asked himself. Are you afraid of something, mate?

He said, "I didn't think to. But now I'm asking."

"You're asking about nothing," she replied. "I'm going back to the kitchen now, Mark. I'm needed to help with Lilybet's breakfast."

She turned to leave him then, with the pawn ticket feeling like something that was searing his palm. Before she was out of the room, however, he spoke.

"Your secret's safe with Paulie," he told her. "He wouldn't tell me. Does *he* know why you've pawned something, then?"

She shook her head. "I've pawned nothing, Mark."

She did leave at that point, but not before he asked himself why she hadn't once looked at him directly after he'd produced the pawn ticket for her to see.

———

HACKNEY
NORTH-EAST LONDON

"I've told you everything, Sergeant. There's nothing more that I can add."

"Happens that's probably not true. Can I come in?"

"Have you *any* idea what time it is?"

"Look. I'm as cheesed off about this as you are, Mr. Carver," Barbara Havers replied. She looked over her shoulder. From the farmyard across the lane, a rooster was raising absolute bloody hell. She said, "You don't actually sleep through that, do you?"

"Silicone earplugs. They were my first investment when I took the flat."

"I hope your second was incense," she said. "Now. Again. Can I come in? I expect you don't want the neighbours to see me. They might get ideas and then—whoops—your reputation goes straight down the drain."

So far, Barbara thought, the only good thing about her morning was that she'd actually been able to sink her gnashers into a Wildlicious Wild!Berry Pop-Tart. Well, two of them if she was being brutally honest about her caloric intake. She went for two in order to make up for time lost, and she served them to herself alongside a very powerful cup of PG Tips. She'd had to eat the Pop-Tarts on the way to Hackney, though, while most of her mug of tea got spilled onto the Mini's floor. The fact that she hadn't spilled tea on herself was mildly cheering, however.

Her mobile had rung as the two Pop-Tarts were coming out of the toaster, filling her cottage with the scent of a thousand and one browned preservatives. So she'd been able to wrap them up in a kitchen towel and grab her tea once Winston Nkata had filled her in on the subject of his early day chin-wag with Rosie Bontempi and her mother. It was this conversation, as reported by Nkata, that had set her on the journey to have another natter with Ross Carver. As the hour was ungodly, she reckoned she'd find him at home, which she had done. And he'd been busy since they'd last spoken. The number of cardboard boxes on his balcony had been reduced by half, no doubt due to the others' being delivered to the Streatham flat.

He said to her, "As I'm up and regrettably awake, you may as well come in," and he left her in the doorway as if allowing her time to make up her mind.

Aside from a pair of sweatpants that hung rather too loosely round his waist, Carver wasn't yet dressed. He had the sort of upper body that came from weight training, though. It was swoon-worthy, as Dee Harriman probably would have put it. He went into the bedroom, but Barbara reckoned she wasn't meant to follow him there. She heard a drawer open and then shut and in under a minute he was back with her, having changed into blue jeans and a T-shirt with the London Marathon's logo on it. His feet remained bare, and his disarranged hair fell in curls about three inches below his ears.

Since the flat was small, the kitchen was three and a half steps from the sitting room. He went to the sink and filled an electric kettle. He grabbed a mug from the cupboard and asked Barbara if she wanted a coffee. She said that she was actually more of a tea girl and wouldn't say no if he had any to hand. He said it would have to be Yorkshire. She said she doubted that a single cup of that would put hair onto her chest, although as far as her armpits went, one never knew.

He opened the fridge and grabbed a large jug of milk. She could see that nearly everything inside consisted of prepared meals. He took one of these, dumped its contents onto a plate, and shoved the plate into a microwave. After he'd set the time, he said to her, "Well? You've not come on a social call. And like I said, I've told you what I know."

"You might have done," Barbara acknowledged. "But does that mean you don't know about Rosie?"

He looked immediately wary. "What about Rosie? Has something happened to her?"

"Yes and no. Depends on how you look at *happen*. She hasn't shared the happy news with you?"

The microwave dinged and he removed the plate. He jerked open a drawer, took out some cutlery, and ate standing up, his arse against the worktop. "What're you on about?" he asked her.

"Pregnancy is what I'm on about."

"Pregnancy?"

"Rosie's in the family way. She says it's yours. She claims it's meant to be; it's written across the heavens, it's a sign of your true and abiding love and all that rubbish. According to her, it's been in the stars just short of forever. You and her, I mean. Not you and Teo."

Ross had ceased eating although he still held his plate. He said, "How could she . . . How did it happen?"

Barbara said, "I expect it happened in the normal way 'nless the angel Gabriel introduced her to the Holy Ghost while she was washing her knickers. You seem gobsmacked, Mr. Carver. Or am I reading you wrong?"

He turned and put his plate in the sink, apparently having lost his appetite. He put a teabag in a mug and then spooned coffee into a press. As she watched him, Barbara went on. "So if Rosie is telling us the truth and you and she were dancing the mattress polka, could be that's what Teo wanted to have a natter with you about. Rosie told her, see. That seems to be what they were shouting about—her and Teo, that is—when the neighbours heard the ruckus. She told my colleague, at first, that they were going at it over visits to their dad. But *now* Rosie's claiming that it was all about the pregnancy and you. She says Teo didn't want you. She says that Teo threw you in the dustbin or to the dogs or whatever. So I need to ask you: Was this Rosie thing a one-off or was it something else? I ask cos we're having a bloody time of it trying to sort her out. Was she your new and true or had you been diddling her on the side while you were married to her sister?"

He went to the fridge again. This time he brought out a glass bottle of some kind of juice, pomegranate or cranberry. He poured himself a glass and drank it down. The electric kettle clicked off but he made no move towards it. He appeared to have forgotten her tea and the coffee press entirely. He said, "Are you always this crude or am I a special case for you?"

"Why don't you give me chapter and verse on your relationship with Teo Bontempi's sister, Mr. Carver? I'll try to be a good girl throughout though I can't promise I'll manage it."

"Fine. Right. Whatever." He began to see to the coffee at last, as well as her tea. He shoved the mug in her direction along with a box of sugar cubes. He used the plunger on the press, taking his time about it. She said his name. He said, "Teo."

"Teo what exactly?"

"It was always Teo. I wanted Teo."

"So how'd you end up with Rosie?"

"She knew it. I was clear. I didn't lie to her."

"What're you on about?"

"Rosalba *knew* it was only Teo for me. Everyone knew it. I've told you this. We'd been together since she was sixteen. But when Teo wanted me to leave, Rosalba felt like . . . I don't know . . . She wanted to be a source of comfort, a shoulder to cry on, whatever you want to call it. She wanted to be, like, a confidante. She proposed herself as a go-between. That's how it started."

"Seems like you used more than her shoulder," Barbara observed.

"I didn't pursue her. She would just show up. Once it started—"

"'It'?"

"The sex, all right? Once it started . . . Each time I told myself, Only this once, I'll do it only this once. And I meant it and I told her I meant it and then she would show up again. What could I bloody *do*?"

"Not letting her through the door comes to mind. But you did let her in, right? Inside this place? Yes?"

He raised his gaze as if looking for assistance from the heavens, a way to make what had happened understandable and himself blameless. Barbara half expected him to cry out *What's a man to do?* Instead, he said, "I let her in. She's beautiful. Everything about her is gorgeous. She wanted me and she made that clear. And I was low. I felt crushed. And this isn't an excuse—all right?—it's just a reason. It's why it happened. I didn't love her. I don't love her. I told her that. I said, 'This isn't love, Rosalba. Don't think this is love. I love your sister.' And she said . . . God help me, she said, 'Pretend I'm Teo, then. Call me Teo.' So that's what I did."

Barbara blinked although what she wanted to do was to strike the side of her head like a cartoon character, making sure she'd heard him correctly. "Are you saying she played a role for you? You did the deed because she was willing to pretend she was her sister?"

"I'm saying that was the how and the why. It gave me an excuse to have her in bed and she knew that for me to do it—which *she* wanted by the way—I would have to have an excuse. And when she told me she was taking precautions, I believed her."

"Yeah. Well. Seems she wasn't. She's told her mum the happy news, by the way. When my colleague was chatting to her, her mum was there. He'd gone to check on some details she'd given him earlier."

"What sort of details?"

"She'd told my colleague that her parents hadn't wanted to adopt Teo, that they'd adopted Teo because it was the only way they could get her—Rosie. She told my colleague the deal from the orphanage was take the sister or you can't have the baby."

"She said that? Rosalba?"

Barbara nodded. "Evidently, her mum set her straight." And then she added, "She also didn't know Teo had been cut."

Ross looked at the floor, drew in a breath, raised his head again to look at her. "Teo didn't want her to know. Only the people who had to know or who knew already: her parents, her GP, me."

"She talked about it on a film, did Teo."

He turned, poured some of the forgotten coffee into a mug with PIAZZA SAN MARCO scrolled on its surface along with the image of a cathedral. He said, "Why would she talk about it on a film?"

"A filmmaker was coaching girls to tell their stories. Their FGM stories? It wasn't working out like she wanted. Evidently, they were freezing up—intimidated probably—when the camera started filming. So your wife told hers. It's not being used in the final film—evidently, the filmmaker promised her—but when I went there to ask about Teo, she showed it me. She seemed . . ." Barbara looked for the right word to convey what she thought she'd seen in Teo Bontempi. "She seemed damaged, did Teo. I don't mean the mutilation. 'Course she was damaged that way. I mean otherwise. It was like part of her . . . her essence? Her spirit? What I mean is that it looked like that had been cut up as well."

Carver took up his mug of coffee and walked out of the kitchen and into the sitting room. He went to the balcony but did not step outside. He stood there looking down at the lane and at the miniature farm beyond it. He said, "Most of the time, she hid that well, what you're saying. It was a part of her—that rupture in her spirit—that I thought might be repaired."

"D'you mean through some kind of counselling?"

"Counselling, yes. But also physically. I've already told you this: I wanted her to see someone. She wouldn't. She kept saying 'What's the point?' It was part of why I couldn't stop insisting and she couldn't take it from me any longer."

Barbara twigged what he might have meant. She said, "We're back to *evaluation*, then, what was written in her diary for July 24."

Carver turned from the window. "Could she possibly have seen someone about what had happened to her?"

"You said earlier that she rang you and wanted to see you. Could that be why?"

"Because she'd been to a surgeon? But if that's what *evaluation* means, why did she wait all those days to tell me? If that's even what she wanted to talk about."

"Could be she wanted to have a word about Rosie, then, about you putting Rosie up the spout. Or both, eh? Along the lines of 'I did this for you, I did this for us, and all the time you were bonking my sister.'"

"I didn't want to. I didn't intend to. I—"

"Right-oh. But why do I think Rosie didn't tie you down and have her way with you? How'd Teo sound on the phone?"

"She didn't ring me. She texted."

"Was that normal?"

"No. Why? What're you thinking? I mean, the text did come from her phone. You're not implying someone else . . . The phone was there in the bedroom. I saw it."

"We can't find it."

"What about cell towers?"

"That takes time. We're on it, but . . ." She lifted her shoulders. "It's a case of wait in line."

"What about records of her calls?"

"We're onto that as well." She fished round in her shoulder bag and brought out one of her business cards. She said, "I expect you watch telly, so you know the routine well enough: You think of anything, you see anything, you hear anything—and believe me, I don't bloody care what it is—you ring me. You hear from her sister, I want to know. You hear from her parents, I want to know. You recall a detail you haven't mentioned, I want to know. D'we understand each other?"

He took the card from her and put it in his pocket. He said, "Yes. We do."

KENNINGTON
SOUTH LONDON

Deborah felt uneasy, her mind running away with thoughts that had the power to intrude upon her work. In this case, those thoughts had to do with the discussion-cum-argument she'd had with her husband and her father, followed by a late-night phone call she had received from Narissa Cameron.

Deborah had thought she intended to talk about her documentary, but as it turned out, Narissa was ringing for another reason entirely. She'd been rumbled by her parents, Narissa said. The police had come calling, having been alerted by a neighbour. She'd got home from Orchid House to find a note on her door in her father's handwriting. Seven words: *Come above please. The police have been.* When she read this, she knew she'd been discovered.

"It was that bloody kitten," Narissa said. "I knew this would happen once I heard about the kitten."

Knowing that the police would hardly have come calling about a kitten, Deborah put the pieces together in short order, aligning them with the hushed conversations she'd heard Narissa and Zawadi having. She said to Narissa, "You've got Bolu Akin."

"They weren't supposed to know. Or, at least, I didn't want to tell them."

"Your parents?"

"I didn't want to risk *anything* that might get me thrown into the street. But, once the cops left, my dad went down to my flat—the basement flat?—and he found her. He'd seen the news. My mum as well. So they knew who she was. My dad's funding the major part of the documentary, and he's made it clear that he'll pull the plug on the project if I don't sort this out. Deborah, I bloody well hate to ask this, but—"

"She won't be safe here," Deborah told Narissa. She detailed her father's news-viewing habits as well as his opinions on the subject of Boluwatife Akin's disappearance. She went on to explain her husband's position in the matter: this is something for the police to handle. "If you bring her here, one of them will ring the local station. I swear it, Narissa. My dad believes Charles Akin, start to finish. My husband doesn't want us involved in what he sees as a police situation. I hope you know I'd take her in an instant, but I can't get either of them on board with the idea of her actually being in danger."

Narissa cursed quietly. Deborah said to her, "What about that woman you ring?"

"What woman? What are you talking about?"

"The woman from your meeting?"

"Victoria?" She was silent for a moment.

"Could she keep her for a night or two?"

"If Zawadi finds out I've moved her, *she'll* pull the bloody plug. Jesus on the Cross, *none* of this would happen if Zawadi would start using protection orders."

"Protection orders?"

"Don't tell me you don't know about them, Deborah. Jesus. Never mind. You're white, you've got buckets of it, so why would you?"

"Buckets of what?"

"Chelsea? Please."

"All right. All right. I'd say *sorry*, but we've been there, haven't we? What's a protection order, please?"

"A weapon against FGM. It puts parents on notice, requires them to hand over their passports, lets them know they'll be arrested, charged, and probably convicted if they cut their daughter or have someone else do it. Anyone can file one, but Zawadi won't use them. If she would do, Bolu could go home straightaway."

"So why won't she—"

"Because she sees protection orders as just another way whites can pretend to be helping while simultaneously doing sod all to improve anyone's life. And in case you haven't noticed, Zawadi does not believe in the 'good works' of white people, anyway—inverted commas. Since it was white people who came up with the idea of protection orders—"

"Hang on. Are you saying that protection orders have the support of *no* Black activists?"

"I don't mean that. There're plenty of Black supporters. But Zawadi believes that far too many people are involved in obtaining a protection order, and they're generally white people. She believes it's easier and quicker to place a potential victim into the home of a supportive anti-FGM family."

"For how long, though?"

"Just till social workers can establish a relationship that ensures the girl won't ever be cut."

But of course that was exactly what Charles Akin and his wife were refusing to do: establish a relationship with a social worker. It was a matter of principle to them, and so far it seemed that they would not relent.

Because she couldn't risk bringing Bolu into her home to ease Narissa's conflict with her parents, Deborah took the decision to speak with Zawadi about Bolu, her parents, protection orders, and the entire situation the very next morning. She managed to get Zawadi's home address from Narissa, and in advance of going to Orchid House for another photography session, she went early to Kennington.

She found the address she was looking for in Hillingdon Street. It was an immense building of grey concrete, with laundry hanging limply on balconies—hoping for a drying breeze—and satellite dishes winking in the sun. She could have been anywhere in town and she'd find these towers. This particular one was set among four others, a stone's throw from Kennington Park and perhaps a quarter hour's walk from The Oval.

Deborah was just getting out of her car when Zawadi drove past her, herself heading towards the tower blocks, not away from them. She braked when, apparently, in her rearview mirror, she saw Deborah waving. She reversed the car, came up alongside her, and lowered her window. Before she had a chance to ask what Deborah was doing there, Deborah herself asked if she and Zawadi could talk about Boluwatife Akin.

Zawadi's eyes narrowed. "What about her? If you're here to pry information out of me—"

"Narissa rang me last night. She wanted to bring her to me, but my dad's siding with Bolu's dad, and my husband . . . It's just that I can't trust either of them." Deborah gave Zawadi the same information that Narissa had given to her: her parents, the advent of the police, the discovery of Bolu in Narissa's flat.

Zawadi greeted all this with an admirable stillness. She contemplated Deborah for a good stretch of seconds before she said, "Come with me." She drove into the car park that served the closest tower. When Deborah parked alongside her, she was grabbing a shoulder bag from her car's back seat. She gave Deborah a glance and said, "I've had to do the school run today. Have you rung the flat?"

"I've only just arrived. I didn't know you had children, Zawadi."

"Ned. He's twelve. So what do you want, exactly? If you can't take Bolu, what've we got to talk about?"

"Actually, I thought . . . perhaps in your flat?"

Zawadi looked at her watch and said, "Ten minutes, then," and she led the way to the tower. Inside the building, she rang for the lift, and while they waited, she said, "I expect your dad saw the television interview."

"He's followed the story from the start. It's to do with my being his only child. He feels for her dad. He believes him."

Zawadi looked at her, head to toe in that way she had, telegraphing disapproval and dislike. "What about you?"

"I'm on your side completely when it comes to FGM. But if you don't mind . . . ?" She indicated the lift, meaning, Can we wait?

The lift arrived and once inside, Zawadi pressed the button for the seventh floor. There, she led the way down a dim corridor. There were lights aplenty hanging from the ceiling, but more of them were burnt out rather than actually illuminating the space. The walls were a bit of a patchwork, where tagging had been painted over without bothering to match the colour exactly or even—in some cases—remotely. Originally, the walls appeared to be yellow—one of those depressing shades that make an appearance in council housing throughout the country—but they were now mottled: cream, beige, mint green, pink, and white doing the honours. Nothing hung on them save a cork bulletin board halfway down. Zawadi's flat was next to this.

Inside, things were in the kind of disarray that attends the presence of a child, a jumble in need of someone to straighten it out. Most of it consisted of items belonging to an active boy: a small drone, a remote-control racing car, Rollerblades, board games, a skateboard, an Xbox, trainers, several footballs. There was a single bedroom with two beds in it. There didn't seem to be an adult male in residence.

Zawadi appeared to read Deborah's mind because she said, "It's the two of us, me and Ned. His dad found someone he liked better."

Zawadi didn't look like someone who was planning to sit, so Deborah remained on her feet and tried to work out how she was going to approach a subject liable to make Zawadi's brain explode. She thought about where and how to begin. She decided upon, "It's this. I find I'm having some doubts about Bolu's parents."

"Good." Zawadi began putting the room back in order, using a large wicker basket to collect Ned's possessions, taking the care of someone who knew that if something broke, it wasn't going to be replaced anytime soon. "You're meant to have doubts. Everyone should be having doubts."

"Yes. Right. But what I mean is that I'm having doubts about—"

"You listen to me, eh? This bloke who calls himself Charles *Akin* used to be Chimaobi Akinjide and he is clever like a fox. He takes in a question and knows from the words and the way they're spoken the emotion he's meant to show. He manufactures that emotion on the spot, he redirects the conversation, and the result is sympathy for what *he's* going through, never mind sympathy for his child. That's what you're feeling, isn't it? Sympathy for Mr. Akin? That's why you've come. Am I right?"

"It's just that I'm not certain it's the right thing: keeping Bolu away from her parents."

"Really? And why d'you think your opinion counts for anything?"

"Because I care that—"

"You listen to me. Mr. Charles Akin, Esquire, knows what he has to do to have her returned because we're not exactly asking for a ransom, are we. But he won't do what it takes to have Bolu back home. He claims it's the principle involved. And I tell you this, until tha' man cooperates, there's nothing more to be said."

"But you can see how he must feel? That he's being targeted?"

Zawadi gave a derisive laugh. "What can you possibly know about being targeted?" She held the wicker basket against her hip and said, "This isn't *about* his precious feelings. This's about a vulnerable child."

"But he's under scrutiny *because* he's Nigerian, isn't he?"

Zawadi grabbed up a sweatshirt and one trainer from the sofa. She shoved both into the wicker basket. She said, "Of *course* he's under scrutiny because he's Nigerian. He'd be under scrutiny if he was So-mali. He'd be under scrutiny if he was from *any* country where girls are still being cut."

"But he's been in the UK forever and his wife's English. *And* she's a doctor. It just seems to me that there's nothing to suggest—"

"Are you forgetting the girl *came* to Orchid House?" Zawadi de-manded. "She walked straight through the doors on her own two feet. Am I meant to ignore that because the television news and half a dozen tabloids see this man as a victim of some sort of injustice while all along the real victims—the hundreds of thousands, the millions of them—don't even arouse enough outrage in people that they stir themselves to do something about it?"

"Narissa did tell me about protection orders."

"We will *not* discuss bloody protection orders!"

"Why not? Listen, Zawadi. Please. I've followed the story in the broadsheets as well as the tabloids. I've seen the story on television news. Everywhere it's the same. Do you not think that could mean—"

"What it means is that child might be in danger. What it means is that she has parents who will say anything to have her back. And hav-ing her parents swear on this or that, having them tell anyone within listening range that they would never do anything to harm their child, this means nothing, because it will not stop them from having her cut once she's back at home if that's the plan. They bloody well know the girl won't turn them over to the cops afterwards. Because if she does, they end up in prison and *then* what happens to Bolu? I'll tell you what happens to Bolu: she goes straight into Care." Zawadi gave Deborah a sharp look. She'd been restacking Ned's board games on a shelf next to a flat-screen television. She rested back on her heels and added, "You *do* know what the cut is, don't you?"

"You know that I know."

"That's good. That's fine. But you've never endured it so you have no place saying that someone else—specifically a child—is *not* in danger. In this, you're just like Narissa at the end of the day. You've got your book. She's got her film."

"Are you trying to say I'm not passionate about this? That Narissa's not passionate about this? That we're using you and Orchid House and the girls?" Deborah felt her face going red. "We wouldn't even be involved, Zawadi, if we didn't want to save these girls."

Zawadi rose from where she'd been kneeling by the coffee table. She'd gathered up the Xbox, the remote-control racing car, and one of the footballs. She said, "Your passions—both yours and Narissa's—are about your projects, and don't think I don't know that. *And* I can see how this part of the entire FGM story—Bolu's part and her parents' part—would make for a nice dramatic twist in the overall story you two are working on. That's what all this is, here and now. It's your attempt to force me into making a decision that'll give both of you a happy ending."

"That's not at all true," Deborah said. "You're starting to see enemies everywhere."

"And with bloody good reason."

"Zawadi, please. I'm *not* your enemy and you *can't* fight this war alone. You've got to know that, so why are you rejecting something that might help put an end to this?"

"Because once a girl walks through the doorway of Orchid House, I'm pledged to help her. And that means, before she's sent home I must be convinced that she will be safe. Bolu's parents have not convinced me and until they do, they're not going to see her."

"If you're arrested for kidnapping, false imprisonment of a child, or *whatever* they're going to call it, then what? How is Orchid House going to go on when you're not there to run it?"

"I expect my solicitor will ask just that question of the magistrate before it's decided to remand me into custody. Now." She looked round the sitting room and seemed to be satisfied with what she saw. "It's time for me to get to Trinity Green. There's work to be done and as you've just pointed out, I'm the only person at Orchid House who knows how to do it."

MAYVILLE ESTATE
DALSTON
NORTH-EAST LONDON

Monifa's assumption was based on what had happened to her when she was taken from the clinic on the High Street. She'd faced police officers. They'd asked questions. She'd answered them. She'd managed to do this without revealing the real reason she'd given the clinic the three hundred pounds that she explained she'd come to fetch back. She'd told them it was deposit money for a "female" procedure she'd wished to have done, but she'd changed her mind, having been told by her husband that they could not afford it, and even if they'd had the money, her body was beloved to him, just as it was. The officers had accepted this. There was nothing inside the clinic to indicate she was lying to them. So they released her, and her belief was that they'd later release Easter Lange as well. Thus the day's plan was to return once again to fetch the three hundred pounds. She took Simisola with her.

Despite the words from the Black detective on the previous evening—that the clinic was closed and, having dodged a bullet when the police showed up, Easter Lange/Mercy Hart probably wasn't going to reopen it in the same location—Monifa was determined to forge ahead because she could not afford to believe that the Black detective was telling the truth. Learning from Tani about the cutter and her presence in their home made everything far more urgent.

When she'd returned to the flat after her conversation with the detective, she'd found Abeo and Tani in the sitting room. Abeo confronted her at once, blocking her way and saying, "You bring even more trouble to this family. What did he want?"

Tani said, "Leave her alone, Pa."

Abeo replied with, "This between us is of no concern to you."

Tani gave a sharp laugh. "Yeah? *That's* what you think? I was *here*. You didn't know, did you?"

"You were here. You were there. What is this meant to tell me?"

"I was here when you brought that bloody witch doctor into the flat. You thought you were alone. You thought you could make all your plans for Simi to be cut and no one would know till it was finished. But it didn't work out that way because I heard it all, and there is no way in hell I'm letting that cow put her hands on Simi." He turned to Monifa, saying, "You tol' the cop, right? About her. The cutter."

Monifa moved her gaze away from her son. He cried out, "You had a bloody cop here to talk to you and you di'n't tell him what's going on? What's *wrong* with you? Why'd you not say—"

Abeo cut in. "Because she knows what must be done."

"*Nothing* must be done," Tani said. "An' if I see that cutter out and about, I handle her myself."

"You will do nothing."

"Don't even bet fifty p on that."

Now, in Kingsland High Street with Simisola, Monifa rang the clinic's bell. She prayed for someone to open the door. Three hundred pounds at this point would serve her well.

"Madam? Madam?"

Monifa swung round. At the doorway of Taste of Tennessee stood a man in a stained, white apron. He gestured to the building in front of which she was standing. "They've bunked off," he said. "Once the coppers came th'other day, that was it. No one's been back but the removals men. Couple more coppers 's well, but tha's the lot of it. You all right? You don't look good. Want me to ring someone?"

Monifa shook her head. She said, "It is fine. We are fine," voicing the lie she'd been telling herself for years. She thought about what she could next do, but she was without a single idea. All she had was two telephone numbers. One belonged to Easter Lange or whoever she was and it didn't matter as she wasn't taking any of Monifa's calls. The other belonged to the Black detective.

WESTMINSTER
CENTRAL LONDON

When Barbara Havers returned to New Scotland Yard, she found a large shopping bag on her desk. She frowned at the sight of it, and although a note was attached, she didn't open it. Instead, she lifted out the contents from the bag and saw that she'd been gifted with a collection of sketching pencils, a fist-size rubber, a small sketchbook, a medium sketchbook, and a ruler. Gazing at this, she knew she didn't have to open the attached note to clue her in as to the giver, but she did anyway. *I reckoned you wouldn't have the time* was written on a sheet torn from a desk calendar featuring Thoughts for the Day. Beneath the thought—"Let your eyes mirror your soul"—was the expected initial: *D*, created with a proud flourish.

Barbara sighed. Saturday was fast upon them. While Dee was not expecting great things from her in the sketching department, she *was* expecting her attendance at the sketching session, where, lurking rather suspiciously round the statue of Peter Pan, both of them would ostensibly meet several prospective men-of-their-dreams.

"Oh bloody hell," Barbara muttered. She replaced the items into the bag and shoved the bag into her desk's kneehole, determined to forget all about it, which, she knew, was going to require her to spend the next few days dodging Dorothea.

She found Lynley at the round table in the corner of his temporary office. He and Nkata were poring over a dozen photographs that formed two neat rows. To one side of these stood a thin stack of more pictures.

She said, "Carver admits it, more or less."

Nkata looked from a photo. He said, "You tell him 'bout Rosie?"

"Did. And either he's treading the boards as Hamlet in his free time or he hadn't a clue she was in the club."

"Do we know if they were actually lovers?" Lynley asked, setting aside a magnifying glass he'd been using to study areas of a picture he was holding.

"Like I said to Winnie. He admits to engaging in the plunge-o-rama with her. But he *claims* she kept after him. He didn't really want to do the business with her—so he says—but she wouldn't take no for an answer and finally, he could resist no more. He says she told him she was taking precautions. He says he told her he only had eyes for Teo, but she didn't mind and she was happy to play Teo if that suited him. Anyway, he seems to believe it's entrapment."

"I got the 'pression Rosie sees it different," Nkata said.

"What d'you think, then, Winnie? Rosie seem like the type who could whack her own sister in the head?"

"Tha's a hard call, innit," Nkata said.

"Take a chair, Barbara." Lynley moved six of the photographs so that she could see them.

"CCTV stills?" she said before she sat. Then, having looked at the pictures, she went on with, "These are rubbish. What're they filming with over there? One pixel an inch? I can barely make out the time stamps."

"They're the best we've been able to come up with so far," Lynley told her.

Nkata added, "Equipment's ancient, is what it is."

"It's what's going on that caught Winston's attention," Lynley said.

"It's not who's doing the what's going on. Admittedly, that part of the equation looks hopeless at the moment."

"Then what . . . ?" Barbara studied the pictures. While four of them showed people who entered the building alone—and, really, one had to assume the killer was alone—two of them showed a woman who'd come to the building's door to speak to the person ringing for her flat, in each case another woman. "Is this . . . Are you saying this is Teo at the door?"

"We think so. The film's gone out to digital forensics. That lot'll work it over and see what kind of improvement can be made. In the meantime, this is what we have to work with. Assuming the woman at the door is Teo—"

"Big assumption, you ask me. She looks more like a blob."

"—we've been mulling over the possibilities attendant to her coming to the door to speak with those two women instead of merely ringing them in."

"Could be she didn't know them?" Barbara offered. "Could be she knew them but didn't trust them?"

"Could be there was someone already inside her flat she didn't want these two to know about?" Nkata pointed out.

"Could be there was some*thing* inside her flat she didn't want these two to know about," Barbara added. "Also could be we bin the whole lot of these because, face it, they don't prove anything."

"Right. But there's this as well." Lynley set aside the pictures that were potentially of Teo at the door speaking to the two women. He brought forward the other pictures he and Winston had chosen. He placed them in front of Barbara.

She saw that in the first of the photos, four people were at the entry to the building, ostensibly waiting to gain admittance. In the second, three of the four people turned as if hearing something or someone behind them. In the third they were joined by an individual in a hoodie who made them five, although it was impossible to tell if the person was male or female. In the last, reduced to four again, they were departing, but without that individual who had entered in their company.

Barbara looked up from the pictures to Lynley, saying, "I'm missing something if I'm supposed to be gobsmacked, sir. Five go inside. Four come out. Could be that Hoodie lives in the building and gave them a shout that prompted them to wait for him. Or her. They all go inside and then along on their separate ways. Four come out again but isn't that explained by what I said: Hoodie lives in the building and had no reason to leave it again?"

"It's possible," Lynley said. "Most anything's possible. But look at the figure closely."

"Look at what's being carried, Barb," Nkata added.

Barbara reached for Lynley's magnifying glass and looked at the photo. She saw that Hoodie was carrying something that looked like a messenger's bag. It bore a light horizontal stripe that could well have been fluorescent at night.

Barbara took up the two photos that they were supposing featured Teo Bontempi at the door to her building, speaking to the visitors. In the second of these photos, the messenger bag appeared in the same position. In both of the CCTV photos, the figure was dressed in black. In both of the photos the figure wore something to cover the head. In this picture it was a baseball cap.

She said the obvious, "Right. Could be the same person. With a bag large enough to hold a head-bashing weapon. But if Hoodie's the one who smashed Teo Bontempi's skull, why never come out of the building once the deed is done?"

"There's a fire exit," Nkata pointed out. "Has to be one. Could be Hoodie left that way, which would've been used only from inside the place."

"But whoever it is would've had to know where it is, right? The killer wouldn't exactly wander round looking for it."

"Nothing to suggest this person hadn't been there before," Nkata said.

"The messenger bag in two of the photos fits that possibility," Lynley pointed out.

"Rosie?" Barb said.

"Could be. And now we know Rosie's pregnant by her sister's husband—"

"Have you pictures of him?" Barbara said. "He says he went to see her. He says he found her on the floor and he put her to bed. Is there corroboration? C'n I have a look through those?" She indicated the other photos, these from the stack that had been printed but rejected. She found one and slid it across the table to Lynley and Nkata. She said, "This looks like Ross Carver. Same height, same weight, same man bun, same—"

"Same what?" Lynley was wearing his reading specs and he looked over the top of them to her. "What is a man bun? Or am I unwise to ask."

"Top knot," Nkata told him. "Bloke's with longer hair . . . ? Like sumo wrestlers?"

"Ah. Fascinating style choice," Lynley commented. "Do we know what time he went there?" He reached for the photo of Messenger Bag entering the building in the company of those who'd held the door open. He compared them. "The time stamp has Messenger Bag entering the building seventy-four minutes before Ross Carver," he said. "Not a great deal of time to get into Teo Bontempi's flat, to distract her enough—with conversation? an argument? some kind of proposal?—to club her, and to leave. All prior to the arrival of Ross Carver, whom she or he—at least we can surmise—did not know was coming."

"But why not finish the job before Carver got there? Only Teo knew he was coming. Her killer wouldn't have known."

"Panic?" Lynley said.

Barbara added, "One of those bloody-hell-what-have-I-done moments?"

"Which suggests that the job on Teo wasn't finished because it wasn't intended in the first place. The killer had gone there for conversation."

"Sounds like Rosie to me," Nkata said.

"But are you saying Rosie is our weapon wielder and she took said weapon with her just in case?" Barbara demanded.

"We got Hoodie with that messenger bag," Nkata pointed out.

"At this point, we could have Colonel Mustard with the candlestick as well."

Lynley set aside all the photos. "It could be the messenger bag actually means nothing, just something Hoodie habitually carries."

"It could also be that both Hoodie *and* the messenger bag mean nothing," Barbara said, and then added, "Have we got anything from the sculptures?"

"Forensics says tomorrow. But they've said that before." Lynley glanced once again at the photos, saying to Nkata, "Do we have the sister on any of the CCTV recordings?"

"DCs're not finished up there," Nkata said. "We been looking at the days leading up to the incident. We'll find her. She's said she was there. It'll help if digital forensics can improve what we gave 'em."

"So," Barbara said, "aside from Rosie we've got two unidentified people having a chat with Teo Bontempi out of doors. She doesn't let them in, right?"

"Tha's it, far 's we can tell," Nkata agreed.

"One of the two shows up again and enters with a group but then doesn't leave. Seems, then, if Hoodie *isn't* Rosie, we're looking for someone who had an agenda in visiting her and a goal in having a natter with her."

"Which takes us where if not to Rosie?" Nkata asked.

"Her job, I daresay," Lynley said. "The one she held at Empress State Building."

"Which means that's where we start?" Barbara asked. "With the team she was on?"

"With that and with FGM."

"Are you thinking it's to do with the clinic?"

"She was largely responsible for shutting it down."

"Mercy Hart, then?"

"We need to find her."

WESTMINSTER
CENTRAL LONDON

"Good news and bad news is what we end up with."

Lynley raised his head from gazing at the computer screen upon which played part of the CCTV film that Nkata's constables had sent over to him for review. Over the top of his spectacles, he saw in the doorway a youthful Chinese woman he didn't recognize, although she wore police identification round her neck. He said, "Sorry?"

She said, "Marjorie Lee. Forensic tech. We've been having a go with that mobile number you sent along."

"Ah." He motioned her to enter. He saw she was carrying a manila folder, and she handed him a document from it.

"Here's the good news," Marjorie said. "We live in a metropolis. Well, really a megalopolis. So we've got thousands of cell towers—literally mobile phone towers—and because of this, the *general* location of any mobile is fairly easy to suss out as long as it's on."

"That's encouraging. And the bad news?" Lynley looked over what she had passed to him. It was a complicated chart resembling—to his unschooled eye—the navigation charts used on ships before the dawn of satellites, computers, and GPS.

"How much do you know about how this all works?" she asked him.

"I know pinging," he said. "Although, to be honest, I've never quite worked out what pinging actually is."

"Simple enough. May I . . . ?" She indicated one of the chairs that sat in front of his desk.

"Please."

She plunked herself into the seat and tucked her hair behind her ears. This bore a streak of burning pink that matched the lozenge-shaped lenses of her wire-rimmed spectacles, which she continually pushed up her nose as she spoke. "Mobile phones are always sending out messages if they're switched on. They communicate with towers that are placed within cells—these are just designated locations—in a community. If you're in the countryside, there won't be a massive number of towers because they're not needed. If you're in a city, it's just the opposite. They're everywhere. We don't see them because we're not looking for them. And mostly, they're on the top of buildings. Anyway, once you know the mobile number, you can work out where it last pinged. You can also work out the route it took to get to the location of that last ping. But the location of the phone itself is only going to be general at best."

"What area was the final ping in?"

She indicated the folder she still held, saying, "We've got its signal from the Vodafone tower in Hackney Downs, as well as from the Vodafone towers in Regal House, and the Cornerstone O2 tower. Triangulating all the relevant data, we can put you within three quarters of a kilometer of Hackney Downs, from its south-east corner." She handed him the folder, which he opened to find more charts. She said, "The difficult bit now is that your lot will have to speak to every mobile owner within the circumference of that circle we've drawn.

At its centre is the south-east corner of Hackney Downs. Where does the owner of that mobile live?"

"Lived. She's been murdered. She lived in Streatham High Road."

"Lived. Sorry. Well, it's possible, if you know her address, to trace the route the mobile phone took to reach the area of Hackney Downs. Is that any help?"

Lynley inserted the materials back into their folder. He said, "I don't think we'll need to do that. I'll let you know."

"Guv?"

It was Nkata at the doorway to Lynley's office. As Marjorie Lee left, Nkata came in, nodding to the woman as they passed each other. He said to Lynley, "Th'other DCs on the team finished up with the folders you and Barb brought from the clinic. Only one of them is someone can be located in London, and she says she never went to that place and why would she as she lives in South Lambeth? She says she's got no clue how her name ended up on a folder there."

"What did the folder say about why she went there? To the clinic, I mean."

"Breast exam then a follow-up exam. But neither thing happened, according to the 'patient.' An' like I said, all the other names on those folders don't belong to anyone at all."

"I daresay we have no reason to be surprised by that. Where are we with the appointment diary from the clinic, then?"

"One of the DCs 's ringing up every one of them listed. They're real enough, that lot. But 'f cutting's going on there, no one's going to talk to coppers about it, mind you. You get anything on the mobile?"

"Hackney Downs is as close as we can get it. We've got a circle drawn from the mobile phone tower in that location."

"For a door-to-door?"

"If we must. But that's a hell of a lot of manpower. I can put in a request, but I don't see Hillier giving it his imprimatur."

"'N other words, no?"

"In other words, no."

"Acting Detective Chief Superintendent Lynley?" came from the doorway, and Lynley didn't need to look in that direction to clock the speaker, since Dorothea Harriman was the sole individual who referred to everyone by full rank and surname.

He said, "Dee?"

"A message from Judi-with-an-i. You're wanted. At once. 'For a chat' is how she put it. But I don't exactly see the assistant commissioner having chats with anyone, if you know what I mean. Especially you. No offence intended."

"None taken." Lynley rose and after telling Winston to check on what was being gleaned from the CCTV recording of cars on Streatham High Road, he headed to see the AC.

Sir David Hillier's face was more florid than usual. The man always looked as if he were teetering on the edge of a life-ending stroke. He greeted him with, "Where the hell are we? What do we know? What's the progress?"

He didn't indicate Lynley was to sit. This meant the meeting would not be a long one, for which Lynley was ardently grateful. He gave the AC line and level: Progress was slow but it was being made. The difficulty was not having enough manpower.

Hillier said, "DCs don't grow on trees. Continue."

They had a fairly good idea about the location of the victim's mobile phone, Lynley told him. They had reached conclusions about the clinic that the victim had been instrumental in bringing to the attention of the local police. They also had discovered that a false identity was being used by the woman who apparently ran the clinic, and they had stills from the CCTV footage during the day as well as on the night Teo Bontempi was attacked.

"Have those ready to give to the Press Office," Hillier said.

"Sir, may I point out—"

"I'm getting hell from above, Superintendent."

Acting only, Lynley thought. Praise God for that.

Hillier continued. "We've got fading interest on the part of the media in this story of the Nigerian barrister and his wife with the missing daughter. If the daughter shows up, there might be one more day of front pages. At that point, the journalists're going to begin sniffing round for fresh meat—especially the tabloids will do—and we both know that the murder of a police officer is exactly that: the freshest, reddest meat there is aside from a decent royal scandal or some MP going at it with an underage girl, a twelve-year-old boy, or a KGB agent. The commissioner *and* the Press Office want to be prepared with something to throw them. CCTV stills are just the ticket, so let's go with that. Photos printed with: 'Have you seen this person? Do you know this person? Do you recognise anything about this person? Contact the Metropolitan Police.' You know the dance."

"We're attempting to improve the quality of the photos first, sir. Without that, they're going to be fairly useless."

"Not important at the moment. That rabid mob—"

Lynley could only assume the AC was referring to the journalists who'd been assigned to the story.

"—will doubtless be quite happy with whatever we give them as long as we give it." Hillier paused for a moment of consideration before he added, "All the better, isn't it, if the photos aren't clear? Demonstrates the constraints we're working under."

After years of labouring daily under the steely gaze of AC Hillier, Lynley knew when further argument was pointless. He'd never been happy when exposed to Hillier's obeisance to the tabloids. Pandering to their collective desire to dictate the course of an investigation was not only illogical, it was also dangerous. He realised, however, that Hillier, the commissioner, and the Press Office—having never seen the images from the CCTV footage—would probably accept anything from him as evidence of their progress. So he said he'd get on it straightaway and he went to inform Winston that they would need to send to the Press Office a few random images of individuals entering the apartment block on Streatham High Road. And it didn't matter who those individuals were.

10 AUGUST

He'd had to wait several hours longer than he'd expected but at last digital forensics had produced greatly improved still photos from the CCTV films. He'd had a very late supper at home as a result, discovering it tightly covered inside the oven in his kitchen. The oven door bore a sign that made a bow to Lewis Carroll as did a bottle of very nice Amarone considerably left open to breathe on the worktop. The former read *Eat me*, the latter *Drink me*. Lynley wondered if Denton had been auditioning for a role as the March Hare or the White Rabbit. He reckoned the Mad Hatter might well be beyond his talents, although he would never have said this to Charlie himself.

He'd had his meal, crawled off to bed, and awakened early, if not refreshed. Showered, shaved, and all the rest, he took a moment to make a phone call before heading downstairs.

"You're up early," Daidre said to him without preamble. "Or is it worse than that? Are you only just at home?"

"The former," he said. "I'm ringing to enquire: Has Wally taken my place?"

"I'm afraid he has. But only for now. He purrs when he's asleep, you know. I'm finding that quite a lovely bit of white noise."

"I can't compete with that, I'm afraid. I sincerely doubt that snoring would be a lovely bit of anything."

"I can attest to the fact that Wally would be most unhappy with snoring, Tommy."

"Damn. My future looks bleak indeed."

"How are things going? Are you making progress?"

"Possibly. We think it might be a female killer. But it's not a typical female crime."

"Is it not? Why?"

"In my experience, women prefer distance when they kill. A hands-on method of murder generally doesn't appeal. Poison, yes. Gunshot, yes. Clubbing someone over the head? Not very likely. But in this case, based—admittedly—largely upon CCTV documentation, it could be that's what we're dealing with."

"Clubbing someone doesn't sound very efficient," Daidre pointed out. She added off to one side, "Just a moment, Wally." And then to Lynley, "Sorry. I must let him out." He could hear the cat meowing and then a door opening as Daidre let him out into the garden. This was followed by the sound of the tap running. She'd be making herself a coffee. A moment and she was back with him. "Do you know what was used? This sounds like a spontaneous thing, not something that was planned. The result of an argument? Something like that?"

"A crime of passion," he said. "It could well be. We have a set of sculptures from her flat being examined by forensics. One of them might have been used."

"That must put paid to any lying-in-wait scenario."

"Hmmm. Possibly. Unless, of course, the killer knew about the sculptures and intended to use one from the first."

"Does that narrow the field or broaden it?"

"It's fairly narrow already."

"I see." Then, "Oh, there's Wally again, ready for breakfast. I swear, Tommy, he eats like someone recently rescued from the Donner Party."

"I expect he knows a soft heart when he comes across one. As do I, by the way. Shall we see each other soon?" He heard the door again, followed by the sound of dry cat food pouring into an aluminium bowl. He could well imagine Wally crouched before it, tail tucked about him, only its tip twitching, triumphant until the moment till Daidre left for work and he was relegated to the garden once more.

She said, "That's rather dependent upon you just now, isn't it?"

He sighed. "I daresay it is. Last night I was there till two. It's astonishing how much information can be gleaned from mobile phone towers, by the way."

"Should I be worried or comforted?"

"If you've recently joined the criminal class, worried. Otherwise, you're probably fine."

They rang off. He went downstairs to see the newspapers laid out in the dining room. *The Times*, the *Guardian*, the *Financial Times*. The front page of each displayed the same photograph and variation on the same headline. An arrest had finally been made in the case of the missing girl Boluwatife Akin.

THE MOTHERS SQUARE
LOWER CLAPTON
NORTH LONDON

Mark Phinney enlarged the first of the tabloid's two CCTV pictures from Streatham as much as he could on his mobile phone. It was going to be virtually useless as a means of identification, he thought. He couldn't work out why the Met had authorised the release of either picture unless it was to keep the hounds from baying for a day or two. For the investigators couldn't possibly hope that someone would come forward to identify the individuals depicted unless the messenger bag carried by the subject of one of the photos was different enough from all other messenger bags so as to make it recognisable, which wasn't likely. He was able to make out what seemed to be some kind of stripe running along the bottom of it, ostensibly making it visible to night-time traffic. Perhaps the hope was that the messenger making a delivery to Teo's apartment block would now step forward.

He enlarged the second picture, with as little success. Everything about it blurred with enlargement. All he could make out was a light shirt and trousers that were possibly jeans. This figure was taller and bulkier than Messenger Bag. It appeared to be a woman but easily could have been a man. The photos were accompanied by the usual announcement from the Met: the police wished to speak to the individuals depicted in the stills from the building's CCTV. If anyone knew who they were . . . et cetera and all the rest.

"Mark?" Pete was with Lilybet. "We're ready for you."

He shoved his mobile into his pocket and went to join his wife. She'd given Lilybet her morning sponge bath—no disasters having occurred during the night—and now she needed his help in dressing her. This was generally Robertson's job, but he'd indicated a later arrival than normal. Part of his journey to them involved London Overground, and a switch had failed between two of the stations along his route, causing a delay. He hadn't known this before he'd set out. Many apologies. No problem, Mark had told him. He could handle things till Robertson arrived.

Mark hated seeing Lilybet naked, though. While he often did see her that way, he liked to avoid it. It wasn't her flaccid flesh that bothered him. Rather it was the indications—still minor at this point but not to be thus for long—that his daughter was maturing. He'd noted a few pubic hairs the last time he'd helped with her nappy. That thrust him into a future that was unthinkable at the moment and would doubtless prove untenable when it arrived.

He found Pete waiting for him, with Lilybet propped up against her. She'd managed to wrestle their daughter into a bright pink Hello Kitty T-shirt. A purple skirt and striped pink and purple socks were laid out neatly next to her. Mark said, "Look at this pretty girl." He took one of her feet in his hands, kissed its toes, said, "We need to give this beauty a pedicure, eh?" and slid the sock onto her foot. He reached for the other as the front door's knocker rapped soundly against the wood.

"Has Robertson forgotten his key again?" Pete asked him. "Perhaps it's time we left one outside."

Mark went to open the door, but it wasn't Robertson. It was the Met detective who'd been to Empress State Building. And if Mark knew anything at all about how the murder squads worked, it was not a good sign when a member of a team—not to mention the head of a team—showed up in the morning upon one's doorstep.

MAYVILLE ESTATE
DALSTON
NORTH-EAST LONDON

Tani had remained in the flat. The place was a tomb in its silence but not in its temperature, and not a breath of breeze made its way through the open window. Even the birds, regular inhabitants of the trees in the play area across the lane, had ceased their songs. He couldn't blame them.

He meant to stay in place. Earlier, he'd found four carrier bags hidden away in a cupboard above the one in which his father hung his clothes. He'd done a deliberate search for them and had been forced to borrow a stepladder from a neighbour to see to the back of the cupboard. Catching sight of the carrier bags, he brought them down and dumped their contents on his parents' bed. If blood could run cold, that was what he reckoned his did.

It all looked perfectly innocent. Had he not been at home when the cutter had shown her face, he probably wouldn't have given the items—as odd as they were in a group—a second thought: bedsheets, a large vinyl tablecloth, two new box cutters, cotton wool, a bottle of alcohol, four packages of gauze. But having been home, he knew exactly what he was looking at. The question, then, was not, What? or, Why? It was, When?

Among the items on the bed, he saw a yellow sheet of paper. On this was the printed list that the cutter had handed over to Abeo. Additional to the list, however, he saw a telephone number. This was beneath the cutter's name—Chinara "Sarah" Sani—centred on the top of the page. Of course, she'd include her name, he thought. This revolting business of cutting little girls was her bread and butter, and she would want other parents of cutting-age girls to know about it. No need to skip off to Nigeria, she was blithely announcing. I offer an in-your-home service and all you need to do is ring for it and demonstrate an ability to pay.

He rang the number. Of course, no human answered. He left a message as requested: "You cut my sister . . . you put a finger on my sister . . . I kill you, bitch. This's Tani Bankole, B-a-n-k-o-l-e. My sister's Simisola, my dad is Abeo, and I mean what I tell you."

He felt no better afterwards, so he gathered up the things that he'd found in his parents' bedroom and he shoved them into one of the enormous metal wheelie bins that served Mayville Estate. He didn't use the closest, but one some distance away from Bronte House. He opened it, dumped the contents of the bags inside, and let the top fall with a satisfying crash. Then, back at the flat, he stuffed the carrier bags with crumpled newspaper and replaced them in the cupboard.

He was going through the chest of drawers in his parents' room to see if there was anything else he needed to be aware of when he heard his name called from outside the flat. Sophie!

She was standing in front of the door, looking hesitant. He went out to her, feeling uplifted for the first time that day, and in a moment he had his arms around her and could feel her heart beating against his chest. It was only a moment's embrace, though, because she pushed him away and said, "I've found a place we can take her."

He said in reply, "Mum's gone off with her. I don't know where an' I don't know why an' I don't know where to look."

She said, "It's all right. Like I said, I've found a place. I read about it online. It's anti-FGM and girls go there if they think they're in danger of being cut. We c'n take Simi there. And, meantime, there're these things . . ." She fished in her large shoulder bag and brought out a sheaf of papers clipped together. She handed them to him, saying, "It's a protection order. We need to get this filed."

He frowned. "But if there's a place—"

"There is, and we'll take her there. But also we've got to try everything. The place to take her is what we'll use first while we're waiting for the protection order to come through."

"Where is it, this place?"

"Whitechapel."

"*Whitechapel*? What th' hell, Soph . . ."

"It's the best solution to get Simi away from here quickly. They stow the girls with families. They *hide* them. It's the same place hid that girl's been in the news? You know which one?"

He'd been far too concerned with what was happening in his own life to consider what might be happening in someone else's, so he shook his head.

Sophie said, "Never mind. She's someone who got taken there and the lady runs the place says she won't budge till she's sure this girl is safe if she goes home."

"Did you talk to her?"

"Didn't need to. All we have to do is to take Simi and explain what's going on. Where is she?"

"Like I said, Soph, I don't *know*. Mum's not letting her out of her sight. *And* I think she found a place could see to Simi—"

"Oh God. Do you think she's having it done *now*?"

"She said there was this clinic, see. She gave them some money, and my dad wanted the money back cos he didn't know she took it in the first place, my mum. And . . . Sophie, I found all this clobber meant to be used on Simi when the cutter shows her mug here again. It was all the shit from the list she left with him. I binned it all."

"Okay. Excellent, that. Now we only got to find Simisola."

THE MOTHERS SQUARE
LOWER CLAPTON
NORTH-EAST LONDON

"May I have a word?" Thomas Lynley enquired politely.

"I'm helping my wife just now," Mark said. "With our daughter."

"Waiting isn't a problem for me," Lynley told him. "And as this is rather important . . . ?"

"Can we not speak later, when I'm at work?"

"I'm afraid not. May I . . . ?" Lynley gestured in a way that indicated he wished to enter.

"She's disabled," Mark said.

Lynley gave him a glance.

"Our daughter's disabled. Her attendant hasn't shown up yet so I'm helping my wife. Which is why if this could wait till later . . ."

It was at that extremely inopportune moment that Robertson showed up. Mark saw him rounding the corner from Sladen Place to enter the square on its western side. The bloke shouted, "Hey ho, I'm here!" and gave a jaunty wave, adding, "Blasted public transport, eh. Her nibs up and about?"

"She is. We were dressing."

"I'll handle that, shall I?" and he stepped past them, with a nod at Lynley, and went to join Pete.

There was nothing for it but to let Lynley inside. Mark did so, saying, "Why here, then? If you want me alone, it could have been like before, in the Orbit."

"I thought you might want this conversation to be more private."

Mark took the detective into the kitchen, the room farthest from where Pete and Robertson were finishing up with Lilybet. The plan had been to strap her into her wheelchair for an outing that morning. It was Mark's hope, now, that the outing would take place sooner rather than later. Pete intended to take her to Hackney Downs, where a path along the edge of the park made manoeuvring the wheelchair easier than in other locations.

He cleared the table of its unwashed crockery and stacked everything on the worktop. This was cluttered already with a coffee maker, a microwave, an upright mixer, and an unwashed blender along with four boxes of cereal, a bunch of overripe bananas, and a large plastic container of milk. At one side of the room stood a rubbish bin that needed emptying as well as a black rubbish bag containing used nappies. These were lending the air a sharp and unmistakable odour. Without wanting to, Mark saw the kitchen as the urbane and well-dressed detective no doubt saw it. He couldn't imagine Thomas Lynley ever having lived in a circumstance even remotely like this.

He offered a coffee, which Lynley declined. He did accept, however, the offer of a chair. He was carrying with him a large manila envelope. From this he took the same two photographs that Mark had seen on the internet via his smartphone. These pictures, however, were far clearer. Someone in digital technology at the Met had vastly improved them since they had been released to the media and used by the tabloids. He wondered as he looked down at them whether that had been a deliberate choice by the Met: to release something too grainy to be useful in order to soothe the photographic subjects into believing they were unrecognisable.

Lynley disabused him of this notion by saying, "These came in quite late last night, which is why they haven't yet been released."

Mark raised his head. He pulled a chair out from the table and sat opposite Lynley. He drew both pictures towards him in a show of giving them his full consideration. He then said, "Is it your thought that I might be able to assist you?"

"You've been to Teo Bontempi's flat. You might well have seen one of these two individuals."

"It seems to me—" Mark had to stop to clear his throat. "It seems to me that you'd get a far better response were you to take these round the flats themselves."

"That's being done," Lynley noted. "In the meantime, do you recognise either of these people? At least one of them appears to be a woman."

He looked at the pictures again. He said, "Why might I know them? Are the photos from the night Teo was hurt?"

"We've backed up a few days. These are from two days before," Lynley said. "They're enlargements of the originals, obviously. The originals feature Teo as well. She's at the building's door."

"With these two?" he gestured to the pictures.

"Speaking with each of them in turn. It appears that in both cases, they rang the entry buzzer. But rather than let them into the building, she came down for a word."

"And then let them in?"

"It doesn't appear that way. But we do need to find them because it's clear each of them went to see her."

Mark shook his head. "I wish I could help," was what he said. "Your trip would have been more worthwhile."

"As to that . . ." Lynley gathered the pictures and returned them to the envelope. He didn't go on.

"Yes?" Mark prompted.

"You have a valuable piece of evidence, and it's that that I've come for, actually."

Mark felt a rush of hot, then cold. "What might that be?"

"Her mobile phone. You have it. Or your wife has it. Or the gentleman who arrived just now to help out has it. The final time it pinged, the mobile was in this area. Of everyone remotely connected to Teo, yours is the address closest to the mobile phone tower that caught her phone's signal. Considering her husband's declaration that the mobile was recharging on her bedside table when he left her, considering that you were the person to find her several days later, and considering that mobile phone tower, it stands to reason that you have the phone. The only real question is when you took it: before the arrival of the ambulance or once Teo was in hospital."

Mark knew that if he denied it, Lynley's next step would be a search warrant. He also knew that he should have tossed the phone in the rubbish and he would have done had he not been such a fool. He said, hearing the heaviness in his voice, "I took it directly I phoned for an ambulance."

Lynley said nothing. He merely watched him with an unwavering gaze.

"I know I should have left it. Or at least turned it over to someone. But I couldn't risk leaving it there." He had the phone with him, on his person. He took it from his pocket and handed it to Lynley. He said, "Someone might have taken it had I left it."

"And you couldn't have that," Lynley noted.

"I reckoned I'd return it to her when she came out of hospital. And then . . ."

"And then she died and you thought you were safe. Especially since you didn't know that her death was actually a murder. But once you knew that . . . There's the rub, DCS Phinney, and I expect you see it. Once you knew she was murdered, you kept the phone. You're a cop, so I know you see how that looks."

"It looks like I lied to you when we first met."

"Did you?"

"She *did* go her own way when she was on the team."

"But that's not why you transferred her, is it? I think the reason might well be more personal. I expect once we get into this phone, we're going to know that reason."

Mark had to look away. His mind was shot through with what Lynley was going to see on that phone: the photos taken and exchanged, the innumerable texts, voice messages, one decidedly raw video. He said, returning his gaze to the other man, "What you'll see is the madness that comes with love, and I expect you'll recognise it as such. I kept the phone because I didn't want you to see it. I didn't want you to know it. No one knew."

"Your wife?"

"No. No. She couldn't have known. There was no way."

"Four," Lynley said.

"Four what?"

"Four denials." From the manila envelope, Lynley removed the photographs he'd already shown Mark. He placed them side by side on the table. He said, "Have another look, please."

"I don't know either one of them. I don't even *begin* to recognise either of them. I don't—" Abruptly he stopped himself. Three denials, he thought.

Darling to be inside you once more, once more.

"Do you want me to know about anything I'm going to see on this phone?" Lynley asked.

"I was mad for her. I was mad *about* her. That's what you'll see. From me, at least. That's what you'll see."

"And from others?" Lynley asked.

"I don't know." Mark recognised that his entire body was going numb. He said again, "I don't know. Once the phone locked, there was nothing else that I could see."

The kitchen door opened and both of them looked in its direction. Pete stood there with Lilybet in her wheelchair and Robertson at their daughter's elbow. Pete said, "We've come to kiss our daddy bye-bye."

Before he could say anything and before he could stop the worst from happening, Pete rolled Lilybet into the room.

LEYTON
NORTH LONDON

Repeatedly, Monifa Bankole had phoned the mobile number given her when she and Simi had first gone to the clinic. Consistently, there had been no reply and, ultimately, there had been no room to leave another message. But the appointment book had been stuffed with names. This being the case, it was inconceivable that the clinic was shut down for good. Indeed, what seemed far more likely was that the operation had merely moved to another area in London. She just had to find out where.

But she'd had no luck, and now she knew she had to take some kind of action. Tani had poured petrol on the fire of her anxiety. Abeo, Tani had informed her, had made the necessary purchases he'd been told to make by Chinara Sani, the Nigerian cutter. Tani had binned them, he'd then shown her the list that the cutter had given to Abeo, and then he'd demanded she hand Simisola over to him so that he could get her to a place of safety because all Abeo had to do was re-purchase the items and arrange to have Simi cut in another location. When she'd declared that she wouldn't hand over Simisola to him, he'd shaken a few papers in front of her face, claiming they constituted a protection order that was going to be handed over to the appropriate authorities if she didn't cooperate.

It was the word *cooperate* that did it for her. It was the very idea that she was meant to cooperate with her own son because she was female. She'd said to him, "You do *not* give me orders."

His tone altered. "Mum. Please. I want to take her someplace safe."

But she wouldn't relent. She knew she was risking Simisola's going into Care by refusing to hand the little girl over to her brother. If he filed the papers on his own, it was probable that Care would be the outcome. But to Monifa, the fear was losing Simi for months upon months and perhaps even permanently.

With Simi's hand in hers, Monifa went in search of Halimah, the mother of Simi's best friend, Lim. She lived on Mayville Estate as well, but at the other side of it, on the second floor of Lydgate House in Woodville Road. Monifa herself had never been there—Abeo did not approve of Halimah, as she was divorced—but Simisola had done, so she knew in which direction to head and to what floor they needed to go in the lift to gain access to Halimah's flat.

Lim had been Halimah's only daughter, her only child. Halimah had not been keen on having Lim cut, but as she herself had been cut, she had sought someone to perform the ritual. For that was how she'd thought it at the time: merely a ritual to be gone through in order to be cleansed and to herald womanhood. She had intended no harm to her child.

No one, least of all Halimah, had expected things to go so very wrong. No one had expected anything but a period of discomfort and, when it was over, Lim clean and pure. But nothing had worked as planned and now Lim was dead by her own hand.

When Halimah opened the door to her knock, Monifa said, "Abeo has found someone. He has brought her to the flat. Tani knows, and I am so afraid that he intends to take Simisola away because of this."

Halimah did not need to ask what was meant in Monifa's words. "He'll look for you here," she said, glancing round as if in the expectation that Abeo would come swinging from one of the nearby trees like Tarzan in order to hurt Monifa and snatch Simisola. "This will be the first place he looks."

"I'm not here for that. I must put a stop to this. I need to know where she lives. I want to talk to her face-to-face."

"Who?"

"You know, Halimah. I *know* you know."

Halimah looked from Monifa to Simisola. After a moment, she said, "Come in."

It was dark inside the flat and slightly cooler than out of doors. Curtains were closed and so were the windows. She was conserving what she could of the night's lower temperatures, but it wouldn't be long before she had to open the place up as the day became stifling.

Halimah left Monifa just inside the door and disappeared into the kitchen where, at least so it sounded to Monifa, she began rooting round in a drawer of cutlery. After a minute or so, she emerged with a folded piece of lined notebook paper. On it was scrawled an address in Leyton. It would not be a simple matter to get there. This couldn't be helped. Monifa nodded her thanks and set off with Simisola.

She found the building in Leyton Grange. It was a tower, faced in brick, with each floor delineated by a band of cream. Its balconies made it different from many other tower blocks throughout London. They were each fronted by a red metal safety barrier with tiny octagonal holes punched into it to allow a freer movement of air. A summer-dead lawn encircled the place, and upon this sat a discarded blue sofa. Shrubbery was dust coated and dropping leaves. Everywhere there were signs of desiccation.

It had taken nearly ninety minutes to reach this place, via several buses and on foot, suffering the airless bus rides first and then receiving two sets of misdirection given by passersby who appeared to be deeply confused by the area. But at last they were standing in front of the building, where Monifa rang the buzzer next to the number of the flat Halimah had included with the street address. Then she waited. Nothing. She buzzed again. This time, a woman's voice said, "What is it?" and Monifa gave her name and asked if she was ringing the flat of Chinara Sani. The shrewd reply to this was, "Are you a relation of Abeo Bankole?" which told Monifa they were at the right place. When she identified herself as Abeo's wife, Chinara said, "And your need is . . . ?" to which Monifa replied, "To speak to you about what Abeo has planned for Simisola."

"A moment, please."

Monifa waited. She imagined Chinara Sani tapping her foot anxiously as she attempted to cook up a plan of escape. After several minutes, she rang the flat again and this time a buzzer sounded and Monifa pushed the door open. She led Simisola to the lift. Chinara Sani, she knew, lived on the tenth floor.

After waiting an interminable length of time as the machinery clanked and groaned, she ushered Simi into the lift and up they rode. Chinara, she thought, must have been standing with her hand on the knob, because no sooner had Monifa's knuckles hit the wood than her flat's door swung open.

She'd expected an extremely old woman, although she couldn't have said why aside from the tradition associated with the cut. She'd also expected native garb. Instead she was instead confronted by a grey-haired professional-looking woman who might have worked in a bank, although her red lipstick seemed out of place and made her mouth look like a gash on her face.

"You're Chinara?" Monifa asked.

"I am. And this must be Simisola, yes?" Chinara flashed a smile. Lipstick was smeared on one of her large front teeth. "Have you brought her to meet me? That makes things easier. How are you, Simisola? Are you ready to become a grown-up girl?"

Simi hung back. Clearly she did not know what to expect of this stranger.

"That," Monifa said, "is what we have come to speak about."

"Have you? Well, this is good. It's not the usual course for a girl's father to make the arrangements while his wife is not at home, eh? Have you concerns, then? Questions?" When Monifa did not reply, Chinara placed her gaze on Simi. "Does Simisola wish to ask me something?" she said. "This is all part of growing into a woman, my dear. You've been told that, yes?"

Monifa felt Simi shrinking into her side. Her little body trembled. She said to Chinara, "There has been a mistake. You will not be needed. There are other arrangements already made. Abeo did not know that when he asked you to come to our home. I have since explained it to him."

"Other arrangements? I am, you know, the only true *Nigerian* cutter you will find in north London. There are Somalis, of course, and they are, admittedly, far cheaper than I am. But I would not allow a Somali cutter to set foot in my house, let alone put hands upon my child. May I ask how you found me today? I mean how you found where I live?"

"From the mother of a girl who killed herself after you cut her. Perhaps you remember her? Lim was her name. She was twelve years old. She used a head wrap belonging to her mother. She hanged herself."

"Twelve years old," Chinara murmured. "It is best if this is done when girls are much, much younger. This is what I tell parents who come to me. I am not responsible for anything that happens if the parents do not listen to me."

"Hear me, then," Monifa said. "If you touch Simisola, I will ring the police. If you come again to my house, I will ring the police."

"I think this is not for you to decide. And your husband has told me that you—"

"I don't care what he's told you."

"—and he are of one mind. Are you saying that he has lied to me?"

"I'm saying that you will not touch my daughter. I'm saying that I will ring the police if you step over the threshold of my house again."

Chinara was wearing large golden earrings and they moved like a hypnotist's watch when she tilted her head. "But what has changed your mind, Mrs. Bankole? When I spoke with your husband, he said you were happy with how we would proceed."

"He was lying to you."

"Why would he lie?"

"Mummy?" Simisola murmured. "C'n I have a wee?"

"Of course, of course." Chinara pointed the way. Monifa started to go with her. The other woman stopped her with, "Surely the girl can manage a wee. No one else is in the flat just now if that worries you."

Everything about Chinara Sani worried Monifa, but she said to Simi, "Go along and be quick about it."

When Simi was gone from the room, Chinara said to Monifa, "You know what will happen, yes? You cannot arrange a proper marriage for her if this isn't done."

"I've told you. I've made other arrangements."

"For a marriage? With a true Nigerian man? He will have expectations . . ."

"None of this concerns you. If Abeo has paid you, keep the money. But do not come to our home again. You understand me in this, yes?"

"Your husband will want to—"

"Only Simisola interests me."

The buzzer sounded. It was loud and long, and Monifa wondered if the length of the ringing comprised a signal of some kind. She felt a rush of fear although she didn't know why, aside from being in the home of a woman whose livelihood could result in a prison term. Having been carted off by the police once already, she didn't wish to engage in a repeat performance.

Chinara did not answer the buzzer. Instead, she walked to where the building's door release was on the wall and she pushed it, admitting someone inside. At this, Monifa knew it was imperative that she and Simi leave. She called to her daughter, telling her to hurry.

The moments passed. Finally, the sound of the loo flushing preceded the running of water into the basin as Simi did as she'd long ago learned: she washed her hands. When she emerged, Monifa went to her, put an arm round her shoulders, and said to the other Nigerian woman, "We will leave you now."

She was heading to the door when three sharp knocks sounded upon it.

"Ah," Chinara said. "Let us find out the truth of the matter."

She walked past Monifa and her daughter. She opened the door, and Abeo entered.

DEPTFORD
SOUTH-EAST LONDON

Leylo and Yasir occupied a flat overlooking Pepys Park in Deptford. It was not overly far from the Greenwich Foot Tunnel, which crossed beneath the Thames, joining forever those oddest of couples: the Isle of Dogs and the Royal Naval College. Leylo and Yasir had good access to Pepys Park itself, Deborah saw. It was open to all, unlike some green areas in London that were available only to those who could afford to hold a key to them. This park seemed quite simple, but as she got out of her car nearby, Deborah could see that it possessed picnic tables, paths, and benches, with a large green—sadly not green at the moment—for playing ball games. It was a pleasant place for reading a book, sunning oneself in a deck chair, or walking a dog, and its trees provided ample shade.

When she'd rung the couple, only Leylo was at home, but she was delighted to know that Deborah St. James was in the vicinity with a photograph to give them. Thus Deborah was knocking at Leylo's door with a large wrapped package under her arm and her camera bag slung over her shoulder.

Leylo, she found, was an altered woman. In another century she would have been referred to as "positively blooming." In the current century, she appeared to radiate good health and energy. She welcomed Deborah with a bright smile, saying, "Oh do, *do* come in. Would you like tea? I would offer you hot, I would, but it seems a bit extreme, yes? This tea is cool."

Deborah told her she'd love a cool tea. She carried her package into the sitting room and found herself wondering where Leylo and her husband could possibly hang the portrait. For above the sofa, on the other walls, and placed upon tables was more African art than she'd seen in her life: paintings, masks, sculptures, stone carvings, baskets, statues, and framed textiles. On a nearby table, there was also a display case sharing space with a sword-wielding statue. Inside the case were curiosities, made of brass in various shapes from figures to abstract swirls and squiggles.

"Those are Yasir's goldweights. He began collecting them as a boy."

"What are they?" Deborah turned to see Leylo carrying a tray that held the promised tea along with a plate of digestives.

"They are for determining the weight of gold dust, for currency, before there were coins and paper notes."

"They're quite beautiful," Deborah told her. "Especially the alligator. Or is it a crocodile? I never know the difference."

Leylo set her tray on a glass-topped coffee table where a collection of catalogues lay open, most of them featuring various styles of bedroom furniture. Seeing Deborah's gaze upon them, Leylo said with a shy smile, "Soon we shall have a new marriage, me and Yasir, yes. He wants a new bedroom to celebrate. Something, he says, that is not bonded with bad memories of suffering and pain."

"That's a wonderful idea," Deborah said. "Your husband seems quite a thoughtful man."

"My husband is very unlike many traditional husbands. I am lucky to have him."

"And he's lucky to have you as well," Deborah said. "I expect he knows that."

"You are married?"

"I am."

"Your husband?"

"He's a man I've loved since I was seven years old."

"Goodness! You were children together?"

"I was a child. He wasn't."

"He is much older, then?"

"No, no. Well, eleven years, but without those years and what occurred during them, we both might be married to other people."

"This is a story," Leylo said as she handed Deborah the glass of tea. It was room temperature, not iced. It was quite refreshing, Deborah found, flavoured with lemon, an antidote to the heat.

"Far too long a story to tell at the moment," Deborah said. "If I can say this . . . ? You look very well. The surgery was a success, then."

Leylo nodded. "I've gone to be checked, and Dr. Weatherall says that soon enough Yasir and I will be able to think about children once again. You have children, yes?"

Deborah shook her head. "I'm afraid not." She indicated the package she'd brought. "Would you like to see the photo I've brought you? I'm on a mission today, distributing them."

"Oh, I would indeed, I would *indeed*, yes, yes."

Deborah nodded at the package, which she'd leaned against the sofa. It was wrapped for its protection, a simple covering of butcher's paper, its ends taped. Leylo made short work of opening it. It was not a typical studio photograph. It was meant for the wall, not to stand on a table or sideboard. Deborah had done it in black and white—as was her preference—and she'd framed it simply, a white mount and a black metal frame. In the picture, Yasir was sitting on the arm of Leylo's chair. He was looking down at her and she up at him. He was in profile. She was in three-quarters view. Deborah liked this particular shot for the nature of their relationship that it revealed and the way the qualities of their partnership could be identified: patience, devotion, compassion, support.

Looking upon it, Leylo clasped her hands beneath her chin. "This is beautiful. You are so kind to bring this to me."

"You were kind to allow me to take the photos," Deborah said. "In fact . . . Would you let me take a few more now? It's only that . . . The change in you is so marked. Would you mind terribly?"

"Here?" Leylo sounded startled. "Now? Without my husband?"

"If it wouldn't make you feel terribly awkward. I have my camera. And the light in here is very good."

Leylo was quiet for a moment, her brow furrowed. But then she smiled and said, "Yes. Where would you like me? Here? Right here?"

She was sitting on the sofa, lit in part by a shaft of sunlight. It would have been interesting to have her placed there because of this light, save for the fact of the wall behind her and the art it held. While each piece was worthy of study, having them in the picture would distract the eye. An adjustment to the depth of field wouldn't entirely solve the problem, but it would have to do. So Deborah said, "If we could move a chair near the window . . . ?"

"Oh yes. That is ever so easy, yes it is." Leylo moved the chair herself and Deborah positioned her. On a table behind her was a lamp that Deborah lit. She turned it slightly and moved from view the statue along with the case of goldweights that the table displayed.

She stepped back a few feet and looked at the arrangement: the woman with ambient light on her cheek, a glow from the lamp on her hair. She said, "This will be lovely, Leylo. I'll bring you a copy. Only . . ." She smiled. "I'll then have to photograph Yasir as well, so you'll have a matched pair of pictures. And then it will be your children, one by one. Perhaps your parents? Brothers and sisters? I'll eventually become such a pest that you'll have no choice but to make me a member of your family."

Leylo laughed at this idea. It was the moment Deborah wanted. She took the picture.

LEYTON
NORTH LONDON

Monifa knew at once that the long pause before Chinara Sani admitted them into her flat had been taken up with her ringing Abeo and asking him what his wife and his daughter were doing buzzing her flat from outside the building. He'd managed to get from Pembury Estate to this place so quickly that she assumed he'd used Lark's vehicle or he'd taken a taxi. There was no other way he could have managed the trip so quickly.

He entered the flat with a face set in stone. He shut the door with care. He walked past Chinara to confront Monifa. He spoke evenly, quietly. Monifa was reminded of a cobra. He said, "What are you doing here, Monifa?" And then with a glance at Simi, who had retreated to a corner of the room, "What is Simisola doing here?"

Monifa drew a steadying breath during which she wondered exactly how much of himself he'd be willing to show in front of a witness who was not part of their family. She said quite reasonably, "I'm here to tell this woman that I will ring the police if she touches my daughter."

"*My* daughter," Abeo countered. "At least that is what you have claimed, yes? And if she is mine, I am who decides what will happen to her, not you. *You* would turn her into what you are: the sour fruit of your father's tree. Come, Simisola."

Simi didn't move.

"Simisola, you must come to me now," Abeo said. "Do not make me fetch you."

"Mummy?" Simi looked to Monifa. "What should I—"

This was not acceptable to Abeo. He crossed the room and grabbed her by the arm. He said to Chinara, "So. We will do it now."

Monifa rushed forward to put herself between Abeo and the cutter. She said, "No! I will not allow—"

Abeo was swift in his release of Simisola and equally swift in capturing Monifa. He shoved her behind him. She stumbled against an armchair and as she was righting herself, he clutched Simi's arm once more and he thrust her towards Chinara. "Now," he said.

Chinara said, "I can't—"

"I have paid you. You can. I will hold her. Assemble what you need." And to Monifa, "You will stay where you are. If you do not, I will—"

"What?" she cried as she moved to confront him. "*What* will you do to me, Abeo?"

He advanced upon her, but he did not get far, for Chinara said tersely, "Stop this! I will *not* do it. You told me she was agreed to the cutting. You lied to me. I do not cut where there is not agreement. I told you that."

"There is agreement," Abeo said. "*I* am the agreement. What you see here in this moment . . . this is about her and me. This is not about making Simisola clean."

"There is *no* agreement when a mother says she will phone the police. This is over. This is done. I will not cut her. Not today, not any day at all."

Abeo's face had gone rigid as Chinara was speaking. To Monifa, it looked like the face of a man having some kind of attack. Simi ran to her then. Monifa knelt beside her.

Abeo was saying in a deadly tone, "I have bought everything you wanted. I have spent money. I have given *you* money. You *will*—"

"I. Will. Nothing. Get out of this flat. All of you. Now."

"I have told you what I want," Abeo declared.

"And I have told you no," Chinara replied. "So you will leave and you will leave now. Or I will be the one who rings the police. And *you* will be the one arrested. Now leave!"

The silence that fell created among them a perilous moment during which Monifa thought Abeo would do violence to the other woman. But after something of a stare-down, he swung round, grabbed Monifa by the armpit, dragged her to her feet, and thrust her towards the door. He grabbed Simisola and did the same.

In a moment they were in the corridor and Chinara had slammed and locked the door behind them. Abeo forced his wife and daughter in front of him to the lift. He said to Monifa, "Now she goes to Nigeria."

WESTMINSTER
CENTRAL LONDON

It was half past ten when Dorothea Harriman said to them both, "I've had a call from Judi-with-an-i. Assistant Commissioner Hillier wants a word."

Winston Nkata swung round from his computer screen and cast a look at Havers. She lifted a shoulder and both hands. He looked at Dorothea and said, "DI Lynley i'n't here."

"I told Judi that. First, she said whenever he arrives et cetera. But then she rang a second time and that's why I'm here."

"You're sayin' he wants a word with one of us?"

Dorothea balanced her right foot on the pin-size heel of her stiletto before she tapped the shoe's toe on the lino. "Straightaway, she said. She also said this couldn't wait for the acting detective chief superintendent. The assistant commissioner wants one of you. You're to go directly."

Havers said, "And this is about . . . what, exactly, Dee?"

"You know Judi never shares that in advance, Detective Sergeant. It robs the moment of its tension. Or surprise. Or whatever. Least, that's what I reckon the assistant commissioner thinks."

Havers said to Nkata, "So. Summoned from on high. What's it to be, Winnie? Three-out-of-five rock, paper, scissors or a coin toss? Choose your pleasure. Praise be that I've dressed with professional flair this morning in case I lose."

"As far as professional flair goes," Dorothea began, giving Havers a head-to-toe, "you've got half of it. *Are* those leopard-skin trainers you're wearing?"

"Please. *Faux* leopard skin. I'm an animal lover. If you'd like a pair, I can tell you—"

"I'll pass for now, Detective Sergeant." And then to Nkata, who'd dug in his pocket and brought out fifty pence, "Well?"

Havers said to him, "Heads, you go. Tails, I go. But keep in mind that I'm not exactly one of Hillier's favourite people."

He flipped it to the floor, where it ended up next to Barbara's chair. She looked down at the coin and then at Nkata. "Enjoy," she said.

Nkata sighed. "I never been."

"No worries," Havers replied. "First time's the best. He'll probably even break out the chocolate bikkies when he sees it's not me."

Nkata gathered up some of his paperwork and sooner than he would have liked it, he found himself standing in front of Judi-with-an-i's desk. He'd never met Hillier's secretary before nor had he been up to this aerie to meet formally with Hillier in a space that was shared with the commissioner as well. He said, "DS Nkata in place of DI Lynley."

Judi-with-an-i looked him over and said, "You're quite tall, aren't you?" in a fashion that told him she had doubts about how things were going to go, considering his height.

"Tha'd be the case," he replied.

"How?" she asked.

"Genetic. Whole family's tall."

She said, "I meant how tall are you, not how did you come to be so tall."

"Oh. Sorry. Six feet, five inches. Near to six. Inches, that is."

Judi-with-an-i nodded. "Right. Well, you look it, don't you." She rang the assistant commissioner and told him DS Nkata had arrived. She listened for a moment, said, "Certainly," and then to Nkata, "Go right in. Attempt to look shorter if you can. It'll help."

Nkata wasn't certain how he was supposed to manage looking shorter, but he hoped for the best, stooped his shoulders a bit, and entered Hillier's office. The first things he saw, aside from Hillier himself, who was standing behind his desk with his knuckles on its surface, were the tabloids. They were spread across his desktop, and it looked to Nkata as if the AC had put his hands on every tabloid in London. No doubt the Press Office had provided them. Behind his desk was an enviable bank of windows from which the tops of the trees in St. James's Park billowed green against a cloudless, pale blue sky.

Hillier looked up from the newspapers. Nkata hadn't yet seen the day's news but he reckoned that if Hillier wanted to see someone and if that person arrived to a collection of London's front pages, the outcome of this encounter was not likely to be hearing the praise of "a job well done."

Hillier's eyes narrowed in his florid face. He said, "And your superior officer is where?"

"Lower Clapton. He's fetching the victim's mobile and having a go with the bloke who had her transferred."

"That's it, is it?"

"He's showing him some pictures 's well."

Hillier gestured to the tabloids, saying, "Let's hope he has improved ones by now. No one is going to ring Crimestoppers over these." He looked up from the tabloids to say, "Did you bring them with you?"

Nkata glanced down at the folders he was carrying. Truth to tell, he wasn't at all sure what he had or why he'd brought it. He said, "The better pictures? The guv di'n't get them from the digital techs till late, sir. Rest of us don't have copies yet."

Hillier evaluated this in silence before he said, "You're loyal, aren't you?"

"Sir?"

"To Lynley. You're loyal to him. That's a fine quality, Sergeant."

Nkata wasn't sure what he was meant to say in reply, so he merely nodded. A phone rang outside the office, probably on the desk of Judi-with-an-i.

"See that you get me copies of the better pictures directly."

Nkata looked away for a moment, evaluating the order. He said to Hillier, "To hand to the media, sir?"

"To do with as I see fit."

"I's only that . . ." Nkata wasn't sure how to play this particular scene.

"That what?" Hillier had a tone, he did. It sounded the way cold steel felt.

"DI Lynley doesn' want the responsible party to know we got better pictures, sir."

"You did hear me, didn't you?" Hillier asked. "I wasn't making a suggestion, Sergeant."

"Oh. Yeah. Right. It's only that if the pictures go out and one or two or whatever number of them do show the killer, we're playing our hand."

"That's one interpretation," Hillier said. "There are others of which I doubt you are aware."

Nkata said, "Yes, sir."

"And may I ask," Hillier enquired, "what is Lynley doing with two DSs when he needs only one? I've asked him but so far he's managed to avoid an explanation. And I can't imagine Sergeant Havers has sought other employment, however that might be ardently wished for."

"Problem 's with the cutbacks." Nkata was grateful to be on firmer ground at the same time as he was determined to lead Hillier away from Barb Havers. "Jus' now? With what's going on with DS Bontempi's murder? We're trying to pull everything together but we got only two DCs on loan from DI Hale. One of 'em 's watching the CCTV from the building where DS Bontempi lived and from two shops 'cross the street. The other's watching film on Streatham High Road for cars and taxis round her building on the day she got attacked. We got a bunch 'f nothing out of that on the day of the attack, so the DC's moved back in time to see what she can see couple of days in advance. She's taking down number plates, sending it off to Swansea, and getting the information from them. There's no ANPR in the area."

"And Swansea?" Hillier said. "Sergeant, I'd prefer straight information to dragging everything out of you."

"Well, the in'eresting thing so far is we got a car registered to Mark Phinney—tha's Teo Bontempi's superior officer before she got transferred—'a few times in the 'mediate area. And he doesn't live anywhere near Streatham. We got him on the CCTV from her building 's well."

"How do the dates match up with what happened to her?"

"Two match up fine with what he's told us. The third and the fourth? They don't."

"Get on it, then."

"I 'spect tha's what DI Lynley's working on, sir. Like I said, he went up to talk to Phinney this morning."

Hillier kept his eyes fixed on Nkata's face in a disconcerting manner that Nkata assumed the assistant commissioner used on everyone he wished to intimidate. "Anything else?" he said evenly.

"We been checkin out an appointment book we found at a closed-down clinic tha' DS Bontempi was associated with. It's all women with appointments, see, which makes sense cause the women who got arrested claimed the place is a women's health practice. But here's wha's in'eresting, sir. Not a single woman was willing to say wha' her appointment was for when we contacted her. And each woman? Right af'er each woman's name is another name in brackets. These're female names 's well. We're thinking our murder victim turned the clinic over to the local coppers as a place was cutting girls, so we reckon that diary has appointments for mums bringing their girls to get cut, and the names in the brackets belong to girls. We don' know that for sure, 'course, but we're looking for the woman who worked there."

"What've you come up with?"

"She's done a runner. She wasn't using her real name, either. Jus' now we're locating the building's owner—this would be where the clinic was—an' soon's we have the owner's name and address, we reckon he'll hand over hers."

"Who's working on that?"

"Barb Havers was . . . is. But . . . well . . . to be honest, we could do with more help. CCTV alone is taking forever, an' we can't weaponise any interview without it."

Hillier's eyes narrowed again. He said, "You've just told me you have two DCs."

"An' they're excellent, they are. Bu' we need more cos ever'time we turn up a name, there's another person got to be looked into. An' we got to show the pictures round, sir, once we get our mitts on copies of the decent ones. You know the drill." He said the last bit without being at all certain. He doubted Sir David Hillier had blazed his remarkably ascendant career through time spent on murder investigations. But it was worth a try to mention this, Nkata thought. Every avenue needed to be greased.

This one paid off. Hillier said, "I can give you two more, and that has to be the limit. You'll have seven people in total working on this, and that's all we can spare. This isn't a serial killer we're dealing with. If DI Lynley can't pull a case together with that number of people, we're in serious trouble and so is he. So get me those pictures, and in the meantime, we all need to pray that something happens that will direct the tabloid press's interests elsewhere. I certainly wouldn't say no to a natural disaster."

Nkata found that he didn't disagree.

MAYVILLE ESTATE
DALSTON
NORTH-EAST LONDON

Sophie went with him when Tani left the flat. Prior to setting off, Tani brought out the rucksack with Simisola's things stowed inside, and he showed Sophie what he'd chosen. She fingered through it and recommended two more T-shirts and sandals if she had them. He took two more T-shirts from a drawer and held up a pair of purple Crocs for her approval. Sophie picked up one of Simi's stuffed animals—a tiger with a missing eye—and that was the last thing that went into the rucksack. After that, and at Sophie's suggestion, they set off to Ridley

Road Market. It was a good possibility, she said, that Monifa had taken Simi there.

They split up at the market entrance. Sophie took the side of the street on which Abeo's butcher shop and fishmonger's stall were situated. Tani took the other. They met at the end thirty minutes later. Neither of them had set eyes on Simisola. When Tani caught a glimpse of the interior of Into Africa Groceries Etc., as well as the butcher's shop, he couldn't see Abeo either. This was far more unusual than the absence of Monifa and Simisola.

"They lef' more'n three hours ago," Tani told Sophie. "What if Simi's getting cut this very minute? Soph, I'm her *brother*. I'm meant to—"

"It's okay," Sophie said. "Tani, it's fine. They probably just went to . . ." And of course, she couldn't come up with a place any more than he could. So she continued with, "They'll be along. Try to stay calm."

"I should've followed 'em," he said. "I heard 'em leave. But I reckoned I couldn't snatch Simi in the street, could I. Only, now I'm thinking why the hell *couldn't* I 've snatched her."

"You've done the right thing. They can't have gone far. They'll be back soon."

Soon turned out to be sooner than Tani expected. He and Sophie were sitting side by side on Tani's bed, not ten minutes after their return from Ridley Road, when they heard the sound of his father's voice. It became louder as he mounted the steps. His words were clipped.

All Tani could make out was, "Now *this*. You will stand aside. You will not—"

"You're hurting her arm, Papa!" from Simisola.

"Close your mouth," Abeo returned.

Tani and Sophie looked at each other. Tani rose from the bed and pushed his bedroom door nearly all the way shut, leaving a crack so that they could hear. He returned to Sophie. The front door opened. Footsteps, and then it closed again.

"Now you examine what you have done," Abeo demanded.

"I've prevented Simisola from being hurt."

"And you know what happens next. I will acquire the tickets today. For this, you may thank yourself."

"I won't allow you to take her out of the country, Abeo. I will stop you."

"Papa, I don't want to go," Simi cried.

"By doing what will you stop me?" Abeo asked.

"I'll ring the police."

He laughed shortly. "And then what? They come, they shake a finger in my face. They say, 'This you must not do, sir,' and they expect obedience. You think you can stop me this way?"

"They'll arrest you."

"Mummy, *where's* he taking me?"

"He wishes to take you to Nigeria. There he will see to it that—"

"You stupid woman!" came in a shout that was followed by the sound of flesh striking flesh, an open palm delivered to the face. "You do not decide what will happen to *anyone* in this family."

"Abeo, you must not—"

"You do *not* speak to me. Enough of your speaking."

"I will never allow—"

"You do not hear me?" The sound of a piece of furniture being shoved across the floor. "*I* allow. *I* do not allow. What must I do to make you understand?"

"Papa—"

"Simisola, please go to—"

"No! She stays where she is. She will watch and learn so that *she* obeys when she is asked to do something."

"Abeo, don't do this."

"Do *not* speak to me of this again."

"Please—"

"What did I just say? Do you not hear me?" The sound of striking once again, followed by a grunt, the sound of striking, a strangled shout of protest, and another cry from Simi of, "Stop it, Papa! You're hurting Mummy!"

"This is what husbands do when their wives will not obey. You listen and you watch . . . *Where* do you think . . . I am *not* finished." The thud of a body falling and then another, heavy on the floor.

Then a cry of "Abeo, stop. You're frightening—"

"I *will* show . . ." Then nothing more from Abeo but grunts and the sound of his fists, of Monifa gasping, of Simi crying, of Simi shrieking, "No! No! Papa!" then from Abeo, "You do *not* intervene in this. You see what you have made of her? Do you *now* see? You ruin what you touch. Simisola, you will *not* . . . you fucking little—"

A shriek from Simi, a scream from Monifa. Tani was on his feet heading for the bedroom door. Sophie grabbed him. She whispered, "Stop, *stop*. If you try to end this, he'll hurt you as well."

Then a roar of "Get to your room and bloody *stay* there or I will kill your mother here and now."

"Papa—" said on a sob.

"Do you want to see her dead?"

And then a rush of footsteps, another sob, and Simi was through the door and shut it behind her. Tani grabbed her and held her to him while Sophie signalled for her to be silent. Crashing and cries from the lounge.

"He's hurting Mummy!" Simisola said into Tani's chest. "Tani . . . !"

Tani whispered, "I know, Squeak. We heard. We know."

"You got to stop him!"

"I will. But you got to come with me and Sophie and you got to do it now."

"But Mummy!"

"No time, Simi," Sophie said. "Your dad wants to hurt you. Your only chance to be safe is to come with us."

"Mum would want you to come," Tani added. He picked up Simi's rucksack upon the roar of "You think I do not know what you *do*? This ends now," and a terrible cry that Tani knew he would not soon stop hearing.

At that Sophie was out of the window. Tani lifted his sister out as well. Sophie took her hand and fled down the steps. Tani was not far behind.

WESTMINSTER
CENTRAL LONDON

Barbara Havers reckoned that Nkata's confab with Hillier—no matter its subject—gave her the excuse she'd been looking for. Once he'd headed in the direction of the assistant commissioner's office, she produced a look as regretful as she could make it and spoke to Dorothea, saying, "It's not looking like the sketching experience is going to happen, Dee. We'll be working straight through, you can bet on it. Especially now Hillier's put a bee in the butter. I reckon the inspector's going to order all hands on deck." She frowned and considered what she'd just said, adding, "I think I mixed metaphors or disagreed my verbs or whatever. But you take my meaning, right?"

Dorothea's perfect posture altered slightly, a deflation of her expectations, as she said, "If I didn't know you better, Barbara—Detective Sergeant Havers, that is—I'd say you're trying to get out of this."

"Never would I dare," Barbara avowed.

"Hmph. Right. But let me ask you: Is it the *sketching* part of it that's putting you off? I did see that you chucked the bag of materials under your desk, by the way."

"Oh. Well. As to that." Barbara wasn't sure where to go from there.

"There's no reason to be nervous about sketching," Dorothea assured her. "I expect three quarters of the people there aren't sketchers at all. They probably don't even want to become sketchers. I reckon they're there for the same reason we are: they're looking for true love."

This was too much. Barbara said, "Dee, you don't actually believe in that, do you?"

"In what? In people looking for true love?"

"In true love, full stop. That only happens in fairy tales."

"And what exactly is wrong with fairy tales?"

"Nothing straight to the end of them," Barbara told her.

"Meaning?"

"Meaning the 'happily ever after' bit. It should've been 'happily enough till something came up.' Believe me: every fairy tale needs a part two."

"Oh pooh," Dorothea said. "You give up too easily."

"Well. Right. You work this job"—with a gesture that took in their surroundings—"you get a bit cynical."

"I intend to cure you of that."

"The job or cynicism?"

"Very funny. I see sketching isn't going to be the thing for you. Give me that bag. I'll take everything back."

"Cheers," Barbara said as she excavated for it beneath her desk and handed it over.

"No worries, Detective Sergeant Havers. I'll find something else that will work a trick. Just you wait." On that note, Dee clicked her stiletto-shod way back to her desk near Lynley's temporary office.

Once she was gone, Barbara placed a call to the forensics lab across the river and, after three tries, she made contact with the tech in charge of the sculptures from Teo Bontempi's flat. There was nothing, she was told, no joy whatsoever. There were a few fingerprints, but they belonged to the victim, and there was no DNA to suggest that any of the sculptures had been used to bash in anyone's head. Another damn nonstarter. Barbara made arrangements to fetch the sculptures back to Streatham, rang off, then looked online for the phone number of Taste of Tennessee.

The phone rang for a bit till someone finally barked, "Yeah? Make it bloody quick. The fryer's ready."

Barbara hastened to cooperate. Did this individual know the name of the landlord for the building next door? The Metropolitan Police were ringing.

"Why the hell would I know that? And why's the Met want it anyway?"

Did he notice the clinic next door had been closed down? Barbara asked him. Yes? Well, the Met was trying to track down the woman who worked there and it was reckoned that the landlord would have her name and address on a lease. But they needed the landlord's name.

"What's she done, this woman at the clinic?"

Nothing, as far as the Met knew. But there were a few questions about the clinic wanting answers, and as this woman worked there, she was the person most likely able to answer them.

"Can't help you," was the reply. "I can try to find out. Were they up to funny business? Got to say there *was* a bit of coming and going from the place, but it always seemed on the up and up. Jesus, this isn't about trafficking is it? Sex slaves? Foreign women believing they were being brought here for decent jobs? You know what I mean. Far as I ever saw, was only ever foreign women going in there."

No, no. It was nothing like that. Barbara recited her phone number so, in case the landlord was identified, someone could notify her at once.

Her listener took the number and promised to ring if he discovered anything. He asked if someone in particular was in trouble and then answered his own question with, "Well, why bloody else is the Met ringing, eh?" before he rang off.

Nkata joined her, fresh from his experience with Sir David Hillier, and on his heels came Lynley. Lynley spoke first with, "What's the joy?"

"Winnie's had to role-play you with Hillier just now."

Lynley looked at Nkata and said, "Ah. Thank you, Winston. That was above and beyond."

"How'd it go?" Barbara asked her colleague. "Did you bend the knee? Bow from the neck? Kiss the ring? I do hope you *backed* out of the office, at least."

"I slouched," Nkata said. He slid his paperwork onto his desktop.

"Slouched?"

"Yeah. Was recommended, it was."

"Judi-with-an-i?"

"It was s'posed to improve his state 'f mind. Bit short, i'n't he?"

"I've always got the impression it was a case of I'm-short-but-I'm-mean with Hillier. Or, p'rhaps, I'm-mean-cos-I'm-short. 'Course, being short has never bothered me, but then I'm the exception to most rules."

"That puts the matter mildly," Lynley noted. And to Nkata, "What did the AC want?"

"The clear ones. Pitchers, I mean. I tol' him the good ones came in late from digital forensics, which is why you gave him th' others. But he wants the new ones."

"Ah. Well, we did manage to buy ourselves a day."

"We need summat to distract his attention," Nkata noted. "I did get us two more DCs, though."

"Excellent work, Winston." Lynley pulled a chair over and sat. He took a mobile phone from his pocket and set it on Barbara's desk. "Where are we, then?"

Barbara said, "Nothing on the sculptures. Teo's fingerprints but no head-bashing DNA. The sculptures could've been washed, 'course. But I don't see how someone could wash off their DNA while leaving someone else's fingerprints in place. I reckon that ticks sudden rage off the list. I'm having the sculptures back at the flat tomorrow. I s'pose I could take a Ouija board with me and hope for the best."

"It may come to that," Lynley said. "Winston?"

Nkata said, "We're down to the CCTV in Streatham High Road. Prior to the killing, this is. And we got Mark Phinney's motor in the area four times. Once two days in advance 'f the attack, once on the day he found her, and two after Teo got taken to hospital."

Lynley frowned. "Taken to hospital? Or after she died?"

"Taken to hospital. How'd you get on with him?"

Lynley nodded at the phone. "It's Teo's. Phinney had it. He says he took it just after the paramedics carried her out of the flat."

"How'd you manage to get it off him?" Barbara asked.

"I asked for it, and he didn't lie about taking it or having it. He claims it was to keep his relationship with Teo under wraps and to protect his wife from knowing anything about Teo."

"Doesn't make much sense, that," Barbara said. "Was he planning to delete details or what? And f'r all he knew, Teo was going to recover, right? She was going to wonder where her mobile had gone to at that point, eh?"

"Unless, of course, he knew she wasn't going to recover," Lynley said.

Nkata added, "Had the phone's code, Phinney?"

"He claims not," Lynley said.

"Why not toss it, then? Why not leave it where it was?"

"Those are the obvious questions, aren't they? But he would have known the mobile would be short work for a cyber kiosk if there was one available and if an officer wanted to download everything."

"Phinney wouldn't want that, eh?" Nkata noted.

"Could be he wanted to hang on to sweet memories of whatever?" Barbara said. "Love in bloom et cetera?"

"There's that, isn't there. Love does make people rather . . ." Lynley paused. "I find myself at a loss for words. *Blind* isn't right for this situation."

"*Stupid* fits," Barbara said.

Lynley stood. "Let me get this down to Marjorie Lee. We'll know soon enough if there are other reasons he took the phone."

As Lynley left to see to this, one of the DCs stepped aside from where she had been lingering nearby.

Nkata said to her, "Got summat?"

"I'm not sure," the DC said. "There's a name I've come across that looks familiar. Monifa Bankole. It's in the appointment book I've been going through from the clinic and I remembered seeing it in one of the activity reports."

"Would be there, yeah," Nkata said. "She's who got arrested 'long with the woman claiming she was Easter Lange. Said she'd gone to collect money she'd given the clinic as a deposit for a procedure she was meant to have."

"Right. There's more. It's to do with the appointment book, if I can tell you."

"Tell away," Barbara said.

"Well, we saw that every name in the diary has another name in brackets beside it and so has Monifa Bankole's. But 'cording to the police report, like you said, she claimed she was there to cancel her *own* appointment and get her money back. It was for a female thing, is how she put it, yes? Was she lying?"

"Since the rozzers arrived to raid the place while she was there, I reckon we can work that out easy enough," Barbara said.

"I s'pose it's time I had another word," Nkata said. And to the DC, "C'n you make a copy of the page has her appointment listed?"

The DC nodded and went off to oblige him, passing Lynley in the corridor. Barbara said to him, "Any joy from you, Inspector?"

"They'll download everything and send it up. If there's as much as I suspect on the mobile, we'll be up to our necks. I'm glad of the extra DCs you've managed to get from Hillier, Winston. We're going to need them. In the meantime . . . ?" He looked from one of them to the other.

"Monifa Bankole," Nkata noted. "She's got a bigger connection than what she said. She wants talking to."

"Aside from Mark Phinney's, have you come up with any other interesting vehicles in the area round the time of the attack, before it, after it?" And when both Barbara and Nkata shook their heads, Lynley directed them to get a decent photo of Mark Phinney and check it against the CCTV on Teo Bontempi's building. They were to use the same dates as those on which his car was in the neighbourhood. Lynley ended with, "We need more movement on this than we're making. But I expect you know that, eh?"

TRINITY GREEN
WHITECHAPEL
EAST LONDON

"What is this place?" Tani asked. "Doesn' look like a safe house for anyone."

"It's here somewhere," Sophie replied. "Trinity Green, the website said. An' this is Trinity Green."

They'd taken forever to get to the place as part of the journey had to be made by National Rail, part by underground, and the rest by foot. Arriving at this walled compound, Tani had noted that nothing identified it as Orchid House, and he felt dizzy at the thought that they'd come to the wrong place. But Sophie pointed out that Orchid House would hardly have a sign on either the brick wall on the pavement's edge or on the wrought-iron gates that separated Trinity Green from Mile End Road. She shepherded him and Simi through the pedestrian gate, where all three paused at the edge of a central summer-brown lawn (the "green," he reckoned) and tried to work out where to go.

Sophie said Orchid House had to be housed inside the distinguished-looking building at the far end of the green. It was the largest, was her reason. It looked like a chapel to Tani, with its arched windows and wide steps leading up to a fancy front door.

There was nothing for it but finding out if there'd been a mistake in Sophie's research. So the three of them walked towards it, past silent accommodations that lined both sides of the green. They were cottage-like and they displayed a variety of belongings in the areas in front of them: everything from a tricycle missing one of its three wheels, to an old croquet set, to a barbecue lacking its grille. The accommodations themselves were in various states of good repair and disrepair, the former a general sign of private ownership and the latter indicating council digs that were going too long ignored by the council.

There were lights on inside the chapel. That was hopeful, as far as Tani was concerned. But when they tried the door, it was locked, and knocking upon it brought forth no one.

"This i'n't good." Tani dropped his arm round Simi's shoulders. She looked up at him, her dark eyes scared. "I thought you said it was always open," this to Sophie who was trying to peer into one of two side windows.

"It's *s'posed* to be open till nine o'clock," she told him. "P'rhaps there's another door?"

Simi pointed to a sign that was fixed to the other window. It was hand-lettered and looked as if it had been done in a rush. *Closed for Now* were the words on it, accompanied by *In Emergency Ring* and a number. Sophie rang, but there was no answer, just an automated voice telling her to leave a message, which she did. Then she descended the steps, signalling Tani and Simi to follow.

They found another door, this one leading to what seemed to be a basement. It bore a brass plate that said *Office*, but this door was locked as well. No sign of life came through its wooden panels.

"Damn," Sophie muttered. "Okay. New plan. We go to my house. Your parents still don't know about me, right?"

Simi looked at her, then at Tani. "Is she your girlfriend?" she asked her brother. "Is she why you said you wouldn't marry that Nigerian girl, Tani?"

Sophie swung round to look at him. "My dad's idea," he told her quickly. "I said I wouldn't do it soon 's he told me it was arranged. I di'n't tell you cos what was the point? If I marry anyone, it's not going to be some woman I never seen, Soph. An' jus' now? I'm not marrying anyone."

They went again to the front of the building. Three girls were at the foot of the steps, about to mount them. Tani told them the place was deserted, and as he was speaking an ancient white bloke came out of one of the cottages. He had scarecrow hair and whatever the scarecrow was meant to protect appeared to be growing from his eyebrows, his ears, and especially his nostrils. In the blazing heat, he was wearing a cardigan, a brushed cotton shirt, and a bow tie.

"You lot," he called to them. "There's no loit'ring round here. So skedaddle." As they approached, he went on. "Tol' her from the first, I did. There can't be loit'ring is what I said. She promised and look where we are, eh? An' she said no boys so what're *you* doing here?"

Tani didn't have to answer because one of the three newcomer girls said, "We got a meeting, we do."

Old gent replied, "Not happenin' today and could be not happenin' never. Cops were here. Got herself arrested is what she did. So, you lot? Like I said? Skedaddle. Off with you now."

"But we got a meeting," protested another of the girls. "Supposably there's someone always here. There's *meant* to be someone. Like all the time, there's meant to be someone."

"Well, I can't help that, can I? And let me tell you, I'm not spending any more of my day telling girls like you lot to run off. I'm missing my telly, I am. I been sitting at the window since the coppers took her. No handcuffs, mind. But when they left, th' place got locked up."

"By who?" Sophie asked.

"By me is by who. I got a key, don't I."

"So you could let us in."

"Could do," he agreed. "And have *no* mind to do. Don' know you, do I. Don' know a single any of you lot. I barely know *her.* Zawadi she's called. Bloody kind of name is that? Made up name, I wager: bunch 'f sounds put together. Now you get yourselfs out of here cause as long as this place's closed up, there's no space here for any of you."

"You know what this place is, though," Sophie said. "Orchid House. You know about the work it does, don't you? You know how it helps little girls. Like this one. Like Simisola here. So you could help if you wanted to."

"I got no idea 'bout any of that," Old Bloke retorted. "An' I'm not about to develop one. Mind my own business is what I do. Long 's I c'n hear the telly, I don' stick my nose anywhere else, do I."

THE NARROW WAY
HACKNEY
NORTH-EAST LONDON

Usually, Mark Phinney waited before heading home. It was a long haul to get there from Empress State Building, so the journey was best made once commuter traffic was no longer an issue. He generally spent the intervening two hours with paperwork or, occasionally, with his colleagues having a pint along Lillie Road, the nearest pub being not far from the police headquarters. His habit, then, was to arrive home round eight, bid goodbye to Robertson, and have dinner with Pete. Lilybet would have long since been given her tea, which was nearly always the same meal, fed to her by either Robertson or Pete: scrambled eggs with cheddar cheese mixed in, along with a bacon toastie. Once she'd eaten, she'd settle in for a nap, which she took in her wheelchair next to the kitchen table. This allowed Pete to make a meal for the two of them to share—often with Robertson joining them. Sometimes this worked well. Sometimes it did not.

On this evening, though, he didn't wait for the traffic to subside. He also didn't journey to Lower Clapton. Instead, he headed north to Hackney, bisecting London diagonally once he reached Holland Park Avenue. This route was like taking an economic tour of the town, as grubby terraces gave way to pristine mansions that gave way to neighbourhoods once considered disreputable but now deemed unaffordable. His objective was one of Paulie's two pawnshops. They were kept open till nine o'clock, so he had plenty of time.

He didn't want Paulie, however. He wanted Stuart, Paulie's brother-in-law.

Mark looked at his watch as he pulled into a space in front of Paddy Power betting shop, across the way from Pembury Estate and a short diagonal walk from one of Paulie's shops. He got out of the car and crossed over to The Narrow Way. Families were out and about in the pedestrian precinct. The open shops provided them with a mild diversion and the evening air was probably cooler than the insides of their houses.

The pawn shop's two neon signs were ablaze, and the bells on the door jangled discordantly as he entered. It was hideously hot inside as there was no air-conditioning and no cross ventilation either. Mark was surprised the walls weren't sweating.

"Moment," Stuart called from the back. He sounded as if his mouth were crammed with something as it no doubt was. McDonald's was just down the way.

"Take your time," Mark called back to him. "'S Paulie around?"

"Mark . . . ? Lemme . . ." Stuart came through the beaded curtain, wiping his hands on a paper napkin, which he then applied to his forehead. "He's down below," Stuart said, by which Mark knew he meant the other shop at the far end of the street. "Sh'll I ring him, then?"

"No. I actually wanted you," Mark told him. "I've already spoken to Paulie." He took from his pocket the claim ticket for the pawnshop that he'd found in Pete's bag. He slid this across the counter to Stuart. "Found this in Pete's wallet," he said.

Stuart said at once, "Oh, I say Mark. If Paulie wouldn't—"

"Could be that I didn't make myself clear enough when I asked him," Mark said. "I'm trying to work out what Pete might have done with the money you gave her in exchange for whatever she pawned. What was it, by the way?"

"I can't tell you that," Stuart said, although he did look slightly uncomfortable, which was gratifying to Mark. "That's between the client and the shop, that is. Why don't you just ask her?"

"Obviously," Mark said. "She'd prefer I didn't know."

"Well, then . . ."

"I don't need to know the amount of money you gave her, Stuart," Mark said. "I don't even need to know the exact item she brought in."

"Items," Stuart said, glancing away from Mark as if in a search for eavesdroppers or listening devices.

Mark decided not to jump on that. He said, "I just need to know— for her sake and for Lilybet's sake—the *category* of item she brought in."

"I don't quite . . . category?"

Mark looked round for something that would explain what he meant. Behind Stuart and arranged on a glass shelf in no particular pattern and with no particular method were six humidors. He pointed them out and said, "Items relating to cigars. And"—with a gaze into the glass case between them, where pocket watches and wristwatches were displayed—"timepieces." He pointed to the wall and said, "Paintings or, if you'd like, art pieces."

Stuart looked thoughtful. Mark didn't push him. Stuart finally said, "I s'pose I c'n tell you that."

He brought from under the counter a volume that would have made Ebenezer Scrooge sigh in delight as he bent over it, scribbling figures by candlelight. Mark couldn't believe Paulie wasn't doing things digitally. Then again, an ancient ledger did have a certain cachet in a pawnshop.

Stuart flipped back two pages and ran his index finger down a column. Mark reckoned he was doing this for the drama of the moment. Stuart drew his eyebrows together and said slowly, "I see . . . How does one say . . . ? Well, I can tell you this at least: jewellery and silver." He looked up at Mark. "I hope that's helpful."

As Pete had virtually no jewellery and as a couple they had absolutely no silver, Mark said, "That's the lot, is it?"

"'Fraid so. But Mark, c'n I say . . . ?" Stuart closed the book and returned it beneath the counter. "I mean, it's none of my business but . . . Why don't you ask her?"

Mark thought about how to reply. "You're right," he said. "It's none of your business."

He left the shop. Stuart was sputtering something behind him, which told Mark that his next action was going to be to ring Mark's brother. That couldn't be helped, and at this point Mark wondered what *could* be helped. He was no closer to knowing what Pietra had pawned than he'd been before. He was no closer to knowing why she wanted money. He was also no closer even to knowing whether she pawned something *because* she wanted or needed money, or whether she had another reason.

11 AUGUST

He woke in the darkness from the kind of dream he'd had far too often in the first six months after Helen's death. In this dream, he'd heard her clearly. She'd said, "Tommy, darling," in that way she'd had of addressing him before she made a request to which she knew he wouldn't want to acquiesce or a suggestion that she knew he would not want to take. There'd been any number of other ways she'd said those words *Tommy darling* in the years they'd been together—both before and during their marriage—and each of them had a separate meaning.

In his dream, he looked up upon hearing her, his heartbeat light and rapid. Her voice had been quite distinct, his name spoken as if she stood directly at his ear. But he couldn't see her in the room, so he went in search of her, knowing that she was nearby, sure that she was in the house. This knowledge raised such a longing within him that he resolved not to stop looking till he found her. He went from room to room, and in doing this, he grew to believe that she was somewhere just beyond his reach, but she *was* there. *There.*

The rooms he passed through were not in London, though. Nor were they the rooms of his family's home on the south-east coast of

Cornwall. He didn't recognise them, and this added to his desperation. He felt a hollow need open within him.

Waking, then, he recognised nothing at first. He saw only the shapes of things, the identity of which he waited to dawn upon him. As he waited, he heard it again, "Tommy?" and he turned his head towards the sound.

He saw that he was in bed with Daidre, but the anguished, hollow loss he'd been experiencing in his dream did not fade. He felt a sense of immense betrayal that told him how unfair he was being. But he could not have said where to apply the unfairness: to the memory of Helen or to the woman he was with, who was facing him, with one of her arms curled under her head and a lock of sandy hair falling across her cheek.

She murmured, "Are you quite all right, Tommy? What time is it? Are you leaving?"

He wanted to. He couldn't imagine feeling any more wretched in his faithlessness. How could he possibly profess his love for this good woman? he asked himself. How could he make love to her and remain with her afterwards—for that was surely where they were, in her flat and not in his Belgravia house—when he felt a groundswell of purist agony upon the thought of Helen. And yet, Daidre was so much his comfort in moments like this. She was a place of resting that he sought out even when, he admitted to himself, he had so little to offer her in return.

He'd arrived in Belsize Park quite late. He hadn't actually intended to come to Daidre at all. With his mind occupied with what they knew about Teo Bontempi, with what they were uncovering about her final weeks of life, and with what all of it might mean, he'd driven to Belsize Park as if on autopilot. Upon arriving, he'd looked round blankly, realised what he'd done, and also realised that he should turn round and head south towards his home. But he'd been incapable of doing that, especially when he saw the sitting-room lights shining from Daidre's flat. He fixed his gaze on that sitting-room window, then, and waited for his mind to clear of all he'd gathered from Marjorie Lee.

It hadn't taken long for her to download everything from Teo Bontempi's mobile using a cyber kiosk. The device had been created for this precise purpose, officers had been trained to use it, and the result was that people's information and their habits, as revealed on their mobiles, were not as secure from the eyes of others as modern technology had led them to believe. Any individual's life became an open book once their mobile phone left their possession and somehow ended up in the hands of the police. With a cyber kiosk, anything that registered on a mobile phone was easily downloaded, generally within twenty minutes. Ordinary people going about their daily lives didn't have to worry much about this. Villains, on the other hand, had to worry plenty.

He'd told Havers and Nkata to go their respective ways while he waited for the documentation to arrive from Marjorie Lee. But neither of them had done so. Havers said, "Really, sir, it's not like I have a hot anything waiting for me at home: man, dog, or jacket potato," while Nkata put in, "I'm ringing my mum, guv. She'll keep a meal warm long 's I promise to eat it eventually."

So they remained. Once the information from the dead woman's phone was transferred to them, they divided it, and there was much to divide. In addition to Teo's texts and a record of her phone calls, they had all of her photos, her recordings, her voice messages, the uses to which she'd put her GPS, her games, her favourite restaurants, her Uber history . . . In short, they had it all and all of it had to be gone through. The DCs on loan would be able to help them, but considering the number of queries and interviews that would be required, everyone was going to be working long hours from now on. For this reason, Lynley had told them all to go home for a rest. They had a real slog ahead of them and God only knew how long it would take.

Now, he heard Daidre say, "Have you slept at all, Tommy?"

"I have," he told her. "But I think that's it for the rest of the night. What time is it?"

"Ten past four," she told him after a moment of consulting the clock on her upended bedside cardboard box.

"Hmmm," he replied. "That's three and a half hours. I've done worse." He swung his legs off the bed and sat up, reaching for his clothes that lay discarded on the floor.

She put her hand on his bare back. "You're very tense," she said. "I wish I could do something to help you."

"Go back to sleep. You've your own workday to consider."

"I do. And I will. But just now, let me make you a coffee."

She reached for her dressing gown, donned it, and padded to the kitchen. He began to dress. He heard a door open and then close, followed by the plaintive mewing of a cat with expectations.

Daidre said, "Have you actually been watching the window?" to which Wally responded with another sad mew. "Yes, well," Daidre told the cat, "you must play second fiddle just now." And then, "Wally, *no*. Not the work top and *not* the table or out you go . . . Oh, all right. Here it is, then."

Lynley smiled as he heard the cat's food being spilled into his bowl. He finished dressing, took up Daidre's spectacles from the cardboard box, and went to the kitchen. Daidre was busy at her coffee machine while Wally munched happily in the corner.

Lynley turned Daidre to him and set the specs on her nose. He smoothed her hair behind her ears. He said, "This is above and beyond, you know."

"In your view, perhaps. But not in Wally's. Will you go straight back to work from here, Tommy?"

He shook his head. "Home first. Shower, shave, change my clothes, and let Charlie know I haven't been kidnapped."

She nodded. He could see, though, that she wanted to say something but was stopping herself. He said, "What is it?"

"Nothing."

"Are you certain?"

"I am."

"We hardly spoke last night."

She smiled. "There wasn't a great deal of time for speaking, was there."

Still and all, he thought. He said, "Daidre, *is* there something . . . ?"

"Something?"

"Something that's happened, something wrong, something that's going on that I should know about?"

"Not at all, Tommy."

"You *would* tell me if there was, wouldn't you?"

She cocked her head and looked at him fondly. "Probably not. At least not just now and certainly not if I knew I could resolve it myself."

"Should I feel insulted? Or perhaps jealous of Wally?"

"Insulted, no. Jealous of Wally? Well, do just *look* at him, Tommy. Who could help telling him all one's secrets?"

Wally raised his head, favoured them with a blank expression, and returned to his food.

Lynley chuckled. "He's certain to be a dispassionate listener, isn't he."

"He's no bleeding heart, that's true enough. But really, when it comes to speaking of one's troubles, is a bleeding heart actually necessary?"

Lynley kissed her. He brought his car keys from his trouser pocket. "I'm not foolish enough to answer that," he told her.

WESTMINSTER
CENTRAL LONDON

He arrived at New Scotland Yard shortly after six, having showered, shaved, and changed his clothes at home as planned. He was at

Barbara's desk when she arrived at seven, followed closely by Winston. She, as usual, was dressed in the height of Havers Fashion: striped drawstring trousers, red high-top trainers, a T-shirt whose slogan was mercifully covered by the pink hoodie she wore. Nkata, as usual, was dressed to impress: blindingly white shirt and tie, suit coat held over his shoulder by his thumb.

Havers carried a Pop-Tart with several bites missing. She saw Lynley clock this over the tops of his reading specs. She also saw Nkata do likewise. She said, "Say nothing, you lot. Especially *you*, Winnie. I don't have a mum whipping up . . . what*ever* your mum whips up in the morning cos I expect it's extra-nutritious, perfectly balanced, and packed with vitamins. And *you*," to Lynley, "what time did you roll in here?"

"Since I wasn't sleeping it was a choice: walking the floor or coming in. Let's have a look at her final days. I've been noodling over some information from her mobile."

"And?" Havers leaned her hip against her desk, where Lynley still sat.

Nkata rolled out his desk chair and offered it to her. "I'm good, Winnie. Ta, though," she said.

"Multiple calls and voice messages from her sister," Lynley said. He rose from her desk chair, gesturing for her to sit. "Only a few returned. Multiple calls to her parents, one voice message from them."

"Wha's the nature of the messages?" Nkata said.

"From her parents, just of the sorry-we-missed-your-call variety. From her sister, it's a bit different."

"Meaning what?" Havers brought a packet of tissues from her large and lumpy shoulder bag. She used one as a napkin, wiping the remains of the Pop-Tart from her fingers and her lips.

"I've only listened to the most recent ones," Lynley told them. "They're messages asking to meet, wanting to talk, urging her— urging Teo, I mean—to tell him the truth."

"*Him* being Ross Carver?" Havers asked.

"Could be. There're four calls to him in the week before she was attacked."

"He tol' Barb she wanted him to come to her for a chat, innit?" Nkata said.

"She texted him, was what he said. Is there a record of that?"

"This corroborates it, yes. But it doesn't eliminate him, as we all know. We've only his word that he found her, helped her to bed, and stayed with her till early morning."

"Other calls?" Havers asked.

"To and from Orchid House, same from someone called Narissa Cameron."

"She's the woman making the documentary film at Orchid House," Havers put in. "She showed me footage she'd taken of Teo as Adaku. She seemed fine to me, Narissa did. And Adaku—Teo, sorry—helped her with the girls, making them more comfortable with talking to the camera. Can't think Narissa would've coshed her for that."

"We got anything from Phinney?" Nkata asked.

Lynley said, "He did tell me to expect to see his relationship with Teo play out on her mobile. He wasn't stretching the truth, by any means. Texts, calls, voice messages, videos, photos. He was besotted. So was she."

"The usual I've-found-my-soul-mate bit?" Havers asked.

"More or less."

"Such tosh," she groused.

"Your day will come," Lynley told her, and Nkata added, "'Specially 'f Dee has anything to do with it."

"Aside from the this-is-bigger-than-both-of-us rubbish," Havers persisted, "'s there anything interesting?"

"He continued to send her text messages after she went into hospital—"

"D'you mean when he had her phone?"

"I do. There are three after she passed as well."

"So he's sending messages to himself, essentially," Havers noted.

"Coverin' his tracks," Nkata pointed out.

"Possibly," Lynley said.

"Sent by someone using Phinney's phone?"

"There's that as well."

"Wife?" Nkata said.

"When I went to Lower Clapton to fetch the mobile, I showed Phinney the improved CCTV pictures. He claimed he didn't recognise either woman, but I saw his wife while I was there speaking to him."

"She's one of the women went to see Teo?"

"One of the two she didn't admit into the building. We'll need to have a word with her. Phinney will be at work, so there's a good chance we can get something out of her."

"She seem the type to bash in a rival's skull, guv?" Havers asked.

"That's always the question, isn't it," he said. "Who knows what's enough to drive people to take an action they otherwise wouldn't consider? There's also a message on the mobile left by a Dr. Weatherall, a woman's voice. She asks Teo to ring her back. She phoned from a landline, though, not from a mobile. The landline's attached to Women's Wellness on the Harbour. Three other calls went from that landline to Teo as well."

"D'we know what Women's Wellness on the Harbour is?" Nkata asked.

"Could it be associated with *evaluation* in her engagement diary?" Havers said.

"We know *where* it is." Lynley bent over Havers's desk and sorted through some paperwork. He said, "Teo used her GPS to find it." He brought out what he'd been looking for and said, "Inner Harbour Square."

"Where's that?" Havers asked.

"Isle of Dogs. You take that, Barbara. I'm going to have another word with Phinney."

MAYVILLE ESTATE
DALSTON
NORTH-EAST LONDON

In the aftermath, she'd managed to go to her bedroom. Since she and Simisola had been sharing it, she'd assumed Simi would run there when Abeo demanded she do so. When Simi wasn't there, she went to Tani's room. But it, too, was empty. The window was open, though, and the obvious conclusion was that Simi had fled. As far as Monifa knew, there were only two places that she could go. She could cross the estate and hide herself in Hamilah's flat. Or she could dash to Ridley Road Market and choose the relative safety of either Masha's Cake Decorating or Xhosa's Beauty.

Monifa knew that she would have to find her daughter and bring her back. But at that moment, she wasn't. Beneath her breasts was pain so severe she could breathe only shallowly, and her jaw sent a searing pain to her head when she opened her mouth, while the rest of her face suggested heavy bruising. The one thing she *could* do was ring Hamilah. But Simisola, Hamilah said, was not with her. Nor had she been.

The only grace given was that Abeo was gone. He hadn't bothered to seek Simisola after his punishment of Monifa was finished. His fury abated, he'd left. She assumed he had gone to his other family or he'd gone to work. It didn't matter. The important bit was that he had not returned home.

Nor had Tani, which gave Monifa reassurance. She told herself that if Tani had spent the night elsewhere, Simi had found him and had told him the tale and now Tani was protecting her from Abeo.

Nothing about any of this had changed by the morning. When she slowly rose, Monifa crept to the bathroom through sheer nerve and by holding on to furniture and pressing against walls. Once there, she looked in the mirror and assessed the damage. She'd tasted blood after one of Abeo's multitude of punches and now she could see that her lip had been split. The skin beneath her eyes looked raw, and it was sore to the lightest touch. Her eyes themselves were very swollen—one of them nearly shut—and her forehead bore a cut that had seeped blood during the night.

As she looked upon her image, Monifa knew she had only herself to blame. She'd gone to Leyton. She'd confronted Chinara Sani with words she'd thought were brave. Indeed, she'd felt quite courageous about what she was doing. She'd not understood that the doing itself was criminally stupid.

Although he did not speak, Abeo's rage had been palpable all the way back to Mayville Estate, but she knew he wouldn't show it in public, so she also knew that she was safe until they reached Bronte House. Once there and inside the flat, though, Abeo had let his fury loose. His cry of "Why do you not obey me?" gave way to the penalty she was meant to pay. At the end, when she was suitably cowed and crumpled, he'd stormed out of the flat, the door slamming shut behind him. Silence swept in, in his wake.

She'd laid there on the floor. Rest, she'd thought. For a moment. Just rest. She thought briefly about how odd it all was: She'd spent so much time trying to work out how to protect Simisola from her father's plans, but she needn't have done. For it was clear that Simi had already worked out how to protect herself.

Finally, when she was able, Monifa moved hesitantly to the kitchen. From the refrigerator, she brought out ice. She was wrapping a few cubes into a kitchen towel when the phone began to ring. She let it go to message and heard, then, her mother's voice. "*Abeg* no vex me, Monifa. You must answer this phone. Abeo has rung me. I know what has happened. Pick up the phone."

Monifa did, as always, what she was told to do. But she said, "What has Abeo told you?"

Her mother's answer was, "You must not be a *mumu* wife, Monifa. You must not oppose Abeo in this. He will kill you, daughter. You must stop this at once."

"I *found* someone to do it," Monifa cried. "It was to be done in a way that Simisola would not suffer the way I suffered."

"Monifa, listen well. Let Abeo bring her to Nigeria. I will tell him he may stay with us so that Simisola can see her granny, yes? I will make the arrangements here. I will see it's done proper way."

"There is no 'proper way' in Nigeria, not where you live," Monifa told her.

"I will see to it."

"Like you saw to me?"

A silence before her mother said, "That was many, many years ago. It is different now."

"How is it different? I won't do it. *No.*"

Her mother's sigh was perfectly audible, even at all this great distance from her. "Monifa, *daina*. I ask you this. What good are you to Simisola if you are dead, eh? What happens to her if you are gone? *Abeg*. Let him bring her to me and I will see she does not come to harm."

Monifa didn't reply. Tears seeped from her eyes, easing beneath the kitchen towels that held the ice and snaking down her cheeks.

"Monifa, are you there? You hear me? I can ring him now?"

Silently, Monifa replaced the phone. She lowered herself painfully to one of the chairs at the table. She returned the kitchen towel and the ice to her face and was sitting there when the door opened. She steeled herself to what would come next.

But it was Tani who spoke, "Mum! Fuck! What'd he *do* to you?"

Hastily she lowered the ice, but that act and what it revealed caused him to cry out, "I'm taking you to A and E. Let's go."

"No," she said. "That will make things worse."

"So what's it going to be?" Tani demanded. "Are you just going to let him kill you? Then, what? I c'n take care of myself, Mum, but Simi can't."

"She managed . . . Yesterday, she went. She knew what to do. She will be—"

"Bloody goddamn hell, Mum. I was *here*. I was in the bedroom. She didn't take herself anywhere. I took her."

"Where?"

"Someplace safe."

"*Where*? You must tell me."

"Tha's not on. No way am I letting him beat it out of you. You won't find her. Neither will he."

Tani had his rucksack with him, and he dropped this on the table where she sat. He opened it. He riffled through its contents and brought out a sheaf of papers. They appeared to be documents that had been filled out. "This's called a protection order," he told her. "It's meant to keep Simi safe. It's all filled out but you got to add information 'bout wha's been going on round here. You got to write that Dad is planning to take her to Nigeria so she can be cut. An' you got to sign it. 'F you do that, I mean if it comes from you direct, we c'n get an urgent order, and Pa doesn't learn 'bout it till it's all done. It means we don't need to wait for papers to go through some government system. It gets done fast—like today, Mum—an' only later is there a hearing."

"A hearing? With a judge? A magistrate? I cannot—"

"Yes, you can. 'Specially if you ever want to see Simi again. An' I mean that. Cos 'nless you fill out these parts of the order I lef' blank, I'm not bringing her back. You got to write *all* of it out. You got to include the cutter here in London. You got to explain how Dad means to take Simi to Nigeria now, how he's going to have her cut there, how he's going to arrange for her marriage, and all the rest."

He brought a biro from the back pocket of his jeans. He put the paperwork in front of her. He clasped her hand and folded her fingers round the biro. He said to her, "Once this's filled out, you got to leave him. Please. You *got* to, Mum."

Monifa bent her head. The paperwork shimmered in her vision. She'd tried. She'd failed. And this would be worse. She knew it because she knew her husband. He wouldn't allow this to pass without his judgement falling upon her. She dropped the pen.

Tani said in a low voice, "Mum, look at what he's done. Please. Think about what more he can do. This . . . this order here? It can protect Simi from him but it can't do that now—straightaway like—unless you fill out your part of it."

He picked up the biro once again. Once again he curved her fingers round it. This time, he guided them straight to the section that wanted filling out. This time, Monifa began to write.

She wrote all of it because she knew that Tani spoke the truth. Even if it meant that she, too, could not now see to Simisola's cleansing—even in the way she'd planned it—she couldn't risk Abeo's taking her away.

When she was finished writing, she placed the biro next to the paperwork. Tani spoke again. "Mum, I got to say this. There're places for women who have husbands like him, blokes who lay into their wives like he does. You don't have to stay here. And you *can't* stay here once I get this filed. You got to know that. Tell me you know that."

But Monifa found she had no words. Her soul felt too heavy. Her body was wounded, true, but her psychic wounds ran deep and they felt permanent.

Tani was folding up the paperwork when the flat's door opened. It was the wrong time of day. They should have been safe. But clearly, Abeo wasn't finished with Monifa.

He looked from Monifa to Tani to the papers Tani was holding. He crossed the room in three steps, so quickly that Tani had no time to stuff the protection order into his rucksack. Abeo grabbed it. It didn't take more than a glance at the bold printing at the top of the first page: Application for a Female Genital Mutilation (FGM) Protection Order. Seeing this, Abeo ripped the papers into pieces, threw them at Tani, and launched himself upon the boy. No matter that Tani was inches taller and possessing the strength that came from Monifa's family, Abeo's momentum knocked him to the floor, with Abeo landing atop him.

"This would you do!" Abeo drew back his fist. He punched Tani's face. Then again. And again. With every blow came another shouted word: "Defy. Disobey. Deny a father his rights."

"Stop it!" Monifa cried.

Tani scrambled for purchase but there was none. He tried to heave his father away, but Abeo knelt upon his arms with his weight on Tani's chest, pinning him to the floor. He raised Tani's head and slammed it down. "You go to the market," he grunted. "You go to Xhosa. You spread lies. You shame me. You shame our family."

"We—"

"I *will* teach you." Abeo drove his fists against Tani's cheekbones, his ears, his eyes, his chin, his mouth, his neck.

"Stop it!" Monifa got to her feet. She stumbled to the kitchen. There had to be something.

"Fucking son of a whore," Abeo grunted. "This time I will . . ."

Monifa grabbed the only weapon in sight, the iron with which she faithfully pressed the wrinkles from Abeo's shirts and from the clothing of his other family. She took it to where he still straddled their son, Tani bleeding so badly that he looked like someone sure to die.

"You will not!" she screamed and the scream unleashed within her a force she didn't know she had. She swung the iron into Abeo's forehead.

_____

TRINITY GREEN
WHITECHAPEL
EAST LONDON

Deborah had no real reason to be at Orchid House, so as she crossed the green and walked towards the old chapel, she decided that she would claim she was there to allow the girls she'd photographed to choose which of their portraits they would like to have as a thank-you for posing. But first she had to speak with Narissa, and she hoped Orchid House was where she would be able to find her.

RESTORED! was what had greeted her on the front page of *The Source* as she descended into the kitchen in Cheyne Row that morning before her departure. The tabloid was being held up by one of the presenters on BBC *Breakfast*. Her dad was tuned in to the show and, when he saw her as he entered the room with a cantaloupe and a honeydew melon in each hand, he said, "They got that little girl back home, they do."

This was an unnecessary explanation, for the next tabloid—with MISSING DAUGHTER RETURNS! as its major headline clarified who had been RESTORED! to whom. The accompanying photographs came onto the television's screen: Bolu with her parents smiling broadly as they all stood together on the top steps of their home, then Charles Akin shaking the hand of one of the officers who had brought the girl home.

The presenters declaimed on the subject of how many column inches were devoted to the story in the day's papers. Many, Deborah discovered. And she knew that while the stories in each would be the same, the approaches to the stories would be completely different: one emotionless, dispassionate, and fact-oriented and the other as sensational as possible. Someone would have used a thesaurus to locate supercharged verbs and adverbs.

Her father placed the melons on the chopping-block table and fetched a knife. He said, "At the end of the day, seems the best happened, Deb," with a nod at the television.

"Why do you say that?"

"Tha' woman got arrested yesterday." He tilted his head towards the television.

"Who? Who was arrested?"

"Her who was interviewed on the telly saying she wouldn't give the girl back till the parents did what she wanted."

"Zawadi? But she had Bolu's best interests at heart. All she wanted was to meet the parents with a social worker present. They were the ones who refused."

"Well, I say she got bloody lucky, she did. Parents've said they're not pressing charges. Said they un'erstand the work this Zawadi person is doing an' they support it one hundred percent. Said they un'erstand young girls're at risk. Said they don' know why Bolu went to that place—"

"Orchid House?"

"—but when Bolu's rested an' happy an' feeling secure, they're talking to her about all of it, they said. All's well that ends well, you ask me."

But there was another consideration in all of this: Had anything happened to Narissa? Deborah had suggested that the filmmaker move the little girl to the home of her twelve-step sponsor, but either someone had seen Bolu during that move or Bolu had not been moved at all. So once in Whitechapel, she went first to the basement. She heard Zawadi speaking to someone. She approached the office door and listened.

"I spent the night in a custody suite!" Zawadi was exclaiming hotly. "D'you know what that's like? And Ned had to stop with his father. He's not even *seen* that bugger in three years."

"I *tried* to explain it to you." To Deborah's relief, it was Narissa speaking. "The police had already been once when she fetched that kitten in from the garden. It was a miracle they didn't find her. But my parents were upset, especially my dad, so I needed to move her. I rang Victoria—my twelve-step sponsor—but she couldn't take her. I'd already asked Deborah—"

"No one places these girls with white people! You don't know that?"

"—but she said Bolu wouldn't be secure because her dad's been following the story and he thinks the parents are in the right. So after Victoria, I had to keep her. Then my parents found out, and my dad rang the cops."

"We see how *that* worked out, don't we? There she is, back at home. And whatever happens next is going to be on you."

"The parents won't lay a hand on Bolu. She's been on the front page of every newspaper, so *who'd* be willing to risk doing anything to her now?" Narissa asked.

"I'm not talking about that. Once that girl was returned, the credibility of Orchid House got flushed down the toilet. Who will *ever* believe me after this?"

"I didn't want this to happen, but I *tried* to tell you what was going on, how dangerous it would be if I kept her. But you told me there was no place else available—"

"Who in the community d'you expect will ever be willing to take an endangered girl into their home on my word alone after all this? And now it's known that all parents have to do to have a child returned is to hold out long enough to garner public sympathy. They do that and wait for pressure to build and wait for someone—someone like *you*, Narissa—to make it easy to tell the coppers where the child is.

So what you've done is this: You've brought the work of Orchid House into disrepute. You've placed hundreds—p'rhaps thousands—of girls in danger."

"I'll come forward, then," Narissa said. "I'll say what's true: that *I* had Bolu with me. I'll say *I'm* the one who talked *you* into hiding her because I believed Bolu would be cut."

"And what good is that? She came to Orchid House. She disappeared from Orchid House. I'm the face of Orchid House and *I* was the one giving the interviews. And what are we now, at Orchid House? We're the ones who shouted wolf when there was no wolf. So the next girl who's afraid she's to be harmed in some way . . . ? Exactly where is she supposed to go now that Orchid House has been thoroughly tarnished?"

There was a moment of silence before Narissa said, "So let me interview you for the film. Zawadi, you can emerge from all this as a heroine if we approach things correctly."

"Oh, too right. This is all about your film, as usual. Everything is about your film. I want no part of it."

"But, Zawadi—"

"No. I'm finished with you. You've done your damage. You stay away."

"I know you're angry, but don't you see how you can channel that anger to—"

"No! Finish your bloody documentary someplace else. I want you gone."

Deborah was compelled to intervene. She went to the door of Zawadi's office. Both of the women were seated: Zawadi behind her desk and Narissa next to a water cooler, as if she needed distance.

Zawadi saw her first and said, "And why are *you* here?"

"Please don't blame Narissa," Deborah said. "I probably could have solved her problem by taking Bolu home with me. But my husband agreed with my dad about returning Bolu to her parents, so I didn't think I could trust them. I didn't want to risk it. Narissa wasn't . . ." Deborah found she didn't know what else to say.

Zawadi, however, did. "Get out of here. I want you *out* of here. People like you think this is a game. People like you haven't got a clue what it's like to be people like me. Or like Bolu. Or like *anyone* who's not lily-white English."

"That's *completely* unfair," Deborah cried.

"I don't care what you think it is. Leave. Both of you leave." Zawadi pushed back her chair and rose to her impressive height, made more impressive by the head wrap she wore. She gestured first to Deborah and then to Narissa as she said, "You've taken your pictures. And *you* have made your film. You both have what you want." She pointed to the doorway.

A few moments of tense silence ticked by. Narissa rose. She came towards Deborah. She slipped past her and into the corridor. Zawadi's eyes narrowed. Deborah joined Narissa.

They didn't speak until they were outside, where Narissa squinted in the sun, her head turned in the direction of Mile End Road. She said, "It's not the end of the world. I've got a lot of footage. But Zawadi's right in one respect. This could kill Orchid House."

"That can't be the case," Deborah said.

"I'm going to need a meeting," Narissa continued, more to herself than to Deborah. "I can make a go of today but tomorrow . . . ? No. I'll need a meeting tonight and another tomorrow morning and then *perhaps* I can work out what to do."

Deborah considered this for a moment before she recalled earlier conversations with Narissa. She said, "Have you found your film's narrator?"

Narissa laughed derisively. "Please. This is not the time."

"Hear me out, just for a moment."

"Look, everyone I've spoken to is on board with the film's importance straightaway and two have offered to do voice-over narration once the piece is edited. But that's not what I want. I want a presence on film, not just a voice."

"Zawadi," Deborah said.

"As narrator? That's a mad idea, that is. I don't see her helping either one of us."

"Oh, I doubt she'd help me," Deborah admitted. "And she won't help you either, if you frame it as help. Thing is, Narissa, she needs you as much as you need her."

Narissa was silent as she took this in. Finally, she said, "Orchid House. Its reputation."

"Isn't Orchid House the real point? Orchid House and the work it does?"

"The real point is to open people's eyes about FGM. *That* it still happens and *how* it happens."

"Right. But, from what I've learned from being here, this seems to be a cultural . . . I don't know . . . is *problem* the right word?"

"It's definitely that. Go on."

"And at the same time, it's something not practised as widely as it once was. Yet it's *still* practised, even today. So girls are still at risk, even today. Which is what the documentary is shining a light upon."

Narissa looked beyond her, to the moptop trees. She said slowly, "Yes. And that being the case—because it is the case—having Zawadi in the film—"

"—articulating those facts—"

"—would make Zawadi part of the solution, instead of having her seen as some angry Black woman with a thorn in her arse," Narissa finished.

"It also brings the work of Orchid House into the picture," Deborah noted.

"Which saves its reputation while it saves Zawadi's reputation."

"Which is good for everyone, if you ask me," Deborah said.

"Especially for young girls," Narissa replied.

EMPRESS STATE BUILDING
WEST BROMPTON
SOUTH-WEST LONDON

Lynley took with him not only the improved CCTV photos—which he'd shown Phinney earlier—but also all of the texts that the DCS and Teo Bontempi had shared. It was quite a number. When she was part of the team, the texts were revealing, but brief. After Phinney had managed her transfer, they were lengthy on his part, brief or nonexistent on hers.

Lynley could tell the DCS wasn't happy to see him but attempting to hide this reaction. He rose from his desk, saying, "One of the team or me?" and when Lynley indicated it was Phinney he wanted a word with, the DCS took him not to the Orbit, but to a nearby conference room, where Lynley said to him, "You'll know we have everything from DS Bontempi's mobile. Not just the texts."

"I reckoned that would be the case. Technology moves with lightning speed."

"From reading her texts, it seems she was as taken with you as you were with her."

"At first, yes."

"Did something other than the forced transfer change things?"

"The pressure didn't help." Phinney gestured to the conference table. It was large, capable of seating more than a dozen people. They sat opposite each other. It was a deliberate egalitarian choice on Lynley's part, signalling to Phinney that they were playing on the same team. For now.

"What sort of pressure?" Lynley asked.

"For sex. We never had . . . ordinary relations. She wouldn't allow it. Actually, she wouldn't allow anything having to do with . . . with that part of her body at all. But I persisted. I thought what every mad fool thinks: I can wear her down. Each time, a little further we'll go until paradise is reached. I expect you know what I mean."

"But nothing changed."

"I thought she was trying to maintain control, that until I left my wife, she was going to deny me. It never once occurred to me that there might be another reason, that there was something about her body she wanted to hide from me. Why would I think that? We were mad for each other. Or at least I was mad for her and she said she felt the same for me. But at this point, who the hell knows."

"So you never had intercourse."

"We didn't. Just . . . what she did to me."

Lynley nodded. He looked through the texts he'd had off Teo's mobile and found the one he wanted. He showed it to Phinney. *Darling to be inside you once more once more.*

Phinney read it but said nothing.

"Given the situation, I expect you didn't send this message. But it came from your phone. Your wife believed you were lovers, didn't she. Not merely emotional lovers but physical lovers as well. What I don't understand is the why of it. Not why you were involved with Teo Bontempi, but why your wife would have sent her this text?"

Phinney said, "I don't know."

Lynley brought out the improved CCTV pictures and laid them out. "She was there, Mark. Two days before Teo was attacked. I believe you recognised her at once when I showed you these yesterday."

"She wouldn't have hurt Teo. She *didn't* hurt Teo."

"Why would she have gone to see her in the first place, then? Teo didn't answer the texts your wife sent, so she had no actual confirmation that you and Teo were involved, had she?"

"She'd told me she knew who it was. I never confirmed anything."

"Perhaps Teo did the confirming when your wife called on her."

"Pete wouldn't have gone to get confirmation. She would have gone to ask Teo to think about Lilybet and what it would mean if I left them. Not that I ever would have done, Teo or not."

"But she didn't know that," Lynley said. "Your wife, I mean."

"I've told her often enough. But there are reasons she wouldn't believe me." And when Lynley said nothing to this, merely waited to hear a further explanation, "We share the same home, Thomas. We share the caring for Lilybet. We share meals and we share conversation and we share a bed. And that's all we share."

"You're saying you live as flatmates? Like brother and sister?"

"Like a brother who sleeps with his sister if *sleeps* isn't a euphemism for anything else. She wants me to have more with someone, something physical. But she wants it to be with nothing attached. No other involvement. No connection."

"Just sex?"

"Yes." Phinney laughed ruefully. He ran his hand along the top of the table, a gesture that stopped him from going on. But he'd not said enough, so he added, "Believe me, I'm completely aware of the irony."

"I'm not sure what you mean."

"I mean that I ended up with the connection but not the sex. Not the *act* of sex. It turned out exactly as Pete feared, but without my having the benefit of sex."

"She knew that there was an emotional connection between you and Teo?"

"I never told her, but she could see the change in me." He looked sharply at Lynley, as if to read him before he asked, "Have you ever been nearly mad with love? Do you know what I mean? Have you ever reached the point when you can no longer think straight because the only thoughts you can muster both begin and end with her? Everything else is obliterated from your mind and only she remains."

"I haven't," Lynley said. "I've been in love, yes. I've badly wanted someone as well. But not driven mad because of it."

"Lucky you. But I expect that's owing to your life rolling along on its expected journey. No need to go mad if what you need and what you want are also needed and wanted by the other."

Lynley didn't illuminate him on the subject of his life rolling along on its expected journey. From age sixteen, that had hardly been the case. It still wasn't. He said instead, "Once you had her reassigned to south London, you continued with her."

"The texts, yes. The phone calls, yes. Teo was the wound I couldn't stop licking. I wanted to do, believe me. I wanted my entire brain erased so that I could just get *on* with my life. If there had been a pill I could have taken that would have removed her from memory, I would have taken it. Instead, I kept telling myself that it would be just once more: just one more message, just one more phone call, just one more conversation. Anything, really. A scrap. A crumb. But she didn't want that. And who could blame her?"

"Your wife must be interviewed, you know."

"She wouldn't have raised a finger to hurt her."

"Perhaps not. But in her mind, she stood to lose a lot. When people are in that position, they'll often do whatever it takes to keep what they have."

MAYVILLE ESTATE
DALSTON
NORTH-EAST LONDON

Monifa Bankole's husband answered the door to Nkata's sharp knock. He held a washing flannel to his forehead, and both the front of his white shirt and his khaki trousers were speckled with blood. Nkata had his warrant card in hand, so although it was unnecessary at this point, he still lifted it and said, "Metropolitan Police."

"You're back, eh?" Bankole remarked. "She rang you, did she? Yes. I see this. What else is there to do on her journey of ruining lives?"

Nkata said, "Happens no one rang me 't all, but looks like someone should've." Beyond the man, Nkata could see a shadowy sitting room where furniture lay in disarray. "I got to speak with Missus Bankole."

"Not here." Bankole began to shut the door.

Nkata stopped him, his hand flat on the wood. "I got to say it, Mister Bankole. Could be you're not telling the truth. So I'll jus' have a look round, eh?"

Bankole turned from the door, leaving it open. Once Nkata had stepped over the threshold, Bankole shouted, "Monifa! You are wanted. Copper's here."

There was no reply and no sound of movement, but that didn't mean no one else was in the flat. Nkata said, "Like I said, I'll have a look," and went in the direction of the kitchen first and from there to the two bedrooms and the bathroom. Bankole was telling the truth, it seemed. He was alone.

Still, he hadn't overturned furniture on his own, and it wasn't likely he'd hit himself on the forehead with the steam iron that lay discarded on the floor near an armchair. The question was whether the blood on him belonged to him, his wife, or someone else.

"Where's she gone to?" Nkata asked him.

"I don't know, do I."

"Wha' happened here, then?"

"My worthless son attacked me. A son. His father. If not for me, that son of a whore would not even exist."

"Looks like he might've got the worse of it, eh?" Nkata said with a gesture at the blood on Bankole.

"He thinks he's far away from the age for discipline. He is not. Now you have seen no one is here, leave me in peace."

"You hurt your wife, Mister Bankole? 'S some of that blood hers?"

"I rule here. That woman does not. No woman will rule here while I live."

Nkata couldn't help himself. He said, "How d'you 'spect that'll work out for you?"

Bankole said only, "Go."

There was nothing to be gained from staying, whether he taunted the man or not. So Nkata left and was checking his mobile phone for potential messages—he'd given his card to Monifa Bankole, after all—when he heard "Ssssst! Policeman! Sssst!"

He looked up. No one was nearby. He gazed round till he saw a woman hanging out of a gaping window on the third floor of Bronte House, some distance from the Bankole's flat. He walked back and stationed himself beneath her. He raised his hands as if saying, "What is it?"

She held up a finger in the universal sign of *wait a moment*. He did so, and in about thirty seconds she was back. She held something in her hand, which she tossed down to him. He caught it and saw that she'd wrapped a piece of paper round a hairbrush. He unwrapped and read the message she'd written. It was the name Halimah Tijani and the words *Lydgate House*. A three-digit number accompanied this. Nkata raised his hand and gave the woman a quick salute, leaving the hairbrush on a nearby step for her to collect later.

He went to the map of Mayville Estate to locate Lydgate House, then made his way there and to the flat numbered 501. A sharp knock on the door brought no response. When he said, "Missus Bankole? Winston Nkata. We spoke before. Metropolitan Police," he heard the murmur of voices.

A bolt was drawn back on the inside of the door, and it was opened by a woman he assumed was Halimah Tijani. She gestured him inside quickly, looking beyond him as if to make certain he hadn't been followed. The flat was unbearably hot and equally stuffy, its closed curtains and windows preventing the relief of air that was fresh if not cool.

Monifa Bankole sat on a plump ottoman in front of an armchair. Nkata blew out a breath when he saw her swollen face and the dark bruises beneath her eyes. When she rose, she did it so carefully that he reckoned chances were good that several of her ribs were broken as well. She said nothing, merely looked at him briefly, then lowered her head.

"He said it was your son he beat," Nkata told her.

She said, "It was. This is . . . Me, this is before."

"You got to come with me, then."

"I cannot. I do not know what Abeo will do to Tani now. But Simisola he will take to Nigeria if I cannot stop him."

"We work this one step at a time, Missus Bankole," Nkata told her. And to Halimah, he said, "She comes with me. *No* one goes back there. Un'erstand?"

Halimah nodded. She said, "Her things? Clothing?" And to Monifa, "What else is there, Monifa? Have you medicines?"

Monifa said, "I *can't*. Tani will return with another order and I will not be there and then I will not know where he is and where Simisola is. Please, you must understand."

"What I un'erstand is that bloke's goin to kill one 'f you. I saw there was something had hit him in the forehead. I clocked an iron on the floor. Did you do that?"

She looked away, made no reply.

"Got it," Nkata said. And then to Halimah, "Give us a minute?"

Halimah nodded and took herself into a corridor and from there into what he assumed was a bedroom. She shut the door.

From his jacket pocket, Nkata took the real reason he'd come to speak to Monifa again: a photocopied page from the clinic's appointment book. He unfolded it, sat in the armchair, smoothed the page across his knee. He said, "I got to ask you to look at this. It's your name, see. And next to your name, there in brackets is another, Simisola, like you just mentioned. You see this?"

Monifa looked dutifully. She nodded in reply to his question.

He said, "What you tol' me before is that you were there to get some money back. You never did explain what that money was for." He didn't wait for her to respond, instead going on with, "But with this name—Simisola's—in brackets next to yours, looks to me like *she* was who was havin' something done. I got tha' right?"

Monifa said nothing, directing her gaze once more to her lap.

Nkata watched her, knowing that she was probably their last hope for verification of what had been going on in the clinic above Kingsland Toys, Games, and Books. Not one of the other women in the appointment diary would give them the information they needed: that FGM was being performed there. Whoever had been operating the establishment was not likely ever to return, but London was vast and it would be a matter of a few months only—perhaps even less—before the clinic was up and running again someplace else.

He said to Monifa Bankole, "You're hopin' for a phone call from this Easter Lange—Mercy Hart, like I told you b'fore—from the clinic on Kingsland High Street. But you got to know that no matter who does it to Simisola, what you got in mind for her is against the law and *if* you do it—no matter where you do it—it ends with you in prison. Or your husband in prison. Or both 'f you, working off prison sentences. See, you're in the spotlight now. And the rozzers? We know 'xactly where to find you. You make any sort 'f dodgy move to hurt your daughter, what happens next is you get arrested and she goes into Care. So what I'm sayin's this: I reckon you want the best for Simisola. But this i'n't the way to go about it. An' 'the best' for Simisola has sod all to do with cutting her up, by th' way."

Monifa looked at him again. It seemed that she was trying to read him. Then her gaze went to the window, still covered by the curtains. She studied this, as if she could see the treetops, their leaves dropping early this year because of the heat and the drought. She spoke so quietly, it was difficult for Nkata to hear at first. He moved closer to her and sat in the armchair in front of which the ottoman stood, with Monifa on its edge, knees drawn up and her breasts resting on them.

"Once I made the appointment, I paid a part of the cost," she said quietly. "I used the family money. I had to have it to secure the appointment and the appointment was the only way to make certain Simi did not suffer. But only Abeo is meant to touch family money, and he found that I'd taken some. So he sent me to the clinic to fetch it back. I was there for that when the police arrived and we were both arrested, Easter Lange and me. I was not able to recover the money."

"Where's she now, Simisola?"

"Tani took her away. He will not say where. He will not return her until a protection order is put in place. That is why he came to Bronte House today: for me to fill out part of the protection order, so that he could make it an urgent request. But Abeo came home. He was already angry, and when he saw Tani, he saw the protection order. He ripped it up. He attacked Tani then. It was not the opposite."

She went on to explain what her husband's plan had been: to have Simisola cut by a Nigerian cutter in London, at much less cost than the clinic would have charged. But as it was the same cutter who'd ruined Halimah's daughter, Lim, Monifa was able to get her address. That in hand, she went to the cutter herself with a threat of phoning the police should she lay a hand on Simisola.

"Chinara Sani will not cut our daughter now, but Abeo knows this so he will take Simisola to Nigeria to be cut. The protection order was meant to stop him doing that. There is no order now and if he finds her, he will take her at once because it is the only way Simisola will be able to fetch a large bride price. Abeo means to get a husband for her in Nigeria."

"How old is she, Missus Bankole?"

"She is eight years."

Nkata took this in fully before he replied. "An' you were okay with that, eh? An eight-year-old gettin set up with a husband?"

"It would be an arrangement only, made formal with the payment of a bride price. But the arrangement could not happen if Simisola was not first cleansed."

"So you want that 's well, eh? Simisola being cleansed, I mean. Which I'm thinking means Simisola being cut up."

She was quiet. She wore a long wrapper in a complicated style, and she began twisting its ends in her hands. Nkata could hear her breathing and it sounded to him like the sound of someone trying not to weep. "I no longer know," she finally said. "It was what I was trying to prevent when I took her to the clinic."

"Well, I got to say it, Missus Bankole: you got me flummoxed," Nkata said. "You took her to an FGM clinic in order to protect her from FGM? Tha' doesn't track."

"Her father would have her mutilated. Like I was mutilated. He would have her damaged. It wouldn't matter as long as it was done. This—what I was trying to do—it was meant to avoid that. It would be done properly, and she would feel nothing. And when it was finished, she would properly heal. But Abeo wasn't going to allow that because it was too costly, and it defied his plans. Twice now he has been defied. There will not be a third time if he can help it. He will take her to Nigeria as soon as he finds her."

"He got a passport? Simisola got one?" And when she nodded, he rose and said, "You come with me, then."

"Please. No. I cannot. I must stop him."

"Tha's something you're not going to be able to do."

"I must."

"I think you might be misun'erstanding wha's happenin here,"

Nkata said. "You c'n come with me cooperatively, Missus Bankole, or I c'n arrest you. The choice is yours."

ISLE OF DOGS
EAST LONDON

Barbara Havers had rung Dr. Philippa Weatherall in advance as there was no sense in making the lengthy journey to the Isle of Dogs from Westminster if the surgeon would not be in. But she was there for the entire day, Dr. Weatherall had confirmed. She was happy to meet with DS Havers between patients. She had a rather full schedule so she couldn't spare a lot of time. "If you could tell me what this is about . . . ?" she'd said.

A deceased woman called Teo Bontempi, Havers told her. "I c'n tell you more when we meet," Barbara said.

After negotiating the drive across central London, she dropped down to the river in the vicinity of Limehouse and made her way from there to Westferry Road, the main route onto the west side of the Isle of Dogs. This was in no way even a remote part of Barbara's regular stamping ground, so from Westferry Road she was forced to use her mobile's GPS. This took her to Millwall Inner Dock, and from there it was a search for parking, followed by a hike to Inner Harbour Square where, she'd been told, she would find Dr. Weatherall's surgery above a takeaway sandwich shop called Our Daily Bread.

That was fortuitous, she thought. She made a brief stop inside the takeaway to purchase a prawn and coleslaw sandwich on brown bread, a bag of salt and vinegar crisps, a snack-size packet of custard creams, and a blackcurrant Ribena. Out in the square she made short work of sandwich, crisps, and Ribena, managing in the midst of this repast to drip coleslaw down the front of her T-shirt. Seeing what she'd done to herself, she cursed and created from the coleslaw drip a very large and—she liked to think—rather artful stain by smearing the mess with a greasy paper napkin. She consoled herself with one of the custard creams and followed this with a deeply satisfying fag.

Thus fortified, she made her way to Dr. Weatherall's surgery. She found the surgeon between patients, in the process of ushering one out while another worked on filling in what looked like a closely printed questionnaire fastened to a clipboard. Barbara would have assumed the woman doing the ushering was an assistant, but she said, "You must be DS Havers?" and when Barbara nodded, she continued with, "I'm Dr. Weatherall. Do come in." She gestured back the way she'd come after saying to the woman with the clipboard, "Fawzia, just knock on the door when you've finished, please."

Barbara waited for her to close the door to the narrow corridor. Three rooms opened off it, one of them the surgeon's office, which was where Dr. Weatherall took her. It was as sparsely decorated as was the physician herself. Office and woman were no nonsense: the walls of the room were hung with her diplomas as well as a few inoffensive prints that one might find on an internet website, and the doctor herself was in a sleeveless black blouse and trousers of black linen—the material a bow to the heat, no doubt, a scarf folded into a headband to hold back her salt-and-pepper hair. Her arms were tanned. They were also toned in a depressingly spectacular fashion, Barbara noted, as were her shoulders. Clearly, she took regular and probably vigorous exercise. She probably watched her diet as well. With this in mind, Barbara nearly felt guilty for her crisps and her custard creams, but as it was only *nearly*, she reckoned she'd get over the feeling quickly enough. She usually did.

Dr. Weatherall sat in one of the chairs in front of her desk rather than behind it, and she indicated that Barbara should sit in the other. Barbara explained to her the death of Teo Bontempi, not how it came about but merely the coma and the hospitalisation, as well as the fact of the police looking into it and the fact of the investigating team's having in their possession the victim's appointment diary.

She said, "Teo wrote *evaluation* on July twenty-fourth, which wasn't helpful. But when we finally got our hands on her mobile and got into its contents, we saw she'd put the address for this clinic into her GPS. She was an FGM victim, and her husband—well, her almost ex-husband—says he banged on a lot about possible reconstructive surgery. We're wondering if that's what you do here."

"That's exactly what I do here," Dr. Weatherall said.

"Did you examine her?"

"I did. It's the first step."

"So you remember her."

"I didn't at first. After you rang me, I looked through my files. I see any number of women in a week, so while I often remember their names, it's difficult to keep straight all the details of an appointment."

"C'n I reckon you've got files for all your patients?"

"Yes. For all of them."

"So you have a file for Teo as well? C'n I get a copy off you?"

Dr. Weatherall steepled her fingers together and looked down at them, as if considering the request. After a few moments, she said, "I don't see why not. But if I may ask . . . If Teo Bontempi has died and if you're the Metropolitan Police, and, as you told me on the phone, there's an investigation . . . with DS in front of your name signifying you're a detective . . . ?"

"Right . . . She's been murdered."

Dr. Weatherall let out a long breath. She said, "I'm very sorry to hear that. How was she . . . Never mind. I suppose you can't tell me." She rose and went to the chair behind her desk. She sat and typed upon the keyboard of her computer. She accessed what she wanted and said, "This will take just a few moments. The printer's . . ." and she indicated the doorway as a way of explaining that the printer was elsewhere. She added, "Shall I fetch everything for you now?"

Barbara told her that could wait till she was leaving, and she asked the surgeon what the result of Teo's examination had been.

Dr. Weatherall gazed at the file she'd brought up on her computer screen. She read a bit, as if to make sure she had the details straight and said, "My notes say she seemed a good candidate for reconstruction. She'd been badly handled by whoever cut her originally, and although she'd been opened as an adolescent there was a great deal of scar tissue. That—the scar tissue—would need to be removed before anything else could be done. It's not difficult, that part of the procedure. It *is* a bit iffy, however."

"Because . . . ?"

"The file I've printed for you includes photos. You'll see the extent to which she'd been disfigured. When the damage is as bad as hers, the first issue is whether she has any nerve endings left beneath the scar tissue. If there are, then I can rebuild a clitoris."

"And if there aren't any nerve endings left?"

"That doesn't make the surgery more difficult. It alters the outcome, though. Whilst I can rebuild what's been removed from a woman's body in that situation, I can't alter her experience of sex other than to eliminate the pain of it."

"Why would a woman go forward with reconstruction if you find that there aren't any nerves left?"

The surgeon pushed back from her desk, resting her hands on the arms of her chair. She said, "For several reasons. Normalcy or at least the degree of normalcy that I can give her. An end to infections as well and, as I said, an end to pain during intercourse. But the woman would, in effect, remain anorgasmic. So: no pleasure for her save the pleasure of being physically close to a sexual partner."

"What was the case for Teo?"

Dr. Weatherall gestured at the computer's screen. "You'll see it in my notes: From examining her, I confirmed that I could definitely *do* a reconstruction. But in her case, as in everyone else's, it would be

only once I'd removed the scar tissue that I could offer a hopeful outcome as to sensation."

"Did you explain all this to her?"

"Oh yes. I always do that, directly after the exam."

"How did you leave things, then?"

"Regarding the reconstructive surgery, my notes in her file indicate
that at first she wanted to think things over."

"That's it, is it?"

"In the notes, yes. But I wouldn't have written down the rest as it's
what I always say: that should she decide to have the surgery, she would
need to find someone willing to accompany her. And if she did want
to go forward with the procedure, she was to ring me and let me know."

"Did she?"

"Not at first. I thought she'd decided against it, which certainly
happens. Sometimes a woman's fear overtakes all other considerations.
Sometimes a husband finds out what a wife wishes to do and he won't
allow it because he fears that being made whole will lead her into
promiscuity. And sometimes a father becomes involved and *he* won't
allow it. A mother as well, for that matter."

"And sometimes they die," Barbara noted.

"I've never lost a patient during surgery, Sergeant."

"Sorry. I was thinking of Teo Bontempi dying before she could
arrange anything."

"When exactly did she die?"

Barbara gave her the date—July 31—and decided to add, "She was
clubbed in the head. She fell into a coma and never came out of it."

"Are you thinking there's someone who didn't want her to have
this surgery, someone she told, someone who . . . I don't know . . .
couldn't bear the news that she might be made whole again?"

"Just now we're looking at every possibility we can come up with,"
Barbara told her. "Did she give you any idea who it was who might
accompany her here if she wanted to go forward with the surgery?"

"No. But that wouldn't be unusual. She was here merely to be evaluated."

"D'you think it's likely she told anyone about her appointment with you? Did she mention anyone?"

"I certainly don't recall her telling me. She might have kept the information about the appointment to herself. That wouldn't have been the first time."

"Why?"

"Consider what it's like for these women. They're almost always married. They come to me because they've heard about my work. When they come, they're holding on to hope for an improvement in their lives with their husbands."

"Sounds natural to me, that."

"It is. But think about what's going on within them when they make the journey here: First, they nurse a hope, then I examine them, then they learn that, whilst I can repair them and put an end to the physical pain, to chronic infections, and to other troubles, the procedure may not alter their experience. It may not give them sensation."

"I'm still not sure why they wouldn't want their husbands or partners to know."

"I think it's one thing for only the woman to have a hope of improvement and for only the woman to end up being crushed by disappointment, but it's quite another to share that hope with a partner and then have to cope with the partner's disappointment as well."

Barbara considered this. She also considered that Teo Bontempi, being separated from her husband, had a good reason for saying nothing to him, especially since by his own account he'd spent so much time trying to heal her spirit as well as her body. How would he have reacted to the knowledge that hers was a hopeless case? Or, for that matter, how would he have reacted knowing about the surgery at all? "I suppose that makes sense," she told the surgeon.

"It's asking a lot of them to talk openly to anyone about what's happened to them, Sergeant. Often, they don't even want to talk to me about it. They just want to be whole again, or at least as whole as I can make them. But as to *how* it happened and when it happened, they rarely wish to speak of it. For some, it's because they were too young to remember. For others, the humiliation is too great. Some of them were tricked into it. Some of them were caught by surprise. Some of them were taught to believe it's a procedure that every girl has done to her. This entire business of FGM is a tightly kept secret in families. Mothers don't pass along to their daughters the truth of it: the crippling consequence of such mutilation, how it will rob them of something that a completely ignorant tradition has dictated they are not going to be allowed to feel. Imagine, if you can, what something like this does to their lives, what it does to their futures, how it reduces them as individuals, how it turns them into saleable *property*." The surgeon's eyes had filled as she spoke, and she grabbed a tissue from a box on her desk. She said, "Sorry. Sorry." She used the tissue beneath her eyes. "I get too wound up."

"No worries," Barbara said. "It's something to be wound up about. Did Teo Bontempi tell you she was on a police team, working to root out and end FGM?"

"She didn't."

"That she was on a police team or that she was a cop?"

"Neither. Do you think that's why she was attacked?"

"Could be. The team's approach is through community outreach and education, generally, that sort of thing, which doesn't much sound like something a copper would be attacked for doing. But from what we've been able to suss out about her, Teo took it further than trying to end it through education and all that. She managed to uncover a cutting place in north London, and she got it closed down. We reckon someone could've gone after her for that."

"You probably know about the Nigerian cutters, then. They're hidden round London. If one of them—"

A knock sounded on the corridor's door and the surgeon called entrance to Fawzia, the woman who'd been filling out the paperwork. Dr. Weatherall took the clipboard from her and said, "Just across is the exam room. Everything below the waist, remove. There's a sheet to cover yourself. I'll meet you in there in a few minutes."

When the woman left them, Barbara said, "So when you examined Teo, you saw she could've been repaired, and you told her that, right?"

"Straightaway. As I've said. Directly we were finished with the exam."

"Would you say the news made her happy?"

"I'm not very good at reading people. But I can tell you that, as a rule, most of my patients are relieved rather than outright happy with the news. And then they generally become thoughtful. It's human nature, I think, not to want to get one's hopes up."

"Is that why you phoned her? We have her mobile."

"I always ring a patient a day or so after the evaluation, to see if there are any questions."

"The phone records show you made four calls to her."

"Do they? Well, if that's the case, I must have done, although I couldn't have said it was four times that we spoke." She paused and her gaze moved to the prints on the walls as she thought about this. "She would have had questions, I daresay. The women generally do."

"Do you normally have more than one conversation with a patient?"

"Frequently. I have as many as it takes to make them comfortable."

Barbara had been jotting all of this in her notebook, and she looked up to ask a final question. "Anything else you can tell me?"

Dr. Weatherall drew her eyebrows together. They were jet black and straight, like underscoring beneath a word. "Just that—and it came to me when I read her file—she seemed troubled."

"D'you mean about the procedure you'd be going through, the steps of the process when she went under the knife?"

"Again, I can't be entirely certain of the memory, but I'd say it was more about having it done at all. She seemed troubled from the moment I examined her, not just when I told her she was a good candidate for reconstruction."

"Someone was pressuring her? To have the reconstruction done or not to have it done?"

"I couldn't tell you, and she certainly didn't say. But *if* she hadn't told anyone about coming to see me, there might be a reason for her being troubled beyond not wanting to encourage a partner to hope for the impossible." As she was speaking, the desk phone rang. It was a sudden, discordant, jarring sound. Barbara waited for the surgeon to answer it, but she instead let it go to message. Then she said, "You must be considering FGM as an element of why she died."

"Just now we're considering everything. Where did you leave things with her, then?"

"She made a decision to have the surgery."

"Had you set a date for the procedure?"

"No. My notes tell me that, as soon as she had the appropriate amount of time off work, she intended to ring me."

"At that point—I mean during the conversation when she told you she'd decided on the surgery—had she at that point told anyone else that she was about to undergo reconstruction?"

Dr. Weatherall shook her head and looked regretful. "I honestly don't know. She may have done. That's all I can say."

BRIXTON
SOUTH LONDON

Monifa understood why the detective had arrested her. She'd told him what her intentions had been. She'd told him what her intentions still were: to have Simisola made pure so that she could proceed into her womanhood. Despite having found a location where Simi could be cut under medical conditions—with anaesthetic, with sterile surgical instruments used by someone trained, and with aftercare—it was still having her cut, and in this country, it was against the law. Monifa had no hope of making this police detective understand any part of what was meant to happen in Simisola's life. He wasn't of their culture, so there were things he would never be able to grasp. She and Simisola were, after all, females. The purpose in each of their lives was to serve the males to whom they were bound through marriage or tied to through birth. This was how it was. Her own mother was living this way, as was her mother-in-law, as had lived her grandmother, her great-grandmother, and the women who had come before them. To their people, this was all part of being a woman. Being cut meant being cleansed. Being cleansed meant being pure. Being pure meant being marriageable. Monifa could no more change this than could she change the order of the months of the year. But this man Nkata at the wheel of the car, he was English, after all, no matter the land from which his ancestors had come. So he would never—could never—understand.

They'd been in the car a while before she finally spoke, saying, "Where you take me is not the police station."

He gave her a quick look. He said, "You got yourself caught up in the middle 'f a murder enquiry, Missus Bankole. Tha's wha' this is. It's being conducted by the Met. So my guv's wanting to talk to you 'bout that clinic where you were arrested. He's 'specially wanting to talk to you about the woman who ran it. Like I already told you, she called herself Easter Lange, but that i'n't her real name. What I 'spect is that if she's not going by a name tha's really hers, she's got no medical licence. 'N other words, you were intending to hand your girl over to jus' 'nother cutter, like the one your husband was goin to use. Only this one made it all look like she was on the up and up."

"This is not what it was," Monifa said.

"You're not tryin to say this *wasn't* about getting your daughter cut, are you? Not af'er you already told me different, eh?"

"What I mean is that it wasn't the same. *She* wasn't the same. Simisola would be safe with her. And when it was over, she would be—"

"I don' care what you *think* she would be," he broke in. "Because, far 's I'm concerned, she wouldn't be anything but cut up and sewn up and wrecked for life."

"You don't understand."

"An' believe me, Missus, I don' want to." He hit the steering wheel with the heel of his hand.

They rode on in silence. Monifa felt upon her the burden of his disgust and his anger. She felt the additional burden of everything she'd listened to for months from her mother, from Abeo, from her mother-in-law. She thought of Halimah's grief at the loss of her precious daughter, her only child. And she felt as if she were bound by lengths of rough cotton that were wound and wound and wound round her body, mummy-like, till movement in any direction was impossible.

Tears came to her eyes. She let them fall. She lowered her head and saw her clasped hands through the shimmer of pain and of pain's legacy that, it had to be said, she'd inflicted on herself and now on her children.

She said nothing more as they drove for a time that seemed longer than forever to her. They crossed the River Thames, passed through areas that she recognised as south-of-the-river gentrification, and at last, they turned off the road they'd been travelling on onto a smaller lane that called itself Angell Road. They came to a stop in the midst of a housing estate.

She said, "This is not a police station."

The detective said, "I lied. You come with me, Missus Bankole."

"You are not a policeman!" she cried. "What is this? Where are we?"

The man Nkata sighed. He reached for the inner pocket of his jacket and took out his police identification, which he'd shown her once before. *Winston Nkata, Detective Sergeant. Metropolitan Police.* His photo was on it. So was his mobile number. But that did not explain where they were or why they'd come here.

He said again, "Come with me. No one's goin to hurt you here."

"Where is this place? You must tell me," she said.

"Loughborough Estate, this is. Brixton. It's where I grew up and where I live."

"Why do you bring me here?"

He took her arm, although his touch was gentle. "'S'okay," he told her. "I got my mum waiting for you."

Monifa recalled that once he'd stowed her into his car, he'd used his mobile before getting in himself. At the time she'd assumed he was ringing his superior officer, but *had* he done that or had he actually rung his mother? And if he had rung his mother, *why*?

He said, "I's a bit of a walk. You c'n take my arm."

The long ride had stiffened her muscles, which were already sore, and her chest wanted to yelp with the pain of movement as she got out of the car. She did as he suggested and took his arm. There was a concrete path leading into the estate, and he followed this, walking slowly to accommodate her pace.

The detective sergeant didn't stop till they came to one of the blocks of flats, where he led her to a door and from there to a stairway. "Lift's gone out," he told her. "Sorry. Bit of a climb."

They went up three flights of stairs, slowly, with every riser causing Monifa to groan, although she did what she could to hide this from the detective. At last, on the third and top floor, he opened a door to a corridor, said, "Not much farther, eh?" and walked her along a lino-clad floor till they reached the fourth door, which he unlocked and opened, calling out, "Mum?" as he did so.

Monifa felt her body shrinking. A woman called back to him, "In here, Jewel," and then there were footsteps and then there was the detective's mother with her hands extended towards Monifa as she said to her son, "You have been a *time*," and adding to Monifa "Alice Nkata's who I am. You come this way, madam. It's Missus Bankole, my boy says. He behaved himself 'cross London, I hope. He drive well coming here? I hope so b'cause there's times, I tell you, he drives like the devil's on his tail."

Monifa saw she'd followed Alice Nkata into a lounge where an old upright piano with yellowing keys shared space with a large African drum, and a three-piece suite with colourful scarves tucked into the chairs, perhaps to hide their age. On the top of the upright piano, a mass of framed photographs stood. A spotless kitchen opened off this room, and a nearby closed door suggested a bedroom, while a short corridor offered other closed doors, presumably to a family bathroom and another bedroom. Monifa said, "I intrude upon you. I am very sorry."

To which Alice Nkata said warmly, "You come with me, Missus Bankole. I brought up two boys and if I don't know anything else, what I do know is how to bind up wounds. Jewel here says you got a few."

A makeshift A and E, Monifa realised, had been set up in the kitchen in advance of her arrival. A worktop held a stack of gauze squares, a tin of Elastoplast, some sorts of unguents in tubes, balls of cotton wool, and a large roll of stretchy ribbed bandaging material. Alice Nkata said to her son, "Jewel, you see to fresh sheets and towels in the bedroom, eh? I couldn't get out of the café as fast as I liked, so I didn't get to that."

"Please," Monifa said in a low voice. "You must not trouble yourself."

Alice said, "This isn't any kind of trouble." She gestured Monifa to a chair and turned to the worktop to make a selection of items. She said, "Jewel and his brother used to share tha' room and often enough,

Stoney—tha's his brother, Harold—wouldn't be in a state fit to sleep in the same room with. That happen, Jewel bedded on the sofa. He got used to it, so you're not to worry about putting anyone out of a bedroom. C'n you take your dress off, Missus Bankole? It's a wrapper, is it? You just lower it, then. That way I can see what's what. Jewel says your ribs're likely damaged. Do they hurt you?"

Monifa cooperated with the policeman's mother, although she required Alice Nkata's help. And then she heard the other woman's clicking of her tongue and her quiet, "Oh my. Jewel said you didn't want th' hospital?"

"I am not that badly hurt."

"You sure about that? Well, okay. But I'm strapping you up just to be safe." Having said that, she began to wind the stretchy bandage beneath Monifa's breasts, round and round and firmly so. "This'll give you some support when you move," she said. "You c'n take it off to bathe, but that's all, mind you. Put it straight back on."

"I cause you trouble. I'm very sorry."

"You're not much trouble compared to my boys. You saw Jewel's scar, I expect. 'Course you did. No one's about to miss it. Now *that* was trouble. An' what's happened to our Stoney is trouble *on* trouble, but tha's a conversation for another time. Can you cook, Missus Bankole?"

"Cooking is one of the few things I can do, Mrs. . . ." She had already forgotten what the woman's surname was.

"Nkata, like Jewel's surname," was the answer to her unasked question. "But you call me Alice."

"I am Monifa," Monifa said.

"Monifa, then. What sort of cooking do you do, Monifa?"

"A little English," Monifa told her. "But mostly Nigerian."

"*Nigerian*?" Alice had opened a bottle of antiseptic and was dousing a ball of cotton wool with it. She called out, "D'you hear that, Jewel?

Monifa cooks Nigerian! Your father's going to be in heaven, that's what it is."

Monifa said eagerly, "He is Nigerian?"

"No. But that won't stop him singing your praises if you can do him *anything* African. He's been in London forever but Africa's where he was born and where he spent his boyhood. Ivory Coast."

"I would be . . . will be . . . pleased to cook for your husband. And you, of course, and . . ." She lowered her voice. "Do I call him Jewel?"

Alice Nkata laughed. "Better not. Tha's my pet name for him cos, obviously, tha's what he is. But I expect he'd like *Winston* from you. Now, let me see to that black eye."

STOKE NEWINGTON
NORTH-EAST LONDON

What Tani really wanted to do was sleep. But he knew this could be a very bad thing, considering the force with which his father had smashed his head into the floor over and over again. If he had a con- cussion from that—and his head *was* pounding—he needed to stay awake till he got looked at. That couldn't happen, though, till Simi was safe. So he stood with Sophie and Simi on the platform of Stoke Newington's railway station. They were waiting for the train that would take them south, in the direction of Whitechapel.

When he'd fled Mayville Estate, he'd made his way back to Sophie, thankful that he'd had the good sense never to tell his parents about her. There were any number of reasons for this, but topping the list was the fact that she was English and, despite having African ancestors, her roots in England were almost three hundred years old, planted at a time when speculative investments in human cargo from Africa sometimes led an Englishman without morals or a conscience to acquire a slave. That sickening fact would not be enough in his father's eyes—and possibly his mother's—to make Sophie suitable for him, however. She wasn't Nigerian, and she definitely wasn't pure: as defined by tradition and his parents. But the happy result of his parents not knowing about Sophie was that they also had not the first clue where she lived. And *this* meant that they also did not have the first clue where he'd taken Simisola.

Sophie's family lived in Evering Road in Stoke Newington, her mum a nutritionist and her dad the sort of tech wizard who invented apps that no one imagined they'd ever need till they started using them. Included in the family were Sophie's two older brothers and her younger sister, and their house was a semi-detached of four floors with a sumptuous garden at the back and a wall in front that enclosed a sunny area of plants and flowers in pots standing outside the glass doors to the basement. The first time Tani had ever seen the place, he'd been staggered by the sheer size of it. Each child had a bedroom, there appeared to be bathrooms in every corner, and the kitchen seemed large enough to hold an orchestra with space left over for dancing. He'd been so intimidated upon entering that fear overtook him just inside the front door. A sudden movement on his part seemed to be enough to upend a china cabinet or another valuable piece of furniture.

Of the Franklin family, only Sophie was at home with Simi when he returned from Mayville Estate. A single look at his condition, and Sophie had dragged him inside and burst into tears. Her cry brought Simi from the lounge to the front door. She, too, began to weep as she flung herself at him.

"'S'okay," he'd said. "Squeak, 's'okay."

He didn't want to say more about what had happened. But he didn't need to, for Simisola herself cried, "Papa hurt you! I hate him!" and began to sob.

Over Simi's head, he said to Sophie, "He showed up and saw the protection order."

"Oh Tani," she cried. "I'm sorry! It was my idea and—"

He cut in, trying to sound as casual as he could, "Think I need some ice for my head, Soph. Or something else cold if you c'n manage it."

Sophie said, "Oh God, of course! In there," and she indicated the lounge. "Lie down, Tani. Simisola, help him," she went on, before she raced deeper into the house. He heard her heading down to the kitchen as Simisola took his hand in hers and led him gently towards a sofa, still crying. She made him sit and she untied the laces of his trainers. She removed them and sat on a low footstool. He said again, "'S'okay, Squeak. Really. 'S'okay. It looks worse than it feels," although he reckoned this probably wasn't the truth. He hadn't yet seen a mirror so he didn't know how bad the damage was, but considering the flow of blood from his face that he hadn't managed to staunch, the raw ache in his throat and round his neck, the pounding in his head, and the lack of vision he was experiencing from one of his eyes . . . He suspected he was a terrifying sight for an eight-year-old girl. Sophie's reaction had been bad enough.

She returned with a washing flannel and a towel, a bowl of ice and a large package of frozen peas. She handed the peas to Simisola, saying, "Can you hold this where his head hurts, Simi?" before she raced off again. She brought back a first-aid kit, which she opened, dumped onto the coffee table, and began to sort through in something of a panic.

Tani saw that her hands were shaking. He said, "Sophie. 'S'okay. 'S'not that bad."

"It was my idea." She dashed tears from her face. "You said no but *I* insisted and *I* made it worse because I wanted the order to be urgent so we wouldn't have to wait till we were called to court and I said your mum was the one who could do that by filling out her part and saying what happened and if I hadn't done, you wouldn't have needed to go there and this wouldn't have happened and you can't go back. Tani, you can *never* go back."

Tani didn't want to tell her that he had to go back. He couldn't leave his mother in his father's hands. She wasn't safe there any more than Simisola was. But he said none of this and instead let Sophie minister to him as Simi held the frozen peas to his head and put her own head on his shoulder. She whispered, "Where's Mummy? Tani, has something happened to Mummy?" to which he murmured, "'S'okay, Squeak. She's okay," although that was something he didn't actually know.

"Pictures!" Sophie ran off again but was back within seconds, her smartphone in her hand. She helped Tani sit up and she snapped him from every angle, taking close-ups of individual wounds, of the fingerprint bruises round his neck, of his swollen-shut eye, of his bleeding forehead, chin, temple, and cheek. These, she told him, would help underscore the need for an urgent protection order. Then she urged him down again and did her best to clean and to bandage him.

After that, they'd set off for Stoke Newington station, which, mercifully, was less than a twenty-minute walk from where Sophie lived. He'd had to take several rests along the way, but with Sophie offering her shoulder to lean on and putting her arm round his waist for additional support, he managed the distance. After that, it was just a wait for the train.

When they finally went through the pedestrian wrought-iron gate giving entrance to Trinity Green, he saw that both of the doors to the chapel stood open, and when they got close, he could hear the sound of voices and laughter coming from within.

"Thank God," Sophie said fervently, although Tani didn't think God had much to do with it. Nonetheless, he followed with Simisola as Sophie hurried across the green to the chapel at its far end. She waited for him at the bottom of the steps and then helped him climb them. Once inside, the first people they saw were two girls standing with a ginger-haired white lady at a long, school dining hall–type table, all of them looking at a mass of photographs spread out on its surface. The white lady was saying, "I like this one, but then I'm not the person who's meant to choose," while one of the girls said, "But I look mad, innit," to which the white lady said, "You look *serious*. There's a difference," to which the girl replied, "Yeah. I look seriously mad," and all three of them laughed.

The white lady was the first to see Tani and his companions. She clocked Tani's appearance, and she quickly said, "D'you need help?" but she didn't wait for an answer. "Follow me," she told them. She came towards them then, descended the stairs, and took them round to the office door that had been locked on their earlier visit.

TRINITY GREEN
WHITECHAPEL
EAST LONDON

Deborah St. James could see how frightened they were, particularly the little girl. She was clinging to the boy's hand with both of hers. Both she and the older girl had clearly been crying. It was the boy's condition, however, that set off the alarum. Someone had beaten him badly.

She swung open the office door and stepped aside to let them enter. There were folding chairs along the corridor, so she unfolded three of them, said, "Let me get you some water," and went to one of the supply rooms across from Zawadi's office. Zawadi herself was inside, she saw, having a conversation with Narissa Cameron. Deborah hadn't realised Narissa had returned to Orchid House.

She popped her head into the doorway. Zawadi greeted this action by saying wearily, "Why are you still here? It's bad enough with her." She lifted her chin at Narissa.

Deborah said, "There's a little girl just come in with two teenagers."

"Who brought them?" Zawadi asked.

"I don't think anyone brought them."

"What do they want, then? Who are the teenagers? What did they say?"

"Nothing yet. The boy is badly—"

"We do *not* allow males inside Orchid House. Do you see what's happening? Orchid House is being set up. *I'm* being set up."

Deborah knew Zawadi meant that the circumstances of the eight-year-old's arrival looked virtually the same as those that had heralded Bolu Akin's arrival: in the company of two adolescents. She couldn't blame her for that reaction in light of all that had happened to her. In a fashion that was only too typical, the tabloids were in the process of dissecting Zawadi thoroughly, every inch of her life and the life of her ex-husband as well. So no matter why the boy and two girls had come to Orchid House, Zawadi was going to be cautious to the tenth degree. Deborah clarified with, "The other is a girl. She's been crying and so has the child. And the boy's been beaten."

"I cannot help beaten boys. He should go to the police." Zawadi's mouth formed a straight line that claimed her decision had been made.

Narissa came into the corridor where Deborah was still standing in the office doorway. She looked in the direction of the little group that had arrived. She said, "Zawadi, they're just in the corridor. I'm going to—"

Clearly, Zawadi wasn't having that. She rose. Deborah stepped back to give her passage. She followed her and Narissa to where the newcomers sat. They all got to their feet at Zawadi's approach. Deborah handed each of them a bottle of water.

Zawadi went to the boy. Her expression changed from hard to wary to alarmed in the time it took her to put her hand on his arm. She said to the older of the two girls, "This one needs A and E."

"He won't go," she said. "His dad did this to him. He's scared the same happened to his mum so he wants to go back to help her."

Zawadi said to the boy, "You've a voice?"

He nodded but he didn't speak. The little girl had tried to hide herself behind him, and he drew her out and put his arm round her shoulders. "This is Simisola," he finally said. "I'm Tani. She's Sophie. Sophie says you c'n help us."

Sophie said, "Simi's dad means to have her cut. He had it all arranged with someone he'd found in town. Tani's mum tried to stop him. But he beat on her. Then we—me and Tani—tried to stop him with a protection order. We had it filled out but it got ripped to shreds by Tani's dad. We mean to fill out another."

"He's setting up to take Simi to Nigeria," Tani said.

"Has he passports?" Zawadi spoke brusquely, as if unwilling to let any emotion enter into her conversation with the kids.

"Yeah."

"You have them?"

He shook his head. "I di'n't have time to look for them, but I think I know where they are."

"Come to my office." Zawadi sounded abrupt, and Deborah wondered if it was disbelief that was triggering her reaction or something else. And while Deborah couldn't blame her for caution, this situation looked straightforward. One didn't counterfeit injuries like those on the boy.

A mobile rang suddenly. Tani dug his smartphone from his jeans. He looked at the screen, apparently saw who the caller was, and said, "I got to take this," and to Sophie, "I's from the market."

They heard only one side of the conversation, which consisted of, "Tiombe, you're back? . . . Oh. Right. No worries . . . I found a place, so—"

And then he listened for a bit to what Tiombe was relating to him. He looked at Simisola. Then he looked at Sophie. He said, "What'd she tell him, then?" and he listened again. Finally, he said, "'S'okay. Really. But I wish Bliss'd rung me before she—"

More listening and then, "Yeah. Guess so. I 'preciate the inf'rmation."

A few more words and the call ended. He said to Sophie, "We got seen in the market couple of times, me and you. He knows 'bout you."

"But not my name!"

"Not yet. Least, that's how it seems."

"I was only ever there with you, Tani. I don't think I ever talked to anyone. No one actually *knows* me there. Did you tell anyone my name?"

He shook his head, and Zawadi said, "What's this going on, please?"

Tani said, "My dad's looking for Simi in Ridley Road Market. He's got two shops there. Tha' was a friend ringing. The person who works with her left her a message that my dad's been asking questions round all the shops 'n' stalls. Simi's pals with them. They got a hair salon."

"That was one of them who rang you?"

"Yeah. Tiombe. She's in Wolverhampton jus' now. Soon's my dad started asking questions round all the stalls and shops, her partner rang her to send me the message." He said to Sophie, "We can't—me an' Simisola—we can't go back to your house, Soph. If he finds out your name and shows up and we're there, it'll be real ugly."

"In my office, please," Zawadi said. "We'll sort through this. You're safe as long as no one knows you've come here."

Zawadi shepherded the three of them inside, and with little ceremony, she shut the office door. Narissa and Deborah were left in the corridor. Deborah said to Narissa, "What generally happens?"

Narissa said, "Same as for Bolu. She'll try to find a safe house for her, for him as well."

"Then what?"

"She'll make contact with their father 's soon as the kids are safe. He sounds like a piece of work, though. So if it's to be face-to-face, with her talking to him, I hope she does the usual and takes a social worker with her. A social worker with big fists. Or one with a cricket bat and the will to use it."

THE MOTHERS SQUARE
LOWER CLAPTON
NORTH-EAST LONDON

Lynley found Pietra Phinney outside, rolling her daughter along the pavement between a line of parked cars and the wrought-iron railings that fronted the crescent of flats in The Mothers Square. He spied her directly he got out of the Healey Elliott, the manila envelope of photos in his hand. She was at the far end of the ellipse, where a large brass plaque hung at the front of the easternmost building. She appeared to be reading aloud from a book balanced across the top of the wheelchair. She did not see him.

As he walked towards her, she placed the book on her daughter's lap and turned the chair in order to lower it from the pavement's kerb. The chair was heavy, and Lynley quickened his pace to assist her as he called out her name. She looked in his direction but did not seem surprised. Doubtless her husband would have rung her to let her know to prepare herself for a visit from the Met.

She was wearing what she'd worn when Lynley had earlier met her: a white T-shirt, blue jeans, and white trainers without socks. Her bow to color was red lipstick. Her black-coffee hair was shoved behind her ears and held in place on either side with tortoiseshell barrettes. Lynley said to her, "Let me help you," and he handed her the manila envelope as he took charge of the chair.

She said, "We were going to sit in the pergola. We were going to read. That can wait, though. Mark's phoned. He said you'd be coming to speak with me."

Lynley wheeled the chair across the narrow driveway that allowed cars access to the flats in The Mothers Square. The central pergola was draped with a mass of wisteria foliage. He ducked beneath an overhanging branch and stopped the wheelchair at the first stone bench.

"What are you two reading?" he asked Pietra. He parked the chair alongside the bench and waited for her to sit before he did likewise, on the bench's mate directly across from her.

"*Matilda*," she said. "We've just reached Matilda's using her power of telekinesis to write on the blackboard. It's one of Lilybet's favourite scenes in one of her favourite books. Isn't it, Lilybet?" She took a tissue from a packet stowed in a side pocket that hung from the arm of the chair. She wiped Lilybet's mouth—unnecessarily, it seemed to Lynley—and adjusted the shawl that was tucked round her legs. Lilybet cooed and waved her hands, and her mother said, "We will indeed, darling. Once I've spoken to this policeman, we'll fetch Robertson and go to Le Merlin, just as I said. What kind of crêpe do you fancy? Chocolate? Chocolate with bananas? Cream with strawberries? You'll have to decide, you know. You must think about it so when we arrive, you'll have made your choice." She put her hands into the girl's armpits and lifted her. During their walk, Lilybet had slid to one side and it was clear she could not right herself.

"Now we can talk," Pietra said to Lynley. She took another tissue and blotted her own face. It was hot, even in the shade, so the tissue made sense.

She'd given the manila envelope back to him before sitting. He opened it now, took out the relevant picture, and handed it across to her. She might have attempted to deny she was the woman in the photo, but she didn't do that. Instead she handed the picture back to him and said simply, "I did go to see her. But it was only once."

"Why?"

"Once was sufficient. She gave her word. I took her at her word."

"I mean why did you go in the first place? I take it you used your husband's car."

"We have only one. And yes, I used it." She looked over his shoulder but seemed not to focus on anything in particular. It was that expression that people had on their faces when they were recalling an incident they'd either seen or been part of. "I wanted to talk to her. I rang the buzzer beneath her name and asked could I come up to her flat, but she said she'd come down. Which was what she did."

"Did she give you the impression that someone was with her in the flat, someone she didn't want you to see?"

"Someone might have been with her. I didn't think that, though."

"What did you think?"

"That she didn't want the wife of her lover to cause trouble that the neighbours might overhear. Or she worried that, once I got inside, she wouldn't be able to get me out again. Or perhaps she thought I intended her harm."

"Someone did."

"I wasn't that someone."

"Tell me, then."

"I waited for her to come down. I thought she might not as it was five or ten minutes before she finally did. We spoke just outside the building, near the buzzers for the flats. She told me she wasn't going to take Mark from me. No intention of doing that, was what she said. And he has no intention of leaving you, was what she added. She pointed out that she was still married, and she didn't have plans to divorce her husband. Not that marriage and divorce matter much in the world any longer, but she obviously had to say something to reassure me. And that's what she chose."

"After that, though, you sent her texts using your husband's phone."

"She'd told me she wasn't seeing Mark any longer. She said she wasn't going to resume seeing him. But saying and doing are two different things, Inspector. Most people can do one but not the other."

"So after you spoke with her, you wanted to check."

"I had to *know*. I couldn't rest easy. He was in love with her, and he'd never before been in love with any . . ." She moved restlessly, reaching once again to adjust the shawl round her daughter's legs before she went on. "Before Teo, there were women, but Mark had never been in love with any of them. They were just . . . just women to him. She was different. She was a real partner. I didn't believe either one of them could give up the other just by saying they'd do so. How could they? Really. How could anyone do that when there's a tie between them? I mean, there's a tie between Mark and me as well. But the tie is . . ." She glanced at her daughter. "Lilybet's the tie, and that's entirely different from Mark's tie to Teo. So once I'd spoken to her, I waited a day or so and I texted with his phone to see how she would reply."

"But she didn't reply."

"Which told me she'd been sincere."

"And Mark?"

"What about him?"

"How did he take the ending of his relationship with Teo?"

"I didn't want to know. Or see. Whatever he was feeling, I couldn't let it get close to me. I just . . . I couldn't. I suppose we started wearing masks with each other. What else, actually, could we do? I had hopes he would get over her and we could go back to how we were before."

"Which was?"

"I expect he's told you. We share only a flat and the care of Lilybet." She swallowed, and Lynley noted how tightly her hands were clasped. "Things like this," she went on, "they don't just begin one day, Inspector Lynley. They develop over time. They're the result of . . . So many things combine to make us who we are and who we become. You understand that, I hope."

Lynley nodded. "I do."

"When Lilybet was born . . . She had to be taken, you see, five months along. It was pre-eclampsia, and things should have worked out well and they *could* have worked out well eventually, I suppose, but they didn't. She . . . there were so many things wrong, so many issues. Her heart, her lungs, one of her kidneys. It was like . . . bits and pieces of her never developed the way they should have done. Every day brought more bad news until there was no news left. Or at least no possibility of *good* news." She crumpled into a ball the tissue she was holding. She began to pick at it restlessly. "I couldn't go through it again. I couldn't face it, take the chance, all of it. I just couldn't do it. And then, after a bit, I . . . I couldn't at all." Her eyes filled. She sought another tissue. "I never would blame Mark if he left. He *should* leave. No one should expect any man . . . What I thought was if I encouraged him to . . . to find someone who understood or not even understood but was at least willing . . . Surely there are women who wouldn't want more than what he had to give."

"You wanted him to find a sexual partner? Is that what you mean? Someone he would hire, perhaps? Someone he would see occasionally and pay?"

"Not pay, not hire. But I thought there *could* be someone for him. Perhaps someone in a marriage gone bad or gone dead, someone who had a physical need that her partner couldn't fulfil, a young widow who didn't want to remarry. I didn't care who the person was or how he found her or even if there were two or three or a dozen of them. I just didn't want him to fall in love. With her, though, with Teo, I saw it happening and I didn't know what to do." She put her forehead on her left hand, which was resting on the wheelchair handles. She murmured, "I'm so sorry," and "Nothing's ever been the way it should be."

Lynley thought about what she had said. He thought about her relationship with her husband. He thought about the secrets people keep behind the closed doors of their homes. He thought about the various destinations to which those secrets could lead.

He said, "Mrs. Phinney, I must ask you where you were on the thirty-first of July. This would be from midafternoon onward."

She didn't reply.

He said, "Mrs. Phinney?"

Still nothing.

Lynley waited. He couldn't think he might have to arrest her, to take her into an interview room and thus compel her into speaking. She was broken in so many ways. It seemed inhuman to break her even further.

"I know this is difficult for you," he told her quietly. "I also know that you see the reality: Everyone connected to Teo Bontempi's death—even remotely—is suffering now, and my responsibility is to uncover what happened to her and through that means bring some wretched form of peace to her family and to those others who loved her."

"Like Mark," she cried.

"Like everyone whose life she touched."

"I didn't hate her." She finally raised her head. Lilybet had coughed and the sound was startling, coming as it did from deep in her chest but strangled at the end with a gasp. Pietra was at once altered. She was on her feet, turning a dial on the canister that hung from the back of Lilybet's wheelchair and fitting a nosepiece into place, holding it there, saying, "Breathe deeply, Lily. Breathe deeply for Mummy."

A man came out of their flat near the entrance to The Mothers Square. He looked round. Lynley recognised him as Lilybet's attendant. He began to walk along the crescent as if looking for Pietra, probably assuming she was having some sort of difficulty with the little girl's chair. It would be only a moment before he saw them.

Lynley said to Pietra, "Whatever you intended towards Teo went in the wrong direction at some point. I believe it was a direction that you never intended. You're frightened now, and rightfully so. But hoping to hide—"

"I didn't," she said. "I wasn't there. I didn't. I saw her once. That was the only time."

"Were you here, then? At home? That late afternoon and early evening?"

In her silence, he had his answer.

"Were you with someone?" and when she didn't reply, "Mrs. Phinney, if someone can verify—"

"There you are!" It was the attendant. He stepped off the pavement's kerb and was coming in their direction. "I thought aliens might've taken the two of you." His gaze went to Lynley, and he added, "Ah. Sh'll I take our Lily off your hands, then, Pete?"

She stood. "No, no. We're coming along, Robertson. I promised Lilybet Le Merlin and we're about to set off. Will you come with us?"

"I'd do myself in if you went without me," Robertson said affably. He reached them, nodded at Lynley, and squatted in front of Lilybet's chair. "Le Merlin! What d'you think of that?" Then to Pietra, "We'll set off, shall we? Me and the princess? If you need the time?"

"We're finished here," she said to him.

Robertson took up position behind the chair and began to push it along the pergola, chatting to the little girl about crêpes and nuts and chocolate. Pietra Phinney blotted her face. For a moment during which seconds ticked by like hours, she looked at her feet.

Lynley waited until she looked up again. He said, "Was it another man, Mrs. Phinney?"

"Have you ever known shame, Inspector Lynley?" she asked him.

"I have," he told her.

"I don't believe you."

"The truth," he said, "is often as inconvenient to one as it is unpalatable to another."

"That," she replied, "I do believe." She began to follow Robertson and her daughter, and he watched her, which she seemed to feel. She turned again and said to him quietly, "Please don't blame Mark for anything. None of this is his fault. It never was."

WESTMINSTER
CENTRAL LONDON

"So she'd gone there for an exam," Barbara Havers said. "Hence 'evaluation' written in her appointment diary. She wanted to know if reconstruction was possible." She had the last custard cream from the packet she'd bought on the Isle of Dogs, and she dug this out of her shoulder bag and delicately set it on her desk, a precious item she would see to momentarily.

"And was it possible?" Lynley had rolled a chair over to join her and Nkata. The four DCs on the team were sitting where they could or otherwise leaning against the nearest wall, notebooks in hand.

"Superficially, it seemed to be," Barbara said. She gestured to the folder of patient information that Dr. Weatherall had printed for her. "She was in excellent health—no surprise there—so there wouldn't have been any problems with the procedure. I mean, she was good for anaesthesia and all that. Good heart, good lungs, blah blah blah." She handed the folder to Lynley, who brought his reading glasses from his jacket pocket.

He said as he opened the folder, "And the phone calls from the surgeon to her?"

"They seem on the up and up. She phoned on the twenty-fifth to ask were there any questions that Teo had once she'd been told she was good for the surgery. She said she always does that with the women who come to her. She said Teo seemed troubled, though, right from the start. So she phoned later, on the twenty-seventh, twenty-eighth, and twenty-ninth. She wanted to reassure her, she said, in case Teo was afraid to go through with it. It's not likely that things actually could've been made worse down there, she told me, but on the other hand, there was also the possibility that things wouldn't've been improved much either."

"Wha's that mean, Barb?" Nkata asked. The faint sound of scribbling came from the DCs.

Barbara explained the situation much as Dr. Weatherall had explained it to her: nerve endings and physical sensation. The rebirth of the latter depended on the presence of the former, and that wasn't guaranteed.

"You think that'd be 'nough to put her off?" Nkata asked.

"I s'pose it's the difference between hanging on to hope and having hope dashed to bits, eh? On one hand, Teo could keep telling herself maybe. On the other, all the maybes could've been done for. Anyway, the real point is—according to Dr. Weatherall—that Teo finally *did* decide to have the surgery. All she needed to do was arrange for someone to be her driver to and from the Isle of Dogs and Bob's your uncle. Or he *would* have been your uncle had things not gone south directly she made her decision."

"Someone stopping her from having the surgery?" Lynley took off his specs and handed the medical folder back to Barbara.

"I wager her sister wouldn't've been chuffed to know about Teo getting operated on," Barbara said.

"'Xcept the sister never knew in the first place that Teo'd been cut," Nkata pointed out. "Either that or she was putting on a bang-up performance when she got told by her mum."

"That seems like a good possibility, considering what you've told us about her," Barbara noted. "Can we look it that way?"

"How do you see it?" Lynley asked her.

"Ross Carver believes he drove Teo off because he couldn't stop banging on about sex, surgery, sex, repairs, sex, sensation, and everything else related to the above, including sex, and she reached the point where she couldn't cope. So . . ." Barbara had ticked items off on her fingers and she went on with, "Teo asks him to leave, and her sister sees the opening she's been waiting for, and she makes her move."

Nkata went on with, "She snares the bloke, she comes up pregnant—"

"And the rest is the rest is the rest," Barbara concluded. "And *then* she discovers that her sister's having surgery, which puts Ross into a picture that Rosie doesn't much want to look at."

"So she clubbed her own sister?" Lynley said.

"Worked for Cain and Abel," Barbara pointed out.

"Yes. But, on the other hand, Rachel didn't kill Leah, and one might say she had far greater cause."

"Who?"

"Ah. Your biblical education didn't stretch far, I see."

"I lost interest with all the knowing and begetting. It was too bloody exhausting. I'm lucky to know who Cain and Abel are, guv."

"Indeed." Lynley looked round at the group. "So Rosie Bontempi remains a suspect. Pietra Phinney denies she was there at any point on the day or night Teo died, although she won't say where she was. What else have we? Winston? Where are we with Monifa Bankole?"

Nkata laid it out for them: confirmation that Monifa Bankole had arranged to have her daughter cut at the clinic above the abandoned toy shop; that she had been going against her husband's wishes in the matter as he had not wanted to spend the amount that the clinic charged; that on the day that the coppers arrived to close the place down, she'd been at the clinic to fetch back her deposit money upon the orders of her husband; that now both her daughter and her son were missing. "The boy—he's called Tani—got beat up bad by

Bankole," Nkata finished. "Over a protection order, this was. Monifa whacked him with a steam iron—Bankole, this is—"

"Ouch," Havers said.

"—and that gave the boy a chance to run off. According to Monifa, Bankole's set on taking the girl—she's called Simisola—to Nigeria and he's going to leave the country with her if their passports aren't grabbed."

"Where did you leave things?" Lynley asked him.

Nkata told the rest quickly: how he'd found Monifa Bankole from information supplied by a neighbour, how he'd got her off the estate entirely, and how he'd taken her home to his mother for her own protection.

"She d'n't want to leave. Th' only way I could get her away was by lyin', 'm 'fraid," he concluded. "I said I was arresting her. Sorry, guv, but otherwise she was intent on finding her kids and she wouldn't've come."

"So she's in Brixton now?" Lynley clarified.

"No way her husband's about to think of lookin for her there."

"You got her chained to the bed or something, Win?" Barbara asked. "Cos if she's set on finding her kids, how're you planning to keep her there?"

"Mum's with her f'r now. She won't let her go. Plus," with a grin, "she's bigger 'n Monifa, my mum is. An' she's used to beating on me and Stoney. We got some work to keep Monifa from her husband, though. An' we need to put our mitts on his passport, which c'n only happen if there's a protection order in place. He strikes me as a bloke who goes his own way no matter what. Which means, no protection order an' he's gone from the country the second he finds Simisola."

"Do we know where she is?"

"Only the brother knows. An' I don't 'spect him to be sharing that information anytime soon."

Lynley directed his next questions to the DCs, saying, "Any joy on finding Mercy Hart?"

"I've got an address," one of them said, a lanky twenty-something who had not yet outgrown spots on his face. He had an impressive patch of them fanning out from the corner of his mouth. "She got herself stopped for speeding in January, this was. She had to give her address and it wasn't the address she'd given to the lads at the Stoke Newington station. I checked to make certain it was still good. It is."

"What do we know about her?" Lynley asked. "Aside from her being associated with a putative women's clinic."

"Not much. Single mum. Three kids. All girls."

"Where does she live?" Lynley asked the DC.

"Stratford," he said. "Rokeby Street."

"Are you certain? That's quite a distance from where she was arrested."

"Could be she's moved house, sir. That's the last known address."

"We'll need to question her, but let's ask the Stratford station to send someone round first. We'll need a photo of her as well. Compare it to the CCTV footage and take it round the flats in Streatham. Even if she's no longer in Stratford, we'll have a leg up if someone recognises her. Check her car's number plates against the CCTV film."

"As to number plates," another of the DCs said, this one a young woman with plaits who looked to Barbara like a twelve-year-old. "Sorry it's been such a time, but there were countless cars on Streatham High Road on the day Teo Bontempi was attacked."

"You've got someone of interest?"

"I'm not altogether certain, guv. Could be it's just a similar name. One of the cars is registered to"—she checked her notes—"a Paul Phinney."

Barbara looked at Lynley and Nkata. Then she shifted her gaze to the young DC. "You're certain?" she asked.

"About who the car is registered to? Yes. 'Course anyone could have been driving it."

CHELSEA
SOUTH-WEST LONDON

He was on his way to the lift that would take him to his car when Lynley was accosted by Dorothea Harriman, whose first words were "Acting Detective Chief Superintendent Lynley? May I ask you something?" When he turned, she went on without waiting for him to reply. "This is . . . Well. Right. I rather need you to clarify something. I can't think who else to ask and since you've worked with her for so long . . ."

"DS Havers, I take it?"

"Yes, yes. Barbara. I thought GroupMeet would be just the ticket, you see. We'd find something beyond our tap dancing. Tap dancing is fine and well—I've lost over a stone and would probably lose more if we didn't go for a curry after almost every lesson—but the thing is it's mostly women. I mean, our instructor's a man. He's quite good, by the way. But the students . . . ? Of course, there *is* a fourteen-year-old boy just joined, but he's not going to do, is he, although I must admit he's an extremely talented dancer. So while we'll continue the lessons—we've learned so much it's pointless to stop—I did feel that another venue would be, as I've said, just the ticket."

"GroupMeet being the venue?" he asked.

"No, no. GroupMeet is merely the *means* to find the venue, although *venue* probably isn't the best word in this case. *I* thought sketching would appeal, but . . . well, it became quite clear Barbara wasn't on board with that. So I thought: badminton, croquet, tennis—not that I play and I seriously doubt Barbara plays either except we wouldn't be there to play, exactly, would we—allotment gardening, cemetery restoration—"

He raised an eyebrow at that.

"I mean, really, *anything*. GroupMeet has it all. We could even learn to judge wine."

"A useful talent," he acknowledged gravely.

"Oh, I know you think it's all foolishness, but have you any idea how difficult it is for a woman to meet someone even vaguely suitable in London?"

"Joining a church choir no longer being of help?" he noted.

"If anyone even *went* to church other than for weddings and funerals, and at Easter and Christmas. And anyway, that's not the point. That's not what I wanted to get clarity on."

She'd been walking alongside him, and she lowered her voice as they reached the lift. "It's this." She looked round to make certain there were no eavesdroppers. "It's occurred to me that perhaps Detective Sergeant Havers—Barbara—might not . . . well . . . you know what I mean . . . men?"

"I'm afraid I'm now the one seeking clarity," he told her.

She sighed. "Do I have to spell it out?"

"Apparently."

"What I mean is p'rhaps Barbara doesn't actually *like* men. I mean p'rhaps she doesn't like men as in *liking* men in the way that, well, women generally like men."

"I see," he said. "At least I think I do. You're asking me if Barbara Havers is a lesbian."

"My God! Shhhh!" Dorothea looked round once again. Then she said to him, "Please! I don't at *all* want her to think . . . *you* know what I mean, don't you?"

Lynley didn't, actually, but to put them both out of her misery, he said, "I've never had the first inkling of anything regarding Barbara's sexual proclivity, Dee. Not that I'm altogether sure what I should be looking for if I *did* have an urge to develop such an inkling."

Her eyes narrowed. "Are you laughing at me, Acting Detective Chief Superintendent?"

"I most certainly am not," he replied.

She tapped her foot, a pensive expression on her face. "It's only that I don't want to put her in the position of *having* to tell me. I mean, she *could* tell me. I'd welcome knowing if she wants me to know. But I don't want her to feel she must tell me if only to stop me banging on about GroupMeet."

"Hmmm. Yes," he said. "But you've forgotten that Barbara could easily meet a woman at GroupMeet, couldn't she? I mean, if women are her interest. And if not, she could meet a man." Or, he thought, she could meet a three-legged hedgehog, but that wasn't likely. "I tend to think you've just not hit on the most appealing activity for her, Dee."

"So you're saying I should continue? I should look for opportunities on the GroupMeet site?"

He wasn't at all saying that—he had a very difficult time seeing Barbara engaged in cemetery restoration—but he didn't want to be the one to dash Dee's hopes or her good intentions with regard to his long-time partner. He settled on saying, "You might want to gauge her level of interest in an activity first."

"She hates them all."

"Not entirely true. She's still tap dancing, isn't she?"

"Well. Yes. But I expect that's due to the curry. I think she sees it as her reward."

"There you are," he said.

"There I am? Where?"

"You've hit on it. She needs rewards. We all do."

"More curry?"

"Probably not." The lift doors opened. He punched for the car park and, lest Dorothea jump inside to continue their discussion, "Dee, I am completely confident you can come up with something."

Once in his car, he made for the river, windows open to catch whatever breeze might be coming off the water. He made good time to Chelsea, and although he was forced to park at the top of Bramerton Street, the walk to the St. Jameses' house wasn't far, and soon enough he was climbing the steps to their door and ringing the bell.

Barking ensued: Peach was causing her usual ruckus. A voice attempted to put an end to her canine greeting, but Peach had never been a dog to be disciplined. She was, after all, a dachshund.

A bolt was withdrawn, the door opened, and Peach dashed out to examine his ankles. Finding them passable, she trotted back inside.

"She's got the devil in her, that dog," Joseph Cotter said, opening wide the door to allow him entrance to the house.

"I daresay she's better than a burglar alarm." Lynley bent to let the dog have a whiff of his fingers, happy he'd thoroughly washed his hands after downing half of a day-old tuna salad sandwich before he left his office.

"Gone out, I'm 'fraid," Cotter told him. "Said he had to speak with someone in Lambeth."

"Ah. There's a trial coming up?"

"Oh aye. Isn't there always a trial coming up? Twenty-four/seven it seems like he's at work. 'Course, Deb's not much better."

"Is she here, then? I've actually come to speak to her rather than to Simon."

"To Deb? Oh. Right, she's above. I c'n fetch her down to the study for you. She's doing something with her photos. Don't ask me what."

Lynley said he would go to her, rather than having to interrupt her work. He went for the stairway and climbed to the top floor of the house. Here, under a huge skylight, both Deborah and Simon often worked, she dealing with her photography, he dealing with requests for his expertise in matters of evidence to be used—or for that matter, discounted—in upcoming trials.

He found Deborah at one of the worktables, a number of photographs spread out in front of her. Her heavy mass of hair was done in whimsical plaits—against the heat, no doubt—and she was wearing a large set of headphones. Her shoulders were moving to the beat of whatever music she was listening to. He didn't wish to startle her, so he crossed the room and put himself on the other side of the table at which she worked. The movement appeared to catch her attention, but she didn't look up. Instead, she lifted a hand in a just-a-moment gesture. She removed two of the photos she was inspecting, filing them in a large accordion folder. That done, she raised her head. She looked surprised and quickly gazed round, perhaps to see if Simon was with him. She removed her headphones—he could hear the dreadful teeth-grinding sound of a rock 'n' roll guitar solo—and she thumbed a small switch to turn the music off.

"What on earth was that?" he asked her.

She laughed. "The Scorpions. 'Rock You Like a Hurricane.' That's just the opening. You're a heavy metal philistine, Tommy."

"And long do I wish to remain. That was indescribable. Aren't you damaging your hearing?"

"With the volume?" She looked at the headphones rather too fondly, in his opinion. "I generally don't listen to anything that loud. But every once in a very long while, only true, metallic rock 'n' roll at maximum volume will do."

"What does it do? Remove tartar from your teeth?"

She laughed again. "I suspect Barbara would approve of my choice."

"Not unless Buddy Holly has left his grave and joined the band."

She waved him off. "Simon's not here, you know. Dad must have told you."

"Is this a bad time?" He gestured to the photos. They appeared to be portraits, all of the same woman, taken inside a home. She was Black, and she had a shy cast to her look. She was seated, and behind her off to one side, a wall was hung with a collection of African art. Mostly masks, he saw. They were deliberately out of focus, but still identifiable as masks. "Who is it?" he asked her.

"She's called Leylo. I'd delivered an earlier portrait to her, but she looked very different when I'd taken it. Seeing her again, I wanted another as contrast. But I'm having trouble deciding which is most effective."

"As what?"

"As a comparison. She was healed from her surgery in these. In the others, the earlier portraits, she was preparing for surgery."

"Surgery?"

"Hmmm. She'd had genital mutilation done to her when she was a child, and she was about to undergo reconstruction."

"That's an extraordinary coincidence." Lynley looked at the photos, one after the other.

"Why 'an extraordinary coincidence'?"

"It appears that Teo Bontempi may have been getting ready for reconstruction surgery as well." He tapped his fingers on the edge of one of the photos, "For what it's worth to your decision making, I like this one."

"Do you not find the background distracting?"

"A bit."

She sighed. "Damn. I thought I'd handled it by moving one of the larger pieces to one side."

"Who did her surgery? Did Leylo tell you?"

"She didn't need to tell me. I was there when she had it. The surgeon didn't want to have her own portrait done, but she'd agreed that I could photograph her during the surgery when she was gowned and masked and all the rest. Unfortunately, that particular group of pictures is . . . well . . . terrible, actually. I should have tried harder to talk her into posing in another location."

"It's a woman, then. The surgeon."

"It is. She's called Philippa Weatherall."

Lynley took this on board with some stirring of the hairs on the back of his neck.

Deborah said, "You look a bit startled, Tommy."

"Her name has come up quite recently," he told her. "Philippa Weatherall."

"Having to do with your case? Is she involved?"

"She seems to be, tangentially. Then she seems not to be." Absently, as he spoke, he picked up a small brass figure that was weighing down a pile of typescript on the edge of the table. He played it back and forth in his hands. He saw it was in the shape of a crocodile.

Deborah saw this and said, "It's a goldweight, that. Leylo wanted me to have it as a thank-you when I gave her a copy of her portrait. I'd never seen one before, and she has a collection of them."

"A goldweight?" he said.

"It was used exactly as the name suggests: to weigh gold dust," she said. "They're from the days before African countries had paper notes. Leylo has all sorts of them."

He set it back upon the papers. He said to her, "How did you manage to locate Philippa Weatherall, Deb?"

"Narissa Cameron told me about her." Deborah reminded him of the documentary Narissa was creating and the booklet Deborah herself was assembling for the Department for Education. Narissa had wished to make Dr. Weatherall part of her documentary through an interview in any form an interview with her would take. She added, "*Are* you thinking she had something to do with Teo Bontempi's death?"

"Only in that having to decide to move forward with surgery, Teo may have given someone a motive to kill her."

Deborah set the photos to one side. She said, "I do know Dr. Weatherall had her own fears about being a target."

"Did she explain?"

"She's worried about reprisals, she said. Husbands, fathers, boyfriends, family. Some people don't want to see FGM's banishment in *any* form, including attempting to help a woman who's had it." Deborah shifted away from the worktable and turned off a fan that had been moving the hot air round in the room. She said, "Shall we go below? It'll be slightly cooler in Simon's study. And knowing Dad, he's making tea for you."

She led the way. A window was gaping in the study, and since his last visit, someone had placed a fan in the opening. Deborah switched it on, but that didn't offer much respite from the heat. She sat on one of the old leather chairs near the fireplace and he took the other.

She looked at him long. He found he suddenly had the half-mad desire to touch her hair—plaited though it was—as he once had done, years in the past, both prelude and promise. It was animal instinct and human desire. One never walked easily away from the passion that goes with love, he thought.

She seemed to feel something as well because she said quickly, "Tell me about Daidre. Have you managed to throw a spanner in the works?"

"You know me too well," he replied with a smile.

"Oh, Tommy. What have you done?"

"Ardent to a fault. That was always my weakness."

"How can that be a weakness? Ardency leads to honesty, doesn't it? What I mean is: It's difficult to be ardent without making ardency known."

"As I said," he replied.

"Oh. I see. Ardency has prompted too *much* honesty? Hmmm. Still, having ardency as a weakness is far better than a weakness for . . . I don't know . . . chocolate sponge?"

"Not if one's true love is a baker, I daresay. However, having revealed what plagues my relationship with Daidre, I must say that I appear to have smoothed things over. For now. I'm sure I shall once again bollix things up in another few days."

Footsteps came along the corridor in their direction. They heard Cotter's voice, saying, "Mind she doesn't get in your way, luv. She will do, when there's food involved."

Deborah glanced at Lynley as she rose from her chair, saying, "We have a guest . . . ," and fell silent as Cotter appeared in the doorway. He was accompanied, Lynley saw, by a small Black girl who was holding a tray of cups and saucers. Cotter himself had a tray that bore the various accoutrements of afternoon tea.

Lynley looked at the girl, then at Cotter, then at Deborah. For the second time that afternoon and this time unaccountably, he felt hairs stirring on the back of his neck.

Deborah said, "Tommy, this is Simi Bankole."

"Bankole," he repeated.

"Yes. She's only just arrived today. She's stopping with us for a bit."

12 AUGUST

Monifa had slept only fitfully. Indeed, it could hardly be called a night's sleep at all. Anxiety had pursued her. Pain had done the same: from her ribs to her bruises, she was a body that throbbed with hurt. As to the anxiety she was experiencing, her children were its centre.

She had more concern for Tani than she had for Simi. She knew very well that Tani would never return to the flat with Simi as long as the situation they were in went unresolved. But Monifa was afraid he would return there alone, either to see to her own well-being or to bring another protection order for her to fill out. If he did this and if Abeo was there, another fight would occur.

There was no way for her to reach Tani, either. He'd long ago programmed her mobile phone with his own mobile's number, but that number was unknown to her. She rang him merely by touching his name on her phone screen, the same phone that was in the flat, left behind when she fled to Hamilah after slamming the iron into Abeo's head.

Monifa sat up slowly, each movement describing a cry for help. It was time for her to be out of bed—on her way to find her children as well—but when she looked at the chair where she'd left her clothing, it wasn't there. Next to the bed, however, was a cup of tea. It wasn't even warm, telling her several hours must have passed since someone— most likely Alice Nkata—had placed it there. She wondered what she was meant to do: remain in the room till someone came for her or call out for assistance?

She saw, then, that a summery yellow dressing gown had been draped over the foot of the bed, a partner to the nightgown that Alice Nkata had lent her. Like the nightgown, Monifa found the dressing gown overly long, but she slowly struggled into it.

There was a built-in clothes cupboard next to the room's door, and she opened this. Inside, there was little enough: one suit, one pair of highly polished shoes, a rack of seven ties, four white dress shirts, two pairs of neatly ironed jeans. Everything was spotlessly clean. Everything could have been hanging in a department store.

She closed the cupboard and went to the door, hearing Alice Nkata's voice as she opened it. Alice was saying, "You ask me, caff's the best alternative, Benj."

"Win says main thing is we're to keep her safe."

"She'd be safe. She'd be with me."

"No doubt she would do," he replied. "But di' you have a word with our Win? Bes' do that before you make any decision. He knows more 'bout this than we do, luv."

It was Benjamin Nkata speaking, whom Monifa had met last night upon his return from his shift driving one of London's double-decker buses. He did the Number 11 route, he told her in an affable fashion. Gen'rally he loved it, he said, but not this summer. This summer it'd been like sitting at the gates of Hades, so hot had it been inside and so foul the humour of even his long-suffering regular passengers. As for the tourists . . . They were worse. And there were crowds of them because the Number 11 bus passed nearly every famous monument and tourist attraction in Central London. He'd heard it *all* from them, he had. Everything from "This is England! It's supposed to rain every day!" to "Haven't you people ever *heard* of air-conditioning?"

Monifa had liked him at once, Benjamin Nkata. She liked the way he interacted with his wife and his son. She liked how they laughed together. She especially liked that he'd asked his wife if she'd had time to see to his dinner. When Alice said she had done and it was jerk chicken with rice and pineapple slices ("tinned, I'm 'fraid"), Monifa liked that he'd declared jerk chicken was his favourite dish and that into his wife's laughter, his son had explained with, "Tha's what he says ev'ry night, no matter what she cooks."

Benjamin's reply had been, "But each time, she goes one better than the last time, so soon 's I taste what she's cooked, it's my new fav'rite."

"You keep talking," had been Alice's response to this, and then to her son, "You takin' notes, Jewel? 'F anyone knows how to beguile a woman, it's your dad."

Monifa eased into the family bathroom, did her business, then looked at herself in the mirror above the basin. Her black eye was only partially open, her eyelid and the space above it were swollen, and her split lip bore an ugly scab. She did the best she could with soap and water, joining the Nkatas in the kitchen when she was finished.

Alice said, "Here she is, then."

"How'd you sleep, Missus Bankole?" Benjamin asked. "That paracetamol help at all?"

"A bit." Monifa told the lie easily in answer to his kindness. "Thank you for being so good to me. I must thank your son as well."

"He went off to work, he did," Alice said. "We've got our orders to take good care of you."

Benjamin added, "Told us to tell you not to worry 's well. If you can, he said. I 'spect that's an impossibility, but you do your best because the one thing I know 'bout Win is he won't let a thing happen to those kids of yours."

Monifa nodded when she heard this, but she wasn't relieved of either anxiety or fear. Tani *would* return to the flat, if she knew him. And, also knowing Abeo as she did, her husband would return as well because he'd have no intention of leaving the flat till he put his hands on Simi.

"I expect you'd like your clothes, eh?" Alice was saying. "They're just over there on the piano bench. I gave them a wash last night and a good ironing this morning."

Monifa was at a loss for what to say. She'd never come across people like this, the sort who would treat a stranger foisted upon them as an honoured guest. "I find I have no way to thank you."

"Tha's not going to be a problem, innit," Benjamin said. "Cos Alice here tells me you're quite a cook."

Alice said before Monifa could reply, "We'd be that happy if you'd do us an African meal, Monifa. And that'll be thanks enough, that will. So if you make up a list of what you need, Benjamin here will fetch the food b'fore he has to be at work. I got someone handling the caff today b'cause I want to watch you cook and I'm taking notes."

Monifa knew that Alice Nkata was under orders from her son to keep watch over her, making sure she remained in Brixton. She meant well, as did her son and her husband. But the truth was that Monifa had no idea how any of them expected to keep her in Brixton if she managed to learn where her children were. Nonetheless, she decided to let them try.

WESTMINSTER
CENTRAL LONDON

What Lynley didn't want to hear on the other end of the phone was Daidre's recorded voice once again: "Awfully sorry. I can't take your call at the moment. Please leave a message." This he had done the previous night, assuming there was some kind of emergency with one of the larger animals at the zoo. But now this morning and despite the early hour . . . ? He was worried enough to consider making the drive to Belsize Park. However, after giving the idea a few minutes' thought as he cleared the bathroom mirror of steam and did his morning shave, he decided against it. If she'd indeed had a very late night at the zoo and as a result was having a lie-in with her phone muted, she wouldn't be pleased to find him on her doorstep.

Still and all . . . There was something not right in Daidre's life at the moment. She'd hinted a bit and he'd read it on her face and in the set of her shoulders. She would tell him when she was ready, he reckoned. Of course, though, that begged the question: When would she ever be ready? He knew the answer—not anytime soon—but that wasn't close to a happy thought.

He'd left her a message, though. "We're both having late nights, it seems. Ring me when you can. If there's anything—" but he changed direction because he knew how she would take his offer of *anything I can do*, so he went on with "—prevents me from answering, I'll get back to you when I'm able."

He'd had his breakfast, then, and as it would probably be his only meal till a late-night dinner left warm by Charlie Denton, he made the most of it. He saw in the *Guardian* a story about a Scotland Yard investigation into the sudden death of a Metropolitan Police officer—Detective Sergeant Teodora Bontempi—and he murmured "Damn," because the brief report could easily prompt more articles at the same time as it could provoke a demand for a progress report from Sir David Hillier. And Hillier was always and ever the last person with whom he wished to converse.

With the additional DCs now on the team, his office had become too small for a gathering, so the whiteboard had been moved to the larger area where the department's detectives had their desks. The entire team was gathered in a semicircle in front of this whiteboard, which displayed a large photo of Teo Bontempi in the uniform all constables wore at the start of their careers. She looked quite solemn in the picture, as if all too aware of the responsibilities she was taking on. But a lift to one corner of her mouth suggested the pride she'd felt.

Beneath the picture, columns had been devised to document actions, the first column bearing information about the various sightings caught by the CCTV cameras: both from the building where she'd lived and from the various shops and other businesses nearby along Streatham High Road. The second column dealt with photos of the individuals who'd known the murder victim and where she lived. These had been shown round the block of flats, and where someone had been sighted by an inhabitant of the building, that was noted. The third and final column had to do with cars, listing what had been seen and to whom it belonged.

"Where are we, then?" Lynley asked as he took his spectacles from his jacket and looked at the columns more closely.

Havers replied, "This lot"—with a nod at the four constables in the room—"finished up showing the photos round last evening, sir. They've got recognition of Ross Carver, which isn't a surprise as he lived there during his marriage to Teo and he's moving back in. Rosie's been. Mark Phinney's been there as well. We got his mug from his police ID. But no one else from our stills was recognised, which could mean no one else got inside to see her."

"Unless no one saw them," one of the DCs said.

"Or someone let them in another way," another pointed out.

"There's that," Havers agreed. "The only other entrance is the fire exit on the north side of the building. No CCTV there."

"Could've been used for something else, that," Nkata said. "It doesn't set off an alarm when it's opened."

"Escape route for her killer?" Lynley asked.

There were murmurs of assent, but no name was offered.

"What do we have from her computer, Winston?" Lynley asked. "Anything yet?"

"I got one of the forensic computer techs giving it to me in dribs an' drabs. He's going for a deeper dive now, but so far what we know tells us a few choice bits." He took up a manila folder from his desk and opened it. "We got emails to and from her colleagues, with a whole pile of them from the DS who took her place."

"DS Jade Hopwood," Lynley said.

"Right. Yeah. Also emails from Mark Phinney—nothing personal in them—"

"They saved the hot and bothered end of their business for their smartphones," Havers added.

"—but a lot about what he wants her to do next and what she's reporting on. There's also emails to and from Ross Carver, her mum, her dad, an' her sister. Most of it jus' like regular correspondence if you know what I mean. But there's an in'eresting bit with the sister. Teo's emailed her asking would she drive her to and from 'a bit of surgery' she's meant to be having. When Rosie responds to say she'll need some lead time to get off work and what's the surgery for, Teo doesn't reply."

"Perhaps she'd found someone else to do the driving?" Lynley asked.

"Or she changed her mind," Nkata said. "Or she didn't want Rosie to know what the surgery was for."

"Or she got herself bashed before she could make any plans," Havers added.

"There's that 's well." Winston went on to list other details he'd had off the computer tech. "She did internet searches, like most of us. In her case, she's gone everywhere from potential spots for holidays—Iceland and Antarctica're both high on her list—to looking for bonsai information websites. There's also a search for anti-FGM sites and anti-FGM groups, as well as a look for genital repair. That one took her to France to the website of a bloke called Ignace Severin, but it was all in French. She also did a search for Philippa Weatherall."

Havers said, "Makes sense, that, if she was thinking about going under the knife."

"What have we uncovered about Mercy Hart?" Lynley asked the detective constables.

One of the women replied with, "The local station rang this morning, guv. She still lives at the address in Stratford. I told them someone from the Met would be coming onto their patch to speak with her."

"Seems to me," another of the constables said, "that if anyone has a motive, it's this one. Teo Bontempi closed down her livelihood."

"But she can easily open another clinic in another part of town," Havers pointed out, and with a gesture towards Lynley, "She's put everything into storage. We got that much from the removal blokes. All she has to do is move all that lumber to a new space when things cool off."

"Right," Nkata said. "But you ask me, Barb, tha's an even better motive, innit. Teo Bontempi's shut her down once and there's nothing to stop her from shutting her down another time. And a time after that. *And* 'less Monifa Bankole's willing to sign a statement 'bout what was really going on in that place, Mercy's in the clear."

"Aren't you working your magic charm on her?"

"Tha' spreads only so far, Barb."

"We may have something to move her," Lynley noted. "I'll get onto that later. Meantime . . ."

He gave them their assignments: Havers to have a go at Rosie Bontempi, he and Nkata to search out Mercy Hart in Stratford, the others to divide up the responsibility for locating the site of Mercy Hart's storage from the removals men, tracking down whatever paperwork there might be on the first property where the clinic was located, and combing through Teo Bontempi's medical file to see if anything might be out of order there.

"No one," he said, "is in the clear."

CHELSEA
SOUTH-WEST LONDON

As long as treats were involved, Peach was perfectly content to sit at Deborah's feet and stay there, despite this involving the dachshund's removal from the kitchen and thus from the potential of bacon somehow falling to the floor. But since the dog also never said no to cheese—the more malodorous the better—Deborah seduced her with fingertips of brie and Peach was content to sit obediently, as well as expectantly, with her. They were on the stairs, waiting just outside of Deborah's childhood bedroom. Simisola Bankole was within, having finally fallen asleep while Deborah read to her a fourth fairy tale from the Brothers Grimm, suitably edited to remove the . . . well . . . the grim bits.

Getting both of the Bankoles under her protection hadn't been accomplished easily, not only because Zawadi did not want them put into the care of a white family but also because Tani had not wanted to be under anyone's protection at all. The only reason Zawadi was finally willing to entertain the idea of Deborah was the intervention of Narissa, who had said impatiently, "See reason, Zawadi. If there's room in Deborah's house, it makes sense they should go with her."

When Zawadi said nothing, Deborah told her, "Only three of us live in the house just now, and we've two spare bedrooms that my husband's family use when they come to town. But no one's coming to town in this weather, and we're just rattling round the place."

Zawadi said, "You have told us your father and your husband cannot be trusted. I won't put these children into the care of—"

"You have no worries there," Deborah cut in quickly. "They'll take one look at Tani and, believe me, they'll be straight on board." She added that while the girl, Sophie, could return to her home, the Bankoles could hardly return to theirs, and since Zawadi herself had declared there were no families available . . .

Tani said at that point that he had no need for accommodation anywhere because he intended to return to Mayville Estate. Zawadi declared this madness, as did Sophie. He was insistent about it, though, and it was only Simisola's clinging to him like a barnacle that garnered his cooperation. She could not abide being separated from him, and who could blame her. She had to be with him, which turned out to be what moved Zawadi to agree to Deborah's offering of shelter and protection for the Bankoles.

She'd introduced herself to both Simisola and Tani, offering each of them a handshake. She'd done the same to Sophie. Then she ushered both Bankoles to her car, Simisola hanging on her brother's hand, Tani scowling at the disruption to his plans, whatever they actually were.

They'd made a stop at the nearest A and E. Deborah wanted the boy to be looked at. She feared a concussion, and when he was taken to be examined, she bought fizzy drinks for all of them, and she waited with Simisola in a sitting area. Engaging the little girl in conversation was a mammoth task, she found. It was only later, when Simisola met Peach, that she even smiled.

The little girl was fine, then. Tani had no concussion, there was a dog to play with, there was also a supercilious cat who *might* thaw out in the presence of an eight-year-old, and everything began to look up until Tani announced that he had to leave.

Simisola became tearful, saying to him, "No, no! Where are you *going*?"

To which he said, "Just over Sophie's, Squeak. I got to check on Mum. I got to try to get her away from there. An' I got to get our passports 's well, especially yours. Tha's real important now. But I'll be back tomorrow. I'll stay with Del's family tonight. It's closer to home. I can be in and out in the morning and back here faster tha' way."

Still, Simisola had not wanted him to go. Neither had anyone else. Simon had said to Tani that this was surely something for the police to handle. But when Tani was insistent, Deborah's father took Tani's mobile and entered a number into it and said sternly that Tani was to push the send button the moment *anything* serious happened. "Give us the address," Simon had added, and Cotter told the boy, "We'll ring the coppers then. An' you don't be shy about using it, eh? And *don't* start thinkin' you c'n handle things you aren't meant to handle. You un'erstand?" So Tani had left them with multiple promises, and Deborah only hoped he would keep them.

The bedroom door opened at last. Simisola stuck her head out. She saw Peach and she sucked in on her lower lip, revealing the little gap between her front teeth. Peach saw her and began to tail-wag. Deborah rose from the step she was sitting on.

She said to Simisola, "Peach was insistent. She would *not* remain below stairs. I went down and she started looking for you and . . . here we are. You'll have to pat her on the head or something very like because otherwise, she'll become intolerable. Would you be willing to pat her head a bit?"

"Oh, I would," Simisola replied, and knelt on the floor to do just that.

STRATFORD
GREATER LONDON

"The St. Jameses have her," Lynley said. "Apparently Deborah was at Orchid House when the girl was brought in. I saw her late yesterday afternoon. So *if* she was taken to Orchid House and from there to Deborah, we must assume the worst about what *both* of her parents' intentions are until we have more clarity. She's certainly not out of danger."

Nkata replied with, "Far as Missus Bankole's concerned, then, I got no idea where Simisola is. She's dead worried, though, guv. 'Bout both the kids."

"I expect she is, Winston. But as long as she's even entertaining the thought of FGM for the girl, that's how it has to be."

"C'n I tell her she's safe, at least? Away from her dad?"

Lynley glanced at him. There would always be some kind of line between them, a divide born of who they were and what comprised their individual histories as well as their shared history as colleagues. So he said, "I'll leave that to your judgement, Winston. Use the information in whatever way you decide is best for everyone."

Nkata nodded. "Ta, guv."

They were heading to speak with Mercy Hart. She lived in Rokeby Street in a nondescript terrace of red-brick-fronted houses with composite roofs manufactured to look like rows of tiles. In front of Mercy Hart's home, a low brick wall defined the property, behind which grew a box hedge in need of trimming. This squared off a patio area where a visible layer of grime and dust lay upon a child's plastic tricycle and a small red chair. These were the only objects on the patio save for a plethora of cigarette dog ends, some of which had been strewn about and some of which were stuffed in a tin, once the home of Heinz baked beans.

A small glassed-in porch had at some time been added to the front of the house, and it looked freshly painted white. They found that its door was unlocked, so they went in, bypassing four pairs of Wellington boots and a wrought-iron stand for holding umbrellas. Lynley knocked on the front door and then, when no one appeared, he rang the bell. This brought a young woman to open it. She was quite attractive, with dozens of braids—shot through with burnt orange— hanging to below her shoulder blades. She was wearing casually-ripped-at-the-knee jeans and a green tank top. She wore two pairs of silver earrings on each ear, a silver ring in one of her nostrils, and she was carrying a toddler on her hip.

Lynley said to her, "Mercy Hart?"

Her reply was, "No. I'm Keisha." She turned in the direction of a narrow stairway behind her and shouted, "Mum. You got company." When she turned back to them, she flashed a smile—directed at Nkata, as far as Lynley could tell—and then with lowered eyelids, said, "Sorry. I can't let you in. Mum's rules. Wait here," and she shut the door. Through it, they could hear children's voices and the clattering of toys on a lino floor.

Out in the street, a motorcycle roared suddenly as someone revved its engine, and a dog nearby began to bark. In the distance, a train clanked in the direction of central London. They weren't far from the railway tracks, although there had been no station that they saw on their search for Rokeby Street.

The door swung open again and they were face-to-face with a woman who didn't look much older than Keisha. Lynley said, "Mercy Hart?" and to her reply of "Tha's right," he concluded that she'd either found what Ponce de Leon had been searching for or she'd had her first child when she was barely out of childhood herself. He showed her his warrant card and introduced himself and DS Nkata. "Metropolitan Police," he added. "May we have a word?"

Mercy's hand reached for the doorknob, forming a barrier. "What about?"

"About the women's health centre that's just been closed in North London. In Kingsland High Street, to be more accurate."

"I don't know about a health centre in Kingsland High Street."

Lynley nodded. "As Mercy Hart, I can see how you wouldn't know it. As Easter Lange, however, it seems you know it quite well. It's called Women's Health of Hackney. We've spoken to your aunt, by the way. May we come in?"

Mercy's eyes narrowed but she stepped back from the door. She didn't move far into the heart of the house, however. Instead, she dug a packet of cigarettes from her trousers, went up four of the stairs, and planted herself there, beneath one of what appeared to be a dozen nicely framed family photographs that climbed the wall. She left Lynley and Nkata standing at the foot of the stairs. She lit up from a plastic lighter, inhaled, and waited.

"A woman calling herself Easter Lange worked at the women's health clinic I've mentioned," Lynley said. "She was also arrested there and taken in for questioning. She was in the company of another woman at the time, Monifa Bankole, and I expect if we show that woman a picture of you, she's going to identify you as Easter Lange."

Mercy took this in without expression. She said, after a moment for consideration, "I used her name. That's it. I didn't take a thing else off her."

Nkata looked up from his notebook and said, "Meaning you di'n't latch on to Easter Lange's identity otherwise?"

"Just her name. So what's she told you? I robbed her bank account? Started up a credit card in her name?" Mercy gave a short laugh. "Not very likely, that."

"Whyn't you use your own name at the clinic, then?"

"I never liked it, my name. So I didn't feel like using it. Hers is nicer. I always thought so."

With very little trouble, they'd manoeuvred her into an admission about the clinic. Lynley gave thought to what else she could be manoeuvred into admitting should they ask their questions carefully enough. He said, "Isn't it more likely that you used her name to keep 'Mercy Hart' safe from the authorities should you be closed down?"

"I don't need to be afraid of the authorities."

"Ah." Lynley altered his position to lean against the wall as Nkata did the same against the wall opposite. Lynley said, "You certainly set up the clinic to look suspicious. You had the medical folders of patients who don't exist. You had an appointment diary with the names of actual mothers and daughters who had an exceptionally good reason not to speak to the police. But, as a rule, it's difficult to"—Lynley sought and finally chose—"batten down every hatch. In this case—in the case of the clinic in Kingsland High Street—one of the hatches was left loose. We have the appointment diary."

She said nothing. She managed to look relatively unconcerned. Clearly, she was waiting for more information.

"Monifa Bankole," Nkata told her. "She paid a deposit to have her daughter cut at your clinic, only her husband sent her back for the money, which was why she was there when you got arrested by the locals."

"On this matter, I have no comment," Mercy said. "I've done nothing wrong, have I. Nothing wrong to anyone, including this . . . this Monifa Bankole."

"But someone's done serious harm to you," Lynley said. "She's called Teo Bontempi and she's responsible for the raid on your clinic and any unpleasantness that followed."

"Teo who? I don't know any Teo."

The ash was growing on her cigarette. Lynley wondered what she would do when it wanted knocking off. He said, "She called herself Adaku Obiaka. She went to the clinic to make an arrangement with you. But she was a police detective and she had no real arrangement to make."

Mercy was motionless. Lynley waited. Nkata altered his position, leaning his shoulder against the wall. He still held his pad and mechanical pencil. He looked interested in what she had to say. Moments ticked by during which children's voices came to them from the garden, one of them calling out, "I wan' to be Mummy! Keisha, tell her *I'm* the mummy! She's too little anyway!"

Lynley said, "Teo Bontempi robbed you of your livelihood, didn't she? You may have walked out of the Stoke Newington police station, but now you were on their radar. More important, you were on the radar of the team Teo Bontempi worked on, investigating and making arrests of parents and practitioners of FGM. Did you see her in the street on that day the clinic was raided, Mrs. Hart? Did you work it out that she had to be the one who turned you in?"

"I make no comment," she told him. She rose at that, coming down the stairs. She opened the front door and then the porch door. She said, "You c'n go," and as if to demonstrate the direction she wished them to take, she threw her cigarette towards the street.

Lynley stepped outside. Nkata followed. But just as she was about to shut both of the doors upon them, Lynley said, "As a point of curiosity, where did you do your medical training, Mrs. Hart?"

"I make no comment," was her reply. She began to close the first of the doors, but Lynley put his hand upon it.

"Are you certain you wish to make no comment?" Lynley asked her. And when she made no reply, he said, "That's unfortunate. Winston, are you happy to do the honours?"

Nkata nodded. "You're being arrested, Missus Hart," and he went on to recite the official caution.

"You can't arrest me if I didn't do anything," Mercy cried. "Nothing, nothing!"

"Performing FGM is hardly nothing," Lynley told her.

"I didn't! I never!"

"And performing any kind of medical procedure without a licence, a degree, or anything else is also hardly nothing."

"I never!"

Nkata said, "Far 's I know, murderin a cop doesn' work as nothing, either. An' jus' now, Missus Hart? You're looking good for that as well."

***

HAMPSTEAD HEATH
NORTH LONDON

Barbara Havers discovered it wasn't going to be quite as easy as she'd anticipated. While Nkata had managed to talk to Rosie Bontempi outside her place of employment—Selfridges in Oxford Street—Barbara was not going to have the same luck. When she rang her, Rosie explained it was her day off work, so if the detective sergeant *did* want to meet up with her for conversation, it was going to have to happen in Hampstead. She was at this very moment walking across Hampstead Heath, and she'd be quite happy to see DS Havers at the Ladies' Pond, where she intended to have a mid-morning swim. The detective sergeant could join her if she wished. It was already quite a warm day, so doubtless she'd find the water blissfully refreshing.

Putting herself into a swimming costume for a round of blissful refreshment was so far down on Barbara's bucket list that she knew she'd never get to it in her current lifetime, so she told Rosie that while she'd meet her at the Ladies' Pond, they'd have to have their conversation upon dry land. To Rosie's "How sad," Barbara informed her that water was not conducive to note-taking. Nonetheless, a plan was laid.

She had no intention of hiking across Hampstead Heath in search of the swimming ponds. What she knew of them—very little—told her they were on the Highgate side of the heath, so she checked the location and saw that parking in the area where Fitzroy Park met up with the far north point of Millfield Lane would put her quite close to a path that should take her to the Ladies' Pond.

Traffic to Highgate wasn't too much of a nightmare, although parking where she'd intended to park required the use of her police placard and the fervent hope that a passing vehicle didn't crush the side of the Mini, although, when she thought about it, crushing the Mini's side might make an improvement to its overall appearance.

It wasn't a time of day during which she'd expected to encounter many people on the heath, but there was more happening than she had expected. Family groups were laying out picnics south of the path, where an impromptu football match was also going on. A number of sun worshippers sat upon deck chairs or had spread themselves supine or prostrate on towels upon the dead lawn. Two young men engaged in throwing a Frisbee (a hugely pointless activity, as far as Barbara was concerned), and a number of pensioners wandered about with sun hats fixed to their heads. There was even a bird-watcher, Barbara saw, although his suspicious proximity to the Ladies' Pond made doubtful his urge to seek out this or that golden-throated warbler.

The pond was tucked among desperate-looking shrubbery, sun-browned lawns, and thirsty trees nanoseconds away from dropping their leaves. When Barbara found it, she also found that the water was teeming with females. More women were relaxing in lawn chairs. Adolescent girls wearing three triangles of material strategically placed were diving into the water from a dock, while others darted in and out of a bathhouse, laughing and chatting to one another.

In some circumstances, finding Rosie Bontempi in this mass of female humanity wouldn't have been an easy task. But since the swimming pond was on the edge of Highgate and since Highgate was a posh area (although, admittedly, not as posh as Hampstead), most of the women present were, unsurprisingly, white. Thus, it didn't take long for her to catch sight of Rosie, who had apparently eschewed swimming in favour of floating round on an inflatable chair. Rosie saw her at the same moment and gave a languorous wave. She hopped off the chair with a splash and swam to the edge of the pond, towing the chair behind her. Out she came like Neptune's second cousin, displaying a body that could only be achieved through genetics, exercise, and a careful diet. She was wearing a yellow bikini with dots of blue. Barbara was very nearly embarrassed that she herself had donned a yellow T-shirt with blue letters proclaiming *Go ahead. Underestimate me. That'll be fun.* She reckoned she'd get over the embarrassment quick enough, although both of them in yellow did rather look as if they'd planned the encounter.

Rosie was gracious enough not to mention the yellow and blue. She said, "Isn't this glorious? Really, you should have planned a swim."

"I should have done lots of things I've managed to avoid," Barbara told her. "Where can we go to talk?"

Rosie gave her a how–would–I–know look, but she glanced round the pond and pointed to the shade of a golden rain tree, with several heroic, albeit now dead, flowers still clinging to it. As they walked towards it, Rosie handed the floating chair over to Barbara and grabbed a towel and a string bag she'd left on the lawn. She said, "I do hope this'll be brief, Sergeant. Mum and I have a luncheon date. I must get ready for that, and anyway, I don't know what else I can tell you."

Loads, Barbara thought. But she shifted her grip on the floating chair and said airily, "This'll be as brief as an English summer," although, given the weather for the past two months, the interview could easily go on forever.

They reached the tree. Barbara plopped the chair onto the shady ground. Rosie plopped onto the chair. But she sat on its edge, leaving room for Barbara, saying, "No need to be less than comfortable."

Barbara took out her notebook and pencil. She too sat on the edge of the chair. But she saw at once that this position gave Rosie the advantage since it kept her face from Barbara's view. Because of this, she clambered back to her feet in a rolling motion that came very near to throwing her onto the sun–crisped lawn.

She said, "I've been going over a few details from our previous natter about the argument you had with Teo two days before she was coshed."

"I don't see why you need to do that. I've told you the truth from the start. What can I possibly add?" She used the towel on one of her legs, raising it, toes pointed heavenward. She went on to the other leg and did the same.

"You could start with explaining why you've changed your story."

"Have I? Really? I don't think I have."

"First, you claimed the argument between you had to do with Teo not showing her face very often in New End Square post your dad's stroke. Then you changed it to an argument due to the fact that you're pregnant by Ross and you gave her the happy news. You claimed that the wedge issue between Ross and Teo was that he wanted children and she wasn't exactly over the moon with the idea, but apparently that's not genuine gold either. So which of the tales is true?"

Rosie draped the towel like a shawl round her shoulders. Barbara noted it was the same pattern as her bikini, with the colours reversed. Rosie used one end of it to dry her ostensibly wet cheeks and forehead after her rigorous swim. She said, "Everything I told you was true, Sergeant. If I can't remember exactly *when* I had which argument with Teo, that means nothing. Sisters argue. Do you have a sister? No? Well, if you had one, you'd know what I mean."

Barbara sought clarity. "Are you telling me that one of your lies is the actual truth or that all of them are?"

"I went to tell her I'm pregnant," Rosie said. "I told her Ross is the father. *Obviously* she didn't take it very well."

"Is that what you were arguing about?" And when Rosie shrugged her acquiescence, Barbara went on with, "What about the thirty-first?"

"What *about* the thirty-first?"

"Teo texted Ross about coming to the flat. I'm thinking she had news for him. I'm also thinking you knew exactly what this news was."

"She wasn't pregnant, if that's what you mean. She and Ross . . . It was completely over between them. He was . . . Please understand, Sergeant. Ross and I had become a couple. We still *are* a couple."

"Got it," Barbara said. "A couple. Uppercase, italics, bold typeface, whatever. But I'm reckoning the ship of this couplehood of yours might've been heading for a reef."

"Why? They were finished with each other. Ross wanted out of the marriage, and so did Teo. He said as much. She said as much."

"Well. Right. Indeed they do and they did and whatever. But the problem with that is that people tend to hear what they want to hear. DS Nkata tells me you never knew your sister was an FGM victim."

Rosie got to her feet. She pulled the plug to deflate her chair. She said, "No one ever told me. She never said a thing about it. Neither did he."

"Would that've made things different?"

"Different for who?"

"Different for you," Barbara said. "For your plan to go after your sister's husband."

Rosie turned to look at Barbara squarely. She said in a voice that seemed under cool control, "I didn't 'go after' anyone. I was someone for Ross to talk to. I was his friend. He's been part of our family for years and I was his . . . I was important to him. What happened between us had nothing to do with Teo being cut. How could it have done when I didn't know? No one told me, ever."

"Like I said," Barbara pointed out, "there're times when people hear only what they want to hear. Did Teo tell you she'd been examined for surgery? Was that part of the argument?"

"I was to drive her to have *a* surgery. That's all I knew. She asked me. I agreed. I wanted to know what sort it was. It worried me that something was wrong, like . . . like cancer or something. But she wouldn't say. I still don't know."

"Reconstruction," Barbara told her. "She was having herself

repaired, putting her female parts back into order as much as possible. Ross Carver—and I assume you know this since you and he are such a couple, eh?—had spent years asking her to see someone who might help her. Fix her. Repair her. Whatever. He wanted her to see a plastic surgeon. She wasn't on board with that idea at first, but eventually she changed her mind. She got herself evaluated and it was all systems go to put her feminine parts right."

Rosie grabbed the chair up and squeezed it. The *whoosh* of air being released sounded like the wheezing of an asthmatic. "How could I have known any of that?" she demanded. "I'd never been told she'd been cut in the first place."

"So when she asked you to be the driver she needed—"

"I asked her why. I sent her a message. She didn't answer. What else could I do? Beat the information out of her?"

Barbara let that one hang there to give the young woman time to hear what she herself had said. Lips pressed together, Rosie began to fold the inflatable chair, reducing its size by half and then a quarter. When still she said nothing more, Barbara spoke.

"Wouldn't a normal sister press on and ask questions about this whole surgery thing?"

Rosie wrapped the towel round her waist. She said, "Teo didn't tell me things, Sergeant. She never told me things. Don't ask me why because I don't know other than to say we weren't close the way some sisters are. We were too different and she was seven years older. Now, if there's nothing else . . . ? My mum's expecting me."

"Right. Your mum-and-daughter luncheon. Got it."

"Good," Rosie said, and she began to head up the slope that would put her on the route back to New End Square.

Barbara attended her, like an unwanted bridesmaid crashing a wedding. She said, "I see how that all would have worked. Unless, of course, Teo did tell you. Unless, of course, *that* was what the overheard argument was about because, let's face it, if she went for the surgery, there was every chance that she and Ross would be together again. Which, of course, makes the future darker for you and your couplehood."

Rosie stopped walking and swung to face her. "Stop saying that. Our 'couplehood.' We were a couple. We *are* a couple. We're lovers and we're having a baby together. D'you really think Ross would've done it with me if he didn't want to be with me? He knew the risks. I knew the risks. We wanted this."

"Right. Got it. Would that be why you had him call you Teo while you and he were rolling round his bed? Would that be why you told him you were taking precautions?"

"Stop it! You don't know how things were. You don't know how things are. You're just some pongy piece of week-old fish. You couldn't pull a man if you and he were the only survivors of a nuclear holocaust. You're jealous, is what you are. We're finished here. You can tag along to New End Square if you fancy that, but I'm not saying another word."

Barbara reckoned Rosie would hold to that promise, so she let her storm off in the direction of Hampstead. She herself turned back towards Highgate and her car. She was on the path leading out of the Heath when her mobile rang. She pulled it out of her bag and saw that the caller was Ross Carver.

She answered it with, "I've just had words with your lady love. Is it me or does Rosie play fast and loose with the truth when the mood strikes her? I've got to ask that because Rosie's stories have turned into something of a moving target."

His response was, "She said sod all to me about blessing anything."

"And yet Teo *did* ask you to toddle on over to the flat for a chinwag, right?"

"Right. That's unchanged. That's what happened. She texted me, she asked to see me, I went there. I'm there now, by the way. That's why I'm ringing. Your forensic people have returned the sculptures."

"Generally, they're good about that kind of thing. They may need them again at some point, so best leave them be till we get everything sorted."

"It's too late for that," he told her. "I've already unpacked them. They're back in place now. But one of them is missing."

MAYVILLE ESTATE
DALSTON
NORTH-EAST LONDON

Sophie had wanted to come with him, but Tani wasn't about to let her. There was no way of knowing what he'd find when he arrived at his family's flat. He *hoped* it would be his mum with her suitcase packed, but if she was still reluctant to make a move, he wanted her to know that Simi was safe, that Abeo would never be able to find her, and that she did not need to remain there for the sake of either of her children. As for Abeo, Tani reckoned his father wouldn't be at the flat, having long since returned to Lark.

He was about to open the flat's door when Mrs. Delfino called out to him quietly from several floors above, her *ragazzo, ragazzo* telling Tani who was speaking before he stepped back and saw her gesturing at him. It was an unmistakable *come here* movement of her right arm that was impossible to ignore. He went to the lift and rode it up. When its door opened, there she was.

He comes for his mama, yes? she said, and when he nodded she informed him, "She leaves Mayville Estate with a Black man very tall." Mrs. Delfino was returning from Ridley Road Market when she'd seen them, she told Tani. They weren't coming from the Bankoles' flat, however. Mrs. Delfino thought they were coming from one of the other buildings on the estate.

She seem very bad, Mrs. Delfino told him, and then after a moment, she corrected herself with, "She look very bad, yes? She look like someone hitted her and the Black man help her to walk. She lean on him, on his *braccio*"—here she pointed to her arm—"and he has a car and he carries her away."

"What'd he look like, this bloke?" Tani asked her.

She repeated, "Very tall. Black. He wears a suit. And his face . . . I remember . . . his face is bad with this . . . this mark down one side. Someone with a knife . . ."

Tani needed no further details. It was the copper who'd been there already. He thanked Mrs. Delfino and she patted his cheek, telling him, "You are a good boy, love your mama. All is good when you love your mama."

Tani wanted to believe that, but he had reached a point from which he reckoned love wasn't going to make anything good. He rang for the lift and went down to the family's flat. He tried the door. It was unlocked. He swung it open and stared at what lay before him.

A rampage had occurred after his departure. It had worked destruction upon the kitchen and the lounge. From where he stood it seemed that every piece of crockery and every drinking glass was broken. The cooker was dented. The cast-iron pan that had done the denting was on the floor. Pots and pans lay helter-skelter, and blanketing some of them were pages of his mother's cookbooks.

In the lounge, the television's screen was shattered and a small table was discarded in front of it. Two lamps had been destroyed and three head wraps were pulled to pieces. In the midst of them, though, Tani saw his mother's mobile. He picked it up and shoved it into his pocket.

He reckoned he knew where the passports were because his father kept a locked fireproof box beneath the bed he and Monifa slept in. Along with the locked box were several plastic containers with Monifa's cool-weather clothes. Tani decided he would take these as well as the passports, so that when he finally saw his mother, he'd be able to encourage her not to return to Mayville Estate.

When he opened the door to his parents' bedroom, what he saw forced him to set aside his plans. Abeo was on the bed. He was fully clothed, asleep, and snoring.

At the sight of his father, Tani's first inclination was to leave at once. But no, he decided. He was done harbouring fear of this man. So he approached the bed, knelt at its side, and found the box where it had always been kept, its key in the single lock.

With his gaze fixed on his father's face, Tani pulled the box slowly from beneath the bed. He turned the key and began sorting through the box's contents as quickly and silently as he could. Inside, he found birth certificates, some paperwork relating to Into Africa and the butcher shop, receipts for rental payments made for Lark's flat in Pembury Estate and this flat in Mayville Estate, and old photographs. He found no passports, and all the family money was gone.

Instantly, Tani felt a burning leap of fire within him. He got to his feet. He stared down at his sleeping father. He realised then that he'd always hated Abeo Bankole. He simply had not allowed himself to feel the strength of it.

Tani took up the fireproof box, stood over his father, and emptied its contents on him. Abeo awakened with a start. He clocked Tani at once, but he didn't seem concerned about his presence, even when Tani snarled, "What've you done with them, you fucking bastard?"

Abeo smiled slowly. "I have learned she is called Sophie Franklin. I am told she's an English whore."

"*Where* are the passports?"

"Stoke Newington, I've been told. Once I learned her name, this was not difficult, Tani, especially when someone has not bothered to take care."

"What d'you think you can do to her? Or to her family? Her mum, her dad, her sister, her brothers? D'you really think any of that lot'll stand round with their mouths hanging open when you try to bully them? Not bloody likely, Pa."

Abeo brushed the various documents and photos from his body. He said, "You should have been left in Nigeria. When I saw you, I knew you were not my son."

"Wishing that doesn't make it true," Tani said. "If it did, I would've been out of here first time you put a hand on me. I would've got myself a ticket to Nigeria and searched him out, whoever my 'real' dad's supposed to be in this fucking fantasy you've got in your head about Mum doing it with . . . Who? Her brothers? The postman? Her own dad? You're pathetic, you are. You're so sodding transparent I feel sorry for you."

Abeo fixed his gaze on Tani. Tani saw one of his fists slowly clench.

He went on, heedless of everything other than what he needed to say. "You could've had a decent family, Pa, but you didn't want that, did you. You didn't want a wife. You didn't want children. You wanted a servant and two slaves to do whatever you said. Well, you've lost us all, you have. And you're never going to find Simi, so give it up."

"Evering Road," Abeo said. "You do nothing, Tani, that I do not know."

He rose, but Tani pushed him back onto the bed. "I want those fucking passports! You're not taking anyone anywhere. I'm not going with you to Nigeria and Simi sure as hell isn't going with you. Fact is, you're not ever seeing Simi again. And you're not seeing Mum because she's *gone*. She left th'estate with that Black detective. An' who can blame her, eh? He's ten times the man you'll ever be and way I hear it, he's lookin for a woman. An' Mum? Well, you can be sure she's lookin for a real man."

Abeo surged up at that. He drew back his fist.

Tani at last had what he'd so long wanted. He punched his father fully in the face. He'd never enjoyed the pain of his knuckles striking someone's bone as he did when he heard the crack of his father's nose. The force of the blow whirled Abeo round. Tani grabbed him then, his arm locked round Abeo's throat. He began to drag him towards the bedroom door and out of the room. But his father was strong. He wasn't going anywhere willingly. He kicked and thrashed. He freed himself. He charged at Tani and knocked him onto the bed. But before he could throw himself on top of his son's body, Tani rolled away so that Abeo's velocity would throw him onto the bed as well, on his stomach this time.

Tani attacked. He straddled his father. He forced his head into the bedding and the mattress beneath it. He held him there. He shouted, "How does it feel? How's the power now? How's the control? You're shit, you are. You're what gets stuck on the soles of shoes. And now . . . now . . ." It felt so very good. It felt like being reborn as who he was meant to be from the first: the new flesh of him, the new muscle of him. Such exultation as the body of his father began to go slack, so slack, so justifiably slack . . .

Tani felt himself being lifted away. He swung round to strike whoever would stop him from doing to this man what he so deserved.

For a moment, he was clueless as he stared at the two women who'd pulled him from his father. Who the *bloody* hell . . . ? But then he recognised them from Orchid House. The one was Zawadi who directed the place. The other was the filmmaker whose name he could not recall.

THORNTON HEATH
GREATER LONDON

"Flats," he said. "They're to run the gamut, in accordance with the council's wishes. So it will be council flats on the ground floor and floors one, two, and three, with luxury on the upper floors. All the mod cons in each flat no matter the floor it's on, and on the premises an indoor pool, a gym, laundries on every floor, parking beneath the building, bicycle lock-ups, extensive garden behind the building, a children's play area, a pitch for games, space allowed for a day care centre should that be desired by residents."

"In other words, gentrification," Barbara said.

"I don't think of it that way," Ross Carver told her.

"Looks to me like a rose by any other name, Mr. Carver. Someone makes a pile of it off buyers and, presto, long-time residents of the area are out on their collective ear."

"I wouldn't have signed on should that have been the desired outcome."

"Right-o. But you'll be long gone before the 'desired outcome' shows its face. Your part is only the structure, eh? Once it's up, you're finished with the project."

"When all is said and done, we'll meet here—you and I—and see which one of us is correct."

They were in the sales office where Ross Carver had told Barbara he would meet her. He couldn't take time away from the job. If she wouldn't mind coming to Thornton Heath . . . ? Barbara hadn't been chuffed by the idea—Thornton Heath was nearly the distance to Croydon—but when she arrived, she espied a Domino's in the High Street. A smallish takeaway (tomato, cheese, mushrooms, and black olives, thank you) was something she could knock back in a tic. Which she did, accompanying it with a Fanta pineapple, enjoying her luncheon as she watched the action in and out of Zenith Halal Butchers.

Now, after a pleasurable smoke as she'd looked for Ross Carver's workplace, she was gazing at an impressive model of the building that would house Thornton Luxury Flats. Nearby on the walls the various floor plans, styles, and sizes of these flats were displayed, while in another room were posted the differing types of lino, carpet, and tiles being offered. All of it was very impressive, and the project was replacing no housing at all but rather an abandoned factory that had been a long-time eyesore in the neighbourhood.

Before committing herself to the journey, Barbara had quizzed Ross Carver about the missing sculpture. As far as she knew, there had been a good number of sculptures taken by the scenes-of-crime officers from Teo Bontempi's flat, so how the devil had he known one was missing when he unpacked them?

The answer to that had been simple: He knew it was missing because he'd given it to Teo.

"Couldn't she have tossed it? Given it to Oxfam or to a consignment shop?"

"She didn't do that and she wouldn't do that," was how he had replied.

Right, Barbara had thought as they spoke. But, she pointed out to him, there were times when a relationship was done for and the aggrieved party—

"She wasn't the aggrieved party," he protested. "If anyone was, it would've been me. I've told you all this. She wanted to separate. I went along with it because what else was I supposed to do? Take her prisoner?"

Stranger things had happened, Barbara thought. She said, "There are times, though, when people decide that a thorough housecleaning of the heart is in order. Everything connected with the relationship is given the ceremonial heave-ho, preparatory to setting it on the barbecue and firing the thing up."

"That didn't happen."

Barbara was curious about his certainty. She said, "How can you know that?"

"Because I gave her three sculptures and only one of them has gone missing. The other two are still with the rest."

"Ah. Well, that colours things a bit differently, that. You're seeing it as the cosh, are you? Teo gets clubbed in the heat of the moment? No attack was planned."

"I don't know how else to see it," he replied. "Do you?"

Barbara scratched her head, considering this. "If someone knew about those sculptures . . . ?"

"Like who?" he asked. "Who could possibly have known they were in the flat?"

Barbara gave him a look but said nothing. He could work out the answer to that on his own. It wouldn't involve any heavy mental lifting. She said, "Or it could be the entire evening was planned down to the last detail, and the sculpture was taken to throw us off the scent, not having been used at all. But again, that would only have been if the killer knew about the sculptures in the first place. Where'd you get it, anyway?"

"There's a gallery in Peckham. They do African art. The piece that's missing from Teo's collection is called *Standing Warrior*. I can't remember the artist's name just now, but all three of the pieces I gave Teo have something like a signature on them."

"Are all three from this Peckham gallery?" And when he nodded, "I'll need the name of the place."

"Padma," he said.

"Got it," she said. "By the way, when I spoke to Rosie this morning, among other delights, she also told me that Teo 'gave her blessing' to the two of you. According to her way of telling of it, Teo was dead chuffed to know that you put our Rosie up the duff. Couldn't wait to be called Auntie by your little bundle of whatever."

"Then that's why she wanted to see me," Carver said, more to himself than to her.

"Teo? Possibly. But there's something else, and Rosie may have known about it."

"You can't be thinking that Rosie—"

"Let's keep the horse, the cart, and the market where they belong. Teo saw a plastic surgeon. That was what *evaluation* in her appointment diary meant. She had an appointment to be checked over in the cause of repairing the damage done to her. She kept that appointment. She was told the results as well. She needed a driver to and from if she was going to have the procedure, so she asked Rosie. But then, well, you know the rest."

He was shaking his head as he took in the information. "Teo didn't tell me," he said. "Why didn't she tell me?"

"Could be that was what she wanted to speak with you about and she wanted to give you the news when you were face-to-face. Could be that was why she asked you to come to the flat. 'Course there's also a bloody high probability that she only wanted to talk to you about Rosie and to give her blessing to this whatever-it-is between you two. Which do you reckon?"

He looked down at his shoes. Barbara could hear him swallow. He said, "I don't know. I wish to God I did. I wish she'd said something, given me a clue, anything. Are you sure she meant to have the surgery?"

"The surgeon herself gave me the word on that. Evidently, it took her—Teo—a little time to decide because the repair didn't mean things would automatically change much for her. Sexually, I mean. As far as her enjoyment went, I mean. She would've needed nerve endings intact for that, and there was no way to tell if there were any unless and until scar tissue was removed. But she was willing to risk it."

"Risk what?" he asked, raising his head to look at her.

"Risk being disappointed."

Three people entered the sales office then, two nicely dressed women and an equally nicely dressed man, who looked at Barbara and Ross Carver curiously. One of the women said, "I'll be just a moment to help you two," which indicated to Barbara that she thought they were a couple eager to buy a flat. This made her lips twitch. What it apparently made Ross Carver do was to say to her, "We ought to . . . ?" and indicate the door.

When they were outside again, he said, "I've made a bloody mess of everything: my life, her life, and now this with Rosie. I should never have . . . And here we are."

Barbara excavated this and came up with Ross, Rosie, and the pregnancy. The news of it must have devastated Teo. She knew that she was meant to say to Teo's estranged husband, "Don't blame yourself. You couldn't possibly have known how things would play out," but the truth as she saw it was that he could have known and he should have known. She said, "Rosie's misinformed my colleague about Teo's adoption by the Bontempis. She's given more than one reason why she and Teo were arguing. She plays fast and loose with the truth when it suits her. That being the case, I'm not on board with the idea that Teo *didn't* tell her what the surgery was for, once she asked her to take her to and from this clinic on the Isle of Dogs where she was meant to have it. But that's what Rosie wants me to believe. What do you think?"

He pressed his fingers to his temples as if this would help him straighten out his thoughts. He said, "I just don't . . . *Why* did she decide to have it now? Why wouldn't she have it earlier? I'd told her surgery existed. I kept asking her to have someone examine her, at least. To talk to a surgeon, if nothing else. To try anything and everything because together we *could* find someone . . ."

"Seems she wasn't ready then," Barbara told him. "Seems by the time she *was* ready, circumstances made it seem too late."

"Unless it wasn't," he said. "Unless she decided it wasn't too late and it was worth trying."

"Well, yes. Right. But you see that puts Rosie straight into it, don't you? She's up the spout, she has expectations, and Teo's about to bollix up everything. She knows—Rosie does—that you've done right by Colton even if you didn't want to marry his mum. She knows you love and haven't got over Teo. And Teo's about to walk back into your life in the way you've always wanted her. Which, let's face it and all things considered, makes the situation look bleak for our Rosie."

He looked skyward, through the smog-stained air. He closed his eyes. He seemed to be trying to make a decision about something, and he finally did just that. He said, "There's something else."

"Something else Rosie knows about you?"

"Something I haven't told you."

"When?"

"When we talked about the night I found Teo. She . . . she said something to me when I got her to her feet. She said, 'She hit me, Ross.'"

To which Barbara sighed and said, "Bloody goddamn hell."

CHELSEA
SOUTH-WEST LONDON

Deborah was working again on choosing portraits, and she had Simi with her as her "assistant." They were on the fifth-floor workroom of the house, Simi perched on one of the room's tall stools, with Deborah next to her but on her feet. They were going through a series of portraits of a thirteen-year-old called Jubilee. Her picture was going to do double duty: as part of the booklet Deborah was assembling for the Department for Education and as one of the images in the larger photo book that she hoped would be her next project. Simon was below, holed up in his study with a colleague from a new independent forensics lab hoping for a contract with the Met. Her father was in a room off the kitchen where he was employing his recently acquired toy—an impressive rotary steam iron—upon freshly laundered sheets, pillow-cases, table napkins, and a tablecloth. This was his new and favourite occupation. He would have ironed the carpets if given his way.

Simisola put her index finger on the edge of one of the portraits and said, "This one. She's pretty, she is."

"I think you've found the best one," Deborah agreed. "She's back with her parents now, and I expect they'll like a copy of this." She glanced at Simi and saw her fingering her spiky hair and looking thoughtful. "She's thirteen years old, is Jubilee, just a bit older than you are, Simi. And the way she's back with her parents? That's what *you'll* be doing when everything's taken care of: going back to your parents. You do know that, don't you? You've nothing to fear on that score."

Simi gazed at her with her wide dark eyes. She said, "Will Mummy come for me?"

"That's something I'm not sure of. I think we must wait for news. No one wants you going anywhere you won't be safe."

A sudden commotion reached them from down below. Peach barking, footsteps in the entry, a door closing, another opening and closing, voices, and more barking from Peach. Deborah didn't like the sound of this, so she helped Simi from her stool and took her into the dark-room. There was a large cupboard where she'd once stored chemicals, empty now and the perfect size for an eight-year-old girl. Deborah told Simi to scoot inside and make no sound. "It's probably nothing," she murmured to the girl. "But we don't want to take chances."

She was on the third-floor landing when she recognised Narissa Cameron's voice. She hurried down the stairs as Simon came out of his study, along with his colleague. Deborah's father had apparently been the one to answer the door. The entry was, as a result, a real mash-up of humanity, because in addition to Narissa, both Zawadi and Tani were there. Who *wasn't* there was the mother he'd gone to his family's home to fetch.

She said, "What's happened? Tani, has something happened to your mum?"

Zawadi said to her, "You *allowed* him to go?" She sounded incredulous.

"Zawadi, she can't tie him to a chair," Narissa countered.

Tani answered Deborah. "She was gone. I got told by a neighbour she left with a copper. It's the same one came to talk to her af'er she got arrested. So now she's arrested *again* and I don't know where she got taken and I got to find her."

"Let us deal with that." It was Simon speaking. "If she's with a policeman, we can sort that quickly enough."

Deborah added, "Simon knows all sorts of police, Tani. He'll start ringing them. We'll find her, and I expect it won't take very long. You need to trust us."

Zawadi rolled her eyes at this but said nothing.

"How do you come to have Tani with you?" she asked both Zawadi and Narissa.

Simon left them then and returned to his study. Deborah heard him say, ". . . some associates of Deborah's," before Narissa claimed her attention, explaining she and Zawadi had gone to north London to make the usual, formal call upon the parents of a girl—in this case Simisola—who was being sheltered by Orchid House. "I went with her because there was no available social worker and no way did I intend to let her go alone, not after what we saw yesterday when Tani showed up at Orchid House with—"

"Wait!" Deborah realised all of a sudden that Simisola was still hiding in the darkroom. "Simi will want to know Tani is well." She ran up the stairs to fetch her.

In very short order, the siblings were reunited, with Simisola dashing down the stairs to fling herself at her brother. She cried, "Did he hurt you more, Tani? Did Papa hurt you?"

Zawadi said in an altered tone, "Opposite's more like it, girl."

Narissa added, speaking to Deborah, "We pulled him off the father. Please don't let him go back there."

"Did he manage to get the passports?" she asked. Then to Tani, "Did you find the passports?"

He shook his head.

Simisola cried, "What about Mummy? Tani, where's Mummy?" and when he said that he didn't know, she began to cry. She buried her face into his stomach.

"I'll find her, Squeak," Tani told her, his hands on the back of her head.

"You," Zawadi said to him, "are to stay well away from both of your parents. After today"—she wore an expression that Deborah couldn't interpret until she went on—"what's next is a protection order. I see that. And, believe me, that doesn't make me happy. But till it's done, you stay right here in this house, Tani. Simisola as well."

"No way is Pa obeying some protection order," Tani said with considerable scorn. "I thought he would. I got talked into it by Sophie. But he won't obey it."

"You listen," Zawadi told him, "because this order that we're going to file, it'll be delivered by a cop and that person—I'm meaning the cop—won't leave the premises without passports. D'you understand me? Your dad's not taking Simisola out of the country and he's not hurting her inside the country. We'll see to that. Now you promise me—you give me your word right here—that you won't go back there. Full stop."

"Wha' about Sophie?" he asked. "He knows her name. He knows where she lives. I don't know how but he knows. And he'll turn up at her house, he will. *Then* what?"

"First, you're going to give her a bell and tell her what's happened. Your dad shows up, she'll ring the police straightaway if she has any sense and she seemed to have sense when I met her."

"An' what about my mum?" he asked.

"We're going to find her," Deborah promised. She sent a prayer heavenward that they could.

***

THE NARROW WAY
HACKNEY
NORTH-EAST LONDON

Mark decided to take a sick day. He knew that the team could function perfectly well on their own. All he had on was a meeting with them in the late afternoon, so he rang DS Hopwood, gave her the word, and told her he'd be back the following morning. Anything you need? was her only question.

Rest is the key, he told her. It was just a summer cold and sore throat.

Lots of fluids, she informed him.

Exactly what he had in mind, he said.

What he also had in mind was Pete: the contradiction that seemed to exist between what she was doing and what she said she was doing. He had to sort it out. Otherwise, the torn-up feeling was only going to become less endurable every day.

He began in their bedroom, and it didn't take long. Pete had never been one for personal enhancements She used no makeup other than lipstick. She wore no jewellery other than her wedding ring and a pair of cultured pearl earrings. She dressed identically every day: white on top and blue denim on the bottom. But as there was always a chance that something more was going on than he was privy to, he quietly went through her drawers, the pockets of jeans and jackets hanging among her clothes, and the medicine cabinet. He advanced to the airing cupboard and from there to the kitchen. But nothing was missing and nothing had been added to their meagre possessions.

She was reading to Lilybet as he did this, children's verses by the sound of it. Robertson was running the hoover. No one was attending to his own activities. As he had given Pete the excuse of a cold, he was free from his duties to Lilybet as well. She couldn't afford to be exposed to anything that might complicate her already compromised condition. So when he called to her, "I'm stepping out, Pete. Need anything from the chemist?" she said that nothing at all was required but to please make certain he stocked up on whatever he needed for that sore throat.

He assured her that he would and set out. Not for the chemist, but for The Narrow Way. There, he went to the pawnshop at the top of the pedestrian street. He looked at the window display before going inside. It comprised, as usual, largely rings, necklaces, brooches, and watches. And of course, none of it had once belonged to Pete because Pete had never owned any in the first place.

One piece, though, caught his eye. It was an intricate, elongated, tear-shaped pendant strung upon a silver chain, something quite easily mistaken for costume jewellery. It shone splendidly beneath the special lighting in the shop window—all jewellery did—and while it might have been a marcasite piece complemented by a large teardrop blue stone and two others fashioned as sashes, Mark knew this was not the case. It was Art Deco, it was white gold, and the stones were diamonds and sapphires. Its value was beyond several thousand pounds. And it belonged to his mother.

He entered and walked directly to the counter, calling out for Stuart. He had to call out two more times when Paulie's brother-in-law did not quickly appear. Finally, he emerged from the back of the shop, a mug of tea in one hand and a piece of well-buttered toast in the other. Without preamble, Mark said to him, "Bring me the jewellery and silver she pawned. I want to see it. And don't mess me about, Stuart. I'm not in the mood."

Stuart didn't bother with a hem or a haw this time. Instead, he nodded and went to the back. He was gone for more than five minutes, which made sense. He would have to remove everything from the shop's safe. He knew what he had—or at least Paulie damn well knew—and while the pendant in the window might be mistaken for something else, there was no way Paulie would risk the entire collection in that way, on view to anyone who happened to walk by.

Mark knew there were fifteen pieces in his mother's collection. She always chose from among them what to wear on special occasions: weddings, christenings, out to dinner for their anniversary, the ballet once a year, the opera twice. His dad had given them to her throughout the years. Mark didn't want to consider how they'd ended up in this shop.

Stuart had four other pieces: a pair of geometric earrings fashioned from platinum and decorated with seven diamonds each; a platinum ring with a large oval jelly opal set between two chevrons fashioned with diamonds; a platinum bracelet with jade and diamonds; an azure-blue aquamarine in an emerald cut, set with diamonds in a platinum ring.

As it turned out, the piece of silver was a small, late eighteenth-century tray, of the sort upon which the well-to-do left their cards when they went calling and found the master or mistress of the house not at home. This, too, belonged to his mother. He couldn't begin to guess what it was worth.

He said to Stuart, "This is the lot, then?"

Stuart nodded.

"Pete brought it to the shop?"

Stuart swallowed, the sound so loud that a frog could have been croaking on the floor nearby. That was acknowledgement enough.

"You didn't ask her . . . ? You didn't wonder . . . ? Jesus, Stuart. What's *wrong* with you? Put the lot of it back in the safe—including the pendant in the window—and don't sell any of it. I don't care if the bloody Prince of Wales walks in and wants to strike a deal. Understand me?" And when Stuart nodded, "And don't tell Paulie I was here."

Stuart nodded again, and Mark left the shop. He walked the length of The Narrow Way to St. Augustine Tower. There he turned into the route that led across the gardens within St. John at Hackney Churchyard. It was blazing hot, so there was little movement within the garden and the only sound was the voices of children at play—heroically, considering the temperature—beyond the wall that sheltered the church. He went past the café, where the air was redolent of frying meat, and from there into Sutton Place.

His mother answered his knock at the door. She smiled, saying, "Boyko! I *thought* I heard something. I'd just come inside for fizzy water or I would have missed you altogether." She inclined her head towards the back of the house, saying, "We're just in the back garden, Esme and I. She'll be that happy to see you."

"No Dad?" he asked.

"Our Eileen's taken him to be fitted for hearing aids, thank the Lord. If I had to spend another week shouting at the man just to be heard I might have murdered him. Go on out to say hello to Esme. I'll fetch you a fizzy water as well."

"That can wait," he said. "It's you I've come to see."

"Me?" Clearly, she read something in his expression because she said, "It's not Lilybet, is it?"

"It's Pete," he said.

Her hand went to her throat. He wondered if all women did that when preparing for what they expected to be bad news, as a way of warding off a coming blow. "She's not . . . ? What's happened?"

"She's taken some of your jewellery: five of the Art Deco pieces. I mean to get them back for you. Considering what she probably got for them, it'll take some time but—"

"You're not thinking Pete has stolen from me."

"She's taken the jewellery and that silver calling card tray to Paulie's upper shop in The Narrow Way. I've just been. I'd found a pawn ticket in her bag, see. I wanted to know . . . I had some ideas . . . It doesn't matter. Stuart showed me."

"He shouldn't have done. That's very naughty of him."

"I didn't give him much choice, Mum."

"Still, he shouldn't have told you or showed you. It's a private matter."

"What's that meant to mean?"

"Obviously, I knew she'd taken the pieces to the shop."

"You knew?" He frowned. "Are you in trouble, Mum?"

"What sort of trouble would I be in?"

"Money trouble, you and Dad."

Her gaze shifted from him to the window. Through its panes he could see Esme spooning compost into a pile of potting soil that stood on the outdoor table. She used a trowel to mix it well, and then began loading a clay pot with the enriched soil.

Mark said, "Look. If there's money trouble, Mum, I can help out. We've not got a pile of ready cash, but there's no need to pawn your jewellery. Besides, Dad gave it you. It's got sentimental value as well. And you meant it all to go to Esme eventually, didn't you?"

She said, "It was just time. Everything has its season, Boyko."

"So it *is* money trouble."

Floss licked her lips and turned her gaze back to him. She said, "There's no money trouble. *And* there are pieces left for Esme. You're to have no fears on either score."

"Then why did Pete . . ."

He watched as misshapen red blotches began to appear on his mother's throat and on her chest where her flowery summer blouse was open at the collar to form a V. He said, "Pete needed the money, not you."

She said nothing. She merely rolled one of the bottles of fizzy water against her palm. Esme, Mark saw, was heading for the door, no doubt wondering why her gran was so long about fetching the fizzy water. He needed to finish this conversation before she came into the house.

He said, "What was it for? Mum, why did Pete need money? Why would she come to you and not to me?"

The door was opening as Floss Phinney said quickly, "I phoned her. We spoke. I gave it to her. More than that, Pete will have to tell you."

"Uncle Mark!" Esme cried as she stepped inside. "Come and see what Gran and I are planting. It's gonna be gor-gee-us in October, isn't it, Gran?"

"Not if we don't get it all planted," her grandmother replied. "Nothing grows where nothing's planted. Best remember that, Esme."

DEPTFORD
SOUTH-EAST LONDON

To Tani's surly, "Where're we going, then?" Deborah responded with, "Deptford."

"Wha's in Deptford? No. Don't say. I c'n answer. *Nothing's* in bloody Deptford."

Simisola said, "Tani, that's rude!"

"We need to find Mum," was his reply.

He wasn't happy and Deborah couldn't blame him. Not only did he find himself part of a household of white people, he also didn't see his remit as swanning about with some white lady in her nearly new Vauxhall Corsa. He saw his remit as finding his mother. Anything short of that rendered him impotent. Deborah would have left him in Chelsea, but Simon had departed for Middle Temple to meet with a silk who was doing duty as the Crown Prosecutor, and her father had gone to do the shop for dinner. She knew it was a fairly sure bet that if Tani had remained in Chelsea with only his promise to stay where he was, he'd vanish five minutes after her departure with Simisola.

Tension was rolling off the boy like steam from a fog machine. Deborah knew she'd made the right decision. She said, "If your mum left with the policeman, Tani, we know she's safe."

"If she left with a copper, we know she's arrested," he replied.

"Even if she is arrested," Deborah countered, "she'll be safer where she is than where she was when she got arrested, wouldn't you agree?"

"Deb'rah's right, Tani." Simisola squirmed round in her seat to look at him. "And anyway, it's not like she did something bad to *get* arrested. If Deb'rah says we'll find her, we will. *I* think we will, anyway. Or she'll find us."

Tani looked at his sister, and in the rearview mirror, Deborah saw his face soften with the beginning of a smile. "At least we're together, you and me, Squeak," he acknowledged. "At least we know each other's safe."

When they reached Deptford, Deborah parked in Millard Road, where she found not only an available space for her car but also a familiar yellow-and-green Super Soft van standing at the foot of the Pepys Park entrance steps. They clambered out and Deborah headed straight for this, with Simisola hard on her heels. Deborah said, "Ah. Potential indulgence," and ushered both of the kids to inspect what the van had to offer. She noted that Tani was attempting to look indifferent, surly not having worked as well as he'd hoped. Indifferent wasn't working much better, however, especially with Simi completely on board with the idea of ice cream. She was chanting "Bunny Ears! Bunny Ears!" to which Deborah said, "And so it shall be, madam. I'm having a single with flake. What about you, Tani?"

He said, "Nothin'," and turned away.

Deborah said, "Hmmm. You look like a mint Cornetto man to me. What d'you think, Simi?"

"I think yes!"

So Deborah made the purchases. As they waited, she said to Tani, "Simi and I will finish yours up, if you don't want it, but both of you are sworn to secrecy. Dad's a proponent of the you'll-spoil-your-dinner school of thought. So we absolutely can*not* tell him." And as she gathered up the treats, handed them to Tani and Simisola, she said "Let's have these in the park."

As they walked up the steps—Simisola at her side and Tani trying to ignore both of them—Deborah sought a way to talk to Tani. The situation he was in was upsetting enough. That he probably also felt powerless to change anything about that situation only made his dilemma worse. It wasn't permanent, of course: where he was and what he was being made to do just now. But at the moment it was likely that it felt permanent.

A beech tree was offering shade to a bench not far from the entrance to the park, so Deborah led them there. She sat with a sibling on either side of her. Simisola was happily doing her Bunny Ears proud as Deborah made short work of the flake and went on to her ice cream. Tani still held his mint Cornetto unopened. "You should eat it," she said to him, but he shook his head. He did begin to remove the wrapping, though. This, Deborah thought, was a good sign.

They watched two little boys kicking a football. They were on the path rather than on the summer-brown lawn. One of them was very good. The other wasn't happy about that fact.

"Do you play?" Deborah asked Tani, and when he shrugged, she said, "Are you sporty at all?"

He blew a breath out between his lips, impatient with her question. Simisola looked at him, then at Deborah. She nodded to indicate he was sporty indeed. Or he played football. But in either case, it might have been something they could talk about, but Tani wasn't having conversation with *her.*

She said, "I thought Sophie seemed quite nice. Have you been together long?"

He gave her a look. He said, "You don't have t' pretend you're in'erested in me an' her."

"Actually," she said, "I *am* interested. But you don't have to answer if you'd rather not."

He was using his thumb to work the ice cream topper off the Cornetto. He studied the resulting chocolate, mint, and vanilla confection. Finally, he spoke to it rather than to her. He said quietly, "She thinks I c'n do whatever I set out to do." He said nothing else, but the set of his shoulders suggested what was going unsaid.

"That's good to hear," Deborah told him. "But c'n I just say . . . ? In this situation, you're not to bear everything on your shoulders, Tani. What I mean is that you don't *have* to bear everything. Aside from your dad, you've got everyone on *your* side of what's been going on. There's no one on your dad's side at all."

He shot a glance at her, then said, "You don't know."

Deborah said, "So tell me. I *want* to know."

"My *mum* was going to do it to her, is what. She was just calling it something diff'rent so Squeak—so Simi—wouldn't know. And both my grans want it done as well. That puts them on his side. Do you see?"

"I didn't know that. But if that's the case, Simi won't go home. She'll stay with me till everything's sorted." Deborah turned to the little girl and said, "Sorry, Simi. We're talking about you in front of you and that's very rude. Can I ask: Are you happy to stay with us till we're absolutely certain you're safe? We'd love to have you stay, by the way. We quite enjoy your company."

With vanilla cream ringing her mouth, Simisola looked from Deborah to Tani. She said, "But wha' about Tani?"

"Tani is very welcome to stay for as long as he wants, *if* he wants to stay. Of course, he'd have to be able to handle Peach and Alaska. D'you think he could do?"

"Oh yes," she said. "He's not afraid of animals at *all*."

"Then if he would like to stay with us—"

"I got to find Mum," he said. "And I got to get those passports, Squeak."

"Won't you allow the police to do it?" Deborah asked him. "Surely, your dad's not going to defy the police, Tani."

Tani gave a look that said she was more than half mad. He said, "You hear me, okay? The coppers can tear the flat from top to bottom. They won't find them cos the passports aren't there. Even if he had them hidden this morning when I was looking, he'll move 'em now. He's got the perfect place to keep 'em till he needs 'em. Unless I c'n get to them first."

Deborah didn't like the sound of this. But how could any of them stop Tani from going his own way? Short of tying him to a pipe or locking him inside a room in their house, she and Simon and her father were powerless to stop him if he wished to leave. He'd learned over time that the only person he could really trust was himself. And perhaps Sophie. But Deborah reckoned he intended to keep Sophie as far away as possible from whatever he was planning to do.

She stood. "I hope I can change your mind. In the meantime, come with me. I must take a photograph to a friend nearby."

Back at her car with the siblings, she removed a package from the Vauxhall's boot. That done, she led them to the building in which Leylo and her husband lived. She'd rung in advance, so they were expected. Leylo was home and, this time, so was her husband.

"Oh this is so very lovely, Deborah," constituted Leylo's greeting when she opened the door to them. "Hello, my dears," she said to the siblings. "I am Leylo and here is Yasir." And when everyone was inside and the door was closed, "I have cool tea and biscuits. And Yasir has only just returned with juice and fizzy water. What may I bring to you? Oh please, do sit."

"I recommend Leylo's cool tea," Deborah told them. "It's very good."

Yasir shepherded them in the direction of the sitting room and

Deborah could see that, at once, both Simisola and Tani were mesmerised by the wealth of African art the room contained. Tani gravitated at once to the masks, Simisola to the glass-topped case of goldweights, much as Deborah had done.

"My guilty pleasure," Yasir said to Tani, referring especially to what hung on the wall.

"These're wicked, man," Tani said. "Where'd you get 'em?"

"Various places in Africa. On many, many travels," Yasir said. "Which do you like best?"

Tani crossed his arms and studied them seriously. "Tha'd be hard to say."

"They are very special, yes." Leylo was entering the room with a wooden tray. She set this on the coffee table. "Please, please. Ah, Simisola, I see you like the goldweights. As did Deborah, you know. You must take one if you wish."

Simi at once hid her hands behind her back. She said, "I mustn't."

"You may if you wish to," Leylo said.

Simi returned to gazing at the goldweights. But she kept her hands behind her back despite Leylo's friendly invitation. Her expression was enchanting: part of her lower lip sucked in as before, the tops of those two very white teeth a pleasing contrast to her skin. Deborah couldn't resist. She hadn't brought her camera, but she had her mobile, so she took the girl's picture. Then she took a second of Tani and Yasir in conversation. Tani was in profile, smiling. It was the first time she'd seen him smile.

She'd placed her wrapped package next to the tray that Leylo had brought into the room and now she said, "You must open it," which Leylo did, crying, "Oh, this is too much. You are too kind," when she saw the photograph Deborah had taken the last time she'd been there. "Yasir, you must look to see what Deborah has brought to us."

He went to her side and she handed him the portrait. He nodded thoughtfully as he studied it. He said to Deborah, "You have caught the difference. I only see it fleetingly on her face, but now I can see it whenever I look at this. Thank you. You are a true artist."

Deborah felt herself going red in the face from the compliment. "I love making portraits. That's all it is. And Leylo is a very good model."

He set the framed photo on the end table near to where Tani was standing. Tani looked at the picture. Then he looked at Leylo, then at Deborah.

"Yasir's right," he said. His expression was not what it had been before. His face had completely softened. He directed his attention to his sister. He said, "She's real good with her camera, Squeak. Maybe she c'n snap you and me sometime, eh?"

"I already have done," Deborah told him. "I'll show you how the printing is done when we get back to Chelsea. If you're interested, I mean."

He was quiet for a moment, perhaps considering her offer and what it meant. Finally he spoke. "That'd be good," he said.

WESTMINSTER
CENTRAL LONDON

"Holiday camp, Barbara! Just think of it. Think of the fun! It's exactly like the holiday camps we all went to as children with our families. You know what I mean. The family goes to a holiday camp on the seaside—that's where these things are generally located—and every little thing is provided for them. All they must do is simply show up."

Barbara had only just arrived back in central London from her tête-à-tête with Ross Carver. Together they'd done a bit of internet research, and she'd had Dorothea make copies of a printout given her by Carver, which had ultimately opened the door to this unfortunate colloquy when Dorothea brought the copies along. Barbara said to her now, "Dee, can we possibly talk about this later?" It was just her luck that she voiced the request as Lynley and Nkata were walking into the room.

Lynley said, as usual, "Where are we? Winston, will you fetch the DCs?" which apparently allowed Dorothea to seize the moment, for she was the one to reply with, "Just *think* of it, Detective Chief Superintendent Lynley."

He looked nonplussed. He said, "Acting only, Dee. And what am I to think of?"

Barbara fairly soared to her feet, saying, "This, sir. Dee's made copies for everyone. Thanks, Dee. This is what we're looking for. It's called *Standing Warrior.*"

Although she started to hand over the stack of duplicated printouts to Lynley, Barbara found that Dorothea was undeterred. She said, "It's a holiday camp for singles! I mean, it's a family camp but every year they do a week for singles only. And it's just the sort of camp we all went to in summers with our families."

Barbara refrained from hooting in derision, but she did manage to say, "I'll wager one hundred quid here and now that the inspector has never darkened the doorway of a holiday camp in his life. With his family or without."

Lynley asked, "Holiday camp?" as he took his reading spectacles from his jacket pocket.

"You *see*?" Barbara said pointedly to the departmental secretary, "He doesn't even know what you're talking about."

Dorothea's enthusiasm was not to be forestalled. She said, "It's like a resort, Detective Chief Super—"

"*Guv* will do for now, Dee," Lynley interposed. He was gazing down at the photo of the sculpture Ross Carver had found.

"You've been to a resort, haven't you? At some point in your life?"

Barbara said, "Does he really seem the type to mix it up with the proletariat?"

"The what?"

"The hoi polloi, the common man, the salt of the earth, the great unwashed, the greater unread, the what*ever*. His accent alone would get him murdered on the first night."

"That's ridiculous," Dorothea declared. "It's for everyone, Barbara. Think of it—"

"Must I?"

Nkata reentered the room, the DCs trailing behind him like ducklings. Lynley gave each of them a copy of the Carver printout. Barbara returned to her desk and plopped into her chair.

"They have swimming and yoga and dance," Dorothea said. "They have badminton, tennis, croquet, crazy golf. There's shuffleboard and even a climbing wall! At night, there's entertainment, in the morning there's exercise classes. And best of all, there's a spa. And a pool. Well, of course, there must be a pool if they have swimming."

"Dee, I hate to dash your dreams, but here it is. I plan to go straight to my death without ever having been to a singles-only holiday camp," Barbara told her.

"Pooh! Ridiculous! This is just what we need. We can hire a caravan, or share a room at the lodge, or we can splurge and try to get one of the smaller chalets. *Or*—and this might be just the very thing—we can sign up to share a large chalet with others. Same sex or mixed."

"And then what?" Barbara asked her. "Sit round in our jimjams having coffee in the morning?"

"Having once seen those jimjams," Lynley noted, looking up from the paper Barbara had handed to him and peering over the tops of his specs, "I do advise using caution, Dee."

Dee started to colour, so Barbara added quickly, "Please. The pyjama remark? It's not what you think. Not that the guv and I don't make the perfect couple. They were a gift from Winston and—"

"Detective Sergeant Nkata!"

"Deep waters here, Barbara," Lynley noted.

"What*ever*," Dee said with a shrug. "But we must move quickly on this, Barbara. It's going to book up or sell out or whatever they call it. It's only today been announced. I was lucky to see the advert."

Lynley said quite solemnly, "You're owed the time off, Barbara," and lowered his head with a smile when Barbara offered him her very best glare.

"*As* to the missing sculpture, sir . . . ," she said with great meaning.

"Oh pooh. I can take a hint," Dorothea announced.

Barbara murmured, "Which God be praised."

"But *you* take these and have a look. And then you can tell me you're not absolutely wild to go." Dorothea extended her hand, which was grasping more printouts, these obviously of the family camps she'd been enthusing over.

There was nothing for it but to take them, which Barbara did. She said, "I'll be on pins and needles till I have time to commit all of this to memory, Dee," and the moment Dorothea had left them, Barbara tossed the lot directly into the wastepaper basket next to her desk.

"She'll only print another set, Barb," Nkata said.

Grousing, Barbara fished them out, but she handed them to him, saying, "Have them. I definitely see a holiday camp for singles in your future, mate."

"Where are we aside from holiday camps?" Lynley said. And gesturing with the printout Barbara had given him, "What are we to make of this?"

"This is called *Standing Warrior*," Barbara said once again. "Ross Carver says he got it from a gallery called Padma, in Peckham. I rang them. They're closed for the day, but you can see the statue's details on the sheet. You ask me, sir, it's the cosh. And the fact that it wasn't with the group that went to forensics suggests the killer took it once Teo Bontempi had been brained with it. And there's a very tasty detail Mr. Carver didn't mention the first time we had a natter, him and me. Teo Bontempi said something to him on the night he found her, but he didn't want us to know what it was. 'She hit me, Ross.' So we've got our confirmation that the killer's a woman."

"'Nless more 'n one person's involved," Nkata pointed out. "I mean, I don't see Teo Bontempi standing round thinking of Jesus while someone goes for a piece of bronze and bashes her with it."

"Could be our skull basher got her when she was walking away from . . ." Barbara thought about this and added, ". . . an argument? a threat? This woman shows up. Teo knows her, so she lets her in."

"Sounds like Rosie," Nkata murmured.

Barbara went on. "They talk, but Teo doesn't agree to whatever she was meant to agree to, so she heads to open the door to give her the boot. She assumes her visitor is following, which she is. Only she's made a detour, and she's picked up the sculpture. She uses it. She knows enough about police work—and who doesn't these days when every other programme on the telly is some police drama or another?—so she takes the cosh with her after the deed is done. She knows that there's evidence on it and that evidence is going to tie her to an assault on Teo and *now* to Teo's death."

"If she took it with her, it's going to be on CCTV, isn't it?" one of the DCs pointed out.

"Unless she left the building via the fire door," another said.

"Or chucked it from a window—the bedroom?—and went round the building to get it afterwards," another pointed out.

"Or it's just a feint," Lynley said.

"Sorry?" This from a DC who looked disturbingly like Charlie Chaplin as the tramp.

"We're to *think* a sculpture was used to cosh her," Barbara said, "so we waste time rushing round to find it."

"Meaning she went there to bash her all along?" Charlie Chaplin asked. "But took something else with her?"

"Not necessarily," Lynley said. "It well could be that she went there only for conversation. It could be that the conversation went badly, and it somehow made Teo Bontempi into a threat."

"That puts Mercy Hart back in the spotlight," Nkata pointed out.

"Rosie Bontempi as well," Barbara noted.

"Also Pietra Phinney," Lynley said. "We have only Mark Phinney's side of the story that his affair with Teo was finished."

All of them took a moment to ponder what they had and what they knew. At last, Lynley listed the next day's assignments:

Barbara would go to the gallery in Peckham for information on *Standing Warrior*; the DCs would split themselves up to continue seeking the location of the lock-up where everything from Women's Health of Hackney had been taken, digging up the paperwork relating to the clinic's location, determining who had let the place initially, ringing every charity shop in London to enquire about a bronze sculpture being donated for sale, and for the same reason, ringing every consignment shop that resold art. Meantime, Nkata would once again try to get a statement from Monifa Bankole about the actual purpose of the Kingsland High Street clinic. Lynley himself would have another go at Mercy Hart before the twenty-four hours during which they could hold her were used up. Barbara would assist with that.

Assignments given, then, Lynley told them all to go home for the night. He wanted everyone back at half-past six the next morning. It was going to be another long day.

—

BELGRAVIA
CENTRAL LONDON

Lynley took his whiskey into the back garden. From the terrace where he sat, he observed the rosebushes and briefly meditated upon the fact that most roses now had little or no scent. In a central bed that was edged in tumbled granite, they weren't far from him and yet they smelled of nothing. This, he recalled, had been Helen's only complaint about the garden. *Darling, roses should at the very least be roses, after all. How on earth has scent been bred from them? Or . . . have I used the wrong word? Are flowers bred? That cannot be right.* She loved the garden otherwise. Her thumb was unfortunately more black than green, but she persisted mucking about in the beds. When the weather was fine, they dined out here. When it was inclement, he often found her looking down upon the garden from the landing window. *I'd love to have been a garden designer,* she'd said to him once. He'd pointed out that she could be that still, that surely there was nothing preventing her from becoming another Gertrude Jekyll, to which she'd replied that her general lack of talent might do the job quite well, Tommy. *But thank you, darling, for displaying such profound confidence in me.* She *had* learned from the internet how to create sumptuous displays of plants in pots. But this, she told him, wasn't more than child's play. *Only three elements besides the soil and asking at the gardening centre which plants actually can be potted together. Now, if I can manage to keep them watered, only the annuals will need replacing.* And they stood, still, the pots she'd created. After she'd died, he'd let them all follow her. It had simply been too much for him to care for them in her place.

From the garden of the house next door, he could hear voices, some laughter, and the accompanying crack of mallets upon croquet balls. "I've got the cocktails ready," a woman called out. "I'm trying something new. Tell me what you think."

The conversation ceased as the cocktail was tried. *Gorgeous* was the first adjective applied.

Lynley smiled at nothing in particular, just the assurance of individuals enjoying each other's company. He listened longer. Too much longer, as it turned out. He began to feel hollow with loneliness.

He'd felt this before, but tonight the loneliness rose from an isolation that grew out of the void in his life. The void was ubiquitous in his world as it was currently put together, although most of the time he was able to fill it with his work. Investigations comprised very long hours, but the reality was that even in the midst of a case, the void was still present because in the back of his mind, and at a level he didn't want to consider, he knew that he was piling action upon action in a fruitless attempt to disguise what he was actually feeling.

He wondered if this was what Daidre sensed in him without being able—or perhaps being merely unwilling—to give it voice. *Did* he love Daidre? he asked himself. Or did he love merely the idea of Daidre, born of his need to be whole again and to love someone as he had loved Helen. After the horrors attendant to Helen's death, how *could* he declare himself free of the grief of losing her when the greater part of that grief came from the decision he himself had made to let her go and to free her spirit from her body?

He drank down the rest of his Macallan. It had come from a bottle of thirty-year-old single malt. He wasn't hungry at all, but he decided to make a go of dinner.

Charlie had left it for him with instructions as to its reheating. As he shut the microwave upon it and set the time, his mobile rang. It was, he saw, Daidre at last. He was happy at this, but cautious as well.

"You've been ringing me, Tommy," she said without preamble.

"I have done, yes," he replied, starting the microwave upon his meal. "I did worry when you didn't ring back. Where are you? Are you quite all right? It seemed . . ." He winced and stopped himself. He hated the needy tenor of his voice, and he knew he was talking too much.

"I'm fine, but I've had to come to Cornwall," she said.

"Is there trouble?" he asked. "Are you at the cottage?"

"Goron has left Gwynder on her own, I'm afraid. *And* without a vehicle, thank you very much indeed. He may have gone back to the caravan, but in any case Gwyn's completely stranded. Well, you know how isolated Polcare Cove is."

He did indeed. The isolation of the cottage was the main reason Daidre had purchased it. Its isolation had also made it the only habitation in sight when he'd needed to find a phone, although there hadn't been one at the time.

"She rang me several days ago, actually," Daidre went on. "I was certain he'd return soon enough. I thought he'd just taken himself off for a pleasant ride in the countryside or a tour of God-knows-where, or something. But he's not returned."

"Could he have come to harm?" Lynley asked.

"That was my first thought as he's not used to driving. But I've rung the hospitals and the various police stations. There's not been an accident. The only place I can come up with as to his whereabouts is the caravan. With . . . well, with his father."

"You did tell me he wasn't happy at the cottage," Lynley pointed out. "Is his leaving such a surprise?"

"Only in that, stupidly, I didn't think he could actually find his way back. I mean to the caravan. And in any event, I'm not sure that's where he is at all. There's no phone and neither of them—Goron or his father—has a mobile, so I can't just give them a bell and ask. Gwyn's become quite frightened something might have happened to him and she's terrified now she's alone in the cottage."

"Not an easy situation," he said.

"Anything but. I'm trying desperately to sort it all out, but I'm not sure what to do. I mean, I can't *force* Goron to remain in Polcare Cove, can I."

"Is that where you are now?" he asked.

"No, no. The reception there's wretched for a mobile. I've had a landline put in for them, but I wanted a bit more privacy in talking to you. I've brought Gwyn up to the inn. I'm in the car park. She's gone inside for a table."

"I expect this is what's been on your mind," he noted.

"The twins? Polcare Cove? Yes. I did think I had them in the very best possible situation. Paying jobs, a place to live, a car to drive. I thought they'd *thrive* away from that wretched place. The caravan, I mean. But now . . . ? I don't know, Tommy. Gwyn's been proposing she go back as well. But really, what sort of life is possible for her there? For either of them? I'm at a loss."

"I can hear that in your voice," he told her. "I'm wondering, though. Could it be that what was good for you—being taken from your parents and adopted into another family—might not be what was good for them? Could it be that the caravan with your—their—father is the best plan after all?"

"How can that be? A future as tin streamers? Living in a caravan? Yes, they have running water and there's a wood stove for heat in the winter, but that's about it."

"Yet we do tend to run to what's familiar," he pointed out. "There's comfort and security in that. Polcare Cove . . . ? It represents the unknown for them, doesn't it? Have you a next step?"

"Admittedly, I'm flummoxed. I'm rather afraid to take Gwyn to the caravan, even to fetch back the car, which, frankly, she's going to need if she's to remain in Polcare Cove. She must have a way to get to work. But if I do take her to fetch the car, she might want to stay at the caravan herself, and then what's to do?"

"Let her stay, I suspect." Lynley paused for a moment. Through the microwave's window, he could see the turntable making its rounds. He fetched cutlery and a placemat for the table in the kitchen, sending an unspoken apology heavenward to his father who, as far as Lynley knew, had never stepped into the kitchen of the family's home in his entire life, let alone eaten a meal there. He went on to say, "I know it's not what you want for her, Daidre. But she's of an age to make her own decisions, isn't she. And she would know that she can reverse that decision at any time. The cottage will still be there."

"I've thought of bringing them both to London. Or at least Gwyn."

"Have you?"

"I can hear the doubts in your voice, Tommy."

"I was merely thinking of the change: from the sea in Cornwall to . . . well, to everything that's London."

"She does like animals. I could see if there's something she could do at the zoo. She'd be among people, she'd be brought out of herself, she might even make a few friends. That's better, isn't it, than what she has now, or rather, what she thinks she wants now, which is to go back to the caravan."

The microwave pinged. He opened its door. The meal sent before it a welcome fragrance of pastry suggestive of steak and kidney pie without the kidneys, which he could not abide.

He took this to the table as he said, "We're back to that point, aren't we. All of that is what you needed and what you wanted, Daidre. It's next to impossible, isn't it, to know what will fulfill the needs of someone else."

He fetched a bottle of ale. Steak pie begged for it. In his opinion, nothing else would do.

She said, "You do always talk sense, Tommy."

He chuckled. "I don't and we're both all too aware of that fact. It's merely that I'm not invested in this situation. I mean, with your brother and sister. With you? That's quite another tale. I'm invested there. Rather too invested at times. I do know that, Daidre. I also know what it's like to watch someone take one decision after another when I very much want them to choose a different course. When that occurs, there are times when it's a difficult admission."

"What is?"

"Accepting and admitting I could well be wrong, that given the circumstances, the individual is taking the very best decision possible at the time and in their frame of mind."

She was quiet again. He wondered what she could see from her car in the car park of the Salthouse Inn: the looming leafy trees behind it, a stony path leading upwards into the woods, the way she'd come on the narrow road from Polcare Cove. He sat at the table, uncovering his meal: steak pie it was indeed, along with courgettes that hadn't quite made it through the reheating process unscathed.

She said, "Do you sometimes feel that you're not fighting hard enough?"

"In my line of work? I expect you know the answer to that."

"I don't. Really. Do you ever feel like that, Tommy?"

"Most days I feel exactly like that, thinking if I only try this, or if I only turned things this way instead of that, if I only considered one more point in addition to everything else I've tried or done . . . surely I'll have the result I want. But that's where we all get lost, I think. With hanging our hats on *what I want* when we could be hanging them on something new. Or something different. Or something unexpected, for that matter."

"I see that. There's no prescription for living, is there."

"If only there were." He ran a knife round the side of the steak and kidney pie sans kidney and let it release its fragrant steam. He upended it onto his plate. He forked up a courgette and examined it for its gustatory possibilities. "I'd offer to come down," he told her, "but I'm afraid I can't."

"No need. But . . ."

He waited. She did not go on. He would have thought they'd been disconnected but he could hear faint noise in the background, probably from the inn's car park.

She finally said, "But I find I would love to have you here, and I don't quite know why."

"Ah."

"'Ah'? That's all?"

"Should there be more?" he asked her.

"That's the question, isn't it."

"Still and always, Daidre."

"Gwyn's just come out of the inn, Tommy. I expect she's wondering what's happened to me. I must join her. But may I say . . . Our conversation? It's been quite helpful."

"Has it? I'm happy you rang, then. I would have been happy in any event, but I expect you know that already."

"I do know that. And thank you for it, Tommy."

"Enjoy your dinner."

"I will."

He hoped he could do the same. The courgette, he reckoned, would provide the answer. To that, if to nothing else.

13 AUGUST

Monifa Bankole wasn't a prisoner, but she felt like one, even if the prison was one of her own making. She could easily leave the Nkatas, true. Alice wished her company at the café today, but she could refuse to go. Or she could walk off on her own on the way to the place and raise a ruckus if Alice tried to stop her. Or, for the matter, she could go along to the café and slip off while Alice was busy with cooking or with customers. But doing any of that did not put her closer to restoring her children to her. There was only one way to gain access to them.

The detective sergeant had made that clear before he left for work. He was going to be honest with her, he said. He told her that Mercy Hart—she who had been Easter Lange—was now in police custody.

Mercy would this morning be questioned for the second time, the detective sergeant told her. The subjects of interest were going to be practicing medicine without a licence and performing female genital mutilation. Now, she'd been clever and the clinic had been— for better or worse—clean of concrete and unassailable evidence of FGM. Because of this, the key to charging her with that part of her criminal behaviour lay at Monifa's feet. This key constituted her statement—from A to Z—written in her own hand about the clinic and her experience there.

"You think about wha's right to do, Missus Bankole," he'd said before he left the flat. "Both for you and for your kids. You got my card so you c'n ring me whenever."

When he was gone, she rejoined Alice and Benjamin in the kitchen. If they'd heard their son's words, they gave no indication. Benjamin was folding the washing. Alice was making him a lunch to take on his bus route. This consisted of what remained from the dinner Monifa had cooked for them the previous night: *efo riro*, *eba,* and egg rice. Benjamin Nkata had taken himself to Peckham's Nigerian and African markets to buy the ingredients.

The dinner had been filled with the sweat and the compliments that generally accompanied a successful Nigerian meal. She'd taken care with her spices and she thought she'd used the heat sparingly, but the first mouthful had sent the detective sergeant to the fridge for milk while his father laughed, saying, "He's one hundred p'rcent English, our Win. You come back here, Winston, an' have some food put hair on your eyeballs."

Now Alice put containers of each dish into Benjamin's lunch bag while Benjamin finished up what he'd started last night. Monifa had never before seen a man in charge of the family's washing, but it seemed the Nkatas were full of surprises. After their dinner, he'd gathered up a basket of towels and sheets and clothing and out the door he went to the building's laundry room, not returning till all of it was both washed and dried.

Alice said to her, "I'm just 'bout ready to head to the caff, Monifa. You okay to go? I decided to try my hand at egg rice first, and I'd be pleased if you watch me and make corrections."

So they set off together. They did a good amount of crisscrossing through the streets, which made Monifa consider whether DS Nkata had advised his mum to take a route guaranteed to confuse her, and on this route they passed Brixton Police Station. This gave her pause and tightened her fight-or-flee muscles, but they went on, and they ended up in Brixton Road. There Alice N's Café was tucked between Launderama and Habeesha Restaurant and Bar. Like most businesses along the road, the front bore a steel roll-up security door that covered both the café's large window and its entrance. It was painted bright blue, and across it the café's name was scrolled in bright red letters. Cartoonish diners sat at tables piled with food. *Morning Coffee*, *Lunch*, and *All-Day Snacks* were lettered in cartoon balloons while *Eat In or Take Away* had been fashioned into the shapes of crockery and cutlery by someone with talent and imagination.

Monifa wondered it had not been tagged. But she saw that the artist had signed his work—Annan Kwame—so perhaps he was a resident nearby and due respect was given to his art.

Alice unlocked the metal door and raised it. Then she unlocked the café itself and motioned for Monifa to go inside. There was an open/closed sign posted on the door's glass, and Alice did not change it from the closed position. She said to Monifa, "Tabby will be along straightaway and I'll want her watching when we get to the cooking. Let's have coffee meantime."

It didn't take long to make their coffees, which Alice carried to one of the café's tables along with a tin jug of cold milk and a basket of various sweeteners. Both of them sat and Monifa said to her, "You have had this café for many years?"

Alice nodded. "When Stoney—our Harold—went inside, I needed a distraction to take my mind off where I went wrong raising him. Benj said I had to do something other than fret as there was nothing more we could do for Stoney, him and me. So I thought about it and since my only talent—other than tatting, and I do like tatting, don't I—was cooking Caribbean, that's what I decided. I did it for Brixton Market at first, just three hours this was, from ten till one. I still have a stall there—Tabby's mum works it—but Benj thought a regular caff would be better as I get older. To keep me out of the weather in winter and the like. So here I am."

Monifa considered what she'd said and asked, "Cooking?"

"What's that?"

"Cooking is your only talent?"

Alice smiled. "Like I said, I do my tatting and I s'pose there's other talents inside me but this is the only one I practise regular. When you've hungry men to cook for, what else is there to do, eh? Plus we always could use the money if I actually *made* any. Which I did *not*, not in the beginning when I was starting out. I overordered, I cooked too much, I served up too much. It took awhile."

Monifa said, "For me, it's the same. Cook, wash, clean, iron, and do the shop."

Alice nodded and took a sip of her coffee, grimaced, then said, "Good Lord, that's strong. You drink that, Monifa, you'll be awake for a week. Let me make another."

"Oh no. Please. This is, I am sure, very fine." Although Alice looked doubtful, Monifa added some milk and sugar, and she brought the cup to her lips. It *was* too strong, but she would never say. "So you have made your talent . . . the work of your life?"

"Life's work?" Alice ran her hand over the table, seemed to find it not up to her standards, and went behind the café's counter. She brought back a spray bottle and a rag and vigorously used them both. "I think it's only my life's work if I'm still learning, you know? That's why I brought you here. I expect you can teach me a lot. You ever thought about teaching Nigerian cookery?"

Monifa cocked her head and studied Alice to see if she was joking. She said, "Me? Teaching?"

"Why not, eh? You're going to teach me today, aren't you?"

"That is different."

"It isn't. You could teach in the evenings easy. Right here in the caff if you want. I expect you could get quite a group together.

'Specially as more and more people with the funds to pay move to this area. You're going to need something."

"I? Why?"

Alice said nothing for a bit. She gave her attention to the Formica topping the table where they were sitting. Finally she seemed to make up her mind, for she straightened her shoulders and looked at Monifa squarely. "I'll say this direct," she said. "You don't appear to be a fool, Monifa."

"I hope not to be," Monifa replied.

"Yeah, I bet you do hope that. But let me tell you something you likely need to hear just now. You'd be a real fool to go back to a man who's beat you. Now, from what I can tell, Jewel's given you a decision today. Am I right?" And when Monifa nodded, "Way I see it, then, you're at a crossroads. It's down to you what happens next."

PECKHAM
SOUTH LONDON

Cynthia Swann and Clete Jensen (Clete? she had thought. *Really?*) were arguing as Barbara made her way to Peckham. Her choice had been to drive from Chalk Farm or to use public transport, but since public transport was going to involve tube, rail, bus, and her feet—not to mention most of her morning—she opted for driving and she'd brought along the audio version of Cynthia and Clete's star-crossed love story to keep her blood pressure steady as she navigated the morning traffic. This had proved to be just the ticket. In the tale of found love/lost love/regained love, things were heating up. Clete had just flung himself from the ranch house that Cynthia had inherited from an uncle long estranged from the family and Clete was the cowboy who'd maintained it, skilfully keeping the ranch above water, both figuratively and literally. Cynthia had come to the ranch to acquaint herself with her inheritance in . . . Barbara could *never* remember the state although the description of it made her think the author had spent too much time in Australia's outback. At any rate, here had arrived Cynthia and here had locked eyes Cynthia and Clete and here had Cynthia and Clete been thrown together by fate and by the fact that there was no other person within fifty miles save a very old former convict who preferred a solitary life. Here had both that fate and that fact decided they were meant to be as one. Within twenty-five pages they had done the deed twice with "unmatchable fulfillment," but the third time had been their undoing—temporary though it was considering the nature of the novel—and now Clete was riding off on his stallion (there was no way he would be riding a gelding, for obvious reasons) while Cynthia sobbed at the window and watched him go. He turned back once as if having second thoughts, allowing their eyes to meet, to hold, to yearn, to soften, to cling to a promise that could not, could never go unrealised . . .

Blah, blah, blah, Barbara thought. She switched the sound off. Clete would be back. One night of unrivalled passion—or two or three nights—would never be enough for either of them. Love regained was just round the corner.

So was Padma Gallery, she discovered, although by that time she was on foot. She was lucky to find it, as it was tucked in an alley that broke off Rye Lane, and it was nearly overpowered by ZA Afro Foods and Ali Baba's Barber. Indeed, she'd walked by it three times before she finally asked at an Asian furniture shop for a clue as to its location.

She should have seen it, she reckoned, but she'd been distracted by the brick wall into which the gallery's door was built. The wall was heavily tagged although the imperative *Feel It* had been rendered with some attention to form and colour. Not that Barbara knew the first thing about art or form or colour, but she could tell *Feel It* was something special, whereas *JOBZ RES!* was clearly the work of a rank beginner.

When Barbara entered Padma Gallery, she was struck by its contrast to everything else in the alley. Inside were all creamy walls that held paintings, white pivoting stands that held sculptures, pristine glass cases that displayed jewellery, and shelves that offered various types of folk art.

A woman wearing African garb and a complicated head wrap looked up from a desk in a corner of the room. She stood and approached Barbara, her hand extended. She was Neda, she said, an associate of the gallery's owner.

Would that be Padma? Barbara enquired.

No. Padma was the mother of the owner, Neda explained.

Barbara took the photocopy of *Standing Warrior* from her bag and handed it over, asking if it had come from Padma Gallery.

"Oh yes," Neda said. "It's called *Standing Warrior*," and she confirmed that Padma Gallery had sold the piece. In London, they were the sole representative of the artist. She was from Zimbabwe. "Would you like to see it?" she asked.

"It's here?" Barbara said, with *jackpot* and *bingo* doing the cha-cha in her skull. "Is it a consignment piece? Did someone bring it in for you to sell?"

"That happens on occasion. But in the case of *Standing Warrior*, I'm afraid not."

Barbara frowned. "I'm not following. You said I could see it?"

"Of course. It's just over here, among several other sculptures. All different artists, but grouped together they look very striking, I think." She led Barbara farther back into the gallery, where a dimly lit alcove had cones of light striking five different pivoting stands. She stopped in front of one of the stands—the largest—and there it was, exact to the photo Ross Carver had pulled from the internet.

The piece stood some eighteen inches tall, a stylised depiction of an African warrior with spear and shield. He was thin and muscular, long-faced but without expression. He wore a necklace of beads and a ring in one ear.

"Artists working in bronze generally do limited editions of their work. This particular artist—Blessing Neube—did fifteen of *Standing Warrior*. She sends them to us two at a time. We don't have the storage for more. When we sell two, she sends the next. This one is number thirteen. You can see the number on the bottom of the piece along with Blessing's initials. May I ask what your interest is?"

Barbara identified herself and explained her interest in *Standing Warrior*: as a murder weapon. While Neda looked concerned at that, she nodded when Barbara asked to pick up the sculpture. It was, Barbara reckoned, perfect for use as a cosh. It was simple to grip round the warrior's ankles, heavy enough to do serious damage, but not too heavy for a woman to wield. She observed the number 13 on the bottom, which prompted her to ask if Neda knew where the other twelve copies of *Standing Warrior* had gone.

Yes indeed, Neda assured her. The gallery kept records of all purchases, not only for purposes of provenance but also to alert buyers should something come to the gallery by the same artist. Barbara gave her Ross Carver's name, and she made very short work on her computer to confirm that, yes, Mr. Ross Carver had bought a *Standing Warrior*. "It was numbered ten," she said.

"I'll need a list of the other buyers," Barbara said. "We'll want to contact them to make certain they're still in possession of the piece they bought."

Neda looked hesitant. She said, "It's terribly irregular . . ."

"So's a search warrant," Barbara told her pleasantly. And she waited a moment before adding, "It's just to make sure we know where the other *Standing Warrior*s are."

Neda gave a small sigh but she printed the list of buyers and handed it over. Barbara gave it a glance. Not a familiar name on it, but it was a box that wanted ticking. She dug one of her cards out of her bag and handed it over, saying, "If someone should bring the sculpture in for you to sell . . ."

"I will let you know at once, of course," Neda assured her.

CHELSEA
SOUTH-WEST LONDON

Tani had not managed to work out why only three people lived in this house, along with a dog and a cat. It was the largest family home he'd ever seen, at least twice the size of the house where Sophie and her family lived. It had rooms for everything: bedrooms, bathrooms, library, kitchen, and those were just the beginning of the place. The previous night had introduced him to the dining room, where all of them had sat at an oblong mahogany table so polished he could see his reflection in it. Eight upholstered chairs followed its curve, and on an ancient cupboard thing against a wall, a big-arse covered soup bowl stood on a tray. To either side of it were framed pictures, all of white people, of course, but then what would you expect? There was among them a wedding picture of the couple who were housing him and Simisola at present, the bride wearing a posh white gown done up to her throat, the groom in a princely grey cutaway, her hand through his arm, his hand covering hers. *We're in love, we're in love*, the picture called out. But at the end of the day, it was just a picture.

They'd passed round plates of food, and they'd engaged in what probably went for typical rich-white-person conversation. Simisola joined in when she was asked a question directly, but when the others were talking, her round-eyed gaze merely travelled among them, as if she couldn't quite believe her bloody good luck in ending up in such a fairy-tale happy ending household.

In the morning, after breakfast, he'd gone into the garden. He began throwing a chewed-up tennis ball for the dog. He wondered why anyone would call a dog Peach, why anyone would call a cat Alaska. Neither name made the least bit of sense to him.

Peach didn't seem to care one way or another *what* she was called. At the moment, she was intent upon the ball. She barked till he threw it, she barked as she went to retrieve it, she barked when she dropped it at his feet. From the central tree, Alaska watched them, the slightest flick of the end of his tail showing he was paying attention.

"We need your opinion, Tani."

He turned to the house. Deborah was at the top of the steps that led down to the basement kitchen. "Simi and I are looking at some pictures. How on earth did you get Peach to fetch that ball for you?"

He looked at the dog. Peach was trotting his way. "I threw it," he said. "All dogs fetch when you throw something."

"I see you've never known a dachshund," was Deborah's reply. "Or perhaps better said: You've never known *this* dachshund. Generally, she'll run after the ball once, drop down to the lawn, and begin to ravage it. I mean the ball, not the lawn. I suppose we could have taught her, using the reward method. You know: bring the ball and get a treat. But none of us have the patience for that, and she's far too wily to act as if she's learned something, because that might prevent her earning more treats. So she's mostly window dressing in our lives, I'm afraid. *Will* you join us?"

She took him to the dining room, Peach on their heels, obviously in expectation of something edible, which she did not get. A laptop was set up on the mahogany table, Simi kneeling on a chair in front of it. She greeted him with, "Deborah's taken ever so many pictures, Tani. You must see. They're from yesterday and we're to choose which one we like the best. They're *ginormously* nice. Come here, come here."

He placed himself behind her chair and Simi began going through the photos. They were good, he thought. In his case, Deborah had used the light streaming into the flat from outside to create shadows hiding how beat up his face was. She'd also managed to isolate a moment when his hard shell had produced the first of its cracks, softening his expression to reveal something vulnerable. *That* picture made him distinctly uncomfortable.

Deborah handed him a small piece of paper. He saw that two other similar pieces had been folded into quarters and lay on the table. She told him that it was now his turn to choose three photos: one of himself, one of Simi, and one of himself and Simi together. "Simi and I have made our own choices," she said with a gesture at the folded papers. "Now it's your turn. We'll compare each other's choices at the end."

"This's a game?" he said.

"No, no. It's a way to narrow down choices without influencing each other."

"What're you doing with them, then?"

"The photos we end up with? I'm going to give them to your mother when I meet her. Whoops. I probably shouldn't have said that. It might influence your choice. Sorry. Try to forget I said it. Although that's stupid, isn't it? How are you supposed to forget what I said thirty seconds ago? Never mind. Do your best."

She was nervous. He could tell. He *made* her nervous. Typical. White lady, Black teenage boy. She probably had the family silver locked up somewhere just in case.

He drew a chair over to sit next to his sister, but he didn't begin going through the pictures at once. Instead, he thought he could actually use her nervousness, so he gave her a look and said, "Did you mean it, about Sophie?"

She looked confused for a moment. But then she said, "About her coming here to see you?" And when he nodded, "Of course. She's very welcome."

"I think Sophie's ever so nice," Simisola said. "She's got two brothers and a sister, Deborah. She's a secret, though, i'n't she, Tani? I mean, Tani was meant to go to Nigeria and marry a girl there which is what he got told by Papa only Papa di'n't know he has a girlfriend already. Only now, we think he does know because someone in the market told him."

Deborah turned her attention to Tani, saying, "I didn't know you were meant to go to Nigeria. Do you want to?"

"Not bloody likely," Tani said.

"What *do* you want? I mean, what do you prefer?"

"You mean what do I want compared to marrying some virgin in Nigeria that I never seen?"

"That's exactly what I mean."

"Sixth form college for a catering certificate and then uni to read business."

"That makes more sense to me than getting married just now. How old are you?"

"Eighteen."

"He can't force you to marry anyone, your dad, can he?"

"He can," Tani told her. "Through Simi. He set it up that way." He took up the piece of paper and jotted the numbers of the three pictures he most liked. When he folded it and put it in the centre of the table, he said, "I want to give Sophie a bell if tha's okay."

"Of course," Deborah said. "Shall I write the directions down for you? So she'll know how to get here, I mean?"

"Just th' address," he said. "She'll do the rest."

And he hoped against hope she would do it soon.

WESTMINSTER
CENTRAL LONDON

Lynley's second interview with Mercy Hart had not gone well. In fact, it had not gone anywhere. In his experience, most people who proclaimed their innocence of any wrongdoing were only too willing to speak with the police wherever and whenever the police thought it necessary, in order to clear their names. They generally were also happy to do this clearing of their names without the presence of a legal representative since they often believed that the request for a solicitor would make them look guilty, which, admittedly, it sometimes did. Thus, because they had no one present to intervene, the police could veer in any unpleasant or unrelated direction they wished to go. Mercy Hart, however, was not such a person. For their second meeting in an interview room, he found she had—in the American vernacular—lawyered up.

She had not requested the duty solicitor. Instead, she had arranged for someone from a private firm. This person was called Astolat Abbott—one of her parents obviously having been a fan of T. H. White, Thomas Mallory, or Alfred, Lord Tennyson—and she handed over her card for him to study, saying with a meaningful glance at her wristwatch, "We're within two hours of the twenty-four you can hold my client without charging her, Inspector, unless you've come up with something new. I'm fairly certain you would have charged her *had* you anything additional to use as evidence of a crime in which Mrs. Hart is involved. From what I've gathered, however, the only *possible* charge in this situation is one of using her aunt's identity at her place of employment and in the purchase of a mobile phone. Would you like to charge her for that so I might arrange for bail, or is there something else my client may do to assist you in your enquiries?"

As Barbara Havers might have said, there was a bloody wheelbarrow of something new, but none of it could so far be supported by anything. Mercy Hart had a motive, certainly. Teo Bontempi had put paid to her source of income, and as members of the team had discussed, she would probably have continued to do so should a clinic be set up in another location. But they could hardly charge Mercy Hart with murder without something to back up that charge, so they were left with either charging her for the crime of FGM or—should that not hold water—practising medicine without a licence. But even there, they had very little to present to the Crown Prosecution Service unless someone was willing to produce a signed statement. Again, as Havers might have put it, they were spitting into a very strong headwind.

So when he arrived at New Scotland Yard, he was the bearer of no good news. There had been nothing for it but to release her once he'd got the word from Winston Nkata that Monifa Bankole was maintaining her silence about the Kingsland High Street clinic.

Everyone was beavering away at their assignments from the previous evening's meeting of the team. It was the sort of work that took hours of slogging. Phone calls were being made to every charity shop and consignment shop in Greater London in an effort to find the missing sculpture; Winston had sent one of the team's DCs to speak to the removals men in order to learn the exact location to which they'd transported the clinic's equipment and furniture so that they could alert the owner to ring the police should those items be removed; he'd also charged another DC with locating the paperwork on the lease agreement for the clinic in Kingsland High Street. Since Lynley had phoned Winston post his extremely brief conversation with Mercy Hart and given him the word, he was now—with the last DC— collecting all CCTV footage in the vicinity of the clinic in an effort to give the lie to Mercy Hart's declaration that she'd never once spoken to Teo Bontempi: as Adaku Obiaka, as Teo Bontempi, or as anyone else.

He'd just finished speaking with Winston when Dorothea Harriman entered the room. She was carrying an embarrassingly large arrangement of seasonal flowers, which she placed with what appeared to be triumph upon Barbara Havers's desk. She looked about, saw Lynley, and said slyly, "There's a card! Shall I . . . ," with a surreptitious glance for eavesdroppers or spies. "D'you think she'd mind if we sneaked a peek at the card?"

Lynley said, "I daresay we can label that as a less than profound idea, Dee."

"But I so want to know . . ."

"Know what?" Havers asked as she entered the room. At once, she saw the flowers and stopped in her tracks. She stared. She approached her desk as if a cobra were coiled upon it. She said, "What is this?" and looked round at them suspiciously. "Who's taking the mickey?"

Dorothea said, "They came only just now. Aren't they lovely? Oh, I do wish someone would send me flowers. It's *such* a romantic statement. Open the card, Barbara. There's a card. You *must* open it. I have a very good feeling about who sent them."

Havers looked at the card poking up from among a group of unidentifiable mop-like fiery orange flowers. She said, "Later."

"But you must open it. You *have* to open it. You won't open it now?"

"Won't. But you'll be the first to know who sent them once I read the card, which will happen later. Much later. Much, *much* later. Super much later."

"Oh pooh, you can't stand the suspense any more than I can, but I know when you're being pigheaded."

That said, she swiveled round on the drawing-pin-size heel of her right stiletto and left them. Havers looked at everyone remaining in the room and narrowed her eyes. "What'd you lot do, take up a collection?"

"For them?" Nkata was the one to speak. "Didn't happen, Barb. Whoever sent them, it was no one from here. 'F *I* send flowers, they go to my mum and no one else, not to offend."

"Hmph," was her answer. She grabbed the card and opened it. She flushed straight to the roots of her hair, something Lynley had never witnessed. Nor had anyone else, because utter silence fell upon them.

Quickly, she shoved the card into her shoulder bag. She seemed to take such care to hide it that her arm went inside the bag nearly up to her elbow. Her immediate delivery of information on the case told the tale of her not wanting to be questioned. Whether she was pleased or not, it was impossible to ascertain.

Her information was all about the missing sculpture and the conversation she'd had at the gallery in Peckham. After her explanation of the source and the revelation of the limited edition that it was part of, she went on to say that she'd "tried it for size as the cosh and you can tick that box straightaway, cos anyone with two hands could've used it: man, woman, child, or organ grinder's monkey. It's tall enough and hefty enough, and if it's not what bashed her, I'll eat these flowers cos there's no other reason for it to go missing. She took it with her when she left or she chucked it out of a window so she wouldn't be caught on CCTV. She either fetched it afterwards and made a wheelie bin its next owner or she's put it somewhere and we need to find out where."

"The DCs are looking at charity shops and consignment shops," Lynley reminded her.

"Wha' about the lock-up where Mercy Hart's got the clinic clobber stored?" Nkata said. "We need a warrant to get into it, but tha's not a problem."

"Damn thing could be anywhere," one of the DCs pointed out.

"Could be but isn't," Havers said sharply. "Look, we've got our suspects. You ask me, we check the boots of their cars, where their spare tyres are kept, the back of their clothes cupboards, under their beds, inside every box we come across. We know it's a woman, we know—"

"We know Ross Carver *claimed* it's a woman," Lynley reminded her. "It's only his word telling us what Teo Bontempi ostensibly said when he found her."

"You're not saying he's the one beat in her head, are you?" Havers said. "Guv, *he's* got no bloody reason to kill her, not one I can see. If you're looking for motives, seems to me Rosie has the best: she's in the family way and Ross is part of that family. Plus, Teo would've let her in the building straightaway, no questions asked. What did she have to fear from her own sister, 'specially since Teo hadn't told her what the surgery was for."

"Which is, as we know, according to Rosie," Lynley pointed out.

"So let's get back to what we can see with our eyes. We've seen the Streatham CCTV from the night she was attacked. We know there's a woman in dark clothes and a hoodie who was careful to be unidentifiable from the building's camera. We know she entered with a group that she was not a part of, and we know she didn't come out the way she went in. She doesn't live there or she would have identified herself—or been identified—when the photographs were taken round the building. I think that's where we start."

"But we've *been* there, sir," Havers said. "And everything you just said applies perfectly to Rosie."

"I think we're missing something," Lynley told her. "Our remit now is to uncover what the something is."

THE NARROW WAY
HACKNEY
NORTH-EAST LONDON

Lynley's part was to speak with Paul Phinney, whose car was among those seen on one of the CCTV cameras in Streatham High Road on the evening of the day that Ross Carver had gone to his estranged wife and found her collapsed on the floor. Paul was the older brother of Mark Phinney, so the box to tick off was who, exactly, was using the car that evening. That detail seemed the connection that wanted making, unless this was the investigation's first indication that Paul Phinney—as well as his brother—knew Teo Bontempi.

When Lynley reached Paul Phinney's place of employment, the pawnshop was locked. There was, however, a hand-lettered *Be Back Directly* sign posted in the window, so Lynley walked across to the McDonald's on The Narrow Way and purchased a coffee—so scaldingly hot that its scent was cleverly disguised by the amount of steam rising from the brew—which he took to one of the few tables inside the place. This allowed him to sit at the window, from which he could see the comings and goings at Phinney Pawn.

Directly did not, apparently, mean what it implied when it was used in the language of Paul Phinney, as Lynley discovered. His coffee had cooled enough to drink by the time the pawnshop showed a sign of life. This sign of life, however, wasn't the return of Paul Phinney. Rather the sign of life belonged to a woman, and she was leaving the shop, not returning to it.

Lynley could see that behind her, still in the shop itself, was a man, and the two of them shared a laugh and a quick kiss at the door. The woman went up The Narrow Way after that. Lynley watched her till she reached what looked like an old church tower. There she turned right and disappeared from view.

He tossed the remainder of his coffee into the bin and crossed over to Phinney Pawn. He entered and was struck by the strong scent of peach air freshener. He caught sight of Paul Phinney, who was employing it more liberally than one would have considered strictly necessary unless the rotting corpse of something had this morning been discovered in the storage room. It was from there that Phinney seemed to be laying a trail of the stuff into the shop.

When Lynley said his name, Phinney stopped his spraying, stood straight, hastily rearranged his hair, and said, "Sorry. Didn't hear you. Can I help?"

"I've been waiting for your return," Lynley told him. "Across the way at McDonald's." He took out his warrant card and presented it, adding, "I hope this is a convenient time."

Phinney gazed upon the card and said, "Sorry about the wait. My wife stopped by for a quick . . . conversation. About our son. I expect you know how these things can go. Families. Discussions. Matters can get bloody well heated, eh? Well, they tend to do with me and Eileen. Heated. You know."

The fact that he was explaining at all suggested to Lynley that whoever the woman was, she and Phinney had not been engaged in earnest conversation about anyone. But he wasn't here to deal with the ins and outs of the Phinney marriage. Instead, he said, "Your car was captured by CCTV camera on Streatham High Road as it drove by a block of flats across the way from a funeral director's. A police detective was attacked in her flat in the building. This was on July thirty-first. Can you tell me anything about that?"

"I don't know any police detective," Phinney said. "I mean, not a woman detective. What was the date you said?"

Lynley repeated it. Phinney frowned. He said, "We none of us have a reason to be in Streatham, far as I know. 'Course, my Eileen could be having it on with some bloke over there, but that's not likely. That was her leaving just now, like I said, and she and I . . . ? We keep each other fairly busy in that department, plus we've got four kids in the bargain. She's not got much free time. Hour here, half hour there. I don't see her driving to Streatham and I sure as bloody hell've never been there myself. I probably couldn't get there even with a road map. Or a GPS, for that matter."

"Someone else with access to your car?"

"My mum has a set of keys. She and Dad live across from us, they do. She knows she can take the car if she needs it, but even then, I can't think why she'd be going to Streatham. And she'd ask me or Eileen first anyway." He was quiet, frowning down at a glass display case holding a large collection of hand-painted enamel trinket boxes. He'd remembered something. Lynley could see it in the way he pressed his hand, fingers splayed, against the glass.

"Someone else, then," Lynley said. "It's only just come to you. I do need the information, Mr. Phinney. This is merely a clearing of the books." Which wasn't strictly true. But it *was* inclined to encourage admissions.

Phinney said, "My brother borrowed it, now I think of it. His wife—Pietra—had taken theirs to meet up with a mate of hers. He needed a car so he asked could he borrow mine and would I stay with Lily till he returned."

"On July thirty-first," Lynley clarified.

Paul Phinney shook his head. "I couldn't say exactly. I wasn't paying attention. It was a simple enough request."

"Was he gone long?"

"That I wouldn't know," Phinney said. "Pete got back before Mark, so I left. The car wasn't there when Eileen and I tucked up the kids and . . . well, did a little personal business in the bedroom. But it was back there in its usual spot in the morning."

"Did he tell you why he wanted to borrow it?"

Phinney shook his head slowly. "He may have done, but I've no memory of that. You'll have to have a chat with him."

Lynley's intention was to do that, at once.

He knew Paul Phinney would ring his brother the moment he himself was out of sight, however, giving the DCS time to prepare mentally for what was coming. There was no help for that aside from tying and gagging the man. It was also pointless to ask him not to notify his brother, for the fact that they *were* brothers made an enormous difference to how they cooperated with the coppers.

PEMBURY ESTATE
HACKNEY
NORTH-EAST LONDON

Tani knew what the real danger was, and this knowledge took him to Hackney. All three of the white people tried to talk him out of it, but he held up his mobile phone and reminded them that Joseph

Cotter had made certain that Tani had the number of his own mobile. Tani set it up so that it was ready to send a message to the man with one tap of his finger, and *if* he sent that message, it would mean he was in danger. Joseph Cotter would ring the police.

Tani said to them, "It's the passports. We *got* to get them. They got to go with the protection order. 'F we don't snatch them away from him, no one's safe."

"But *you're* not safe if you go back there," Deborah St. James had said. "At least let Dad go with you."

"That's a good idea, Tani," Deborah's husband said. He gestured to his leg. Tani had already seen the metal bar that went through the heel of his shoe. It was obviously connected to a leg brace of some kind that made him walk unevenly, and the poor bloke probably couldn't run at all. Simon went on with, "Obviously, I wouldn't be much help if you ran into your father again. But Joseph would be."

Simi watched them all from the lowest step on the stairs. They were in the entry of the house, and Tani had his hand on the doorknob. She said, "*Please* don't go, Tani. I'm scared something bad'll happen."

The three white people looked at him meaningfully. Tani turned to his sister and he felt himself weakening. But this one last action had to be taken. All of them knew it at one level or another, even Simi. If someone didn't put hands on the passports, their father's power over them would never end. Tani said to his sister but also for the benefit of the white people, "By the time I get there, he'll be in the market, Squeak. You know that. He lef' the shops alone yesterday, but no way he's doing that two days in a row."

"Oh, please, *please*." Simi clutched her hands prayerfully at her chest. From where Tani stood, he could see that her eyes were brimming.

"I *got* to, Squeak. An' I'll have my mobile. See?" He held it up for her. "I c'n get help easier 'n anything if I need it. But I'm not going to need it. He got what was due from me yesterday anyway. He won't try again."

Simi looked to the white people beseechingly. Joseph Cotter said, "Best idea's for me to fetch you there and back. You got to know that, lad."

He did and he didn't. He understood better than any of them that his mission could turn tits-up in a very bad way. But he also understood that having a white person with him was the perfect match to set fire to the box of tinder.

They finally reached a minor compromise. Deborah would drive Tani to the underground at Victoria Station. If he took the tube north from there, he would have to change only once for the overground rail to take him to Hackney Central. The trip would be quicker.

Aside from having to cope with the hordes at Victoria Station, the journey was easy and uneventful. Tani disembarked at Hackney Central. Up The Narrow Way a few minutes from the station and he was looking at Pembury Estate.

When he rang the buzzer for the flat, Lark's voice replied. He identified himself and there was a pause. Then the silence that bore no hollow sound within it, telling him she'd broken their connection. He rang again. She answered with, "Do I need to ring your dad or what?"

Which was exactly what he needed to know. Lark was alone, as he'd suspected she would be. Or her children were with her. But in either case, Abeo wasn't there.

He used the old trick, then. He pressed the buzzer for every flat but Lark's. Someone in one of them released the lock without question. People, he thought, never learned.

Lark opened the door when he knocked. She seemed resigned to his presence. She stepped back and let him enter.

She looked hugely pregnant, and he wondered at this. She hadn't seemed so pregnant when last they'd met. So Abeo's newest offspring was soon to make an appearance. He wondered what the kid's life would be like.

She said, "I've rung your father. You'll want to be gone when he gets here."

"What I'll want," he said, "is the passports. Hand them over and I'm out of here."

"What passports? Whose passports?" Lark pressed her fingers into the small of her back and grunted. She looked hot, tired, and dispirited.

"Mine, Simisola's and Mum's passports," Tani said. "They weren't at home and you and me know there's only one other place they'd be."

"Is that the case? Then the location should spring into my brain. But it hasn't and it's not going to." She walked into the kitchen where she opened the fridge's freezer, saying, "This *bloody* heat." She stared inside before she shifted things round, and in a moment she took out an icepack of the sort used by athletes after a workout or a sporting match of some kind. She put this on the back of her neck and walked to the dining table, where she sat. The table held crayons and a colouring book, opened to images from a Disney cartoon in which every hero was white and every heroine needed rescue. What shit, he thought.

He waited. He wasn't lit up by the idea of tossing Lark's flat to find the passports. He'd do it if he had to, but he took her at her word when it came to ringing his dad. And Abeo wasn't about to come on foot from Ridley Road Market, not with his plans hanging in the balance. He'd be here within minutes, and Tani wanted to be gone before then.

Lark moved the icepack from the back of her neck to her chest. She gave Tani a glance. She looked surly. She moved the icepack to the back of her neck again. As she did this, she directed her gaze to a thirsty-looking potted plant beneath the lounge window, and she held it there. Then it was the sofa that interested her, and she held her gaze there.

Tani knew she was trying to misdirect him. She was trying to buy time as well. The question was, Where did she not want him to look? The answer was in that moment of hesitation she'd displayed, the one in which she realised she'd unwittingly made the wrong decision and quickly had to cover it.

Tani went to the fridge. Lark's chair scraped the floor as she pushed back from the table. He thrust his arm into the freezer and began sweeping everything in it onto the lino. And there it was.

Along with frozen chips, three plastic trays of ice, two bags of veg, premade dinners, a package of crumpets, and two boxes of fish fingers, a small freezer bag of the sort used for sandwiches lay at his feet. Inside were the passports, their dark covers a contrast to the frost that had built up on the bag. They had probably been here for months, Tani thought. Perhaps for years.

He picked up the bag. Lark, on her feet now, said, "Leave them." And when his reply consisted of opening the bag and drawing from it all of the passports, she said, "I told you to leave them. *Leave* them."

He ignored her. He opened each to make sure whose they were. He tossed the plastic bag onto the floor into the freezer's detritus. She took a step towards him and then another, one hand raised.

He shoved the passports into the back pocket of his jeans. He said, "I don't fancy hitting you, but I will. You got that?"

"I don't care. Do it."

"Don't be stupid."

"*Do* it! He says that's what you're like. He's told me. You'd do anything to get what you want."

"That i'n't the case," Tani told her. "But you be wise and listen cos I *will* do this. You're not likely to win against me if you wan' to go at it. He's prob'ly told you I fight dirty 's well."

She made a grab for the passports, but he stepped back. She came towards him. He stepped to the side. She snatched at his arm and her nails dug in. He shook her off. She blocked his route out of the kitchen and began to scream: for help, for the police, for his father. She was being brutalised. Intruder! Intruder! Burglar! Rapist! Murderer! Thief!

The only way out of the flat was the way he'd come in and she was blocking him. He had to move her out of his way. She was rock solid and screaming bloody murder into his face. He did what he had to do. He shoved her to one side. She crashed to the floor.

He didn't stop to see how she landed or where she landed or if she needed help. He had to get out of there. That was what he did.

EMPRESS STATE BUILDING
WEST BROMPTON
SOUTH-WEST LONDON

His Met identification had been enough to get him through security and to the lifts this time round. When Lynley finally arrived from north London and rode up to the seventeenth floor, he found Mark Phinney seated at DS Jade Hopwood's desk. As Lynley entered, DS Hopwood was shaking her head and saying, "Look, if you want my opinion, guv . . ."

"I do," Phinney declared.

"Then here it is. No amount of enforced education is going to work for women if the men don't start speaking up. You ask me, they're the key, not the women. I'm talking about Nigerian men, not just Black blokes off the street. Until they begin stepping forward to declare they're willing, happy, and eager to marry a woman who *hasn't* been cut, there i'n't going to be a change."

"An entire paradigm shift," was Mark Phinney's response.

"Whatever you want to call it. And, if I can suggest . . . ?"

"Go ahead."

"You need *Black* officers to take the messaging and sermonising where they need to go because these white blokes you've got now? It's ludicrous, it is, to have them preaching *anything* about how Black men—Nigerian or not—need to start viewing Black women." The detective sergeant saw Lynley then and said, "I expect DCS Lynley'll take my side."

"It makes sense," Lynley said. "But I only heard the last minute of your conversation. I'm clueless about what went before." And then to Mark, "I need a word, if you will."

The DCS told DS Hopwood to carry on and took Lynley to his office. There, Lynley asked him about his brother's car. He was in luck when it came to this, he discovered. Because Phinney had been meeting with Jade Hopwood, he hadn't checked his phone. He did so at the mention of the car, however. But first he shut his office door.

"I did borrow it." Phinney moved behind his desk but he didn't sit. Instead, he went to the window, where the time of day allowed him to be backlit, his face made much more difficult to read. "I didn't see that I had a choice. I was afraid she intended to confront Teo again, and there wasn't a point to her doing that. It would upset her. It would upset Teo. I'd reassured Pete more than once. I'd said it was over, and it *was* over. I told her I would never leave her and Lilybet, and I wouldn't have done. How could I and still live with myself? So in my mind, there was nothing left to say. About Teo, I mean. About myself and Teo. I could repeat myself again and again into eternity, but what was the point?"

His office window was large and he leaned against its sill. Behind him the blue of the sky was washed by smog and bore a growing yellow hue, another declaration that London—indeed, the entire country—was desperate for rain.

Phinney said, "For a few years, she's been going out weekly to meet a friend of hers. It's the only thing she's willing to do, socially. She's called Greer, the friend. She was to be the midwife when Lilybet was born. That wasn't how things turned out, but she and Pete became quite close. Sometimes they have a two-person book discussion group, sometimes they go out for a drink or a meal or a film. This time, Pete said, they were meeting at a wine bar."

"The meeting didn't occur, I take it?"

"What occurred was a knock on the door and Greer on the front step. Coming along to say hello, she told me. She'd been in the area. First, I thought she'd mixed up their meeting place or p'rhaps Pete had. But it turns out they'd stopped meeting altogether. Pete had called a halt to it some three months ago. I wondered at this. Who wouldn't? It seemed to me that if she'd stopped meeting with Greer but was still going out weekly, there were only two other possibilities as to where she was and where she'd been on those nights when she'd gone out. She either had a lover or she was . . . I don't know . . . stalking Teo? Watching Teo? Waiting to see if I would turn up somehow?"

"That's rather a leap, isn't it?" Lynley asked.

"Why?"

"It seems you would have concluded there was someone else, a lover, before you jumped to the idea of her stalking Teo Bontempi."

"It just didn't seem likely to me: that she'd taken a lover. She gave no sign of that, and I reckoned there would have been signs. A new way with her hair? More makeup? Hasty phone calls? Messages on her phone? And she was so consumed—she *is* so consumed—with Lilybet. I couldn't see her having something on the side. But, on the other hand, she *knew* there was something between Teo and me, so I thought . . . Like I said, I didn't know. I thought she might have gone to Streatham. If she'd been doing something else—taking a class, perhaps? visiting the library? joining a choir? God knows what—why wouldn't she have told me? But she'd never once said a word other than she was having a night with Greer. So when she left me—Greer, I mean—I rang Paulie. He stayed with Lilybet and I used his motor. I went to see if Pete had gone to Teo another time."

"So Teo told you your wife had been there once before?"

"She had done, yes. But you know that, don't you. You've her photo from the CCTV film. You've known it was Pete since you saw her that morning."

Lynley didn't reply to that, merely saying, "Why didn't you just ring her mobile?"

"I did. But she'd turned it off, so I didn't have a clue. I still don't have a clue." Phinney turned to look at the view. For a moment, he spoke to it, rather than to Lynley. "While I was there, waiting in Paulie's car and thinking what to do next, Ross Carver turned up. I'd seen photos of him. I'd . . . I'd looked him up on social media and whatnot when Teo and I first became, you know, involved. He let himself into the building, and that was that."

"He had a key, then. Did you?"

"Never. Like I told you, I had to ring the concierge when I went there to see why she hadn't reported for her new assignment."

"How long did you stay there? Parked, I mean."

"Probably a quarter-hour. Bit less, p'rhaps. I waited to see if Pete would emerge. I couldn't think she'd want to stay there once Carver arrived."

"Did she emerge?"

"No. And as far as I could tell, she hadn't been there in the first place. By the time I got back home, she was in bed and Paulie was gone. Asleep or faking it, I don't know."

"Did you ask her where she'd been, on the following day?"

He looked down at his feet. He shook his head. "I reckoned Greer would tell her that she'd been rumbled and she'd come to me and . . . What do I call it? Confess? But she didn't. I suppose I don't really want to know where she was. And the fact is . . ." He looked up at Lynley. His face bore a look that suggested the pain he'd been carrying round for so long.

"The fact is . . . ?" Lynley prompted him.

"I never saw the car. I mean our car. It wasn't nearby and, believe me, I looked. I can't see her hiding it. Why would she have done? She wouldn't have known Greer blew the gaff. She wouldn't have known I'd show up in Streatham. She had no reason to hide the car, did she."

On the other hand, Lynley thought, she was a copper's wife. She'd know the game better than most. And there was another consideration as well. She could have gone to Streatham *and* left Streatham in the time that it had taken her husband to arrange borrowing his brother's car and driving to south London himself. He didn't point this out to the DCS, however. Phinney wasn't thick. He would have already worked this out.

"We're going to ask for her fingerprints, Mark," Lynley said. "DNA as well. If she did get into Teo's flat somehow, no matter what occurred between them that night, we'll need to eliminate her from the list of possible suspects."

Phinney nodded. His expression was bleak. "I'll let her know. But please understand. She wouldn't have hurt Teo. That's not who she is. That's not her way."

Lynley made no response to this. It was, after all, what most husbands would say.

BRIXTON
SOUTH LONDON

Monifa knew there was only one real choice. She could cook a thousand dinners for the Nkata family. She could add twenty Nigerian dishes to the menu at Alice N's Café; she could add fifty Nigerian dishes if she thought that might work. She could join Alice there as a cook or she could teach Alice and her assistant Tabby how to go about creating the Nigerian dishes themselves. But none of that was going to get her closer to Simisola and Tani.

Once Alice and Tabby had mastered the egg rice, Monifa joined Alice in the café's kitchen, where the cooker elevated the temperature so much that they draped wet hand towels over their heads and when the towels were dry, they dampened them again and each took another to wear around her neck. Throughout the day, Tabby worked behind the counter, taking customers' orders for takeaway food, serving customers' orders for eating in. There were plenty of both, and Monifa discovered that Alice as well as Tabby knew most of the clientele by name. Indeed, Tabby was able to order for most of them on her own, so regular were their habits. As cheerful Jamaican music played, conversation and laughter dominated the eating area.

The cleanup required two hours, delivering her back to Loughborough Estate just before six. Alice chose a different route to take them there from the one she'd used in the morning. Again, it served to confuse Monifa. She had no way of knowing exactly where they were once they made the first turn at the second corner beyond the café.

"Now you sit down and put your feet up, Monifa," Alice told her as they entered the family's flat. "I'm making us a pot of tea. Or p'rhaps you'd want a fizzy water?"

Tea, Monifa told her, would be very nice, thank you. She went on to ask Alice if there was any blank paper to be had in the flat. Alice thought there was a yellow pad inside the piano bench, from the long-ago days when Benj fancied himself a composer, she added. "There's prob'ly a pencil or biro 's well. But you say the word if there i'n't and I can get you one."

"I must write for the detective sergeant," she said.

"Mind you make it legible, then. Jewel's a stickler when it comes to penmanship. You ever see his, Monifa? No? He writes like it's going into some museum, he does. Watch your *q*'s, specially. Jewel can't abide *q*'s that look like *g*'s not able to make up their minds."

Monifa lifted the piano bench and found the yellow pad. A biro was attached to it by its own clip. The top page of the pad did indeed hold some bars of music.

She thought about what she needed to write. She wanted to consider how she might state what she knew without damaging anyone. If the clinic was indeed closed as the detective sergeant had told her it was, then the only worry she actually had was what her statement would do to Mercy Hart. She *could* lie about Mercy Hart. She could swear that Mercy Hart had nothing to do with any part of whatever went on in the clinic. She could write that, as far as she knew, Mercy Hart's job consisted of taking in down payments or full payments, making appointments for women and their daughters, and dealing with body temperatures and blood pressure. There would be no way for DS Nkata to have any other information. If he was trying to get it from her, it stood to reason that he hadn't got anything from Mercy herself. But would lying bring Tani and Simisola back to her? It didn't seem so.

When Alice came into the lounge with a teapot and cup, Monifa had not yet written a word. She was staring at the yellow pad as if it could remove her from the dilemma she faced. When Alice said, "Sugar and milk, Monifa?" Monifa didn't register that she was being asked a question. Alice went back to the kitchen and returned with a white jug in the shape of a cow as well as a bowl of sugar. Monifa felt her light touch on the shoulder. She looked up.

"My Jewel's a good man," she said. "Whatever he's said to you, I just want you to know you can trust him. I never knew him to lie about anything. Full stop. He doesn't have it in him."

When Alice returned to the kitchen and began removing items from the fridge for dinner, Monifa finally picked up the biro and put it to paper. She began the statement that Alice's son required of her.

She started with her name: Monifa Bankole. She started with the fact of discovery: conversation with a customer at the stall selling dried herbs and spices. She herself was seeking Cameroon pepper, dried bitter leaf, *yaji*, *ata Jos*. She'd been listening to a woman next to her complaining about the scarcity of uziza leaves when, from behind her, a woman's low voice said, "They do it different. There's someone knows how to do it clean and sterile."

Monifa glanced over her shoulder and saw two women having this low-voiced chat. She joined them, said her name, told them she had a daughter who was of age. The women had been reluctant to bring her into their circle till Talatu walked by and called out, "Tell that Simisola of yours that I'm still waiting for those head wraps, the special ones, she'll know what I mean. Hope I don't have to wait till next hols to get her back on board."

This had been sufficient. It tagged her with a school-age daughter. The two women drew her to one side and gave her the information she wanted.

That was, she wrote, how she came to know of the clinic in Kingsland High Street. She took Simisola there to arrange for her to be cut. That was how she came to know a woman called Easter Lange who was Mercy Hart. At this clinic, Mercy examined Simisola and told Monifa that her daughter was fit to have the procedure. She would be unconscious while it was done. Awakened later, she would remain for one night at the clinic to monitor her well-being. The procedure was expensive, yes. It required three hundred pounds just to reserve an appointment. But it was also guaranteed painless.

So, everything the police suspected about the clinic in Kingsland High Street was true. While she had not been an actual witness to any procedure, Mercy Hart—or Easter Lange, as she'd called herself—had understood why she was there with Simisola and why she'd brought along three hundred pounds.

Monifa signed her name. She added the date. She had to believe that Alice Nkata was right about her son. She had to hope that he was a man of his word.

STOKE NEWINGTON
NORTH-EAST LONDON

"Is someone out there, Tani? Who're you looking for?"

Tani flicked the sheer curtain back into place and turned to the bed. Sophie was sitting up, her back against the pillows and the headboard, her breasts sweetly balanced on the arm she held across her body. Beneath the sheet pulled up to her waist, she was starkers.

He'd known it was not a particularly good idea to come to Stoke Newington once he left Lark. Thus, he needed an excuse for not returning to Chelsea directly as he'd told everyone he would do. He used the passports as this excuse.

Sophie had been surprised to see him, but she was quickly on board when she saw the passports. She took a thin, sharpened knife and, up in her bedroom, cut her mattress along its seam at the foot of her bed. The cut she made was just slightly larger than the width of the passports. She slid them inside. She offered to sew the seam back together, but Tani sidetracked her. It was her bedroom that had done it, it was the mattress, it was the opportunity.

Upon his arrival, he'd told Sophie briefly where he'd been and what had happened.

"She *fell*? She's all right, isn't she?" and when Tani lied and said Lark was fine—because, after all, he did not know—she went on with, "Are you sure your father didn't follow you here?"

That was something Tani also didn't know, although he said that he was sure about everything. Once Abeo arrived at Lark's flat, Tani declared, his father would stay with her *because* she fell. No way would he leave till he'd rung the midwife or taken her to A and E to have her checked. His first priority would be Lark and their baby.

But, he'd explained, he needed to leave the passports with her, with Sophie. Because of Lark, his dad would now be searching for him. He reckoned it wasn't beyond belief that his dad would also ring the coppers to charge Tani with assaulting Lark. So he didn't want the passports to be anywhere near him. Could Sophie hide them where Abeo would never think to look even if he somehow managed to get inside the Franklins' house?

Sophie said, "But you said he didn't follow you."

"He knows the street, Soph. He named it last time I saw him."

She'd thought about it and decided upon the mattress in her bedroom. When she had it all seen to, though, Tani couldn't bring himself to leave her. With the bed just where it was, they put it to use and dozed afterwards. When he awakened, he saw that two full hours had passed.

Quickly, then, he'd swung out of bed and gone to the window to flick the sheer curtain to one side, to look at the street, to gaze at each house and each car and each potential place where his father might lurk. Abeo had had more than enough time to see to Lark's well-being and then to start the search for his son.

So when he turned from the window to answer Sophie, what he said was, "He's not out there." He began dressing. She did the same.

She followed him down the stairs to the door. He kissed her, his fingers dipping into her baby-soft hair. Then he eased the door open to check the street once again. He gave her a nod and set off on his way.

He dug his mobile from the pocket of his jeans as he walked towards the station. It was more than time to let his sister—not to mention the occupants of the big house in Chelsea—know that he was safe, fine, and on his way back.

When he looked at the mobile's screen, he saw that he had missed several texts and a phone call. He paused on his way to the Stoke

Newington rail station to see what was what. Two texts from Deborah St. James, one from her father, one from Zawadi at Orchid House. There was also a voice mail, so he listened to that as he resumed his walk to the station.

"You think you can do this to the woman I love? To the mother of my children? Now you are finished. I will find you, Tani. And whoever protects you will be sorry they ever gave you shelter or said so much as your name."

Tani listened to the message once again. The fact that his father had rung Tani's mobile did not surprise him. The fact that he'd threatened Tani's life surprised him even less. But that everyone who knew him faced real danger was something he had not foreseen. If his journey to Pembury Estate had begun with his search for the passports, it had ended with something else entirely.

CHALK FARM
NORTH LONDON

Of course, Barbara Havers thought, they only had it from Ross Carver that his estranged wife ever said "She hit me, Ross" when he found her on the floor in her flat. Or, more precisely stated, when he found her on the floor of what would now go back to being *his* flat. He *had* to be bloody well chuffed that he was leaving the malodorous environs of Hackney City Farm, not to mention the morning cacophony of the place, courtesy of its resident rooster. Still, Barbara couldn't bring her mind to the task of viewing him as a viable suspect. He'd gone round to Teo's flat at her invitation, hadn't he? Her mobile phone confirmed that she'd texted him. So what could have happened between them while he was there that might have prompted him to whack her with *Standing Warrior*? If—as Barbara suspected—he'd gone round at her request because he'd put her own sister up the spout, wasn't it more likely that Teo would have whacked *him*? After all, she was committing herself to surgery that might restore her to sensation, that might indeed have restored their marriage, restored them to each other, and now *this*. Her husband and her sister and baby makes three? All of them living some bizarre form of happily-ever-after together?

That did put Rosie Bontempi into the picture, though, didn't it? She'd been to see Teo relatively often, they'd had a loud and awful row heard by all of the neighbours shortly before Teo's death, she knew there was CCTV at the entry to Teo's building, so *if* she returned to whack her sister, she wasn't going to do the macarena in front of the building's security camera before she entered. Instead she was going to make herself unrecognisable when she entered, she was going to find a way to get into the building without alerting her sister, and she was going to leave by the fire door, which she bloody well would have known was there.

Still . . . What sort of person kills her own sister? And just like the situation with Ross, wasn't it more likely that Teo would have whacked *her*? Teo knew Ross better than anyone, didn't she? That being the case, she would have twigged at once that Ross would do his duty by Rosie. He might not marry her, true, just like the outcome of his doings with Colton's mother. But that baby Rosie was carrying would be a fact of his life and Rosie herself would be a fact of his life and if Teo hoped or planned or intended to resume her marriage to Ross post-surgery—always a big if, Barbara admitted to herself—that meant Rosie-as-Mum-and-Ross-as-Dad would forever be part of her life as well.

Yet, there were others who benefitted from Teo's death in one way or another, specifically DCS Mark Phinney and his wife, specifically Mercy Hart/Easter Lange if she had plans to set herself up with another clinic. But at their final meeting of the day, they were no closer to fingering anyone for the crime than they'd been that morning.

Lynley's appearance was brief. Judi-with-an-i had rung him with the usual message that she passed along at this time of the day. The assistant commissioner wanted a word with Acting DCS Lynley before he left. So after letting the team know what he'd learned from Paul Phinney and then from his brother, Mark—it *was* beginning to look as if everyone in London had been desperate to take a drive to Streatham that evening—Lynley left them. He'd said before setting off to speak with Hillier, "Carry on, for now, especially with the CCTV from Kingsland High Street. There's got to be something on it we're missing."

Since it *was* a high street and not a residential area or even a side street with a few shops on it, there was plenty of CCTV to view. Most shops had security cameras. Some had more than one security camera. The borough itself had security cameras, as did the Met. This was the reality of life in London, where people were documented going about their business hundreds of times each day.

Two hours of footage later and Barbara decided she had done her bit. She made a stop for a takeaway at a small Greek restaurant, where the chef stuffed two halves of pita bread with lamb, a few bits of lettuce, tomato for colour, and plenty of *tzatziki*. This came with either a side salad or an order of chips, and as far as Barbara was concerned, nothing said "your arteries are shot" better than an order of steaming, fresh chips, blisteringly hot from the oil, dashed with malt vinegar or, in a pinch, a Matterhorn of ketchup.

She carted all of this home. She carried the bag of food along the path at one side of the conversion behind which she lived. She noted, as she always did, that the ground-floor flat attached to the yellow house showed no sign of life, but she told herself as she always did that circumstances made it unlikely that the flat would be occupied anytime soon. More likely, it would be offered for sale or to let.

Once inside her garden shed of a cottage, she plopped her dinner onto the small table that served many uses in the kitchen, which itself also served many uses, especially when it came to her smalls that twice a week got washed in the sink. She returned to the Mini and pulled out the flowers she'd been sent. She felt a perfect fool parading them along the path to the cottage, but she knew that out of sight was out of mind. Dorothea wasn't about to stop wheedling for the name of the sender as long as the flowers were within her view, and Barbara's colleagues would love to take the piss for a few more days with the flowers as good a prompt for their humour as any.

Then there was the fact of the card and the question of how to respond. When someone wrote *We must meet again soon*, was that person extending an invitation or merely being polite? When Barbara thought about that—an invitation or an act of courtesy—it seemed to her that the former was probably the case. They had not met in three weeks and that meeting—at the far extreme, she *supposed* one could call it a date—had gone well, full of conversation and not a few laughs.

But she would eat first, before taking this any further, wouldn't she? Yes. She would.

She opened a bottle of Newcastle brown ale. Greek food and chips with ale to wash it down? Sounded perfect to her. She unpacked her food, delved for ketchup in the fridge, excavated for malt vinegar from a selection of what she liked to refer to as "rescue condiments" that she kept in a cupboard. Then she went at it. She had nothing to follow save a bag of boiled sweets. She'd bought them the previous Easter, thrown them in the freezer, and rewarded herself with two or three or ten of them on the nights she managed to have a healthy meal, *healthy* being a relative term, of course. This meal seemed to weigh in on the healthy side of the health-o-meter, so she allowed herself two. She unpeeled each from its cheerful foil wrapper and set it down in order to meditate upon the flowers.

Then she dug her mobile from her bag and spent two fags trying to come up with what she wanted to say. Finally, deciding that straightforward was always best, she found the number and tapped it.

The mobile rang four times with no one picking up. Then five times. She told herself she'd end the call at six—Why hadn't it already gone to message? she wondered—when she heard his voice.

"Lo Bianco," he said. "*Pronto.*" Then as if remembering where he was, "Sorry. Hello?"

"Salvatore?"

"Barbara! How nice! To me, it pleases . . . No. No. *Ho torto.* This is not correct. I am happy at your call."

"How's the English coming along?"

"I wish to have learned it when I had five years."

"When you were five years old? That would've been nice, eh? Well, you're doing better with English than I'd ever do with Italian, I can tell you that."

"To speak it—Italian—is best to live it . . . best to live *there.* It goes similar for most languages, I'm thinking. Unless one is a genius for language, like my Marco. His mother has a television with many, many . . . *canali* is the word in Italian."

"Channels?"

"Yes, yes. She has many channels; therefore Marco watches English. He likes the crime dramas."

"That'll give him an interesting vocabulary, eh?"

Lo Bianco laughed. "Also I should watch such programmes. Marco likes to teach English to me, what he learns from the programmes, this is. *Dodgy.* He likes this word. And 'the nick.' He tells to me, 'Papa, when you return to the nick?' I do not know what this means so he must explain. So now I can ask you. Barbara, how is all . . . no, not that. How is everything happening at this nick where you are?"

"We're up to our ears. A cop was murdered."

"I am sorry to know that. A friend of yours?"

"No, no. She worked for the Met but in a different part of town. We got the case *because* she's a cop, though. The AC—the assistant commissioner, I mean—isn't exactly chuffed when a copper is cracked on the head and ends up dead. So here we are."

"We are where?"

"Sorry. Just an expression. It doesn't mean anything, really."

"Ah. Yes. In Italian also we have this."

Then there was a little silence between them. He *had* seemed pleased to receive her call. She was doing her part, wasn't she, to encourage him? Or at least not to inadvertently *dis*courage him. She wondered what he was doing, as they spoke. She knew he had found a room not far from Dagenham East station, where his landlady in a B & B served him the full English every morning, but that was all she knew about his accommodation. She also knew that he boarded the train each day and spent that day attending his English classes as well as getting out and about in London. But that was it. She could picture him taking his meals alone, but then she wondered why he would be alone. He was an affable bloke. He wanted to learn. He would know he couldn't learn by maintaining himself in some kind of isolation. He was practising his language skills somewhere. Perhaps that was what he'd been doing when she rang him and at this very moment his impatient language partner was sitting across from him waiting to carry on as they had been doing moments before she'd rung him. And then there was the question of what *carrying on* actually might mean, no matter the language being practised.

She mentally slapped herself across the face. Bloody hell. Just thank the man, for God's sake.

She said, "Actually, I was ringing to thank you for the flowers. Dead unnecessary that, but thank you all the same. And to reply, more or less, to the note. I agree, Salvatore. We ought to meet. I could do dinner. Not here. I mean, a restaurant. Should I dig up a place? Not Italian, of course. I wouldn't do Italian. But Indian's easy if one likes curry. It's on me, by the way, as you paid last time."

His reply caught her entirely by surprise. "Flowers?"

"Late this morning was when they came. Brave of you to send them to the Yard and all that. They could've been munched by some X-ray machine going through security. Anyway, thanks. I've brought them home and they cheer the place up."

"Ah. Yes," he said.

"You've not seen my digs but, you c'n trust me, they're in bloody desperate need of cheering, they are."

"I am happy, then," he said. But he sounded off.

There seemed to Barbara only one reason for this. She said, "I've rung you at a bad time, right? There's someone with——"

"No, no. I am quite alone. I've had dinner nearby and am doing a walk." He cleared his throat. "It has done hot, this month? This was what I did not expect. I always thinked . . . no, thought, yes, *thought* the English have very bad weather. But this is similar to Lucca in summer."

"Without Lucca's atmosphere," she said.

"True," he said. "This is very true." And then, in a rather hesitant voice, "Barbara, to me it is pleasing to dine with you. But it would not be right if I let you——"

"No arguing, Salvatore. I am treating you."

"This means . . . ?"

"I'm paying and you're not arguing."

"Yes, I understand. But I must not——"

"Don't be bloody-minded about this. It's probably not the Italian way, but it's my way."

"It is the flowers," he said.

Which was when the penny dropped. Or perhaps, better said, it was when the anvil dropped. On her head. Barbara said, "Oh."

Salvatore's reply was gallant. "It would not be proper for me to take credit for such a gesture. You have another admirer who has sent you flowers."

She felt a bloody stupid fool. She wanted to sink straight through the floor and keep going till she hit the centre of the earth. She managed to say with a laugh, "Good Lord. Another? They're beginning to come out of the woodwork, they are."

He picked up on this as a gentleman would do. "You must take care, then. Soon you will be covered in flowers."

"Which'll wreak bloody havoc with my allergies."

They laughed together. Barbara kept up the pretence for another very long minute. For his part Salvatore seemed to do the same.

BRIXTON
SOUTH LONDON

When Winston Nkata arrived at Loughborough Estate, he sat in his car for some ten minutes, adjusting the seat to recline a bit, using the headrest, and closing his eyes. He was dead knackered. Who, he thought, would've predicted that watching footage from a plethora of CCTV cameras would have affected him in such a way that it seemed his head was splitting in two? In other circumstances, what he would do was swallow two paracetamol tablets and wait for relief and hope it would come quickly. In other circumstances, he would have retreated to his bedroom and sunk directly onto the mattress with his head embedded in the pillow. He might have joined his parents for dinner later. He might not have joined his parents at all. However, aside from being free to swallow as many tablets as he liked, he could do none of this. He had no bedroom at the moment, and having brought her to his parents' home, he couldn't avoid seeing to Monifa. All he had was these few minutes, and he would take advantage of them.

At least the efforts of his DCs and himself had not been entirely in vain. Although there was more footage to view, they'd managed to find Teo Bontempi—in African dress—on the pavement in Kingsland High Street. Indeed, they even had footage of the detective sergeant crossing the street to walk towards the clinic. It didn't look as if anything sinister were happening, though. Continued viewing of the CCTV footage from several other nearby shops had found Teo Bontempi ringing a buzzer next to the door to the building in which the clinic did its business. That might have been argued away as inconsequential—despite there being no businesses in the building aside from the clinic—but additional viewing of the footage in question showed the door opening and someone in the shadows giving the detective sergeant access to the place. It wasn't enough to tie Mercy Hart to Teo Bontempi, but it was at least a start.

When he could stand the idea of moving his body, Nkata opened his car door and unfolded his long legs. He set off in the direction of his parents' flat and was approaching it when his mobile rang. A glance told him the caller was Barb Havers. Her first words to him were, "I bloody well want to bloody well know if you're in on it." He could tell she was in a serious lather.

"Say wha', Barb?" he asked her.

"You know what I mean, Winston. Don't pretend you don't. Are you in on it? Simple question with a simple answer of *yes* or *no*."

"Must be *no* then cos I don't know what you're talking about."

"You swear? *Swear.* Swear that you don't." She sounded on the verge of tears. "I just made a *sodding* fool of myself. One of you or the whole lot of you set me up, and I want to know who."

He couldn't work anything out of what she was saying. He gave her the only response he could. "Swear, Barb. You all right, there?"

"Of course I'm not all right. Do I sound all right? I just rang Salvatore Lo Bianco. I could 's well have pulled down my knickers in public."

"Inspector Lo Bianco? I di'n't know he was still in London. I only met the bloke one time, Barb, at that tap-dancing event. You want to tell me wha's happenin?"

What she apparently wanted was to cut off their conversation, which she did. He was left saying her name several times, then punching her mobile number, then ringing her landline and leaving a message. He texted her *Ring if you want to talk more* and then he went to his parents' flat.

Inside, he heard their voices first: his mother's rhythmic pattern of speaking and Monifa's hesitant responses. He found them in the kitchen where the scents were of beef and chicken and three pots were covered both with foil and then with lids. His mother saw him first and said, "Monifa's done us *ewedu* soup, Jewel. And *Buka* stew. She's also made *fufu*. The *fufu* is cassava, but Monifa says it can be made from . . . what did you say, Monifa?"

"Many things," Monifa said. "Plantains, cassava, yams . . ."

"Can he look, Monifa?" Alice asked. "He won't have ever seen *fufu* before."

Monifa nodded and offered a smile. "Yes, yes," she said. She lifted the lid of one of the pots.

Nkata checked out its contents. The *fufu* turned out to be a cream-coloured loaf that wasn't bread, that wasn't potatoes, that wasn't anything but *fufu*. It was, Alice explained to him, used to dip into or to scoop up soup. No cutlery allowed, she informed him. And if you eat it the way Monifa says it's eaten, you don't chew the *fufu* but swallow it whole.

That sounded like their pudding was guaranteed to be the Heimlich manoeuvre. Monifa apparently read this from his expression and said, "No, no. You must chew if you have never eaten *fufu* before now."

Nkata was ready to try nearly anything that was presented to him—he had skipped lunch although he wasn't foolish enough to let Alice know it—so he went for the paracetamol, downed two, and rejoined his mother and their guest. His dad would eat when he arrived home from his late shift on the Number 11 bus.

He found that several sheets of paper from a yellow pad were folded lengthwise in half and tucked to one side of his plate. He sat and unfolded them. He quickly saw what they were.

She'd written the history of her dealings with Women's Health of Hackney. She identified the individual she had met there: Mercy Hart posing as Easter Lange. She explained why she had taken her daughter to this place. What she described was what was being called medicalised FGM in those countries where doctors had begun offering the procedure in a sterile setting. Still, what she described was illegal in the UK no matter how it was performed or by whom. Finally, then, the Met had what it needed to finish off Mercy Hart and seal her fate.

This brought them no closer to making an arrest in the investigation of Teo Bontempi's death. But it needed doing.

He looked up from reading it. He saw that Monifa was watching him. Her expression was earnest and he knew what she wanted: his assurance that she would be taken to her children or that her children would be brought to her.

"Is this . . ." Monifa gestured towards the papers he held as Alice brought the *fufu* and the stew to the table. "Do I write enough? For Simisola? For Tani?"

He said, "I 'spect you have done, but I got to clear it with my guv. This Mercy Hart? She's on the pitch for more 'n one investigation, see. What you wrote here . . . ? This hammers down the first and gets her hauled back to the nick and charged. But the other we're needing more time to wrestle to the ground, an' I can't do somethin' might jeopardise where we are."

"You will ring him, though? You will ask him tonight? You *can* ring him."

"Can an' will," he said. "Af'er I see what this *fufu* is like."

Alice had fetched the *ewedu* soup, which she began to dish up to each of them. Monifa presented him with his own small mound of *fufu*, placing it next to the other food while Alice added stew to his plate. She did the same for Monifa and then for herself and then joined Nkata at the table.

"You sure I c'n chew it?" Nkata asked Monifa. "I mean the *fufu*.

I'm thinkin' I can chew the stew. But the *fufu*? It's not some kind of taboo, is it? I mean chewing it b'fore I swallow."

Monifa assured him with, "It is not a taboo and as you've never encountered a swallow before, yes, yes, you must chew it as you will."

"This lady here, Jewel," his mother said as she broke off a portion of the *fufu* and used it as a scoop, "she cooks like a dream. I maintain she should offer lessons. You taste it an' try to tell me I'm wrong."

He did as she asked. Alice wasn't wrong. But even if she had been straight out of her mind when it came to the food, Nkata knew the wisdom of not saying so.

14 AUGUST

While Lynley understood the importance of the Press Office, and while he was on board with all attempts to manage how information was presented to the press—not to mention *which* information was presented to the press—he hated being part of the show. He knew his presence was considered a necessity, especially now he was standing in for DCS Ardery while she was on the Isle of Wight. In her place as the putative leader of any investigation under what would have been her purview, he was meant to have his fingers on every beating pulse, and it was expected that he'd be able to relay how many beats per minute each of those pulses was exhibiting. So on the previous day when he'd arrived for his afternoon colloquy with AC Hillier and Stephenson Deacon, head of the Press Office, he should have known what was coming. But with other things on his mind, he had not. Judi MacIntosh's direction—that he was to meet the assistant commisioner and chief press officer in a location that was *not* Hillier's office—didn't even get through to him. He was inside the large conference room and confronted by the sight of at least twenty journalists, three camera crews, and a dais on which Hillier and Deacon were seated behind a long table before he twigged that he'd been tricked.

"Ah yes. Here he is now. Detective Chief Superintendent Lynley will be able to amplify on all of this." Hillier made the proclamation with a meaningful affability that signalled an unspoken order for Lynley to cooperate. At his words, twenty other heads swung in his direction, along with cameras, and his every move was documented as he proceeded unsmiling to the dais.

In very short order he discovered the reason behind the hastily called news briefing. On the table in front of Hillier and Deacon lay the country's most scurrilous tabloid, *The Source*. It was apparently flame-fanning through the use of an enormous IS THIS WHY? headline, a photograph of Teo Bontempi that took up most of the front page, a subheading reading *Racial Bias = Lack of Progress*, and a paragraph beneath this, the subject of which was beyond doubt. The story made a jump to page three, where doubtless there were more photos and further stories. Racial divisions when it came to policing was a topic that *The Source* would be only too happy to exploit.

Lynley's reply to the first question had neither endeared him to anyone nor appeased anyone. "That's rubbish," was not what the reporters were seeking. And "Do you honestly *believe* the Met would drag its feet on the murder of one of its officers?" soothed no feathers whatsoever. Indeed, it opened the door to the policing of Black-on-white murders versus Black-on-Black murders. Did the DCS have any comment he wished to make about the scrutiny given to one and not to the other? And then followed the relative rates at which cases were closed, the relative rates at which the CPS took up the prosecution of offenders, the rates of conviction, and the rates of incarceration.

By the time the press briefing was over, Lynley's jaw was clenched so tightly that his ears had begun to pound. He said nothing till he,

Hillier, and Deacon were out of the room and on their own. Then it was, "If you *ever* do that to me again—"

Which Hillier cut off with a sharp, "You'd do well to remember who you're talking to."

To which Lynley concluded with, "—I'll walk off this job so quickly, your head will spin."

"Now see here," Stephenson Deacon began.

At which point, Lynley had walked away. But it had taken two doses of the Macallan and a deep immersion into Tchaikovsky before he'd felt capable of speaking to another soul. And even then, it was only Charlie Denton with whom he'd been willing or able to exchange words. Did he want wine with dinner? Denton wanted to know. It was *boeuf bourguignon*.

Yes, Lynley wanted wine. He probably could do with an entire bottle.

He'd managed to recover his equilibrium by morning. He was rather later than usual to New Scotland Yard, a very long hot shower followed by a very brief cold shower having eaten up a good bit of time, so everyone was assembled when he arrived. They'd divided into two groups. Nkata was talking to some of them while Havers was talking to the others.

His "Where are we?" brought them into order.

The first report concerned *Standing Warrior*. All consignment shops had now been contacted, and the bronze sculpture was not in any of them nor had it been in the weeks between Teo Bontempi's death and now. This proved true for all the charity shops as well. To this Barbara Havers added that all owners of the other twelve editions of the warrior were still in possession of them. It was only number 10 that remained missing, the sculpture that Ross Carver had given his estranged wife. That would be before the estranged bit, she added. She said all this in an unusual tone, Lynley thought. He looked at her curiously and caught her in the midst of what he could only receive as a hostile glare, directed at him.

"Is there something else?" he asked her.

"It can wait," she said shortly.

Nkata's group of DCs had been busy, both with CCTV footage and the location of the lock-up to which Women's Health of Hackney's contents had been taken. They also had made contact with the building's owner and uncovered the lease on the clinic. The name on the lease was Easter Lange. It turned out that Easter Lange had also signed for the storage unit. She'd paid in cash as well, for three months of storage. They would need a search warrant for Mercy Hart's lock-up, then, Lynley told them. If *Standing Warrior* had not been found in any of the shops, that was where it well might be, tucked into everything that had been removed from the clinic.

"Monifa Bankole's given us a statement, as well." Nkata handed a manila folder to Lynley. "She's fingered Mercy Hart, guv. She admits it was FGM she was there for."

Lynley took his spectacles from his jacket, opened the folder, and gave it a look. He read a bit of it and then flipped to the final page, where he saw her signature and the date. "We'll want her picked up again," he said. "Mercy Hart, that is. Arrange for that, Winston. If we can get her into a custody suite closer to town, that would be helpful. I expect her solicitor would appreciate that as well."

Nkata nodded and then said, "She's asking to see the kids, Monifa Bankole, guv."

"Arrange that, then. But the kids stay where they are for now. There's no telling where she'll disappear to if she's allowed to take them, and we're going to need her. The CPS is going to need her as well." To the rest of them, he said, "All eyes on the CCTV footage, then. We want anyone Teo as Adaku speaks to in Kingsland High Street. I daresay that footage remains the best route to her killer."

He left them to it and headed for his office.

WESTMINSTER
CENTRAL LONDON

Barbara followed him. She'd been shooting daggers at him from the second he'd walked into the meeting. She knew he'd seen them hurled in his direction. She knew he was aware that something was off with her. Now she was going to let him know exactly what it was.

He hadn't sat down at his desk before she was on him with, "I want a word with you. Now."

He set the manila folder with Monifa Bankole's statement on his desk. He said, "Something's happened."

"Oh, too right, that. Something's *bloody* well happened. I thought you would probably want to know how it all turned out."

Frowning, he gestured to one of the two chairs in front of the desk. He would, Barbara knew, never take a seat himself while she was standing. His sodding lordship was too *infinitely* well bred for that. If he sat, he'd be struck by lightning. A meteor would fly through the office window and obliterate him. The hand of God would pinch off his head. Not that she would mind that last one. Or, really, any of the others.

He said, "I'm not certain what you're talking about, Barbara."

"Bugger that for a lark. You're not only 'certain,' you're about to be chuffed straight out of your mind. And *that's* what you've been waiting for, isn't it?"

He said nothing. She wanted to pull out his eyeballs with her fingernails.

"Stupid me," she said. "I took it seriously. I actually thought . . . But we *both* know I've got bubbles for brains, eh? And you . . . You couldn't stay out of my life, could you? You couldn't stand to pass by a chance to play me for the complete fool that I am."

He cocked his head and Barbara saw his eyes go quite dark. His lips parted, he let out a breath upon which she thought she heard him say, "Good Christ."

So she said, "Yeah. That's it. Good Christ. And let me tell you, it worked *such* a trick it would've got him down off the Cross just to listen in. You understand that?"

"Listen in to what? Barbara, I'm—"

"I rang him, all right? I thanked him. I made a loon-job of myself and it's down to you that I did it. It's. Down. To. You. The note? Oh, *that* was a brilliant touch. And you knew just enough—didn't you—to use the right words."

He lowered his head. He put the tips of his fingers on his desk. He said, "You might want to close the door, Barbara, if we're going to have this conversation."

"Oh, we're bloody well having this conversation, In*spec*tor Lynley, and I don't care who hears what I've got to say. Because if you think from your high, mighty, and silver-spooned mouth you can *possibly* produce words to excuse yourself for invading other people's lives and playing puppet master to watch everyone—like me, like miserable little me—dance to your tune, you're—"

"Mixing your metaphors," he said.

"Shut up! I don't care! I'll mix my metaphors and be happy as the dickens to shove them straight up your—"

"Guv?"

Barbara swung round. Nkata stood there. "Leave us alone!" she shrieked. "If you're trying to make all of this go away, try something else. It's not going away. It's *never* going away. This isn't the first time but I swear to God it's going to be the last because—"

"Not that." Nkata held up his hands—palms towards her—to stop her words. "We finally got it on film," he said. And then to Lynley, "We got Mercy and Teo Bontempi on CCTV footage, guv. Not jus' once but twice. In Kingsland High Street. She's in African dress like before, Teo is, so there's no doubting it's Teo."

CHELSEA
CENTRAL LONDON

Sophie made good time to Chelsea. And unlike him, she didn't walk into the house with eyes the size of Frisbees. She probably knew baskets of people who lived in houses like this one, Tani reckoned. Her parents' lives were way far different to the lives of his own parents, different to *his* life as well, so when Mr. Cotter opened the door to her, what she said had to do with the dog who dashed out on the front step doing what she apparently always did: barking, sniffing, barking, and turning circles until Sophie finally took note of her.

"What's *your* name?" she asked Peach, quite as if the dog could answer her. "You rule the roost here, I expect."

"She does, that." Joseph Cotter was the one to answer. He'd not been willing to open the door until Simi had dashed above stairs and Tani ducked into the study, determined to stay out of sight. But Tani came out at once when he heard Sophie's voice.

She was extending her hand to Mr. Cotter, and she gave her name and identified herself as "Tani's friend Sophie Franklin."

Hearing her voice, Simi dashed down the stairs, crying out, "It's Sophie! Sophie!" as she ran to her and threw her arms round her waist.

Mr. Cotter said, "Best come in," as Tani reached her side and kissed her. Then he did that English white person thing, did Cotter. He offered tea.

So far the day was working out.

It had begun when he responded to the message from Zawadi, which he had largely forgotten in his haste to be back in Chelsea after his two hours with Sophie on the previous afternoon. When she answered and said brusquely, "I text you asking you to ring me, you ring me straightaway. We clear?"

"Sorry. I got caught up—"

"Well, don't *get* caught up."

"Sorry."

"I got a place for both of you. Just happened this morning. It's not why I'm ringing you, but we'll get to that. There's a family in Lewisham happy to have you and Simisola. Bit crowded, this place, but you'd be safe. And you'd be in a normal situation."

Tani knew that what she meant by "normal" was changing their placement to one in the home of a Black family. He considered this. These people in this house . . . ? He knew they meant well. He also knew they were committed to protecting both Simisola and him. They were do-gooders, the lot of them—especially Deborah—but at least they were putting themselves . . . well, *out* there. More than that, Simi was enjoying herself: a dog, a cat, a garden to run round in, Bunny Ears if a Super Soft van happened to be in the area. Things could be a bloody sight worse.

He said, "We're good. Prob'ly best thing is for us to stay where we are. This lot here? They're decent enough."

"What's that mean? 'Decent enough'? They're not treating you right?"

"I mean they're okay. They're nice, for white people."

"If that changes even one degree, I want to know. You ring me." When he said that he would do, she went on. "I've got the urgent order," she told him. "The protection order."

He was definitely not expecting this bit of news, all things considered. He said, "Did Mum—"

"Didn't need her. We filled it out here at Orchid House and took it to the authorities."

"But I thought her part of the application was the important bit."

"Still is. They'll want her story soon 's we can get it. For now, I used the photos of your face after your dad beat on you. That did the job of illustrating the sort of bloke he is."

"Are you . . . You're not takin' it to him, are you? The protection order? That's bats, innit."

She wasn't, she told him. "Like I said before, th' order goes to the coppers now, the station nearest where you live. Someone there will take it soon 's it's in hand. It'll be delivered to your dad personally and he'll be told to hand over the passports."

"Passports were never there. But I found 'em." He related the story to her.

Her reaction was to tell him that—Sophie or not—she still needed those passports. Only once they were in the hands of the police and thus inaccessible to Abeo would Simisola be safe.

So he'd rung Sophie and she'd come to Chelsea as soon as she was able. She took the passports out of her shoulder bag and was handing them over to Tani when Deborah St. James joined them in the entry.

Simi cried, "Look who's here, Deborah! Sophie's here! Your dad's making tea!"

"I see her," Deborah said to the little girl. She saw the passports. She said to Tani with a nod at the passports, "You'll want to ring Zawadi now they're here, yes? The police will want them?"

That was the case indeed, but Tani wasn't sure he wanted to hand them over. Now they were in his possession, he knew that he could keep them safe, which meant he could keep Simisola safe. He didn't fully trust anyone else to do that.

They were rejoined by Cotter, who also spied the passports. He said, "Tea in the kitchen or in the garden?"

"I want Sophie to see the garden!" Simi cried. "Is Alaska in the garden? Is Peach?"

"Can't say about that cat," Cotter told her, "but you know Peach by now, eh? Once she smells a teacake, she'll be underfoot quick as quick can be. You want to show Sophie the way?"

Simi grabbed her hand. Tani wanted to do the same, but Cotter spoke to him next, saying, "D'you want me to have those?" with reference to the passports. "I got places in this house no one's *ever* looking. Tear it down brick by brick, and they still wouldn't find 'em. I promise to hand them over soon 's you ask for them."

This seemed like the best idea, Tani thought. Until he or Zawadi could get the passports to the police, Joseph Cotter's hiding them sounded to him like the safest way to go. None of them would know where they were. Which meant, naturally, that none of them would or could tell anyone else.

BETHNAL GREEN
EAST LONDON

Mercy Hart had been taken to a custody suite in Bethnal Green, certainly closer than the station nearest to her home but inconvenient nonetheless. There, she'd been placed under arrest. There, she'd been waiting in a cell pending the arrival of her solicitor as well as the detectives on their way from Central London to interview her. She'd been in the hands of the police for more than three hours by the time everyone was assembled.

In Lynley's experience, only career criminals or repeat offenders were unbothered by the quite particular sound of a cell door slamming shut upon them. As Mercy Hart was neither of these, she'd become a bundle of nerves by the time Lynley and Havers entered the interview room where she and her solicitor were waiting.

She had a great deal to be nervous about. The first bit of CCTV footage that Lynley and Havers viewed had come from Taste of Tennessee's security camera. Teo Bontempi in the native dress of Adaku Obiaka had passed directly beneath this camera in close conversation with Mercy Hart. Mercy had been the one talking, Teo Bontempi listening intently with her hand through Mercy Hart's arm. They might have been two friends having a chat as they strolled along had the woman in native garb only been someone else. That she was a detective on a team bent upon eliminating FGM in London and beyond gave the conversation a different colour than it might otherwise have had.

The second bit of footage was more damning still. It had come from one of the Met's surveillance cameras in the high street, this one perched on the edge of Rio Cinema's roof, with its wide-angle lens taking in the street for a good thirty yards in either direction. The CCTV was state of the art, so the picture was clear. It also could be enlarged. So Mercy Hart was quite identifiable when she opened the ground-floor door and admitted Teo Bontempi into the building where the clinic was located.

Mercy had been charged with lying to the police, practicing medicine without a licence, and performing female genital mutilation. She was now teetering on the edge of being charged with homicide as well. To Astolat Abbott's demand for evidence, Lynley assured her that evidence regarding FGM was well in hand in the form of a full statement made by a woman who'd arranged to have her daughter cut at the Kingsland High Street clinic. This procedure would be performed by one Easter Lange, an identity adopted by Mercy Hart, who was the niece of the owner of that name. This same "Easter Lange" had placed her signature upon the lease for the clinic, as well as upon the paperwork attached to hiring a lock-up in a storage facility where the clinic's contents had been taken after the local police had raided it. A picture of Mercy Hart was being taken to the storage facility, and the lessor of the lock-up would be looking at her photograph as well. As far as performing FGM went, Ms. Abbott's client was finished and soon to be imprisoned.

"Do you have any comment you'd like to make?" Lynley asked Mercy.

Mercy looked at her solicitor. Astolat Abbott communicated with her digitally, in the true sense: she raised the fingers of her left hand slightly and then lowered them.

Mercy looked back at Lynley and said, "I do what I'm told."

"What's that meant to tell us?" Havers asked.

"It tells you that you're wasting your time with my client," Astolat Abbott said. "Whatever you think has gone on in that clinic, it has nothing to do with her. She was only employed there to book clients and to pass out paperwork for them to complete."

"That doesn't quite explain her conversations with Adaku Obiaka," Lynley noted.

"I told you," Mercy said sharply. "I don't know that person. I've never met that person."

"So that's not you on Taste of Tennessee's CCTV footage?" Havers asked. "You and Adaku having a natter while you shimmy down the street together?"

"You admitted her into the clinic," Lynley added. "The Met's CCTV has a very good record of that."

"I didn't," she said. "None of that. Nothing."

"How do you explain the films, then?" Havers asked.

"These things . . . ? Everyone knows they can be altered. If you have a laptop, you can do that."

"Got it," Havers said. "Any clue why Taste of Tennessee would be interested in altering their video?"

"The films would've been altered after," Mercy said.

"After what, exactly?"

"Once you got your hands on the films, then they would have been altered."

"Ah. Got it. Like the Met's tech people—with nothing else to do aside from gazing at their smartphones, mind you—would have set everything aside to tinker about till they were able to put Teo Bontempi's head—that's Adaku to you—on the body of a woman wearing ethnic garb just like hers, which, by the way, was hanging in her clothes cupboard. So who was it, then, all kitted out like Adaku?"

"I would have to see the film."

Havers blew out a breath.

Lynley observed the woman. She licked her lips. He could see her swallow. She reached for a plastic cup on the table between them, began to lift it, but set it down quickly. Her hands, Lynley saw, weren't steady enough that she'd want them to be noted.

He said to her, "What is it you're afraid of? Or should I ask *who* are you afraid of?"

"I never hurt anyone," was her reply. "No FGM, no murder, nothing. Nothing like that. Nothing. If someone wrote and accused me of whatever it is, what they wrote is a lie. That's all I'm saying." And to her solicitor, "I want to leave now."

"You've been charged," Havers said. "You can leave like you want, but where you'll go when you do leave is straight into remand. That would be up in Bronzefield Prison, that would. So how do you reckon your Keisha's gonna do, playing mummy to the little ones?"

"I have no comment," Mercy said.

"I'd like a word with my client." This from Ms. Abbott.

Lynley rose, switching off the recorder that was documenting their interview. He said they would wait in the corridor, and he opened the door for Havers to precede him out of the room.

Once the door was closed behind them, Havers said to him, "She's playing for time. She's holding together, but you ask me, she knows she's at the end of her rope when it comes to FGM."

"Possibly. But I daresay her solicitor will be telling her the signed statement we've got merely constitutes someone's word against her own. We could study the films and find Monifa Bankole on CCTV entering the clinic with her daughter to support her written statement, but when it comes to what occurred inside, we'd be down to what a jury will believe. And we can't set aside the fact that Monifa might yet decide it's in her best interest to back away from what she wrote, claiming her statement was coerced. Her children are missing and, as far as she's concerned, we're the people who know where they are and are keeping the information from her."

"Forget FGM, then. What about Teo's getting the clinic closed down? She's got motive in spades, Mercy Hart."

"She does. But that's the beginning and end of what we have on her, Barbara. If she says nothing, we're down to CCTV film of Mercy and Adaku talking. You and I know that amounts to very little unless we put her at the crime scene or find the murder weapon with her DNA on it."

The door to the interview room opened then. Astolat Abbott stepped into the corridor. Mercy Hart, the solicitor informed them politely, had taken her decision, so there would be no need for further conversation at this time. She was ready to be remanded to Bronzefield Prison.

CHELSEA
CENTRAL LONDON

Their destination was a leafy canyon of a neighbourhood, its north-west side occupied by tall brick houses, all attached to each other, all fronted by shining iron railings to prevent passersby from tumbling into the area in front of their basement windows. Its south-east side was less distinguished looking and indifferent to a uniform appearance, with its mishmash of construction materials and building styles. Both sides were lined with dusty-leafed trees, though. Where there were window boxes, nearly all contained flowers, many of which were drooping in the heat.

Monifa couldn't imagine herself in this place, let alone her children.

When she got out of the car, it was into utter silence save for the twittering of birds and someone coughing beyond the open window of the house in front of which DS Nkata had parked his car. Monifa said to him, "What is this place?" and when he told her it was called Chelsea, she'd never heard of it other than as the name of a football team. And that was only something she knew because of Tani's devotion to Tottenham.

The sergeant led her to one of the tall brick houses, this one on a street corner. There were window boxes here, planted with red geraniums on all three sides of the ground floor bay, and there were four steps up to a sheltered porch. A tall umbrella stand stood to one side of the door, the curving handles of its contents attesting to the fact that the house's occupants didn't expect these to be snatched up by a thief strolling along the pavement.

When the detective sergeant used the brass door-knocker, no one answered. He frowned at this and Monifa felt her heart begin to pound in her temples. She didn't entertain the thought of Abeo discovering their children here—they might as well have been on the moon—but the fact that they appeared to be elsewhere made her palms sweaty and her upper lip damp.

After another application of door knocker to door did nothing, nor did ringing the bell, the detective sergeant told her to follow him, which she did. Round the corner and just along the street perpendicular to the one that the front door faced, they found a gate. Beyond this a dog was barking and a child was crying out happily, "You mustn't give her a treat 'nless she brings it back, Sophie."

Simisola. Monifa grabbed the gate's handle and shoved upon it. It opened and there they were: Simisola, Tani, and a shapely Black girl with a display of flesh only made possible by her immodest clothing: blue jeans cut off near the top of her thighs and a cotton shirt without sleeves, possessing a neckline that displayed the pronounced curve of her breasts.

A long-haired sausage dog was running back and forth from the girl, Sophie, to Simisola. Watching this from deck chairs were Tani and a white lady with masses of flaming hair.

She was the one who espied Monifa and the detective sergeant, and it was instantly clear that DS Nkata was known to her. She got to her feet and said, "Winston! Hullo."

"Brought a visitor," he said.

The two girls looked over their shoulders, whereupon Simisola dropped the ball she was holding and ran to Monifa, shouting, "Mummy! Mummy!"

Monifa held out her arms. The sweet weight of her daughter's body pressed into hers. She extended her hand to Tani, and he came to her. He was still bruised from the beating his father had given him. She put her hand on his cheek and his handsome face blurred in her vision.

"I'm Deborah St. James," the white lady said. She added with a smile, "Something tells me you're Mrs. Bankole."

Monifa could only nod as she absorbed what she felt, having her two children with her again.

The sole person who said nothing was the immodest girl. And she—this girl—looked at Tani. She was expecting something and Tani was not loath to give it apparently because he said to Monifa, "Mum, this is Sophie, my girlfriend. She's been helping us. Me and Simi."

The kind of help the girl was giving Tani was all too simple for Monifa to work out. She glanced at her son but made no mention of what Sophie's clothing suggested about the probable consequences of Tani's continuing to have anything to do with her. There would be time for that later.

For her part, Sophie came to join their little group. Monifa wanted to push her away, but she knew the wisdom of saying only, "I give you thanks."

"I'm that happy to help," Sophie said, and she added, "I'm glad to help all of you."

"Sophie's special," Simisola said. "She took pictures of Tani after what happened so we could get a . . ." She screwed up her face in confusion and said, "Tani, what'd we get?"

"An urgent protection order, Squeak," Tani told her. He then said to Monifa, "So your name doesn't have to be on it, Mum. If anyone takes a fall from this, it'll be me and I'll make sure he knows it."

Monifa didn't want this. Tani had been through too much already. Simi had been through too much as well. She—Monifa—was meant to take the steps necessary to send her children somehow into a future that was bright with promise.

"Where're you staying, Mummy?" Simi asked her. "Have you come to stay here?"

"I am with Sergeant Nkata's family," Monifa answered.

"Can't you be with us? Deborah's ever so nice. Oh, and this is Peach, Mummy. Tani's been teaching her how to fetch. And I think Alaska's in that tree. Least, that's where he *was*. Alaska's a cat. *Can* you stay, Mummy?"

Deborah St. James said, "You're very welcome to stay, Mrs. Bankole."

"Oh please, Mummy. Please." Simi clasped her hands together beneath her chin.

The detective sergeant interposed. "Not jus' now, Simisola. She's teaching my own mum how to do Nigerian food, she is. We need to keep her for a bit."

"But that'll take for*ever*," Simisola said in protest.

"My mum learns real fast," he said affably.

"And in the meantime . . ." Deborah said. "I've something to give your mum, Simi. D'you want to fetch it? D'you remember where it is?"

Simi gave a little gasp, loosed her grip on her mother, then clamped her hand over her mouth. Monifa could see she was stifling a smile. She couldn't, however, quite stifle her giggle.

"Oh yes!" she cried. "Sh'll I . . . now?"

"Please," Deborah said. "We'll wait right here."

Simi trotted off in the direction of the stairs. She hopped down them and the basement's door banged shut behind her as she entered. Deborah said to Monifa, "I've made something for—"

Which was when it happened. The gate swung open with a bang against the garden wall. An inarticulate cry cut into the neighbourhood's stillness. It came from the man who charged across the lawn in their direction. Abeo had found them.

"Where is she?" he roared. He grabbed Monifa. He punched her fiercely in the temple. He dragged her in the direction of the gate. "Where's Simisola?" he shouted. "Where've you taken Simisola?"

All of it happened in a matter of seconds. DS Nkata sprang into action. Three steps and he'd overtaken Abeo. He said quite clearly, "We're not havin' that, man," and Monifa felt Abeo release his hold on her. Deborah and Sophie raced to her side. Tani was advancing on his father. But Nkata still had Abeo in a grip round the neck and he kept it there till Abeo sank to the ground.

Nkata fished in his pocket and brought out keys, which he passed to Tani, saying, "Red Fiesta. Jus' up by the church. Glove box'll have plastic cuffs inside."

As Tani dashed out of the garden, DS Nkata brought out his mobile and punched in three numbers. Nine-nine-nine, Monifa thought. But *he* was the police, so—

"Mummy? Mummy!"

Simisola was back, a manila envelope dangling from her fingers. Abeo could not be allowed to see her, but Simisola saw him and she stopped in her tracks. Sophie was the one to take quick action. She raced to Simisola, scooped her up, and carried her down the stairs and into the house as DS Nkata identified himself into his phone and said, "Got a bloke with me just assaulted a woman . . . Can you . . . Yeah. Got it," and he recited the address of the house.

Abeo stirred. He opened his eyes. He began to rise. The detective was too quick for him, though. He grabbed both of Abeo's arms and had them behind him before Abeo had got to his knees.

"Inside the house," the detective said to Monifa. He began to haul Abeo towards the garden gate. By the time he'd reached it, Tani was back. The last Monifa saw of them, Tani was helping put the plastic handcuffs round his father's wrists.

CHELSEA
SOUTH-WEST LONDON

Deborah found Sophie and Simisola huddled next to the basement door when she and Monifa went inside. They'd not made it even into the kitchen. Simi was weeping as she clung to Sophie's arm and Sophie herself looked like someone who'd managed to walk away unscathed from an accident fatal to everyone else.

Monifa grabbed her daughter, saying, "It's over, Simi. He will not hurt you. He will not take you."

Sophie covered her mouth with her hand. Deborah saw the girl's gaze move towards the door to the garden and said to Monifa, "Is Tani all right?"

"He did not touch Tani. Tani helped Sergeant Nkata. The police are coming. We are . . . all of us. We are safe."

Sophie's voice broke as she said. "I was so careful . . . How *could* he have . . . He must have followed me. But I never saw him. I didn't think. I'm so sorry, so *sorry*. He wanted the passports, didn't he. He must have known. Why didn't he just snatch them from me?"

"He wanted Simisola," Monifa said. "The passports, of course. But they are useless to him without Simisola."

The door opened and Tani entered. He said, "He's in the front. The detective . . . Sergeant Nkata's got him. They're waiting for the police."

Monifa said, "But *he* is the police. Why can he not . . . ?"

"He said it's safer for a patrol cop to do it," Tani said. "But I think he doesn't want to leave us."

They were indeed alone in the house, or at least as alone as five people could be, Deborah thought. Simon wasn't there and neither was her father. And although there *were* five of them should something more happen at this point, they'd all just had their nerves shattered by Abeo's sudden appearance in the garden and by his attack upon Monifa. She was grateful that Winston had taken the decision to stay with them.

Still, she excused herself for a moment and rang Simon, merely to have the comfort of his voice. He'd left them that morning for a meeting to do with the family's business in Southampton. His intention had been to spend two nights in order to see his brothers and their families as well as his mother.

"I'll come home straightaway," he told her now, as soon as she told him what had happened. "Where's your father?"

"No, no," Deborah said. "No need to come back. We're fine now, Simon. Dad's not here. I think he's doing the shop for dinner. But Winston's with us—he's just outside waiting for the police to come for Simi's father—and if we're not safe with Winston, we're not safe with anyone. I . . . it's childish. I just wanted to hear your voice." She added after a brief pause, "I do love you, Simon." It seemed silly but at the same time necessary to tell him so.

They both knew the underlying truth of the matter although neither of them would ever speak it. Had he been with them, there was very little he could have done to stop a man like Abeo Bankole—in a rage that gave him enormous strength.

He said, "And I you, always. Will you ring your father? I'll be easier about what's happened if I know he's with you."

She promised she would do, and they rang off after promising to speak later. She heard Nkata's deep voice from the kitchen, then, and he sounded so calm, so reassuring, that everything felt as it had been before Abeo's sudden arrival.

He was saying, ". . . busy for a bit of time, that will. Good I was here, though."

"He's gone?" Deborah said as she rejoined them. They were gathered round the central chopping table.

"He'll be 'xplaining himself at Belgravia Station for a bit, he will."

"He followed me here," Sophie said. "Tani, I'm so sorry. I thought I was careful. I *tried* to be careful. I—"

Tani went to her, put his arm round her waist, kissed the side of her head. He said, "He worked out I took the passports to you. It's my fault, not yours. If I'd kept them once I had 'em off Lark . . . It was an excuse to see you. And even when Zawadi texted me, I could've told her to fetch them from you."

"Tha's what this 's 'bout?" Nkata said. "Beyond ever'thing else this is also about?"

"There's a protection order now," Deborah told him. "When it's served on Tani's father, he must hand over the passports so he can't take Simi out of the country."

"Best give them to me, then," Nkata said. "I'll see they go where they're meant to go and meantime—even if Belgravia doesn't hold him for twenty-four—he's not coming to Brixton to fetch 'em, I 'xpect." He added with a quick smile, "Even I wouldn't want to tangle with my mum."

Deborah agreed with Nkata's plan. It made much more sense that he would have the passports. She said she would ring her dad to learn where he'd hidden them.

This was a process that took very little time since Deborah didn't tell her father anything other than Winston Nkata being with them and asking for the passports in order to give a protection order against Abeo Bankole its full weight.

"Fixed up Alaska a nice place to do his business," Joseph Cotter replied.

Deborah said, "You've put them in the garden?" to which he said with a chuckle, "Didn't use the garden when he was a kitten, did he? Check under the sink in the old scullery, Deb."

She did so. Admittedly, it was—as her father had told her—an excellent place to hide something. The old litter box had been unearthed from wherever her father had stored it and, ever economical, he'd apparently kept fresh litter as well. He'd even added two patches of water so it appeared that the box had been recently used.

Deborah dug through all this and at the bottom beneath the litter, she found the passports, well wrapped individually in cling film and put together inside a plastic freezer bag. She removed them from the bag, washed her hands of the dust, and took the passports to Winston.

"Good hiding place like he tol' us?" Tani asked.

"Oh yes," Deborah said. "Only a very brave heart would have found them. I'd no idea my father was so ingenious."

Nkata put the passports into the inner pocket of his jacket. He also fished out one of his cards and handed it to Tani. If Tani would ring the woman with the protection order and tell her the coppers—in the person of Nkata—now had the passports . . . ?

Tani promised to do so.

THE MOTHERS SQUARE
LOWER CLAPTON
NORTH-EAST LONDON

Their conversation was overdue. He had been avoiding it despite his mother's direction to ask Pete if he wanted to know why she had pawned some of Floss's Art Deco jewellery. So when he arrived in

Lower Clapton—earlier than usual for once, and wasn't that a blessing—he took a moment to gather his thoughts. He forced those thoughts to remain on a single topic. Why had his wife wanted or needed money?

Greer had said that Pete had called off their weekly girl encounters some time ago. Yet she was going somewhere and doing something once each week. After Teo's death, his own guilt in the matter of their affair had led him to assume Pete had merely been waiting for the perfect moment to put a plan into action that would rid her life of the worry that her husband might leave her for another woman. But there were other reasons—and certainly more likely ones—that Pete was engaging in a secret activity.

It wasn't probable that she was hiding an addiction from him: heroin, cocaine, methamphetamine, one of the pain medications that were as addictive as they were deadly. The mental picture of his wife lolling about on a mattress in a den of addicts or making clandestine drug purchases under a railway arch was as inconceivable as it was laughable. Besides, even *if* she was using something, Robertson would have picked up on it, wouldn't he? Unless, of course, she'd been using something for so long that how she was when she was using looked perfectly normal to the male nurse. That certainly ruled out heroin and the various pain medications that could render users virtually immobile. And meth would have long begun to exact its price as well.

An affair didn't seem likely, considering Pietra's fears. But then, that would be an affair with a man, wouldn't it? An affair with a woman seemed much more possible. But it would have to be a woman completely unknown to him, because as far as he knew, the only woman his wife saw was Greer, who was either very good at demonstrating confusion or not at all involved in whatever Pietra was up to.

Gambling? he asked himself. Could she have taken up gambling in one of the many forms it took in London? He couldn't picture her in a William Hill or one of London's casinos, so his thoughts took him to bingo. But . . . bingo? Of course, there were people who played it religiously, but again he had a difficult time visualising Pete lining up twenty bingo cards, hot upon winning. She *could* be purchasing lottery tickets, of course, but why would that take her out at night?

No, he had to go back to the idea of Pete meeting someone. It was someone she hadn't wished to speak about to him, so aside from an affair, that left what?

At the edge of what he wanted to think about was that Teo had died. Pete had discovered the woman with whom her husband had fallen in love, and she'd traced her to where she lived. There, she'd spoken to her. While he wanted to believe that was the end of the story, the money received for his mother's jewellery made another claim. What was to prevent Pete from hiring someone to do what had been done to Teo?

But that, too, seemed absurd. He was going to have to speak with her and both of them were going to have to be truthful.

He'd arrived at The Mothers Square earlier than usual. DS Hopwood had been engaged in speaking with five DCs of colour—two of them women—about her design for working with and upon the attitudes of Nigerian and Somali immigrant men instead of confining their efforts to women. As Mark left, he'd seen all of them gathered in the conference room, and the detective sergeant was using a Power-Point projection.

When he put his key in the lock of the door, he could hear music coming from within. He recognised it as part of the recording of a children's book about polar bears that Lilybet was fond of listening to. Each chapter was broken by cheerful music and song.

Inside, he went to the sitting room. There, Pete and Robertson had Lilybet up on her feet "dancing." This consisted of both of the adults holding her upright and swaying to the beat of the music as they sang along with it. Lilybet was smiling. She emitted the gurgle that was her laugh. It was blisteringly hot in the room, however, and Mark watched the three of them: the adults sweaty, rings of perspiration on their shirts; Lilybet scantily clad in diaper and overlarge T-shirt.

Robertson saw him first and gave a nod in his direction. Pete then looked his way and said, "Here's Daddy! Here's Daddy!" to urge Lilybet to look at her father. But the story had begun again, and Robertson lowered Lilybet to her chair while Pete came to his side, saying, "You're so early. I'd no idea. I've not even popped out for the makings for dinner."

"I'll fetch us takeaway," he told her. "But before that, I need a word, Pete."

He set off to their bedroom. He didn't look back to make sure she was following. He reckoned she would follow due to the tenor of his voice, and he was not wrong. When she was in their bedroom with him, he shut the door.

He said to her, "Mum's decided to keep your secret. At least, that's how I interpret what she's said to me."

Pete looked so confused by this that he knew his mother had not phoned her in advance to give her time to cook up a story. "Sorry?" she said.

"The Art Deco jewellery Mum gave to you. You know my dad gave it her over the years, only when he could afford to set a piece aside instead of putting it on display when its time ran out. You know that, right?"

"I didn't ask your mum for it, Mark. She wanted me to take it."

"But she didn't need the money it would bring. You did."

She faced him squarely but didn't look at him directly. She spoke to whatever she could see beyond his shoulder: most probably the curtains. "I wasn't going to use it. But your mum said I must. She said if nothing else I must at least try. She said it wasn't fair as things were, not to Lilybet, not to me, but most of all not to you. She asked me how long I expected our lives to go along the way they were going along. She said everything's a matter of time, even this. Especially this."

Mark could see how miserable this little speech made her. But he couldn't tell if the misery rose from guilt or simply from being caught out. He said to her, "I'm in the dark, Pete. I'd rather not be. When I found the claim ticket in your bag, I didn't know what to think. But I did know we own nothing worth pawning. If I hadn't seen the one piece of jewellery in the shop window, I still wouldn't know what was going on. And as it is, I know half only. Or perhaps two thirds. Mum gave you the jewellery and that silver calling card tray in order to pawn them. You pawned them, but the money wasn't for her."

She rubbed her hands down the front of her jeans. She pushed her dark hair away from her face and behind her ears. She finally said, "It's therapy."

"Therapy?" In the way of a mind hopping quickly from one idea to another, he went first to physical therapy and he thought she intended it for Lilybet, save for the fact that when Pete was gone from home, Lilybet wasn't. Then it was physical therapy for herself because she wouldn't want him to know if she'd hurt herself lifting their daughter's dead weight. And that certainly made sense since Pete was forever lifting Lilybet instead of waiting for him or Robertson to help her.

"Yes," she said. "I would have tried for a meeting during the day, but she had none. She had only the evening, so that's what I took and that's where I've been when I said I was with Greer. I made the appointment at the same time and on the same day as I'd meet with Greer. I told her—Greer—that I couldn't manage meeting her for a while, at least not in the evening and not while you were so busy. She doesn't know where I've been, though. You mustn't think she ever did."

This wasn't getting them closer to the truth, though. He pressed her with, "The police know you've been to Streatham. You're on CCTV where Teo lived. She came to the door to speak with you. At some point you're going to have to tell the truth. I'd be that grateful, Pete, if you'd start with me."

She was silent. She lowered her head and seemed to be studying the tops of her white trainers. Finally, she said, "I know I told you that I wouldn't be bothered by it, by what you did because of how I am. But I found that wasn't the truth."

"You must mean with my finding someone for sex, that you wouldn't be bothered by that."

She nodded. Still she didn't look at him. She said, "At first I wasn't. How could I be? That wouldn't have been either right or fair. And how could I be angry and how could I blame you when I'd *told* you to take care of yourself. I just didn't think, ever, that . . . Then there she was and I knew everything was different and it would stay different unless I did something."

"About Teo?" His throat was tight. It was difficult for him to manage the words. The music resumed in the sitting room. The audiobook, it seemed, had very brief chapters. He was suddenly afraid that she might walk out, leaving him once again in the dark so that she could see to Lilybet, but she didn't move.

Instead she said, "About me, not Teo. This therapist, Mark. It's . . . She's the kind of therapist who takes people with problems . . . with issues. Like mine. Your mum found her."

"My *mum*?"

"She knew. She knows. You must have said something at some point and I don't blame you for that. Because that's what sent your mum on a"—she looked up and gave a small, sad smile—"a mission, I think. She gave me the name and the number and she said not to worry because she would pay and if I could ever return the money, that was fine, and if I could never return the money, that was also fine.

So I rang for an appointment but she—the therapist?—only sees people whose problem isn't physical. I mean, it doesn't have a physical cause. If there's a physical cause, she won't take the patient. So one sees a GP first and if there's nothing physically wrong, one is referred. It's not on NHS, though. Your mum knew that. Well, it wouldn't be, would it."

He put together everything she'd said since they'd first begun talking. That his mother knew, that his mother wanted to help make it more understandable. He said, "Pete, are you seeing someone about sex?"

She dropped her head again. But having done so, she also nodded. She was fingering the seam on her jeans, working a thread loose, pinching and tugging it. She looked small and sad and tired, like someone who'd been carrying a burden alone, unwilling to ask for help. He felt what he hadn't expected to feel as the outcome of this conversation. He felt his heart open, and something of himself flowed towards her. He couldn't identify what it was, exactly. Love? Empathy? Sadness? Loss? He only knew she'd been by herself in the dark, while he'd been too consumed not only by need but also by a hundred and one unspoken feelings, the existence of which he'd long denied.

He said to her, "Pete, you *never* had to—"

"I know that." She looked up then. "But I just didn't want to be that person any longer. I wanted to stop being so afraid all the time. It's eaten me up inside till there's almost nothing left of the me who was me, the woman you loved. It's felt like a slow disappearing, and I was just so *tired*—"

He crossed to her. He touched her hair. "Loved and still love, Pete," he said. When she didn't move away, he put his arms round her and drew her to him.

She rested her head against his chest. "I'm trying to find the way back to you," she told him.

"Ah, girl," he said in return. "Good God, Pete, what courage you have." He pressed his lips to the top of her head. "Let's find our way back to each other, Pete. Let's discover together if we can do that."

WESTMINSTER
CENTRAL LONDON

All the way back to New Scotland Yard from Bethnal Green, they talked about the case: the ins, the outs, the ups, the downs, the evidence, the lack thereof, the suspects, the motives, and the question of access. During all this, Barbara waited. She wanted to see if Lynley was going to bring up the subject that needed to be brought up between them. She wanted to know if she was the one who was going to have to broach it. She was about to do so as he pulled into his parking bay, and said, "Hang on, Barbara, if you don't mind."

She was desperate for a fag, but she remained in the car. She glanced in his direction and saw that he was watching her, tapping his fingers against the steering wheel of the Healey Elliott. He seemed to be thinking so she let him think.

He finally said, "I want to explain the flowers."

"No. You want to excuse," she replied.

"I want to tell you the reason."

"There's a difference?"

"Of course there's a difference. I have no excuse for doing it. An excuse would be 'I meant them to be sent to my mother for her birthday, but somehow they came here by mistake.'"

"With my name on them. Oh bloody yeah, I see how that could've happened."

"I'm just using my mother's birthday as an example, Barbara. I think you know that."

"And *was* it her birthday?"

"No. Of course not. But that's hardly the point."

"What is the point, then, when it's home with its mother?"

"Dorothea's the point."

Barbara frowned at him. He had an expression on his face that indicated she was supposed to be following some kind of impeccable logic that he was laying before her.

He went on with, "We talked about it, you and I. You mentioned Charlie temporarily playing the role of your suitor so that Dorothea—"

"My 'suitor'? We're not living inside a Jane Austen novel last time I looked, Inspector."

"A gentleman caller. Your lover. Your boyfriend. Why does *boyfriend* sound so strange? A new prospect destined to alter your life? We talked about Charlie taking up that role—I mean *playing* the role—so Dorothea would give you up as a project. Is any of this sounding familiar, Barbara?"

Barbara sighed. She picked up her bag and rooted out her fags and a plastic lighter. She saw his expression, and said, "I'm not bloody stupid."

"Thank you," he said. "Dorothea came to me and I could see that she wasn't about to let anything go when it comes to your love life. So do you see . . . ?"

"You had someone write the note. That was cruel. That was bloody hardhearted. What was I supposed to think once I read it?"

He moved in his seat so that he was facing her more directly. He said, "That was merely to make it authentic but—"

"What a rotten thing to do."

"Hear me out," he said. "You were meant to arrive in advance of the flowers. I intended to take you aside and tell you to expect them and to expect the card. But they arrived first. Dorothea brought them to your desk. Then there you were and so was she and I wasn't able . . . Christ. What a dog's dinner I've made of it."

"Too right, that," Barbara said.

"And then you opened the card, and I saw your expression. At that point, I felt that I couldn't tell you. Not then, at least. I should have, of course. There is no excuse. I have no excuse. But I want you to know that it wasn't meant to . . . *I* didn't mean to . . . It was all in the cause of . . ."

Barbara realised that, in the years she'd known him, she'd never seen Lynley in such a state and she'd never once heard him say anything that was less than well thought out and completely articulate. "Is that all, then?" she said to him.

"No. Of course that's not all. I want to apologise. I want to admit how utterly stupid I was. Not only did I not think it through, I also didn't pause to consider the effect the flowers and the card would have on you. I hurt you when I wanted to help you. It just seemed, at the time, the only way to derail Dorothea from her chosen path."

"You're mixing your metaphors," she pointed out.

He thought for a moment before saying, "Yes. I am."

"That's somewhat reassuring, Inspector. An imperfection here and there? It always goes miles in making someone look a bit more human. Mistakes do the same."

"At this point, I daresay you have a catalogue of my imperfections and another catalogue of my mistakes."

"I could say the same."

"You could do, yes." He looked away from her for a moment, at the grey expanse of wall that served the underground car park. "But imperfections and mistakes are only part of the whole, aren't they. And it's the whole we connect with although, to be frank, it would be easier if we could pick and choose and build relationships only from the parts we like." Then he put his frank brown-eyed gaze upon her again. "I'm humbled and contrite," he told her. "Truly I am. I ask you to forgive me."

Barbara thought about this. She thought about the damage he'd done. She came to the conclusion that the damage was to her pride alone, and like all the blows to her pride in the past, she'd get over this one if she chose to do so.

"Right," she said. "Okay. I forgive you. Go in peace. Sin no more." She opened the car door then and lit up her fag as she was getting out. She'd not lit up since before they'd set off for Bethnal Green. She took four deep and altogether blessed hits of the cigarette.

Lynley, out of the car as well, said, "You've got to give that up, Barbara. It's going to kill you if you don't."

"Can't," she said.

"Whyever not? I was able."

"It's not that," she said, going for hit number five.

"What is it, then?"

"I don't want to lose any of my imperfections."

He laughed. Together they headed for the lift, Lynley careful to stay out of the contrail she was creating. She dropped the fag, crushed it out with the toe of her high-top trainer, picked up the dog end, and stowed it in her bag. Lynley's phone dinged. He took it from his jacket pocket. He read the message and said, "We're wanted."

"Oh God, not Hillier," Barbara said.

"It's Winston. One of the DCs just texted him. She's found a bit of CCTV footage. She wants us to take a look at it."

"Has Winston seen it?"

"He's on his way."

"Where is he, then?"

"Coming from Brixton."

The lift arrived in silence and its doors slid open. Soon enough they were back with the team, and the DC in question—name tag identifying her as June Taylor—was waiting for them. Winston had sent her a message as well, so she was ready with the footage. She said, "It might be nothing at all, but DS Bontempi—in her African clothes—is in it so I reckoned you might want to see it."

"We do," Lynley said. "What's the location?"

"More of Kingsland High Street. It comes from the day the clinic was raided. She must have been watching from somewhere nearby."

"Close to the clinic?"

"Some number of buildings away, from what I can tell. On the High Street but not terribly close to the clinic."

"And you're certain . . . ?"

"Certain that it's DS Bontempi? Oh yes. I'm totally certain, sir."

The footage was high quality, identifying itself as having come from one of the Met's security cameras. DC Taylor had stopped it and refocused it on two figures in a conversation. They spoke for two minutes and forty-three seconds, DC Taylor said. This particular still shot of their talking was fifty-two seconds into it.

DS Bontempi, operating as Adaku Obiaka, was unmistakable not only by her clothing and her headgear but also by her height and stature. She was caught in the act of speaking to the other figure in the footage, another woman. She was dressed in black, she was much smaller than the detective sergeant, and she was white.

Barbara leaned into the screen as did Lynley. Lynley asked DC Taylor to move the footage slowly forward, which she was able to do. A woman with a toddler in a pushchair glided by, as did three men dressed for a building site. Teo Bontempi and her companion moved out of their way, and in doing so the companion's face was captured perfectly by the CCTV camera.

Barbara drew a breath and said, "Bloody hell in a bun."

"Do you recognise her?" Lynley asked.

"That's Philippa Weatherall," she said.

15 AUGUST

The plan for the day was, as before, that Monifa would go with Alice to the café. There were several recipes that interested Detective Sergeant Nkata's mother, and she believed they would be popular with those of her customers who were African born. She had the ingredients for at least four snack dishes. They could, she told Monifa, begin with *alkaki*. She revealed that in anticipation of this, late the previous afternoon while Monifa was visiting her children, she had prepared the wheat and the yeast, and the mixture had sat—covered—for the required ten hours. She happily continued, saying that she also wanted to learn how to make *donkwa*. She'd read about its popularity as a street food, and since Alice N's offered takeaway food, she believed this too would be something that would sell quite well.

Monifa had no doubts about Alice's enthusiasm. Indeed, she could almost picture herself joining Alice N's as a permanent part of the establishment. Alice had, after all, suggested cooking lessons as a way for Monifa to establish a new life for herself and her children. But Alice was of a different culture, so things that seemed simple and logical to her were neither simple nor logical for a woman like Monifa.

Still, Monifa agreed to the plan. There was little else she could do at this juncture. She was in a waiting mode and had no power to change that. She did say, however, "These are so simple, *alkaki* and *donkwa*. You do not need me to guide you, Alice."

"But I *want* you to guide me," Alice responded. "Tabby and her mum will watch as well. We'll sell them from the market stall at first and if they can be made at home—"

"They can. They are so very simple."

"—then Tabby's mum can have them ready when she opens the stall in the mornings. Jewel, is it safe for Monifa to be at the café today?"

"Long 's Abeo's being held, yeah." He was just coming out of the bedroom Monifa was using, where he'd excused himself from their breakfast to dress for the day since Benjamin Nkata was working an extra shift in less than an hour and had taken up occupancy of the bathroom. "But charges need to be filed to keep him there, innit." The detective sergeant gave Monifa a meaningful look. He said to her, "We need to talk that over, you 'n' me."

Monifa had known this would be coming. She was the only person Abeo had touched at the St. Jameses' house. Even if she made a report, though, she had no idea if Abeo would be charged for what he'd done to her, his wife. Since his assault of her had ended within seconds, was there truly anything sufficient to keep him out of her way and away from Tani and Simisola? And if she did agree to make a report against her husband, what would he do in return? And who would suffer afterwards?

She nodded, though, and kept her thoughts to herself. She said, "Yes. I understand."

Nkata smiled and nodded in turn, then said, "Tha's good. Now, have you shown Mum those pictures of your kids? I 'spect she'd like to see 'em, specially Simisola," and to his mother, "Deborah St. James—you recall her, yes?—she did three pictures that Monifa's got. I want to see 'em 's well."

Monifa reckoned he'd made the request simply to get her out of earshot so that he could speak quietly to his mother. She wasn't wrong. For as she was fetching the manila envelope of photos she heard the murmur of their voices and she caught the sound of the name Zawadi, so she knew they were talking about the protection order as well as the passports. She reckoned, then, that Zawadi had made her phone call to Sergeant Nkata, just as he'd spoken about to Tani on the previous afternoon.

She returned to them with the manila envelope, and she drew from it the three pictures she'd been given. She handed them to Alice, saying, "They are my life's true blessings."

Handsome and *so sweet* were the words Alice used. She passed the photos one by one to her son, who also admired them, saying, "That Simisola . . . She's something special."

"This is so true," Monifa said. "Everyone who meets her sees this."

Nkata was gazing upon the final photo his mother had handed him. He cocked his head as he examined it, but his features became puzzled and his smile faded. He looked up and said to Monifa, "Did she say where these pictures got took?"

"I did not ask," Monifa replied. "Should I have asked? Is something wrong?"

He drew his eyebrows together, but he said, "No. Nothin's wrong. Tha's not it. But c'n I take this? Just this one and I'll bring it back to you soon's I can?"

She nodded. She handed him the manila envelope to protect the picture when it was in transit, wherever he was taking it.

His mother said, "There's something important in the picture, Jewel?"

"Maybe something, maybe nothing," he told her. "But either way, I got to check it out."

EEL PIE ISLAND
TWICKENHAM
GREATER LONDON

They arrived quite early in Twickenham and parked directly across the river from Eel Pie Island. An arched footbridge led them to a glassed-in noticeboard at its end, standing at a point where two paved footpaths met. On the noticeboard was pinned a map of the island's cottages, with the name and the location of each noted. Unfortunately, Mahonia Cottage wasn't listed.

"Damn and blast," was Lynley's reaction to this.

Barbara's was, "I dunno, guv. How hard can it be? We just need to find the cottage with no name on it, right?"

"Presupposing there's only one without a name on it, which I doubt."

They quickly walked the shorter path, which shot off to the right, with cottages strung along the water. All save one of them showed a name, and the nameless one had its windows boarded and a broken-down ramp leading to its door. These suggested there had been no habitant for quite some time, so they returned to the noticeboard and set off along the longer path that curved and disappeared beneath the poplars and willows creating pools of shadow.

They hadn't got far along when they encountered a cyclist walking his bicycle in the direction of the footbridge. When they asked him if he knew which of the cottages on the island was Mahonia, his response was an unhelpful, "They have names?"

"This one belongs to Philippa Weatherall," Barbara said.

"Oh! Pips!" He used his thumb to gesture over his back, in the direction from which he'd come. "It's along the way. It's got a blue roof. You'll see it on the right."

They thanked him and began to set off, pausing when he said, "But she's not there. She's on the river. I came off . . . p'rhaps ten minutes ago? She was heading towards the boathouse, but it takes a bit of time to replace everything, so she's probably still there." He turned now, using his arm to point in the direction he'd just indicated with his thumb. He said, "Go along and you'll see it on the left. Can't miss it. It's the only one on the island."

That said, he mounted his bicycle and went on his way, leaving them to sort out which of the buildings they came across served as a boathouse. But it turned out that his description was accurate. They couldn't miss it, especially since it bore a sign that identified it as the island's rowing club. Unfortunately, it was also fenced and gated, and the gate bore a lock of the sort that demanded a code. There was nothing for it but to leave and track the surgeon down later in the day or to wait for her to come out of the gate. They chose waiting.

The twenty minutes before the gate opened seemed much longer. And then, it was a young man who came through it.

"'S Dr. Weatherall still on the river?" Barbara asked him.

"Philippa?"

"We need to speak with her," Lynley said.

"She's sorting her gear. Should be finished up in—"

Lynley showed him his warrant card. "We need a word now," he clarified.

The young man's eyes widened. He held the gate open for them. "Hope no one's in trouble," he said as the gate swung shut behind them.

When they found her, Dr. Weatherall was replacing the scull she'd been using. She was wearing black: a neoprene one-piece with reflective stripes following the seams. She whirled round when Lynley said her name. "Good Lord, you startled me," was her greeting. And then to Havers, "Another meeting? I've nothing else to offer, I'm afraid."

"It's not for me," Barbara told her. "This is my guv, DCS Lynley."

Dr. Weatherall looked from Barbara to Lynley and back again to Barbara. "Why at this time of day?" she asked.

"Early birds and worms . . . ?" Barbara said with a shrug. "You're something of an early bird yourself."

"I am. But I don't show up to speak with people at ungodly hours, as it happens."

Lynley said, "We'd like to ask you a few questions."

"And we reckoned you'd be more comfortable answering them at home than at the clinic," Barbara told her.

Dr. Weatherall shoved the scull's oars onto a metal bar with a line of others. They clipped nicely into a vacant holder. "I can only spare a few minutes," she said. Her tone was brusque. She glanced at her watch. "I've a patient at half past eight."

"A few minutes is all we need," Barbara said affably. "Are you finished up here or can we help you?"

"I'm finished. I do need to shower before I head to work, though. So if you intend to take more than five or ten minutes, we'll need to schedule this for another time."

"Ten minutes should be adequate," Lynley told her. He extended his hand to indicate the way they had entered, adding, "If you will."

The surgeon seemed to Barbara more like someone to whom *if you won't* applied, but she cooperated. They walked in silence back along the path to her cottage, where a cat was crouched in anticipation of breakfast, near one empty bowl and another filled with water.

"Looks like you're expected," Barbara said in note of him.

"Oh, yes," Dr. Weatherall said. "He knows a soft touch when he encounters one, that cat." She let them inside the cottage, where she flipped on overhead lights. She handed a bag of dried cat food to Barbara, saying, "If you'll give him some, we can get going on the purpose of your visit here. I'm having a coffee. Either of you . . . ?"

Lynley demurred. Barbara said coffee sounded like the very thing.

The surgeon set about the job with an electric kettle and a coffee press. Barbara poured food into the cat's bowl on the front step and returned inside. Lynley was looking at a group of framed pictures that sat on a shelving unit along with a flat-screen television. They were older photos, Barbara saw when she joined him, and most of them looked as if they'd come from Dr. Weatherall's childhood. They generally depicted a family in various happy locations at different seasons of the year. Although there were half a score of childhood pictures, the adolescent Philippa Weatherall was in only one of them, skeletally thin with cadaverous cheekbones and eyes so sunken they might have been marks made by a felt-tip pen. Anorexia, Barbara thought. Considering how she looked in the photo, she was lucky she was still alive.

"It took ten years of my life." The surgeon was still in the kitchen, but the cottage was quite small and she could easily see what they were studying. "It's why my mum died young."

Barbara said, "How's that?" as Lynley replaced the picture.

"Ovarian cancer. She ignored the signs because she was taking care of me. I was in and out of hospital for a decade, and I think she blamed herself. No reason, but she couldn't see that." She was quiet a moment before she cleared her throat and went on with, "I've found mothers take on blame whether there's cause or not."

"That's certainly been my experience," Lynley said. The surgeon glanced in his direction as if to gauge his sincerity.

The kettle clicked off. She saw to the coffee, asked Barbara if she wanted milk and sugar, and then joined them. She handed a mug to Barbara, and with her own, she indicated a photo of two men in formal dress—perhaps ten years her junior—with their arms slung round each other. She said, "My brother and his partner. Well, his husband now. And this"—she gestured with her mug to a shot of a beret-wearing soldier—"is their older son Elek."

"Unusual name," Lynley noted.

"Greek, like one of his fathers. It means 'defender of mankind.' It was apt. He died in Afghanistan."

"I'm sorry to hear that," Lynley said.

"Yes. Well," Dr. Weatherall replied. "Please do sit. There's no reason for us to stand for this conversation, is there?"

She went to a modern-looking armchair: two cushions and slim arms and legs of chrome. Lynley and Barbara took the sofa, which was nearly buried in brightly coloured decorative pillows. Barbara brought out her notebook and pencil. The surgeon saw this but said nothing.

Lynley said, "We'd like to learn about your relationship to the women's clinic in Kingsland High Street."

"Women's Health of Hackney? It's been closed," the surgeon said. "So I have no current relationship to it."

"But you did have."

"Yes, indeed. I volunteered there when I was free."

"You volunteered as a surgeon?"

"No. Your sergeant has probably told you already that I perform my surgeries in a clinic on the Isle of Dogs. In Kingsland High Street, I did exams, mostly screening for cancers: breast, uterine, and ovarian. I did some counselling as well, about birth control, prenatal care, postpartum issues, and the like. Why?"

"Couldn't women get all that from their GP?" Barbara asked her. "Or from their midwives?"

"They could do, yes. But some of these women are here illegally. Others—too many others, in fact—have male GPs and no wish to be examined intimately by a man. These things cause difficulties, and I try to ease those where I can."

"None of that seems to apply to Teo Bontempi," Lynley said.

Dr. Weatherall frowned. "Sorry? What does Teo Bontempi have to do with my volunteering at the clinic?"

Barbara told her. "She's the reason the place was raided. Only . . . I think you know that. We both think you know that."

Dr. Weatherall looked from one of them to the other before she said, "How on earth would I know that? She'd come to see me on the Isle of Dogs, but—"

"She confronted you in Kingsland High Street, the very day the place was raided, within thirty minutes of the raid, in fact. It's on film, by the way. CCTV. You're speaking to her."

"Is that why you've come to see me at this hour? Because I spoke to her in Kingsland High Street? But why on earth wouldn't I speak to her? I knew her. She'd come to see me about reconstructive surgery. I did tell you about this, Sergeant Havers."

"That's one way to interpret what we saw on the film," Lynley said. "Two acquaintances happen to come across each other in a part of town entirely unrelated to where they'd met."

"Is there another way to interpret it?" the surgeon asked. "If, as you say, you have our encounter on film, I daresay you can tell from my expression that I was astonished to see her. At first I didn't know who she was, by the way. She was dressed ethnically, but when she and I met on the Isle of Dogs, she'd worn . . . what would I call it? Ordinary clothing? British clothing? Western clothing? So suddenly there she was in front of me dressed as an African, saying my name, and it took me a moment to recognise her."

"Did she ask what you were doing there?"

"I don't recall. Probably. It would make sense, wouldn't it?"

"And you?" Lynley asked. "Did you ask her?"

"I hadn't memorised her home address. For all I knew she lived in the area and wore ethnic clothing whenever she wasn't on duty." She stood then, although Barbara and Lynley remained seated. She said, "Now. If there's nothing else, I've patients to see on the Isle of Dogs and not a lot of time to get there."

"That's quite a jaunt from here," Lynley said. "Wouldn't Twicken-ham have been more convenient for your clinic?"

"I go by motorboat. I don't own a car. And no, Twickenham

wouldn't have been more convenient, certainly not for the women I see. But they can get to the Isle of Dogs by the docklands railway. I expect you know this."

"Kingsland High Street would have been more convenient for them, wouldn't it? As there's a clinic in the high street and as that clinic has—or at least had—a small room for surgery, why wouldn't you do your reconstructive work there?"

She looked at him impatiently. "Obviously because it wasn't *my* clinic, Superintendent. And I require a larger operating theatre."

"Mercy Hart claims the clinic's not hers, either."

"Who?"

"Mercy Hart. As you volunteer there, surely you know Mercy Hart, Dr. Weatherall."

"I do not," she said. "I've never heard of her. And now I'm going to shower and change as this conversation has gone on quite long enough."

"You probably know her as Easter Lange," Barbara said.

"Easter? Yes, I do know Easter. It's Easter's clinic. She's how I came to be there in the first place. She read about my work—and don't ask me where or how because I don't know—and she rang me about volunteering a bit of time if I could. She called herself Easter. But you're saying she's who?"

"Mercy Hart. Easter Lange is her aunt."

"So between the two of them—Mercy Hart and Easter Lange—is where the answers to your questions lie. Either Mercy Hart is using the name Easter Lange or Easter Lange is behind whatever is going on in that place that got it shut down."

"FGM got it shut down," Barbara said.

The surgeon's mouth opened then shut. She seemed to take a few moments to put herself back together before she said, "That has to be nonsense."

"Unfortunately, it's not," Lynley told her. "We've a statement from the mother of a prospective patient confirming it."

"And you're thinking that I'm involved with cutting? I've been working for *years* repairing the damage done to these women through FGM." She raised her hands as if to ward off anything else they might want to say. "Please leave now," she said. "As I told you, I want to shower and get to the Isle of Dogs. You've kept me from both of those objectives quite long enough."

WESTMINSTER
CENTRAL LONDON

"Seems like they were on the same side, guv," Havers said as they walked to their cars. They'd come separately, each of them from their homes to Twickenham. "Seems they were going after FGM each in her own way. And what she said makes sense. She didn't know Teo Bontempi was a detective working on a special team. Seeing her out of place like that—in her African togs as well—she would've been surprised, wouldn't she? By the coincidence if by nothing else." She lit up a Player's. He gave her a look. She said, "We're out*doors*."

"You might have waited till you were in your car," Lynley pointed out.

Havers said to the sky, "Reformed smokers are the worst, aren't they?" No answer came from above, so she went on with, "If she's also counselling women in the Kingsland clinic, she's in a position to talk down FGM 's well. I can see her doing that, especially on the sly when Mercy's busy with something else."

"And yet she claims to know nothing about it at the same time as Mercy claims she was merely an employee of the place, and that someone else was cutting girls."

"D'you believe her? Mercy, I mean. Not Dr. Weatherall."

"She's willing to be inside Bronzefield Prison rather than open up further. What does that tell us?"

"Tells me she's worried about being banged up for a bucket of offences, after which she goes back to Bronzefield to while away a few years perfecting her macramé. What's it tell you?"

"Perhaps she's afraid."

"Right. She's afraid of ending up in the dock. She has motive, guv. In spades. In diamonds. In what you will. No wonder she doesn't want to talk to us or to anyone else within reach of the silver bracelets."

They separated then and headed in the direction of central London. It was still fairly early, so the traffic had not yet begun its sluggish crawl. They made good time, but only till they reached the Great West Road, where the battle with buses, taxis, and cars daily tested one's patience, endurance, and driving skills.

Lynley lost sight of Barbara's Mini in Chiswick. But however she had managed it, she pulled into a parking bay beneath New Scotland Yard moments after he emerged from the Healey Elliott, its copper paint job still pleasingly unscathed.

They went up in the lift together, Havers reeking of cigarette smoke and completely unapologetic about it when he cast an unappreciative look at her. There was no point to commenting upon the possibility of spraying herself with air freshener, so he said nothing save good morning to Dorothea Harriman as he followed Havers to join the others.

They were gathered round Winston Nkata's desk, passing among themselves what appeared to be a photograph. There was a decided air of something in the room. Under other circumstances it might have been an air of excitement had there actually been something about which one could get excited at this point.

Nkata clocked them first, saying, "You got to look 't this, guv. I had it off Monifa Bankole before I left Brixton."

Lynley joined them, as did Havers. "What is it?" He put on his reading spectacles and took the photograph that one of the DCs was extending in his direction. In it, a good-looking Black teenager was caught half in shadow, half in light. He wore a white T-shirt with a small hole in the neck. His arms were crossed but the light struck him in a way that defined his muscles. Lynley knew who had taken the picture before he turned it over and saw the small gold seal with Deborah's name upon it.

"Who is this?" he asked.

"Tani Bankole. Tha's Monifa's son. He's with Simisola in Chelsea."

Lynley looked at the picture again and said, "This wasn't taken in Chelsea, was it." He handed it to Havers and removed his glasses. "It's significant somehow?" he asked Nkata.

"Bloody hell," Havers muttered. "Bloody bleeding hell." She raised her head and went on with, "Winnie, I'd ravish you on the spot but I don't think either of us would live through it."

"Thought you'd say that," Nkata said. "Well, not *that* 'xactly. But I figgered you'd wan' to see it."

Lynley drew his eyebrows together. Obviously, he'd overlooked a significant detail that the picture displayed.

Havers tapped the picture, a tap not on the boy but on the background. Lynley returned his glasses to his nose. He saw that Deborah had adjusted the depth of field so that the background was little more than a series of shapes, rendering it more like a cubist painting than whatever it actually was. He could tell it was a wall behind the boy and he assumed the wall held objects of some sort, none of which were particularly definable. But because of its position—which was closer to the camera and not on the wall but instead upon a table close behind Deborah's subject—one of these objects was more defined, albeit not perfectly. From what Lynley saw, the object looked tall. It looked angular. It also looked bronze. But more than that and above it all, the object looked like *Standing Warrior*.

Lynley understood then why the excitement in the room was muted. There were, after all, thirteen copies of *Standing Warrior* in various collections of African art located by Havers, with one of them gone missing from Teo Bontempi's own collection. This sculpture in the photo *could* be the missing sculpture they sought. But even if it was *Standing Warrior*, it just as easily could be one of the series sold by Padma, a piece belonging to an individual on the list Barbara Havers had produced from that gallery in Peckham.

"This could be pay dirt," Havers said. "We need to know where Deborah St. James took this picture."

"We need to be certain this is *Standing Warrior* as well," Lynley told her.

"Sir, you can *see*—"

"We can see the shape, and yes, I agree, it looks very much like *Standing Warrior*. But let's begin with the owner and go from there. I'll ring Deborah. The rest of you, soldier on."

WESTMINSTER
CENTRAL LONDON

Deborah laid out the photographs she thought would be best suited to the booklet that Dominique Shaw had in mind for the Department for Education. The undersecretary had brought along a mock-up of the final project, so together they were able to see which of the photographs seemed to fit best on those pages that were going to require pictures.

Narissa Cameron and Zawadi were there as well. Narissa had presented the undersecretary with a rough cut of the twenty-minute film that, when completed, would be shown to schoolgirls. The longer film—the actual documentary, she'd told Deborah—was at least a year away from completion. But the good news was that Zawadi had agreed to be the narrator in both.

By phone late the previous evening, Narissa had confided to

Deborah that, with her reputation trashed by the tabloids in the wake of "the Akin affair," as she called it, Zawadi understood that only a defiant stance and a head-held-high presence in the fight against female abuse was going to prove to the public that she was undaunted by mistakes she might have made with regard to the Akin family. "She came to understand that fading from view would be unwise," Narissa had said to Deborah. "Personally, I intend to suggest she also get a publicist to do whatever it is they do when people want a better public image. But it's early days for that, and in the meantime, I don't want anything to put her off narrating the films."

"I'm glad to know you're going to narrate," Deborah said to Zawadi when she joined them. "You're a good choice."

"You think so, eh?" Zawadi said in her usual manner when speaking to Deborah. "This big Black woman's actually got something worth saying?"

Deborah flushed. She said, "I didn't intend . . . I'm so sorry. Was I racist without intending to be? I only meant—"

Zawadi cut in with a laugh, saying to Narissa, "Yeah. Right. She does."

"I . . . what?"

"Apologise. Say 'sorry' for everything. No need. I don't need to be besties with you to know you 't least mean well." She gestured at the photographs. "These're good for what they're going to be used for. I'm not saying there's no Black photographer couldn't have done the same, but these're good. I c'n see that."

Deborah knew how reluctant was the other woman's praise. She couldn't blame her. For the truth was that she'd trod ignorantly into Zawadi's world with her camera, her tripod, and her good intentions when she could easily have insisted the job go to a Black photographer. But she hadn't done that, had she, because she'd instantly seen that out of this particular spate of employment could come another photography book like *London Voices*. She hadn't considered the cost.

The three of them left together once Dominque Shaw had expressed her pleasure with the outcome of their work. They would meet again once the booklet was assembled and the film was ready to be shown. They would meet another time when both projects were presented to the head teachers whose schools would receive the booklets as well as see the film.

They were outside and about to go their separate ways when Deborah's mobile rang. She saw who it was, said to the two others that she must take the call, and bade them farewell. She stepped back inside Sanctuary Buildings to receive the call, saying, "Tommy?"

"Where are you?" he asked.

"Great Smith Street," she said.

"Are you free?"

"Yes. I've just left a meeting at the Department for Education. Why?"

She heard him say to someone, "She's just in Great Smith Street. You'll find her at the Department for Education," before he returned to her with, "We have a photograph you took, a picture of Tani Bankole. Winston brought it from the boy's mother this morning."

"Right," she said. "I took a photo for his mum."

"Where?"

"In Deptford."

"It looks like you're inside someone's home."

"We were. I'd already taken a photograph of the woman who lives there. You saw it, Tommy. Remember? She and her husband have a large collection of African art."

"Ah. The cluttered background. Of course."

"Don't please bury me in praise," Deborah said. "It makes me blush."

"Oh. Sorry. You're right. Apologies."

"Anyway, I took Tani and Simisola to see the collection. It was meant to be a break from being in Chelsea? Tani especially seemed to need one. I don't think I'd had ten words out of him at that point."

"Her name?"

"She's called Leylo. Her husband is Yasir. I'm not sure of their sur-name." He said to someone with him, "Leylo and Yasir. She doesn't know the surname. Check the list."

She said, "The list? Tommy, what's going on?"

"She and her husband have a sculpture—we can see it in the picture of Tani—that could well be the one we're looking for. Have you the address?"

"I don't know it off the top of my head. I'd need to get to my GPS. It overlooks Pepys Park, though, the building they live in. I can tell you that much. D'you need a closer look at it? Would you like me to fetch it?"

"Nkata will do it." Again he spoke to someone else and then when he was with her again, "Since the woman knows you, will you ac-company him, Deborah?"

"Of course. Shall we do it now?"

"He'll be there directly. He's on his way. What do you know about the couple who have the sculpture? Barbara's just indicated that they're not on the list of people who purchased editions of it from the gallery, if indeed it's the same sculpture we've been trying to find. How did you come to know the woman and her husband?"

"Through the project I'm doing for the Department for Education."

"Through Orchid House, then?"

"No, no. This was something quite different. It had its genesis at Orchid House. I was taking photos at a clinic on the Isle of Dogs and Leylo and her husband were there. She's an FGM victim, and she was going to have reconstructive—"

"Dr. Weatherall?" Lynley cut in.

"Do you know her, Tommy?"

"I do. So did Teo Bontempi."

Deborah listened to his explanation of details as well as the proof they'd come up with regarding the acquaintance of the two women:

Teo Bontempi and Philippa Weatherall. Deborah was silent as she took this in. She finally said, "Are you thinking Dr. Weatherall had something to do with Teo Bontempi's death? But why would she have done?"

"We're not sure what to think at this point, which is why we need to put hands on that sculpture. If it's *Standing Warrior*—as it's called—and if it's the tenth of the series, then it's the one taken from Teo Bontempi's flat and it must go to forensics."

She promised him that she would see to it that the sculpture ended up where Lynley wanted it to end up. That seemed to be in the hands of Winston Nkata, and they rang off just as DS Nkata pulled to the kerb in his red Fiesta.

CHELSEA
CENTRAL LONDON

Tani was waiting for news about his father. He was trying to remember how it all worked when it came to being hauled off by the coppers. He knew very little about the Metropolitan Police, and what he did know came from television dramas. But it seemed to him that someone like his father would be held in custody for a period of time, although he wasn't sure what that period of time was.

They'd passed twelve hours with nothing occurring to indicate where Abeo Bankole was. This resulted in Tani's assuming the police could hold him for twenty-four. There was always the possibility, however, that Abeo hadn't been put into custody at all. Tani was only sure about one part of what had gone on during and after his father's appearance at the St. Jameses' house: It wasn't likely his mum was going to press charges against her husband. She never had done before. What was so different about this time that she would do so now?

Tani didn't understand his mum, but he'd never understood her.

She'd been a presence in his life, of course. He knew she *was* his mum. Yet it seemed to him that she'd deposited her loyalty into the Bank of Abeo the day she married him, and although Tani tried to tell himself that she'd known no better, that she'd been brought up by her own parents to serve and obey the husband who would pay the bride price her father was asking, he could not help thinking how different his entire life would have been had Monifa . . . what? he asked himself. What did he want his mother to have done? The fact that he had no answer to that aside from "stand up to him," which would have garnered her a beating, told Tani that he couldn't place blame upon his mother. He could come up with a list of actions she *might* have taken, yet was there a single one of them that would have kept Abeo away from what he saw as his rightful place at the head of the family? This position gave him unlimited power over the rest of them. In his earlier years, this fact hadn't troubled Tani, who'd assumed that, in the future, he'd wield power as well. But he'd misjudged Abeo's determination to keep everyone under his thumb and that had been a chilling mistake.

Abeo had been able to dig up Sophie's identity although Tani had not named her to any person in Ridley Road Market. Abeo had been able to discover where she lived. Once Abeo had followed her to where Simi was hidden, Tani had understood his father's power in ways he'd never been able to assess in the past. And if he—Abeo's son— recognised exactly what this meant in their lives, Monifa probably saw Abeo's turning up in Chelsea as proof positive that no matter what she tried, she would fail to free herself from Tani's father. She could run and hide and run and hide and run and hide again, and at the end of the day it would be for naught.

"Tani, Tani, Tani!"

At least, he thought, Simisola was safe for now. "Down here, Squeak," he told her. He'd taken himself to the kitchen, where Joseph Cotter was looking at recipes online. He'd said earlier that he intended to give Tani and Simi a proper Nigerian meal. He'd taken note of how little they were eating, and he'd assumed it was his cooking and not their fear and anxiety about what was happening to their lives. He'd been defeated by the ingredients, though. He had his doubts that the local supermarket carried either *daddawa* or ground crayfish.

Simi came down the stairs with the St. Jameses' cat slung over one shoulder. "Alaska wanted attention," she confided. "I could tell by how he was looking at me."

"Doesn't like to be held much, that one," Cotter said, looking up from his laptop. "Mind he doesn't scratch you, wanting to get down."

"He's purring, though," Simi said. "He was purring most all night. *That* means he's happy."

"You let him sleep with you? An' he stayed the night?" Cotter sounded amazed. "Looks like you're his chosen, then. That cat never sleeps with anyone. Truth is, I don't know where he gets himself off to at night."

"Where's Peach, then, Mr. Cotter?" she asked. "Tani, you need to find Peach so we'll both have someone an' we can snuggle with them."

Excited barking gave them the answer. It came from above stairs. What followed it was the ringing of the front door's bell. What followed that was rapid knocking on the door.

Cotter said to them, "You two stay right there. Lemme see what's what."

Off he went up the stairs and soon enough Peach had stopped barking, which had to mean that the dog was busily sniffing someone's ankles and shoes or that Mr. Cotter had sent the person away. Simi had allowed Alaska to leap onto the floor and came to Tani, her eyes dark and fearful. The cat disappeared from the kitchen, cat door flapping as he went into the garden.

Then there were footsteps on the stairs and Mr. Cotter was saying, "—just in the kitchen with me."

The response was a fervent "Thanks to God," and Tani recognised his mother's voice.

Simi barely had time to say "It's Mummy!" before Monifa was with them and Simi was running to her. She flung her arms round Monifa's waist and hung there, looking up at their mother with undiluted joy.

Monifa's gaze sought Tani. She said, "They phoned me. Thanks to God, at least they phoned me."

"What's—"

She cut Tani off with, "They have released him. They told me he spent the night and was no longer a threat to any of us. But how can they say this? They do not know him. They know only what he tells them and they see only how he acts when he is with them. But now he will come here, and nothing will stop him."

"Lemme ring the coppers," Mr. Cotter said. "He c'n show up. But he's not getting into this house."

"No!" Monifa cried. "Please. It will not matter. He will bide his time. He will come again. You must let me . . . Simisola, you must come with me. Tani, you must remain. You must speak with him so that he thinks Simi is here and you will not let him see her. But she will not be here. She will be in Brixton with me and with Sergeant Nkata's family. Tani, will you do this? Please. *Will* you do this? After yesterday, what he might do now . . . Simi must not be here. He must not discover where she is."

Tani nodded wordlessly. He felt fear grip him. He didn't want to believe Abeo would try another time to invade their safety, but he knew his father. In addition to his unaltered plans for Simisola, there were scores he would want to settle with Tani.

"Mum, how will you—" he began.

"I have a taxi," she told him. "Simi, we must leave at once."

"But I got to go upstairs and get my—"

"There is no time, Simisola. Tani will bring your belongings later. You must come with me now."

Simi looked imploringly from Tani to Cotter and back to Tani. He said to her, "Go with Mum, Squeak. I'll bring anything you want later."

She ran to him then and hugged him. She did the same to Mr. Cotter. Then she clasped Monifa's extended hand and Monifa took her quickly up the stairs. Tani followed.

Before his mother opened the door, Tani stepped in front of her. He said, "Let me check. If he's out there and he sees you . . . and he sees Simi . . ."

"Yes," Monifa said. "Yes, yes. Please."

Tani opened the door. The taxi—a minicab, not a black taxi—waited in the street. He went to it. He looked in every direction, even up into the trees. His father was nowhere in sight. He gestured to his mother and she hustled Simisola out of the house and down the steps. She urged Simisola into the car and got in after her. Then she said to Tani through the open window, "You are the best of sons. But you *must* be careful. You must not let him into this house. He wants to hurt you, Tani."

Tani's hand was on the base of the window. She took it and kissed it and pressed it to her cheek. Then, releasing it, she said to the driver. "Please go quickly. As quick as you can."

The vehicle drove off, to the end of Cheyne Row before it paused for a break in the traffic, then turned left and disappeared from view.

ISLE OF DOGS
EAST LONDON

Lynley waited in his office for the call from Nkata. As he did so, Havers was directing the DCs who were engaged in several haystack searches. One of these involved every minicab company south of the river as well as every car-hire service and every black taxi, a task that would take forever to accomplish if the investigation wasn't able to bring things to a conclusion in another manner. The other of these involved the name and location of every pier or wharf on the south bank of the Thames between King's Stairs and London Bridge, as well as the location of every CCTV camera for each of them, should there even be a CCTV camera nearby. It was grueling work. But it was also critical, and Lynley made that clear the moment Winston Nkata had left them to accompany Deborah St. James to Deptford. At this point, and barring something truly conclusive, he didn't anticipate an admission of guilt from anyone when it came to Teo Bontempi's death. There were far too many moving parts in the investigation to be hopeful about anything.

It was two and a quarter hours into the slog being carried out by the DCs when the phone call from Nkata finally came. After speaking with him, Lynley rang the Met's station in Westferry Road, arranged for an interview room for questioning, and told his colleagues there to expect him, along with DS Barbara Havers. With thanks, he said. Sometimes necessary conversations with suspects worked quite well in their own environments, and sometimes they did not. This, he reckoned, was going to be one of the latter.

He collected Havers, who asked him sardonically if he had the first idea how many docks and piers there were along the river. Dozens, he expected. But if the DCs perused the map *and* made contact with their colleagues at Wapping River Station, that should go some distance towards telling them which of the piers and docks were most easily used by casual boaters. She passed the information along to the DCs and joined him at the lift.

They set out in Lynley's car. It was midafternoon and neither of them had taken time for lunch. Havers fished in her bag, saying she was bloody well famished. After a dedicated search, which involved removing an astonishing number of belongings from her shoulder bag, she brought forth a Twix and, after casting a speculative glance at him, handed over half of it. They munched companionably, after which she dug a flapjack from among her belongings, and they munched again.

She followed this up with a packet of custard creams. She was again generous with it, and he half expected her to produce a Pop-Tart next. It certainly wouldn't be something more wholesome like—in an utter change of culinary character—a piece of fruit. She didn't disappoint, although it turned out that, post custard creams, she had only four Starburst sweets left in her cache, two of which had come unwrapped and bore a disturbing fur-like evidence of this. He demurred on these as his teeth were beginning to ache, and although he assumed this was psychosomatic, he thought it best to heed their warning. By the time they reached the station in Westferry Road, they admitted to each other that short of murder, they would both do anything for a cup of tea. Havers's suggestion was stopping at "the nearest wherever, guv," as she put it. For Lynley's part, he said with certainty that the station would doubtless have a suitable canteen that would be available to them.

The station was large, its entrance taking up a street corner, the wings of the building stretching in both directions. Once they parked and made themselves known at reception, a uniformed constable came to fetch them. All was ready, they were informed.

They went first to the canteen—called Peeler's, what else?—where they ordered three cups of tea to take away. Havers availed herself of the opportunity to replenish her stock of pre-packaged comestibles, after which they followed the constable to the interview room that had been set aside for their use.

She was waiting inside, and she wasn't happy.

She said, "You two. I should have guessed. Is this really necessary?"

"You've not asked for a solicitor?" Lynley asked. He and Havers took seats opposite Dr. Weatherall. He switched on the tape recorder, gave the time and each of their names, and repeated his question as Havers passed one of the three takeaway teas to the surgeon. She'd also stowed several thimbles of milk and four packets of sugar in her bag, which she also produced.

"D'you know that I was about to begin a reconstruction?" Dr. Weatherall said. "That I was told by two completely indifferent constables it would not be allowed? I was informed that, surgery or not, I must come at once. And now I've been sitting here in this goddamn bloody room for"—she glanced at her wristwatch—"the same amount of time it would have taken me to perform most of the surgery in the first place."

"Which type of surgery would that be?" Lynley asked her.

"What is that supposed to mean? You know exactly what I do. And if, for some reason, you do not understand it, there are enough details available through any number of internet sources to clarify matters."

"Yes, we're familiar with that. But it's the other procedures we're interested in."

"It's a women's clinic. I deal with women's health issues. I don't intend to sit here and list them for you. We've been over this already. I assume your sergeant has all of this in her notes."

"She does indeed," Lynley said. "But we'd like to expand on what you've told us. Are you certain you don't want a solicitor? We can easily have a duty solicitor brought in for you."

Her eyes narrowed. Lynley had kept his voice as affable as possible, but this repeated offer of a solicitor was sending her a message, and he could see she didn't like it one bit. He waited. Ultimately, she refused his offer of a solicitor once again. Next to him, Havers brought forth her tattered spiral notebook and a mechanical pencil. This second item he recognised as belonging to Winston Nkata. He looked from it to her. She produced an innocent smile. She was, as always, incorrigible.

He said to the surgeon, "A woman called Leylo was one of your patients, I understand. Is the name familiar?"

"Of course it is. She underwent a successful reconstruction not long ago. She'd had a good result. Is this about her?"

"We've learned that it's your practice to give a gift to each woman who undergoes the surgery. Was this true for Leylo?"

"I give them a token," she said. "It may be hard for you to believe, but having the surgery after what's been done to them takes a great deal of courage, Detective Lynley . . . Sorry, I can't remember your rank."

"Detective is fine," Lynley told her. "What sort of token?"

"What?"

Havers said, "You said you give them a token. What would that be? Box of chockies? Stationery? Lotion? Scent? A scarf? Gift certificate to McDonald's?"

"It varies." She reached for her tea for the first time. She added two thimbles of the milk. There was nothing with which to stir it, so she swirled the liquid in the cup.

"But that's a bit odd, isn't it," Havers said. "I'd think it would go th' other way round. Them giving *you* a gift and not the opposite. I mean, you're saving *them*, right? You're improving *their* lives. Why wouldn't they want to thank you with a gift?"

Dr. Weatherall lifted a shoulder in reply. "It's odd to you, perhaps. But you've never been in their position. They've been betrayed by the people they love. These are people they trusted, the people who were supposed to protect them. They've been failed by their entire society, so when they decide to hand themselves over to me—a complete outsider *and* a white woman—they're engaging in an act of trust. For some of them, this is the first time they've trusted anyone since they were cut. So the gift I give them . . . it's a reward. It's a thank-you from me for the privilege of helping them."

Lynley was struck by this. She was utterly sincere, and he could feel it. This was her passion. She'd probably spent her professional life putting all she had and all she was into it. Which made everything else so much more difficult to understand. Out of the manila envelope into which it had been put, he brought the photo that Deborah St. James had taken of Tani Bankole. He laid it on the table and slid it to Dr. Weatherall. She looked at it, drew her eyebrows together, then looked at him.

"Am I meant to know this young man?"

He shook his head. "If you look beyond him, you can see there's a sculpture on the table that stands next to the sofa." He waited for her to note this and acknowledge its presence. She did so. He went on with, "Leylo has identified the sculpture as the gift you gave to her, the thank-you for placing her trust in you."

To this, she made no immediate reply, but she dropped her gaze to the photo and said hesitantly, "It could be the same."

"You did give her a sculpture, did you not?"

"I did. But this photo—"

"Yeah, it's a bit blurry, eh? I expect this'll help." Havers took a folded paper from the back of her notebook. It had become dog-eared, but when she unfolded it, she smoothed its edges with some ceremony before she slid it next to Deborah's photo of Tani Bankole. It was the picture of *Standing Warrior* that Ross Carver had produced from the internet. "Would this be it?"

Lynley watched Dr. Weatherall as she gazed at it. He could tell she was considering her answer. The alternatives she faced were tricky. She could brazen it out with a denial that could easily be checked or she could brazen it out with an admission that could cause her infinite difficulties. The nature of these difficulties constituted the unknown for her. So she was going to have to go with her gut.

She made her choice. "Yes." She gestured to the printed copy from the internet. "This is very similar to the piece I gave her."

Lynley said, "Thank you," and then to Havers, "If you will, Sergeant . . ."

Havers recited the caution. Dr. Weatherall—he could tell—knew at once she'd made the wrong choice. She said, "What's going on?"

Lynley said, "You've been told that anything you say can be used as evidence against you. At this point, let me ask you again: Would you like a solicitor?"

"Why would I need a solicitor? I've done nothing. This is absurd. What's my crime supposed to be?"

"Are you again refusing a solicitor?"

"I am. I have no idea what I'm doing here, and I'm beginning to think you've no idea either."

Lynley raised his fingers from the table, accepting her allegation as something that could be true. He said, "Where did you get the sculpture you gave to Leylo?"

"I don't recall. I purchase items to use as gifts for my patients whenever I happen to see them. This could have come from anywhere. A street market, a secondhand shop, a car boot sale, a charity shop."

"Teo Bontempi's flat?" Lynley asked.

"What?"

"Teo Bontempi had a collection of African sculptures," Lynley said.

"And you're implying . . . what? That I stole this from her to give to Leylo? I haven't the first idea where Teo Bontempi lived."

"Except that wouldn't be the case, would it?" Havers pointed out. "You've got every one of her details in her file."

"I'm not sure what that signifies, Sergeant. I don't memorise my patients' files. And even if I went to call upon her, which I did not, why on earth would I take one of her sculptures?"

"Once you brained her with it, you didn't have any other choice."

She stared at Havers. Then she moved her gaze to Lynley. She said, "That's completely mad."

"What's been challenging is to work out why," Lynley said. "We've got the *how* sorted. You told us yourself. You don't own a car, and you come here to the Isle of Dogs by motorboat. That explains how you managed to get to Teo Bontempi's flat without a car of yours being caught on CCTV in Streatham High Road. From the Isle of Dogs you motored to the dock or pier closest to a route to Streatham. By taxi or minicab you went from that dock to Streatham High Road.

Then back to the pier by cab. Once into the boat, you motored on the river to Eel Pie Island. We'll find the relevant CCTV eventually. We'll do the same with the cabs."

She said, "These are fairy stories. I'd like a solicitor now."

"Your own or will the duty solicitor do?"

She accepted his offer of the duty solicitor. This was quickly arranged, although they had to wait forty minutes for the duty solicitor's arrival. She was young, Chinese. She hid her youth by wearing a grey pinstriped trouser suit, a severe white blouse so starched it might have stood up on its own, and very large black-framed spectacles. She needed the air of gravitas these items lent her. Dressed otherwise and without the glasses, she easily could have been mistaken for an adolescent. Vivienne Yang, she introduced herself. She would, she told them, need some private time with her client before they resumed their questioning.

Lynley gave her his mobile number and he and Havers returned to Peeler's. They had just sat at one of the tables when his mobile rang. Havers was saying, "That was bloody fast," when Lynley saw it was Winston ringing him. He had the bronze sculpture in hand, he said, suitably placed in an evidence bag. It was definitely the one they'd been looking for. He was taking it to forensics in hopes it could go to the top of the stack of jobs awaiting results. He did not, however, sound particularly hopeful. To the naked eye, the piece looked quite clean.

"There might well be DNA still on it: Teo's or Dr. Weatherall's," Lynley said. "And there are other facts about that piece that will prove impossible to argue away. So long as we have *Standing Warrior* in hand, we've got more than one route from it to the person who wielded it."

Within twenty minutes after his exchange with Nkata, Lynley received the message from Vivienne Yang. They returned to the interview room, where Lynley once again engaged the tape to record their interview, formally reminding Dr. Weatherall that she was still under caution.

He said, "As we've established on your own word, the sculpture depicted in the photograph taken in the home of your patient Leylo is the one you gave to her."

"I said the sculpture in the picture is very *like*, Detective Lynley. I have no way of knowing if it's the actual one that I gave her."

"Are you suggesting that she has another identical to it? Or that she bought another somewhere in order to have a matched pair?"

"I'm not suggesting anything. I'm merely saying that what's depicted in the picture is very like what I gave to her. You yourself can see that the midpoint of the photo isn't perfectly sharp. And the background of it is merely shapes."

"Hmmm. Yes. That's largely why I sent my sergeant to have a look at the piece himself. He's confirmed that it's *Standing Warrior*. He's also confirmed it was once in the possession of Teo Bontempi."

"That's absurd. He has no way of confirming that, and you know it."

Lynley said, "I'm afraid that's not the case. The statue's on its way to forensics, and what will come of that is something we won't necessarily know for a few days. A few weeks, even, depending upon the laboratory's workload. However, there's another way that the sculpture can be placed inside Teo Bontempi's flat. It was a gift from her estranged husband, and when he returned to the flat, he saw that it was missing."

"You and I both know that she could well have rid herself of it. She could have given it away as a gift. She could have tossed it in the rubbish. There are dozens of explanations, Detective. And even if it *was* missing as you say, you can hardly claim that the piece missing from the woman's flat somehow ended up in the hands of one of my patients."

"And yet it did." Havers was tapping her pencil against her pad, and her tone was impatient. "It made a direct journey from Streatham to Deptford, and it was in your possession nearly all the way."

"I don't see how—"

"It was number ten," Lynley cut in.

"What?"

"*Standing Warrior* is a limited edition of fifteen bronze sculptures, Dr. Weatherall. Ross Carver—that's Teo Bontempi's husband—bought edition number ten of the twelve that have been sold from a gallery in Peckham. The artist numbered it when she signed her name. She does this, apparently, on the bottom of her pieces, so unless you looked for it, you wouldn't know it's there."

The surgeon said nothing at this. Vivienne Yang folded her hands on the table. Voices came from the corridor. Above their heads, the whir of the building's ventilation system sent a sudden blast of icy air into the room.

Lynley said, "So far, Mercy Hart has been holding her tongue, but you can't expect her to do that much longer no matter what you're paying her, which I expect is quite a bit. When we go to Bronzefield Prison to have another word with her—"

Dr. Weatherall's glance sharpened when Lynley said Bronzefield Prison, but she still didn't speak.

"—there's a very good chance she'll explain your association with the Kingsland High Street clinic once we tell her you're in custody."

"I have no further comment," Dr. Weatherall said.

"You don't need to comment at this point, do you?" Havers asked her. "Aside from that tenth copy of *Standing Warrior*—which is going to make things bloody difficult for you—and aside from Mercy Hart's decision to loosen her lips—which *is* going to happen once she learns you've been arrested and charged—we've got the phone calls you made to Teo Bontempi *after* she confronted you on the day the clinic was raided. The first of those calls was made that very evening. And all the rest lead directly up to the night she was attacked."

"When you phoned Teo, you were trying to persuade her not to report you," Lynley said.

"Report me for what? Helping mutilated women become whole again? Has that become illegal, Detective?"

"We thought at first it was Mercy Hart doing the cutting on little girls and using the name Easter Lange. But it wasn't, was it? It was you and you were on your way there—to the clinic—when Teo Bontempi in her African clothing saw you. I expect she was shocked at first, trying to work out what you were doing in that part of town. But it didn't take long for her to reach the only conclusion possible. It was where you performed medicalised FGM."

"I have no comment, *no* comment," Dr. Weatherall said. And to Vivienne Yang, "Do I have to sit here and listen to this?"

Vivienne Yang murmured the answer that Lynley and Havers already knew: exactly how long they could hold her before they charged her with a crime. It was a stretch of time that the surgeon more than likely did not want to spend with the likes of them.

"Not all women you operate on can pay for the reconstruction, can they? And the sort of surgery you offer isn't covered by the NHS. You need a reliable source of funding to keep your health centre going here on the Isle of Dogs and to pay Mercy what I expect is a hefty wage. It's likely you receive contributions from anti-FGM organisations and from individuals, but Women's Health of Hackney is how you top up your income. What I don't understand—and I wager Sergeant Havers doesn't understand this either—is why you chose medicalised FGM as a means of supporting your work. Not only is it against the law, but it's the very thing you're fighting against."

Havers said, "Not actually, sir. She's fighting against the *way* it's been done, not the fact of the doing in the first place. I say she's reckoned that, if parents want their daughters cut up, at least she can keep them from having someone incompetent butcher them. Which is also why there's no bloody way she'd let Mercy Hart do the cutting. But she needed it to *look* like Mercy was doing it, so I expect she'd show up only when Mercy gave her the word that a cutting was scheduled. Would that be how it was, Dr. Weatherall?"

"I have no comment, no comment," she said. Her voice was lower now as, moment by moment, she was being bled of bravado.

"Where Mercy fits in is the puzzle piece, though," Lynley said meditatively. "She had to know what was going on and she had to know it's against the law."

"She needs the money, guv. She's got those kids, no husband or boyfriend to help out, life's expensive, and all the rest."

"Yet she's run an enormous risk. Just for the money?"

"Could be Mercy's a believer, sir. Not in FGM but in using medicalised FGM to support what Dr. Weatherall's trying to do for the women who've been mutilated by it."

Dr. Weatherall said nothing at this. But along the lower part of her eyes a liquid brightness appeared. Vivienne Yang spoke quietly in her ear. Dr. Weatherall nodded after a moment. The solicitor said, "We'd like some private time, Detective."

Back into the corridor they went, after pausing the interview's recording. Havers left him with, "Got to have a bloody fag or you don't want to know me," and went in the direction of the police station's main door. Lynley checked his mobile phone and saw there were two messages. A text had come from Dorothea Harriman, three words only: *It's China Wharf.* The other was a voice message from Daidre. "I'll be back tonight, Tommy. I've missed you terribly. Will you ring me, please?" He did so at once, only to be directed to her own voice mail. His message was brief. They were closing in on the finish of the investigation, he told her, and he added that he was very happy she was due back in town. What he didn't add was that he hoped she'd resolved all the issues plaguing her siblings. He reckoned she'd tell him when he saw her at last.

Post-cigarette, Havers smelled like the remains of a campfire, but on the other hand, she was in a decidedly better frame of mind. They remained where they were for another quarter of an hour. Vivienne Yang finally opened the door and said, "We're ready for you now."

They resumed their seats, and Lynley once again set the recording in motion. Havers reminded Dr. Weatherall she was under caution. She nodded, glanced at Vivienne Yang, drew in a fractured breath, and said, "I'd like to explain what happened."

BRIXTON
SOUTH LONDON

Winston Nkata first returned Deborah St. James to her car, which she'd left in a car park not far from the Palace of Westminster. He hadn't gone into any detail with her about why the tenth edition of *Standing Warrior* in the possession of Leylo was important, and she hadn't asked. But she wasn't married to an expert witness in the field of forensic science for nothing. She merely said, "I expect that's the cake's icing," when Nkata fetched an evidence bag from the boot of his car in order to remove the sculpture from the flat in Deptford. He said to her, "We're hopin', innit," and that was the limit of their discussion. Once they parted, he took *Standing Warrior* to the forensic lab they'd been dealing with during the course of the investigation, and he did his best to charm the technicians into a willingness to put this particular job at the head of the queue. He was told "no guarantees, mate," but he found hope when the comment was made in a sympathetic tone.

He was walking back to his car when his mobile rang and, when he saw an unknown number and answered, a woman's voice said, "Is that Winston Nkata?" and when he said yes, she went on to identify herself with the name Zawadi and then to tell him, "Tani Bankole's told me you have the passports. We've the emergency protection order in hand and I need them off you. Stoke Newington Police Station'll hold them. That's where the order will be."

"I got 'em safe," he said.

"I expect you do, only they need to stay with the protection order so when it's lifted, if it ever is, the passports can go back to the family."

He told her they were stowed at his home but he could fetch them, as he wasn't far. He'd take them to Stoke Newington if that was helpful. She said she'd come to fetch them. She told him that, given the address, she would set off at once.

So he went home to his parents' flat. No one was there, but no one would have been there at this time of day. His dad was at the wheel of a Number 11 bus while his mum would be at Alice N's, probably doing the post-lunch clean-up with Tabby and Monifa.

He'd left the passports in the breast pocket of the jacket he'd worn on the previous day. He went to his bedroom, where a set of perfectly folded sheets and another of towels formed a neat stack at the end of the bed Monifa was using. Inside the clothes cupboard, his jacket hung. He took it out and slipped his hand into the jacket's inner breast pocket. But what he brought forth was a single passport where there should have been four. He opened it to see it belonged to Tani. He looked through the other pockets in the jacket, and, finding nothing, he frowned and returned to the cupboard, where he looked on the floor although he couldn't work out how the other passports might have fallen there. He could, of course, have somehow dislodged three of the documents when he placed his jacket in the cupboard, although he didn't see how. Nonetheless, he checked the floor to make sure they weren't lying in the shadows.

They weren't. He lowered his head. He thought back carefully. He knew he'd been given all four. Deborah St. James had wiped each off individually once she'd removed them from the wrapping that had protected them at the bottom of the cat's litter box. She'd given all of them to him and he'd put all of them into his jacket. He'd known they'd be perfectly safe there. Abeo Bankole was in the hands of the Belgravia police at that point, so it was impossible that he'd somehow not only concluded that Nkata—whose name he did not even know—had the passports, but that he'd also managed to discover where Nkata lived, broken into this flat, and found the passports without leaving the slightest indication that he'd been there in the first place. Even had that been the case, it stood to reason that only two passports would have been missing: his and Simisola's.

In his peripheral vision, Nkata saw those sheets and towels, and he considered them in an entirely different light. He'd concluded at first that his mum had left them for Monifa's use later that night, but now he saw them as something that could be quite different. He went to the head of the bed, pulled back the thin, striped summer duvet, and saw that the bed had been stripped. He touched the towels and found them still slightly damp from use. He moved them, examined the sheets, and realised they'd been used as well.

He fumbled for his phone and punched in the familiar number. Tabby answered at the café. He asked for his mum. In a moment, he heard her say, "Jewel, you all right, love?" and his mouth was like a sandpit when he replied. "'S Monifa with you, Mum?"

"She's left to fetch Simisola, love," Alice said. "She had a phone call. She was told that Abeo—that's her husband's name, yes?—had been released. She was in such a state that he'd go straight down to Chelsea that I arranged a taxi for her. To fetch Simisola here, that is. She was meant to come back directly, Jewel. Hang on, love. Let me ask Tabby . . ."

Nkata heard his mother ask Tabby if she recalled the time that Monifa had left the café. Tabby could only guess at it. They'd been so busy with the lunch crush, hadn't they. He knew how it was at the café during lunch: packed with people eating in with a queue for takeaway meals stretching out of the door and down the pavement past at least two shops.

"It's been several hours, Jewel . . . Oh, Lord. Now I think, Abeo could have managed to get to Chelsea before her . . . What, Tabby?"

As Nkata felt the sweat break out on his forehead, Tabby said something he couldn't hear. Alice filled him in with, "Tabby *thinks* she got the phone call round half past twelve?" There was a pause and then— as if she'd looked at the wall clock or her watch—"Oh dear. She should have been back before now. I let you down. Jewel, I hope . . . If the husband did get to her, I'll never forgive myself. I am so, *so*—"

"'S'okay, Mum," Nkata told her. "I 'spect he didn't get to her."

They rang off on that reassurance. It was, Nkata knew, absolute. Still, he proved this to himself by ringing the Belgravia station. Yes, he was told, Abeo Bankole was still in custody. If no charges were filed, he would be released at the end of the twenty-four hours they were allowed to hold him.

Nkata rang the St. Jameses next. He spoke briefly and as calmly as possible to Joseph Cotter. From him, he gathered the limited information that Monifa had come for Simisola. When he asked to speak with Tani, he learned the rest from the boy, and it was the same as he'd learned from his own mother. Monifa had been there, and she'd told them about Abeo's release. Tani knew his father would never give up a single one of the plans he had for them, so he'd remained behind to face off with Abeo once he showed up, while Monifa hid Simisola away. But Abeo hadn't returned to Cheyne Row, at least so far he hadn't.

Did Tani know where Monifa had intended to take Simisola? Nkata asked him.

"To Brixton, was what she said. She tol' me my dad wouldn't know how to find her there."

"An' if she didn't go to Brixton?"

"But she did. Tha's what she told us, me an' Mr. Cotter." His voice altered then as he seemed to understand that something had gone wrong and perhaps badly so. "Wha's . . . Did he *get* her?"

"Let me check on all that," Nkata said.

"But *did* she go to Brixton like she said?"

"Lemme check on that 's well, Tani. You stay with Mr. Cotter, yeah? Is Mrs. St. James back?"

"Yeah."

"Mr. St. James?"

"No. But—"

"Okay, then." Nkata cut in. "You all stay there in Chelsea. I got to make some phone calls. I'll be in touch soon 's I know something 'bout where your mum is. Just in case, any place else she might go?"

"We got cousins in Peckham."

"You ring them and check for me, eh?"

Nkata rang off quickly before the boy could ask more questions that he couldn't answer, with either truth or falsehood. He did have phone calls to make, though, and the first of these went to Zawadi in order to give her the news. She didn't answer her mobile phone, which told him she was as good as her word: she was on her way to Brixton for the passports. He left her a message to ring him as soon as she could, and then he connected to Lynley. Before he could explain what had happened, Lynley told him that China Wharf was the location on the South Bank that the DCs had marked as having the highest potential for docking a motorboat. It was just east of Tower Bridge, with easy access from the river to its bank via steps at either end of the wharf. There was CCTV across the street on a building not far from a tunnel that gave access to the river. The tunnel itself was between China Wharf and Reeds Wharf, both of which were situated in Bermondsey Wall. As the warehouses in the location had long since been converted to flats, there was every chance that more CCTV cameras would be located there for the buildings' security.

Nkata hoped the good news Lynley had imparted would outweigh the bad news about the missing passports. He shared the information and then went on to explain what had occurred at his mum's café.

He ended with, "Tabby—tha's mum's helper in the caff—says there was a phone call that Monifa took, giving her the information that her husband's been let go. Only that call wasn't from the Belgravia cops, cos Abeo Bankole's there till half past three if no one wants charges filed against him."

Lynley said nothing. Nkata could hear voices in the background. After a few moments for thought, Lynley said, "So it *could* be she's taken the girl back to . . . what was the name of the housing estate?"

"Mayville. But why tell Tani she was bringing the girl to Brixton, guv? And why'd she take those passports with her?"

"Does she have a credit card?" Lynley asked. "Access to cash? Enough to take the girl somewhere out of the country?"

Nkata said, feeling hollow, "I bloody don't know. She's got a cousin in Peckham she might've gone to and Tani's checkin'. But . . ."

"It's unsettling," Lynley said.

"Wha's happenin' with Weatherall? Anything?"

"She's giving a statement. She could have come up with a dozen tales, hoping that Mercy would keep silent as she's done so far. But she couldn't explain away the tenth edition of *Standing Warrior*. You did good work there, Winston."

"Barb did the work, guv. I jus' saw the picture Deb St. James took."

"Nonetheless," Lynley said. And then, "Stay in touch regarding the Bankole woman. Check with Belgravia. She may have gone there to give a statement."

Nkata thought that unlikely. But he agreed, although he knew he couldn't do anything until he'd had the necessary word with Zawadi. He rang her again, and this time she answered. She was there in Brixton, she told him, wandering round Loughborough Estate and, "Where the devil *are* you?"

He said that he would come to her straightaway and where was she? She identified her location as "some kind of bloody crescent," which was unhelpful as there were streets named *crescent* in every direction.

Send him a photo of the nearest building, he told her. That should do it.

It did. He hadn't a clue what she looked like, of course, but when he saw the woman on the corner of St. James's Crescent and Western Road, he recognised Zawadi by what telegraphed her impatience: crossed arms, tapping foot, glances at the watch on her wrist, fingering a necklace of African beads. He introduced himself.

She gave a nod, said her own name, and then, "The passports?"

"They're gone, Simisola's and her mum's and her dad's. I've still got Tani's. But tha's all."

She stared at him, her expression altering from blank to incredulous, as if he'd suddenly sprouted another head. "How're they bloody gone?" she demanded.

"Monifa . . . Simisola's mum. I think she took them. I can't see anyone else doin' it."

"You didn't keep them with you? Once you had them, you didn't lock them up? *What* in God's name . . ." She clenched her fists in front of her. Nkata reckoned she wanted to punch him and he couldn't blame her. She said, "Without a protection order, the girl's not safe. And without the passports *and* a protection order, she can be carted off to Nigeria as soon as there are tickets available. You stupid, bloody . . . Are you a cop or not?"

"I'm sorry," he said. "I di'n't think—"

"Too right, that. You didn't *think*. I'm dead glad we've established that. So does Monifa have any clue where we've put Simisola and Tani?"

Nkata could feel himself cringe inside. He was only happy he didn't do so outwardly. He said, "She knows, yeah. She fetched Simisola from there."

"Bloody *God*. How did she discover where they were?"

It was worse and worse, but he owned it, so he told her. Monifa knew where Simisola was because he'd taken her there once she'd done her part in a murder investigation the Met was conducting. She'd written a statement about a clinic that the coppers had shut down in Kingsland High Street. She'd confessed that she had intended to have Simisola cut there, but to have it done medically.

"And that didn't tell you *anything*?" Zawadi cried. "She's been showing her intentions from the very first, you fool, and it's down to us to stop her."

ISLE OF DOGS
EAST LONDON

"People say, 'We're ending this,' and they set off on a crusade," Philippa Weatherall said. "They believe that they can stop the tide. But they can't. No one can. This thing that some of them still do to girls . . . ? It's a remnant of their culture and that's how it's defended. Well-meaning individuals, the law, courts . . . nothing stops it. Do you know where we are with this now, today, here, at this point in time, Detective Lynley? Mostly it's done in infancy now, only occasionally is it still done to a prepubescent girl. An infant can't speak, she can't report what's happened or what's being threatened. She can't tell a school-teacher, the police, anyone. She's pre-verbal and pre-memory. What I'm saying to you is that the entire ugly business of cutting girls has been driven deeply underground."

They were back in the interview room. They had more tea and Havers had decamped briefly to Peeler's, where she also purchased two bowls of cut-up fruit, four bananas, and four sealed packages of cheese and biscuits. The surgeon was delineating the why of how she'd been making herself "useful" to the mothers who continued to believe and to insist that their daughters would be able to marry only if they were clean and pure, with their virginity not only guaranteed but forcibly maintained.

A great deal of what she'd said so far had made perfect sense, at least to her. The hideous practice of mutilating girls was not going to end simply because there were people who wanted it to end. She'd learned as much after she'd begun to study with the French surgeon who'd developed a way to restructure the genitals of FGM's victims. She learned his technique and brought it to London, but she'd soon realised she could do more than merely reconstruct what had been badly, incompetently, and gruesomely damaged. She could prevent irreparable harm in the first place, by circumcising the girls herself so if, in the future, they wanted the surgery to reverse what had been done to them, the work involved would not deprive them of a sexual life that offered them more than pain.

The word went out once she opened Women's Health of Hackney. She performed hundreds of procedures in its tiny operating theatre. Not a single girl among those she circumcised died, and she appeared quite proud of that statistic. That it was grisly and disfiguring—no matter how nicely she did it—didn't seem to occur to her.

Everything went well, she said. Mercy Hart's part was to promote what the clinic had to offer, to encourage word-of-mouth among mothers of daughters, and to hand out cards—with only a phone number on them—wherever she could. Mercy handled the clinic's day-to-day business and Dr. Weatherall had taught her how to conduct an initial exam. When there was an appointment set up, the surgeon would spend the necessary time in Kingsland High Street. Patients and their mothers did not see her face. She was masked and gowned on the day of surgery when she met them, and she stayed that way until she left the premises.

Then, Teo Bontempi.

"She put it together: the clinic and my unexpected presence in Kingsland High Street on the morning the police showed up. She wanted to know what I was doing there, of course. I talked about being a volunteer. She asked me how I could possibly be a volunteer without knowing what was going on in the place. She accused me of being involved in cutting girls. I denied it, of course. Outrageous and ridiculous, I said. She had no real evidence that FGM was being provided at the clinic at all. But she was committed to getting the evidence—I could see that—and I realised that eventually someone was going to tell her the truth. Someone always tells the truth, she said. It would only be a matter of time. And if everything came together as she wanted, I would be struck off."

"You had to stop her," Lynley said quietly.

"I phoned her that very night. And then again and then again."

"Were you not worried that Mercy would confess as to what was going on in the clinic?"

She shook her head. "Mercy believes in the work we're doing."

"Cutting babies?" Havers asked. "Cutting little girls?" She looked disgusted.

"Safeguarding their lives, Sergeant. Do either of you have any idea how many native cutters there are in London? No? Neither do I. But I've seen enough of the harm they've done, with their razor blades and their kitchen knives and their box cutters and whatever else they use, to know that, until immigrant women have enough education-based facts to put a stop to this, it's going to continue. It continues because they *allow* it to continue. It will stop when they refuse to carry it on."

"Teo didn't see it that way," Lynley said.

"She saw black and white, cause and effect, right and wrong."

"So you went to Streatham and you killed her."

"No. *No.* That was never my intention. We talked, but I couldn't make her see . . . She said I'd had her final word on the subject and she began to walk to the door of her flat and there was this moment—this one single blinding moment because I couldn't make her *understand*. I hit her with the sculpture. I didn't even think about it first. It was a blind reaction. That's all it was, and once I'd done it and she'd fallen and she wasn't moving . . ." Dr. Weatherall had been gazing from one of them to another. Her solicitor sat quietly, letting her talk as she wished. Lynley wondered what advice Vivienne Yang had given the surgeon while he and Havers had been out of the room. No sooner had he entertained that thought, the potential answer came with what she said next. "I was going to help her at once. I was horrified at what I'd done. I dropped the sculpture and knelt by her side. But then I heard several knocks on the door and the door started to open and I . . . I . . . hid."

"Where?" Havers asked this. "Not a lot of places to hide, you ask me. We've been in the flat."

"There was a clothes cupboard."

"In her bedroom? A bit risky, that."

"What choice did I have? There're two large cupboards for storage near her door, but I couldn't get to them, and I wasn't thinking straight. I couldn't claim I'd just come upon her. She'd name me when she regained consciousness. I didn't know who was about to walk in and I didn't know what else to do. So I hid and I waited and I hoped who-ever it was would leave."

"Without coming to her aid?" Lynley asked.

"Yes. No. I don't know," she said.

"But that didn't happen, did it?" Havers asked. "He didn't leave."

"He didn't . . . ?" She looked confused. "It wasn't a man," she said.

CHELSEA
SOUTH-WEST LONDON

When he rang off from talking to DS Nkata, Tani sat on the edge of the bed in the St. Jameses' spare room that he had been using. He stared at his trainers, their laces untied. He rocked slightly. He didn't want to think. He'd tracked down the Peckham cousin, who was astonished to hear from him, so long had it been since their family had become estranged. How was Tani? How was Aunty? How was Simisola? Did Tani know about the marriage of his sister Ovia? Had Tani been told? We got to get together, we do, Tani. What're you doing these days? Have you taken up with any fine ladies?

It was clear that Monifa and Simisola weren't there. His cousin in Peckham hadn't heard from any member of the Bankole family in at least five years. So he rang Halimah just in case, but she'd not seen Monifa since Monifa had left Mayville Estate with the police detective. She'd not spoken to her either. Nor had she spoken to Abeo.

Halimah asked if there was something wrong, but Tani didn't tell her the truth for a simple reason. He didn't know what the truth was.

He developed a few ideas, though. When he rang the detective sergeant and told him what he'd learned about the whereabouts of his mum and his sister—nothing—Nkata's response was not reassuring. "I'm on it," he said. "Heading to the Belgravia Station," and to Tani's "D'you think—" Nkata cut him off with, "Lemme get back to you. But stay there, yeah? I need to know where you *are*, at least."

Tani said he'd remain in Chelsea with the St. Jameses, but that was very low on the list of what he truly wanted to do. Every nerve ending in his body was shouting at him to take some kind of action. His mother was not a resourceful person. There was a limit to what she'd be able to do when it came to protecting Simi. If—and he was forced to think it—she intended to protect Simi at all.

He rang Sophie. He said to her, "Mum came for Simi. I don't know where they are."

"But that's good, Tani. Isn't it?" Sophie said. "I mean, she'll keep her away from your dad."

"Right. Yeah. But, Soph, here's what it is. She said she was takin' Simi to Brixton, to stay with the fam'ly of that cop. Only, she di'n't."

Sophie was silent. He could see her in his mind, considering the question, twisting a lock of her short hair round her index finger in that way she had. "But that's positive, isn't it?" she said. "What I mean is if your dad turns up like she thinks he will, he can't force you to tell him what you don't know. That's what she's thinking, your mum. She's got to do everything she can do to keep Simi away from your dad. And once he turns up in Chelsea . . . Are *you* still in Chelsea?"

He told her he was. He told her that the police detective Nkata had rung him asking about Monifa. He told her Nkata had asked about places his mother might have taken Simi. He said at the end, "Soph, I think there's something gone wrong. When Mum came, she said the police'd let my dad leave the station and there was a taxi waiting—"

"But Tani, what else could she do but take a taxi? If your dad was on his way, she had to be quick."

"Tha's what it is, Soph. He never came here."

"Then he probably went to see . . . what's her name?"

"Lark."

"Right. Lark. I mean, last time he was there in Chelsea, he got hauled off by the police. Makes sense he wouldn't do the same thing twice. He's with Lark and he's making a new plan. You wait and see."

Tani wanted to believe that. It did make sense. His father's first appearance in Chelsea hadn't gone well, so why would he want to make another? The answer to that, however, was one he knew already, without needing to consider various possibilities. Abeo knew that Tani had taken the passports from Lark. And there were also scores to settle regarding Tani's shoving his father's pregnant mistress to the ground.

He tied the laces of his trainers and got to his feet. Downstairs on the ground floor of the house, he found Deborah St. James in the study. She was sitting in one of the leather chairs. She was listening to someone on her mobile phone. She was saying, "But that's so difficult to believe . . . Why . . ." She listened for a bit once again. "Do you think that's the best idea? . . . Can you control things? I mean, obviously, you've already shown that you can, but that was before—" She caught sight of Tani standing in the doorway. She nodded at him and held up a finger, which told him he should remain there and wait. "Dad's not here, nor Simon. He's not due back till later this evening . . . Southampton, for a meeting with Andrew and David and then to see his mum . . . Yes, yes . . . And, Winston, did having the sculpture help at all? . . . Well, at least that's good news, isn't it?" Soon after that, she ended the call.

She stood and came across the room to Tani. She put her hand lightly on his shoulder and said, "You're not to worry," and he was about to demand to know what was going on because it was clear to him that something was happening when she went on with, "That was Winston. DS Nkata. Tani, you're not to be concerned with this, but he's going to the Belgravia Police Station to speak with your father when he's released."

BELGRAVIA
CENTRAL LONDON

It took very little time to discover that Monifa Bankole had not put in an appearance at the Belgravia station to file a charge of assault against her husband. That being the case and because they were very close to the hour at which the man would be released anyway, it was a matter of conversation and paperwork to put Nkata in the company of Abeo Bankole. There was no surprise in the fact that Bankole was not happy to see that the person awaiting him was the same one who'd rung the coppers to remove him from Chelsea on the previous day.

He was the worse for wear after his night in custody. His clothing was crumpled and his face was unshaven. He smelled rank, as if several days had passed since his arrest instead of only one. He clocked Nkata and said, "You," with an expression of disgust on his face.

Nkata said, "We need to have a talk."

"I have nothing to say to you."

"Happens I don' think tha's true. I've a car jus' outside."

"I will go nowhere with you."

Nkata paused. They were on the pavement. He'd left his Fiesta a short distance away in Ebury Square, but Abeo was under no obligation to follow him there. From this point forward, he needed the man's cooperation, and he had limited means to gain it. He said, "I'll take you where you choose, Mister Bankole, long 's you talk to me on the way. Now, I can't make you do that, and we both know it. But Simisola's gone missing, her mum's taken her, and since their passports're missing as well, I got some concerns where they might've gone."

Abeo's face went completely still for a moment. Then a pulse began beating in his temple. He said, "Tani and that whore girl of his—"

"This i'n't about them. They di'n't have a thing to do with it. I'm the one, Mister Bankole. Me. You got that?"

"You."

"Me. So you an' me, we can go at it just here, in this spot if tha's wha' you want. It'll take some time, an' you'll be the worse for it—which I expect you know—or you c'n come with me and help sort this out, cos I'd like to take you back to Chelsea. Lemme say, though, that Tani's still there an' if you put a hand on him, you come back here straightaway. You got that, Mister Bankole?"

A muscle moved in Abeo's jaw. He breathed in deeply. He jerked his head to indicate acceptance. Nkata said, "Right then," and directed Abeo towards the corner of Semley Place and Buckingham Palace Road and from there along the pavement and the side of the police station till they reached Ebury Square, where enormous London planes provided some welcoming shade for the benches that surrounded a fountain.

They didn't speak. Nkata reckoned that a spark in the tension between them could have set his car in flames as they made their way to the Thames. It was no great distance, for which he was grateful, as time was spinning away from them. They got caught briefly behind a number 44 bus, but Nkata managed to zoom past it—illegally—at an intersection and got them onto the Embankment, where soon enough they were in sight of Albert Bridge. He rang Deborah St. James to prepare Tani for his father's arrival.

She was waiting for them near the door, it seemed, for Nkata had knocked once only before she opened it. She had Peach in her arms and the dachshund was ecstatic at the idea of visitors, squirming to be put onto the floor where—doubtless—she would soon be snuffling round their feet. Deborah had thought to provide them with cool drinks, which she'd placed in her husband's study. If she noticed the odour emanating from Tani's father, she gave no sign of it.

Tani was already in the room waiting for them. He'd apparently been at the window keeping watch, because he stood there still and faced his father. He was the first to speak and Nkata had to admire him for that.

He said, "I didn't mean to shove Lark. I jus' needed the passports, Pa. That's what it was. I'm that sorry I pushed her."

"You know nothing," was Abeo's curt reply.

To his credit, Tani replied with, "Could be tha's the case and I don't doubt it."

Abeo looked away from his son. When Deborah gestured to one of the two leather chairs in the room, he walked to it and sat. He adopted a dominant posture, his legs spread, his hands on his thighs, his arms akimbo. Tani seemed to read it for what it was and remained by the window.

"We got transport police working on this," Nkata said. "Rail, underground, and overground. Far as we know, she doesn' have much in the way of funds but if she's got a credit card—"

"Her mother," Abeo said. "Or mine. Or any of her relations. Or any of mine."

"Meaning what?" Nkata asked.

"Meaning money," he said. "She has the passports but she needs the money to use them. One of them will have purchased the tickets for her."

"That would be the phone call," Nkata said, after a moment.

"What phone call?"

"Someone rang her when she was with my mum. She said it was Belgravia police telling her you were released. You were on your way to Chelsea, she said. But I expect that was a call from whoever it was bought the tickets, letting her know where she could fetch them. Where's she going, then?"

Abeo barked a laugh. "She has the passports! Where *would* she go, you stupid sod?"

"Nigeria," Deborah St. James murmured, and added, "No. Really. That can't be."

At Deborah's word *Nigeria*, Nkata went to the doorway, taking his mobile phone from his jacket. The number was connecting as behind him he heard Tani cry, "Pa, no! No way, *no* way did anyone buy her tickets. Tha's not true. And *you* were the one. You said—"

"*What* did I say?"

"You talked about that girl in Nigeria I was meant to marry and the bride price you would get for Simi."

"And this means what?"

"You brought that woman meant to cut her to the flat. You bought all that clobber for her to use."

"How else do I make it seem to your worthless mother that *I* will be the one to declare what happens to Simisola? Monifa will *not* be that person who makes decisions for our family."

Tani grabbed his own head as if this movement could clear his thoughts. He cried, "No. *No.* It doesn't make sense."

"You heard her yourself," Abeo said sharply. "You *know* what she wanted with that clinic of hers. You heard me try to stop her. You knew I sent her to fetch back that money. I told her not to come home without it. Why did I do that if not to stop her?"

"Are you're saying this is down to Mum? That everything's been down to Mum all along?"

"What is 'everything'? Do you mean the cutting of your sister? That?" Abeo laughed sharply in affirmation. There was no amusement involved.

Nkata returned to the room, letting them know that the word was going out as fast as possible. Airports would soon be covered, the airlines were receiving the information, the gate agents would be told, Passport Control would not allow them through.

Abeo stood then. He said, "You . . . All of you . . . You pretend to know and you do not. I will find them and put an end to this."

He moved towards the study door. Deborah said quickly, "Winston, do you not think . . . ?" and Nkata saw the appeal on her face. But he also saw reason in what the Nigerian man had said. And what he knew as a certainty was that he had neither purpose nor grounds to stop Abeo Bankole from leaving them and setting off to find his daughter and his wife.

WESTMINSTER
CENTRAL LONDON

"Why'm I not chuffed about how it all turned out?" Havers asked him.

They were on their way back to New Scotland Yard, having made the arrangements to remand Dr. Weatherall into custody at Bronzeville Prison pending her first appearance at a hearing. This would take place once the CPS decided upon the various charges the surgeon would face: those that were related to the clinic in Kingsland High Street and those that were related to her attack upon Teo Bontempi.

Lynley understood the sentiment Havers was expressing. He felt it as well and he considered *unsettled* the best term to use to describe it. He said, "It's easier, isn't it, to see things as Teo Bontempi did: in black and white. If there's no grey area to think about, a decision appears simple."

"Except seeing the situation as a black-and-white issue got her killed, didn't it."

"And yet, what was she to do once she understood what was happening in the Kingsland clinic?"

Havers squirmed in her seat. He could sense her looking at him and he glanced in her direction. "Seems to me that where it all went to hell was when Philippa Weatherall tried to talk Teo out of having her arrested. After all, Teo thought Mercy was the cutter. She brought the coppers in because of that, not because of Dr. Weatherall. She didn't even know about her. So if she had just kept up with her story about volunteering, how was Teo ever going to prove that she was anything more?"

"Could be that Dr. Weatherall reckoned at some point Mercy would crack once she was arrested. No matter how much she believes in the work, I can't think Mercy would have wanted to go on trial in the real culprit's place. FGM, assault, murder? I expect at some point Mercy was—and still is—going to make a deal with the CPS. Her testimony in exchange for a lighter sentence, a suspended sentence, or no sentence at all. Dr. Weatherall has to know that. Mercy has three children, after all."

Havers was quiet for a moment. Finally, she said, "C'n I say she meant well?"

"Dr. Weatherall? Christ, that's difficult, isn't it. Perhaps she started out meaning well, but she took a wrong turn more than once. And that was badly done. A jury may see it otherwise, of course. I have to say that I hope you don't."

They were quiet. They were heading into the end of the day, and with every tenth of a mile the traffic increased. They were approaching Tower Hill station when Lynley's mobile rang. He fished for it in his jacket and handed it over to Havers. She glanced, said, "It's Winston," and answered with, "We're on our way back. Dr. Weatherall's admitted it. But, Winnie, there's—"

He evidently interrupted her because she began to listen intently. She said, with a glance out of the window, "We're just at the Tower. Where are you? . . . How the hell did that happen, Win? . . . So what are they saying? What are they telling you? Anything? . . . Okay. I'll let the guv know . . . Hey . . . Winston . . . *Win*ston, hang on. We'll sort it." She listened for a bit more and then said, "We'll see you back there, then."

Lynley looked at her, one eyebrow raised.

"Win's lost the Bankole woman," she said.

"Lost . . . ?"

"She's done a runner."

Lynley cursed under his breath. They needed her. They had her statement, true. But ultimately they needed her to fill in the gaps by telling her story to the CPS and then to a jury.

Havers continued with, "It gets a bit worse, sir. She's got the passports with her. She's also got Simisola, the little girl."

"What in God's name . . . ?"

"Her husband thinks the family in Nigeria got tickets for her, to take Simisola to them."

"The husband?"

"I don't know, sir. Could be he's come over from the dark side. Could be he's telling porkies as fast 's he can 'n order to get his maulers on the girl. Either way, Winston's put the word out. He's got everyone possible on the alert. If she *does* try to leave the country, she'll be stopped. He hopes."

"Why 'hopes'?"

"She had a few hours' head start."

"Did he say how she managed to get the passports?"

Havers didn't reply at once. Lynley glanced at her and said her name. She replied with, "He hadn't secured them, guv."

"Winston hadn't secured the passports?" Lynley had heard her clearly, but he simply did not want to believe what she'd said.

"Yeah. That's the case, according to Win. She took them from his jacket."

Lynley hit the steering wheel with his fist. "What in the name of God was he thinking?"

"He feels rotten, sir."

"As he damn well should."

"She pulled the wool, is what it is. Seems she did that to everyone."

They said very little else as they made their way through the congestion. It was one of those times when only a helicopter would have sufficed to get them anywhere quickly. Once they reached New Scotland Yard, Havers announced baldly that only a fag would settle her nerves. She lit up as they made their way to the lifts. He made no comment.

Nkata was waiting for them as the lift doors opened. He apologised three times in a single sentence.

"Have you heard anything from the airlines or airports?" Lynley asked him.

Nkata shook his head. "I don't wan' to think she's got her out of the country, guv. This's down to me."

"To me as well, Winston," Lynley said. "I did tell you where the children were, as you should recall."

"Tha's good of you to say, but all the same—"

"Let's take everything one step at a time. Get the team together."

Nkata nodded, and he went to collect them, bringing them to Lynley's office. Lynley brought the DCs up to date and gave them what he hoped would be their last assignment. Philippa Weatherall had confessed but in her confession she claimed to have heard someone enter Teo Bontempi's flat. Whoever it was knocked and, without waiting, opened the door, found Teo on the floor, probably saw the sculpture lying next to her, said a few words, and left. "She says it was a woman," Lynley told them. "If she's telling the truth—and God knows she may not be—chances are very good it was the sister."

"Not DCS Phinney's wife out to eliminate a rival?" Havers asked.

"Phinney looked for her there but never saw her. He did see Ross Carver arrive. I've asked for his wife's fingerprints and a DNA sample, but I daresay she's going to be in the clear. What we know is that—if Dr. Weatherall is telling the truth, which is admittedly a moot subject, all things considered—whoever it was, she didn't have a key and she didn't ring below to be allowed into the building."

"She must've got in in someone's company?" Nkata said.

"The woman with the messenger bag?" one of the DCs offered. "The one who entered with that group?"

"I believe we're going to find that was Dr. Weatherall," Lynley said.

"That leaves the sister," Barbara pointed out. And with a glance at Nkata, "Sorry, Win. I know she warmed the cockles et cetera."

"She could easily have got inside in the company of someone she knew from the building, someone who knew her well enough to understand she'd be calling on Teo."

"Back to CCTV, then?" a DC asked with very little enthusiasm, and who could blame her?

"Back to it," Lynley agreed. "But what you'll be looking for this time round is a woman leaving the building on her own. This should be between the time Messenger Bag arrives and the time Ross Carver arrives at . . . What was the time, Barbara?"

"Round eight forty. Messenger Bag was just after seven."

Lynley repeated the times and turned to Nkata to say, "Winston, you'll need to be here to identify her should a woman alone appear on film."

"Guv, you don't think I should . . . the airports . . . Monifa Bankole?"

"I can identify Rosie Bontempi, sir," Havers said.

"I want you dealing with the airports and St. Pancras," Lynley said. What he didn't add was that they couldn't afford another cock-up. He saw Havers glance apologetically at her fellow DS. He added, "I'll want word at once if Monifa Bankole surfaces, Barbara."

BELSIZE PARK
NORTH-WEST LONDON

By half past ten, Rosie Bontempi had finally been spotted twice: once on the CCTV film from the building in which her sister lived and once—for good measure, according to the DC who did the honours—on Streatham High Road, where she'd cooperatively parked within viewing distance of the CCTV camera on the funeral director's business across the street. But nothing had yet come of the airlines, the airports, or St. Pancras and the Eurostar. Since there were hotels near all of these locations, Nkata directed that the team turn to that. Lynley left them to it and went on his way.

He thought briefly about going home—considering the hour, tossing back two fingers of the Macallan and dropping into his bed sounded quite good to him—but seeing Daidre sounded better, and he reckoned she would have long since arrived back in London from her trip to Cornwall. So he drove through the night to Belsize Park.

Had the flat been in darkness, he might have turned for home as she'd had a difficult time in Cornwall followed by the drive back to London, and she probably would have been just as happy to have an undisturbed night of sleep. But there were lights on, so he found a spot he deemed safe for the Healey Elliott, and he walked back to her building.

He used his key this time, and once inside the building, he heard conversation and music. The television, he thought. Daidre wasn't a daily or nightly viewer of anything in particular, but it was a way she could relax with a glass of wine and—no doubt—Wally lounging next to her. He reckoned that was what she was doing. He unlocked the door, opened it, and said, "Has that animal completely supplanted me?"

A woman's cry of surprise came from the sofa. But it was not Daidre. Lynley had not seen her in nearly two years, and she was much changed. Then she had quite short hair, its colour altered by peroxide to an unattractive shade of orange. Then she had worn no makeup and had a squint that suggested her eyes badly wanted correction. Now, however, her hair was dark, it fell to just below her ears, in a curve that enhanced the shape of her face, and—like Daidre—she wore spectacles. Daidre's were frameless; these were tortoiseshell and round.

"Gwynder," he said to her. "Sorry. I didn't expect—"

"Tommy!" Daidre had come to the doorway of the bedroom. She carried sheets, blankets, and a pillow in her arms. She said, "You've met Tommy, Gwyn. He came to the caravan with me once."

She'd taken him there because his suspicions about her had encouraged him to force her hand, making her reveal the truth about her childhood, the childhoods of her siblings, and the lives they'd led with their parents. He'd assumed that both Gwynder and her twin, Goron, knew about his involvement with their sister. From Gwynder's expression, though, it seemed that this was as unknown to her as Daidre's early life had once been unknown to him.

She said, "You're the policeman."

He said, "I am."

"Edrek never said."

This, he knew, was Daidre's birth name, discarded by her when she'd been adopted into her Falmouth family. There was very little answer he could make to this, aside from, "Ah. Did she not?" which he said as kindly as he could manage, for he could see how ill at ease Gwynder was in his presence. He wanted to add to Daidre, "We appear to be faced with something of a dilemma, don't we?" but she was quickly moving to the sofa, where she placed the linens and the pillow, after which she put her hand on Gwynder's shoulder.

"It's quite all right, Gwyn. You've nothing to . . . It's quite all right."

Lynley wondered what she'd been about to say: Nothing to fear? Nothing to worry about? Nothing you need to say to the man who loves me? What? But she'd glanced in his direction and had clocked his raised eyebrow and had apparently decided that some thoughts were best not given voice.

He said as pleasantly as he could manage, "Welcome to London. I hope you find the change from Cornwall isn't too drastic for you."

Gwynder fingered the neckline of the sundress she was wearing, rolling it nervously between her fingers. She looked from him to her sister and back to him. She said, "Do you live here? With Edrek?"

"No, no," Daidre said.

"He's got a key, though."

"Well yes, of course. Tommy's . . ." Daidre looked at him in a way that suggested she was unequal to the moment. This was completely unlike her. Lynley had never known her to be unequal to anything.

He said, "I'm here occasionally. Sometimes I arrive before your sister. Sometimes I arrive quite late. It seemed easier if I had a key."

"You sleep with her, then. You're her lover. Edrek, why didn't you tell me you have a lover?"

Lynley reckoned he knew the answer to that well enough. Had Daidre informed her sister that she and Lynley were involved, Gwynder would not have come with her to London. He knew how unlikely it was that Daidre would admit this, though.

Instead, she said, "Tommy and I are . . . Well, I'm not quite certain how to define us. Tommy, are you?"

"I thought I was," he said, after a moment to collect himself. "Perhaps it's something worthy of discussion. May I fortify myself with a glass of wine?"

"Of course," she said brightly. "Shall I . . . ?" She indicated the kitchen.

"I'll find it," he told her.

She followed him as he reckoned she would. He heard her say to her sister, "Gwyn, I must—"

But he heard nothing else because, at that juncture, what he could hear mostly was the blood roaring inside his head. He wanted to tell himself he wasn't angry. He wanted to say how petty a thing it was to be angry over . . . what? A slight? An omission? An embarrassed inability to reveal a relationship with a man? He didn't know what it was. But he did know that he'd not been so angry, disappointed, or whatever he was with a woman in years. Indeed, he couldn't remember ever feeling about a woman's actions what he was feeling in the moment.

"Tommy." She'd come up behind him. "Try to understand, please."

He held his hand up to stop her. If they were to have this conversation, he thought, they weren't going to have it with her sister sitting in the next room. He went to the garden door. When he opened it, Wally dashed inside. The presence of the cat—his previous supplanter—made him want to laugh rather too insanely.

"Would you prefer to feed him?" he asked Daidre.

"Don't," she said. "That's not worthy of you."

She followed him into the garden, still very much a work in progress. He heard her shut the door. She came down the steps behind him. She placed her hand lightly on his back as if to urge him to turn, which, at the moment, he did not want to do.

"You did know I was going to bring her to London," she said. "I couldn't leave her there. She was frightened to stay at the cottage alone. I didn't want her to go back to the caravan. There was no other choice. And besides . . ."

In her long pause, he turned to her. The light from the kitchen window fell upon the side of her face, but the rest of her was in shadow as was he. "Besides?"

"I wanted to bring her, Tommy. It was the right thing to do. And I must do what I decide is the right thing to do."

"Have I stopped you from that in some way?" he asked her.

"You've . . ." She sighed. She unclipped her hair, which bought her time. The gesture was habitual with her and it generally didn't bother him because he knew she needed and wanted to sort through her thoughts.

Normally, he couldn't blame her for this. Her life was complicated in ways his wasn't. Tonight, however, he found in her hesitation a truth that she didn't want to admit and he didn't want to see. But she was going to have to speak that truth. He couldn't and he wouldn't do it for her.

"You've made it clear," she said. "What you want. How things ought to be. What you need. You've made it all clear."

"Have I?"

"Tommy, you *know* you have. There's something you want from me, some quality you think you sense within me, something that you believe I can give you if I only . . . You see, I don't know. If I only try harder? If I only open up to you? If I only pour out my heart, spill out my soul, cut open a vein? And I can't do any of that because I don't know how and I don't know if there's anything else inside of me anyway. I keep trying to tell you: Here, here, right here, standing in front of you . . . This is Edrek Udy. This is Daidre Trahair. This is who I am and what I have to give. And you and I know it's not enough. I'm not enough. I'll never be enough."

"Is bringing Gwynder to London like this . . . ? Was that particular action supposed to give me that message?"

"No, of course not."

"Then why did you not simply tell me?"

"I've tried to tell you. You can't possibly say I've not tried to tell you."

"You misconstrue. The part of this that's you and I? That's not what

I'm talking about, and I think you know that. Why didn't you say 'This is how it has to be. Gwynder must come with me to London'? I could have lived with that. We could have worked with that. But this . . . Daidre, you must see how it seems."

"I couldn't," she said, and her voice broke on the second word. "And that goes to the core. I couldn't."

She began to weep and he took a step towards her. But at the same instant she took a step away.

That movement on her part created the separation from her that he needed. Had she allowed him to do what he wanted to do, which was to take her into his arms, he would have neither seen nor understood what she was trying to say. He realised then that allowing him to hold her, to find a way to soothe her, was, for Daidre, taking the easy route, and she was not a woman who did that. He realised then that by defining her rather than allowing her to define herself, he was asking her to live the image he had of her instead of living as who she was.

Gwynder was the only way she saw to do this. Indeed, bringing her sister to London was the only way she could show Lynley the woman she actually was. Nothing else would have worked because nothing else *had* worked, from the moment she'd come upon him inside her cottage in Cornwall, uselessly looking for a telephone. Indeed, wasn't *that* oddly appropriate? he thought. He'd fallen in love with her because she was so unlike anyone in his world. And then he'd set about making her into someone he thought she needed to be.

He said quietly, "Daidre." He waited. He said her name again. And then a third time until she raised her head to look at him. "I am," he told her, "gravely at fault here. Please know that I finally see it. You are in no way to blame for my failure to understand before now what you've been trying to tell me from the moment we met. I'm so bloody sorry for what I've put you through. Truly, I am."

He fished in his pocket and brought out the key she'd given him. He recalled that he'd asked for the key. He recalled that at first she'd hesitated, but then she'd complied. Even that memory seared his conscience. Twenty-five different ways he'd been a fool.

He handed it to her. He closed her fingers round it.

"Know that I love you," he said. "You, Daidre, here and now, as you are. When you can—if you can—welcome me into your life, I'll be waiting. I'll hope that time comes, but if it doesn't, please believe I shall do my best to understand."

16 AUGUST

NEW END SQUARE
HAMPSTEAD
NORTH LONDON

On this, his third trip to the Bontempi house, Winston Nkata felt a weight on his shoulders like a yoke worn by an ox. He'd been up all night, not because he was at work but because he was waiting for word about Monifa Bankole. None had come.

The only person who seemed to feel worse than he did about her disappearance was his mother. She blamed herself for not asking more questions of Monifa and for not ringing her son at once to explain what was going on. And she *could* have done that, she kept insisting. All she'd had to do was ring him and ask him to check with the Belgravia police about the release of Abeo Bankole. But she hadn't thought to do that because she'd not seen a reason that Monifa would lie. Nor had he, he reassured her. He'd been taken in by the Nigerian woman's apparent helplessness. He reckoned he wasn't the first person to find himself in that position.

Now pulling into New End Square, the idea of being taken in seemed to have a second application. He'd not wanted to think of

Rosie Bontempi as responsible in any way for her sister's death, and he had to admit that a large part of his disbelief had to do with Rosie's beauty and sensuality. And the truth was that she *wasn't* responsible for Teo's death. What she *was* responsible for was leaving the flat without ringing 999 to ask for assistance. With her sister unconscious and the discarded sculpture lying nearby, Rosie hadn't had a single reason for walking away and leaving her on the floor. Yet, she had done so. The why of it needed to be admitted to and explained.

He arrived early, as before. His ostensible reason was to let the family know that Teo's body would be released to them, and the arrangements for her funeral could now be made. But his other reason was the conversation he needed to have with Rosie. And that was something he wasn't anticipating with the slightest degree of pleasure.

As before, Solange Bontempi opened the door to him. Unlike his earlier visits, however, she was not wearing professional attire. Rather, she was in linen: navy trousers and a bright pink top, colour-blocked with navy and grey. Her feet were bare, but her toenails were the pink of the top she wore. Her only jewellery consisted of her wedding ring, a gold chain with a navy stone held by gold filigree, and small gold hoops for earrings. Seeing him, she smiled and said, "Detective Sergeant. Good morning. You have arrived just as we were setting off. Cesare insists that he return to the hospital today."

"He's had a turn?" Nkata asked her.

She gave a charming laugh and said, "No, no. I mean the animal hospital. I have agreed to this, and as I have two days away from my own work, I'm taking him, watching him, and generally hovering over him. He will not like this, of course, but as he cannot drive to Reading on his own, he must either call a car service or have me as his driver. He—wisely, may I say—chose me. Please come in."

She directed Nkata to the sitting room, where he found Cesare Bontempi sitting in an armchair, casually dressed, like his wife, but in jeans and jumper. He had a Zimmer with him, but he also had a medical walking stick. Nkata reckoned having both constituted a compromise he'd reached with his wife.

"What have you to tell us?" Cesare demanded in the same brusque manner he'd used before. "Can you tell us about our Teo or not?"

"I can do," Nkata said. "'F Rosie's here, she'll want to hear as well, I 'xpect."

"Let me fetch her," Solange said. "Please. If you will sit . . . ? It will be a moment only."

Once she had left them alone, Cesare turned to Nkata and said, "It is over, this? Are we having our Teodora back? You come here in person with news, no? Otherwise you do not return."

"Tha's right," Nkata told him. "An' your news is you're returning to work, innit?"

"I am. Enough of this at-home time. I am needed elsewhere, and between you and me, I wish to be elsewhere for at least part of every day. Me, I love my family, yes? But not twenty-four hours every day and every week and on and on. That? It makes me . . ." He pointed to his head and rolled his eyes dramatically.

"Hear you," Nkata said. "I 'xpect tha's the case for most people, eh?"

Solange reappeared at the doorway. She said, "Rosie is coming. She works earlier today so she was just dressing. Can we begin without her?"

"Can do, yeah. But I got to say: Rosie's needed to clarify a few details."

"Rosie?" Solange asked.

Cesare added, "Why? What is this she clarifies?"

Nkata didn't need to answer because he could hear Rosie coming down the stairs. The sound suggested she was in her stilettos and ready to leave. He stood as she entered the room, as striking a woman as he'd ever seen and today was no different. She wore a fashionably tailored coverall in pumpkin orange with a forest-coloured cardigan over her shoulders. The stilettos were, as before, a few strips of leather that left most of her weight balancing on her toes.

"*Maman* says you need me. So there's news?"

"We've made an arrest and we've got a confession," he said. "Your sister was gone after by a woman called Philippa Weatherall, who was due to repair her FGM damage."

This was met by silence. All of them looked stunned to varying degrees. It was Solange who said, "But Teo had already been repaired. What was this?"

"Teo'd been cut open," Nkata said. "But tha's diff'rent from being repaired. Repaired means getting her close to what she was, or 'least as close as possible. So she got examined by a surgeon and she got the go-ahead. Only problem was the surgeon was performing FGM on the side to make money to help with the cost of women getting repaired. Teo worked that out *after* she'd seen her to be checked for surgery. She wanted to stop her doing FGM, but the surgeon didn't want to be stopped. And there wasn't any way she wanted to be struck off, which was what would've happened if Teo turned her over to the police."

Solange raised her fingers to her lips. Against them, she murmured, "Did no one know?"

"Which part?"

She shook her head. "I . . . I don't know which part I mean."

Cesare said, "She tells no one about this? That she will have surgery to be . . . what?"

"Made normal-looking far as a surgeon could make her. Made so she could feel something again if that was possible."

"What is this 'to feel something'?" Cesare asked. "How did she not feel something?"

Solange looked as if she wanted to ask the same question. As for

Rosie, her gaze was on her stiletto-shod feet, which suggested she knew exactly what 'to feel something' meant.

"To enjoy herself more," was how Nkata put it. "Seems she never enjoyed it at all."

"Sex," Rosie finally looked up and spoke to her parents. "I think he means that Teo couldn't enjoy sex with Ross."

"This was why they divorced?" Solange said.

"They hadn't divorced, *Maman*. You know that. They hadn't even begun the process. If you ask me, they never would have. They would have continued in some sort of mad limbo with neither one of them wanting to escape."

"But . . . You and Ross? What was that?" Solange asked.

"What's this of you and Ross?" Cesare said. "How do we have a you and Ross?"

Rosie looked to her mother, and it was clear to Nkata that the news about the coming grandchild via Rosie and Ross had not reached Cesare. He wondered why mother and daughter were keeping it from him. Would he react with too much passion? Too much emotion? Too much of something that might bring on another stroke? They were afraid to tell him, and Nkata could see it. He reckoned it was not his place to shed any light on the subject.

He said, "We'll need to know where you want her body taken. To prepare her for . . . whatever you're considering. You c'n ring me to let me know or you can ring the morgue." He'd written down both numbers on a page from his notebook and he handed this over to them. Solange took it, folding it neatly in half.

She said, "Ross. What does he know?"

"My colleague's informing him of ever'thing jus' like I'm inform-ing you."

Rosie said, "I should ring him, then. He'll be quite upset."

"Af'er I have a word with you," Nkata told her.

"With me? Why?"

"Toss it round your head and I 'xpect you'll work that out," he told her.

——————

STREATHAM
SOUTH LONDON

Barbara Havers had rung him on the previous evening, so she knew that Ross Carver had completed his move back into his former home. Over the phone she'd told him that they'd made an arrest and they had a confession. Any more than that, she said, she would prefer to tell him in person. So after leaving her Mini in front of Maxwell Brothers Funeral Directors, she crossed the road and used the buzzer next to the name *Bontempi* on the building, giving thought to when he would change it from *Bontempi* to *Carver* once again.

He said, "Sergeant Havers?" through the intercom.

"With bells on," she replied, and he buzzed her in.

She found him dressed for work but having a final cup of coffee. He offered her one from what looked like a new espresso-and-everything-else maker, but she shook her head. She said, "It was the surgeon, I'm sorry to say. The woman who was on board to repair her."

He'd been lifting his coffee to his mouth, but he lowered it. He gestured her to the table where they'd sat before. She noted that the tenth edition of *Standing Warrior* had not been returned yet. So that was where she began.

"We found *Standing Warrior*. Teo's edition of it, I mean. It had been given to a woman who was one of the surgeon's patients. We saw it in a photo, went to check it out, and there it was. That took us straight to the surgeon. It's with forensics now."

"Why?" he said. "Why the hell did she club her?"

"Teo discovered she had two clinics, not just one: a clinic where she performed repairs and another where she practised FGM."

"What the . . . ? What was she doing? Lining up future patients for repairs?"

Barbara shook her head. She said, "Mind if I open . . ." and gestured to the balcony and its door, to which he said, "Have at it," so she did. Despite the fact that it was still early morning, the sunlight streaming through the balcony doors and the dining-room window had already transformed the flat into a sauna. She returned to the table, saying, "It's called medicalised FGM in some countries. FGM performed with all the mod cons of an operating theatre—like general anaesthetic— and post-surgery care. In some countries, it's actually legal. Here, no. Teo had been watching a clinic in Dalston. When she'd seen enough, she had the local coppers shut the place down. She was there when it happened."

"So she saw the surgeon there?"

"More or less, that. This's a woman called Philippa Weatherall. She—the surgeon—wasn't in the clinic when the local cops arrived, so that was why she didn't get arrested. But she came along directly and Teo saw her. She put it together, and she let the surgeon know she put it together. Once Teo turned her in, that was going to mark the end of her career—Dr. Weatherall's, I mean—and she couldn't let that happen. She rang several times to try to speak to Teo about it."

He dropped his gaze to the coffee cup. He swirled the coffee within it, but didn't look like a man who wanted to swill it down. He said, "Why the hell did Teo let her into the building? At that point, she must have known the risk. She wasn't a fool."

"She didn't let her in," Barbara said. "We're fairly sure Dr. Weatherhall managed to get inside the place with a group who were entering. I'll be taking her picture round when I leave here. Someone is going to recognise her."

"But even the flat . . . I don't understand why Teo let her in?"

"She might've been surprised to see her, but obviously, she didn't think Dr. Weatherall was dangerous. And according to the surgeon, she came only to talk to her again. But she got desperate when Teo refused to give in. She whacked her with the bronze piece before she had a chance to think it through."

"Then why not finish her off? She's a doctor, after all. She'd check for vital signs, wouldn't she?"

And here they were, at the tricky part. Barbara hated what she had to tell him.

NEW END SQUARE
HAMPSTEAD
NORTH LONDON

"You knew she was hurt," Nkata said to Rosie. They'd gone outside, into the large garden at the front of the house. He'd led her down the steps from the porch, beneath the massive wisteria vine, and along a path that edged the lawn. Midway was a weathered teak bench spotted with lichen and growing grey moss. He'd gestured to it and she'd sat cooperatively. So had he. "The sculpture was on the floor, and she was unconscious, and tha's how you let her stay."

Rosie met his gaze with her own although she didn't reply.

He said, "What I can't work out is why you di'n't ring 999."

She said, "I don't know what you're talking about."

He'd brought a copy of the shot they had from the digital film, catching her as she exited the building. He said, "I 'xpect you know what night this was taken."

She took it from him and examined it. She said, "I don't, actually. Why don't you tell me?"

"The night she got the cosh on her head is when. Tha's when this was taken. DS Havers—you met her already—she's taking a copy of this round the flats in Streatham. Tha's just a formality, though. You were there and you saw her on the floor."

"If she was unconscious, isn't that going to be difficult for you to prove?"

"Would've been," he admitted. "But happens Teo wasn't alone. The woman who coshed her with the sculpture was still in the flat."

"I don't believe you. You're trying to—"

"She heard you knock, Rosie. Then she heard the door. Then she heard you come in, but by then she'd got herself into the bedroom and hidden herself. She heard you come upon Teo and then she heard you say her name, couple of times this was. What she di'n't hear was a call being made to 999. What she di'n't hear was you doing anything at all to help your sister. What she *did* hear was you leaving. Which is wha' she did herself soon 's you were safely gone, cos she di'n't want to risk someone else walking in on her."

"Even if I did that, even if I left Teo where she was, it wasn't a crime."

"Not coming to someone's aid? You've got tha' right, you do. I's not a crime, that. But I got to say it takes a special kind of person to leave someone—an' a sibling at that—like you did. It makes me wonder what you were . . . I dunno . . . afraid of? I got guesses but not much more 'nless you tell me."

Rosie looked away from him then. She raised her hand to acknowledge the greeting of another inhabitant of New End Square. She finally said, "She was going to have him back. How d'you think that felt?"

"You're speakin' of Ross Carver?"

"Who else?"

"An' how did you know this? She tell you 's much?"

"I could tell."

"From her?"

"From Ross. She texted him that she wanted to speak to him and I could see everything on his face. I could see that the moment she crooked her finger, he would go to her and that was how it would always be. She knew I was pregnant by him, and she was intending to destroy my life. So yes, when I saw her on the floor, I left her there and allowed fate to decide things."

"You got lucky, then, di'n't you? Very badly wrong is what it was and the luckiest part of all for you was that Ross Carver di'n't understand what was happening to Teo cause she came round when he found her. 'Nstead of calling emergency, he helped her to bed. An' the rest is the rest."

"I didn't hurt her," Rosie said. "I didn't even touch her." She reached for his hand and covered it with her own. "I didn't want her to die. How could I have done? She was my sister." Her voice quavered and he reckoned her eyes were about to drop tears down her cheeks and onto her coverall. He found that he felt stony at this. He didn't like what this said about him: that someone's anguish did not touch him.

Then she cleared his conscience with a single question, "You won't tell my parents what I did, will you?" and he knew that the quaver in her voice and the tears in her eyes were part and parcel of the performance art at which she so excelled.

STREATHAM
SOUTH LONDON

"My colleague's gone to talk to the family," Barbara concluded. "He'll talk to Rosie as well. But there's not much doubt that it was her." She handed him the still of Rosie from the CCTV footage. "Doesn't make sense that she'd be here to have a stroll round the building, does it. And according to Dr. Weatherall, the woman knocked first, and when there was no answer, she came inside. She didn't need a key as Teo hadn't locked the door when she'd let Dr. Weatherall in."

"If Rosie had done something when she saw her . . . ?"

Barbara sighed. "D'you mean if she'd tried to help? That's a tricky call, that is. Could be had Teo been taken straight to hospital, nothing that came from there would be different. Also could be she'd've lived through it once the pressure was taken off her brain."

"But to do nothing. To say nothing. Just to leave her. How am I meant to interpret that aside from understanding that Rosie wanted her dead?"

"Answering that . . . ?" Barbara replied. "Too bloody far above my pay grade, that is. Except to say what I expect you already know. She had hopes of you. For years she'd had them and now she was pregnant by you. It might've taken a saint not to think how different things might become if she just left Teo where she was. P'rhaps she thought she'd just wait and see how things developed."

"Still and all," he said. He fell into silence then, and Barbara allowed the silence to hang there. If Rosie had cocked up, so had he. Barbara expected he knew that.

He finally spoke with, "I'll do for the baby what I've done for Colton: money for support and my personal involvement with the child. But I won't marry her. I can't."

"Something tells me things between you won't be so easily resolved as that," Barbara said.

"People need to marry for love. Don't you agree?"

"People marry for all sorts of reasons. There're times and situations when love's got nothing to do with it."

"Not for me. And I don't love her. I'm fond of her. I've always been that. But what I did with her . . . ?" He looked from Barbara to the bronze sculptures that sat upon the credenza. "I took her suggestion," he said. "I thought only of Teo. I acted the part. I made love to Rosie and listened to her moan and sigh and felt her come while I was inside her and through it all, I pretended she was Teo, as Teo would have been had she only been whole."

Barbara nodded, but she found it difficult to sympathise with Carver. No matter Rosie's part in what had happened between them, he'd gone along with it. The why of it was truly on him: No matter his claims about his indifference to Teo's disfigurement, he couldn't cope with her not feeling the way he—Ross Carver, not Teo herself—wanted her to feel. That inability on his part had started all of them down this road. As well intentioned as he might have been and as well meaning as he no doubt saw himself, he'd not allowed his wife to forget for an instant what she most wanted to forget about herself.

CHELSEA
SOUTH-WEST LONDON

Sophie believed none of it. Tani had rung her and had got as far as "Mum's got the passports," when Sophie said, "I'm coming to Chelsea," to which he'd replied, "There's nothing you c'n do, Soph. Everyone reckons she's taking Simi to Nigeria and—" which she'd interrupted with, "She *isn't.* She can't be. I'm coming." She'd then rung off.

She made very good time from the college. She'd been in a lecture when she'd seen he was ringing her, she told him. She'd ducked out of the hall to take the call. She'd arrived so quickly upon the conclusion of their conversation, she might have been transported through magic.

Tani was waiting for Sophie with Deborah St. James in her husband's study. They had both been there for hours, in anticipation of Monifa being located at one of the airports, inside a nearby airport hotel, at St. Pancras International, or at a hotel in the train station's vicinity. DS Nkata had told them that he would ring the instant he knew anything at all. Tani had been waiting in the study since long before dawn, joined by Deborah St. James, who'd appeared round half past seven with a tray of breakfast for him, which he hadn't been able to eat. Sergeant Nkata hadn't rung, however, and as the hours passed, Tani's hopes for his sister's safety faded. Either his mother had made an escape from the country or his father had found her. He didn't want to think of the outcome of either possibility.

Tani had been taken in at first by his father's performance on the previous day. But after a sleepless night during which he'd considered everything that had gone on with his family and everything he'd learned about his parents since the night Abeo had revealed the arrangement he'd made for Tani to marry a girl he didn't know, he'd had to conclude that Abeo no more wanted to find Simi to keep her from harm than he wanted to renew his marriage vows—whatever they'd been—with Monifa. First and foremost, he wanted Simi made pure and clean and whatever else was required because nothing had changed: he wanted to offer her for a hefty bride price to some bloke with funds in Nigeria. And he wanted *that* because at the end of the day he wanted what he'd always wanted—once he had whatever *else* he wanted—which was money and control over every person who touched upon his life.

When Sophie arrived, she joined him and Deborah St. James in the study. She said, "Anything yet?" to both of them. She flopped into one of the two leather chairs.

"We've not had a word from anyone," Deborah told her.

Sophie looked at Tani, and he could tell she was trying to evaluate his state. He wished she wouldn't, but he didn't want to try to act as if an unrealistic hope was bolstering him. There'd been enough acting in his family. Having reached a conclusion, Sophie turned back to Deborah and said, "Can't you ring someone?"

"I could do if that will ease your mind. But—"

"Not my mind. Tani's."

"—I would only be able to ring Sergeant Nkata or his superior, and there's little point to that because they'll be waiting for word as well."

"Sergeant Nkata's not seeing to this on his own?"

"He's working on a murder case," Deborah told her. "He won't have been able to place himself at any of the locations we're waiting to hear from. But you're not to worry. He'll get the word at once if they find her. Or his superior will. One of them will ring if that happens."

"Could be she's left already," Tani noted. "If she went straight to an airport from here?"

"I think we'd have heard by now," Deborah said. "They would have checked that first and her name would be on a passenger list along with Simi's."

"So where is she, then?" he demanded. "Where are they? 'Cause if my dad's found them . . ."

"Is anyone checking hospitals?" Sophie asked.

"That's something I *can* find out." Deborah had placed her mobile on the table that stood between the leather chairs. She unlocked it and was about to tap in a number when Tani's mobile rang, and he dug it from his pocket and looked at the screen. There was no identification of the caller, just the number of a landline he didn't know.

When he answered, a woman's voice said, "Is that Tani?" and he instantly thought his father had found them and this was a hospital ringing to tell him that his mother had been admitted with broken bones or worse. He steeled himself and said that yes, it was Tani. The woman then said, "I've got him," to someone who was apparently with her. After a moment he heard, "Tani? Are you still with the ginger-haired lady?"

For a moment Tani couldn't reply. It was his mother's voice, and when he said nothing, she went on with, "Tani? You are there? You've been kept safe?"

He felt dazed. His mother sounded as she always sounded except there was no stress or tension in her voice and he didn't know what this meant. He managed, "Mum." Then, "Pa's been. Only he came with Sergeant Nkata because he hadn't been let go from the police and you lied to us. Just like Pa. You *lied*, Mum."

"Tani, I am sorry that—"

"Where's Simi? What've you done with her? I'm not speakin' another word to you till you tell me what you've done to Simi and where she is and why you lied to me and—" To his complete humiliation, his voice broke. He gave the mobile to Sophie and raised his arm to hide his face.

Sophie quickly put the mobile on speaker. She said, "Mrs. Bankole, is Simi with you?"

Monifa's voice said, "Where is Tani?"

"He's just here next to me, but he's got upset. I've put you on speaker. If you can tell us where you are . . . ?"

"This is something I am not allowed to do, Tani," Monifa said. "I could not tell you yesterday. They phoned me and said they were ready for me but I was not to tell you or anyone."

It was Deborah who twigged what Tani's mum meant. She said, "Have you found a safe house, Mrs. Bankole?"

There was silence for a moment and then the phone apparently changed hands because a woman's voice said, "This is Dorcas. I'm not able to give you my surname. Monifa and her daughter are with me, and they are both fine. We're a shelter for abused women. Please don't ask me to name the shelter or to tell you where it is because I won't do that."

"I want to talk to my sister," Tani said. "I want to know she's safe."

"Of course," was Dorcas's reply, and after a moment, Tani heard Simi's voice. "Tani! Tani! I *wanted* to ring once we got here, but it's not allowed. Not the first day. Dorcas says it's better that way."

"No one's hurt you?" he asked her.

"No one's touched you, Simi?" Deborah asked.

"Only Mum," Simi said. "She had to fix my hair."

"Oh, I hope I didn't hurt it too badly," Deborah said.

"Well . . . no. *Your* kind of hair's different to mine is what it is. See, yours is sturdier. Mine's more—" Someone in the background spoke.

Simisola said to that person, "She wants to know did she wreck my hair . . . She didn't have proper product, you see . . ." And then back into the phone, "Anyways, Mum fixed it but she's the only one touched me, Tani."

"Tha's good, that is," Tani said.

Another moment as, apparently, the receiver on the other end switched hands again. Monifa said, "I have destroyed the passports: Simisola's, mine, and your father's. Yours I left with Sergeant Nkata. You must finish what needs to be done for the protection order, Tani. I still have what remains of the passports. They will go with the protection order."

"But what're you . . . Why did you . . . ?" Tani wasn't sure what he wanted to ask.

Sophie put it for him, and she did it baldly. "Mrs. Bankole, are you leaving Tani's father? That's what he wants to know only he doesn't know how to ask you."

"We will have a new life when this is sorted, Tani," his mother said. "It will be the three of us. We will have a life. And you will finish college and attend university."

"No," he said. "I need to work now, Mum. I need to have a job. And I will. And, Mum . . . ? I *know*—"

But his mother interrupted to tell him that Tani was not responsible for her, for Simisola, or for the decision she'd made to leave his father. She was, she said, finished with everything that related to her marriage to Abeo. He had Lark and another family and now they would be the only individuals he was meant to support. As for Monifa herself, she had a job waiting for her at a café in Brixton, where she would cook Nigerian dishes during the day and teach Nigerian cookery at night. She would remain at the women's shelter until she had the funds for a flat. She would find one among their own people. When she had the flat arranged, they would all be together.

Tani said, "There's the family money, Mum. He has to give you half of it. You can find a flat now if you have that money. You can find one today."

"I wish to do this my own way," she said.

"Mum, no. It is not right that he keeps it."

"It is right for me. And this . . . everything is different, Tani, which I hope you will one day understand." She went on to say that she wished an ending to their time of distress could be sooner. She wished it could be now. But it would be soon and when the time arrived, they would be their own small family again.

"Tani is welcome to stay with us, Mrs. Bankole," Deborah said. "Until you're ready for him, I mean. I promise not to put even a finger on his hair."

"Or he can stay with my family," Sophie said. "My mum and dad know him. It would be perfect. It would be fine."

"This is for Tani to decide," Monifa said. "I thank you both."

At this point, the phone voice was Dorcas's again. She asked for the details that would tell her who had the protection order, who would file it, and what police station would present it to Simisola's father. All of that, she reassured Tani, would now happen as quickly as possible. In the meantime, he was to stay away from his father. Could he promise to do that.

"Easy as anything," Tani said. "I promise."

CHELSEA
SOUTH-WEST LONDON

"I react to the tone," Deborah said to her husband. "Honestly, Simon, I know you mean well, but when you speak to me with that certain tone—the way you spoke when the subject was Bolu and her parents—it's as if you're attempting to guide my seven-year-old self to some kind of behaviour that you've decided I need to adopt. And then I just see red."

"I never intend that," he told her. "Not the seeing red part, but the other. The lecturing part."

"I don't mean to imply that you intend it. But intentionally or not, you step out of the role of husband and *into* the role of father figure, and . . . well . . . I really do just want to punch you in the face when you do that."

"I'm glad you've managed to restrain yourself."

"I'm not joking, Simon."

"Nor am I."

They were in the garden. It was evening, and they'd carried with them a jug of Pimm's. Deborah's father had taken Peach for her final stroll of the day. She reckoned this would involve a visit to the Kings Head and Eight Bells, where the dog would busily search the floor for anything edible that might have dropped there and her father would probably have a pint of cider. Cider, like Pimm's, always mitigated the heat.

She had brought her husband up to the minute on everything that had occurred during his absence. Once she'd concluded with Monifa, Tani, and Tani's departure with Sophie, she'd felt the uneasiness that told her there was something she had to address with Simon, something that had gone on too long between them. Hence, this conversation.

She said, "I do understand how it happens. You were rather a father figure to me early on, albeit quite a young one. You did have to decide how to interact with a seven-year-old, didn't you. But you see, I never saw you that way, as a father figure. Yes, you were Mr. St. James because I was trained to call you that. In here, though"—she tapped her chest lightly—"you were never other than Simon to me. You didn't really see me, and that was logical, wasn't it, considering the difference in our ages. But I always saw you." She reached for her drink. Simon was adding another spear of cucumber to his, having eaten the first one. She watched his hand cradling the bowl that held the spears, and she wanted to say that she loved his hands and that it was likely his hands were what she had fallen in love with first. But instead she tried to clarify who he was to her by saying, "Simon, I have one father. I don't need another. I don't want another. But if I must have a second one, if that's truly my fate, I don't want him to be the man I sleep with."

He gave her a look. In the evening light, his eyes had grown dark. "I hope I'm not meant to take that as a threat."

"Of course not," she said. "Not that a threat would move you. But I think love might do that job. And God knows I love you, even at your most maddening."

He smiled. "That's reassuring, as I feel likewise."

"When I'm at my most maddening?"

"Especially then. And believe me, you can be quite maddening, Deborah. No one is quite as maddening as a ginger in high dudgeon. And you mustn't argue the point because I have a great deal of experience in the matter."

"It only happens when I'm provoked," she said in defence of herself.

He laughed then. "If that's what you want to believe, my love."

The garden gate opened then. Both of them looked towards it. Deborah assumed it would be her father with Peach in tow, but it was Tommy. He said, "I thought I'd try my luck back here. I rang the bell and when Peach didn't raise a ruckus, I reckoned you might be taking in some cooler air."

"I think the weather's about to break," Simon said.

"Ever the optimist, isn't he?" Deborah added. "You look quite tired, Tommy. Have you had your dinner? Would you like to join us? We'll get to it eventually. In the meantime, there's Pimm's."

"Charlie will have something waiting at home. He's been quite patient with me, so I won't stay long." He pulled one of the deck chairs over to where they were sitting, not on the lawn but on the flagstones that served as a patio at the top of the basement stairs. He said, "We've had a confession from Dr. Weatherall. It all made perfect sense to her." He explained the rationale behind the confession he'd taken from the surgeon. "We've spent the day tying up loose ends. It's quite a blessing you had the photo, Deb. The tenth edition of *Standing Warrior* was what sealed things. Once she understood the sculpture was part of a series, and numbered as well, there was little more for her to say."

"Did she tell you why?"

"She did." He went on to explain. It took a bit of time. His explanation involved not only the surgeon, but also the woman who assisted her at Women's Health of Hackney. He added the sister of the murder victim along with Teo Bontempi's husband. The time frame of events was quite nearly incredible. Everything related to the attack on Teo Bontempi seemed to have occurred within two hours.

When he'd completed his recitation, Deborah told him about Monifa Bankole, Tani, the passports, and the women's shelter. His reply was, "I'm glad of it. Winston will want to know."

Then he was silent. He was looking at the flagstones. Slowly, he blew out a breath. Deborah knew him well enough—as did Simon—to understand there was more.

Simon was the one to say, "None of this appears to unburden you."

"Except it's not the investigation, is it, Tommy?" Deborah said.

"I think I may have lost my way," he admitted.

"Daidre," Deborah said. And when he acknowledged this with a tilting of his head, she went on with, "Has something happened? Well, how stupid of me. Obviously something's happened. Can we help?"

"She's moved her sister to London to share her flat. I find I'm at a loss. It's the oddest thing."

"That she's moved her sister to London?" Deborah asked.

"No. That I can successfully run a murder investigation to its conclusion but I'm utterly incapable of reading between the lines when a woman is trying to tell me something."

"Are you meant to read between lines?"

Simon said before Lynley could reply, "You're not alone in that, Tommy. I'm hopeless as well. Deborah will be only too happy to attest to that fact."

Lynley chuckled wearily. "It seems I'm Pygmalion without an Aphrodite to pray to. When I'm in the midst of things, I don't see that. It's only when they're at an end that I'm able to take a few steps away and realise what I've been trying to do. I don't intend to—"

"We never do," Simon added.

"—but it happens to me nonetheless. I think in terms of someone—Daidre in this case—being what I want, what I need, what will fill the . . . the chasm. But then some part of me that, as of now, I can't control begins to engage in a game of here-is-what-will-make-you-perfect-for-me. That's what I've been doing to her. She's made it clear and I can't blame her for how she feels."

"How *does* she feel?" Deborah asked.

"At her wits' end. Is that a feeling?"

"Perhaps she needs time," Simon said.

"I can tell myself that," Lynley replied. "If nothing else, it's an excellent way to avoid examining what I've been up to. I've gone badly wrong and it's not the first time. God knows I did it to Helen as well."

At her name, they fell silent. She was there, in the quiet: the terrible darkness—the infinite cavern—that her death had brought into his life. All of them had loved her. All of them missed her. But only Tommy had to bear the weight of the decision he'd been forced to make to let her go.

Deborah said, "And Helen always forgave you, didn't she?"

"She did. Yes. She always did."

"Daidre will as well, Tommy. But I think there's something you've lost besides Helen and until you recapture it, the women you love will float away."

"What's that, then?" he asked her.

It was Simon who replied. "I daresay it's your biggest lesson when it comes to . . . what did you call it? . . . going badly wrong. You have to learn to forgive yourself."

CHALK FARM
NORTH LONDON

Barbara's conversation with Dorothea had taken longer than she thought it would do, but it was nonetheless both crucial and necessary, if not completely satisfying. She liked Dee. Indeed, she always enjoyed the time she spent with her and, it had to be admitted, she actually found pleasure in their tap-dancing lessons, which was the last outcome she'd ever expected. Still, there was something that had to be said between them.

Before she left the Yard, she cornered the department's secretary in the ladies', engaged in repairing her makeup before she set off on a mercy date—as she named it—with a bloke who had nearly toppled her as she came out of Westminster tube station. In a film, Dorothea told her, it would have been called "a 'meet-cute'." In reality, she'd badly scuffed her stilettos, cried "Oh no! Watch where you're going, you bloody fool," and this had apparently endeared her to him. He would not be brushed off. He insisted upon drinks. He assured her that he was not a serial killer, that he was a bloke who had only honourable intentions "towards any lass," and since he bore a startling resemblance to one of the royal princes—"when he had all of his hair"—she finally decided to have a go.

"Taking a lot of care for a 'mercy date,' aren't you?" Barbara asked her. Dee was using a small mirror in an attempt to see the back of her hair. Barbara stepped behind her, said, "It looks smashing and even if it didn't, he's not going to be evaluating your hair . . . or is he?"

She replied to Barbara's first remark. "He seems rather nice in a horsey kind of way."

"You did mention the royal princes," Barbara pointed out.

"I meant in personality," Dee told her. She applied lipstick, stepped back, observed her image, applied a second colour. In the mirror, she said to Barbara, "What's to come of your evening? No celebration?"

"I'm thinking Welsh rarebit with a side of chips and another of baked beans."

Dee cast her a disapproving look. "We *need* to book the holiday camp, Barbara. You do see that, don't you?"

What Barbara saw was the opening, so she took it. "As to that, Dee."

Dee raised a shapely eyebrow. "No arguments," she said. "We're doing it. That's done."

"I appreciate all of this. I really do," Barbara told her. "But . . . Bloody hell. I don't know exactly how to say this."

Dee dropped her lipstick-wielding hand. "Oh Lord. He was wrong. He *was* wrong, wasn't he? You are and I've been very, very stupid."

"I am?"

"*Is* there someone I've not met? Have you not wanted to say? You can't have been afraid you'd be bullied. Lord, Barbara. Who on earth would have the nerve to bully you? And anyway, aren't we past that? I don't mean you and me. I mean society in general. Aren't we past that kind of intolerance?"

Barbara was so far out to sea she began to think they were speaking in foreign—and decidedly different—tongues. She said, "Dee, the thing is, I'm not looking for a man."

"I know, I know."

"You do?"

"Isn't that what you've been trying to tell me?"

"More or less," Barbara admitted. "But what the hell are *you* trying to tell me?"

Dee turned from the mirror. She'd taken a case of makeup from her bag, and she shoved this back where it belonged as she said, "That you . . . Well, that you prefer—and believe me I don't care in the *least* except, obviously, I'm not available . . ."

Barbara twigged. "Women," she said.

"Well, yes. I mean, I asked the inspector . . . I mean the acting detective chief—"

"Got it," Barbara cut in. "You asked Lynley if I'd rather be with a woman. For the sake of my own interest, what did he say?"

"He didn't actually know. I mean, how could he when you think about it. But he said he doubted it. Or words to that effect. Or something. And then those flowers came—"

"Right," Barbara said. She wasn't about to reveal the source of the flowers. "The answer is no. I don't prefer women. At least I don't think I prefer women."

"Yet you still don't want to . . . Let's do the holiday camp, Barbara. I'm mad to do it. Aren't you?"

"Dee, only having my teeth pulled sounds worse."

"That means no, does it?"

"It means I'm fine. As I am. Who I am. Do I look like someone who's spending her life moping round waiting for a bloke to shove a glass slipper onto my foot?"

Dee crossed her arms, leaned against the wash basin, gave Barbara an up and down. She said, "To be frank?"

"Please."

"No. You don't. You never have actually." She sighed then and arranged the strap of her shoulder bag so that it didn't cause a wrinkle in her cotton dress. "But can I ask you one question." And before Barbara could say yes or no, she went on with, "We'll still tap dance, won't we?"

"I didn't buy tap shoes to give it up now," Barbara told her. "Especially when I can, at long last, do a bloody Shirley Temple."

Now, Barbara had finally reached Chalk Farm. She wasn't as late as she so frequently was, so she was able to park in front of the house behind which she lived. She'd not stopped for takeaway although she reckoned she might regret the omission. Despite what she'd said to Dorothea, she wasn't certain she had the required comestibles for Welsh rarebit, and while she'd left a tin of Heinz baked beans open in the fridge, she couldn't have sworn to its suitability for consumption as she'd completely forgotten when she'd deposited it there. But there would be something edible in her little habitation. If nothing else, she had plenty of Pop-Tarts.

She walked along the side of the house. She'd given a glance at the empty basement flat—it was habit—and she saw that it was as it had been for quite some time, silent and empty. She heaved a sigh, turned the corner of the house, and realised there was someone sitting on the single step that served as introduction to her front door.

It was Salvatore Lo Bianco, and when he espied her, he rose at once. He'd been using his smartphone, which he shoved into his pocket. He said, "Finally, she is here. *You* are here." He walked to her swiftly. He was smiling. He did that European cheek kiss thing, where the cheeks might meet accidentally but the lips touch nothing but air.

She said, "What the bloody hell . . . ?" and then with narrowed eyes she added, "Who sent you here, Salvatore?"

"I am not sent," he said.

"You swear to that?"

"I swear? You think I am sent? *Che pazza*, Barbara. Who would send me?" He took her arm. "Still, you are looking very well. But you have hungry, yes? No. This is wrong. You are hungry, yes? You have not ate?"

"Eaten," she said. "Not yet. Why?" And then she saw what she hadn't noted before. Two Waitrose carrier bags were on the ground next to the step on which Salvatore had been sitting.

He gestured to these flamboyantly as he urged her gently towards the door. "I am very happy for your hungry," he told her. "Me? I am cooking your dinner."

"My dinner? D'you actually *know* how to cook?"

"*Madonna mia*," he said to the sky. "Barbara Havers asks can I cook."

"Well, *can* you, Salvatore?"

He laughed in delight. "Barbara, Barbara, what do you think? For the love of God, I'm Italian."

Acknowledgments

Several years ago, a conversation with my goddaughter's aunt planted the seed for this novel. A great deal of reading on my part was the result of that conversation. The reading was followed by interviews with various people who guided me in my initial steps in putting together the book.

Detective Inspector Allen Davis and Detective Sergeant Karen Bridger of Empress State Building gave me a crash course in what their Strategic Development department does to put an end to the various forms of abuse perpetrated upon girls and women in the Somali and Nigerian communities in London, from female genital mutilation to forced marriage. From them came the idea for Women's Health of Hackney and for "medicalized" FGM. From them also came the information about ritualized abuse, protection orders, and the criminal charge of failure to protect a child.

The individuals at my US and UK publishing companies made contributions of all sorts, especially Nick Sayers, my UK editor, who connected Deborah Balogun to my work in order to ensure that the details in the lives of the Bankole family were correct. It would be impossible for me to thank Deborah enough, not only for her careful reading of the manuscript but also for her willingness to offer her frank commentary, which allowed me to make the necessary changes in Nigerian tribes, their clothing, their food, their attitudes, and their names.

Once again, Nick Sayers teamed up with my US editors to provide me with a single and thoughtful editorial letter and a list of proposed changes. Once again, the indefatigable Swati Gamble contacted the people I wanted to interview and then set up those interviews for me.

Brian Tart and Gretchen Schmid in the United States proved to be insightful and—perhaps more important—flexible when it came to accepting the extended timeline I needed to finish this book. Gretchen especially was flexible about the potential difficulties I would face with editing and then proofreading online. I am a dinosaur when it comes to technology, and I don't see that changing anytime soon. So I thank Gretchen for accommodating me when it came to proofreading and I thank Brian for accommodating me when it came to everything else.

Ben Petrone and Bel Banta from Viking have done soldiers' work when it comes to publicizing in the time of COVID; Kate Kehan from Hodder & Stoughton has done the same.

When it comes to things digital, I must thank Nicole Robson of Trident Media Group for her efforts on my behalf, as well as my digital goddess Cindy Peterson and my digital god Clay Fourrier.

Robert Gottlieb of Trident Media Group has been guiding the ship of my career for more than twenty years, and I thank him for never putting a single thing on the back burner. Erica Silverman of Trident Media Group may well have pulled a rabbit out of the hat, but that remains to be seen. Fingers crossed.

The current board of trustees of the Elizabeth George Foundation have, for years, done much to free up my time to write: Patricia Fogarty, Barbara Fryer, Blake Kimzey, Chris Eyre, Elaine Medosch, and Jane Hamilton. Charlene Coe has done the day-to-day work of the foundation, taking care to make sure everything gets done when it needs to be done.

My husband Tom McCabe has been a rock of support from the get-go, and I'm deeply grateful for his patience, love, and abiding belief in my ability to finish a journey once I've set out upon it.

The subject matter in this book is sometimes difficult to grasp. A spotlight needs to be shone upon it so the suffering ends as does the ruin of women's lives in the cause of making them "pure" and "chaste" and hence suitable to become someone's wife.

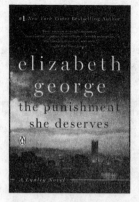

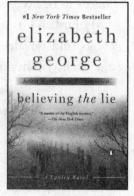